# Darkness Visible

# Darkness Visible

by

## WILLIAM GOLDING

FABER AND FABER
London & Boston

First published in 1979
by Faber and Faber Limited
3 Queen Square London WC1N 3AU
Printed in Great Britain by
Lowe and Brydone Printers Limited
Thetford, Norfolk

© William Golding 1979

British Library Cataloguing in Publication Data

Golding, William
Darkness visible
I. Title
823'.9'1F     PR6013.035D/
ISBN 0-571-11454-7

SIT MIHI FAS AUDITA LOQUI

# Part One
# MATTY

# CHAPTER ONE

There was an area east of the Isle of Dogs in London which was an unusual mixture even for those surroundings. Among the walled-off rectangles of water, the warehouses, railway lines and travelling cranes, were two streets of mean houses with two pubs and two shops among them. The bulks of tramp steamers hung over the houses where there had been as many languages spoken as families that lived there. But just now not much was being said, for the whole area had been evacuated officially and even a ship that was hit and set on fire had few spectators near it. There was a kind of tent in the sky over London, which was composed of the faint white beams of searchlights, with barrage balloons dotted here and there. The barrage balloons were all that the searchlights discovered in the sky, and the bombs came down, it seemed, mysteriously out of emptiness. They fell in or round the great fire.

The men at the edge of the fire could only watch it burn, out of control. The water mains were broken and the only hindrance in the way of the fire was the occurrence of firebreaks here and there where fires had consumed everything on other nights.

Somewhere on the northern edge of the great fire a group of men stood by their wrecked machine and stared into what, even to men of their experience, was a new sight. Under the tent of searchlights a structure had built itself up in the air. It was less sharply defined than the beams of light but it was far brighter. It was a glare, a burning bush through or beyond which the thin beams were sketched more faintly. The limits of this bush were clouds of tenuous smoke that were lit from below until they too seemed made of fire. The heart of the bush, where the little streets had been, was of a more lambent colour. It shivered constantly but with an occasional diminution or augmentation of its brightness as walls collapsed or roofs caved in. Through it all—the roar of the

9

fire, the drone of the departing bombers, the crash of collapse—there was now and then the punctuating explosion of a delayed-action bomb going off among the rubble, sometimes casting a kind of blink over the mess and sometimes so muffled by debris as to make nothing but noise.

The men who stood by their wrecked machine at the root of one northern road that ran south into the blaze had about them the anonymity of uniform silence and motionlessness. Some twenty yards behind them and to their left was the crater of the bomb that had cut the local water supply and smashed their machine into the bargain. A fountain still played in the crater but diminishingly and the long fragment of bomb-casing that had divided a rear wheel lay by their machine, nearly cool enough to touch. But the men ignored it as they were ignoring many small occurrences—the casing, the fountain, some fantasies of wreckage—that would have gathered a crowd in peace time. They were staring straight down the road into the bush, the furnace. They had positioned themselves clear of walls and where nothing but a bomb could fall on them. That, oddly enough, was the least of the dangers of their job and one almost to be discounted among the falling buildings, trapping cellars, the secondary explosions of gas and fuel, the poisonous stinks from a dozen sources. Though this was early in the war they were experienced. One of them knew what it was like to be trapped by one bomb and freed by another. He viewed them now with a kind of neutrality as if they were forces of nature, meteors it might be, that happened to strike thickly hereabouts at certain seasons. Some of the crew were wartime amateurs. One was a musician and now his ear was finely educated in the perception and interpretation of bomb noises. The one that had burst the mains and wrecked the machine had found him narrowly but sufficiently sheltered and he had not even ducked. Like the rest of the crew he had been more interested in the next one of the stick, which had struck further down the road, between them and the fire, and lay there now at the bottom of its hole, either a dud or a delayed action. He stood on the undamaged side of the machine, staring like the others down the road. He was muttering.

"I'm not happy. No. Honestly chaps, I'm not happy."

Indeed, none of the chaps was happy, not even their leader whose lips were set so firmly together. For by some kind of

10

transference of effort from them, or by a localized muscular effort, the front of his chin trembled. His crew were not unsympathetic. The other amateur, a bookseller who stood at the musician's side and who could never put on his wartime uniform without a feeling of incredulity, could assess the mathematical chances of his present survival. He had watched a wall six storeys high fall on him all in one piece and had stood, unable to move and wondering why he was still alive. He found the brick surround of a window on the fourth storey had fitted round him neatly. Like the others, he had got beyond saying how scared he was. They were all in a state of settled dread, in which tomorrow's weather, tonight's Enemy's Intention, the next hour's qualified safety or hideous danger were what ruled life. Their leader carried out within limits the orders that were sent him but was relieved even to tears and shudderings when the telephoned weather forecast indicated that a raid was impossible.

So there they were, listening to the drone of the departing bombers, estimable men who were beginning to feel that though everything was indescribably awful they would live for another day. They stared together down the shuddering street and the bookseller, who suffered from a romantic view of the classical world, was thinking that the dock area would look like Pompeii; but whereas Pompeii had been blinded by dust here there was if anything too much clarity, too much shameful, inhuman light where the street ended. Tomorrow all might be dark, dreary, dirty, broken walls, blind windows; but just now there was so much light that the very stones seemed semi-precious, a version of the infernal city. Beyond the semi-precious stones, there, where the heart of the fire was shivering rather than beating, all material objects, walls, cranes, masts, even the road itself merged into the devastating light as if in that direction the very substance of the world with all the least combustible of its materials was melting and burning. The bookseller found himself thinking that after the war if there ever was an after the war they would have to reduce the admission fee to the ruins of Pompeii since so many countries would have their own brand-new exhibitions of the broken business of living.

There was an episode of roaring, audible through the other noises. A red curtain of flame fluttered near the white heart of the fire and was consumed by it. Somewhere a tank of something had

11

exploded or a coal cellar had just distilled out its own coal gas, invaded a closed room, mixed with air, reached flashpoint—That was it, thought the bookseller knowledgeably, and now safe enough to be proud of his knowledge. How strange that is, he thought, after the war I shall have time—

He looked round quickly for wood; and there it was, a bit of lath from a roof and lying close by his foot so he bent, picked it up and threw it away. As he straightened up he saw how intently the musician was attending to the fire with eyes now rather than ears and beginning to mutter again.

"I'm not happy. No, I'm not happy—"

"What is it old chap?"

The rest of the crew were also staring more earnestly into the fire. All eyes were aimed, mouths drawn in. The bookseller swung round to look where the others were looking.

The white fire, becoming pale pink, then blood-coloured then pink again where it caught smoke or clouds seemed the same as if it were the permanent nature of this place. The men continued to stare.

At the end of the street or where now, humanly speaking, the street was no longer part of the habitable world—at that point where the world had become an open stove—at a point where odd bits of brightness condensed to form a lamp-post still standing, a pillar box, some eccentrically shaped rubble—right there, where the flinty street was turned into light, something moved. The bookseller looked away, rubbed his eyes, then looked again. He knew most of the counterfeits, the objects that seem endowed with life in a fire: the boxes or papers stirred into movement by localized gusts of wind, the heat-induced contractions and expansions of material that can mimic muscular movement, the sack moved by rats or cats or dogs or half-burnt birds. At once and violently, he hoped for rats but would have settled for a dog. He turned round again to get his back between himself and what he was sure he had not seen.

It was a remarkable circumstance that their captain was the last to look. He had turned from the fire and was contemplating his wrecked machine with the kind of feeling that kept his chin still. The other men drew his eyes to them by not meaning to. They turned away from the fire far too casually. Where there had been a whole set of eyes, a battery of them staring into the melted end

12

of the world, that battery now contemplated the uninteresting ruins from a previous fire in the other direction and the failing jet of water in the crater. It was a sheer piece of heightened awareness, a sense sharpened by dread that made the captain look at once not where they were looking but where they were not.

Two-thirds of the way down the street, part of a wall collapsed and spilt rubbish across the pavement so that some pieces went bowling across the road. One piece struck, of all things, a dustbin left standing on the other side and a metallic clang came from it.

"Good God!"

Then the others turned back with him.

The drone of the bombers was dying away. The five-mile-high tent of chalky lights had disappeared, been struck all at once, but the light of the great fire was bright as ever, brighter perhaps. Now the pink aura of it had spread. Saffron and ochre turned to blood-colour. The shivering of the white heart of the fire had quickened beyond the capacity of the eye to analyse it into an outrageous glare. High above the glare and visible now for the first time between two pillars of lighted smoke was the steely and un-touched round of the full moon—the lover's, hunter's, poet's moon; and now—an ancient and severe goddess credited with a new function and a new title—the bomber's moon. She was Artemis of the bombers, more pitiless than ever before.

The bookseller contributed rashly.

"There's the moon—"

The captain rebuked him savagely.

"Where did you think it would be? Up north? Haven't any of you got eyes? Do I have to notice everything for everybody? Look there!"

What had seemed impossible and therefore unreal was now a fact and clear to them all. A figure had condensed out of the shuddering backdrop of the glare. It moved in the geometrical centre of the road which now appeared longer and wider than before. Because if it was the same size as before, then the figure was impossibly small—impossibly tiny, since children had been the first to be evacuated from that whole area; and in the mean and smashed streets there had been so much fire there was nowhere for a family to live. Nor do small children walk out of a fire that is melting lead and distorting iron.

"Well! What are you waiting for?"

13

No one said anything.

"You two! Get him!"

The bookseller and the musician started forward. Half-way down the street the delayed-action bomb went off under a warehouse on the right-hand side. Its savage punctuation heaved the pavement across the road and the wall above it jerked, then collapsed into a new crater. Its instantaneity was dreadful and the two men came staggering back. Behind them the whole length of the street was hidden by dust and smoke.

The captain snarled.

"Oh—Christ!"

He ran forward himself, the others at his shoulder, and did not stop until he was where the air cleared and the heat from the fire became a sudden violent attack on the skin.

The figure was a child, drawing nearer. As they picked their way past the new crater they saw him plain. He was naked and the miles of light lit him variously. A child's stride is quick; but this child walked down the very middle of the street with a kind of ritual gait that in an adult would have been called solemn. The captain could see—and now, with a positive explosion of human feeling—why this particular child walked as it did. The brightness on his left side was not an effect of light. The burn was even more visible on the left side of his head. All his hair was gone on that side, and on the other, shrivelled to peppercorn dots. His face was so swollen he could only glimpse where he was going through the merest of slits. It was perhaps something animal that was directing him away from the place where the world was being consumed. Perhaps it was luck, good or bad, that kept him pacing in the one direction where he might survive.

Now they were so near that the child was not an impossibility but a scrap of their own human flesh, they became desperate to save and serve him. Their captain, indifferent now to the slight dangers that might ambush them in the street, was the first to reach the child and handle him with trained and devoted care. One of the men raced in the other direction without being told, to the phone a hundred yards away. The other men formed a tight and unprofessional knot round the child as he was carried, as if to be close was to give him something. The captain was a bit breathless but full of compassion and happiness. He busied himself with the kind of first aid for burns which is reversed by the

14

medical profession every year or so. In a very few minutes an ambulance came, the team was told all the nothing that was known about the child and he was driven away, the ambulance bell ringing, perhaps unnecessarily.

It was the dimmest of the firemen who expressed the general feeling.

"Poor little bugger."

All at once they were talking to each other enthusiastically about how incredible it was, a kid walking out of the fire like that, stark naked, burnt but going on, steadily making his way towards a glimpse of safety—

"Plucky little bugger! Didn't lose his head."

"They do wonders now. Look at them pilots. Getting faces as good as new they say."

"He might be a bit shrivelled like, down the left side."

"Thank Christ my kids are out of it. And the missus."

The bookseller was saying nothing and seemed to be staring at nothing. There was a memory flickering on the edge of his mind and he could not get it further in where it could be examined; and he was also remembering the moment when the child had appeared, seeming to his weak sight to be perhaps not entirely there—to be in a state of, as it were, indecision as to whether he was a human shape or merely a bit of flickering brightness. Was it the Apocalypse? Nothing could be more apocalyptic than a world so ferociously consumed. But he could not quite remember. Then he was deflected by the sounds of the musician being sick.

The captain had turned back to the fire. He looked down a street that in the event had proved neither as hot as they supposed nor as dangerous. He jerked his attention away from it and back to the machine.

"Well. What are we waiting for? They'll want to tow us if we can be towed. Mason, try the steering and see if you can free it. Wells, come out of that trance! Start tracing the brake lines—quickly now and cheerfully !"

Under the machine, Wells swore horribly and profoundly.

"Now then Wells, you're paid to get your hands dirty."

"The oil went straight into me fucking mouth!"

A burst of sniggering—

"Teach you to keep your mouth shut!"

"What's it taste like, Wellsy?"

15

"Can't be worse'n the canteen!"

"All right lads, turn it up. We don't want the breakdowns to do our work for us do we?"

The captain turned back to the fire. He looked at the new crater half-way down the road. He saw quite clearly in a kind of interior geometry of this and this and that and that how things had been and how they might have been and where he would have been running if he had set off at the very first moment he had realized the child was there and needed help. He would have run straight into the space where now there was nothing but a hole. He would have run into the explosion and he would have disappeared.

There was the clatter of a part falling under the machine and another burst of cursing from Wells. The captain hardly heard it. The skin had seemed to freeze on his body. He shut his eyes and for some sort of time saw that he was dead or felt that he was dead; and then that he was alive, only the screen that conceals the workings of things had shuddered and moved. Then his eyes were open again and the night was as normal as that kind of night could ever be, and he knew what the frost was on his skin and he thought to himself with the cunning immediacy that was part of his nature that it just didn't do to examine such things too closely and anyway the little chap would have suffered just as much and anyway—

He turned back to his own smashed machine and saw that the tow was coming. He came, silent and filled in an extraordinary way with grief, not for the maimed child but for himself, a maimed creature whose mind had touched for once on the nature of things. His chin was quivering again.

The child was called number seven. After the kind of holding operations that had to be performed while he recovered from shock, number seven was the first present he got from the world outside him. There was some small doubt as to whether his silence was organic or not. He could hear, even with the ghastly fragment of ear on his left side, and the swelling round his eyes soon subsided so that he could see well enough. He was contrived a position in which he did not have to be doped very much and spent days and weeks and months in it. But, though the burnt area reckoned as a percentage of the whole made it improbable, he did in fact survive, to begin a long progress through hospitals of one sort of expertise or another. By the time he had come to speak his occasional word of English it was impossible to discover whether it was his native tongue or whether he had picked up the word in hospital. He had no background but the fire. He was known in successive wards as baby, darling, pet, poppet, sweetie and boo-boo. He was at last given a name because a matron put her foot down, a thing of power. She spoke roundly.

"We can't go on calling the child number seven behind his back. It's most improper and injurious."

She was an old-fashioned matron who used that kind of word. She was effective.

The appropriate office was working through the alphabet in rotation, since the boy was only one among the wreckage of that childhood. The office had just presented a baby girl with the name "Venables". The young wit who was given the job of using "w" suggested "Windup", her chief having displayed less than perfect courage in an air raid. She had found she could get married and still keep her job and she was feeling secure and superior. Her chief winced at the name and drew his pen through it, foreseeing a coven of children all shouting "Windup! Windup!" He made his own substitution, though when he looked at what he had written it seemed not quite right and he altered it. There was no obvious reason for doing so. The name had first jumped into his mind with the curious effect of having come out of empty air and of being temporary, a thing to be noticed because you were lucky to be in the place where it had landed. It was as if you had sat silently in the bushes and—My!—there settled in front of you the rarest of butterflies or birds which had stayed long enough to be seen and had then gone off with an air of going for ever, sideways, it might be.

The boy's current hospital accepted "Septimus" as a middle name but made no use of it. Perhaps it had overtones of "Septic". His first name, Matthew, became "Matty"; and as "Seven" was still written on all the relevant papers, no one used his surname. But then, for years of his childhood, all visitors had to peer among sheets and bandages and mechanisms to see any part of him but the right side of his face.

As the various aids to recovery were removed from him and he began to speak more, it was observed that his relationship to

17

language was unusual. He mouthed. Not only did he clench his fists with the effort of speaking, he squinted. It seemed that a word was an object, a material object, round and smooth sometimes, a golf ball of a thing that he could just about manage to get through his mouth, though it deformed his face in the passage. Some words were jagged and these became awful passages of pain and struggle that made the other children laugh. After his turban came off in the period between the primary work and what cosmetic work was possible, the ruin of his half-raw skull and blasted ear was most unappealing. Patience and silence seemed the greater part of his nature. Bit by bit he learnt to control the anguish of speaking until the golfballs and jagged stones, the toads and jewels passed through his mouth with not much more than the normal effort.

In the illimitable spaces of childhood, time was his only dimension. Adults who tried to establish contact with him were never successful with words. He accepted words and seemed to think long about them and sometimes he answered them. But it was a dissociated traffic out there. He was, at this time, to be approached by a method beyond conceptual artifice. Thus the nurse who squeezed him with her arms, knowing just where his body could bear the contact, found the relatively good, relatively undamaged side of his head burrowing against her breast in wordless communication. Being, it seemed, touched being. It was natural that this girl should discount what further thing she had noticed, since it was too delicate, even too private a perception to be called awareness of a symptom. She knew herself not to be particularly intelligent or clever. So she allowed the awareness to float in the back of her mind and paid no particular attention to it, only accepting that she, more than the other nurses, now knew the Matty-ness of Matty. She found herself saying things to herself that would mean one thing to others but something quite different inside her.

"There's Matty thinking I can be in two places at once!"

Then she would find what she had noticed was blown away or rendered massively inaccurate by the words her mind had accidently wrapped round it. But it happened too often and it settled into a pattern of belief that she accepted as a kind of definition of his nature.

Matty believes I'm two people.

Then later and even more privately—*Matty believes I bring someone with me*.

There was a delicacy in her mind that knew this belief to be unique to Matty and not to be discussed. Perhaps she felt a certain delicacy about the nature of her own mind in its surely unusual working. But she felt nearer this child than the others and she showed it in a way that the other children resented because she was pretty. She called him, "My Matty". When she did that it was the first time since his emergence from the furnace that he was observed to employ the complex musculature of his face in a communicative way. The rearrangement was slow and painful as if the little mechanism was in need of oil, but there was no doubt about the end-product. Matty was smiling. But his mouth remained lopsided and closed all the time, which made the smile unchildlike and seemed to concede that though smiling was possible, it was not a common practice and a wicked one if indulged in often.

Matty moved on. He suffered this in animal patience, seeing this was what was going to happen and there was no escaping it. The pretty nurse hardened her heart and told him how happy he would be. She was accustomed to partings. She was young enough to consider him lucky to be alive. Besides, she fell in love and that deflected her attention. Matty went one way and she went the other. Presently the delicate perceptions ceased, for she did not or could not use them on her own children. She was happy and forgot Matty for years until middle age overwhelmed her.

Matty was now fixed in a different position so that skin could be transferred from one part of his body to the other. It was a condition of some absurdity and the other children in the burns hospital, none of whom had much to laugh at, enjoyed his plight. Grown-ups came to entertain and console him but no woman held his undamaged side to her breast. She would have had to contort herself to do so. His smile went unused. There was rather more of him visible now to the casual visitor; and these, hurrying to their own unfortunates, were repelled by the sordid misery in which Matty passed his days, and they flashed sideways at him an uneasy smile which he interpreted with absolute precision. When at last he was cut loose, and having been as much as possible repaired was set on his feet, his smile seemed to have gone for good. The blasting of his left side had given him some contraction of the sinews that growth had not yet redressed, so he limped. He had hair on the right side of his skull but the left side was a ghastly white, which seemed so unchildlike it was an invitation by its appearance of baldness to discount his childishness and treat him as an adult who was being stubborn or just silly. Organizations ground on round him for his benefit but there was little more that could be done with him. His background was probed and probed without result. For all that the most painstaking inquiries could find, he might have been born from the sheer agony of a burning city.

# CHAPTER TWO

Matty limped from hospital into his first school; and from that into a school maintained by two of the biggest trade unions in Britain. Here, in the Foundlings School at Greenfield, he met Mr Pedigree. They could be said to have converged on each other, though Matty was going up and Mr Pedigree was going down.

Mr Pedigree had declined from teaching at an ancient choir school through two less historical foundations and a considerable period which he accounted for by foreign travel. He was a slight and springy man with hair of faded gold and a face that was thin and lined and anxious when it was not vexed or arch. He joined the staff at Foundlings two years before Matty got there. The Second World War had, so to speak, disinfected Mr Pedigree's past. He lived therefore, unwisely, in a top room at the school. He was no longer "Sebastian", even to himself. "Mr Pedigree", a figure of the unimportant schoolmaster, was what he had become, and grey was beginning to appear streakily in his faded hair. He was a snob about boys and found the orphans generally repellent with some notable exceptions. There was no use found here for his Classics. He taught elementary geography mixed with elementary history and elementary English Grammar thrown in. For two years he had found it easy to resist his "*times*" and he lived in a fantasy. He pretended to himself that he was always the owner of two boys: one, an example of pure beauty, the other, an earthy little man! His personal charge was a large class into which boys who had given some evidence of having reached their educational ceiling were thrust, there to mark time until they could leave. The headmaster considered that with this lot he could do little harm. This was probably true except in the case of the boy with whom Mr Pedigree had his "spiritual relationship". For there appeared, as Mr Pedigree grew older, an extraordinary kink in the relationship

21

beyond what a heterosexual person might think extraordinary. Mr Pedigree would lift the child on to a pedestal and he would make himself all in all to him, oh yes, all in all; and the little boy would find life wonderful and all things would be made easy for him. Then, as suddenly, Mr Pedigree would turn cold and indifferent. If he spoke to the child it would be sharply; and since it was a spiritual relationship, with not even the touch of a finger on a vellum cheek, what had the child, or anyone else, to complain of?

All this was subject to rhythm. Mr Pedigree had begun to understand that rhythm. It was when the beauty of the child began to consume him, obsess him, madden him—bit by bit, madden him! During that period, if he were not very careful he would find himself taking risks beyond what was common sense. He would find himself driven—the words bubbling over his lips before some other person, a master perhaps—driven to say what an extraordinarily attractive child young Jameson was, one really had to consider him a beauty!

Matty did not immediately go into Mr Pedigree's group. He was given a chance to exhibit his intellectual potential. But hospitals had taken too much of his time as the fire had taken any gloss there might have been about him. His limp, his two-toned face and ghastly ear hardly concealed by black hair swept over the baldness of his skull made him a natural butt. This may have contributed to his development of a faculty—to give it a name—which was to increase throughout his life. He could disappear. He could become unnoticeable like an animal. He had other qualities too. He drew badly but with passion. Leaning over the page, encircling it with an arm as his black hair swung free, he would sink into what he drew as if about to dive into a sea. His outlines were always without a break and he filled each space with colour of absolute evenness and neatness. It was a deed. Also he would listen devotedly to anything told him. He knew large portions of the Old Testament and small portions of the New Testament by heart. His hands and feet were too big for his thin arms and legs. His sexuality—and this was brilliantly perceived by his fellows—was in direct proportion to his unattractiveness. He was high-minded; and his fellows considered this to be his darkest sin.

The Convent School of Saint Cecilia was a hundred yards down the road and the grounds of the two establishments were separated by a narrow lane. On the girls' side was a high wall with

22

spikes on top. Mr Pedigree could see the wall and the spikes from his top room and it brought back memories from which he flinched. The boys could see it too. From the landing and the great window three storeys up outside Mr Pedigree's room you could look over the wall and see the blue dresses and white, summery socks of the girls. There was a place where the girls could get up and peer through the spikes if they were naughty enough or sexy enough, which of course was the same thing. There was a tree on the boys' side that could be climbed and the young creatures could see each other face to face with only the lane between them.

Two of the boys who had taken particularly against Matty's high-mindedness, mostly because they were of exceptional low-mindedness, set out with the directness and simplicity of genius to play on all his weaknesses at once.

"We been talking to the girls, see?"

And later—"They've been talking about you."

And later—"Angy's sweet on you, Matty, she keeps asking about you."

Then—"Angy said she wouldn't mind a walk in the woods with you!"

Matty limped away from them.

Next day they gave him a note, which in a confusion of ideas from the adult world they had printed then signed. Matty inspected the note, torn from a rough workbook like the one he had in his own hand. The golf balls emerged from his mouth.

"Why didn't she write it? I don't believe it. You're having me on!"

"But look, it's got her name there, 'Angy'. I expect she thought you wouldn't believe her unless she signed it."

Shrieks of laughter.

If Matty had known anything at all about girls of school age he would have seen that they would never send a note on such paper. It was an early example of sexual differentiation. A boy, unless deflected, would apply for a job on the back of an old envelope. But if girls got hold of stationery the results were liable to be frightful, purple, scented and strewn with flowers. Nevertheless, Matty believed in the note torn from the corner of a rough workbook.

"She's there now Matty! She wants you to show her something—"

Matty stared from one to the other under lowered eyebrows.

23

The undamaged side of his face flushed red. He said nothing.

"Honestly Matty!"

They crowded in on him. He was taller than they were but stooped by his condition. He laboured at words and got them out.

"What does she want?"

The three heads came as close now as they could get. Almost at once, the redness sank away in his face so that the spots of his adolescence seemed even more definite against their white background. He breathed his answer.

"She didn't!"

"Honestly!"

He looked at each face in turn, his mouth left open. It was a strange look. So a man swimming in the deep ocean might lift his head and stare before him in search of land. There was a trace of light in the look, hope struggling with a natural pessimism.

"Honestly?"

"Honestly!"

"Cross your heart?"

Once more shrieks of laughter.

"Cross my heart!"

Again that aimed, imploring look, movement of a hand that tried to brush aside banter.

"Here—"

He thrust his books into their hands and limped quickly away. They held on to each other, laughing like apes. They broke apart, clamorously collected their fellows. The whole troupe clattered up the stone stairs, up, up, one, two, three storeys to the landing by the great window. They pushed and shoved against the great bar that ran from one end to the other at boy-height, and held the verticals that were less than a boy's width apart. Fifty yards away and fifty feet down a boy limped quickly towards the forbidden tree. Two little patches of blue did indeed show above the wall opposite it on the girls' side. The boys along the window were so entranced they never heard the door open behind them.

"What on earth is all this? What are you men doing up here?"

Mr Pedigree stood in the doorway, nervously holding the doorknob and looking from one end of the row of laughing boys to the other. But none of them minded old Pedders.

"I said what's all this? Are there any of my men here? You, the lad with the lovely locks, Shenstone!"

"It's Windy, sir. He's climbing the tree!"

"Windy? Who's Windy?"

"There he is, sir, you can see him, he's just getting up!"

"Oh you are a feeble, nasty, inky lot. I'm surprised at you, Shenstone, a fine upstanding lad like you—"

Scandalized, gleeful laughter—

"Sir, sir, he's doing it now—"

There was a kind of confusion among the leaves of a lower bough. The blue, sexy patches disappeared from the wall as if they had been knocked off by shot. Mr Pedigree clapped his hands and shouted but none of the boys paid any attention. They went cascading down the stairs, and left him there, flushed and more agitated by what was behind him than in front. He looked after them down the well of the stairs. He spoke sideways into the room and held the door open.

"Very well my dear. You can run along now."

The boy came out, smiling confidently up at Mr Pedigree. He went away down the stairs, assured of his own worth.

When he had gone Mr Pedigree stared irritatedly at the distant boy who was coming unhandily down the tree. Mr Pedigree had no intention of interfering—none whatever.

The headmaster heard from the Mother Superior. He sent for the boy who came limping and spotty and anxious. The headmaster was sorry for him and tried to make things easy. The episode had been described by the Mother Superior in such words as hid it behind a veil which the headmaster knew he must lift; and yet he viewed the lifting of a veil with some apprehension. He knew that lifting any veil was liable to uncover more than the investigator bargained for.

"Sit down there, will you? Now. You see we've had this complaint about you. About what you did when you climbed that tree. Young men—boys—will climb trees, that's not what I'm asking you about—but there may be considerable consequences coming from your action, you know. Now. What did you do?"

The unmended side of the boy's face became one deep, red flush. He looked down past his knees.

"You see, my dear boy, there's nothing to be—frightened of. People sometimes can't help themselves. If they are sick then we help them or find people who can help them. Only we must *know*!"

25

The boy neither spoke nor moved.

"Show me, then, if that's easier for you."

Matty glanced up under his eyebrows then down again. He was breathing quickly as if he had been running. He took his right hand across and took hold of the long lock dangling by his left ear. With a gesture of absolute abandon he ripped the hair across and exposed the white obscenity of his scalp.

It was perhaps fortunate that Matty did not see how the headmaster shut his eyes involuntarily, then forced them open and kept them open without any change of expression in his face. They both said nothing for a while until the headmaster nodded understandingly and Matty, relaxing, brought the hair back across his head.

"I see," said the headmaster. "Yes. I see."

Then for a while he said nothing but thought of phrases that might go in his letter to the Mother Superior.

"Well," he said at last, "don't do it again. Go along now. And please remember you are only allowed to climb the big beech and even then, up to the second bough. Right?"

"Sir."

After that, the headmaster sent round the various masters concerned to find out more about Matty and it was obvious that someone had been too kind—or perhaps unkind—and he was in a stream that was too much for him. The boy would never pass an examination and it was silly to make him try.

It was for this reason, therefore, that one morning when Mr Pedigree was dozing in front of his class as they drew a map, that Matty came clumping in, books under his arm, and stopped in front of the master's desk.

"Good God boy. Where have you come from?"

It seemed the question was too quick or too profound for Matty. He said nothing.

"What d'you want, boy? Say quickly!"

"I was told, sir. C.3, sir. The room at the end of the corridor."

Mr Pedigree gave a determined grin and wrenched his gaze away from the boy's ear.

"Ah. Our simian friend swinging from branch to branch. Don't laugh, you men. Well. Are you house-trained? Reliable? Brilliant intellect?"

Quivering with distaste, Mr Pedigree looked round the room. It

26

was his custom and entertainment to arrange the boys in order of beauty so that the most beautiful occupied the front row. There was no doubt at all in his mind as to where the new boy should go. At the back of the room on his right, a tall cupboard left enough space for a desk that would be partly concealed by it. The cupboard could not be shifted flush against the wall without blocking a window.

"Brown, you exquisite creature, I shall want you out of there. You can sit in Barlow's place. Yes, I know he'll be back; and then we shall have to do some more arranging, shan't we? Anyway Brown, you're an imp, aren't you? I know what you get up to at the back there when you think I can't see you. Stop laughing, you men. I won't have you laughing. Now then, what's your name, Wandgrave. Can you keep order, mm? Go and sit in that corner and just keep quiet and tell me if they don't behave, mm? Go along!"

He waited, grinning with determined cheerfulness until the boy was seated and partly out of sight. Mr Pedigree found that he could divide the boy by the line of the cupboard so that only the more-or-less undamaged side of his face was visible. He sighed with relief. Such things were important.

"All right everybody. Just get on. Show him what we're doing, Jones."

He relaxed, dallying now with his agreeable game, for Matty's unexpected arrival gave him an excuse for another round of it.

"Pascoe."

"Sir?"

There was no denying that Pascoe was losing what had never been a very high degree of attractiveness. Mr Pedigree wondered in passing what he had ever seen in the boy. It was fortunate the affair had gone very little way.

"Pascoe, dear friend, I wonder if you would mind changing places now with Jameson so that when Barlow comes back—you don't mind being just a *little* further from the seat of judgement? Now, what about you, Henderson. Eh?"

Henderson was in the middle of the front row. He was a child of bland and lyric beauty.

"You don't mind being close to the seat of judgement, do you, Henderson?"

Henderson looked up, smiling, proudly and adoringly. His star
27

was in Mr Pedigree's ascendant. Moved inexpressibly, Mr Pedigree came out of his desk and stood by Henderson, his fingers in the boy's hair.

"Ghastly, dear friend, when did you last wash all this yellow stuff, eh?"

Henderson looked up, still smiling and secure, understanding that the question was not a question, but communication, brightness, glory. Mr Pedigree dropped his hand and squeezed the boy's shoulder, then went back to his desk. To his surprise the boy behind the cupboard had his hand up.

"What is it? What is it?"

"Sir. That boy there. He passed a note to him, sir. That's not allowed is it sir?"

For a while Mr Pedigree was too astonished to answer. Even the rest of the class were silent until the enormity of what they had heard penetrated to them. Then a faint, increasing booing sound began to rise.

"Stop it you men. Now I said stop it. You, what's your name. You must have come straight out of a howling wilderness. We have found a cop!"

"Sir you said—"

"Never mind what I said, you *literal* creature! My goodness what a treasure we've come across!"

Matty's mouth had opened and stayed open.

It was odd indeed after that, that Matty should adopt Mr Pedigree. It was a sign of the poverty of his acquaintance that he should begin to dog the man and irritate him, since attention from Matty was the last thing he wanted. In fact, Mr Pedigree was on the slope of his rising curve and had begun to recognize where he was in a way that had not been apparent to him in the long distant days of the choir school. He knew now that points on the curve signalled themselves precisely. As long as he admired beauty in the classroom, no matter how overt his gestures of affection, everything was safe and in order. But there came a point where he began—*had* to begin—to help boys with their prep in his own room, forbidden as it was, dangerous and delirious; and there again the gestures would be innocent for a time—

Just now, in the last month of this term, Henderson had been elevated by nature herself to that pre-eminent beauty. Mr Pedigree himself found it strange that there was such a constant supply of that beauty available, and coming up year after year. The month was strange both for Mr Pedigree and Matty, who dogged him with absolute simplicity. His world was so small and the man was so large. He could not conceive of a whole relationship being based on a joke. He was Mr Pedigree's treasure. Mr Pedigree had said so. Just as some boys spent years in hospital and some did not, so he saw that some boys did their bounden duty and reported on their fellows and some did not, even though the result was desperate unpopularity.

Matty's fellows might have forgiven or forgotten his appearance. But his literal-mindedness, high-mindedness and ignorance of the code ensured that he became an outcast. But baldy Windup yearned for friendship, for he did not only dog Mr Pedigree. He dogged the boy Henderson too. The boy would jeer and Mr Pedigree would—

"Not now, Wheelwright, not now!"

Quite suddenly Henderson's visits to Mr Pedigree's room became more frequent and unconcealed and the language in which Mr Pedigree addressed the class became more extravagant. It was the top of the curve. He spent most of one lesson in a digression, a lecture on bad habits. There were very, very many of them and they were difficult to avoid. In fact—and they would find this out as they grew older—some of them were impossible to avoid. It was important however to distinguish between those habits which were thought to be bad and those which were actually bad. Why, in ancient Greece women were thought to be inferior creatures, now don't laugh you men, I know what you're thinking, you nasty lot, and love reached its highest expression between men and between men and boys. Sometimes a man would find himself thinking more and more about some handsome little fellow. Suppose for example, the man was a great athlete, as it might be nowadays, a cricketer, a test player—

The handsome little fellows waited to find out what the moral of this discourse was and how it related to bad habits but they never did. Mr Pedigree's voice trailed off and the whole thing did not so much end as die, with Mr Pedigree looking lost and puzzled.

People find it remarkable when they discover how little one man knows about another. Equally, at the very moment when people are most certain that their actions and thoughts are most hidden in darkness, they often find out to their astonishment and grief how

29

they have been performing in the bright light of day and before an audience. Sometimes the discovery is a blinding and destroying shock. Sometimes it is gentle.

The headmaster asked to see the report books of some boys in Mr Pedigree's class. They sat at a table in the headmaster's study with the green filing-cabinets at their back. Mr Pedigree talked volubly about Blake and Barlow, Crosby and Green and Halliday. The headmaster nodded and turned the reports over.

"I see you haven't brought Henderson's along."

Mr Pedigree lapsed into frozen silence.

"You know, Pedigree, it's most unwise."

"What's unwise? What's unwise?"

"Some of us have peculiar difficulties."

"Difficulties?"

"So don't give these private lessons in your room. If you want to have boys in your room—"

"Oh but the boy's welfare!"

"There's a rule against it, you know. There have been—rumours."

"Other boys—"

"I don't know how you intend me to take that. But try not to be so —exclusive."

Pedigree went quickly, with heat round his ears. He could see clearly how deep the plot was; for as the graph of his cyclic life rose towards its peak he would suspect all men of all things. The headmaster, thought Pedigree—and was half-aware of his own folly—is after Henderson himself! So he set about devising a scheme by which he could circumvent any attempt on the part of the headmaster to get rid of him. He saw clearly that the best thing was a cover story or camouflage. As he wondered and wondered what to do, he first rejected a step as impossible, then as improbable, then as quite dreadful—and at last saw it was a step he would have to take, though the graph was not falling.

He braced himself. When his class was settled he went round them boy by boy; but this time, beginning with awful distaste at the back. Deliberately he went to the corner where Matty was half-hidden by the cupboard. Matty smiled up at him lopsidedly; and with a positive writhe of anguish, Pedigree gave a grin into the space above the boy's head.

"Oh my goodness me! That's not a map of the Roman Empire

my young friend! That's a picture of a black cat in a coal cellar in the dark. Here, Jameson, let me have your map. Now do you see Matty Windrap? Oh God. Look I can't spend time loitering here. I'm not taking prep this evening, so instead of going there you just bring your book and your atlas and the rest of it to my room. You know where that is don't you? Don't laugh you men! And if you do particularly well there might be a sticky bun or a slice of cake—oh God—"

Matty's good side shone upwards like the sun. Pedigree glanced down into his face. He clenched his fist and struck the boy lightly on the shoulder. Then he hurried to the front of the classroom as if he were looking for fresh air.

"Henderson, fair one. I shan't be able to take you for a lesson this evening. But it's not necessary is it?"

"Sir?"

"Come here and show me your book."

"Sir."

"Now there! You see?"

"Sir—aren't there going to be any more lessons upstairs, sir?"

Anxiously Mr Pedigree looked into the boy's face, where now the underlip stuck out.

"Oh God. Look, Ghastly. Listen—"

He put his fingers in the boy's hair and drew his head nearer.

"Ghastly, my dear. The best of friends must part."

"But you said—"

"Not *now*!"

"You said!"

"I tell you what, Ghastly. I shall be taking prep on Thursday in the hall. You come up to the desk with your book."

"Just because I did a good map—it's not fair!"

"Ghastly!"

The boy was looking down at his feet. Slowly he turned away and went back to his desk. He sat down, bowed his head over his book. His ears were so red they even had a touch of Matty's purple about them. Mr Pedigree sat at his own desk, his two hands trembling on it. Henderson shot him a glance up under his lowered brows and Mr Pedigree looked away.

He tried to still his hands, and he muttered,

"I'll make it up to him—"

Of the three of them only Matty was able to show an open face to the world. The sun shone from one side of his face. When the time came for him to climb to Mr Pedigree's room, he even took extra care in the arrangement of his black hair so that it hid the livid skull and purplish ear. Mr Pedigree opened the door to him with a shudder that had something feverish about it. He sat Matty down in a chair but himself went walking to and fro as if the movement were an anodyne for pain. He began to talk to Matty or to someone, as if there were an adult understanding in the room; and he had hardly begun when the door opened and Henderson stood on the threshold.

Mr Pedigree shouted,

"Get away, Ghastly! Get away! I *won't* see you! Oh God—"

Then Henderson burst into tears and fled away, clattering down the stairs and Mr Pedigree stood by the door, gazing down them until he could no longer hear the boy's sobs or the noise of his feet. Even then, he stayed where he was, staring down. He groped in his pocket and brought out a large white handkerchief and he passed it over his forehead and across his mouth and Matty watched his back and understood nothing.

At last Mr Pedigree shut the door but did not look at Matty. Instead, he began to move restlessly round the room, muttering half to himself and half to the boy. He said the most terrible thing in the world was thirst and that men had all kinds of thirst in all kinds of desert. All men were dypsomaniacs. Christ himself had cried out on the cross, "Διψῶ!" The thirsts of men were not to be controlled so men were not to blame for them. To blame men for them would not be fair, that was where Ghastly was wrong, the foolish and beautiful young thing, but then he was too young to understand.

At this point Mr Pedigree sank into the chair by his table and put his face in his hands.

"Διψάω."

"Sir?"

Mr Pedigree did not reply. Presently he took Matty's book and told him as briefly as he could what was wrong with the map. Matty began to mend it. Mr Pedigree went to the window and stood, looking across the leads to the top of the fire-escape and beyond it to the horizon where the suburbs of London were now visible like some sort of growth.

Henderson did not go back to his prep in the hall nor to the

32

lavatories that had been his excuse for leaving it. He went towards the front of the building and stood outside the headmaster's door for whole minutes. This was a clear sign of his misery; for it was no mean thing in his world to bypass the other members of the hierarchy. At last he tapped at the door, first timidly, then more loudly.

"Well boy, what do you want?"

"See you, sir."

"Who sent you?"

"No one, sir."

That made the headmaster look up. He saw the boy had been crying very recently.

"What form are you in?"

"Mr Pedigree's, sir."

"Name?"

"Henderson, sir."

The headmaster opened his mouth to say *ah!* then closed it again. He pursed his lips instead. A worry began to form itself at the back of his mind.

"Well?"

"It's, it's about Mr Pedigree, sir."

The worry burst into full flower, the interviews, the assessment of blame, all the vexations, the report to the governors and at the end of everything the judge. For of course the man would plead guilty; or if it had not gone as far as that—

He took a long, calculated look at the boy.

"Well?"

"Sir, Mr Pedigree, sir—he gives me lessons in his room—"

"I know."

Now it was Henderson's turn to be astonished. He stared at the headmaster, who was nodding judiciously. The headmaster was very near retirement, and from tiredness as much as anything switched his determination to the job of fending the boy off before anything irremediable had been said. Of course Pedigree would have to leave, but that could be arranged without much difficulty.

"It's kind of him," said the headmaster fluently, "but I expect you find it a bit of a bore don't you extra work like that on top of the rest, well, I understand, you'd like me to speak to Mr Pedigree wouldn't you, I won't say *you* said so, only say that we don't think you're strong enough for extra work so you needn't worry any

33

more. Mr Pedigree simply won't ask you to go there any more. Right?"

Henderson went red. He dug at the rug with one toe and looked down at it.

"So we won't say anything about this visit to anyone else will we? I'm glad you came to see me, Henderson, very glad. You know, these little things can always be put right if you only talk to a, a grown-up about them. Good. Now cheer up and go back to your prep."

Henderson stood still. His face went even redder, seemed to swell; and from his screwed-up eyes the tears jetted as if his head was full of them.

"Now come along, lad. It's not as bad as that!"

But it was worse. For neither of them knew where the root of the sorrow was. Helplessly the boy cried and helplessly the man watched, thinking, as it were, furtively of what he could not imagine with any precision; and wondering after all whether fending off was either wise or possible. Only when the tears had nearly ceased did he speak again.

"Better? Eh? Look my dear boy, you'd better sit in that chair for a bit. I have to go—I'll be back in a few minutes. You go off, when you feel like it. Right?"

Nodding and smiling in a matey kind of way the headmaster went out, pulling the door to behind him. Henderson did not sit down in the offered chair. He stood where he was, the redness draining slowly from his face. He sniffed for a bit, wiping his nose with the back of his hand. Then he went away back to his desk in the hall.

When the headmaster returned to his study and found that the boy had left he was relieved for a bit since nothing irremediable had been said; but then he remembered Pedigree with much irritation. He debated speaking to him at once but decided at last that he would leave the whole unpleasant business until the first hours of morning school, when his vital forces would have been restored by sleep. Tomorrow would be soon enough, though the whole business could not be left longer than that; and remembering his earlier interview with Pedigree the headmaster flushed with genuine anger. The *silly* man!

However, next morning when the headmaster braced himself for an interview he found himself receiving shocks instead of

34

delivering them. Mr Pedigree was in his classroom but Henderson was not; and before the end of the first period, the new master, Edwin Bell—already "Dinger" to the whole school—had discovered Henderson and suffered an attack of hysterics. Mr Bell was led away but Henderson was left by the wall where the hollyhocks hid him. It was evident that he had fallen fifty feet from the leads or the fire-escape that was connected with them and he was dead as dead. "Dead," said Merriman, the odd-job man, with emphasis and apparent enjoyment, "Dead cold and stiff," which was what had touched off that Mr Bell. However, by the time Mr Bell had been quietened, Henderson's body had been lifted and a gymshoe found beneath—with Matty's name in it.

That morning the headmaster sat looking at the place where Henderson had appeared before him and faced a few merciless facts. He knew himself to be, as he expressed it colloquially, to be for the high jump. He foresaw a hideously complicated transaction in which he would have to reveal that the boy had come to him, and that—

Pedigree? The headmaster saw that he would never have carried on teaching this morning if he had known what happened during the night. It might be what a hardened criminal would do, or what someone capable of minute and detached calculation would do—but not Pedigree. So that who—?

He still did not know what to do when the police came. When the inspector asked about the gymshoe, the headmaster could only say that boys frequently wore each other's gear, the inspector knew what boys were; but the inspector did not. He asked to see Matty just as if this were something on the films or television. It was at this point that the headmaster brought in the solicitor who acted for the school. So the inspector went away for a while and the two men interviewed Matty. He was understood to say that the shoe had been cast, to which the headmaster said in an irritated way that it had been thrown, not cast, it wasn't a horseshoe. The solicitor explained about confidentiality and truth and how they were protecting him.

"When it happened, you were there? You were on the fire-escape?"

Matty shook his head.

"Where were you then?"

They would have known, if they had seen more of the boy, why

35

the sun shone once more, positively ennobling the good side of his face.

"Mr Pedigree."

"*He* was there?"

"No, sir!"

"Look boy—"

"Sir, he was in his room with me, sir!"

"In the middle of the night?"

"Sir, he'd asked me to do a map—"

"Don't be silly. He wouldn't ask you to bring a map to him in the middle of the night!"

The nobility in Matty's face diminished.

"You might as well tell us the truth," said the solicitor. "It'll come out in the end you know. You've nothing to fear. Now. What about this shoe?"

Still looking down, and plain rather than noble, Matty muttered back.

The solicitor pressed him.

"I couldn't hear that. Eden? What's Eden got to do with a gymshoe?"

Matty muttered again.

"This is getting us nowhere," said the headmaster. "Look, er, Wildwort. What was poor young Henderson doing up that fire-escape?"

Matty stared passionately up under his brows and the one word burst from his lips.

"Evil!"

So they put Matty by and sent for Mr Pedigree. He came, feeble, grey-faced and fainting. The headmaster viewed him with disgusted pity and offered him a chair into which he collapsed. The solicitor explained the probable course of events and how a heavier charge might be abandoned in favour of a lesser if the defendant pleaded guilty to render unnecessary the cross-examination of minors. Mr Pedigree sat huddled and shivering. They were kind to him but he only showed one spark of animation during the whole interview. When the headmaster explained kindly that he had a friend, for little Matty Windwood had tried to give him an alibi, Mr Pedigree's face went white then red then white again.

"That horrible, ugly boy! I wouldn't touch him if he were the last one left on earth!"

His arrest was arranged as privately as possible in view of his agreement to plead guilty. Nevertheless, he did come down the stairs from his room with policemen in attendance; and nevertheless, his shadow, that dog of his steps was there to see him go in his shame and terror. So Mr Pedigree screamed at him in the great hall.

"You horrible, horrible boy! It's all your fault!"

Curiously enough the rest of the school seemed to agree with Mr Pedigree. Poor old Pedders was now even more popular among the boys than he had been in the sunny days when he gave them slices of cake and was quite amiably ready to be their butt so long as they liked him. No one, not the headmaster nor the solicitor, nor the judge ever knew the real story of that night; how Henderson had begged to be let in and been denied and gone reeling on the leads to slip and fall, for now Henderson was dead and could no longer reveal to anyone his furious passion. But the upshot was that Matty was sent to Coventry and fell into deep grief. It was plain to the staff that he was one of those cases for early relief from school and a simple, not too brainy job was the only palliative if not remedy. So the headmaster, who had an account at Frankley's the Ironmongers at the other end of the High Street down by the Old Bridge, contrived to get him a job there; and like 109732 Pedigree the school knew him no more.

Nor did it know the headmaster much longer. The fact that Henderson had come to see him and been turned away could not be condoned. He left at the end of term for reasons of health; and because the tragedy had been what pushed him out, in his retirement in a bungalow above the white cliffs, he went over the dim fringes of it again and again without understanding it more deeply. Only once did he come across what might be a clue, but even so could not be certain. He found a quotation from the Old Testament, "Over Edom have I cast out my shoe." When he remembered Matty after that he felt a little chill on his skin. The quotation was, of course, a primitive curse, the physical expression of which had been concealed in the translation, like "Smiting hip and thigh," and a dozen other savageries. So he sat and thought and wondered whether he had the key to something even darker than the tragedy of young Henderson.

He would nod, and mutter to himself—

"Oh yes, to *say* is one thing: but to *do* is quite another matter."

# CHAPTER THREE

Frankley's was an ironmonger's of character. When the canal was cut and the Old Bridge built, it diminished the value of all the properties at that end of Greenfield. Frankley's, in the early days of the nineteenth century, moved into rickety buildings that backed on the towpath and were going dirt cheap. The buildings were indeterminate in date, some walls of brick, some tile-hung, some lath and plaster and some of a curious wooden construction. It is not impossible that parts of these wooden areas were in fact medieval windows filled as was the custom with wooden slats and now thought to be no more than chinky walls. Certainly there was not a beam in the place that did not have here and there notches cut, grooves and an occasional hole that indicated building and rebuilding, division, reclamation and substitution, carried on throughout a quite preposterous length of time. The buildings that at last were subsumed under Frankley's management were random and seemingly as confused as coral growths. The front that faced up the High Street was only done up and unified as late as 1850 and stayed so until it was done up all over again for the visit of His Majesty King Edward the Seventh, in 1909.

By that time, if not earlier, all the lofts and attics, galleries, corridors, nooks, crannies had been used as warehouses and were filled with stock. This was over-stocking. Frankley's held from each age, each generation, each lot of goods, a sediment or remainder. Poking about in far corners the visitor might come across such items as carriage lamps or a sawyer's frame, destined not for a museum but for the passing stagecoach or sawyer who had refused to turn over to steam. True, during the early days of the twentieth century, Frankley's made a determined effort to get as much of the contemporary stock downstairs as possible. This, by a kind of evolution with no visible agent, organized itself into sections or departments devoted to various interests as it might be tools, gardening, croquet or miscellaneous. After the convulsion of the First World War the place grew a spider's web of wires along which money trundled in small, wooden jars. For people of all ages, from babies to pensioners, this was entrancing. Some assistant would fire the jar—clang!—from his counter and when the flying jar reached the till it would ring a bell—Dong! So the cashier would reach up, unscrew the jar, take out the money and inspect the bill, put in the change and fire the jar back—Clang! . . .Clang! All this took a great deal of time but was full of interest and enjoyment, like playing with model trains. On market days the noise of the bell was frequent and loud enough to be heard above the lowing of the cattle that were being driven over the Old Bridge. But on other days the bell would be silent for periods that grew longer as the years revolved. Then, a visitor wandering in the darker and farther parts of Frankley's might find another property of the wooden jars. Tricks of construction might muffle the sound of the bells themselves, and a jar would hiss over the customer's head like a bird of prey, turn a corner and vanish in some quite unexpected direction.

Age was the genius of Frankley's. This complex machinery had been designed as a method of preventing each shop assistant from having his own till. The unforeseen result was that the spider's web isolated the assistants. As a young Mr Frankley took over from the late Mr Frankley and became old Mr Frankley and died, his assistants, kept healthy, it may be, by the frugality and the godliness of their existence, did not die but remained static behind their counters. The new young Mr Frankley, even more pious than his forebears, felt that the overhead railway for money was a slur on these elderly gentlemen and removed it. He was, of course, the famous Mr Arthur Frankley who built the chapel and whose name was shortened to "Mr Arthur" by those gentlemen in their corners whose speech remained uncontaminated by times that were seeing the spread of the horseless carriage. Mr Arthur gave each counter back its wooden till and restored dignity to separate parts.

But the use of the overhead railway had done two things. First, it had accustomed the staff to moderate stillness and tranquillity; and second, it had so habituated them to the overhead method of money sending and getting that when one of these ancient gentlemen was offered a banknote he immediately gestured upwards

39

with it as if to examine the watermark. But this, in the evolution or perhaps devolution of the place, would be followed by continuing silence and a lost look while the assistant tried to remember what came next. Yet to call them "assistants" does their memory scant justice. On bright days, when even the dim electricity was switched off and the shop relied on plate-glass windows or wide, grimy skylights, some of which were interior and never saw the sky, there were restful areas remaining of gloom—corners, or forgotten passageways. On such days the loitering customer might detect a ghostly winged collar gleaming in an unvisited corner; and as he accustomed his eyes to the gloom he might make out a pale face hung above the winged collar, and lower down a pair of hands perhaps, spread out at the level where the invisible counter must be. The man would be still as his packets of bolts and nails and screws and tags and tacks. He would be absent, in some unguessable mode of the mind, where the body was to be left thus to pass life erect and waiting for the last customer. Even young Mr Arthur with all his goodwill and genuine benevolence believed that a vertical assistant was the only proper one and that there was something immoral in the idea of an assistant sitting down.

Since young Mr Arthur was devout, by one of the spiritual mysteries of the human condition it is undeniable that during his reign the assistants became more and more holy. The combination of age, frugality and devotion made them at once the most useless and dignified shop assistants in the world. They were notorious. Young Mr Arthur was exhausted by his Napoleonic decision about the spider's web. He was one of nature's bachelors, less by distaste or inversion than by a diminution of sex drive; and he proposed to leave his money to his chapel. During the Second World War the establishment ceased to pay its way; but minimally. Mr Arthur saw no reason why it should not continue to do so, for the rest of his life. The holy old men were to be supported because they could do nothing but what they were doing and had nowhere else to go. Taxed on this unbusinesslike attitude by the progressive grandson of his father's accountant, Mr Arthur muttered vaguely, "Thou shalt not muzzle the ox that treadeth out the corn."

It is not possible now to discover whether the reintroduction of separate tills had any effect on the speed of the shop's decline. All that is certain is that as the decline became more perilous, by an apparent spontaneity the place made convulsive efforts to save itself. It did not shake off its honourable commitment to the elderly gentlemen who had stood so long and sold so little. But in a first convulsion, it bundled an unimaginable load of oddments away from one loft to another and opened a showroom upstairs! Here was to be seen cutlery and glass; and as all the elderly gentlemen were busy behind their counters, new blood had to be imported. At the time there was none of the right age or cheapness available, so with an air of coming clean and bursting out into the twentieth century, the shop hired—the word "employ" had a masculine dignity—hired a woman. In this long upstairs showroom the electric light—and what is more, with more powerful bulbs than anywhere else in the building—was not turned off, no matter how bright the day, until the front doors had been shut at six. The very way up to this glittering room betokened a basic frivolity that was suited to the goods on display and the sex of their guardian. It was a drumheaded, plaster-moulded survival from the late seventeenth century and there was no way of discovering how anything like that had found itself indoors rather than out. After a short while, to the cutlery and tumblers were added decanters, wine glasses, china, table mats, napkin rings, candlesticks, salt cellars and ashtrays in onyx. It was a shop within as well as above a shop. Yet it seemed a flighty thing, that lighted, drumheaded entrance with the carpeted stairs, the rugs and polished floor, the flash of glass or silver under the wastefully bright lights. Below it the broomsticks remained, the galvanized iron buckets, the rows of wooden-hafted tools. It did not accord well with the pigeon-holes of stained and broken wood, that were filled with nails or pins or tacks or iron or brass screws and bolts.

The old men ignored it. They must have known that it would fail, since the shop, as they were, was in the rip of something uncontrollable, an inevitable decline. Even so, after the upstairs showroom, plastics burst in and would not be denied. Plastics committed enormities in the way of silent buckets and washing-up bowls, sink-baskets, watering cans and trays all of blinding colour. Plastics went even further after that and blossomed as a range of artificial flowers. These all grouped themselves as a kind of bower in the centre of the downstairs showrooms. The bower flung out an annexe of plastic screens and trellises that demanded whimsical garden furniture. Once more, it was a feminine place.

41

Once more, a female was its guardian; and not just a female, but a girl at that. She had a till like everyone else. She experimented with coloured lights and hid herself inside a fantasy grove.

It was into this complex disorder of ancient and modern, this image in little of the society at large, that Matty was projected by the headmaster. His status was ambiguous. Mr Arthur explained that the boy had better come until they found out what use they could make of him.

"I think," said Mr Arthur, "we might make use of him in Deliveries."

"What about the future?" asked the headmaster" — his future, I mean."

"If he does well enough he can go into Despatch," said Mr Arthur, with, as it were, a far-off glance at Napoleon."Then if his head for figures is good enough, he might even move up to Accounts."

"I don't conceal from you that the boy seems to have little ability. But he mustn't stay at school."

"He can start in Deliveries."

Frankley's delivered for ten miles round and gave credit. They had a boy with a bicycle for parcels in Greenfield and two vans for longer or heavier journeys. The second of these vans had a driver and a porter, as he was called. The driver was so crippled with arthritis that he had to be inserted in his seat and left there as long as he could stand it and sometimes longer. This was another of Mr Arthur's unimaginative kindnesses. It kept a man in a job that was a constant trial and terror to him and ensured that two people did one man's work. Though the phrase was not yet widely used, Frankley's was Labour Intensive. It was what was sometimes called "a fine old establishment".

Tucked away at the bottom of the yard that ran along by the small garden of GOODCHILD'S RARE BOOKS, and kept in what was still called the coachhouse, was a forge, complete with anvil, tools, fire, and of course ageing blacksmith, who spent his time making trifles for his grandchildren. This area took Matty and absorbed him. He received pocket money, he slept in a long attic under the rosy, fifteenth-century tiles. He ate well, for this was one of the things Mr Arthur could measure. He wore a thick, dark-grey suit and grey overall. He carried things. He became the Boy. He carried garden tools from one part of the place to another and got customers to sign for them. He was visible part of the time among stacks of packing-cases outside the smithy—packing-cases which he prised open with an instrument like a jemmy. He became adept at opening things. He learnt the measure of sheet metal and metal rod, of angle iron, girders and wire. He could be heard, some-times, in the silence of business hours tramping unevenly overhead through the lofts and attics among the stock. He would deliver to it strange objects the name of which he did not know, but which would be sold at the rate of perhaps one out of every half a dozen ordered, while the other five rusted. Up there, the occasional visitor might find a set of jacks for an open fireplace or even a deformed packet of the first, snuffless candles. Matty swept here sometimes—swept those acres of uneven planking where all the brush did was to raise the dust so that it hung about invisibly in the dark corners but sneezily palpable. He began to reverence the winged collars in their places. The only boy of his own age or slightly older, there, was the boy who did the local deliveries either on foot or on the bicycle which he regarded as his own. It was already older than he was. But this boy, thick-set and blond with oiled hair that gleamed as seductively as his boots, had perfected a way of remaining away from the establishment that made his visits seem more like those of a customer than a member of the staff. Where the winged collars had achieved, it seemed, a perfect stillness, the other Boy had discovered perpetual motion. Matty, of course, remained too naive to bend circumstances in his direction as the blond Boy had done. He was perpetually employed and never knew that people gave him jobs to get him out of their sight. Ordered by the blacksmith to pick up the cigarette ends in a corner of the yard where he would be hidden, Matty did not grasp that no one would mind if he loafed there all day. He picked up the few cigarette ends and reported back when he had done it.

It was not many months after his arrival at Frankley's that a pattern from his days at Foundlings repeated itself. Already he had passed the bower of artificials and smelt it with a kind of shock. Perhaps it was the intolerable and scentless extravagence of the flowers that made the girl inside so determined to smell sweet. Then, one morning he was told to bring a bundle of new flowers to Miss Aylen. He arrived at the bower, his arms full of the plastic roses on which it had not been thought necessary to imitate the thorns. He looked forward through a gap between his own roses, a leaf meanwhile interfering with his nose. He found that she had made a gap in the wall of the bower by shifting the rose already there from a shelf in front of him. For this reason he was not only able to see through his own roses but into the bower.

He was aware first of a shining thing like a curtain. The curtain was ogival at the top—for she had her back to him—spread very slightly all the way down until it passed out of sight. The scent she wore, obeying its own laws, came and went. She heard him and turned her head. He saw that this creature had a nose that curved out a very short way as if conferring the absolute right of impertinence on its owner, even though at that moment the curtain of hair was caught under it by the turn of her head. He saw also that the line of her forehead was delimited by a line of brow beyond mathematical computation and that under it again was a large, grey eye that fitted between long, black lashes. This eye noted the plastic roses; but she was engaged with a customer in the other direction and had time for no more than a monosyllable.

"Ta."

The empty shelf was under his elbow. He lowered the roses and they cocked up, hiding her from his view. His feet turned him and he went away. "Ta" spread, was more than a monosyllable, was at once soft and loud, explosive and of infinite duration. He came partly to himself near the smithy. Brilliantly he asked if there were more flowers to deliver but was not heard for he did not know how faint his voice had become.

Now he had a second preoccupation. The first, so unlike the second, was Mr Pedigree. When the Boy was sweeping clouds of dust in the loft and when his face had more anguish in its right, expressive side than the occasion would warrant, Mr Pedigree would be there in his mind. When his face contorted with sudden pain it was not the dust nor the splinters. It was the memory of the words screamed at him in the hall—"It's all your fault!" In one very private experience, he had seized a spike and stuck it clumsily into the back of the hand that held the broom. He had watched, a little paler perhaps, the blood turn into a long streak with a drop at the end—and all this because the soundless voice had screamed at him again. Now it seemed to him that this glimpse of part of a face, this fragrance, this hair, filled with a similar compulsion all the parts of his mind that the memory of Mr

44

Pedigree did not inhabit as of right. The two compulsions seemed to twist him inside, to lift him up against his own wishes and leave him with no defences and no remedy but simply to endure.

That morning he drifted away from the yard and climbed the stairs into the lofts. Familiarly he picked his way among packing-cases bursting with shavings, past piled paint, through a room where there was nothing but a set of rusting saws and a heap of hip baths stacked one inside the other, down through rows of identical paraffin lamps and into the long room for cutlery and glass. Here in the centre there was a great skylight of ridged glass that was supposed to let daylight down into the main show-room from a second skylight above it. Looking down, he could see the irradiated glow of coloured lights, could see them move among the ridges as he moved. He could see also, his heart quickening, a vague mass of colour down there that was the flower counter. He knew at once that he would never come this way again without a sideways and downward look at that blurred mixture. He went forward and into yet another loft, empty this one, then a step or two down some stairs. These led down the wall at the farthest point from where the yard was. He put a hand on the guard rail, bent down and peered along under the ceiling.

He could see the mass of artificial flowers but the opening where the customers were dealt with was to one side of him. He could see flowers on this side, and the roses he had stacked all too quickly on the other. All that was visible in the middle was the very top of a light brown head with a white, centre-parting down it. He saw that the only way to do better was to walk along the shop and glance sideways as he passed the bower. He did think for a moment to himself that if one were sufficiently knowing—like for example the blond Boy—one might stop and chat. His heart jumped at the thought and the impossibility of it. He went quickly therefore, but his feet seemed to get in his way as if he had too many of them. He passed a yard from the counter that was not stacked with flowers and looked sideways without moving his head as he passed. But Miss Aylen had bent down and the bower might have been empty for all he could see.

"Boy!"

He broke into a shambling trot.

"Where've you been, Boy?"

But they did not really want to know where he had been,

45

though they would have been amused and liked him better for it if they had known.

"The van's been waiting for about half an hour. Load her up!"

So he hauled the bundles into the van, bundles of metal flung shatteringly into the corner, put down half a dozen folding chairs and finally swung his clumsy body into the seat by the driver.

"What a lot of flowers we've got!"

Mr Parrish, the arthritic driver, groaned. Matty went on.

"They're just like real aren't they?"

"I never seen 'em. If you had my knees—"

"They're good, those flowers are."

Mr Parrish ignored him and set himself to the craft of van-driving. Matty's voice, practically of its own accord, went on speaking.

"They're pretty. Artificials I mean. And that girl, that young lady—"

The noises that Mr Parrish made dated from the days of his youth when he had driven one of Frankley's three horse-vans. He had been transferred to a motor van not many years after such an innovation became available and he took two things with him—his horse-van vocabulary and a belief that he had been promoted. There was no sign at first, therefore, that Mr Parrish had heard the Boy. He had heard everything the Boy said, however—was waiting for the right moment to wrap up his silence, roll it into a weapon and hit Matty over the head with it. He did so now.

"When you address me, my lad, you call me 'Mr Parrish'."

This may well have been the last time Matty ever tried to confide in anyone.

Later that day he was able to go once more through the lofts over the main shop. Once more he glanced sideways at the coloured blur in the ribbed skylight and once more he peered along under the ceiling. He saw nothing. When the shop closed he hurried to the empty pavement in front of it but saw no one. Next day at the same time he got there early, and was rewarded with an exhibition of light-brown hair with honey lights, the apparently naked crooks of knees and the gleam of two long, shining stockings as they disappeared from the platform of a bus to the interior. The next day was Saturday—a half-day—and he was kept busy all morning so that she had gone before he was free.

On Sunday he went automatically to morning service, ate the

large, plain dinner that was served in what Mr Arthur called the Refectory, then wandered out for the walk he was ordered to take for his health. The winged collars snoozed meanwhile on their beds. Matty went along, past GOODCHILD'S RARE BOOKS, past Sprawson's and turned right up the High Street. He was in a curious state. It was as if there was a high, singing note in the air from which he could not detach himself and which was the direct result of some interior strain, some anxiety that could—if you remembered this thing or that thing—sharpen into anguish. This feeling became so strong that he turned back to Frankley's as if sight of the place where one of his problems lay would help to solve it. But though he stood and looked it over, and the bookshop next to it and Sprawson's next to that, he was given no help. He went round the corner of Sprawson's to the Old Bridge over the canal and the iron loo at the root of the bridge flushed automatically as he passed. He stood, and looked down at the water of the canal in that age-old and unconscious belief that there is help and healing in the sight. He had a moment's idea of walking along the towpath, but it was muddy. He turned back, round the corner of Sprawson's, and there was the bookshop and Frankley's again. He stopped walking and looked in the window of the bookshop. The titles did not help him. The books were full of words, physical reduplication of that endless cackle of men.

Now some of the problem was coming into focus. It might be possible to go down into silence, sink down through all noises and all words, down through the words, the knives and swords such as *it's all your fault* and *ta* with a piercing sweetness, down, down into silence—

On the left in the window, below the rows of books (*With Rod and Gun*), was a small counter with a few items on it which were not in the strict canon of bookishness at all. Such was the alphabet and the Lord's Prayer in a hornbook. Such was the carefully mounted scrap of ancient music on parchment—music with square notes. Such was the glass ball that lay on a small stand of black wood just to the left of the old music. Matty looked at the glass ball with a touch of approval since it did not try to say anything and was not, like the huge books, a whole store of frozen speech. It contained nothing but the sun which shone in it, far away. He approved of the sun which said nothing but lay there, brighter and brighter and purer and purer. It began to blaze as when

47

clouds move aside. It moved as he moved but soon he did not move, could not move. It dominated without effort, a torch shone straight into his eyes, and he felt queer, not necessarily unpleasantly so but queer all the same—unusual. He was aware too of a sense of rightness and truth and silence. But this was what he later described to himself as a feeling of waters rising; and still later was described to him and for him by Edwin Bell as entering *a still dimension of otherness* in which things appeared or were shown to him.

He was shown the seamy side where the connections are. The whole cloth of what had seemed separate now appeared as the warp and woof from which events and people get their being. He saw Pedigree, his face contorted with accusation. He saw a fall of hair and a profile and he saw the balance in which they lay, the one the other. The face he had never fully seen of the girl among the artificials was there in front of him. He knew it familiarly but knew there was something wrong with the knowledge. Pedigree balanced it. There was everything right with this plain knowledge of Pedigree and his searing words.

Then all that was unspeakably hidden from him. Another dimension from low on his right to higher on his left became visible with huge letters written in gold. He saw that this was the bottom of the window of the bookshop and that it had GOODCHILD'S RARE BOOKS written in gold. He found that he himself was leaning to one side and, after all, the golden words were horizontal. The glass ball on its stand of black wood had retreated behind the condensation of his breath on the window. The sun no longer blazed in it. Confusedly he remembered that all that day there had been no sun but solid cloud from which rain pricked every now and then. He tried to remember what had happened, then found that as he remembered he changed what had happened. It was as if he laid colours and shapes over pictures and events; and this was not like crayoning in the spaces of a crayoning book where the lines are all set out but like wishing things and then seeing them happen; or even *having* to wish something and then seeing it happen.

After a while he turned away and began to walk aimlessly up the High Street. The rain prickled down and he hesitated then looked round him. His eye fell on the old church, half-way up the left-hand side of the street. He walked more quickly towards it, first thinking of shelter, then suddenly understanding that it was what he had to do. He opened the door, went in and sat right at the back under the west window. He pulled up his trouser-legs carefully and knelt down without really thinking what he was doing. There he was, almost without his volition, in the right attitude and place. It was Greenfield Parish Church, a huge place with side aisles and transept and full of the long, undistinguished history of the town. There was hardly a slab in the floor without an epitaph on it and not much more unlettered space on the walls. The church was quite empty and not merely of people. It seemed to him empty of the qualities that lay in the glass ball and had found some kind of response inside him. He could not make any connection and there was a lump in his throat too big to swallow. He began to say the Lord's Prayer then stopped, for the words seemed to mean nothing. He stayed there, kneeling, bewildered and sorrowful; and while he knelt the painful and extraordinary necessities of the artificials and the brown fall with the honey lights came flooding back.

*The daughters of men.*

He cried out silently to nowhere. Silence reverberated in silence.

Then a voice spoke, quite clearly.

"Who are you? What do you want?"

Now this was the voice of the curate who was clearing up certain things in the vestry. He had been submitting himself to an austerity of which his vicar knew nothing. He was surprised in this by the sound of a choir boy scrabbling at the vestry door and trying to get in to retrieve a comic he thought he had left. But the voice sounded right inside Matty's head. He answered it in the same place. Before the balance with its two scales, the one with a man's face, the other with a fire of anticipation and enticement, he had a time that was made of pure, whitehot anguish. It was the first exercise of his untried will. He knew, and it never occurred to him to doubt the knowledge, or worse, accept it and be proud of it, that he had chosen, not as a donkey between carrots of unequal size but rather as the awareness that suffered. The whitehot anguish continued to burn. In it was consumed a whole rising future that centred on the artificials and the hair, it had sunk away from the still-possible to the might-have-been. Because he had become aware he saw too how his unattractive appearance would have made an approach to the girl into a farce and humiliation; and thought, as he saw, that it would be so with any woman. He began to weep adult tears, wounded right in the centre of his nature, wept for a vanished prospect as he might have wept for a dead friend. He wept until he could weep no more and never knew what things had drained away from him with the tears. When he had done he found he was in a strange position. He was kneeling but his backside was touching the edge of a bench. His hands were grasping the top of a pew in front of him and his forehead lay on the little shelf where the prayer and hymn books were. As he opened his eyes and focused them he found he was staring down into the wetness of his own tears where they had fallen on stone and lay in the grooves of an ancient epitaph. He was back, in dull, grey daylight with the faint whisper of rain above him on the west window. He saw the impossibility of healing Pedigree. As for the hair—he knew that he must go away.

# CHAPTER FOUR

It was typical of Matty's jagged and passionate character that once he had decided to go away he should go as far as humanly possible. It was part of the strange way in which circumstances were apt to adjust themselves round him as he went—as if for all his jaggedness he was fitted for the journey with streamlined farings—that his way to Australia should be made easy. He met what seemed like compassionate officialdom where there might have been indifference; or perhaps it was that those who winced at the sight of his shrivelled ear speeded him out of their sight. It was no more than months before he found himself with a job, a church, a bed in the Y.M.C.A. in Melbourne. All three were waiting for him downtown in Fore Street by the London Hotel. The ironmonger's was not as large as Frankley's but there were storerooms overhead, packing-cases in the yard at the side and a machine shop to stand in for a forge. He might have stayed there for years—for a lifetime—if it had lived up to his innocent belief that by going far and fast he had outdistanced his troubles. But of course, Mr Pedigree's curse came with him. Moreover, either time or Australia or the two together quickly sharpened his vague feelings of bewilderment into downright astonishment; and this at last found words somewhere in his head.

"Who am I?"

To this, the only answer from inside him was something like: you came out of nowhere and that is where you are going. You have injured your only friend; and you must offer up marriage, sex, love, because, because, *because*! On a cooler view of the situation, no one would have you, anyway. That is who you are.

He was also someone who lacked more skin than he knew. When he had come at last to realize just how great an effort even the kindest people had to make not to be visibly affected by his appearance he ducked away from any intercourse he could. It was not just the unattainable creatures (and pausing for forty minutes at Singapore, that doll-like figure in its glittering clothes and standing submissively by the passenger lounge) but a minister and his kindly wife, and others. His Bible, on India paper and in squashy leather, gave him no help. Neither—though in his innocence he had thought it might—did his English voice and emergence from the Old Country. When they were assured that he did not think himself special and did not look down on Australia and did not expect preferential treatment, his work-mates were unkinder than they might have been through sheer annoyance at being wrong and missing a treat. Also there was a quite gratuitous confusion.

"I don't care what you're bleeding called. When I say 'Matey' I mean 'Matey'. My bleeding oath!"

—And turning to the Australian equivalent of Mr Parrish—

"Telling me how to speak the King's bleeding English!"

But Matty left the ironmonger's for a very simple reason. The first time he had to take some boxes of china to the Wedding Gifts Department he found it presided over and rendered unspeakably dangerous by a girl both pretty and painted. He saw at once that travel had not solved all his problems and he would have gone back to England there and then except that it was impossible. He did the best he could, which was to change jobs as soon as there was one to be had. He got work in a bookshop. Mr Sweet who ran it was too short-sighted and vague to grasp what a handicap Matty's face would be. When Mrs Sweet, who was not short-sighted or vague, saw Matty she knew why nobody browsed in the shop as they used. The Sweets, who were much richer than English booksellers would be, lived in a country house outside the city and soon Matty was established there, in a minute cottage that leaned against the main building. He was odd-job man; and when Mr Sweet had had him taught to drive, chauffeur between the house and the shop. Mrs Sweet, her face averted, pointed out that his hair would keep in place better if he wore a hat. Some deep awareness of self rather than awareness of identity made him choose a black one with a broad brim. It suited both the mournful, good side of his face, and the lighter, but contracted and more formidable left side where the mouth and eye were both pulled down. It lay so close to the purple knob of his ear that people seldom noticed his ear was anything out of the ordinary. Piece by piece—jacket, trousers, shoes, socks, roll-neck sweater, pull-over—he became the man in black, silent, distant, with the unsolved question waiting on him.

"Who am I?"

One day after he had taken Mrs Sweet to the shop and was waiting to bring her back, he stood by the tray of battered books that were displayed outside the shop and all at fifty cents or less. One seemed curious. It had wooden covers on either side and the back was so worn the title was illegible. Idly he picked it out and found it was an old Bible, heavier in wood than squashy leather, though the paper was much the same. He leafed through the familiar pages, stopped suddenly, turned back, then forwards, then back again. He bent his face nearer the page and began to mutter under his breath, a mutter that died away.

One of Matty's characteristics was a capacity for absolute inattention. Speech would wash over him without leaving a trace in his mind. It is likely that in the Australian churches he attended less and less—and in the English churches, and far back in class, at Foundlings—there was talk of the difficulty of moving from one language to another; but explanations must have failed before the present fact of black print on a white page. In the very middle of the twentieth century there was a kind of primitive grating between Matty and the easy world of his fellows that sorted out, it seemed, filtered out, ninety-nine per cent of what a man is supposed to absorb and gave the remaining one per cent the shiny hardness of stone. Now, therefore, he stood, the book in his hands, lifted his head from it and stared aghast through the bookshop.

*It's different!*

That night he sat at his table with both books before him and began to compare them, word by word. It was after one o'clock in the morning when he stood up and went out. He walked the straight and endless road up and down until the morning when it was time to drive Mr Sweet into the city. When he got back and put the car away it seemed to him that he had never heard before how the quality of bird-noise in the countryside was a kind of mad laughter. It disturbed him so much that he cut a lawn quite unnecessarily, to hide in the noise of the machine. When they heard the first whirr! the flock of sulphur-crested cockatoos that haunted the tall trees round the low house took off, crying and circling, then fled away across the sunburnt grass where the horses grazed—fled to and filled a solitary tree a mile off with their whiteness and movement and clamour.

That evening after high tea in the kitchen he took out his two books and opened them both at the title-page. He read each title-page several times. At last he sat back and shut his book of squashy leather. He took it, went out, across the nearer lawn and along through the vegetable garden. He came to the fence that lay between the garden and the way down to the pool where the yabbies swam. He looked at the miles of moonlit grass that swept away to where there were dim hills on the horizon.

He took out his Bible and began to tear the pages out, one by one. As he tore each, he let the breeze take it, fluttering from his hand to blow away turning over and over into the distance where it was hidden at last among the long grass. Then he went back to his cottage, read in the other Bible between wooden covers for a time, said his mechanical prayers, went to bed and to sleep.

That was the beginning of what was mostly a happy year for Matty. He had a time of conflict with himself when the new girl who served in the village store proved to be pretty; but she was so pretty that she quickly moved on to be replaced by one to whom he could be peacefully indifferent. Happily he moved round the grounds or through the house, his lips moving, the good side of his face as cheerful as one side of a face can be. He never took his hat off where other people could see him and this led to rumours in the village that he slept in it, which was not true. It was not the kind of hat he could sleep in, being broad-brimmed, as everyone knew very well; but the story suited him, matched his withdrawal. The early sun, and always the moon, would find him in his bed, the long smear of black hair lying all ways to one over the pillow, the white skin of his skull and left face disappearing and reappearing as he moved in his sleep. Then the first birds would jeer and he would jerk upright, to sink back for a few moments before he got out of bed. After the bog and the basin he would sit and read, in the book with the wooden covers, his mouth following the words, his good side frowning.

During the day his lips would continue to move, whether he was driving the rotavator through the dust of the vegetable patch, or laying out the hoses, or waiting at traffic lights, the engine idling, or carrying parcels or sweeping, dusting, polishing—

Sometimes Mrs Sweet was near enough to hear.

"—one silver charger of the weight of an hundred and thirty shekels, one silver bowl of seventy shekels, after the shekel of the sanctuary; both of them full of fine flour mingled with oil for a meat offering: 56 One golden spoon of ten shekels full of incense: 57 One young bullock, one ram, one lamb of the first year for a burnt offering: 58 One kid of the goats—"

Sometimes she would hear him in the house as his voice got louder and louder, stuck like a scratched gramophone record.

"21 And he said unto them—said unto them—said unto them—said unto them—"

Then she would hear a few quick steps and know that he had gone into his own place to look at the book lying open on the table. He would come back after a few moments; and through the rub and squeak of the window being polished she would hear him once more.

"said unto them Is a candle bought to be put under a bushel or under a bed? And not to be set on a candlestick?
22 For there is nothing hid, which shall not be manifested; neither was anything kept secret, but that it should come abroad.
23 If any man—"

A happy year, all things considered! Only there were things—as he said to himself once in a moment of quite brilliant and articulate explanation—there were things moving about under the surface. If things moved about *on* the surface there was something to be done. For example, there were explicit instructions as to conduct if a man should defile himself. But how if the thing that moves beneath the surface is not to be defined but stays there, a *must* without any instructions? *Must* drove him to things he could not explain but only accept as a bit of easing when to do nothing was intolerable. Such was the placing of stones in a pattern, the making of gestures over them. Such was the slow trickling of dust from the hand and the pouring of good water into a hole.

It was during this year that Matty ceased to go to a church which had made only perfunctory efforts to retain him. Ceasing to go to church was as much a *must* as the other gestures, and positive. Yet the change from that year to the next, which might have slipped by in the usual well-oiled manner leaving no trace anywhere but on the calendar, came to creak for Matty like a rusty hinge. Mrs Sweet's widowed sister came from Perth to spend the Christmas break and the New Year and brought her daughter. Sight of the girl with her fair hair and a skin to match sent Matty walking the road again until the small hours and it turned his eyes to the sky as if he might find some help there. Then lo! high in the sky he saw a familiar constellation. It was Orion the hunter, glittering, but with his dagger bursting fiery up. Matty's cry stirred the birds awake like a false dawn; and in the silence after they had settled again he understood the roundness of the earth and the terror of things hung in emptiness, the sun moving the witchway, the moon on its head; and when he added in the ease with which people lived in the midst of majesty and terror then the rusty hinge creaked round and the question which went with him always, changed and came clearer.

Not—who am I?

"*What* am I."

There on the open road in the small hours at New Year a few miles from the city of Melbourne he asked it aloud and stayed for an answer. It was silly, of course, like so much that he did. There was no one awake and up for miles; and when at last he turned away from the spot where he had cried out and then asked his question, though the sun was already lightening the hills on the horizon he still had no answer.

So the winter and the summer and the spring and the autumn were the second year only there wasn't any winter, not really, and not much spring. It was the time when the question seemed to get warmer and warmer under the surface of his mind and his feelings, and then hotter and hotter until he dreamed it night after night. Three nights running he dreamed that Mr Pedigree repeated his awful words and then asked for help. Only Matty was dumb three nights running, struggling under the bedsheet and in his mouth trying to explain—*How can I help until I know what I am?*

After that, when he woke up he found that saying his portion aloud was not the thing to do. It was bad enough having to talk or listen to talk when you had the question there all the time; and because he could not answer the question or know what it meant or how to ask it, certain consequences began to come clear in much

56

the way that the question itself had creaked into a new form. He saw that he must move; and he even had a time of wondering if this might not be the real reason why people moved, or wandered the way Abraham did. Certainly there was desert enough to hand if you drove a few miles, but whether consciously or not, no sooner did Matty understand that he must move, than he saw the necessity of moving *north* to where the fiery jet of Orion's dagger might lie at least more level. A man who moves because he cannot stand still needs a very small impulse to settle his direction. All the same he spent so much time hung up in the sheer impossibility of understanding anything that he had broken into his fourth Australian year before he did what he thought of as shaking the dust of Melbourne from his feet. Because he could not tell, really, why he went, nor what he hoped to find, he spent much time making small arrangements for simplifying life. With some of the wages he so seldom spent he bought a very small, very cheap and hence very old car. He had his Bible between its wooden covers, spare pants, spare shirt, shaving gear for the right-hand side of his face, a sleeping-bag and a spare sock. This was his most brilliant rationalization and he proposed to change one sock a day. Mr Sweet gave him some extra money and what used to be called a "character" which said he was hard-working, scrupulously honest and absolutely truthful. It is some indication of how unattractive these characteristics are when unsupported by anything else, that after Mrs Sweet had said goodbye to him she went into the kitchen and danced a few steps in sheer relief.

As for Matty, he drove off with what he felt was really sinful pleasure. The road led away over the known routes by which he had sometimes taken Mr and Mrs Sweet for Sunday drives but he knew there would come a moment when his wheels would take him away from the prints the Daimler might have left, into a new world. When it came, it was a moment, not so much of pleasure as of sheer delight—all the more sinful of course, since that was his nature.


Matty worked for more than a year after that for a fencing company near Sydney. It got him some more money and kept him away from people for most of the time. He would have left the company earlier only his small car broke down so badly it took him six months' extra work to pay for repairs and get on the road again. The question continued to burn and so did the weather as he moved on towards Queensland. Near Brisbane he needed another job and got it. But he kept it a shorter time than any other he had ever had, including the ironmonger's in Melbourne.

He started as a porter in a sweet factory which was small enough not to be mechanized; and what with the heat, for it was summer, and his appearance, the women swarmed all over the manager demanding his dismissal on the ground that he kept looking at them. In fact they kept looking at him and whispering "No wonder that lot of cream went sour," and so on. Matty, who must have thought himself invisible like an ostrich if he did not look at anybody, was called before the manager and in the process of being given his cards when the door opened and the owner of the factory rolled in. Mr Hanrahan was about half Matty's height and four times his width. His face was fat, with little, darting black eyes always on the watch for something in the corner or behind the door and when he heard why Matty was being dismissed, he looked sideways up into Matty's face, then round at his ear and after that all the way down to his feet and up again.

"And isn't he just the man we've been looking for?"

Matty felt his questions were about to be answered. But as it was, Mr Hanrahan led the way outside and told Matty to follow him up the hill. Matty got into his ancient car, Mr Hanrahan got into his new one and started it, then leapt out again, dashed back to the door, flung it open and stared into the office. He backed away slowly, closing it carefully but watching always, even through the last crack.

The road wound away from the factory through woods and fields and up, a zig-zag up the side of the hill. Mr Hanrahan's house hung on the hillside among strange trees that dripped with orchids and moss. Matty parked behind the new car and followed his new employer up an outside staircase to an enormous living-room that seemed to be walled completely with glass. On one side you could look right down the hill—and there was the factory, looking like an architect's model of itself. Directly he entered, Mr Hanrahan seized a pair of binoculars from the big table and levelled them at the model. He blew out his breath fiercely. He grabbed a phone and shouted into it.

"Molloy! Molloy! There's two girls skulking out at the back!"

But by the time he had said that, Matty was rapt, gazing at the glass on the three other walls. It was all mirror, even the backs of the doors, and it was not just plain mirrors, it distorted so that Matty saw himself half a dozen times, pulled out sideways and squashed down from above; and Mr Hanrahan was the shape of a sofa.

"Ha," said Mr Hanrahan. "You're admiring my bits of glass I see. Isn't that a good idea for a daily mortification of sinful pride? Mrs Hanrahan! Where are you?"

Mrs Hanrahan appeared as if materialized, for what with the window and the mirrors a door opening here or there was little more than a watery conflux of light. She was thinner than Matty, shorter than Mr Hanrahan and had an air of having been used up.

"What is it, Mr Hanrahan?"

"Here he is, I've found him!"

"Oh the poor man with his mended face!"

"I'll teach them, the awesome frivolity of it, wanting a man about the place! Girls! Come here, the lot of you!"

Then there was a watery conflux in various parts of the wall, some darkness and here and there a dazzle of light.

"My seven girls," cried Mr Hanrahan, counting them busily. "You wanted a man about the place did you? Too many females were there? Not a young man for a mile! I'll teach you! Here's the new man about the place! Take a good look at him!"

The girls had formed into a semicircle. There were the twins Francesca and Teresa, hardly out of the cradle, but pretty. Matty instinctively held his hand so that they should not be frightened by his left side which they could see. There was Bridget, rather taller and pretty and peering short-sightedly, and there was Bernadette who was taller and prettier and wholly nubile, and there was Cecilia who was shorter and just as pretty and nubiler if anything, and there was Gabriel Jane, turner-of-heads-in-the-street, and there was the firstborn, dressed for a barbecue, Mary Michael: and whoever looked on Mary Michael was lost.

Cecilia clasped her cheeks with her hands and uttered a faint shriek as her eyes adjusted to the light. Mary Michael turned her swan's neck to Mr Hanrahan and spoke enchanting words.

"Oh Dad!"

Then Matty gave a wild cry. He got the door open and he tumbled down the outside stairs. He leapt into his car and wrenched it round the curves down the hill. He began to recite in a high voice.

"The Revelation of St John the Divine. Chapter One. I. John writeth his revelation to the seven churches of Asia, signified by the seven golden candlesticks. 7 The coming of Christ. 14 His glorious power and majesty. The Revelation of Jesus Christ, which God gave unto him, to show unto his servants—"

So Matty went on, his voice high; and it lowered bit by bit and it was normal as ever it was by the time he had got to— "19 And if any man shall take away from the words of the book of this prophecy, God shall take away his part out of the book of life, and out of the holy city, and *from* the things which are written in this book."

With the "Amen" at the end he found he needed petrol which he got; and while waiting, a kind of after-image of Mary Michael came floating through his mind so he started off again at random, both on the road and in the book—

"22 And Kinah, and Dimonah, and Adadah.

23 And Kedesh and Hazor and Ithnan,

24 Ziph, and Telem, and Bealoth.

25 And Hazor, Hadattah, and Kerioth, *and* Hezron, which *is* Hazor.

26 Amam and Shema—"

And Matty came in the evening unto the city of Gladstone which is a great city. And he sojourned there for many months at peace, finding work as a grave-digger.

But the pattern repeated itself, the question returning and the restlessness and the need to move on to some place where all things would be made plain. So Matty began to think; or perhaps it would be better to say that something began to think itself in Matty and presented the result to him. Thus without his conscious volition he came across the thought; *Are all men like this?* Then there was added to that thought; *No. For the two sides of their face are equal.*

Then; *Am I only different from them in face?*

*No.*

"What am I?"

After that he prayed mechanically. It was strange about Matty. He could no more pray than he could fly. But now he added a bit in after the petitions for all the people he knew, to the effect that if

60

it was permissible he would be glad if his own particular difficulty could be made easier for him and directly following on that another thought performed itself in his mind, a quotation and a horrible one—*Some have made themselves eunuchs for the sake of the kingdom of God*. He had that thought in a grave, which was the best place for it. It got him out of the grave in a kind of instant resurrection and he was miles up the coast in a land of violent and wicked men before he could put the quotation out of his mind. The wicked men did it for him. He was stopped by police who searched him, and the car, and warned him that murder had been done on the road and would be done again, but he went on because he did not dare go back and there was nowhere else to go. He had looked at a map in a petrol station but his years in the land had not taught him the difference between a country and a continent. He went ignorantly expecting the journey to Darwin to be a few miles and with convenient petrol stations and stores for food and wells for water. He had no interest in acquiring knowledge and the Bible, though it was full of wildernesses and deserts, did not mention the incidence of wells and petrol stations in the outback. So he turned off what was already no major highway and he got thoroughly lost.

Matty was not frightened. It was not that he was brave. It was that he could not realize danger. He was not *able* to be frightened. So he lurched and bumped on, juddered and slid and thought he would like a drink but knew he had none, watched the needle of the fuel indicator drop lower and lower until at last it bounced on the pin, and still there was nothing but the merest track and then the car stopped. It did not do so dramatically or in a position of apparent drama. It stopped where scrubby thorns fledged a soil that looked rather like sand and where the only break in the prickly horizon was the low hump of three trees, not all together, but spaced all along on the north hand and seeming distant. Matty sat in the car for a long time. He saw the sun go down ahead of him and the sky was so cloudless that even down at the edge of it the sun mixed and clotted for a while among the thorns before it managed to lug itself down out of sight. He sat and listened to the noises of the night but by now they were familiar enough and even the thumping passage of a large animal among the thorns was not at all frightening. Matty composed himself in the driver's seat as if it were the proper place and went to sleep. He did not wake up until the dawn; and what woke him was not light, but thirst.

He could not be frightened; but he could be thirsty. He got out of the car into the chilly dawn and walked round as if he might come across a pool or a snack bar or a village store; and then, without any preparation or much thought he began to walk forward along the track. He did not look round until a strange warmness on his back made him turn and stare at the rising sun. There was no car under it, only scrub. He started to walk again. As the sun rose, so did his thirst.

The literature of survival had passed Matty by. He did not know about the plants that hold water in their tissues, nor about digging holes in the sand or watching the behaviour of birds; nor did he feel the excitement of adventure. He just felt thirsty with a burning back and the wooden covers of the Bible bouncing against his right hip-bone. It may not even have occurred to him that a man could walk and walk until he dropped and still not find water. So he went on in the same stubborn way that he had done everything all his life, even back at the beginning of it.

By midday strange things were happening to the bushes. They were floating about sometimes as if Mr Hanrahan had got them into his strange living-room. This interfered with Matty's view of the track or what he thought was the track and he stopped for a bit, looking down and blinking. There were large, black ants running round at his feet, ants that apparently found the heat encouraging and an incentive to work for they were carrying huge burdens as if about to achieve something. Matty considered them for a while but they had nothing to say to his condition. When he looked up again he could not see which way the track went. His own footprints were no help for they curved out of sight and the scrub lay all around. He examined the close horizon as carefully as he could and decided that in one direction there was a thickening of its texture or additional denseness and additional height. It might be trees, he thought; and with trees there would be shade so he decided to go in that direction if it lay anywhere in the sector to the west. But at midday, that near the equator, even with a sextant it is very difficult to take your bearing from the sun and all that happened was that Matty, looking up, took a step to the rear and fell flat on his back. The fall made him breathless and for a moment among the wheeling rays and flashes from the meridian there seemed to be a darkness, man-shaped and huge. He got to his feet and of course there was nothing, just the sun falling vertically so that when he got his hat on again the shadow of the brim lay on his feet. He found the direction of the thickening and tried to think whether it was the sensible direction or not but all that came into his mind was a stream of Biblical injunctions about the size of seas of brass. They set him seeing water in flashes and this got mixed into the mirrors in Mr Hanrahan's room and his own lips out there felt like two ridges of rock in a waste land. So then he was pushing through scrub that came up to his shoulders and beyond it was a tall tree full of angels. When they saw him they jeered and flew and circled and then streamed away through heaven so that he saw clearly that they meant him to follow and jeered because he could not fly. But he could still move his feet and he pushed on until he stood under the tree that held its leaves sideways to the sun and gave no shade and all there was round the tree was a little space of bare and sandy soil. He got his back against the trunk and winced at the pain for he was burnt through his jacket. Then there was a man standing at the edge of the bare sand and he was an Abo. He was the man, Matty saw, who had been there, up in the air and between him and the sun when he fell. Matty now had the chance to examine him all over and carefully. The man was not so tall, after all, really rather short. But he was thin and this seemed to make him taller. The long, wooden stick with the burnt black point which the Abo held upright in one hand was taller than either of them. The Abo, Matty saw, had a cloud in his face, which was reasonable enough, seeing how he had materialized in the air under the sun. He was bollock naked too.

Matty took a step away from the tree and spoke.

"Water."

The Abo came forward and peered into his face. He jerked his chin up and spoke in his language. He gestured hugely with the spear, tracing out a great arc in the sky, which included the sun.

"Water!"

Now Matty pointed into the cloud that hid the Abo's mouth, then into his own mouth. The Abo gestured with his spear towards the densest of the scrub. Then he took out of the air a small, polished stone. He squatted, put it down on the sandy soil and muttered to it.

Matty was appalled. He scrabbled his Bible out of his pocket and held it over the stone but the Abo went on muttering. Matty cried out again.

"No, no!"

The Abo looked impenetrably at the book. Matty thrust it back into his pocket.

"Look!"

He scuffed a line in the sand and then another that crossed the first. The Abo stared at it but said nothing.

"Look!"

Matty flung himself down. He lay, his legs stretched down the first line, his arms held wide on either side along the second. The Abo at once leapt to his feet. The cloud in his face was split by a wide flash of white.

"Fucking big sky-fella him b'long Jesus Christ!"

He leapt into the air and landed with a foot on either outstretched arm, a foot in the crook of either elbow. He stabbed down on this side and that with his fire-hardened spear into the open palm. He jumped back high, and he landed with both feet in Matty's groin and the sky went black and the Abo disappeared into it. Matty rolled up like a leaf, like a cut worm, screwed his body up and the waves of sickness increased like the pain until they carried his consciousness away.

When he came to he knew he was badly swelled up so he tried to move on hands and knees but the sickness swamped him again. So it being his nature, he got upright with the world reeling and he kept his legs apart and his belly dragged so that he held himself in with both hands so as not to lose anything down there. He went towards the place where he seemed to remember there had been some thickness beyond the scrub. But when he was through the thickness he came into an open space with trees a little further off. In the open space and stretching all along from as far that way to out of sight on this was an electrified fence. He turned, mechanically, to go along it but a car hooted behind him. He stood still, humbly and dumbly and the car was a Land Rover that came by his left shoulder slowly then stopped. A man got out and came across. He wore an open-necked shirt and jeans and a digger's hat turned up at the side. He peered into Matty's face and Matty waited like an animal not being able now, to do anything else.

64

"My oath. Been done have you? Where's your cobber? Mate? Matey?"

"Water."

The man manoeuvred him gently towards the Land Rover, hissing between his teeth now and then as if Matty were a horse.

"You have been done my old son oh dear oh dear. What *has* been at you? Gone ten rounds with a roo? Drink this. Easy!"

"Crucified—"

"Where's your oppo?"

"Abo."

"You seen an Abo? Crucified? Here. Show us your hands. That's no more than scratches."

"A spear."

"Little thin man? With a little fat woman expecting and two nippers? That'll be Harry Bummer. The bleeding sod. I expect he let on he didn't know English didn't he? Moved his head like this, didn't he?"

"Just one Abo."

"They'll have been grub-hunting likely, the others I mean. He's never been the same since they made that film about him. Tries it on all the tourists. Now let's have a gander at your doolies mate. You're in luck. I'm the vet, see? What about your chum?"

"Alone."

"Oh my word. You been in there by yourself? You could go round and round in there you know, just round and round. Now careful, easy does it, can you lift up? Let me get my arm under and then pull your pants down. Oh my word as we say in Aussieland. If you was a bullcalf I'd say someone hadn't done a neat job. Oh dear. We'll put 'em in a sling. Of course in my line of business I'm generally moving in the other direction if you follow me."

"Car. Hat."

"All in good time. Let's hope Harry Bummer doesn't find it first, the ungrateful sod. After all the education he's had. Keep 'em wide apart. I expect after all they'll find he hasn't spoilt your chances, ruined the family jewels, clumsy it was. I've often looked at a bullock and wondered what he'd say to me if he could. What's this in your pocket? Oh, a preacher are you? No wonder old Harry—Now you lie still. Try to brace yourself with your hands. It'll jolt a bit but we can't help that and the hospital isn't far, not really. Didn't you know? You were nearly in the suburbs. You didn't think you were really in the outback did you?"

He started the engine and moved the Land Rover. Very soon Matty lost consciousness again. The vet, looking back at him and seeing that he had passed out, put his foot down and bumped and slewed through the sandy soil and on to the side road. As he went he talked to himself.

"Got to tell the police I suppose. More bleeding trouble. Not that they'll catch old Harry. He'll have an alibi with a dozen of them. This poor Pom could never tell them apart."

# CHAPTER FIVE

Matty came to in hospital. His legs were strung up and he had no pain. There was pain later on but nothing his stubborn soul could not cope with. Harry Bummer—if it had been he—never found the car, which was brought in for Matty with his spare shirt, pants and third sock. His wooden Bible lay on the night table by the bed and he went on learning his portions from it. He had a period of fever when he mouthed inarticulately, but when his temperature was normal he fell silent again. He was calm, too. The nurses who attended to him so intimately found his calmness unnatural. He lay, they said, like a log and no matter how sordid the necessity he submitted to it with a still face and said nothing. The ward sister at one point gave him an aerosol to keep his privates cool, explaining delicately why it was touch and go with some vessels, but he never used it. At last his legs were cut down and he was allowed to sit out, be wheeled out, to limp out with sticks and finally to walk. His face had acquired an immobility in hospital on which the disfigurements seemed painted. From long stillness his move-ments had become more deliberate. He no longer had a limp, but he did walk with his legs kept slightly apart as if he were a freed prisoner whose body had not yet rid itself of the memory of chains. He was shown photographs of various Abos, but after a dozen, he spoke the great Caucasian sentence.

"They all look the same to me."

It was the longest sentence he had spoken for years.

His adventure was publicized and a collection taken up so that he had some money. People thought he was a preacher. Yet those who got in touch with him were baffled by a man of so few words, so awful and grave a face yet who did not seem to have opinions or a purpose. Yet still inside him the question pressed, altering now and becoming more urgent. It had been *who I*, then become *what am I*; and now through the force of his crucifarce or crucifiction by the black man leaping on him out of the sky it changed again and was a burning question.

*What am I for?*

So he moved round the curious tropical city. Where he walked now, clad in black and with a face that might have been cut out of particoloured wood, the old men sitting on the iron seats under the orange trees fell silent until he had passed towards the other end of the park.

Convalescing, Matty wandered round and round. He sampled the few chapels and those who moved towards him to ask him to take off his hat, came close, saw what they saw and went away again. When he could walk as far as he liked he would go and watch the Abos in their lean-tos and shacks round the edge of the city. Most of the time their actions were only too easily to be understood; but now and then they would do something, no more than a gesture, it may be, that seemed to interest Matty profoundly, though he could not tell why. Once or twice it was a whole mime that absorbed him—a game perhaps with a few sticks, or the throwing of pebbles with marks on them, then the absorbed contemplation of the result—the breathing, the blowing, the constant blowing—

The second time he saw an Abo throw the pebbles, Matty hurried back to the room he had been found in the Temperance Hotel. He went straight through into the yard and picked up three pebbles and held them—

Then stopped.

Matty stood for half-an-hour, without moving.

Then he laid the pebbles down again. He went to his room, took out his Bible and consulted it. Then he went to the State House but could not get in. Next morning he tried again. He got no further than the polished wooden information desk where he was received courteously but got no understanding. So he went away, bought matchboxes and then was to be seen, day after day, arranging them before the door of the State House, higher and higher. Sometimes he would get them more than a foot high, but they always fell down again. He gathered groups for the first time in his life, children and layabouts and sometimes officials who stopped on their way in or out. Then the police moved him away from the door out on to the lawns and flowerbeds; and there, perhaps because he had moved away from officialdom, people and children laughed at him louder. He would kneel and build his tower out of matchboxes; and sometimes, now, he would blow at them like an Abo blowing on the pebbles and they would all fall down. This made people laugh and that made children laugh; and now and then a child would dart forward while the tower was abuilding and blow it down and everyone would laugh and sometimes a naughty boy would dart forward and kick it over and people would laugh but also cry out and object in a friendly manner since they were on Matty's side and hoped one day he would manage to get all the matchboxes balanced one on the other since that seemed to be what he wanted. So if a naughty, energetic boy—but they were all naughty, energetic boys and quite capable of saying "Go up Baldhead!" except that they did not know what was under the hat and there are no bears in the Northern Territory—kicked, struck, spat, jumped and knocked the matchboxes over, all the grown-ups would cry out, laughing, shocked, nice women out to do the shopping, and pensioners, cry out—"Oh no! The little bastard!"

Then the man in black would move back on his knees and sit on his upturned heels and he would look round slowly, round under the brim of his black hat sweeping round at the laughing people; and because his face like particoloured wood was inscrutable and solemn, they would fall silent, one by one on the, by now, watered grass.

After seven days Matty added to his game. He bought a clay pot and gathered twigs; and this time when everyone started laughing at his matchboxes, Matty put the twigs together with the pot on top and tried to light them with the matches but could not. Crouched down in black by his twigs and pot and matchboxes he looked silly and a naughty boy kicked his pot over and all the grown-ups cried out "Oh no! You little sod! That's *reely* naughty! You might have broke it!"

Then, as Matty gathered his matchboxes and twigs and pot together, everyone drifted away. Matty went away too, watched absently by a park-keeper.

The next day, Matty had moved out to where the twigs would not be damp from the water that the automatic jets sprinkled on the grass lawns by the State House. He found a kerb near the central parking lots, a kind of nonplace with rank grass and seeding flowers, rank under the vertical sun. Here it took him a little longer to gather a group. In fact he was an hour at his building and might have got his matchboxes all vertically arranged the way any game of patience will come out at last given enough time but there was a little wind and he could never get more than eight or nine on top of the other before they fell over. However, at last the children came and stopped and then the adults and he got his attention and his laughter and a naughty boy and "Oh no, the wicked little sod!" So then he was able to lay his twigs and put the pot on top and strike a match and light the twigs and he got more laughter and then applause as if he was a clown who had suddenly done something clever; and through the laughter and the applause you could hear the crackling of the twigs under the pot and the twigs blazed and grass blazed and the flower seeds went bang, bang, bang and a great flame licked across the wasteland and there were shrieks and screams and people beating each other out and the children and people scattering and the screech of brakes as they ran into the road and the crash as cars shunted each other and cries and curses.

"You know," said the secretary, "you mustn't do it."

The secretary had a thatch of silver hair that was as carefully arranged, as carefully wrought as a silver vessel. He had the same accent, Matty could hear, as old Mr Pedigree had had all those years ago. He spoke mildly.

"Will you promise me not to do it again?"

Matty said nothing. The secretary leafed through some papers.

"Mrs Robora, Mrs Bowery, Mrs Cruden, Miss Borrowdale, Mr Levinsky, Mr Wyman, Mr Mendoza, Mr Buonarotti—an artist do you think?—You see when you singe as many people as that—and they are very, very angry—oh no! You really must not do it again!"

He put the paper down, laid a silver pencil on it and looked across at Matty.

"You're wrong, you know. I believe your sort of person always has been. No, I don't mean in the, the content of the message. We know the state of things, the dangers, the folly of taking a meteorological gamble; but we are elected you see. No. You are wrong in supposing that people can't read your message, translate your language. Of course we can. The irony is—the irony always was—that predictions of calamity have always been understood by the informed, the educated. They have not been understood by the very people who suffer most from them—the humble and meek—in fact, the ignorant who are helpless. Do you see? All Pharaoh's army—and earlier than that the firstborn of all those ignorant fellahin—"

He got up and went to the window. He stood looking out of it, his hands clasped behind his back.

"The whirlwind won't fall on government. Trust me. Neither will the bomb."

Still Matty said nothing.

"What part of England do you come from? The south, surely. London? I think you would be wise to return to your own country. I can understand that you won't stop what you are doing. They never do. Yes. You had better go back. After all—" and he swung round suddenly—"that place needs your language more than this one."

"I want to go back."

The secretary sank easily into his chair.

"I'm *so* pleased! You are not really—You know, we felt what with that most unfortunate episode with the native, the Aborigine—did you know they *insist* on being called Aboriginals as if they were adjectives?—but we did feel that perhaps we owed you something—"

He leaned forward over his clasped hands.

"—And before we part—tell me. Do you have some kind of, of perception, some extra-sensory perception, some second sight—in a word, do you—*see*?"

Matty looked at him, mouth shut like a trap. The secretary blinked.

"I only mean, my dear fellow, this information you feel called on to press on an unheeding world—"

For a moment or two Matty said nothing. Then slowly at first but at the last with a kind of jerk, he got himself upright on the other side of the desk and stared not at the secretary but over him out of the window. He convulsed but made no sound. He clenched his fists up by his chest and the words burst out of his twisted lips, two golfballs.

"I feel!"

Then he turned away, went out through one office after another

71

and into the marbled hall then down the steps and away. He made some strange purchases and one, a map, that was not so strange and he put everything he had into his ancient car, and the city knew him no more. Indeed Australia knew him no more as far as eccentricity is concerned. For the short remainder of his stay he was noticed for nothing but his black clothes, and forbidding face. Yet if human beings had little more to do with him in Australia there were other creatures that had. He drove for many miles with his curious purchases and he seemed to be looking for something big rather than small. He wanted, it seems, to be low down and he wanted to find some water to be low down with and he wanted a hot and fetid place to go with it all. These things are specific and to be found together in known places but it is very difficult most of the time to get close to them by car. For this reason Matty took a winding course in strange places and often enough had to sleep in his car. He found hamlets of three decaying houses with the corrugated iron of their roofs grinding and clanking in a hot wind, and not a tree for miles. He passed by other places of Palladian architecture set among monstrous trees where the red galahs squawked and lilies loaded the tended pools. He passed men riding round and round in little traps drawn by horses with a delicate high step. At last he found what no one else would want, looked at it in the bright sunlight—though even at noon the sun could scarcely pierce through to the water—and he watched, perhaps with a tremor that never reached the outside of his face, the loglike creatures that slipped one after another out of sight. Then he went away again to find high ground and wait. He read in his Bible with the wooden covers and now, for the rest of the day he trembled slightly and looked closely at familiar things as if there was something in them that would bring comfort. Mostly of course he looked at his Bible, seeing it as if he had not looked at it before and noticing for what that was worth how the wood of the cover was boxwood and he wondered why and thought aimlessly it might be for protection which was strange because surely the Word did not need it. He sat there for many hours while the sun took its wonted way over the sky and then sank and the stars came.

The place he had looked at now became additionally strange in the darkness which was thick as the darkness an old-time photographer thrust his head into under the velvet. Yet every other sense would have been well enough supplied with evidence. Human feet would have felt the soft and glutinous texture, half water half mud, that would rise swiftly to the ankles and farther, pressed out on every side with never a stone or splinter. The nose would have taken all the evidence of vegetable and animal decay, while the mouth and skin—for in these circumstances it is as if the skin can taste—would have tasted an air so warm and heavy with water it would have seemed as if there was doubt as to whether the whole body stood or swam or floated. The ears would be filled with the thunder of the frogs and the anguish of nightbirds; and they would feel too, the brushing of wings, antennae, limbs, to go with the whining and buzzing that showed the air too was full of life.

Then, accustomed to the darkness by a long enough stay and willing—it would have to be by sacrifice of life and limb—to trade everything for the sight, the eyes would find what evidence there was for them too. It might be a faint phosphorescence round the fungi on the trunks of trees that had fallen and were not so much rotting as melting away, or the occasional more lambent blueness where the flames of marsh gas wandered among reeds and floating islands of plants that lived as much on insects as on soupy water. Sometimes and suddenly as if they were switched on, the lights would be more spectacular still—a swift flight of sparks flashing between tree trunks, dancing, turning into a cloud of fire that twisted in on itself, broke, became a streamer leading away which incomprehensibly switched itself off to leave the place even darker than before. Then perhaps with a sigh like a sleeper turning over, a big thing would move washily in the unseen water and loiter a little further away. By then, feet that had stayed that long would have sunk deep, the mud moving to this side and that, the warm mud; and the leeches would have attached themselves down there in an even darker darkness, a more secret secrecy and with unconscious ingenuity, without allowing their presence to be felt would have begun to feed through the vulnerable skin.

But there was no man in that place; and it seemed impossible to one who had inspected it from far off and in daylight that there ever had been a man in the place since men began. The sparks of flying life came back as if they were being chased. They fled in a long streamer.

A little while later the reason for this flight in one direction was evident. A light, and then two lights, were moving steadily behind the nearer forest. It showed treetrunks, hanging leaves, moss, broken branches in silhouette, lighting them and bringing them into a brief local visibility so that sometimes they seemed like coals or wood in a fire, black at first, then burning, then consumed as the twin sidelights wound onward through the forest to the marsh, each light bringing with it a dancing cloud of flying things, papery and whiteish. The old car—and now its engine had warned away everything but the flying creatures so that even the frogs had fallen silent and dived—stopped two trees away from the mysterious darkness of the water. The car stopped, the engine died, the two sidelights faded just a little but were still bright enough to light up the flying things and a yard or two of mould on this side of what must have been a track.

The driver sat for a while without moving; but just when the car had been silent and motionless long enough for the noises of the place to begin again, he jerked open the right-hand door and got out. He went to the boot, opened that and brought out a number of objects that clanked. He left the boot open, came back to the driver's seat and stood for a while, staring towards the invisible water. After he had done that, he became suddenly busy and incomprehensible. For he was pulling off his clothes so that his body appeared in reflected light from the sidelights, thin and pale, and to be investigated at once by some of the papery flying things and a great many of those that hummed or whined. Now he brought a curious object from the boot, knelt down in the mould and began, it would seem, to take the object apart. Glass clinked. The man struck a match, brighter than sidelights, and what he was doing—but there was no one to see—became comprehensible. He had on the ground before him a lamp, an antique practically, he had the globe and the chimney off and he was lighting the wick and the papery things whirled and danced and flared and were consumed or crawled away half burnt. The man turned the wick right down, then put on the tall funnel and the glass globe. After that, when he was sure the lamp stood straight and safe in the mould, he turned to the first set of objects. He worked at them and they clanked and everything was inscrutable except inside of the man's head where his purpose was. He stood up, no longer quite naked. There was a chain round his waist and on this chain, heavy steel wheels were slung; one, and that the one of greatest weight,

74

lay over his loins so that he was absurd but decent even when nothing could see him but the natural creatures that did not matter. Now he bent down again but for a moment had to steady himself by clutching at the door of the car because the heavy wheels made kneeling straight down a very difficult business. But at last he was there, kneeling, and slowly he turned up the wick; and now the white globe of the lamp took over from the sidelights and the trees and the undersides of the leaves. The mould and moss and mud came solid like things that would still be there in daylight and the white, papery things went crazy round the white globe and across the gleaming water, so flat, so still, a frog stared at the light through two diamonds. The man's face was close to the white globe and it was not the light that made a difference on this left side where the eye was half closed and the corner of the mouth twisted.

Now he lifted the lamp and got himself up, slowly, by holding onto the door. He got upright, with the clanking wheels round his waist and the lamp, now held high, the foot of it even, above his head. He turned and walked slowly, deliberately, towards the water. Now the mud did feel human feet, the warm mud moving away to this side and that as this foot pressed and sank and then that foot. The man's face was additionally contorted now as if with unutterable pain. His eyes flickered shut and open, his teeth gleamed and gritted, the lamp shook. He walked in, his feet went, his calves, his knees, strange creatures touched him underwater or snaked away over the rippled surface and still he went, down and in. The water rose past his waist and to his chest. The frog broke out of the hypnosis of the light and dived. The water at past this midpoint of the pool was at the man's chin; and then suddenly, higher. The man floundered and the water washed. For a yard it may be, he was out of sight and there was nothing to be seen by whatever was watching but an arm and hand and the old lamp with its bright white globe and the dancing crazy creatures. Then black hair floated wide on the water. Down there underneath he was thrusting strongly into the ooze with his feet and he got his head up and grabbed a breath. After that he rose steadily towards the other side and the water ran from him and from his hair and his wheels; but not from the lamp. Now he stood; and though the air was hot and the water steamed he began to shudder, shudder deeply, convulsively, so that he had to hold the lamp with both

75

hands to keep it upright and from falling in the mud. As if this shuddering was some kind of sign, thirty yards away across the water, a huge lizard turned and loitered off into the darkness.

The man shuddered less and less. When he was no more than trembling he picked his way round the pool and back to the car. It was all solemnity and method. He held the lighted lamp up carefully, heaved it four times at four points of the compass. Then he turned down the wick and blew it out. The world returned to what it had been. The man loaded the lamp and the wheels and the chain into the boot. He dressed. He arranged his curious hair and set his hat firmly on it. He was quiet now, and a drift of fireflies came back and danced over the faint gleam of the water each to its own image. The man got into the driver's seat. He pressed the starter and had to do it three times. It was perhaps the strangest noise of all in that wilderness, the suburban sound of the starter and then the engine catching. He drove slowly away.

Matty set out, not by air, though he could just about have afforded the cheapest one-way fare, but by sea. It may be that the air was too presumptuous and high for him; or it may be that hidden away at the back of his mind was not the sight of the dollgirl in Singapore with her glittering clothes, but just an unease over the whole question of Singapore Airport, a gleaming Wickedness detached from any substance. For certainly he now moved easily among women as among men, looked and was struck no more by the one than the other, and would not have avoided the Wanton with her cup of abominations in fear for his peace of mind or virtue.

He gave his car away but took what other few things he had. He tried to ship as a seaman; but there was no place for a man of his age whatever it was, who was skilled in odd-jobbing, sweet-packing, grave-digging, car-driving in difficult circumstances and, pre-eminently, in Bible-studies. Nor did it matter that he had testimonials from many kinds of people, all of whom wrote of his probity, reliability, honesty, fidelity, assiduity (Mr Sweet), discretion, without mentioning that they had found these qualities really rather repulsive.

So he went at last to the docks with his small suitcase which contained the shaving material for the right side of the face, one spare pair of pants, one spare shirt, one spare black sock, one flannel, one bar of soap. He stood for a while looking up at the side of the ship. At last he looked down at his feet and appeared to be lost in thought. At last he lifted the left foot and shook it three times. He put it down. He lifted his right foot and shook it three times. He put it down. He turned round and looked at the port buildings and the low line of hills that was all a continent could muster from its inside to bid him farewell. He seemed, or would have seemed, to look through those hills at the thousands of miles over which he had travelled and at the hundreds of people that for all his care he had, if not met, at least, seen. He stared round the quay. In the lee of a bollard there was a pile of dust. He went to it quickly, bent down, took a handful and strewed it over his shoes.

He climbed the ladder, away from the many years he had spent in Australia, and was shown the place he had to sleep in with eleven others, though none of them had arrived. After he had stowed his one suitcase he went back up again to the deck and stood again, still, silent and staring at the continent he knew he was seeing for the last time. A single drop of water rolled out of his good eye, found a quick way down his cheek and fell on the deck. His mouth was making little movements, but he said nothing.

# CHAPTER SIX

While Matty was in Australia Mr Pedigree came out of jail and was cherished by a number of societies. He had a little money coming to him from his mother's will, for that ancient lady had died while he was still inside. It gave him, not so much freedom, as a degree of mobility. He was able therefore to break away from those who were trying hopelessly to help him and made for central London. He very soon went straight back to jail. The next time he came out he had aged many more years than the period of his sentence for his fellows had, as he said to himself, weeping with self-pity, *cottoned on*. He had never had any spare flesh and now a little of what he could not well spare was worn away. He was lined, too, and bent and there was no doubt about the grey that was spreading through the faded straw of his hair. He had sat to begin with on a bench in a London terminus and had it up-ended under him by the police at one o'clock in the morning and it may be that this experience removed any magnetism there was in London, for from that time he worked his way to Greenfield. That was, after all, where Henderson had been; in death Henderson had been subsumed into Mr Pedigree's mind as the desired perfection. He found that there was a hostel in Greenfield that he had never known of before—would not have had to know of before. It was heartlessly clean and the large rooms were divided into separate cubicles, each with a narrow bed, a table and chair. Here he lived and from here he made his expeditions: one to the school where he gazed through the gate and saw the place where Henderson had fallen and the fire-escape above it and the edge of the leaded roof. There was no reason in law why he should not go closer; but he had joined or was in the process of joining the wall-creepers, men of decayed appearance who keep a wall at their side so as to be sure there is at least one direction from which trouble will not come. He was now the sort of man whom a policeman feels in his bones should be moved on; and consequently he began to feel himself that he ought to be moved on and whenever he saw a policeman, moved himself on or sideways round a corner as soon as possible.

Yet he still had his little income and except for his compulsion—which in many countries would not have got him into trouble—he was without vice. He had next to nothing and lived on it without feeling any hardship. He owned what he stood up in. His Victorian paperweights had gone, sold alas before the market blew up, and his few netsukes—though they had fetched more—all gone except one. This was a netsuke he called his lucky charm and kept in his pocket so that it was always there to be fingered, smooth ivory, the whole thing no larger than a button which of course it really was, the two boys merging so excitedly and excitingly. Sometimes the netsuke burned his fingers. It was after one of these burnings that he made what was now becoming one of his regular trips to jail. This time the possibility of an operation was put to him; at which he began to scream on and on, piercingly and mindlessly, so that even the Home Office psychiatrist gave up. When he came out he went back to Greenfield again; and it was as if his brain had now settled into simple patterns, rituals both of action and belief. On the first day of his arrival he came down the High Street, noting as he did so how there were more and more coloured people about. He crept down until he found himself facing the front of Sprawson's with the bookshop and Frankley's on one side of it and the Old Bridge humped up on the other. There was an antique public lavatory on the root of the bridge this side. It was a cast-iron structure, pictorially impressive, not so much stinking as smelly and not so much dirty as with the appearance of dirt (that black creosote) rather than the substance. Here, too, by a technological marvel of the eighteen-sixties the cistern filled and flushed, filled and flushed night and day, sure as the stars or the tides. It was the scene of the moderate triumph that had sent Mr Pedigree back to jail on the last occasion; but he did not return solely with a rational hope or desire. He came back because he had been there before.

He was developing. Over the years he had moved from a generous delight in the sexual aura of youth to an appreciation of all the excitement attendant on breaking taboos if the result was

79

sufficiently squalid. There were public lavatories in the park of course, and more by the central car stack, there were some in the market—oh there were public lavatories dotted round the place, far more of them than anyone without Mr Pedigree's specialized knowledge would guess. With school barred for ever, they were the next step in some direction or other. He was now about to leave the protection of the wall at the end of Sprawson's when he saw a man come out of the house and walk up the street. Mr Pedigree peered after him, then looked back at the urinal, then back at the receding man. He made up his mind and loped, bending and swaying up the High Street. As he went he straightened up. He passed the man and turned.

"Bell, isn't it? Edwin Bell? Aren't you left from my time? Bell?"

Bell faltered to a stop. He gave a kind of high whinny.

"Who? Who?"

The years, all the seventeen of them, had made a great deal less difference to Bell than to Pedigree. Though Bell had also had his troubles, they had not included the awful problem of putting-on weight. He had kept, too, the singular garb of an undergraduate of the late thirties, all except the Bags, and there was about him, the carriage of his snub nose, the tiny evidence of authority exercised and assertion without contradiction.

"Pedigree. Of course you remember me! Sebastian Pedigree. Don't you remember?"

Bell jerked upright. He drove his fists deep into his overcoat pockets, then brought them together in panic in front of his privates. He gave a kind of wail.

"Hu—llo! I—"

And fists driven deep, nose up, mouth open, Bell began to tiptoe, as if by this simple tactic he could lift himself above his embarrassment; and so doing was nevertheless reminded that to pass by on the other side was not the action of a liberal person and therefore he came down again which made him stagger.

"Pedigree, my dear fellow!"

"I've been away you see, rather lost touch. Retired and thought—oh yes, I thought I might as well look up—"

Now they were facing each other, the crowd in its many colours moving round them. Bell stared down into the old man's face, the lined and silly mask that looked up at him so anxiously.

"I might look up the old school," said the lined face sillily and

80

piteously. "I thought you'd be the only one left from my time. Henderson's time it was—"

"Oh I say, Pedigree—you—I'm married you see—"

Insanely he began to ask Pedigree if he was married too and then managed to stop himself. Pedigree never noticed.

"I just thought I'd look up the old school—"

And there, floating in the air between them was the quite clear and specific knowledge that if Sebastian Pedigree put his foot inside the school buildings he would be taken up for loitering with intent; and the equally clear and specific knowledge that if Edwin Bell took him in arm-in-arm the law would stand back for the time being and it wasn't worth it for either of them only Pedigree would think it was; and taking Pedigree in was what a saint would do probably, or Jesus or maybe Gautama and certainly Mahomet, let's not think of Mahomet in this instance as it will get me into deep waters and *Christ* how am I going to get rid of him?

"So if you were going that way—"

Edwin jerked up on his toes again. He struck his buried fists together convulsively.

"Oh bother! I've just remembered! My, my—I must go back at once. Look Pedigree—"

And now he had turned, striking a vivid coloured female with his shoulder.

"—I'm so sorry, so sorry, so clumsy! Look Pedigree, I'll keep in touch."

He turned to tiptoe down the street and knew without looking that Pedigree was coming after him. So then there was a kind of confused charade in which Edwin Bell, his privates still concealed by fists as well as clothes, ducked and wove through the saried marketeers, followed as closely as possible by Pedigree while both of them talked at once as if silence would allow something else to be heard, something deadly. It turned in the end—when they had reached Sprawson's and there was a clear danger of Pedigree coming right upstairs, past the solicitor's office, right up to the flat—into a naked avowal, a terrified prohibition from Edwin Bell, hands out, palms facing outward and his voice high—

"No, no, *no!*"

He broke away as if there was a physical bond between them and fled away up the stairs, leaving Pedigree alone in the hall and still talking about the possibility of coming back to the school and about Henderson as if the boy were still there. Then, when Pedigree stopped he became aware of where he found himself, in a private building with that glass door there leading down to the garden, stairs leading up both sides, and doors, one at least for a firm of solicitors. So Mr Pedigree became once more a wall-creeper, moving out and down two steps to the stone pavement in front of Sprawson's. Then he hurried across the street to the comparative safety of shop fronts and looked back. He glimpsed Edwin's face at an upper window with Edwina's beside it and then the curtain hurriedly pulled back.

It was thus that Mr Pedigree on his return became a problem not merely to the police who knew something about him, if not all, not merely to the park-keeper and the young man in a grey raincoat whose duty it was to head off the likes of Mr Pedigree, but precisely to Edwin Bell, the only man left from the old times in Greenfield. The process by which Mr Pedigree felt himself connected to Bell defied reason. Perhaps he needed a link with what passed for normality, since now his rituals began, bit by bit, to consume him. Thus, after leaving Bell, or rather after Bell left him, Mr Pedigree went towards the seductive urinal on the Old Bridge and would have gone in but a police car shoved its nose over the crest of the bridge and he went nimbly for his age down the steps and sheltered on the towpath under the bridge as if from rain. He even held out a palm in a dramatic gesture, then examined it for possible drops of water before walking away along the towpath. He did not want to walk along the towpath but he was facing in that direction and the police car had made the road behind him painful. So Mr Pedigree went widdershins round a circle that was in fact a rectangle. He went along the towpath, past the old stables behind Sprawson's, past the jumble of roofs that was the back parts of Frankley's the Ironmongers, past the long wall that cut off the almshouses from the perils of water; and coming then by a kissing gate on his left (with Comstock Woods on his right) through the footpath to the side streets and then left again, past the almshouses, Frankley's, Goodchild's and Sprawson's in reverse order; then left once more and in furtive triumph, the police car defeated, to the roots of the Old Bridge and the black urinal again.

What was strange and sad and sane was not his abortive meeting with Bell—a meeting which Bell, having backed away,

82

took very good care not to have repeated—but the fact that there were no meetings at all. Sim Goodchild had been dimly visible beyond the books in his shop window. As Pedigree came past Sprawson's for the second time there had been the sound of a woman's voice raised high, where Muriel Stanhope was embarking on the quarrel that would send her finally to Alfred and New Zealand. High walls, less penetrable than brick, than steel, walls of adamant lay everywhere between everything and everything. Mouths opened and spoke and nothing came back but an echo from the wall. It was a fact so profound and agonizing, the wonder is there was no concert of screaming from the people who lived with the fact and did not know that they endured it. Only Sim Goodchild in his bookshop whimpered occasionally. The others, Muriel Stanhope, Robert Mellion Stanhope, Sebastian Pedigree, thought it was their individual and uniquely unfair treatment by a world that was different for everyone else. But for the Pakistanis, the men in their sharp suits, the women in gaudy colours with a corner snatched across the face, but for the Blacks, the world *was* different.

So Mr Pedigree came out of the urinal and walked back up the High Street, keeping as close as possible to any convenient wall. He glanced back at the upper window in Sprawson's but of course the Bells were no longer visible. He made for the park. He went in, past the notice-board with its list of necessary prohibitions, with what for him was an air of complete security. He was near the bottom of his graph after all. He was able therefore to find a seat and sit on its iron slats and finger the netsuke in his pocket as he spied out the land. He was, as he sometimes said to himself, window-shopping. The children were in groups, some with balls, some with balloons, some trying not very successfully to fly kites in the light wind. The adults were dotted about on the seats—three pensioners, a courting couple with nowhere to go and the young man in a grey raincoat whose presence was not unexpected to Mr Pedigree. In the far corner were the lavatories. Mr Pedigree knew that if he got up and went there the young man would follow and watch.

Regularly, since now there was the possibility of meeting Bell as well as visiting the Old Bridge, Mr Pedigree rotated, day after day, through his own rounds of Greenfield. It was at this time that there was a curious kind of epidemic in the town. People only thought of it as an epidemic when it was past its height and nearly over. Then they thought back, or some of them did and felt they knew where the blame was to be laid, right back, even to the first day, because the first day was so soon after Mr Pedigree met Bell on his latest emergence from retirement. It was a young woman seen, a white woman trotting from Pudding Lane into the High Street. She wore platform shoes and that made her trot even more comical than it might have been, because she was the sort of young woman who can only run with her hands up at either side and with her feet kicking out this way and that—a method of progress which allows of no acceleration. Her mouth was open and she was saying "Help, help, oh help!" in a die-away voice almost as though she was talking to herself. But then she found a pram by a shop with a baby in it and that seemed to quieten her because after she had examined the baby and jogged the pram for a bit she wheeled it away without saying anything, only looking round her nervously or perhaps sheepishly. The same day Sergeant Phillips had a real cause to look sheepish because he found a pram with a baby in it outside Goodchild's Rare Books and neither Sim Goodchild nor his wife Ruth had any idea of how it got there. So Inspector Phillips had to push the pram all the way up the High Street to his car and then radio a description. The mother was soon identified and had left the pram complete with baby outside the Old Supermarket next door to the Old Corn Exchange. There were a few days then and it started all over again. But for a month maybe, prams were moved as if someone was trying to draw attention to himself and using this as a kind of sign language. Mr Pedigree was watched; and though he was never caught at it, the pram-shifting stopped and that month simply became the one people remembered when you couldn't leave a pram unattended. They forgot a rather nasty confrontation between Mr Pedigree (entering the Old Supermarket in search of cereal and carrying the minute pot of Gentleman's Relish he had obtained from George's Superior Emporium) and some ladies who saw him threading his diffident way between the prams that were parked outside like boats moored at a landing stage. As Mrs Allenby remarked to Mrs Appleby over coffee when they discussed the affair in the Taj Mahal Coffee Shop, it was lucky for Mr Pedigree this was England. Of course she did not call him Mr Pedigree but that ghastly old creature.

There was nothing to connect Mr Pedigree with the pram-pushing. But as Sim Goodchild agreed with Edwin Bell, people of Pedigree's sort often had a degree of cunning in the pursuit of their perversions that was the result of not being able to think about anything else. It was true. In this respect, except for the fleeting interests that Mr Pedigree's expensive education sometimes gave him, he was like Matty and dedicated to one end only. But unlike Matty he knew only too well what that end was, what it had to be; and watched it approach or found himself compelled to approach it, with a perpetual kind of gnawing anxiety which aged him far more than the mere flow of time. It is not recorded anywhere if there was a single person living in Greenfield who pitied him. Certainly those ladies at the supermarket who were prevented from scratching his eyes out would have screamed a rebuke at anyone who had suggested it was possible he had never touched a pram at all. And after he had got away from them it could not be a coincidence that Greenfield prams seemed to be safe from interference thereafter.

So Mr Pedigree kept out of the High Street for a while, going no nearer it than Foundlings, round the corner, where he sometimes hoped to see Edwin Bell, who took care not to be visible. The old man, stuck like a broken gramophone record, would stand outside the railings, mourning for the perfected image of little Henderson, and cursing the boy with the mended face, who at the time had landed at Falmouth in Cornwall from a Greek cargo boat and had gone back to ironmongering, locally, the Bible when consulted having told him to make no more than a Sabbath journey. It was the same day that the ladies tried to maim Mr Pedigree that Matty in Cornwall, and for a most extraordinary reason, started to keep the following journal.

# CHAPTER SEVEN

17/5/65

I have bought this book to write in and a biro because of what happened and I want to keep the book for evidence to show I am not mad. They were not like the ghost I saw in Gladstone it was a ghost it must have been. These appeared last night. I had read my portions and then repeated them from memory and I was sitting on the edge of my bed taking my shoes off. The time was eleven forty I mean eleven forty when it began. At first I thought it is cold for May and then my room is cold but it got colder and colder. All the warmth went out of me like being drawn out. Every hair on my person, I mean every short hair not the long hair on my head which prickled but every short hair stood up each on a lump. It is what people call being frightened and now I know it is awful. I could not breathe or call out and I thought I should die. Then they appeared, to me. I cannot properly say how. Remembering changes it. I cannot say how. But I am not mad.

18/5/65

They did not come back tonight. No, last night I must say now. I waited until twelve o'clock and when it struck I knew they would not come. What can it all mean I ask myself. The one was in blue and the other in red with a hat on. The one in blue had a hat too but not as expensive. They appeared and stayed I do not know how long from eleven forty just looking at me. It was awful. The ghost was without any colour at all but these were red and blue like I have said. I cannot say how I see them when I see them I just see them but it is different remembering. Is it a warning I ask myself, have I left something undone. I searched back and could not find any except of course my great and terrible sin, which I would undo if I knew how but the Bible sent me here and he is not here so what am I to do. It is all hidden. I gave many signs nearly two years ago in Darwin Northern Territory and nothing has happened. It is to try my faith.

17/5/66

I take up my pen a year after to say they came again. I knew they would as soon as I felt the cold and the warmth drawing out of my person. I waited but they did not speak but still looked at me. I cannot tell when they went away. They came at after eleven and went away before the clock struck just like a year ago. Perhaps they come every year. I think perhaps it is something to do with my feeling that I am at the centre of an important thing and have been always. Most people do not live into their thirties without knowing what it is to be frightened and most people are afraid of ghosts and do not see spirits.

21/5/66

I was reading at the table Revelations when I understood. At once it was like when the spirits appear but they did not. I went cold, shivering and the short hairs on my person stood up. I saw that a FATEFUL DAY is coming by reason of the calendar. At first I did not know what to do. This must be why the spirits appeared before me. They must come again to tell me what to do. My waiting on them is a wave-offering. I must make a heave-offering but have so little it is difficult to see what I have left for a heave-offering.

22/5/66

I thought in the shop what would be a heave-offering but it is so awful I am holding it back.

23/5/66

I bind to lift up more of what I eat and drink then place it on the altar. I bind to lift up all of what I speak except what must be spoken. There is almost no time left. I pray all the time I can.

### 30/5/66

At first with eating so little I felt great pain and weakness but then I found a way of seeing all that I had not eaten offered up on the altar and this helped me. Also cold water is alright to drink but I have a great and live memory of tea hot tea with milk and sugar like in Melbourne. Sometimes I can even smell the tea and feel how hot it is. I wondered then I might be being ministered to as it is said. Mr Thornbury tells me I should see a doctor but he does not understand. Because I have made a heave-offering of my talking it is not right for me to explain to him.

### 31/5/66

I have been among the Baptists and Methodists and Quakers and the Plymouth Brethren but there is no dread anywhere and no light. There is no understanding except sometimes when I repeat my portion inside from memory. When I go among these different people they question me sometimes. Then I lay my hands over my mouth and see by the way they smile that they understand a little. Now I have been cold all day, thinking of the calendar. I thought in these exceptional circumstances the spirits might come back but now it is past twelve and though I got colder as the clock struck nothing happened because I tell myself the cup is full but not yet *pressed* down and overflowing. Also I said to myself it would start perhaps when it started first down under and then remembered it is said *in the twinkling of an eye* so it would be in Melbourne, Sydney, Gladstone, Darwin, Singapore, Hawaii, San Francisco, New York and Greenfield also in Cornwall at the same instant.

### 1/6/66

It is terrible to see the days pass, the cup already full and waiting to be *pressed down*. I eat nothing and only drink a little cold water. Today as I came upstairs to my room I stumbled for weakness but it is no matter with the time so short. It came to me in a flash, a great opening while I was just writing those last words, a hand was laid on me and I understood what I must do on THE DAY. It is my task to give Cornwall ONE LAST CHANCE!!

There are no preparations to make. Tomorrow I will watch all night *lest we be taken sleeping*. It seems to me that on 1/6/66 a voice told me what to do but I cannot be sure. It is all mixed up like when the display counter was turned over by that great dog.

I watched all night having put everything ready the day before. It was much harder to cut myself than I had thought but I made an offering of it. A bird sang at first light and I had the dreadful expectation that it had sung for the last time. I took blood and wrote on the paper in letters each as long as my thumb the awful number 666. I put the paper as instructed in the band of my hat so that the number was to be seen from in front. I repeated my portion as I thought I should not have the opportunity later but be in judgement and was in great dread at the thought. Then I walked out. The streets were so empty that at first I thought judgement had already been done and I left of all the world alone but later I saw it was not so as people were bringing food to market. I believe some were stricken and some even brought to recollection when they saw me bearing the awful number through the streets on my head and written in blood. I went through all the churches and chapels in the town with my hat on except those that were locked. At each of these I knocked three times then shook the dust of the threshold off my feet and walked away. All this time I was very tired and in such terror I could hardly walk. But when it was dark I went back to my room, on hands and knees up the stairs and waited until midnight when I began to write this so that not to make a lie of it the number should be 7/6/66. Many people will know the carnal and earthly pleasures of being alive this day and not brought to judgement. No one but I have felt the dreadful sorrow of not being in heaven with judgement all done.

I have looked for the judgement that was to be done on the sixth but cannot find it. Sara Jenkins died, may she rest in peace, and a son was born to the doctor's wife in the cottage hospital. There was a slight accident at the bottom of Fish Hill. A boy (P. Williamson) fell off his bike and sustained a fracture of the left leg. His will be done.

15/6/66

It is a great relief to me to think that all these people have time now in which to repent. Yet in that relief I feel a great grief and when not a grief I feel a great emptiness and my question comes again. What am I for, I ask myself. If to give signs why does no judgement follow. I will go on because there is nothing else to do but I feel an emptiness.

18/6/66

They came back. I knew they would as soon as I felt the cold and my hairs rise up. I was more ready this time because I had thought while serving in the shop what to do. I asked them in a whisper so as not to be heard through the partition by Mr Thornbury if they were servants of OUR LORD. I expected them either to say nothing or to speak out loud, or perhaps whisper, but it was a mystery instead. For when I had whispered I saw they held a great book between them open with HIS NAME there in shining gold. So it is alright but still dreadful of course. The hair on my person will not lie down all the time they are there.

19/6/66

They will not speak in a common way. They hold out beautiful white papers with words on or whole books faster than newspapers being printed like you see on the television. I asked them why they came to me. Then they showed on a paper: We do not come to you. We bring you before us.

2/7/66

They came again tonight, the red spirit with the expensive hat and the blue spirit with a hat but not so expensive. They are hats of office I cannot say what I mean. Also the red robes and the blue

90

robes. I do not know how I see them but I do. I am still frightened when they come.

11/7/66

Tonight I asked them why they brought me before them out of all the people in the world. They showed: You are near the centre of things. This was what I had always thought but as I felt the pride of it I saw them both much dimmed. So I hurled myself down inside, down as far as I could and I stayed like that. But they went away, or as I should say, put me from them. Now my fear is not just the cold, it is different. It is deeper and it is everywhere. I got cold when they came but not like I did when they first came and my hair just prickles a bit.

13/7/66

The fear is everywhere and mixed in with it is being sorry, grieving, but not me only being sorry but everything. This feeling is there even when they are hidden from me.

15/7/66

There is too much to put down but I must put it down for evidence. Great things are afoot. They have been four times, always after I have repeated my portion. The first time they brought me before them I asked them why they brought me before them. They showed: We work with what we have. I was put in great satisfaction by this reply and asked what I was for, my old question. They showed: That will appear at the appointed time. The next time they were there I asked what I was, the older form of my great question and they showed: That will appear too. The third time they brought me before them was very terrible to me. I asked them what they would have me do. Then the red one showed: Throw away your book. I thought he meant this book and I started up from the edge of the bed—for that is where I seem to be sitting when they bring me to them—and reached out for the book to tear it. But as I did so the red one showed very plainly: Let the record of our meetings alone. We mean you are to throw away your Bible. At this I think I cried out and they thrust me away from them so that they were hidden. I could not sleep all night I was so frightened, and next day in the shop Mr Thornbury asked me what was the matter. I said I had a bad night which is true. I wondered all day if they had thrust me away from them for ever as being unworthy of a place near the centre of things and I thought that if they came back—or rather I must remember it is difficult—if they bring me before them I will have some questions to test them. Satan may appear as an angel of light so much more easily as a red or blue spirit with hats. They did come that night, the fourth time it was in a row. I asked them at once, Are you both true servants of OUR LORD? At once they held up between them the great book with HIS NAME in shining gold. I watched very closely for I knew that THAT NAME would strike Satan down and burn him like an acid. But the beautiful paper was the same as ever and the gold too. Then, for I had determined not to be mistaken, I said though frightened and cold, What do you mean by HIM. Then they showed: We worship HIM THE LORD OF THE EARTH AND THE SUN AND THE PLANETS AND ALL THE CREATURES THAT ARE ON THEM. At that I flung myself down inside myself and whispered, What does HE want of me? I am willing. Then they showed: Obedience and to throw away your Bible. It was a quarter to ten. I put on my charity greatcoat and took my Bible and walked out into the night all the way to the headland. It was very dark with clouds and there was a sound all the time of wind and sea that got louder as I got nearer. I stood right on the edge and saw nothing in the dark but some white patches down below where the water was moving round the rocks. I stood there some time in fear to throw and in fear to fall though I think to fall would have been easier. I waited for a while hoping that the order would be cancelled but there was nothing but the sound of the wind and sea. I threw my Bible as far out into the sea as I could. Then I returned very weak and thirsty and failed at the knees as I climbed the stairs. But I managed at last and came at once into their presence. I whispered, I have done it. Then they held out the great book between them and I saw that it was full of the comfortable words.

17/7/66

They brought me before them and showed: Though every letter of the book is from everlasting to everlasting the great part of it that

92

you have learnt by heart is what your condition needs and was laid down for you from the beginning. I said it was terrible knowing what to do or what not to do in such a matter. It was like being on a tightrope high up over a street. Then they showed: Be obedient and you shall not fall.

25/7/66

Tonight they showed at once when I came before them: Now you are to go on a journey. I said I am willing, where am I to go? Then they showed: That will be revealed to you presently. But we are pleased with your ready acceptance and as a reward we allow you to ask us what you like provided you have not asked it before and been answered. Then I thought for a while and asked them why they did not come or rather bring me before them every night. They showed: Know that we see your spiritual face and it so badly scarred by a sin that we have to summon up great courage to look at you. But all the same you are the best material that can be obtained in the circumstances. I asked at once what had scarred my spiritual face and I wept bitter tears when they showed me what I had already guessed. For however ignorant a man is he always knows his sins until he is lost if there can be any like that. Yes it is the terrible wrong I did my dear friend though perhaps I should not call him that he was so high above me, Mr Pedigree. Indeed, not a day passes but at some time of it I hear what he said to me as they took him away. No wonder my spiritual face dims the light the spirits bring with them, and that lies around them.

27/8/66

They have not brought me before them for a long time. When they do that I am cold and frightened but when they do not I am lonely even with people about. I have a great wish to obey them in this journey they talk about. Is my wish to go away from Cornwall a being led by them, I ask myself. Sometimes when the spirits do not appear and I remember my Bible floating away in its wooden covers or sinking down my hair prickles a bit still and I go cold but it is not the same cold. But then I remember I am at the centre of things and must be content to wait no matter how long.

93

I take up my pen to write that they have not brought me before them for more than a period of three weeks. I know I must wait but worry sometimes in case they do not bring me before them because I have done something that is wrong. Sometimes when I am far down I wish dearly that I had a kind wife and some little children. Sometimes I have a great wish to return to what I may call my home, that is, Greenfield, the town where Foundlings was.

25/9/66

They came again. I said I did not know whether the saying to me that I was to go on a journey was all or that it was right to wait for more instructions. They showed: You are right to wait. You are now to eat and drink more to get up your strength for the journey. You are to go to Curnow's Store and choose among the second-hand bikes you saw there for one to ride. You are to learn to ride it.

3/10/66

They showed: We are pleased with your progress in strength and in riding the bike. In a little while we shall send you on your journey. We are pleased with you and allow you to ask us any questions you like. Then I was bold to ask something that had been on my mind for several months. When I was at a stand for progress I offered up speaking as a heave-offering. Now I said they allowed me to eat and drink more. Could I perhaps speak more too for in my young days I was a great talker and not ever content with yea and nay but spoke many unsanctified words. When I had said this to them I saw their light dimmed and there was a silence in heaven for a space of half an hour. So I offered myself up on the altar. At last they showed: You are so often in our thoughts familiarly that we do not always remember how naturally wicked you earthly creatures are. Then the spirit dressed in red (I think he is some kind of president) showed: Your tongue was bound so that in the time of the promise which is to come you shall speak words like a sword going out of your mouth. I thanked them both very much but mostly the spirit in red as he is a higher spirit than the other. Then they showed: Seeing you are a friend of ours in the spiritual kingdom for all your terrible face and earthly wickedness we will allow some relief to your wish to talk. You may if the pain of not talking is past putting up with (and as it is a spiritual pain we know it is three times worse than an earthly pain) you may, in a dark place preach a sermon to the dead. But let no living person hear. I was much comforted by this and thanked them again.

### 7/10/66

It is easier to drive a car than to learn to ride a bike when you are a grown man but today my knees and elbows seem better and the bruising has gone down. I am much stronger and do not fail on the stair as I did or when carrying boxes in from the yard.

### 11/10/66

They came and showed: You are to ask Mr Thornbury for a rise and when he refuses it you are to shake the dust of Cornwall off your feet and go to Greenfield to the employment exchange there. You are to take no thought for what kind of work there is but accept what is offered.

### 12/10/66

Mr Thornbury refused the rise. He said I was worth it but with business as it is he could not afford it. He gave me a testimonial to whom it may concern saying I had worked for him for two years was sober, hard-working and scrupulously honest. I feel bad that he is not a Godly man. What will become of him I ask myself.

### 19/10/66

Exeter is not a good place to stop. It is better to choose B and B in the country but a woman by herself would not let me in because of my face. My bike stands up to it. If the spirits had not told me to buy the bike I should have gone by train and it would have been cheaper. I am spending money like a rich man. The weather continues fine.

The country is very open between Salisbury and Basingstoke with a great deal of long straight road. All day I saw rainstorms on every side but they did not come nigh me. I take it as a sign that my journey is a hallowed one and the spirit of Abraham encloses it.

28/10/66

Greenfield is much changed. I had a thought to go to Foundlings but of course my dear friend Mr Pedigree would not be there since he was despised and rejected. No one would know what had become of him. I may do so later. There is much new building and crowds of people. There are many more black and brown men and women, the women wear all kinds of costumes but the men not. There is a heathen temple built right next door to the Seventh Day Adventists!! When I saw this and also the mosque I was torn by the spirit. I had a great desire to prophesy Thou Jerusalem that slayest the prophets and sitting on the saddle with one foot on the pavement I had to clap both hands over my mouth to keep it in. But the church is still there. I went in and stayed for a time in the same seat where it happened how many years ago I ask myself. Also looking in Goodchild's Rare Books but the glass ball is gone and that part is filled with books for children, two of them stories from the Bible. The employment exchange was shut for the day so I found a bed and cycled round a bit. Then I came back here to repeat my portion.

29/10/66

In the employment exchange the man took all my testimonials and read them and thought well of them. He said he thought he had a place for me in a school. I felt very strange at once, thinking of Foundlings and Mr Pedigree and all that sad story, but no. He said it is Wandicott House School which is some way out in the country wait while I ring them. He telephoned the school and read out my references to the man at the other end and they laughed with each other which surprised me for there is nothing in my references to laugh at even by carnal men. But then the man said the bursar wanted me to come straight away for an interview and bring my references. I rode down the High Street and over the Old Bridge over the canal where there are a lot more boats than there used to be. I rode along through Chipwick then up a bridle path in a deep groove under trees. (I did not ride up, that would be a lie, I pushed my bike up.) Then I went down the other side of the downs into Wandicott village where the school is, and where I am now. It is six miles from Greenfield with the downs in between. Captain O. D. S. Thomson D.S.C. R.N. Rtd. interviewed me. He asked me how much money I wanted. I said enough to keep soul and body together. He mentioned a sum and I said it was too much and would cause me trouble. He was silent for a while and then explained about inflation and that I could leave the spare money with him and think no more of it unless needed. I am to be at every man's beck and call. When he said that I understood with joy that it was exactly what the spirits wanted and that my task is to be obedient unless asked to do what is wrong.

### 30/10/66

I have a room with the head gardener but he is gruff and sullen and does not want me to use his toilet as there is one by the harness room about fifty yards away. I do not use a toilet often since I have given up so much of my earthly living.

### 7/11/66

The spirits have not brought me before them since the night of 11/10/66. They have put it all on me. As they showed it is my responsibility to always remember how I am near the centre of things and all things will be revealed. This evening I spent sewing a patch on my rough trousers (the spare pair of army surplus) where the saddle had worn it.

### 12/11/66

This school is not at all like Foundlings. I did not know there were schools like this. The boys are rich and noble and have more people looking after them than there are children. You can walk for a mile and still be inside the grounds although some of them are fields with cattle. You would think that the drive from the gates to the school was an ordinary road it is so long with trees over it. I have nothing to do with the children of course but only with the lowest people. Mr Pierce the head gardener has a down on me. He takes a delight I think in giving me hard things to do and humble things too but it is the only way I may learn what I am for. I have a half-day off every week. Mr Braithwaite says I can have evenings off by arrangement but I would sooner work.

20/11/66

I help the gardeners weeding and picking things. Mr Pierce is still gruff and sullen and gives me jobs to dirty me it is his nature. I have helped Mr Squires in the garages. We have our own pumps.

22/11/66

I have nothing to do with the boys but the masters speak to me sometimes and the headmaster's wife, Mrs Appleby. She does not seem to mind my face but inside she does and I daresay speaks about it when I am not there.

24/11/66

I fetched a rugby ball for the boys from some bushes and they did not mind me at all but looked and thought me strange I believe but did not mind.

26/11/66

At last I got up my courage even though the spirits had not told me and cycled to Foundlings. I stared through and could see the place where all the hollyhocks used to be and S Henderson fell. All is as it was. While I looked someone opened Mr Pedigree's window (I mean the one at the top that opens on to the leads and where I saw S Henderson come away after I had followed him and waited). It was a woman I saw by the shape of her arm. Perhaps she was cleaning the room. Of course I could not see my poor friend. But what I did see was the young master who discovered Henderson's body after he fell. It was Mr Bell and he is much much older. I was

98

sitting on my bike by the pavement when Mr Bell dressed the same way as he used to be, with his big scarf came out of the front door just by the headmaster's study then came out of the gate and walked away down the High Street. I was moved to follow him and he went into Sprawson's by the Old Bridge. It was a great grief to me that he passed me where I sat on my bike without recognizing me that is the truth. It seems I have no part left in Greenfield which was what I came to think of as my home, not supposing my one friend was still there but in my mind seeming to connect him with it.

31/12/66

Tonight while I was waiting for the clock in the Wandicott church to strike twelve (and then some of the masters who have stayed on for the holiday will ring a peal for the New Year it is done not for godliness but in fun) I read through this book from the beginning. I began it as evidence of the spirits visiting me in case I should be thought mad and taken up and put away in a mental hospital as happened to R. S. Jones in Gladstone but I see I have recorded much else as well. Also I find in myself that I have written down words instead of speaking them and it is a little comfort. The spiritual life is a time of trial and without the comfortable words and the spirits telling me I am at the centre of things and all shall be made plain I should be tempted to do as R. S. Jones and do a mischief to myself. For the question that I now ask, what am I and what am I to do is still unanswered and I must *endure* like a man holding up a heavy weight. The peal is ringing and I wish I could weep but it does not seem possible.

5/2/67

A wonderful thing has happened. The weather has been so cold the playing fields are frozen and the boys not playing. They go for walks in the estate instead. I was cleaning out a corner by the harness room (for Mr Pierce will find work for me even when the air is freezing and the earth not to be turned even by a pick) when three boys came by and stopped. It is rare for them to be near me but they stood and watched. Then the biggest who was white asked me why I wore a black hat! I had to think very quickly because though I do not speak more than is necessary these were children which He said must be suffered etc. I decided that it was a part of obedience to do as they asked and they asked me to reply to them. So I said to keep my hair tidy. This made them laugh and one said I was to take off my hat. I did and they laughed so loud I had to smile and I saw they did not mind my mended face at all but thought someone had had a joke with me. I was a clown for them. So I lifted the hair away from the bald side showing them my bad ear and they were very interested and not a bit frightened or horrified. After they went away I felt more happy than at any other time. I put my hat back on and continued to clean the corner but I thought that if only I could put all right with my friend Mr Pedigree I would then prefer to live among children and in this very school than anywhere else. Can it be that what I am for is something to do with children I ask myself.

13/4/67

I helped the groundsmen taking down the rugby posts. They did not work as hard as they should. One was telling the others how Mr Pierce makes money by selling garden produce on the side when it ought to be used for the school. They also told me about some of the parents of some of the boys but soon stopped talking to me when they found out how little I answered. They said two of the men about the place were detectives and one of the gardeners I wonder which it cannot be Mr Pierce surely. But it is not my business I remind myself. I am much troubled as to whether I should tell Captain Thomson D.S.C. R.N. Rtd. about Mr Pierce and the garden produce.

20/4/67

I have a bad cold and a temperature making all things move about and shake. But when I was repeating my portion the spirits came again they were just the same as ever, the red one and the blue one. They showed: We are pleased with your obedience to Mr Pierce though he is a bad lot. He will be paid out for it. However to comfort you we allow you to ask what you like and if it is lawful we will answer. I asked what had troubled me off and on for a long time, which is why so little effect was visible in Cornwall when I carried the awful number written in blood through the streets. They showed: Judgement is not the simple thing you think. The number did much good not only in the town but as far afield as Camborne and Launceston. Ask on. Then I thought and asked if my spiritual face was healed or still ugly for them. They then showed: No it is still dreadful to us but we bear it cheerfully for your sake. Ask on. Then I said, hardly knowing what I did, Who am I? What am I? What am I for? Is it to do with children? Then they showed: It is a child. And when you bore the awful number through the streets a spirit that is black with a touch of purple like the pansies Mr Pierce planted under the rowan was cast down and defeated and the child was born sound in wind and limb and with an I.Q. of a hundred and twenty. Ask on. At this I cried out What am I? Am I human? and heard Mr Pierce turn over in bed with a great honk of a snore and the spirits removed me from them but gently. It seems to me that perhaps this night I do not need sleep.

22/4/67

It must have been nearly three o'clock in the morning I think that quite suddenly I sweated streams and streams and felt a great need of sleep after all. So I slept and next day was hard put to it to do the work that Mr Pierce laid on me. But I am happy to think that what I am for is to do with these little boys though Mr Pierce tries to keep me away from them. 120 was the I.Q. of Jesus of Nazareth.

2/5/67

Today I went into Greenfield on my half-day. Mrs Appleby the headmaster's wife who often speaks to me asked me to get her some things and it was so strange when she said, You can get them at Frankley's! So I went in. Then I looked at GOODCHILD'S RARE BOOKS and was a little sorry that the glass ball was not there any longer, sold I suppose or I might have bought it. Only also when I was looking in the window two little girls came from Sprawson's where I took the fireirons all that time ago and looked in the window at the children's books. They were so beautiful like angels and I was careful to turn my bad side away. They went back into Sprawson's and the door of the shop was open so I heard a

101

woman inside say that Stanhope's little girls were everything to each other. I got on my bike and rode away but I could not help wishing that they were who I am for. I do not mean I looked at them in the way I looked at Miss Lucinda or the daughters of Mr Hanrahan all that is done with I think, gone out of my mind as if it had never been. It is very strange all the events of 20/4/67 are cloudy so that I cannot remember clearly if the word in the book was child or children. Perhaps I am to do not with the children of this school but the little girls, Stanhope they are called or one of them but I would like it to be both. While waiting to find out what I am for I shall keep an eye on them on my half-days. The next time the spirits call me before them I shall ask about the little girls. One of them is dark and one fair. I add them to my list for praying for.

9/5/67

The spirits have not brought me before them. Today on my half-day, I went in to Greenfield again to see if I could see the little girls but they did not appear. I may not see them very often but that will be as God wills of course. I looked at their house. It is a big one but a firm of solicitors lives in one part and there is a flat.

13/5/67

The spirits came again. I asked at once about the little girls and they showed: That will be as it will be. I then had a sudden fear that I was in danger of committing a sin by preferring these little girls to anything else. They did not wait for me to whisper this to them but showed at once: You are right. Do not go into Greenfield unless you are sent. They seemed a bit severe with me I thought. They thrust me away from them quickly. So I am once again in the position of doing a hard thing. I must be content with my lot and talking now and then to the little boys and trust that there are good spirits (angels) looking after the little girls which of course there are. And as they are everything to each other they do not need me.

102

# Part Two
# SOPHY

# CHAPTER EIGHT

What Mrs Goodchild had said to Mr Goodchild was quite true. The twins, Sophy and Toni Stanhope, were everything to each other and they hated it. If they had been identical it might have been better but they were as different as day and night, night and day you are the one, night and day. Even when Matty saw them, within a week of their tenth birthday, Sophy had a sharp idea of how different they were. She knew that Toni had thinner arms and legs and a less smooth, pink curve from her throat right down to between her legs. Toni's ankles and knees and elbows were a bit knobbly and her face was thinner like her arms and legs. She had big, brown eyes and ridiculous hair. It was long and thin. It was not much thicker than—well if it had been any thinner it wouldn't have *been* at all: and as if preparing for disappearance it had entirely got rid of its colour. Sophy on the other hand knew that she herself lived at the top end of a smoother and rounder and stronger body, inside a head with dark curls all over it. She looked out through eyes that were a bit smaller than Toni's with masses of long, dark eyelashes round them. Sophy was pink and white, but Toni's skin, like her hair, had no colour in it. You could see through it in a way; and Sophy, without bothering to know how she knew, knew pretty well the Toni-ness of the being who lived more or less inside it. "More-or-less" was as near as you could get because Toni did not live entirely inside the head at the top, but loosely, in association with her thin body. She had a habit of kneeling and looking up and saying nothing that had a curious effect on any grown-up present. They would go all soppy. What made this so maddening was that at these times, Sophy knew Toni wasn't doing anything at all. She wasn't thinking and she wasn't feeling and she wasn't being. She had simply drifted away from herself like smoke. Those huge, brown eyes, looking up from the falls of lintwhite hair! It was magic and it worked. When it happened, Sophy would disappear inside herself if she could, or remember the precious times when there had not been any Toni. There was one with a whole roomful of children and music. Sophy could do the step and would have liked to do it for ever, one, two, three, hop, one, two, three, hop; calm pleasure in the way that threeness always brought the other leg for you to do a hop with, and for some reason, no Toni. Pleasure too because some of the children could not do this simple, lovely thing.

There was also the long square. Later she thought of it as the rectangle, of course, but what was remarkable was that she had Daddy to herself, and Daddy had actually proposed a walk, thus causing her such a confusion of delight that only later had she understood why he did it. She might have been a trouble to him if she had missed Toni! But for whatever reason, he actually took her by the hand, she reaching up and looking—bah!—with a simple trust in that handsome face and they had descended the two steps, passed between the small patches of grass and were on the pavement. He had wooed her, there was no other word for it. He had turned them right and shown her the bookshop next door. Then they had stopped and looked in the huge window of Frankley's the Ironmongers and he had told her about the lawn-mowers and tools and said that the flowers were plastic and then had taken her on past to the row of cottages with the words on a shield over them. He had told her they were almshouses for women whose husbands had died. Then he had turned her right down a narrow lane, a path it was and then through a kissing gate and they were on the towpath by the canal. Then he had explained about barges and how there used to be horses. He turned right again and stopped by a green door in the wall. Suddenly she understood. It was like taking a new step, learning a new thing, the whole place came into one. She saw that the green door was at the bottom of their garden path and that he was already getting bored in a princely way, standing there on the towpath before the blistered paint. So she ran on, getting too close to the water and he caught her as she intended but angrily, just at the steps up to the Old Bridge. He positively lugged her up them. She tried to get him to stop by the public convenience at the top but he would not. She tried to take him straight on after he had turned right again, tried to make him go with her up the High

106

Street but he would not and they did turn right and there was the front of the house. They had come round and back to it and she knew he was angry and bored and that he wished there was someone else about to take charge of her.

It was in the hall that the little conversation had taken place.

"Daddy, will Mummy come back?"

"Of course."

"And Toni?"

"Look child, there's no need to worry. Of course they'll be back!"

With her mouth open she had looked after him as he disappeared into his column room. She was too young to say the thing in her mind that would be like killing Toni. *But I don't want her back*!

However, on the day when Matty saw them they were indeed being more or less everything to each other. Toni had suggested they ought to go to the bookshop next door and see if there were any of the new books there that would be worth having. With a birthday next week it might be worth dropping hints to the current auntie, who needed prodding. But when they got back from the shop Gran was in the hall and the auntie was gone. Gran packed for them and took them away in her little car all the way down to Rosevear, her bungalow near the sea. This was such an excitement it put books and aunties and Daddy clean out of Sophy's mind, so that their tenth birthday flew by without her noticing. Besides, at that time she discovered what fun a brook was. It was much better than a canal and moved with a chatter and pinkle. She walked by it in the sun among tall grasses and buttercups, the buttery petals with their yellow powder so real at head height making distance itself, space so real. There was so much green and sunlight coming from everywhere at once; then when she parted the greenness which was what the grasses were, she saw water between here and there, that farther bank, outland, water moving between, Nile, Mississippi, trickle, dabble, ebble, babble, prick and twinkle! And then the birds that stalked through the jungle down to the edge of outland! Oh that bird all black with a white keyhole on the front of its head, and the tweeting, squeaking, chirping brood of fluffies climbing and scrambling and tumbling among the grasses at its back! They came out into the water, mother and chicks all ten on a string. They moved on with the brook and Sophy went right out

107

into her eyes, she was nothing but seeing, seeing, seeing! It was like reaching out and laying hold with your eyes. It was like having the top part of your head drawn forward. It was a kind of absorbing, a kind of drinking, a kind of.

The next day after that, Sophy went looking through the long, buttery flowers and grasses of the meadow to the brook. As if they had been waiting for her all night, there they were the same as ever. The mother was swimming away down the brook with the string of chicks behind her. Every now and then she said, "Kuk!" She was not frightened or anything—just a bit wary.

This was the first time Sophy noticed the "Of course" way things sometimes behaved. She could throw a bit but not much. Now—and this was where the "Of course" thing came in—now there was a large pebble lying to hand among the grasses and drying mud, where no pebble had any business to be unless "Of course" was operating. It seemed to her she did not have to look for the pebble. She just moved her throwing arm and the palm of her hand fitted nicely over the smooth, oval shape. How could a smooth, oval stone be lying there, not under the mud or even under the grass but on top where your throwing arm can find it without looking? There the stone was, fitted to the hand as she peered past the creamy handfuls of meadowsweet and saw the mother and chicks paddling busily down the brook.

When you are a small girl, throwing is a difficult thing and, generally speaking, not something you practise for fun, hour after hour, like a boy. But even later on, before she learnt to be simple, Sophy could never quite understand the way in which she saw what would happen. There it was, a fact like any other, she *saw* the curve which the stone would follow, saw the point to which the particular last chick would advance while the stone would be in its arc. "Would be", or "Was"? For also, and this was subtle—when she thought back later it did seem that as soon as the future was comprehended it was inescapable. But inescapable or not she could never understand—at least, not until a time when understanding itself was an irrelevance—how she was able, left arm held sideways, upper arm rotating back from the elbow past her left ear in a little girl's throw—was able not merely to jerk her upper arm forward but also to let go the stone at the precise moment, angle, speed, was able to let it go unimpeded by the joint of a finger, a nail, pad of the palm, to follow—and really only half

108

meant—to follow in this split and resplit second as if it were a possibility chosen out of two, both presented, both foreordained from the beginning, the chicks, Sophy, the stone to hand, as if the whole of everything had worked down to this point—to follow that curve in the air, the chick swimming busily forward to that point, last in line but having to be there, a sort of silent *do as I tell you*: then the complete satisfaction of the event, the qualified splash, the mother shattering away over the water, half flying over it with a cry like pavements breaking, the chicks mysteriously disappearing, all except the last one, now a scrap of fluff among spreading rings, one foot held up at the side and quivering a little, the rest of it motionless except for the rocking of the water. Then there was the longer pleasure, the achieved contemplation of the scrap of fluff turning gently as the stream bore it out of sight.

She went to find Toni and stood tall among the meadowsweet with the tall buttercups brushing her thighs.

Sophy never threw at the dabchicks again and understood why not, perfectly well. It was a clear perception, though a delicate one. Only once could you allow that stone to fit itself into the preordained hand, preordained arc, and only once do so when a chick co-operates and moves inevitably to share its fate with you. Sophy felt she understood all this and more; yet knew that words were useless things when it came to conveying that "More", sharing it, explaining it. There, the "More" was. It was, for example, like knowing that never, never would Daddy walk again with you round the long square, the rectangle, past the other side of the outer stable door. It was like knowing, as you did, certainly, that the wooing Daddy would not be with you because he wasn't anywhere, something had killed him or he had killed himself and left the hawk's profile stuck at the top of the calm or irritated stranger who spent his time with an auntie or in the column room.

Which was perhaps why Gran's and the brook and the meadow were such a relief, because despite the fact that the meadow was where you learnt about "More", you could use it for sheer pleasure. So as the holiday lengthened, in the cheerful, buttercup-plastered enjoyments of the water-meadow and butterflies and dragonflies, and birds on boughs and daisy chains, she thought *rowdily* of that other thing, that arc, that stone, that fluff as no more than a slice of luck, luck, that was what it was, luck explained everything! Or hid everything. Making a daisy

109

chain with little Phil or being Indians in a wigwam with Toni, the
two of them in a rare state of oneness, she knew it was luck. In
those times, dancing times, singing times, times of going to a new-
ness and meeting new people who should not be allowed to go
away (but did)—the tall woman with red hair, the boy only a bit
younger than herself who let her put on his blue denims with the
red animals sewn on them, the big hat, party times—oh, it was
luck and who cared if it wasn't? It was also, that summer, the last
time they went to Gran's and the last time Sophy inspected
dabchicks. She left Toni looking for small insects in the grass by
the lane and waded away through the longer grass, meadowsweet
and docks of the meadow and when she saw the mother with her
chicks she chased them along the brook. The mother uttered her
warning cry, harsh, staccatissimo and swimming faster, the chicks
too, faster and faster. Sophy ran beside them until at last the
mother took off with her shattering noise and foam and the chicks
disappeared. They disappeared instantly, as it were into thin air.
At one moment there was the fluffy string of them straining to go
faster, necks out, feet whipping under the water; then the next
instant there was a *phut!* sound and no fluffies. It was so astonishing and baffling that she stopped running and stood watching for
a while. Only after she had seen the mother come part-way back
and swim busily in the brook, brandishing her cry like a hammer,
did Sophy find that her own mouth was open, and close it. After,
it may be, half an hour, the mother and chicks came back together
and Sophy chased them again. She found that the chicks did not
vanish into thin air but thin water. There was a point in their fear
where it turned into hysteria and they dived. No matter how small
they were—and these were about as small as chicks could be—if
you chased them, at last they would dive and get clean away from
you no matter how fast you ran and how big you were. She
brought this astonishing news back across the field to Toni, half in
admiration of the chicks and half in irritation at them.

"Silly," said Toni. "They wouldn't be called dabchicks if they
didn't."

That reduced Sophy to putting out her tongue and waggling her
fingers beside her head, thumbs in ears. It was unfair the way Toni
behaved, sometimes, of being miles away, certainly nowhere near
her thin body with its empty face; and then proving carelessly, to
be present. She would come down out of the air and be inside her

110

head. Then with what you could only call a wrench, she would bring things together that no one else would have thought of, and there you were with something decided, or even more irritating, something seen to be obvious. But Sophy had learnt to qualify her early dismissal of the Toni-ness of Toni. She knew that when the essential Toni was seated, perhaps a yard above her head and off-set to the right, it was not always doing nothing or sliding into sleep or coma or sheer nothingness. It might be flitting agilely among the boughs of invisible trees in the invisible forest of which Toni was the ranger. The Toni up there might be without thought; but then, it might equally be altering the shape of the world into the nature it required. It might, for example, be taking shapes from the page of a book and turning them into solid shapes. It might be examining with a kind of remote curiosity the nature of a ball made from a circle, a box from a square or that other thing from a triangle. Sophy had discovered all this about Toni without really trying. After all, they were twins, kind of.

After Toni had pointed out the connection between the behaviour of the dabchicks and their name, Sophy felt cheated and annoyed. The magic disappeared. She stood over Toni wondering whether she should go back and chase the dabchicks again. She saw in her mind, that the thing to do was not to chase the dabchicks down the brook but up it. In that way the movement of the water would help you and hinder them. After that, you could keep up with them and watch them carefully under water and see where they came up. After all, she thought to herself, they must come up somewhere! But really, her heart wasn't in it. The secret was no longer a secret and of no use to anyone but the silly birds themselves.

She pulled her hair out of her ears.

"Let's go back to Gran."

They laboured through the bursting fertility of the meadow towards the hedge and as they went, Sophy wondered whether it would be any use asking Gran how explanations took the fun out of things; but two things put the whole matter out of her head. In the first place, they met little Phil from the farm—little Phil from the farmhouse with his curls, just like little Phil in *The Cuckoo Clock*, and they went off to play with him in one of his father's fields. There, little Phil let them examine his thing and they showed him their things and Sophy suggested they should all get

111

married. But little Phil said he had to go back to the farm and watch telly with his mum. After he left, they found a red pillar-box at the crossroads and had fun posting stones in it. Then, in the second place, when they got back to the bungalow Gran told them they were going back to Greenfield next day because she was going into hospital.

Toni pulled some unexpected knowledge out of whatever place she kept it in.

"Are you having a baby then, Gran?"

Gran smiled in a kind of tight way.

"No I'm not. Nothing you'd understand. I'll probably come out feet first."

Toni turned to Sophy with her usual air of speaking from a height.

"She means she's going to die."

After that Gran did a bit of packing for them which seemed mostly to be flinging things about. She seemed very angry, which Sophy thought unfair. Later when they were in bed and Toni in that sleep where she seemed not to breathe at all, Sophy lay thinking, until it was so late it was quite, quite dark. The hospital and Gran and dying, made the darkness shivery. She examined, despite herself, the whole process of dying as far as she knew about it. Oh indeed, it was shivery—but exciting! She flung herself round in bed and spoke out loud.

"I shan't die!"

The words sounded loud, as if someone else had said them. They sent her down under the bedclothes again. It was down there that she found herself, as it were, forced to think of the place, the bungalow, as if it were now all part of this new thing, Gran's dying—Gran's bedroom where the bed seemed almost too big for the floor, the huge furniture crammed into the little rooms as if a great house had been contracted; the huge, dark, sideboard with carved squiggles and the cupboards you were not to open as in Bluebeard, the present darkness, that was like some creature sitting in each room; and Gran herself, made mysterious, no, dreadful, by coming out of hospital, monstrously feet first. It was at that very point that Sophy made her discovery. The mystery of things and Gran coming out feet first drove Sophy in on every side into herself. She understood something about the world. It extended out of her head in every direction but one; and that one was secure because it was her own, it was the direction through the back of her head, *there*, which was dark like this night, but her own dark. She knew that she stood or lay at the extreme end of this dark direction as if she were sitting at the mouth of a tunnel and looking out into the world whether it was dusk or dark or daylight. When she understood that the tunnel was there at the back of her head she felt a strange kind of shiver that shot through her body and made her want to escape from it into daylight and be like everybody else; but there was no daylight. She invented the daylight, there and then, and filled it with people who had no tunnel at the back of their heads, gay, cheerful, ignorant people; and presently she must have fallen asleep because Gran was calling them to wake up. At breakfast in the kitchen Gran was very cheerful and said they mustn't pay too much attention to what she said, everything would be all right probably and nowadays they could do wonders. Sophy heard all this and the long chat that followed without listening to it, she was so interested to see Gran, couldn't take her eyes off her because of this enormity, Gran was going to die. What made everything odder was that Gran didn't understand. She was trying to cheer them up as if *they* were going to die which was silly and to be dismissed in view of the plainly visible outline that now surrounded Gran, cutting her off from the rest of the world in her movement towards coming out of the hospital feet first. However, there was more of interest to be extracted and Sophy waited impatiently for all the things Gran was saying to cheer them up and as soon as there was a pause in the long explanation of however much they loved her they were young and would find other people which was what she had been meaning to tell them—in the subsequent drawing of Gran's breath, Sophy managed to get out her question.

"Gran, where are you going to be buried?"

Gran dropped a plate and burst into some quite extraordinary laughter which turned into other noises and then she positively rushed out and slammed the door of her bedroom. The twins were left at the kitchen table not knowing what to do, so they went on eating, but in respectful silence. Later Gran came out of her bedroom, kind and sunny. She hoped they wouldn't be too sorry for their poor old Gran and would remember the good times and what fun they had had all three together. Sophy considered that they had had no fun at all, all three of them and that Gran could

113

snap if you got your shoes too dirty but she was beginning to learn what not to say. So she watched Gran who still had that curious outline round her, watched with solemn eyes over her mug while Gran talked sunnily. They were going to be very happy when they went back to Daddy because a new lady would be looking after them. Gran called her an au pair.

Toni asked the next question.

"Is she nice?"

"Oh yes," said Gran, in the voice that meant the opposite of what she was saying, "she's very nice. Your Daddy would see to that, wouldn't he?"

Sophy was not concerned to think about the new auntie because of the outline round Gran. Toni went on asking questions and Sophy was left to her own thoughts and observations. There was nothing particular about Gran (except the outline) to show that she was going to die so Sophy altered things round a bit to consider what the result would be. It was with disappointment and a little indignation that she saw how Gran's dying might very well cut her off from the buttery meadow and the dabchicks and little Phil and the pillar-box. She very nearly put this point to Gran, but thought better of it. And there—Toni must have said something! Gran was off again, the bedroom door slamming. The twins said nothing but sat; and then, simultaneously they caught each other's eyes and burst into a fit of the giggles. It was one of those rare moments when they really were everything to each other and enjoyed it.

Gran came out later, not so sunny, put their luggage together and drove them to the station in complete silence. This move towards home deflected Sophy into a consideration of the future. She asked a question which carefully avoided any point of contact with Gran and Gran's future.

"Shall we like her?"

Gran understood that one.

"I'm sure you will."

Then after a while and two traffic lights she spoke again in that voice which always meant the opposite of what it said.

"And I'm sure she'll be devoted to the two of you."

When they got back to Greenfield they found that the "au pair" was their third auntie. She appeared to have come out of the room across the landing like the other two, as if that bedroom produced

114

aunties like butterflies in warm weather. This third one was certainly more like a butterfly than the other ones had been. She had yellow hair, she smelt like a ladies' hairdressers' and she spent a long time each day putting things on her face. She had a way of speaking that was unlike anything the twins could hear, either in the house, or down in Dorset, or in the street from white, yellow, brown or black faces. She informed the twins that she came from Sydney. Sophy thought at first that Sydney was a person and that caused some confusion. However, the au pair, Auntie Winnie as she was called, was cheerful and quick once she was satisfied with her face. She whistled and sang a lot and smoked a lot and though she made so much noise she did not irritate Daddy in the slightest. When she wasn't making a noise herself, her transistor radio did it for her. Everywhere that Winnie went the transistor was sure to go. By listening to the transistor you could tell where Winnie was. When Sophy understood that Sydney was a big city on the other side of the world, she was encouraged to question Winnie.

"Isn't New Zealand on the other side of the world too?"

"'Spose so, dearie. Never thought of it like that."

"An auntie a long time ago. Our first auntie she was. Well she said Mummy was gone to God. Then Daddy said she'd gone to live with a man in New Zealand."

Winnie screamed with laughter.

"Well, it's the same kind of thing me old sweetheart, innit?"

Winnie changed things a lot. The stables down at the end of the garden path were now officially the twin's own house. Winnie persuaded them that they were proud and lucky to have a house of their own; and they were young enough to believe her for a time. Then later, of course, when they got used to it, there was no need to change anything. Daddy was particularly pleased and pointed out to them that they would no longer be annoyed by the sound of his typewriter. Sophy, who had sometimes been lulled to sleep by the secure sound of the typewriter, saw this as just another indication of what Daddy (Daddy out there, through there, along there, Daddy at a distance) of what Daddy really was. But she said nothing.

Winnie took them to the sea. This was going to be a great thing but it went all wrong. They were on sand among a huge crowd of people, most of them in deck-chairs with children scattered

115

between. The sun wasn't shining and it sprinkled rain now and then. But what went wrong was the sea itself, and it went wrong even for the grown-ups. The twins were inspecting a rippled inch or two at the very edge of the water when there were shouts and people started to run away up the beach. The sea had a line of foam on it which came near and turned into a green hollow of water and this fell on them and there was a time of screaming and choking and Winnie wading with them both under her arms, then leaning forward and straining while the water tore at them and tried to take them away. So they all three went home at once. Winnie was so angry and they were all shivering and the transistor had stopped working and Winnie seemed quite different without it. The first thing she did when they were home again and dry was to take the transistor to be mended. But the wave—and no one could explain it, not even grown-ups, though they talked on the telly about it—the wave had a nasty habit of returning when you were asleep. Toni seemed unaffected by it but Sophy suffered. She woke several times to hear herself screaming. It was odd about Toni, though. Just once, when the two of them were squatting in front of the telly and watching a fun thing about all the various adventures you could get up to, as for example, hang gliding, there were included some shots of people surf-riding in the Pacific. At one moment the screen was full of a wave approaching, and the camera zoomed right up, right in, so you were right inside the immense green hollow. Sophy felt a terrible pang in her stomach and a fear of everything and she shut her eyes to keep out the sight though she could still hear the wave, or some wave, or other, roaring and roaring. When the telly said now how about a change from water to air and she knew it would show pictures of parachutes she opened her eyes again to find that her untwinlike twin, Toni of the bleached hair and indifference to everything, had fainted clean away.

After that, for a long time, weeks and weeks, Toni was more often than not up in the air in her private forest or whatever it was. Once, when Sophy mentioned the wave (it being absent) to give herself an agreeable shiver there was a long silence before Toni answered.

"What wave?"

Winnie's transistor came back from the shop and went every-where with her again. Once more you might hear a tiny orchestra

116

playing in the kitchen or a man's voice coming down the garden path at knee height. When the twins were taken up the High Street past the new mosque to the school and introduced to the milling children, the small man's voice went with them and left them there holding each other's hands as if they liked each other. Winnie fetched them after school which made some of the children laugh. Some of them were men, almost, at least, some of the black ones were.

Winnie lasted much longer than the other aunties, seeing how different she was from Daddy. She moved into his bedroom, transistor and all. Sophy disliked this but could not really tell why. Winnie arranged that the twins could use the old green door from the stables onto the towpath. She said to Daddy that they had to get used to the water.

This meant that for a time that summer and autumn the twins explored the towpath, from the Old Bridge with its tablet saying that someone had built it—though not perhaps with the stinky-poo urinal on the top—all the way, oh a mile or two perhaps by a path narrowed between brambles and loosestrife and stands of reed, all the way to the other bridge right out in the country. There was a wide pool by that bridge with a decaying barge in it, a boat much older than the line of motor boats and rowing boats and converted (but decaying) thises and thats across the canal from the green door. Once they even went so far they climbed up a track on the other side of the canal, up and up along a deep groove with trees hanging over on either side, up and up till they came out on the very ridge of the downs and could see the canal and Greenfield on one side and a valley full of trees on the other. They were late home that time but nobody noticed. Nobody ever noticed and sometimes Sophy wished they would. But then Sophy knew in a direct sort of way that Winnie had pushed them down the garden path into the stables—and very comfortable they were, what lucky children!—simply in order to get them out of the way and as far as possible from Daddy. They could do what they liked in the stables, dressing up from among the ancient trunks that seemed to hold the spillage of all history, the Stanhope family from way back, curling irons and hoops, dresses, shifts, materials, unbelievably a wig, faintly scented and with a trace of white powder lingering in it, shoes, and they lugged all this around and tried most of it on. Only they were not allowed to

117

have other children in without permission. By the time the business of the wave had settled down a bit and sunk away into the place where occasional nightmares came from, Sophy began to think that she and Toni were being forced to be everything to each other again. She thought this so clearly one day that she tried pulling Toni's hair to prove that they weren't. But by now Toni had evolved her own way of fighting, flailing wildly with thin arms and legs and all the time looking nowhere with her big brown eyes, that it seemed she had escaped and left her thin and lengthening body behind her to inflict whatever it could of random injury and pain. Sophy began to find fighting unsatisfactory. Of course, at the school there were such tough children, men almost, it was best to keep out of that sort of trouble and leave the centre of the playground to them. So they played in the stables, parallel, so to speak, or walked primly in the High Street, conscious of difference among the black and yellow and brown, or went for quite wild walks along the towpath between the canal and the woods. They found a way of getting on the old barge, which was very long inside and had cupboards. It had an old sort of lavatory in a cupboard right up at the front end, so old it was no longer stinky-poo, or at least no more than the rest of the barge was.

So that year wore away unnoticed, what with school and living in the stables and having Mr and Mrs Bell to the stables for tea in a very grown-up way; and then they were out of thick trousers and sweaters and into jeans and light shirts and their eleventh birthday showed up on the horizon. Toni announced that it would be a good thing to go looking for books that they might like for their birthday. Sophy understood completely. Daddy would give them money, it was easier than thinking about them. Books chosen by Winnie would be ridiculous. They would have to make her mind up for her without her knowing since there was all this pretence of secrecy about birthday presents and she had to think it was her own idea. They went, therefore, from the stables at the bottom of the garden up the path under the buddleias, up the steps to the glass door into the hall, past Winnie who was playing her transistor in the kitchen, past Daddy who was playing the electric typewriter in his column room, then down the two steps to the front of the house where it looked up the High Street. They turned right to GOODCHILD'S RARE BOOKS and there they were, between the two boxes outside Goodchild's window, the sixpenny box and the shilling box, all full of books no one would ever think of buying.

Mr Goodchild was not in the shop but Mrs Goodchild was at the back doing some writing at the desk by a door that led somewhere. The twins paid no attention to her, even after they had got the door open and been ever so slightly startled by the ting! of the shop bell. They looked round the books for children but had most of them in the stables anyway because books were the kind of thing that seemed to come from every direction, and though often interesting were not particularly precious. Sophy soon saw these books were too simple and she was about to go when she saw that Toni was examining the old books on the shelves with her particular silent attention so Sophy waited, turning over *Ali Baba* and wondering why anyone would want it when there were the four thick volumes in Daddy's column room to be taken away if you felt like it. Then the old man who was so helpful to little boys in the park came in. Toni ignored him because by then she was right inside a grown-up book but Sophy greeted him politely because though she did not like him she was curious about him; and the one thing all the aunts and cleaning women and cousins were keen on was being polite to everybody. Certainly he came under the interdict of not-talking-to-strange-men-in-the-street, but Mr Goodchild's bookshop wasn't a street. The old man poked about among the books for children, then he went up the shop to where Mrs Goodchild was sitting. At the same time old Mr Goodchild came in ting! from the High Street and immediately talked in a joky kind of way to the twins. But before this had got properly under way he saw the old man and stopped. In that silence they all heard the old man who was holding out a book to Mrs Goodchild say, "For my nephew, you know." Then Toni, who had had her nose in a grown-up book but had seen him out of the back of her head, said helpfully that he had forgotten the one he had put in the right-hand pocket of his raincoat. After that things were fast and mixed. The old man's voice went shrill as a woman's, Mrs Goodchild stood up and talked angrily about police and old Mr Goodchild walked up to the old man and demanded the book now and no nonsense or else. The old man came in a sort of dance, a twisting of the body, inward movement of the knees with arms almost flailing but not quite, and his high woman's voice complaining, down the shop by the shelves and under the cases and Sophy opened the door for him ting! and shut it after him, because that too had a bit of the *meant* about it that sometimes happened. Mr Goodchild's face stopped being red quite quickly and he turned towards the twins but Mrs Goodchild talked to him first in the voice and words they were not supposed to understand.

"I can't think why they've let that man out of you-know-where again. He'll simply do it all over again, and there'll be some other poor little mite—"

Mr Goodchild broke in.

"Well at least now we know who's been taking the children's books."

After he had said that he became silly again, bowing to the twins.

"And how are the Misses Stanhope? Well, I trust?"

They answered him in beautiful unison.

"Yes thank you, Mr Goodchild."

"And Mr Stanhope? He is well?"

"Yes thank you, Mr Goodchild."

There was no question of being well as Sophy realized already. It was a thing people said, just as wearing a tie was something they did.

"I think, Mrs Goodchild," said Mr Goodchild in a more than usually silly way, "that we can offer the Misses Stanhope some liquid refreshment?"

So they went with comfortable Mrs Goodchild who was never silly, but calm and matter-of-fact, into the shabby sitting-room through the door at the back of the shop, where she sat them side by side on a sofa in front of a television set that was switched off and went away to get the fizzy drinks. Mr Goodchild stood in front of them, smiling and rocking on his toes and said how nice it was to see them and how he and they saw each other most days, didn't they. He had a little girl of his own, well she was a big girl now, a married lady with two little children but a long way away in Canada. It was half-way through his next sentence, which was about how much pleasanter a house was with children in it—and of course he had to add something silly like, "or not children precisely, let us say a pair of delightful young ladies like you," whereas when they left home if they went a long way away—half-way or somewhere in this twisting sentence Sophy had a naked realization of her own power should she care to exercise it, to do

120

anything she liked with Mr Goodchild, that large, old, fat man with his shopful of books and his silly ways, she could do absolutely anything she liked with him only it would not be worth the trouble. So they sat, toes only just reaching the old carpet and gazed at things over their fizzy drinks. There was a large notice on one wall that said in big letters how BERTRAND RUSSELL would address GREENFIELD PHILOSOPHICAL SOCIETY in the Assembly Rooms on HUMAN FREEDOM AND RESPONSIBILITY at such and such a date. It was an old notice and getting dim and seemed odd since it was stuck or hung where most people would put a picture; but then in the rather gloomy light Sophy saw under the big BERTRAND RUSSELL, in small print, Chairman, S. Goodchild, and understood, more or less. Mr Goodchild went on talking.

Sophy asked what interested her.

"Mrs Goodchild. Please, why was the old man taking books?"

After that there was quite a long pause before anyone spoke. Mrs Goodchild took a long drink of her instant before she said anything.

"Well dear, it's stealing, you see."

"But he's old," said Sophy, looking up over the rim, "He's old as old."

After she said that, Mr and Mrs Goodchild looked at each other over their instant for quite a time.

"You see," said Mr Goodchild at last, "he wants to give them to children as presents. He's—he's sick."

"Some people would say he's sick" said Mrs Goodchild, meaning she wasn't one of some people, "and needs a doctor. But others—"and it sounded as if Mrs Goodchild might be one of the others—"just think he's a nasty, wicked old man and that he ought to be—"

"Ruth!"

"Yes. Well."

Sophy could feel and almost see those shutters coming down that grown-ups had in constant supply when you wanted to know something really interesting. But Mrs Goodchild went off round a corner.

"What with W. H. Smith taking over and ruining the assembly rooms and the supermarket giving away paperbacks it's hard enough keeping the place together without nasty old Pedigree helping us on the road to ruin."

121

"At least we know now who's been doing the shoplifting. I'll have a word with Sergeant Phillips."

Then Sophy saw him change the subject behind his face. He became fatter, rosier, beaming with his head a bit sideways. He spread out, his cup in one hand and the saucer in the other.

"But with the Misses Stanhope to entertain—"

Toni spoke in the pause, using her faint, clear voice in which every syllable was as precise as a line in a good drawing.

"Mrs Goodchild. What is Tran-scend-en-tal Phil-os-oph-y?"

Mrs Goodchild's cup rattled in her saucer.

"God bless the child! Does your daddy teach you words like that?"

"No. Daddy doesn't teach us."

Sophy saw her fly away again and explained the thing to Mrs Goodchild.

"It's the name on a book in your shop, Mrs Goodchild."

"Transcendental Philosophy, my dear," said Mr Goodchild in a jokey voice that had nothing to be jokey about, "might on the one hand be called a book full of hot air. On the other hand it might be considered the ultimate wisdom. You pays your money as they used to say and you takes your choice. Beautiful young ladies are not generally considered to stand in need of an understanding of Transcendental Philosophy on the grounds that they exemplify in themselves all the pure, the beautiful and the good."

"Sim."

It was evident that nothing was to be learnt from Mr and Mrs Goodchild. For a little while longer Sophy and Toni did their "remarkable children" thing, then said together—it was one of the few benefits of twinship—that they must go now, got down, did their "thank yous" demurely, to hear as they retreated down the shop old Mr Goodchild going on about "enchanting children" and Mrs Goodchild breaking in—

"You'd better have a word with Phillips this afternoon. I think old Pedigree is having one of his beastly times again. They ought to put him away for good."

"He wouldn't touch Stanhope's little girls."

"What difference does it make whose child it is?"

That night in bed, Sophy did a long brood that was almost a Toni, a drifting away up into the boughs. "Stanhope's little girls?" It seemed to her that they weren't anyone's little girls. She sent

122

her mind round the circle of people who impinged; Gran, who had disappeared together with Rosevear and all that, Daddy, the cleaning women, aunts, a teacher or two, some children. She saw clearly that they belonged to each other and to no one else. As she didn't like belonging to Toni and contrariwise, it was clear she wouldn't like belonging to anyone else either. And then—that personal, that wholly isolated direction at the back of your head, the black place from which you looked out on things so that all of those people, even Toni, *out there*—how could the creature called Sophy who sat there at the mouth of the tunnel behind her belong to anyone but herself? It was all silly. And if belonging was like being twin with a lot of people out there the way Daddy had lived with aunts and the Bells with each other and the Goodchilds with each other and all the others—but Daddy had his column room to disappear into and when he had disappeared into his column room—she saw suddenly, knees up to her chin—he could go further, do a Toni and disappear into his chess.

When she thought that, she opened her eyes and the room came into view with a glimmer from her dormer so she shut them again, wishing to stay inside. She knew she was not thinking the way grown-ups thought and there were so many of them and they were so big—

All the same.

Sophy became very still and held her breath. There was the old man and the books. She saw something. She had been told it often enough but now she *saw* it. You could choose to belong to people the way the Goodchilds and Bells and Mrs Hugeson did by being good, by doing what they said was right. Or you could choose what was real and what you knew was real—your own self sitting inside with its own wishes and rules at the mouth of the tunnel.

Perhaps the only advantage of being everything with a twin and knowing the exact Toni-ness of Toni was that in the morning Sophy had no hesitation in discussing the next step with her. She suggested they should steal sweets and Toni not only listened but contributed ideas. She said they would use a Paki shop because the Pakis couldn't keep their eyes off her hair and she would hold the man's attention while Sophy did the actual stealing. Sophy saw the reasonableness of this. If Toni let her hair fall over her face, then tried in a deliberately baby-way to get it clear and looked up through the tresses it was like doing a bit of magic. So they went to the shop kept by the Krishna brothers and it was simply too easy. The younger Krishna was standing in the doorway and talking in a liquid voice to a blackie—"Now you go off you black fellow. We are not wanting your custom." The twins sidled past him and inside the shop the older Krishna came forward from between sacks of brown sugar that were open for the scoops and said the shop was theirs. Then he positively forced curious sweets on them and added some curious sticks which he said were incense and refused to be paid for anything. It was humiliating and they abandoned the project, seeing that if they tried it on Mr Goodchild's books it would be much the same; and the books were silly anyway. There was another thing that now presented itself to Sophy. They had more toys than they wanted and more pocket money than they wanted. All Daddy's cleaning women and cousins ensured that. Worst of all, they found there was a group of kids at their school who were doing the same thing only on a larger scale, *really* stealing and sometimes breaking in and then selling the loot to those children who could afford to buy it. Sophy saw that stealing was wrong or right according to the way you thought, but both ways it was boring. Being bored was the real reason for not stealing, the reason that counted. Once or twice she thought about this matter so piercingly, it was as if right and wrong and boring were numbers you could add and subtract. She saw, too, in this particularly piercing way that there was another number, an x to be added or to be subtracted, for which she could find no value. The combination of the piercingness and the fourth number made her panicky and would have settled into a chilly fear, if she had not had the mouth of the dark tunnel to sit at and know herself to be not Sophy but *This*. *This* lived and watched without any feelings at all and brandished or manipulated the Sophy-creature like a complicated doll, a child with all the arts and wiles and deliberate delightfulness of a quite unselfconscious, oh a quite innocent, naive, trusting little girl—brandished her among all the other children, white, yellow, brown, black, the other children who surely were as incapable of inspecting this kind of sum as they were of doing the others in their heads and had to write them down laboriously on paper. Then, suddenly, sometimes, it would be easy—flip!—to go out there and to join them.

This discovery of what-is-what might have seemed very

important except that their eleventh birthday was the start of a really dreadful month for Sophy and perhaps for Toni, though Toni did not seem to be as affected. It was on the birthday itself. They had a cake, bought from Timothy's and with ten candles round the top with one in the middle. Daddy actually came all the way down from the column room to share in the tea and he was jokey in the way that did not suit him or his hawk's face that always made Sophy think of princes and pirates. He told them after only the slightest many happy returns and before they'd even blown out the candles. He told them he and Winnie were getting married so they'd have what he called a proper mother. Sophy knew a lot of things in the burning moment after he stopped speaking. She knew the difference between Winnie keeping her clothes in the aunties' room and paying Daddy visits; and Winnie going straight in there to undress and get in bed and be called Missis Stanhope and perhaps (because it happened in stories) having babies that Daddy would want the way he didn't want the twins, his twins and nobody else's. It was a moment of deadly anguish—Winnie with her painted face, her yellow hair, her strange way of speaking, and her smelling like a ladies' hairdressers'. Sophy knew it couldn't happen, couldn't be allowed to happen. All the same, that was no comfort and she couldn't get her mouth together to blow but it went wider and she began to cry. Even the crying was all wrong because it began in sheer woe but then because she was exhibiting it before Winnie, and worse, before Daddy, thus informing him how important he was, it got mixed up with rage. Also she knew that even when she had done with crying, the fact would still be there, massive and unbearable. She heard Winnie speak.

"Over to you, cobber."

Cobber was Daddy. He came and said things over her shoulder, touched her so that she twisted herself away and there was silence after a time. Then Daddy roared in a terrible voice.

"Christ! Children!"

She heard him thumping down the wooden stairs into the coachhouse and then hurrying up the garden path. The door into the hall slammed so hard it was a wonder the glass didn't break. Winnie went after him.

After she had got rid of all her tears without improving the situation she sat up on her divan bed and looked across at Toni on hers. Toni was the same as usual except that she was a bit pink in the cheek—no tears. She simply said in an offhand voice;

"Cry-baby."

Sophy was too miserable to answer. She wanted nothing so much as to get right away and abandon Daddy, forget him and his treachery. She rubbed her face and said they should go along the towpath because Winnie told them not to. They did this at once though it seemed weak and nowhere near a reply to the awful news. Only by the time they had got to the old boat by the broken lock Winnie and Daddy did seem a bit smaller and farther away. They mooned about on the boat for a bit and they discovered a clutch of duck's eggs that had been left there a long time. When she saw the eggs, everything came quite clear in Sophy's head. She saw how she would torment Winnie and Daddy, go on and on tormenting them till she had driven them both mad and away, both taken away like Mr Goodchild's son in the mental hospital.

After that things happened the way they were intended to happen. They fell together in a kind of "Of course" way, as if the whole world was co-operating. It was meant that when they got back to the birthday cake and ate some of the icing—there was no sense in leaving it—they should decide to open the old leather trunk they had been told not to and find the bunch of rusty keys there. The keys opened everything usually kept shut. That night, sitting up in bed, her knees against her new breasts, Sophy saw clearly that one of the old eggs was meant for Winnie. She found herself overcome with a passionate desire in the darkness to be Weird—there was no other name for it, Weird and powerful. She frightened herself and curled down in the bed but the dark tunnel was still there; and in that remote security she saw what to do.

Next day she found how easy it was. You just looked for the areas of inattention with which grown-ups were so liberally supplied and walked through them. You could do it quite briskly and no one could see or hear you. Therefore, briskly she unlocked the drawer in the little table by Daddy's bed, broke the egg in it and walked away briskly. She put the key back with the others on the heavy ring that quite obviously had not been used for years and felt it was the nearest she could get to being Weird but not really satisfactory. That day she was so preoccupied in school that even Mrs Hugeson noticed and asked what was the matter. Nothing of course.

126

That night in her bed under the dormer in the stables she brooded about being weird. She tried to join things together about weirdness but could not. It was not arithmetic. Everything floated, the private tunnel, the things that were meant and oh, above all, the deep, fierce, hurting need, desire, to hurt Winnie and Daddy up there in the bedroom. She brooded and wished and tried to think and then brooded again; and presently her feelings made her want so desperately to be weird for this occasion that she saw in a kind of supposing that burnt, how it should have been. Now she saw herself glide up the garden path, through the glass door, up the stairs, gliding through the bedroom door to the big bed where Daddy lay and Winnie curled, her back to him. So she went to the little table which now had three books on it by the bedside lamp and she thrust her hand with the egg through the locked wood and she broke the egg beside the other one, so eek, so stinky-poo, so oof and pah and she left the two messes there. Then she turned and looked down and she aimed the dark part of her head at sleeping Winnie and gave her a nightmare so that she jerked in bed and shrieked aloud; at which the shriek kind of woke Sophy—though it could not wake her as she had never been asleep—and she was in her own bed with her own shriek and she was deadly frightened by the weirdness and she cried out after her own shriek, "Toni! Toni!" But Toni was asleep and off away wherever it was so Sophy had to lie for a long time, curled up, frightened and shaking. Indeed she began to feel that going on being weird would be too much and that grown-ups would win after all, because too much weirdness made you sick. But then Uncle Jim appeared from fucking Sydney.

At first everyone had fun with Uncle Jim, even Daddy, who said he was a natural comedian. But not more than a week after the birthday party that had gone wrong Sophy noticed how much time he was beginning to spend with Winnie; and she wondered about it all and was a bit scared that she might have produced him by being weird. After all, he did kind of dilute the situation, she said to herself, proud of having found a word that was even better than just the right word, he diluted everybody's feelings and made them—well, dilute.

On the seventh of June, that being approximately a fortnight after the birthday, when Sophy was already accustomed to thinking of herself as eleven, she was behind the old rose bush and squatting down, and watching the ants being busy about nothing when Toni came flying down the garden path and up the wooden stairs to their own room. This was so astonishing that Sophy went to see. Toni wasted no time in explanations.

"Come."

She grabbed Sophy's wrist, but she resisted.

"What—?"

"I need you!"

Sophy was so astonished she allowed herself to be led. Toni went quickly up the garden path and into the hall. She stood outside the door of the column room and put her hair straight. She held on to Sophy's wrist and opened the door. Daddy was there, looking at a chess set. The Anglepoise light was switched on and lowered over it, though the sun was shining outside.

"What do you two want?"

Sophy saw that Toni had gone bright red for the first time in memory. She gave a little gasp, then spoke in her faint, colourless voice.

"Uncle Jim is having sexual relationships with Winnie in the aunties' bedroom."

Daddy stood up very slowly.

"I—you—"

There was a pause of a kind of woollen silence, prickly, hot, uncomfortable. Daddy went quickly to the door, then across the hall. They heard him on the other stairs.

"Winnie? Where are you?"

The twins ran, Toni white now, ran to the glass door down into the garden, Sophy leading. Sophy ran all the way down to the stables again, she hardly knew why or why she was excited and frightened and scared and triumphant. She was up in the room before she saw that Toni had not come with her. It was perhaps ten minutes before she came, slowly and still even whiter than usual.

"What happened? Is he angry? Were they doing that? Like in the lectures? Toni! Why did you say 'I need you?' Did you hear them? Did you hear him? Daddy? What did he say?"

Toni was lying on her tummy, her forehead on the backs of her hands.

"Nothing. He shut the door and came down again."

After that, there was a pause of about three days; and then

128

when the twins came back from school in the afternoon they walked through a furious grown-up row. It was high above their heads and Sophy walked away from it down the garden path, half hoping that weirdness was working but wondering in a gloomy sort of way if all that really worked was what Toni had done, in letting Daddy know a secret. But whichever it was, that was the day it was all done with. Winnie and Uncle Jim went away that very evening. Toni—who did not, it appeared, concern herself with the idea of being weird at a distance—had stayed as close to the grown-ups as she could and reported helpfully to Sophy what she had heard without trying to explain it. She said Winnie had gone with Uncle Jim because he was a digger and she was sick of fucking Poms it had all been a mistake anyway Daddy was too fucking old and the kids were a consideration and she hoped there were no hard feelings. Sophy was half-sorry and half-glad to know that she had not got rid of Winnie by being weird. But Uncle Jim was a real loss. Toni dropped one piece of information which did show Sophy how carefully her twin had planned and gone about the whole scheme.

"She had a passport. She was a foreigner. Her real name wasn't 'Winnie'. It was 'Winsome'."

This struck the twins as so funny they were happy with each other for quite a while.

There were no more aunties after Winnie, and Daddy spent regular times in London at a club and doing his chess broadcasts. There was a long series of cleaning ladies who did the bit of the house that wasn't occupied by the solicitors and the Bells. There was also a sort of cousin of Daddy's who stayed every now and then, overhauled their clothes, told them about periods and God. But she was a colourless character not worth being friends with or tormenting.

In fact, after the disposal of Winnie time stopped. It was as if after climbing a slope they had both come to a plateau, the edges of which were out of sight. Perhaps this was partly because their twelfth birthday went unnoticed by Daddy, there being no Winnie or other auntie to remind him. Both twins were made aware in the course of that year that they had phenomenal intelligence, but this was no news, really, except that it did explain why all other children seemed so dim. To Sophy the phrase "phenomenal intelligence" was a useless bit of junk lying in her mind and not really connected to anything that would be worth having or doing. Toni seemed the same, unless you knew her the way that Sophy did. It showed, perhaps, in the way that they quickly found themselves in different classes for certain subjects, though not all. It showed itself more subtly in the way that Toni would sometimes say things offhand that settled a question for good. You could tell then that long thought had preceded the words; but there was no other evidence for it.

Periods, when they happened, hurt Sophy and enraged her. Toni seemed indifferent to them, as if she could leave her body to get on with its job and be away somewhere herself, out of the whole business of feeling. Sophy knew that she herself had these long, still times; but she knew they weren't thinking, they were brooding. It was when she had a period and it hurt that she began to brood again—for the first time since Winnie—on the whole business of being weird and what there was in it. She found herself doing some strange things too. Once, near Christmas, she went into the deserted aunties' room and then had to think—why did I come here? She brooded some more—standing by the head of the stripped single bed on which the ancient electric blanket, creased and stained with iron mould, seemed ugly as a surgical appliance—brooded on the *why* and decided that she had had some vague wish to find out what an auntie was and what they had in common; and then, with a shiver of a kind of dirty excitement and also disgust she knew that she wanted to find out what there was about them that made Daddy summon them to his bed. While she was thinking that, she heard him come out of the column room and run up the stairs two at a time if not more, slam the bathroom door—and then there was running water and all that. She thought of the duck's egg by his bed and wondered why no one had ever said anything about it; but with him in the bathroom there was no chance of going in his bedroom to see. She stood there by the single bed and waited for him to go down.

Any reasonable auntie would have been glad to get out of that room. There was an old rug by the bed, a chair, a dressing-table and large wardrobe and nothing else. She tiptoed to the window and looked down the garden path to the dormers of the stabling. She opened the top drawer of the dressing-table and there was Winnie's little transistor lying in the corner. Sophy took it out and

130

examined it with a comfortable feeling of security from Winnie. She felt a bit of triumph as she switched on the set. The battery was still live so that a miniature pop group began to perform miniature music. The door opened behind her.

It was Daddy, standing in the door. She looked at him and saw why Toni had such a white skin. There was a long silence between them. She was the first to speak.

"Can I keep it?"

He looked down at the little leather-sheathed case in her hands. He nodded, swallowed, then went away as swiftly as he had come, down the stairs. Triumph triumph, triumph! It was like capturing Winnie and keeping her caged and never letting her out—Sophy sniffed the case carefully and decided that none of Winnie's scent had clung to it. She took it away, back to the stables. She lay on her divan bed and thought of a tiny Winnie shut there in the box. It was silly of course, to think that—but as she said that to herself she had a thought to go with it; having a period is silly! Silly! Silly! It deserves to have a duck's egg, a stink, some dirt.

After that Sophy became addicted to the transistor with Winnie inside it. She thought it likely that all transistors had their owners inside them and so it was lucky this one was already tenanted. She listened often, sometimes with her ear against the fairing of the speaker, sometimes pulling the earplug out of its niche and being private to herself. It was that way she heard two talks which spoke not to the little girl with her smiling face (little friend of all the world) but directly to the Sophy-thing that sat inside at the mouth of its private tunnel. One was about the universe running down and she understood that she had always known that, it explained so much it was obvious, it was why fools were fools and why there were so many of them. The other talk was about some people being able to guess the colour of a greater percentage of cards than they should be able to, statistically speaking. Sophy listened enthralled to the man who spoke about this nonsense, as he called it. He said there was no magic and how if people could guess these so-called cards more than they ought, statistically speaking, then fiercely, oh so very fiercely, the man's eyes must be popping out, *statistics must be re-examined*. This made even the Sophy-creature giggle because she could swim in numbers when she wanted. She remembered the duck's egg and the little

131

Sophy-child walking through those areas of inattention; and she saw that what they missed out of their experiments in magic which gave them no or little result, was just the stinky-poo bit, the breaking of rules, the using of people, the well-deep wish, the piercingness, the—the what? The other end of the tunnel, where surely it joined on.

In the evening when these things came together, she jumped clean out of bed and the desire to be weird was like a taste in the mouth, a hunger and thirst after weirdness. It seemed to her then that unless she did what had never been done, saw something that she never ought to see, she would be lost for ever and turn into a young girl. Something pushed her, shoved her, craved. She tried to get the rusty dormer open and did so, just a crack; then more than a crack as if the door of a vault were grinding on its hinge. But all she could see in the evening light was the canal shining. But then there were footsteps on the towpath. She did a violence to her head, thrusting it sideways in the crack and yes, she could see now what was never before oh not by living people seen from this angle, not just the towpath and the canal but along the towpath to the Old Bridge, yes, more of the Old Bridge and yes, the filthy old stinky-poo urinal, whiff whiff; and there was the old man who stole books from Mr Goodchild going in and she kept him there she did! She willed him to stay in the dirty place, like Winnie in the transistor, would not let him come out, she bent her mind, frowning, teeth gritted, she brought everything down to one point where he was in the dirty place and kept him there; and a man in a black hat went cycling primly out over the Old Bridge into the country and a bus heaved this way over it and she kept him there! But she could not hold on. The man in the black hat went cycling out into the country, the bus went on into Greenfield High Street. Her mind inside her let go so that she could not tell whether she was keeping the old man in the dirty place or not. All the same, she thought as she turned away from the dormer, he stayed in there and if I can't be sure I kept him in, I can't be sure I didn't. Then all at once because she had let go of her mind and become the Sophy-child again in her pyjamas out in the centre of the moony room, fear descended over her like a magician's tall hat and froze her flesh so that she cried out in panic.

"Toni! Toni!"

But Toni was fast asleep and stayed that way even when shaken.

In their fifteenth year at a specific hour or even instant, Sophy felt herself come out into daylight. She was sitting in class and Toni was the only other girl of her age in the room. The rest were seniors with lumpy breasts and big bums and they were groaning as if the algebra was glue they were stuck in. Sophy was sitting back because she had finished. Toni was sitting back because she had not only finished but evaporated and left her body there with its face tilted up. That was when it happened. Sophy *saw* as well as knew, that there was a dimension they were moving through; and as she saw that she saw something else too. It was not that Toni was Toni the wet, though she *was* a wet hen and always would be, but yes, she was beautiful, a beautiful young girl—no, not beautiful with her smoke-grey hair afloat, her thin, no slim body, her face that could be seen through—she was not just beautiful. She was *stunning*. It was a pang clean through Sophy to see that so clearly; and after the pang, a kind of rage, that wet hen Toni of all people—

She asked to be excused, went and examined herself urgently in the grubby mirror. Yes. It was not like Toni's beauty but it was alright. It was dark of course, and not to be seen through, not transparent, but regular, pretty, oh God, *healthy*, outdoor, winning, inviting, could be strong and yes that would be the best side for a photograph; in fact very satisfactory indeed if you didn't have always at your side the wet hen for which or whom there was now no easy word—So Sophy stared into the grubby mirror at her reflection, seeing all things in the daylight that had brightened and cleared so suddenly. That evening after the French verbs and American history she lay on her divan and Toni on hers. Sophy wrenched up the volume of her new transistor so that it blared for a moment, a challenge perhaps, an insult even, or at least a rude jab at her silent twin.

"Do you mind, Sophy!"

"Doesn't make any difference to you does it?"

Toni half knelt, changing her position. With her new, daylight eyes, Sophy saw the impossible curve alter and flow, from the line of the forehead under the smoky hair, down, round the curve of the long neck, the shoulder, include the suggestion of a breast, sweep round and end back there where a toe moved and pushed off a sandal.

"It does as a matter of fact."

"Well you'll have to go on minding then, my deah, deah Toni."

"I'm not Toni any more. I'm Antonia."

Sophy burst out laughing.

"And I'm Sophia."

"If you like."

And the strange creature drifted away again, leaving her body to lie there, as it were, untenanted. Sophy had a mind to blow the roof off with the radio but it seemed an action out of that childhood which they had so suddenly left behind. She lay back instead, looking at the ceiling with the big spot of damp. With another jolt of awareness she saw that this new daylight made the dark direction at the back of her head all the more incredible yet all the more evident; because there it was!

"I've got eyes in the back of my head!"

She sat up with a jerk, conscious of the words spoken aloud, then the turn of the other girl's head and the long look.

"Oh?"

Neither of them said anything after that and presently Toni turned away. It was impossible that Toni should know. Yet Toni did.

There are eyes in the back of my head. The angle is still there, wider, the thing called Sophy can sit looking out through the eyes, the thing which really is nameless. It can choose either to go out into the daylight or to lie in this private segment of infinite depth, distance, this ambushed separateness from which comes all strength—

She shut her eyes with sudden excitement. She made a connection that seemed exact between this new feeling and an old one, the one of the rotten egg, the passionate desire to be weird, to be on the other side, desire for the impossibilities of the darkness and the bringing of them into being to disrupt the placid normalities of the daylight world. With her front eyes shut it was as if those other eyes opened in the back of her head and stared into a darkness that stretched away infinitely, a cone of black light.

She came up out of this contemplation and opened her daylight eyes. There the other figure was, curled on the other divan, child and woman—and surely expression too, not of the futile pinpricks

134

of light with its bursting and efflorescence, but of the darkness and running down?

It was from that moment that Sophy ceased to make many of the gestures that the world required of her. She found a measuring rod in her hand. Look at "ought" and "must" and "want" and "need". If they were not appropriate at the moment to the sweet-faced girl with the optional eyes at the back of her head, then she touched them with her wand and they vanished. Hey presto.

When they were fifteen-and-a-bit, the staff said Toni should go to a college but Toni wasn't certain and said she might prefer to model. Sophy didn't know what she would do but saw no point in going to college or loading your body with someone else's clothes day after day. It was while she was still in the position of not really believing that it would come to the point of living in the outside world that Toni went off to London and was away quite a time, which infuriated the school and Daddy. The thing was that after a few days, girls being supposed to be a fragile commodity, Toni became a genuine missing person and listed by Interpol, as on the telly. The next anybody knew was that she turned up in Afghanistan of all places, and in deep trouble because the people she had accepted a lift from were running drugs. It seemed for a while that Toni might have to stay in jail for years. Sophy was astonished by Toni's daring and a bit jealous, and decided to get on with her own further education. The first thing she did, being certain that by now Toni must have got rid of her virginity, was to examine her own by means of a strategically placed mirror. She was not impressed. She tried a couple of boys who proved incompetent and their mechanisms ridiculous. But they did teach her the astonishing power her prettiness could wield over men. She examined the traffic situation in Greenfield and saw the best place, by the pillar-box a hundred yards beyond the Old Bridge. She waited there, refused a truck and a man on a motorbike and chose the third one.

He drove a small van, not a car, he was dark and attractive and he said he was going to Wales. Sophy allowed him to pick her up by the post-box because she thought he was very likely telling the truth and never seeing him again would be that much easier if it was what she wanted. Ten miles out of Greenfield he drove down a side road, parked in the skirts of a wood and enveloped her,

135

breathing heavily. It was she who suggested they should go into the wood and there she found there was no doubt about his competence at all. He hurt her more than she had thought possible. When he had ended his part of the affair he pulled out, wiped himself, zipped himself and looked down at her with a mixture of triumph and caution.

"Now don't you go telling anyone. See?"

Sophy was faintly surprised.

"Why should I?"

He looked at her with less caution and more triumph.

"You were a virgin. Well. You aren't, now. I've had you, see?"

Sophy took out the tissues she had brought with her for the purpose and wiped a trickle of blood from her thigh. The man said, in high humour and to no one in particular.

"Had a virgin!"

Sophy pulled on her pants. She was wearing a dress rather than jeans, which was most unusual but another bit of foresight. She looked curiously at the man who was now evidently delighted with life.

"Is that all?"

"What d'you mean?"

"Sex. Fucking."

"Christ. What did you expect?"

She said nothing, since it was not necessary. She then had a lesson in the extraordinary nature of men, if this specimen was anything to go by. This instrument of her initiation told her what a risk she had run, she might have been picked up by anyone and lying there at this very moment strangled, she must never, never do such a thing again. If she were his daughter he would take the strap to her, letting herself get picked up and she only seventeen, why she might, she might—

By this time Sophy lost patience.

"I'm not sixteen yet."

"Christ! But you said—"

"Not till October."

"Christ—"

It was a mistake. She saw that at once. It was another lesson. Always stick to the simplest lie like the simplest truth. He was angry and frightened. But then as he blustered about deadly secrets and how he'd find her and cut her throat she saw how

136

slight and silly he was, all this about never letting on, forgetting him, if she said a word—if she mentioned *anyone* had picked her up. Bored, she broke it to him.

"I picked you up, silly."

He made for her and she went on quickly before his hands touched her.

"That card I posted when you stopped by me. It had the number of your van on it. It's to my Dad. If I don't pick it up—"

"Christ."

He took an uncertain step among the leaves.

"I don't believe you!"

She recited the number of his van to him. She told him he was to take her back to where he had found her and when he swore, mentioned the card again. Finally, of course, he drove her back, because, as she told herself, her will was stronger than his. She liked that idea so much that she broke her recent resolve and told him in so many words. It made him very angry all over again but pleased her. Then what was the most extraordinary part of the whole thing, he got positively wet, telling her she was a lovely kid really and she shouldn't waste herself on this sort of thing. If she waited for him at the same place and time next week, they'd go together regular. She'd like that. He had a bit of money—

To all this Sophy listened silently, nodding occasionally, since that was what kept him planning. But she would not tell him her name or give him her address.

"Don't you want to know my name then, kiddy?"

"As a matter of fact, not."

"'As a mattah of fact not.' Christ stone the fucking crows. You'll be murdered one of these days. Straight, you will."

"Just put me down by the post-box."

He shouted after her that he would be at the same place, same time, next week and she gave him a smile to get rid of him and then walked a long way home by all the sidestreets and alleys she could think of so that the van could not follow. She was still in the grip of her astonishment at it meaning so little. It was so trivial an act when you subtracted the necessary and not-to-be-repeated pain of the first time. It meant nothing at all. There was little more sensation to it than feeling the inside of your cheek with your tongue—well, there *was* a little more but not much.

137

They said too, whoever it was said, that the girl cried afterwards.

"I didn't cry."

At that, her body gave a long shudder, all on its own, and she waited for a bit, but nothing more happened. Of course, the sex lectures always added in the bit about pair-bonding and about achieving orgasm which might not happen to a girl for quite a long time—but really so trivial an act and significant only in the possible, though quite unbelievable outcome. It seemed to her, walking home by way, at last, of the towpath, vaguely right that this thing they made so much fuss about—wrestling with each other on the box or grunting at it on the wide screens, all the poetry and music and painting and everybody agreeing it was a many-splendoured thing, the simplest thing, well it *was* very nearly the simplest thing and so much the worse, yes, vaguely right in view of how the whole thing is running down—well, it was silly.

She agreed mildly with Daddy's cleaning lady that she was home early from school, listened for the electric typewriter then remembered it was the afternoon of his school broadcast, and went to the bathroom where she washed herself out as in the films and was faintly repelled by the mess of blood and spunk, and—reaching far in, her lower lip hurting between clenched teeth—she felt the pear-shaped thing stuck inside the front of her stomach where it ought to be, inert, a time bomb, though that was hard to believe of yourself or your body. The thought of the possible explosion of the time bomb started her even more elaborately probing and washing, pain or not; and she came on the other shape, lying opposite the womb but at the back, a shape lying behind the smooth wall but easily to be felt through it, the rounded shape of her own turd working down the coiled gut and she convulsed, feeling without saying but feeling every syllable—*I hate! I hate! I hate!* There was no direct object to the verb, as she said to herself when she was a little more normal. The feeling was pure.

But washed and cleaned out, menstruated and restored, this active hate sank down like a liquid to the bottom of things and she ·
was a young girl again, felt she was; a young girl conscious of listening to the sound of space, confused over the possibilities of weirdness since the word was used in several ways, conscious of

resisting the proposal of teachers that you should make one last effort to use your unquestioned intelligence; or—and suddenly—a giggly girl about clothes and boys and who was going with whom and yes isn't he gorgeous and catch phrases and catch music and catch pop stars and catch and catch as catch can be simple.

All the same, with Toni not yet retrieved and staring into her own bland face, she was worried over it meaning nothing, even though that in itself was about as simple as you could get. She thought round the whole circle of people she knew, even dead Gran and forgotten mother and she saw they were shapes and it worried her. It was almost better being forced to be everything with someone you didn't really like than this living with yourself and to yourself. With a confused and fundamentally ignorant expectation that wealth and sophistication would make a difference—and besides, now she was sixteen!—she picked up an expensive car, only to find that the man inside was much older than he looked. This time the exercises that took place in the wood were not painful but more prolonged and she did not understand them. The man offered her more money than she had ever seen before to perform various actions for him, which she did, finding them a bit sick-making but not more so than the inside of her own body. It was only when she got home—Yes, Mrs Emlin, school *is* out early—she thought; *Now I am a whore!* After the bathroom she lay on her divan, thinking about being a whore, but even if she said it out loud it didn't seem to change her, didn't seem to touch her, just was not. Only the roll of blue five-pound notes was real. She thought to herself that being a whore didn't mean anything either. It was like stealing sweets, a thing you could do if you wanted, but boring. Not even rousing the Sophy-creature to say—*I hate!*

After that she put sex on one side as a discovered, examined and discarded bit of triviality. It became nothing more than playing with yourself lazily in bed to the accompaniment of quite unusual or what seemed like quite unusual imaginings, very private indeed.

Antonia was flown home and had terrific cold rows with Daddy in the column room. There was a little, a very little, communication in the stables but Toni was not inclined to give a blow by blow account of her life. Sophy never knew why or how Toni and

Daddy worked it, but before long Toni was living in a hostel in London which was official and would keep her safe from everything. She said she was an actress and tried for it, but the odd fact was that despite her intelligence and her transparency she wasn't any good. There seemed little for her but the university but she swore she wouldn't go and began to talk wildly about imperialism. Also freedom and justice. She seemed to have even less use for boys or men than Sophy had, though they swarmed after her remote beauty. No one was really surprised when she disappeared again. She sent them a defiant postcard from Cuba.

Sophy got a job that demanded nothing. It was in a travel agent's and after a few weeks she told Daddy she was moving up to London, but would keep her bit of the stables.

He looked at her with evident dislike.

"For God's sake go and marry somebody."

"You're no advertisement for marriage, are you?"

"Neither are you."

Later when she thought that one over and understood it, she had half a mind to go back and spit in his face. But as a remark the farewell at least served to confirm her in her understanding of how deeply she hated him; and even more than that—how much they hated each other.

# CHAPTER NINE

Runways Travel was boring but undemanding. Despite what she had told Daddy she travelled up to it every day for a bit, and then the manager's wife found her a room which was good but expensive. The manager's wife produced plays for a small amateur group and persuaded Sophy to act but she wasn't any better than Toni. She went out with boys a few times and fended them off from the boring sex stuff. Really what she liked was to lie in front of the television and watch programmes indifferently, advertisements or even the Open University, and let it all go by her. She went to the flicks sometimes, usually with a boy and once with Mabel, the lanky blonde who worked next to her, but without much enjoyment. Sometimes she wondered why nothing mattered and why she felt she could let her life trickle out of her hand if she wanted to, but most often she did not even wonder. The thing at the mouth of her tunnel brandished a pretty girl who smiled and flirted and even sounded earnest now and then—"Yes I *do* see what you mean! We're destroying the world!" But the thing at the mouth of the tunnel said without sound—*as if I cared*.

Someone—Daddy? a cleaning woman?—sent on a postcard from Toni. This time the print round the picture was Arab writing. All Toni said was, "I (and then she had crossed out the I) We need you!!" Nothing else. Sophy put it up on the mantelpiece of her bedsitter and forgot all about it. She was seventeen and not to be fooled by the pretence that they were everything to each other.

A ponderously respectable person began to visit her desk and ask questions about voyages and flights she suspected he had no intention of taking. At his third visit he asked her to come out with him and she did in an exhausted kind of way since it was what was expected of a girl who is seventeen and pretty. He was Roland Garrett, and after the first two times she went out with him—once to the flicks and once to a disco where they didn't dance because he couldn't—he said she should take a room in his mother's house. It would be cheaper. It was. She got it almost for nothing. When she asked Roland why it was so cheap he said his mother was like that. He was protecting a girl, that was all. It seemed to Sophy that the protecting came from Mrs Garrett but she did not say so. Mrs Garrett was a haggard widow with dyed brown hair and little substance to her body other than its skeleton. She stood in the open doorway of Sophy's room, leaning against the doorpost with her skinny arms folded and a dead fag-end hanging from one corner of her mouth.

"I expect you have trouble being so sexy dear, don't you?"

Sophy was folding underwear in a drawer.

"What trouble?"

There was a long pause then, which Sophy did not feel inclined to break. Mrs Garrett broke it instead.

"Roland's very steady you know. Very steady indeed."

Mrs Garrett had large eye-hollows that looked as if they had been charred. Her eyes, deeply set in them, seemed extra bright, extra liquid by contrast. She put up a finger and touched one hollow delicately. She elaborated.

"In the civil service dear. He has very good prospects."

Sophy understood why she had got the room for next to nothing. Mrs Garrett did her best to thrust them together and quite soon Sophy had shared his narrow bed with that freedom which stemmed from the pill; and he performed correctly as if it were a bit of civil service work or bank business or duty. But he seemed to enjoy himself, though as usual there wasn't much in it for Sophy. Mrs Garrett began to keep on at Sophy to consider herself engaged. It was fantastic. She saw that Roland couldn't get himself a girl and his mum had to do it for him. Being tied to Roland with his prospects was a thought that made her shudder and giggle. Of course there was a bit of warm pleasure in it, and on her side a faintly pleasurable contempt for them both, as she said to herself, putting words to what wouldn't really go into them. Roland had a car and they looked at places and pubs and she said why not this new thing, hang gliding, you know. He said I'd never let you do a thing like that it's dangerous. She said of course not I mean you. However, he taught her to drive, more or less, complete with L-plates; and he wanted to meet her father.

142

Amused, she took him to Sprawson's and of course it was Daddy's day in London. So they went through to the stables. Roland displayed a kind of automatic interest in the layout as if he were an architect or archaeologist.

"It'll have been for the coachman and the grooms and ostlers. You see? They must have built it before the canal because now you couldn't get a coach out. That's why the house went downhill."

"Downhill? Our house?"

"There'll have been other stables along there—"

"They're just warehouses for storing things. When I was little there used to be a big ironmonger's. Frankley's, I think."

"What's beyond that door?"

"Towpath and canal. And the Old Bridge just along with the dirtiest loo in town."

Roland looked at her sternly.

"You shouldn't say things like that."

"Sorry, dad. But I live—lived here you know. Me and my sister. Come and see." She led the way up the narrow stairs.

"Your father could do this place up and let it as a cottage."

"It's our place. Mine and Toni's."

"Tony?"

"Antonia. My sister."

He peered about.

"And this place was yours."

"Belongs to both of us—belonged to both of us."

"Belonged?"

"She hasn't been home for ages. Don't even know where she is."

"All these places where pictures were stuck up!"

"She had a religious thing. Jesus and all that. It was *so* funny. Christ!"

"And you?"

"We aren't alike."

"Twins, though."

"How did you know?"

"You told me."

"Did I?"

Roland was picking over the pile on the table.

"What are these? Girlish treasures?"

"Don't men have treasures?"

143

"Not this sort."

"That's not a doll. It's a glove puppet. Fingers in here. I used to do this a lot. Sometimes I felt—"

"Felt what?"

"It doesn't matter. I made this thing in pottery. It rocks all the time because I didn't get the bottom quite flat. All the same, they fired it. To encourage me, Miss Simpson said. I never made any more. Too boring. It does for tidying things into."

Roland picked out a tiny pearl-handled knife with a blade of soft silver folded into it. She took it from him and when she opened the blade to show him, the whole thing was still no more than four inches long.

"This is for protecting my honour. It's the right size."

"And you don't know where."

"Where what?"

"Toni. Your sister."

"Politics. She got politics the way she got Jesus."

"What's in that cupboard?"

"Skeletons. Family skeletons."

All the same, he opened the cupboard door just as if she had told him he could; and that pointless freedom annoyed her so that somewhere in her mind a question was asking itself—why is he here? Why do I put up with him? But by that time he was pawing all her old dresses, even the ballet one, and all still faintly perfumed. He took hold of a handful of frills, then suddenly turned to her.

"Sophy—"

"Oh not now—"

All the same, he put his arms round her and began making swooning noises. She sighed inwardly but laid her arms round his neck since she had found that in this business it was less bother to comply than to exercise will. She wondered resignedly what the order of service would be this time and of course it proved to be Roland's usual routine, what you might call his ritual. He tried to put her on the divan and at the same time remove both their essential clothing without interrupting the kind of swooning eagerness he thought most seductive. She was obedient, since he was relatively young and strong, passably good to look at, with wide, flat shoulders and a flat stomach. Yet even so as she complied, somewhere or other the question was asking itself—as

144

if *this* was murmuring from where it lay ambushed, even in day-light, at the mouth of the tunnel—a question concerning life which they said was so important, you must live your life, you only have one life to live, et cetera—life so trivial if it must be organized round such pointless activities as Antonia's Jesus or politics or ponies or this grunting and heaving. So she lay, clamped down by flesh and gristle and bone. The thing was face-less, no more than a mop of hair shaking by her left shoulder. Now and then the mop paused, turned into a puzzled face for a moment or two and went back to the shaking mop again.

"I do what you want, don't I?"

"There's more to it than that—"

And he set to again, if anything, with a more determined energy. So lying there with his weight on her she tried to find out what more there was to it. The weight was—pleasant. The move-ment was natural and—pleasant. Just so, even the varying degrees of obedience she had experienced with the old man in the big car had been pleasant in some way, like the money; a kind of entry into an area not of secrecy but—outrage. And this prolonged and rhythmic activity about which there was so much talk and round which such a—social dance—was organized? This—ludi-crous—intimacy which must be sort of intended since the parts fitted so well? and Roland, irritating Roland, and suddenly exasperating Roland was moving faster and faster as if this were some sort of athletic activity, a private dance after the public one. There *was* sensation, no doubt of that; and she made some words in her head to describe that sensation which surely would be of more interest, more intensity, with a different head to shake by her shoulder.

The words pleased her so much that she said them aloud.

"A faint, ring-shaped pleasure."

"What?"

He collapsed on her, gasping, and angry.

"You meant to put me off—and when I was—and for you, too!"

"But I—"

"For Godssake, girl—"

Some deep rage boiled out of her. Her right hand found it still held the familiar shape of the little knife. She jabbed it fiercely into Roland's shoulder. Distinctly she felt the skin resist, then puncture and give way as a separate substance from the flesh

145

into which the blade slid, a meaty moment—Roland gave a howl, then jerked away and went bending and doubling up round the room cursing and groaning with one hand clapped to his shoulder. She lay still, spread on the divan and felt inside her the breaking of the skin and the smooth slide of the blade. She held the tiny thing up before her eyes. There was a thin, red smear on it.

Not mine. His.

Something strange was happening. The feeling from the blade was expanding inside her was filling her, filling the whole room. The feeling became a shudder then an unstoppable arching of her body. She cried out through her clenched teeth. Unsuspected nerves and muscles took charge and swept her forward in contraction after contraction towards some pit of destroying consummation into which she plunged.

Then for a timeless time there was no Sophy. No *this*. Nothing but release, existing, impossibly by itself.

"I'm still bleeding!"

Sophy came back, sighing gustily, drowsily. She got her eyes open. He was kneeling by the bed now, hand still clapped to his shoulder. He whispered.

"I feel faint."

She giggled then found herself in a yawn.

"So do I—"

He took his hand from his shoulder and peered into the palm.

"Oh. Oh."

She could see his shoulder now. The wound was so small and faint and blue. The blood had come out mostly from the pressure of his palm. By contrast with the tiny puncture there was so much of him, such muscle, such a silly, square, male face. She felt almost affectionate in her contempt.

"Have the bed for a bit. No. Not Toni's. Mine."

She got off it and he lay there, hand once more covering his shoulder. She dressed and sat for a while in the old armchair that they had talked of re-covering but of course had never re-covered. Stuffing was still coming out of one arm. Roland began to whiffle and snore but faintly as if he had swooned in his sleep. Sophy returned to contemplating the upheaval in her own body that had changed so much, lighted up so much, calmed so much down. Orgasm. That was what the sex lectures called it, what they had all talked about, written about, sung about. Only no one had said what a help a knife would be—kinky?

All at once a world fell into place. It was all part of—a corollary? Extension?—of that axiom discovered when sitting in a desk ages and ages ago. It was all part of being simple. With *their* films and books and things; with *their* great newspaper stories of hideous happenings that kept the whole country entranced for weeks at a time—oh yes, of course, all outraged and indignant like Roland, and perhaps all frightened like Roland—but all unable to stop reading, looking, going with the feel of the blade sliding in, the rope, the gun, the pain—unable to stop reading, listening, looking—

The pebble or the knife to the hand. To act simply. Or to extend simplicity into the absolute of being weird whether being weird meant anything or not—as it must when magic efforts *fester* with dirt—

To be on the other side from all the silly pretence. To be.

Roland made a honking noise, then sat up.

"My shoulder!"

"It's nothing."

"I must get one, quick."

"Get what?"

"Anti-tet."

"Anti-what?"

"Tetanus. Lockjaw. Oh Christ. Injection. And—"

"Of all the—!"

But it was what he did. She only just managed to get a seat in his car, he was so preoccupied and violent.

"What happened when you were a boy if you fell down?"

But he was too busy driving. He took his large and violated body to the hospital not caring whether she came or not. He came back from the room where it had been punctured—more expertly perhaps—and slid in a dead faint to the floor. When he had recovered a bit, he drove her back in silence to his mother's house and went into his room without a word.

Sophy mutinied. She went out by herself, back to the disco called The Dirty Disco, which was supposed to be a joke, but it was actually filthy. Even her jeans and the sweatshirt she had pulled on with BUY ME stencilled on it seemed sweet by comparison. The noise was solid but she had not been there for more than a few seconds when a young man pushed through the dancers

147

and pulled her to her feet. He proved to be everything, marvellous, inventive, and oh so strong without thinking about it; and he lifted them to a level where Sophy discovered she was marvellous, too. Soon there was a space round them so that in their twoness they were wilder and wilder, going from one extravagance to the next endlessly. All the place began to applaud so that there was as much clapping and cheering as music, except the beat of course, the beat in the floor. When the beat stopped they stood looking at each other, panting. Then he muttered *see you* and went back to his table where there was another man, and a nignog grabbed her and dragged her into the dance. When he let her go she went looking for the young man and they met half way like old friends and he shouted to her (his first words!) "Two minds without a single thought." It seemed the sun rose or something. This time, by an agreement that neither of them needed mention, they put virtuosity on one side and shouted their whispered inquiries at each other. She glimpsed the other man sitting at the table but she knew this one, Gerry, oh yes, this one was no more queer than she was and everything had happened at once.

He shouted.

"How's your father?"

"My father?"

As she said that, the beat stopped—stopped more suddenly than Gerry was able to—so that his reply was shouted into the silence.

"The bloke you were with the other night—the elderly gentleman in the lounge suit!"

When he heard himself he clapped both hands over his ears but took them away at once.

"Oh my God! But what's a girl like you, etc.? There—they're off as the monkey said. We fit like the hand and the glove."

"Mm?"

"Consummate."

"Well of course."

"Promise?"

"Necessary?"

"Still. Bird in the hand, you know. No? Not tonight Josephine?"

"It's not that. Only—"

Some sort of necessary preparation. Wash Roland off me. Wash them all off me.

"Only?"

"Not tonight. But I promise. Faithfully. Cross my heart. There."

So they sat and he gave her his address and they sat and at last Gerry said he was falling asleep and they parted for the time; and only when they had parted did she remember they had no special date for meeting. A black man followed her back to the house so she rang the bell since the door was not only locked but bolted. After the briefest of pauses Mrs Garrett unlocked and unbolted and let her in; and glanced across at the black man loitering on the other pavement. After that she followed Sophy up to her room and stood in the doorway, not leaning against the doorpost but upright this time.

"You're learning, aren't you?"

Sophy said nothing but looked back good-humouredly at the eyes gleaming so liquidly in their charred cups. Mrs Garrett licked her thin lips.

"It's one thing with Roland. Boys will be boys. Men, I mean. And then, he'll settle down. I know things are different nowadays—"

"I'm tired. Goodnight."

"You could do worse, you know. Much worse. Settle down. I wouldn't say anything about him."

"Him?"

"The nig."

Sophy burst out laughing.

"Him! But after all—why not?"

"Why not indeed! I've never heard—"

"And then—I *do* like to be able to see what I'm doing."

"You like to *see*!"

"Just a joke. Look. I'm tired. Really."

"Have you and Roland had a tiff?"

"He went to the hospital."

"He never! Why? On a Sunday? Was he—"

Sophy scrabbled in her shoulder bag. She found the little knife and took it out. She began to laugh but thought better of it.

"He got cut. With my fruit-knife. Look. So he went to get a what d'you call it. Anti-tet."

"Cut?"

"He thought it might be dirty."

"He always was—but what was he doing with a thing like that?"

149

The words *peeling fruit of course* formed in Sophy's mind and rose to her lips. But looking at those liquidly glistening eyes she understood suddenly how easy it was to deny them any-thing—any entry. They could not look in. All this Sophy in here was secure. Those eyes in Ma Garrett's face were no more than reflectors. All they saw was what light gave them. You could stand, allowing your own eyes to receive and bounce back the light; and the two people behind, each floating invisibly behind her reflectors need not meet, need give nothing. Need say noth-ing. All simple.

But then, still looking, she saw more. In immediate contra-diction, whether it was from knowledge of the world up to that moment, whether it was to be read in the subtlest changes in the woman's stance or in her breathing or in the arrangement of her face, Sophy saw more than those twin reflectors intended. She saw the words approach Ma Garrett's lips, *You'd better leave*, and hang there, inhibited by other thoughts, other words, *What would Roland say, she might just do, and if he's hooked on her—*

Sophy waited, rembering simplicity. Do nothing. Wait.

Ma Garrett did not precisely slam the door, but closed it with such an elaborate absence of noise it was just as good an indica-tion of anger. After a moment or two, listening to quick steps on the stairs, Sophy let her breath out. She went to the window and there was the nig still standing on the other pavement and looking across inscrutably at the house; but as she watched, he glanced to one side then ran away round the corner. A police car cruised down the street. Sophy stood for a while, then undressed slowly and remembered the fullness, the clearing out of want and urgency like the fall of a great arch; and it was easier to give the credit for it not to Roland at all but to nameless masculinity. Or if it must have a name, give it Gerry's name, Gerry's face. There was tomorrow.

150

# CHAPTER TEN

All that day it seemed to Sophy that nothing could be sillier than having to tell people what it would cost them to fly to Bangkok or how to get to Margate from Aberdeen; or how to get from London to Zürich with a stop-off somewhere, or how to take a car to Austria—not only silly as could be but more and more boring as the day dribbled away. When the job was done she hurried back to the house and watched the clock till it was just possible the disco would be open and away she went. Every now and then she ran a few steps, as if afraid she would be too late rather than too early. But Gerry wasn't there. And Gerry wasn't there. And Gerry still wasn't there. At last she danced a bit and fended off mechanically with a smile like on a statue. She saw it was all intolerable, all quite, quite impossible too; and short of being weird—how the old thoughts could come back!—if a man won't be where you want him, there is only one thing to do.

Next morning, instead of going to work she went straight to the address that Gerry had given her. He woke, late and frowsty, to hear her at the door. He fumbled to let her in with eyes half-shut. She edged in sideways with her load of belongings in shopping bags. She had an apology for her own untidiness on the tip of her tongue but abandoned it when she saw the room and smelt it.

"Phew!"

Despite himself he was ashamed.

"Sorry about the mess. I haven't shaved either."

"Don't shave."

"You want me without or with?"

It was a hangover. With a kind of automatic libidinosity he reached out at her but she swung a carrier bag in the way.

"Not now, Gerry. I've come to stay."

"Christ. I must go to the loo. And shave. Oh hell. Make some coffee will you?"

She got busy in the dirty corner where the sink was. It could be considered a flat if you shut one eye and—she thought this as she cleared a space for the kettle—if you could shut your nose. They said men were less sensitive to smells anyway.

Gerry himself cleaned up astonishingly well. When he was dressed as well as shaved, she sat on the chair and he sat on the unmade bed and they looked at each other over the mugs of coffee. He was satisfactorily taller than she was but on the slight side and loosely put together, with a head and face that in daylight was—well, pretty was wrong and handsome wouldn't do either, so why bother? Rhythm—and as if he saw the word in her head, having looked in right past the reflectors—he began a sort of tone-less whistling, the sketch of a tune and one finger beat on the side of his coffee mug—rhythm was everything to him, which was why—

"Gerry, I'm out of work."

"Sacked?"

"Left. Too boring."

The sketched tune stopped, to be replaced by a whistle of surprise that did achieve some tone. Overhead, a brief argument flared and there were a couple of thumps then comparative silence.

"Desirable neighbourhood. Hang on a moment."

Gerry put down his coffee, pulled out a cassette player and switched it on. The air swingled. Relieved, he took up the rhythm, nodding his head, eyes closed for the time being, ripe lips pursed; lips that would—that would avoid the four-letter word which she never used herself so that this could not be pair-bonding as with ducks, was it?

"What bird were you with, then."

"No bird, dear thing. Chap I know."

His eyes flicked open, large, dark, and he smiled at her round them. What girl could pass up that smile, those eyes, that dark hair with its forward flop—?

"Yeah?"

"Fairly thick night."

"Is that all?"

"Word of an officer and gentleman."

152

"So *that's*—"

"That's. Care to see my commission? Once you have it, you have it even when you've declined a posting. Second lieutenant. Imagine being shot at in Ulster. Paff!"

"Have you been shot at? Really?"

"Well. I would've been if I'd stayed in."

"I wish I'd seen you in uniform."

He pulled her to the bed and hugged her. She hugged him back and kissed him. His gestures became more intimate.

"Not now, Gerry. It's too early. I wouldn't be fit for anything later."

"There's nothing to do later. Not till they open."

All the same he took his hands off her.

"Look, dear thing. You'll have to sign on for social security. But I was looking to you for the occasional hand-out."

She doted down at him in recognition of what they shared right from those first few seconds; the complete acceptance of what each was; or what each thought the other was.

"We'd better not let on we're living together."

"Oh. So we're living together are we?"

"Sheer gain, mathematically."

"And you could always earn a bit on the side."

"Mm?"

"Red lamp in the window."

"Too much like work. I've—well. What about you?"

"Dodgy market. Know any rich old ladies?"

"No."

"Used to be loads of them. We were talking about it last night. Nowadays they're all poor old ladies. Unfair to junior officers. No, dear thing. It's social security or paff paff."

"Paff?"

"Mercenary. Make you at least a captain if you can produce evidence of being an O and G in herself's forces. Loads of lolly."

"That's all very well for you—"

"Oh is it my God? Not so hot if you get wounded or captured. Time was, you used not to get wounded or captured. Nigs had a decent sense of who was who. Now you get shot like those poor bastards. Then again, I've got prospects, sort of—no. I'm not telling you, sweet thing, chubby prattler."

She took him by the arms and shook him.

153

"No secrets!"

"You trying to get rid of me? You need my social security as much as I need yours."

She collapsed, giggling on his chest. The words popped out.

"Thank God I don't have to pretend any more!"

For a day or two, what with the Employment Exchange and trying to make Gerry's flat habitable for two people, she had some time away from him and spent it thinking about him. No indeed, they did not, must not use that four-letter word, the many-splendoured, but all the same, when you are young and have told yourself what nonsense so much is, you cannot help an occasional glance at the current situation and say to yourself—is this it? You examine the curious fact that this twin, this discovered twin, could outrage and yet not annoy. There were those moments when a funny struck them both and they fell towards each other, hugging and giggling and not needing to say anything—also those moments when a smile round those big eyes, or fall of a lock of hair on his forehead could be a sweetness in the stomach—oh, he was sweet!

And there standing at the pigeon-hole, with the faceless servant of the unemployed public behind it, her soul said aloud, "You are sweet!" only to come plummeting down as the face flashed into an amazed smile then blushed scarlet. Moreover, she thought, as she handed in the completed form, moreover I know he doesn't work because he can't work, it's not in him. How can a child work? Now he has all of me and my body, he is waiting without knowing it for the box of bricks or the train set—

The fourth night, Gerry told her about his friend Bill.

"Quaint character. He was shot at as it happens. They got his C.O. so he opened up and knocked off half a dozen of them."

"He really shot people?"

"So they slung him out! Imagine! What in hell do they think soldiers are for?"

"I don't know what you're talking about."

"He said it was tops. Smasheroo. Stands to reason, doesn't it? All those millions—wouldn't be done if it wasn't natural to do it. For God's sake. Christ. I mean!"

"Oh you—yes, yes!"

"Bloody silly the whole thing."

"This friend of yours, Bill—"

"He's a bit thick mind you. But then you don't want privates to go thinking, do you? Perfect other rank, I'd have said. End up in a red coat at Chelsea. And then they go and chuck him out!"

"But *why*?"

"Didn't I tell you? He enjoyed it you see. He likes killing. The natural man. So they told him he didn't ought not to have done it, as he put it. Said he supposed they thought he should have had tears in his fucking eyes. Pardon his French."

"He sounds like Uncle Jim. Was he an Aussie?"

"British to the backbone."

"Fun to meet him."

"Well you will. He's not a handsome chap like me, my sweet, but remember whose doggie you are."

"I bite."

So she did.

They met Bill in a pub. He had some money, only just enough for the three of them and he was vague about the source. He was much older than Gerry but treated him with awful respect and even called him "sir" once or twice, which made Sophy smile. He was physically rather like Gerry, but with less forehead and more jaw.

"Gerry's told me about you."

Bill sat very still. Gerry broke in.

"Nothing you'd mind old sport. That's all over—"

"Of course he doesn't mind, do you Bill?"

"She really all right sir, Gerry?"

"What's it like, Bill?"

"What's what like Miss, Sophy?"

"Killing people."

There was a long silence. Gerry gave a sudden shudder then took a long drink without stopping. Bill surveyed her, stonily.

"They give us ammo."

"Bullets, you'd call them, dear thing. Live rounds."

"I mean—was it sort of led up to? Was everything arranged, so that when you did it, it was like finding a stone ready for throwing—kind of?"

"We was briefed."

Now it was her turn to be silent for a while. What do I want to know? I want to know about pebbles and the hissing in the

155

transistor and the running down, running down, endless running down!

"I'm sick of all the things they say. Pretending life is what it isn't. I want—I want to know!"

"Nothing to know, dear thing. What is. Bed and board."

"That's right sir, Gerry. You got to look at the facts."

"And what happens?"

"Bill. I think she means when you knock one off."

Then there was more silence. Staring at him, Sophy saw a faint smile come in Bill's face. The direction of his gaze altered. Slid over her body, came back till he glanced at her eyes again. Then he looked away. She knew, with a tiny prickle of the flesh, what was happening. She said the words inside her head. *He fancies me!* Oh how much he fancies me!

Bill was looking at Gerry.

"Tarts is all the same."

He looked back at her with the faint smile of his awareness round the mouth.

"You squeeze, see? Pip! He falls down."

"All fall down, dear thing. Nothing to it. Ringa ring."

"Does it hurt? Does it take long? Is there any—is there much—"

The smile widened into one of more accurate comprehension.

"Not if it's a neat shot, see? One wriggled. I give him another. Finee."

"It's a highly technical matter, Sophy dear. Don't trouble your pretty head. Leave it to us splendid male beasts. Yours not to reason why."

Bill was nodding and grinning into her face as if they understood each other. Oh how he fancies me; and no you don't, she said to herself, not with a bargepole as they say, you dumb animal!

She looked away.

It soon became evident that the two men had not met merely to drink. After a certain amount of allusive talk, they stopped, with Bill looking at her again. Gerry patted her shoulder.

"Honeybunch. Wouldn't we care to go and powder the little nose?"

"Powder your own, dear thing!"

"Haw," said Bill with his best imitation of a debby voice. "Powdah your own. Sorry, miss. Sophy, I mean."

156

But she went, for all that, because it didn't much matter and she smelt a secret to be worked out later.

The next day Gerry said he had a date and he was very excited and shivering a bit. That was when she found out that he was on pills, tiny black things that could be hidden under a thumbnail or lost in a crack between two boards. He came back very late at night. He was white and exhausted and she made a joke of it, saying it must have been some bird, *some* bird he'd been with. But she knew what it was all about when he slipped a gun, real or model, back in the drawer. She had sex with him and ended in their single bed with his head on her naked breast. All the same, he was Gerry again next day and produced a wad of notes he said he'd won at the dogs, having forgotten, apparently, that she had seen the gun. So it all came out. He and Bill did a job now and then. They had a high old time for a day or two. Once they met Bill and his current girlfriend. She was a card, Daisy, a punk, six-inch heels, cheap trouser-suit, dead white face, dead black eye make-up, straw hair like a rick, plastered down on one side and sticking straight up on the other. It seemed to Sophy that one meeting was enough, but it turned out she had something to do with Gerry's black pills.

Gerry took her to another party with no Daisy and no Bill, but some very odd types. It was a party in a real flat with several rooms. There was much music and chat and drink and they went just the two of them, as Gerry said Bill's face wouldn't fit. He meant her to be debby and straight because of the man he was contacting, but things went wrong in a very odd way. Somehow as the noise increased into a party roar some of the people began playing a silly game with a piece of paper with a blotch of ink on it. You had to say how many things it was like and some of the answers were wonderfully dirty and witty. But when Sophy had her turn she looked at the black shape in the middle of the paper and nothing happened at all. Then without any kind of intermission she found she was lying on the sofa and staring at the ceiling and there was no party roar and people were standing round and looking down at her. She got up on one elbow and saw the woman who was giving the party standing by the open door of the flat and talking to someone who was outside it.

"Nothing my dear Lois, nothing at all."

"But that dreadful screaming and screaming!"

157

Gerry took her away, explaining that she had fainted from heat, and it was a day or two before she worked the whole thing out and knew why her throat was sore. But that night, after they had left the party, Gerry said they needed some calm. So the next evening they sat, drinking quietly in a pub, and watching the telly that was fastened high up in one corner. Indeed, Sophy, puzzling over the darkness inside her, began to find it a bit too quiet and suggested they should move on. But Gerry said to hang on. He was watching the box intently and smiling.

"Christ!"

"What gives?"

"Fido! My old friend Fido!"

It was indoor athletics. A young man bulging with sinew and muscles was performing on the high rings. To Sophy he seemed like every other young competitor in the hall; but perhaps that was because he wore a face of such stern dedication.

"Fido! He was in with me—"

"Was?"

"Teacher now. PT. Some posh school or other. Wandicott."

"I know Wandicott. Knew of Wandicott. It's out our way, beyond Greenfield."

"Oh good show, Fido! Splendid fellow! Dear God he's sweating like the Sunday roast."

"What do they do it for?"

"Showing off to their girls. Winning prizes. Getting promotion. Health, wealth, fame—show's over."


Sophy persuaded Gerry and Bill to let her help. Daisy didn't come, didn't want to come, it wasn't her scene. They did three shops and came away with just over two hundred pounds. The risk seemed appalling to Sophy and she persuaded them to try Paki shops. It was certainly job-satisfaction for a bit. Pakis dwindled when Gerry pointed his fake gun at them. Sophy improved their technique by making Bill tell them that the organization would bomb the shop if there was any trouble. It was fun to see how the Pakis bundled money into the bag as if it was sweets or incense. They couldn't get rid of it fast enough.

Sophy did some arithmetic with it, putting risk on one side of an equation and the money on the other. She talked to Gerry in bed.

"It's no good, you know."

158

He yawned in her ear.

"What isn't?"

"Robbing the till."

"Old soul! Have you got religion?"

"Too much chance of being caught."

"One in a hundred."

"And when you've done a hundred shops?"

There was a long pause.

"I mean—who's got the money? The real money, I mean. The stuff to set you up for life, set you free, go where you like, do what you like—"

"Not banks my poppet. They've learnt too much. Advanced technology."

"Arabs."

She felt him shaking with laughter.

"Invasion is just not on. We'd need all three services. Good night, gorgeous."

She put her lips close to his ear and giggled at the sheer outrage of her idea.

"Where do they send their children to school?"

This time the pause was even longer. Gerry broke it at last.

"Christ all bleeding mighty. As Bill would say. Christ!"

"Wandicott School, Gerry. Where your friend is. It's stiff with them. Princes—the lot."

"My God. You—you really are—"

"Your friend—what was it—Fido? Gerry—we could grab a boy and hide him and ask—we could ask a million, a billion and they'd pay it, they'd have to pay—they'd have to pay or we'd—Gerry kiss me right now yes feel me fuck me we'd have a prince in our power to bargain with and if that's good more he'd be hidden and tied up and gagged and if oh if ah nothing nothing nothing on and on and on and on oh oh oh—"

So then there was another time of lying side by side, she with her arm across the chest of a Gerry who seemed wrecked and confused in the darkness. Then when he did breathe evenly she shook him—shook him hard.

"I wasn't joking or pretending. It wasn't just a thinking to come with. I mean it. Not this fiddling with shops! We might as well be stealing milk bottles!"

"It's too much."

159

"It isn't too much for us, Gerry. It's just enough for me. We'll be caught if we go on doing shops because it's small. But this—We need one big thing, a thing so monstrous no one would bother to defend against it—"

"It's too much. And I want to kip."

"I want to talk. I'm not going on with shops. That's flat. If you want me, you'll—We could be rich for life!"

"Never."

"Look Gerry. At least we can go down and see what the school's like. Meet your friend Fido. Get him in, perhaps. We could go and see how things are—"

"Not bloody likely."

"We'll drive down there and see what's possible."

"No we won't."

There was a long silence which she did not choose to break this time. Then when he was breathing evenly again, she spoke to herself, silently.

*Oh yes we will, my sweet. You'll see!*

# CHAPTER ELEVEN

They parked the car where the tree-covered track led up to the crest of the downs. They walked up and found that the old road along the top was deserted and windy. Clouds and bright sun succeeded each other, like takes in a film, across the rounded greennesses and indigo horizon. Nothing moved but the clouds. Even the sheep seemed to prefer motionlessness. A mile ahead of them the downs rose to a blunt top. The track led over the top then on, bump after bump away into the remote centre of the country. Sophy soon stopped.

"Wait a minute."

He turned to her, grinning. He had plenty of colour and the hair was flopped over his forehead. She thought dizzily, as she got her breath back, that he had never been so beautiful.

"Not a natural walker are you, my beloved?"

"Your legs are longer."

"Some people call this fun."

"Not me. I wonder why they think so."

"Beauties of nature. You are a beauty of nature and so—"

She twisted out of his arms.

"We're doing a job! Can't you keep your mind on it?"

They walked on, side by side, a country-visiting pair. Gerry pointed to the concrete stand at the top.

"That's a base for triangulation."

"I know."

He looked at her in surprise. But unfolded the map.

"We spread this out on the plate and look round."

"Why?"

"Sheer pleasure. Everybody does it."

"Why?"

161

"Actually I *am* enjoying it quite a lot, you know. Takes me back to all that 'Forward men!' and so on."

"What do we look round at?"

"We identify six counties."

"Can we?"

"It's always done. Great British tradition identifying counties. Never mind old thing, I won't press it. Notice anything about the air?"

"Should I?"

"But they've written whole books about it!" And standing by the concrete pillar, his hair and the map fluttering, he began to sing, " 'Give to me the life I love, let the lave go by me—' "

From deep inside her she was shaken by a gust of sheer rage.

"For God's sake Gerry! Don't you know who—" She caught herself up and went on quickly. "I'm edgy. Can't you see? You don't know what it's like to be—Sorry."

"OK. Look, Sophy. This isn't going to work, is it?"

"You said. You agreed."

"A recce."

They stared at each other across the pillar. It seemed to her that something, the air perhaps, was reminding him of other places and other people. He was firm and drawing back almost as if he might—escape.

The man in the van. *My will is stronger than his.*

"Gerry dear. We aren't committed to anything. But we've spent three days on the job already. We know he uses the right of way and that we'll meet him there by accident. We'll make contact, that's all. Argue later."

He still stared at her from under his fluttering hair.

"One thing at a time."

She moved round the pillar and squeezed his arm.

"Now then, map-reader. Where is it?"

"The right of way leads down from this place—see the dotted line? Down there is what you saw from the other side of the valley yesterday. He brings the boys up this dotted line towards us then turns to his left and circles back. Healthy country run."

"Just about right. Come on."

The right of way led down at the side of a wire fence that seemed to stretch without a break into clumps of trees in the bottom of the valley. Sophy pointed to a huddle of grey roofs.

"That's it."

"Over there on the other side where the trees are is where we were yesterday."

"And there they are!"

"Christ yes. Dead on time. And there he is. Tell him a mile off. Well. He is a mile off or near enough. Notice his high-stepping action? Come on."

The boys were coming up from the hollow with its glimpsed leaden roofs. They were a string of bobbing red objects, small boys in some sort of red sports outfit, and a larger bit of red bounced up and down in pursuit of them. The whole string trotted up the hill and the patch of red behind it became a wiry young man in a scarlet tracksuit who ran with an exaggerated knees-up action and now and then shouted at the boys in front of him. Gerry and Sophy stopped and the boys ran past, looking at them and grinning. The young man stopped too and stared.

"Gerry!"

"Fido—we saw you on the box!"

The young man called Fido gave a bellow that halted the boys. He and Gerry slapped each other's backs, punched ribs and exchanged badinage. Fido was introduced. Fido was, or had been, Lieutenant Masterman but pointed out at once that he answered to the name of Fido or Bow Wow or Doggie but Fido mostly.

"Even the boys," he said triumphantly. "They all call me Fido."

Though Fido was only of average height he was splendidly developed. He had less head than face and his features were weathered by exposure. Sophy knew, from what Gerry had said, that Fido's chest had been expanded by weight-lifting, his legs by assiduity on the trampoline and his balance by hair-raising exploits on any rock face within reach. His hair was dark and curly, his forehead low and his manner imperceptive.

"Fido is a positively national athlete," said Gerry, with what Sophy recognized as malice. "You'd never believe his snatch."

"Snatch?"

"Weight-lifting. D'you know how much?"

"I'm sure it was enormous," cried Sophy, curving at Fido. "It must be marvellous to be able to lift as much as that!"

Fido agreed that yes it was rather marvellous. Sophy emitted

163

some perfume at him and allowed all the lines to stretch in his direction. There was a mutual expansion of pupils. Fido's eyes were rather small and the expansion improved them. He told the boys to stay where they were but jump about a bit. Gerry said they'd seen the name of the school on the map and having seen Fido on the box thought that they might look him up—and now here he was!

"Keep warm, you men," shouted Fido. "We'll be going on in a jiffy."

"You must be an inspiration to them, Mr Masterman."

"Fido, please. I come when you whistle."

He danced, fisted the air a bit then gave an ejaculatory laugh that really was rather like a bark. He went on to say that she could whistle for him when she liked and it would be a pleasure.

Gerry broke in.

"How's the job, then, Fido?"

"Schoolmastering? Well, you can see I manage to keep fit on it. Do a lot of this stuff. Of course, it's not the same as proper road-work. You can't have the little men really going at it. So most days I carry weights. Besides—" He glanced round them cautiously, inspected the downs, bare of all but sheep and boys. "I have to keep a careful eye on them you know."

Sophy trilled.

"Oh Fido! You're stuck away here at the end of nowhere—"

He leaned towards her, reached out a hand to grasp her arm, then thought better of it.

"That's just it. You see the little fellow there? No—don't let him know you're looking. Be subtle about it like me. Out of the corner of your eye."

Sophy looked. The little boys were just little boys, that was all, except that three of them were black and two brown. Most were the usual sort of whiteish.

"The one thumping the nig?"

"Careful! He's *royal*!"

"But Fido, how thrilling!"

"His parents are really nice people, Sophy. Of course they don't get down here much together. But she actually spoke to me, you know. She said, 'Build him up, Mr Masterman.' She has a marvellous memory for names. They both have. He follows weight-lifting with keen interest, you know. He said 'What d'you

164

reckon your limit'll be in the snatch?' I tell you, as long as we have them—"

Gerry tapped him on the shoulder and turned him from his exclusive attention.

"And you have another job as well as running the P.T.?"

"I'm not saying, am I? The little men don't know, you see. But it's such a load—why, good Lord, the lad his little highness was toughing up—and take that little brown fellow for example—he's the son of an oil sheik. Got to call him a prince, though of course it's not the same. More like a laird who's struck it lucky when deer-stalking or something. His old man could buy this country."

"I expect he has," said Gerry with uncharacteristic feeling. "Nobody else would."

"You mean his father's really rich, Fido?"

"Billions. Well. Mustn't let the old gluteus maxima get a chill!. Sophy, you two—I'm free for a bit round about four. Tea in the village? Scones? Home-made stuff?"

Before Gerry could answer, Sophy accepted.

"Super, Fido!"

"The Copper Kettle then. About half an hour. See you."

"We'll be there."

Fido gave her a last expanded pupil then bounded off up the track. He chased the little boys about and made noises like a dog tormenting cows. The little boys responded with mooing and shrieks of laughter. Fido was evidently popular. Sophy stared after him.

"They actually spend their time lifting up weights?"

"For God's sake, you saw them on the box!"

"So I did."

"Dear thing, you're not into the modern scene."

She saw that for all his twinship he was irritated by the traffic in pupils and she was pleased and amused.

"Don't be dumb, Gerry. It couldn't have happened better."

"I'd forgotten what a thick oaf he is. Christ."

"He's our way in."

"Yours, you mean."

"You agreed to it."

"I'm only just beginning to find out what we've taken on. You heard what he said. They'll have the works here, the complete works! We're probably on tape already."

"I don't believe it." She moved close to him. "You don't know about being invisible, do you?"

"I'm a soldier. Try and find me when I want to hide."

"Not just hiding. I've known it for these last three days. *We're invisible.* No, not because of some magic or other—though perhaps—but anyway; not because of magic; but just *because.* That he's here and you know him. That I can—manage him—Sometimes there are coincidences; but sometimes the arrangement of things is—deliberate. I know about that."

"Well I don't."

"When I was in the travel agency I did a lot of looking-up tables and things, and dates and numbers. I understand them. I really *do* understand them, you see, the way Daddy understands his chess and all that. I'm just not used to putting that kind of knowing into words. Perhaps it won't go anyway. Listen. Those numbers. The girl who was there when I first got there. Well. She was a dim blonde. She was a smasher too. The manager knew how to pick them. Not all that good for business, but why should he worry? You'd have popped your eyes at her, my dear. But she, she was dim. D'you know? I watched her use tables to work out what ten per cent of a bill came to!"

"Just the way she should be. Keep a lot of chaps very happy."

"The point is this. She had to fill in a date and it went, the seventh day of the seventh month of the seventy-seventh year; so it was seven, stroke, seven, stroke, seven, seven. Well. Alice filled it in, looked at it with her bulging great blue eyes, gave her idiotic laugh—the one the manager said was like a bird-trill—he was wet, he couldn't keep his hands off anything; and she said, 'It's quite a coincidence, isn't it?' "

Gerry turned away and began to walk down by the wire.

"So it was."

"But—"

She ran after him, caught his arm and pulled him round.

"Don't you see, dear, my, my lovely—it wasn't! A coincidence comes out of the, the mess things are, the heap, the darkness and you can't tell how—But these four sevens—you could see them coming and wave goodbye to them! It was the system—but coincidences—more than coincidences—"

"Honest to God, Sophy, I don't know what you're on about."

"Everything's running down. Unwinding. We're just—tangles.

Everything is just a tangle and it slides out of itself bit by bit towards something that's simpler and simpler—and we can help it. Be a part."

"You've got religion. Or you're up the wall."

"Being good is just another tangle. Why bother? Go on with the disentangling that will happen in any case and take what you can on the way. What it wants, the dark, let the weight fall, take the brake off—"

A truth appeared in her mind. *The way towards simplicity is through outrage.* But she knew he would not understand.

"It's like the collapse of sex."

"Sex, sex, there's nothing like sex! Sex for ever!"

"Oh yes, yes! But not the way you mean—the way everything means, the long, long convulsions, the unknotting, the throbbing and disentangling of space and time on, on, on into nothingness—"

And she was there; without the transistor she was there and could hear herself or someone in the hiss and crackle and roar, the inchoate unorchestra of the lightless spaces.

"On and on, wave after wave arching, spreading, running down, down, down—"

The leaden roofs of the school came back into focus then moved out of it as she stared up into Gerry's worried face.

"Sophy! Sophy! Can you hear me?"

That was why this vast body she inhabited was being moved backwards and forwards; and becoming known now as a girl's body, and man's hands shaking it by the shoulders.

"Sophy!"

She answered him with lips that could hardly move.

"Just a moment can't you? I was speaking to—of—I was someone—"

His hands stilled but held her.

"Take it easy then. Better?"

"Nothing wrong." As the words fell out of her mouth she saw how funny they were and started to giggle. "Nothing wrong at all!"

"We need a drink. My God, it was like—I don't know what it was like!"

"You're so wise, my dear!"

He was peering closely into her face.

167

"I didn't approve one little bit, old soul. It was damned weird, I can tell you."

With that, there was clear daylight, sun, breeze, downs, a known date and place.

"What did you call it?"

"Bloody worrying for a moment."

"You said 'Weird'."

All things flowed together. Power filled her.

"You talked about guards round this place and about tapes. But we're in a special time. They come, you see. It's not that they can't see us. It's that they don't. Why when I was small—It's the tangle untangling, sorting itself, slipping and sliding. You must be simple. That's the real thing."

"I'm beginning to realize you're an oddball. Not sure we ought to go on. There are things I just don't—"

"We'll go on. You'll see."

"Not if I say no. I'm in charge."

"Of course, dear."

"I'll go exactly as far as things are—possible. When we reach the impossible we'll stop. Understand?"

She gave him an especially brilliant smile which he kissed in a protective kind of way. He took her hand and they walked down the wire in silence. Lovers out walking.

The Copper Kettle was empty except for its fake eighteenth-century furniture and fake horse-brasses. Here they sat, viewed indifferently by a cretinous girl, and waited for Fido. He came breathlessly. Gerry played up, acting out sparks of at first amused jealousy; and then, she saw, putting a little more than acting into it. Fido was soon barking. He had brought some photographs with him. One showed him receiving a medal on a rostrum. Sophy saw to her surprise that he had not won the event but come third. Encouraged by her intense interest in his activities he took a sheaf of photographs out of his breast pocket and exposed them to her. Here was Fido, all gleaming muscle and sinew and lifting weights. Here was Fido rock-climbing and suspended, grinning over a hideous gulf. Here was Fido at the trampoline, caught upside-down in mid-air. When Sophy admitted provocatively that she had some small doubt as to the importance of all these activities, Fido simply didn't understand her. Did she mean it was dangerous? A girl might well feel that—

Sophy took her cue.

"Oh but it *must* be terribly dangerous!"

Fido meditated.

"Took a tumble rock-climbing."

Gerry spoke nastily from the place where they were ignoring him.

"Wasn't that when you fell on your head?"

Fido responded with a precise catalogue of his injuries. Sophy broke in, hoping to conceal her giggles.

"Oh but it's not fair! Why can't we—?"

Gerry gave a positive guffaw.

"You! Christ!"

But Fido was already pointing out those areas of sport in which he thought female participation was allowable.

"And croquet," said Gerry. "Don't forget croquet."

Fido said he wouldn't; and gave Sophy a conquering look from his expanded pupils. After tea he walked them some way to the bus that would take them to Gerry's car. They received a pressing invitation from him to return; and the fact that it was directed wholly at Gerry was the only false thing about it.

Sophy kissed Fido goodbye so that he barked again and she willed her scent into him. When at last they were alone in the car, Gerry looked at her, half in anger, half in admiration.

"You were half-way up his flies. Christ!"

"He might be useful. He might even come in with us."

"Don't be wet, dear thing. You may be fatal but you can't do miracles."

"Why not?"

"Think you're something out of history, don't you?"

"I don't know any history."

Gerry revved the engine viciously.

"Don't need to. Whore's instinct."

He was silent after that and she considered his point of view. It was, she saw, peculiarly male. Here was Gerry—who would quite calmly suggest she should keep them both by using men and had been serious about it, she was certain—getting worked up by her approach to ridiculous Fido. Brooding on this she found it all rooted in men's need to see. Possible customers were faceless. But Gerry knew Fido.

Two days later they had a letter from Fido repeating his

invitation. Gerry was all for ignoring it, they must have been out of their minds. When Sophy said she had to think, she saw Gerry take this as meaning, "I want to do nothing." He patted her, got pilled up and went off with Bill to arrange a job. Sophy rang Fido from a callbox. She said she didn't think she and Gerry should come down. Interrogated insistently by Fido she admitted she had thought they weren't easy together and Gerry had been, well, not difficult but thoughtful. She couldn't bear the idea of breaking up an old friendship that way. No! For her part she would have liked nothing better. In fact—

She refused to be drawn on the fact. But then she heard along the miles of wire how Fido barked as a brilliant idea came to him. He invited her to a meeting in South London where she could watch him lift weights and afterwards they could discuss the situation.

The weight-lifting competition, in which Fido won his section, struck her as so funny that that side of it was almost compensation for the pervading smell. Afterwards Fido, breathing quickly, conveyed to her that he found her exceptionally desirable. She waited for the pass; and it was an invitation to come to the school on parents' day. Sophy, who had expected a straightforward proposition, found this as comic as weight-lifting.

"I'm not a parent."

He explained it was the day when parents saw how agile he had made their little men. She allowed herself to be persuaded and began to suspect that the actual proposition when it came might be a moral one. Married—to a weight-lifter! Fido obviously thought that Gerry once out of sight would be out of mind as well. She listened as he, with a kind of egotistical innocence, displayed his life before her—his grandmother's money, and that line out to the royals on which he placed such weight, intimating that one day he might be able to present her to them, or to one of them, if she agreed to come.

"Mind," he said. "I'm not promising anything. I can only present you if I'm commanded."

So she went to parents' day, conspicuously inconspicuous in a cotton dress and straw hat. No royals were present and this cast a profound gloom over Fido, only lightened by a word or two with Lord Mountstephen, and the Marquis of Fordingbridge. Sophy inspected Fido's bedsitter and found that it resembled an annexe to the gym except for the rows of photographs. She knew now that any idea of getting Fido in with them would be pointless. It was not that he would find it wrong. He would find it dangerous in a way that did not apply to rock-climbing. It would not be his scene. Nor was there any future for his girlfriend or wife. Fido's offer of companionship and sex would be limited to what was unavoidable between the competitions. The sex would be a quick use of the body, healthy when taken in moderation. The only other use he had for a woman was as an audience for his physical perfection. Most masculine of men—how narrow his hips, how tucked in behind him the hard rondures of his bum! How wide his shoulders and glossy his skin!—He had all the narcissism of a woman or a pretty boy. He enjoyed the beauty of his flesh more than Sophy enjoyed the beauty of hers. She knew all this, even while he put his arms round her, and the school drum-and-fife band made noises on the playing fields outside the window and the summery parents drifted round the various exhibitions. Nevertheless, she let him have her on his narrow, bachelor bed, and the exercise was only a little less boring than resisting him. But he had yet another surprise for her, announcing when he had finished that they were engaged. On the way back to London it seemed to her more and more incredible that these valuable children should be so freely available to inspection once you had joined the peculiar club that surrounded them. But she thought to herself—it's simple—I'm inside!

Daisy's bloke came out of jail so Bill had to move on quick. He came to tell them all about it so the three of them held a council of war in Gerry's unkempt, uncleaned room that they called his flat. The last job had been a flop—much danger and little money. The two men were inclined to listen to Sophy if only for the sake of a little harmless fantasy. But when she began to describe the school and suggest routes, Gerry patted her as if she were a child herself.

"Sophy, like I said, they'll have gadgets you just wouldn't believe. For example. You walk along a path. A chopper with a gadget could follow you half an hour after you passed just by the bit of warmth where you'd walked. If you hid in a wood they could spot you by the lovely warmth, yum, yum, of your body. On the screen you'd look like a fire."

"He's right, see? You got to be careful."

171

"Let's plan a smack at a bank, old soul. That's dicing with death, but not *absolument* daft."

"But this is new, don't you see? And who cares about gadgets? Once we'd got him—Fido showed me the layout. I can find out anything we want. *Anything*. That's—power. He introduced me to the headmaster's wife. You see, Daddy's fearsomely well thought of, the last of the Mohicans and all that—last of his family, I mean Bill, never mind. And after all, I mean—chess!"

"None of them would tell you everything, Miss. There's always something. He wouldn't even know."

"Couldn't have put it better myself, old thing. Covering fire. Think you're in the clear, then paff! All fall down. Besides—wrong league."

"Look, Gerry. It's new. That's why it'll work. We—me and 'Toinette, my sister Toni—we did their tests. You think too highly of people's intelligence. They aren't you know. They're mostly the ones who fail or score about a hundred. We did the tests without trying. Well, *I* know what an asset we've got with me inside. We'll need more people, more information—I'll get it. We'll need weapons, explosives perhaps, we'll need safe places to hide ourselves or him. This place? Maybe—and the stables and the old barge. There's a cupboard, an old loo—"

"We'd need a safe way of getting out ourselves—Christ!"

"Fuck me, sorry Miss."

She reached for the transistor. It was no longer Winnie's ancient machine. This one fitted easily into the palm of her hand. She switched it on and voices from some other life filled the room.

*Yes. It's a black one. Moving your way. Over.*

Gerry laughed.

"You don't suppose they'd use a channel you could get at with that thing?"

It's not ridiculous, she thought. Why am I so certain I am not being ridiculous? Under her arm the flat voices were talking at intervals. *Yes, if you say so. No, I said it's a black one.* Perhaps they were not police. Perhaps—what? Inside a radio and out there in infinite space that included the world there was audible mystery and confusion, infinite confusion. She moved the control, destroying the voices, passed through music, a talk, a quiz, a burst of laughter, some foreign languages, loud, then faint. And she moved the control back and found the point between all stations;

172

and immediately in the uncleaned room which seemed always to smell of drains and food, and to be organized, or disorganized round an unmade bed—the very light from the window seeming dusty and dim as if the whole world were no more than an annexe to the room—immediately there came the voice of the darkness between the stars, between the galaxies, the toneless voice of the great skein unravelling and lying slack; and she knew why the whole thing would be simple, a tiny part of the last slackness.

Running-down. Dark.

A voice came back faintly on the verge of the hissing. *I couldn't get the number. I said it's a black one.*

A wave of happiness and delight went over and through her.

"It's going to be simple."

"Who says so?"

"Think."

It was a triumph of the will. As if a hand was on them the two men began to discuss the operation they so plainly did not believe in. They began to isolate problems and put them aside unsolved. Sophy thought of the school as she knew it and the people there. She became indifferent to the ineffectual and random kind of suggestions that they tossed from one to the other. She heard nothing of what they said but the tone, understanding by it how they felt themselves to be pawing at a steel wall that surrounded such a centre of the privileged and valuable. In the end they came to a full stop. Bill went off at last. Gerry got the whisky out of the drawer in which he had hidden it. They drank bit by bit as they undressed and then had sex, Sophy absently.

"Your mind's not on your work."

"Have you noticed, Gerry, how through this thing we understand each other more?"

"No I haven't."

"Well. We're closer."

Then there was a time in which he convulsed and gasped and grabbed and groaned and she waited for it to be over. She patted his back and ruffled his hair in a companionable sort of way.

He grunted into her shoulder.

"Can't be closer than two-in-a-bed."

"I said 'understand'."

"Do we?"

"Well. I understand you."

173

He purred.

"Tell me about myself, doctor."

"Why should I?"

"It's this recurrent nightmare I have, doctor—may I call you Sigmund?—about a disgusting wench—"

"I wonder. I'm sure you don't dream, Gerry. You daydream about money, you lovely man. Masses of money."

"My oh my. I ought to beat you up to satisfy the neighbours. But remember, by the way, that I'm in command."

"You?"

"Well fo' lan's sake honey chile! Sleep time."

"No."

"Insatiable."

"Not that, it's the school. It's those questions—"

"Dead end."

She said nothing for a while, thinking how easily he gave up and how he must be pushed.

"I shall go back."

He rolled over on his back, stretched, yawned.

"Sophy, pet. Are you getting a thing about him?"

"Fido? My God, he's such a bore! Only after the three of us talked about it, I can see how much I'll have to find out. That's all."

"Remember whose doggie you are."

"Wuff wuff O my God. Still—if he ever got me into bed it would be out of sheer boredom. Premarital sex."

He smiled at her sideways, boyishly, winningly.

"If it's absolutely necessary. But please, please dear thing, don't enjoy it."

She felt a certain pique.

"My fiancé is not like that. He's in training. All the same, Gerry, I think you might at least pretend to be jealous!"

"We all have to make sacrifices. Tell him if he'll sell us a boy he can have me too if he wants, the splendid male thing that he is. Has he improved his snatch?"

"You don't know what I put up with. The headmaster's wife thinks that as soon as we're married we should start a family straight away. She's all for families straight away. I'll need more money."

"We're short. You know that."

"I have to dress the part. Phyllis isn't too keen on slacks."

"Phyllis?"

"Phyllis Appleby. Headmaster's wife. Cow."

"It's all a lot of nonsense. Nighty night."

"Fido? Bless you my love, divine to hear you! Oh super! I was afraid you might be out with the little men. Yes I know it was going to be Saturday but oh my sweet good, good news! There's been a rearrangement at the agency and do you know it gives me three extra days—yes *with* pay! I'm coming down to you right away!"

"Oh that's jolly good, Sophy, jolly good! Bow wow!"

"Wuff wuff!"

"It'll be great! Of course, by the way, you know I'll be working and I'm in training."

"I know dear. I think you're marvellous. You're doing what? Sorry, I can't hear you, it's this line—you're doing what? You're developing what? You're developing your deltoids? Oh super darling, where are they? Can I help?"

Inside the receiver a tiny voice began to talk about deltoids. She held it away from her and looked at it with distaste. The tiny voice continued to talk. She waited, idly watching a man walk past with a horrid, two-tone face. The tiny voice called her—

"Sophy! Sophy? Are you there?"

"Sorry darling. I was looking for more change. You'll be glad to see me?"

"Rather! Mrs Appleby was asking after you. Listen. I'll try and get you a room in the school."

"Oh super. Then we could—"

"Training! Training, dear!"

"Can you fix it? Ask matron. I'm sure she fancies you."

"Oh go on, Sophy, you're pulling my leg!"

"Well I'm jealous darling. That's why I'm coming down early now I have the chance to keep an eye on you."

"You don't need to. I'm not like Gerry."

"No. True."

"You haven't seen him?"

"Good heavens no! If a girl's got you—"

"And if I've got a girl—bow! wow!"

175

"Wuff! Wuff!"

(Christ.)

"The usual bus?"

"The usual bus."

"Sophy darling, I must go—"

"Until this afternoon then. I'm sending you a great big kiss along the wire."

"And one back for you."

*"Darling!"*

She put down the receiver and stood for a moment looking at it and the tiny figure of Fido beyond it, physically so attractive if you fancied a kind of a statue. She spoke in her outside girl's voice.

"Eek!"

So she got the bus and it humped over the Old Bridge and along to Chipwick and then round the downs into the next valley and Wandicott village where Fido managed to meet it. She put outrage, whether successful or not, out of her mind. Yet she had to act and could not entirely live her part. For though the five days were too full to be unpleasant actively, yet there was a constant kind of glee in her (a song in my heart) that she had a list of things to find out about the school and could tick them off in her mind one after the other, though some had to be approached carefully as a bird sitting on a nest. If Fido had had an ounce more wit or been slightly less preoccupied with the splendours of his own anatomy he might have questioned her insistence on knowing who looked after what. The little boys pleased her too and they were desirable, edible, even. They did not call her 'Miss' or 'Sophy'. Solemnly, from the biggest down to the smallest, they called her 'Miss Stanhope'. They opened doors for her, picked up anything she dropped. When she asked a boy a question he did not say 'How should I know?' but 'I'll find out for you, Miss Stanhope,' and ran off to do so. It was most peculiar. While Fido was working she quite enjoyed watching these edible little boys, so bland and pretty. Watching one of these infinitely precious objects she found herself saying inside herself. *Lovely my pet! I could eat you!*

As for Fido, it was a relief that he was in training. But they did have sex once. He came to her where she sat under the dying elms and watched the little boys play cricket.

"Come along Sophy to my room after lights-out. I'll leave the door ajar."

176

"But you're in training darling!"

"It's good for the system once in a while. Besides—"

"Besides what?"

"Well. We're engaged and all that."

"Darling!"

"Darling! Oh well played Bellingham!"

"What did he do?"

"But wait till lights-out as I said."

"What about the duty master?"

"Old Rutherford?"

"I don't want to run into him going his rounds and be taken for a wicked woman."

Fido looked cunning.

"You'd be going to the loo, he'd think."

"Well then, Fido, why don't you come to my room?"

"You'll get me the sack."

"What! In this day and age? For God's sake Fido, they think—I mean, look at this ring! We're engaged! We're in the nineteen-seventies!"

Fido displayed an unusual perceptivity.

"No we aren't, Sophy. Oh dear no. Not here."

"Well. You could be going to the loo as convincingly as I could."

"You know as well as I do it's not in your direction."

So annoyed, but resigned and thinking it a reasonable price for the precious information that was stored unforgettably in her pretty head, she agreed that she should go to his room; and that night did so. She had never felt so indifferent, so divorced from sensuality or emotion. She lay like a log; and this, it seemed, was just as agreeable to Fido as a fuller co-operation would have been. After he had pleased himself, and, as she thought, relieved himself, she could hardly make the smallest token gesture of affection. She spoke to him in the whisper that the place demanded.

"Finished?"

It was a real pleasure to be back and alone in the room that the headmaster's wife had found for her. The next day, as if sex were something that drove them apart rather than united them, they parted with the merest of pecks.

"Goodbye, Sophy."

"Goodbye Fido. Have some good deltoids."

This time, she went straight to the flat. Gerry was there, turned in after a session at the pub that had taken him far into the dreary reaches of the afternoon. He lifted his head off the pillow and looked at her blearily as she flung her four plastic shopping bags on the bed.

"For Christ's sake!"

"God, Gerry, you do look a mess!"

"Got to go to the loo. Make some—"

"Coffee will you?"

It was instant coffee and ready by the time he came out of the loo. He pushed both hands through his hair and stared into the shaving mirror that was propped on the shelf over where the open fireplace had been.

"God."

"Why don't we leave this filthy place? Get a better pad. We don't have to live in Jamaica."

He slumped on the edge of the bed, took the coffee and engrossed himself in it. Presently, one hand supporting his bowed head, he held the empty mug out to her with the other.

"More. And the pills. Twist of paper, top left-hand."

"Are they—"

"You're making my head ache. Keep quiet, will you, playmate?"

This time she brought some coffee for herself as well and sat on the bed by his side.

"I think it's Phyllis."

"Mm? Phyllis?"

"Mrs Appleby. Headmaster's wife."

"What's she got to do with it?"

Sophy smiled to herself.

"She's training me. I've passed the first inspection good as gold. Schoolmaster's wife. Now she's on to—you just wouldn't believe. Women, particularly with small boys about, have to be so careful of their person."

"Rape?"

"No, you grotty thing!"

"I know that word. You've been talking to small boys."

"Listening. But personal hygiene, dear. That's what she's on about."

"She thinks you stink. B.O. they used to call it."

178

"Perfume. That's what she's on about. 'I wear the merest trace, Sophy, dear.' "

She lay back on the bed and laughed at the ceiling. He grinned and straightened up as if the coffee or the pills or both, were working for him.

"All the same I know what she meant."

"Do I reek?"

He reached out absently and began to mould her nearer breast.

"Lay off Gerry. It's the wrong time of the day."

"Exhausted by Fido's enormous sex drive. How many times did he have you?"

"He didn't have me at all."

Gerry put his mug on the floor, took hers from her, set it down, then turned over so that he was lying partly on her. He smiled into her eyes as he spoke.

"What a liar you are, old soul."

"If it comes to that, dear thing, how many times have you had it off while your little girl has been unavoidably absent?"

"Nary a once, honest to God, marm."

Then they were both laughing at each other, twins. He bowed down and laid his head by hers, face down. He nuzzled his face into her hair and murmured so that his breath tickled her ear.

"I've got such a hard-on I could get right up between your tits and make your teeth rattle."

But he didn't. He lay there, breathing lightly, lighter than Fido. She freed a curl that was pulling and murmured back.

"I've got all the answers to those questions."

"Goldfinger would be pleased with you. You do keep on, don't you?"

"Will Bill have a hangover too?"

"He never gets a hangover. God is too good to him. Why?"

"Well Christ! Another council of war!"

He looked at her, shaking his head wonderingly.

"Sometimes I think you're—you never give up, do you?"

So once more the three of them met in the gloomy room and the two men went about it and about. She made no suggestions herself, only answered questions they asked her about the set-up. But it became clearer and clearer to her that they were drifting away from the real world into fantasy. For a while she went with them, and then, bored, she began to invent fantasies for herself, pictures inside her mind, impossible daydreams that she knew for what they were. They would have a helicopter which lowered a hook and snatched one of the black, brown or white highnesses literally. They dug a secret tunnel. They got themselves invulnerable bodies and irresistible strength so that they strode in with bullets bouncing from their skin and the hands of men sliding from their more-than-human flesh. Or she became all-powerful and could alter things as she pleased so that the boy was snatched out of his bed and through the silent air to the place—what place? With a shiver of waking she saw what the place was, and where it was; and as if that place thought rather than her mind, the idea came with it.

The two men were silent, looking at her. She could not remember speaking but smiled sleepily from the one to the other. She could see how relieved they were to have proved the whole thing impossible. When she spoke, her words were as gentle as her smile.

"Yes. But what would they do in the night, if there was a big bang and a fire?"

The silence went on and on. At last Gerry spoke, in a voice that was carefully controlled.

"We don't know about that. We don't know what would burn. We don't know where the kids would go. We don't know anything. Not about that. For all you've told us."

"He's right, miss. Sophy."

"Well. I'll go back. I'll go back as often as necessary. We've started this thing and we won't—"

Bill stood up abruptly.

"Well then. Till you've been back. Cor."

The other two waited until he had gone.

"Cheer up, Gerry! Do a daydream about money!"

"Oh my oh my. Is Bill chicken? Honey chile, just be very, very careful!"

"Trouble is I haven't a good excuse for going back."

"Passion."

"I'm suppose to be working at Runways, clot."

"Say they sacked you."

"Spoil my image."

"You sacked them. Better yourself."

"But I can't go rushing back to Fido—"

"Go down in a panic and say he's knocked you up."

180

"Knocked me up?"

"Enceinte. Preggers."

Pause.

"Like I told you, field-marshal, I didn't have it off with him."

"Tell him I've made him a father."

Then they were rolling over and over each other with explosions of sniggers and giggles that turned suddenly into sex, pre-occupied, wounded, experimental, libidinous, long, slow and greedy. When their unsynchronized orgasms had let them down, back into the crumpled bed and into the grey light from the grimy window, Sophy could not even be bothered to repair her lips but lay there in a kind of trance of consent.

"One day, Gerry, you'll be the filthiest old man."

"Filthy old woman yourself."

The grey light washed through Sophy like a tide.

"No. Not me."

"Why not you?"

"Don't ask me. You wouldn't understand anyway."

He sat up abruptly.

"Psychic are we? Snap out of it. What do I keep you for?"

"In all this luxury?"

"I'll say one thing for you, angel. You aren't a libber."

That made her laugh.

"I like you, twin. I really do! I think you're the only person for whom—"

"Yes yes?"

"Never mind. Like I said, I'll go. I could have left my ring down there. So precious my dear and besides it's not just the money it's the sentimental value—oh Fido darling I've done a terrible thing can you ever forgive me? No it's not Gerry—but dearest I've lost our ring! Well of course I've been crying! Oh darling it must have cost at least two pounds fifty—where shall we ever find that sort of money again? You know, Gerry he's—what's the meanest thing there is?"

"You're pretty mean with hand-outs."

"One of these days I shall swipe you."

"Yum yum."

"Will you keep this bloody ring for me? No—come to think of it, I'd better find it somewhere in the school, hadn't I? More convincing."

"Don't forget to look under Fido's pillow."

"You are *the*—"

And then out of the complications too vast for understanding, out of the lies not admitted but nevertheless known to be lies, out of the surmises and the complexities and the seamy side they collapsed in each other's arms, shaking with mutual laughter.

So she took her ring back to Wandicott House and got a shock. For one thing, when Fido heard the ring was lost he was very angry indeed and told her what it had cost. It was considerably more than two pounds fifty and some of it was still outstanding. For another thing, the news that pretty Miss Stanhope had lost her engagement ring flashed through the school and brought it to a full stop. The whole place reorganized itself. Masters whose names she did not know revealed themselves as leaders of men. As for the boys—! But of course the operation, though it was ideal for her purpose, was not without a certain degree of embarrassment. Dr Appleby, the headmaster, impressed on everyone the first thing to do was to establish with precision Miss Stanhope's exact movements during every moment of her previous stay; and though Phyllis Appleby with practised ease turned his remarks in the direction where they would sound as little silly and suggestive as possible, he had nevertheless sown a seed. The news, therefore, that Miss Stanhope had visited her fiancé's room to inspect his photographs was greeted with a solemnity that creaked. Sophy managed to weep and this was a huge success. Fido was told gently by Phyllis what a lucky man he was, that a ring was only a ring and that what a girl really *needed* was to be assured by her fiancé that she was ten thousand times more precious than any mere object. The headmaster came near to ticking Fido off.

"You know, Masterman, what it says in the Bible. 'The price of a good woman is above rubies.' "

"It was an opal."

"Ah well. We're not superstitious, are we?"

It was a great relief when Sophy or the odd-job man—this bit was not quite clear—found her ring under one of the dying elms. It must have been the odd-job man because she was heard thanking him effusively and smiling at him sweetly for all his awful face. But when she told Fido he ought to reward the man, Fido appeared never to have seen or heard of him. The only real drawback after that was that Phyllis insisted they should take her car and go for a drive together. Oh never mind the reading lesson! She would take it herself, so long as the little men didn't have to be told how to spell "accommodation". Now you two young people go off and be alone for a bit. Fido don't sulk! And don't be a brute! Girls aren't like your soldiers you know! They need—Sophy, take him off and pull his ears for him. Go over to have a look at the abbey, the west front is simply marvellous!

So they drove off. Fido doing it moodily and unhandily but gradually thawing and simmering down, then heating up a bit so that he became amorous. Sophy happy in the knowledge that this was the last time she would have to put up with him, explained that it wasn't any good today. He did know that about girls, didn't he? Apparently he did; but not much else; and the information made him moody again.

All at once Sophy's boredom with him flowed over. It even spilled out to Gerry and Bill and Roland and the whole world of men. She thought to herself, I won't go back to the flat tonight. I'll ring the pub and ask them to give Gerry a message and I'll sleep in the stables and to hell with it. I need something bigger, I—need something I—

Respect? Admire? Fear? Need?

She made him drop her in Greenfield High Street and because she was in such a temper with him, the outside girl was even more flashing as she walked briskly down the street to Sprawson's. Jauntily she swung her plastic bags past the laundromat, the Chinese takeaway, Timothy Krishna, Portwell Funeral Directors, Subadar Singh's Gent's Best Suiting. Gaily she greeted Mrs Goodchild as she crossed to the front door, still so splendid in its eighteenth-century manner. She nudged sideways through the door into the hall and a solicitor's clerk proceeding in the other direction hoped she was a client but feared not; and Edwin Bell, climbing the stairs to his flat over the solicitor's office thought—I know that positively breezy way of coming in—Sophy, dear Sophy is back!

Sophy listened outside the column room but heard nothing, so walked straight in to use the telephone.

"Daddy!"

He accepted a peck but cried out as her arm brushed the table.

"Mind what you're doing! Damn it must you girls be so

183

confoundedly clumsy? You're supposed to be—where's the other one—Antonia?"

"How should I know? Nobody knows."

"Oh of course. Well. Neither of you need think I'm going to pay for more flips by air. If it's a question of money you might as well know straight away—"

"It isn't a question of money, Daddy. I just came to see you. After all, I'm your daughter. Forgotten?"

"You want to use the phone."

Pause.

"Later perhaps. What's this thing?"

He looked down at the scattered pieces and began to arrange them again on the little machine.

"They call it a computer but it isn't really. More what I'd call an adding machine. It works through a few variables and then—"

"Can it think?"

"Did they teach you nothing at school? There! Look at that for a move. The thing's moronic. I've worked out a way of mating it with white to move, in eight moves. And you're supposed to pay hundreds of pounds for it!"

"Why bother?"

"I'm supposed to review the thing. There's a certain mild interest in working out from what it does how they've made it. Takes me back to my code-breaking days."

She picked up her bags to leave and was amused to see how he sat back and with a conscious effort set himself to show a little interest, like a father in a book.

"Well. How are things, er, Sophy?"

"The agency was too, too boring."

"Agency? Oh yes!"

"I'm thinking of looking for something else."

He had set his fingertips together, legs stretched under the desk, was looking sideways at her. He smiled and his face lit up, was conspiratorial—was—and she saw at once with what ease he must have persuaded the aunties to come one after the other out of the bedroom across the landing.

"Have you got a boyfriend?"

"Well. What do *you* think?"

"I, mean, are you—going steady?"

"You mean am I having it off with a bloke?"

184

He laughed soundlessly up at the ceiling.

"You won't shock me, you know. We used to have it off too. Only we didn't call it that and we didn't talk about it so much."

"All those aunties after Mummy—went. When Toni pushed off with the Butlers she was looking for Mummy, wasn't she?"

"That crossed my mind."

The awareness at the mouth of the tunnel spoke but used the voice of the outside girl.

Lightly.

"I hope it didn't come between you and your toys."

"Toys? What are toys? How would you define toys?"

"Mummy didn't like chess either, I suppose."

He became restless. It was not so much movement as a kind of deliberate stillness out of which his voice came a tone higher and with a hint of strain in it.

"Use the phone if you like. I'll go. Private I suppose. Only I don't ever want to talk about her. Understand that."

"But I *do* understand that!"

He blared out at her.

"Like hell you do! What do you know, any of you? This, this romantic stuff, this, this—"

"Go on. Use the word."

"It's like stinking treacle. It swallows, drowns, binds, enslaves—*that*—" and he gestured sweepingly over the desk with its litter of papers and games—"that's life. A meanwhile, a what the man said, a surcease, even a cleanness in the stink in the wetness, the milk, nappies, squallings—"

He stopped; then went on in his normal, cold voice.

"I don't want to seem unwelcoming. But—"

"But you're busy with your toys."

"Precisely."

"We're not very wholesome are we?"

"That's a good word."

"You, Mummy, Toni, me—we're not the way people used to be. It's part of the whole running down."

"Entropy."

"You don't even care enough about us to hate us, do you?"

He looked at her and moved his body restlessly.

"Push off, er, Sophy. Just go away."

She stood there, half-way to the door, between her plastic

shopping-bags full of gear. She looked back at his frown, the old-fashioned hair-do with its side parting, the collar and tie, the grizzled sideburns, the lines on his stripped face, his eagle's face that nevertheless was so wholly male. All at once she understood. It had been so, always so, back beyond the birthday when she had lost him for ever, back to the time of the rectangle and the tiny girl looking up and *woo'd*, yes woo'd for those few minutes, that half hour; was so even now, not in a Gerry way or Fido way or Bill way or, or—but in a wide passion rooted beyond the very stars in which *I fancy you* was trivial as a single bubble on a stream, a nothing, a joke—

Her mouth began to talk in a cover-up, partly arch girl, concerned daughter, partly fugitive from this last piece of outrage.

"But look Daddy, you can't go on living by yourself. You'll get old. You'll need, I mean you can say sex is trivial but what do you do about it, I mean—"

And then, facing him, unable to take her eyes off his face, the severe, masculine mouth, the eagle's beak, the eyes that surely could see as far as she through a brick person—*then*, both hands trapped by her sides by the swinging bags, her splendid, idiotic body took charge, and before him, her unbra'd breasts rose up, their vulnerable, tender, uncontrollable, enslaving points hardened, stood out and lifted the fabric of her shirt in a sign as clear as if it had been shouted. She saw his eyes move their focus from her own, move down, past her flushing face and throat until they stared straight at the overt signal. Her mouth opened, shut, opened.

"What do you do—"

At these words that she could only just hear over the pounding of the blood in her ears she saw his eyes lift to hers. There was a redness in his cheeks too. His hands had shifted back and were clutching the arms of his revolving chair. His nearer shoulder was hunched as if to get between them and he was staring at her round it. Then, as if to demonstrate his freedom, boldness, his power to say anything that might be thought unsayable, he spoke directly into her face. He even swung his chair round a little to show there was no concealment, not even from his shoulder. His words were like blows, driving them apart, destroying them, hurling her away from the toy room, the column room, the room that was so secure from people.

186

"What do I do?" Then with a hissing kind of hatred—"You want to know? You do? I masturbate."

So there they were, he, crouched in his chair, trapped between his hands, she by the door, trapped between her bags. With great deliberateness, as if he himself were a lay figure, a puppet which he was rearranging, he shifted his position, his head moved to look down at the chess machine, body moved round and forward, the hands lifted one after the other from the arms of the chair; picture of a man absorbed in his study, his job, his business, his all, his. What a man is for.

She stood there; and for once the presence at the mouth of the tunnel was not able to make itself felt. There was too much of outside girl. Her face felt swollen and water was building up under and behind her eyes.

She swallowed, looked at the window, then back at his indifferent profile.

"Don't we all?"

He did not reply but stayed where he was, looking down at the chess machine. He picked up a biro in his right hand and held it ready but for nothing. The hand and the biro stayed there, shaking slightly. She felt full of lead, full of pain unexpected and not understood; and this storm of emotion that filled the room was like a physical thing and must surely be confined to a cuboid shape by the walls, not understood, only one thing understood, the great slash he had made between the two of them, through what had not existed, oh no, could never have existed, and where there was severance, goodbye and good riddance, cruel and contemptuous act of will.

"Well—"

Her feet seemed stuck to the floor, stuck in it. She pulled them out of the floor with an effort that made her stagger, turned, and was swung at least partly by the weight in her either hand and went through the idiotic business of getting the door wider open, then pulling it to with one foot behind her. It closed on the silent figure with the quivering hand and she hurried through the hall, got the glass door open somehow, then pulled it to with one foot behind her, like the other door, more or less fell down the steps, hurried along the asphalt under the buddleias, past the riot of rosemary and mint and the straggling roses that were overtaken by their own stock. She climbed the narrow stair to the old room

187

with the dormers and collapsed on the cold comfort of her divan. Then she began to cry, and rage against everything. It was in the middle of this rage that she heard an unspoken sentence from her own inside that the secret of it all was outrage; so she looked among her hot tears, her rage and hatred for the outrage that would go with the unravelling, and there it was right in the front of her mind so that she stared at it. There was a girl (oh not with an addled egg in her hand) going up the garden path with her girl's body, her scent and her breasts, laughing she went, back to the hall, the door, flung it open and there laughing offered what she had to him; and now a real, solid girl's body staggered down the stairs and along the path after the phantom girl, up the steps, got open the glass door; and the electric typewriter was going and going, chattering the apegame in the column room and she could not, *could not*, her body would not, *would not*, and she came away, tears streaming and she got back to the unaired divan and lay there, failed in outrage, and seething with the hatred that was a thing all on its own, bitter in the mouth and the belly, worse than bitter, acid burning.

At last she lay without either thought or feeling, and with a sentience that neither commented nor criticized but was a naked and unemotional "I am" or perhaps "It is". Then the interior, nameless thing was there again, the thing that had sat from ever-lasting to everlasting, staring out. Now, for an aeon at the mouth of its tunnel it stared out and was aware, too, of that black angle, direction behind that stretched, widening, as far as there was to stretch. The thing examined the failure to outrage, noted it; was aware that there would be some other occasions for outrage; even said (but silently) a word.

*Presently*.

Sophy became aware of the divan, the place, her body, her ordinariness. She felt how diagonally across her right cheek a wrinkle in the coverlet had pressed it and had done so with more effect than usual because the flesh of that cheek was pulpy with a suffusion of the blood of rage and hatred and shame. She sat up and swung her feet off the divan. She went to the mirror, and there it was, the crease mark on a face that tears had reddened round eyes even redder.

*Sewn in with red worsted*.

Who had said that? An auntie? Toni? Mummy? Him?

188

She became very busy talking to herself.

"This will never do, my old soul! We must repair the damage, mustn't we? A girl's first duty is to get herself up as a lollipop a nice bit of crumpet what would our dear fiancé think or our dear boyfriend? Or our dear—"

Someone was coming very softly up the wooden stairs. There was almost no sound from the feet and only the faintest of creaks from the weight. She saw a head appear, a face, shoulders. It was a dark head of hair and curly as her own. The eyes under it were dark in the delicate face. A scarf, a long raincoat open, to show a trouser-suit too sharp for Greenfield, trousers tucked into the tops of long, high-heeled boots. The girl drew clear of the stairs and stood looking across at her expressionlessly. Sophy stared back. Neither of them said anything.

Sophy felt in her shoulder bag, got out her lipstick and mirror, busied herself repairing her face. It took quite a time. When she was satisfied, she put the things back in the bag and dusted off her hands. She spoke conversationally.

"I couldn't get mine under a wig as easily as that. Contact lenses too. Or did you cut it?"

"No."

"Palestine. Cuba. And then—I know where you've come from."

A faint, far-off voice from behind the face on which a new face had been marked out by make-up.

"Obviously."

"England's turn, is it? The superior, blinding bastards!"

"We're considering. Looking round."

As if to demonstrate this, Toni began to move round the room, peering at the places on the wall where the pictures had been. All at once, Sophy felt a kind of glee that awoke in the depth of her body and bubbled up, not to be quelled.

"Have you seen him?"

Toni shook her head. She picked at a scrap of a picture still sticking to the plaster. The glee bubbled up and up.

"You said 'We need you.' Well?"

"Well?"

"You have men. Money. Must have."

Without moving her feet, Toni sank down and sat on the end of the divan, very slowly. She waited. Sophy stared out of the

189

dormer and at the blind windows of the old house.

"I have access. And a project. Know-how. It's saleable."

Now she, in her turn, sank down on to the divan slowly and faced the enigmatic contact lenses.

"My deah, deah Antonia. All over again! We're going to be everything to each other."

# Part Three
# ONE IS ONE

# CHAPTER TWELVE

Next door to Sprawson's, in Goodchild's shop, Sim Goodchild sat at the back and tried to think about First Things. There were no people browsing along his shelves so it should have been easy. But as he told himself, what with the jets soughing down every minute to London airport and the monstrous continental trucks doing their best to break down the Old Bridge, any thought was impossible. Moreover he knew that after a moment or two on First Things (getting back, he sometimes called it) he knew he would be likely to find himself brooding on the fact that he was too fat, also as bald as bald and with a cut at the left corner of the chin, acquired in the process that morning of shaving a jowl. He said to himself you could work of course. You could do a bit of rearranging and fool with the job of reticketing so as to limp after inflation. It was really the only sort of thought possible in all the town-racket, what with being bald and old and breathless. You could also brood on what to do in the large sense, as a business-man. The oil shares were all right and would last their lifetime. They provided the bread and butter; but no jam. The shop wasn't providing any jam either. What to do? How bring in the Pakis? How the Blacks? What brilliant and unique stroke of the anti-quarian bookseller's craft would prise that crowd of white people away from the telly and bring them to read old books again? How to persuade people of the essential beauty, lovableness, human-ity even, of a beautifully bound book? Yes. You could brood on that for all the rumpus, but not on First Things.

This was the point in his daily brooding when he was accustomed to finding himself stood on his feet by a kind of interior pressure. The pressure was the memory of his own short-comings and he stood up because if he did not the memories would take on time and place, which was intolerable. He stared at

Theology, Occult, Metaphysics, Prints, the *Gentleman's Magazine*—and flash! the very episode which he had stood on his feet to avoid shot bang into awareness.

About a month ago, the auction.

"£250, £250. Any advance? Going for the last time at £250—"

That was when Rupert Hazing from Midland Books had bent to him.

"This is where I step in."

"What? With one year missing?"

Rupert's mouth had stayed open. He had glanced at the auctioneer then back at Sim. It had been enough. While Rupert hesitated the books had been knocked down to Thornton's of Oxford.

That was sheer wantonness, not helping the business but hindering Rupert. For fun. The diabolical *thing* down there disporting itself. And you could not embark on the long voyage of reparation that could make all well, could not give Rupert Hazing all the volumes of the *Gentleman's Magazine* for £250 with, say, ten per cent on top for himself—could not do it because, to change the metaphor, this latest piece of wantonness was only a bit on the top of the pile. The pile was a vast heap of rubbish, of ordure, of filthy rags, was a mountain—it did not matter what one did, the pile was too big. Why pick the last bit of filth off the top?

Sim blinked and shook himself as he always did at this point and came up out of the pile to the modified daylight of the shop. This was the bold, the cynical point in his mornings when he walked down between Novels, Poetry, Literary Criticism on the one hand and Bibles, Prayer Books, Handicrafts and Hobbies on the other. It was the point where he sneered at himself and his ancestors and the good old family business now going so inexorably to the dogs. He was accustomed even to sneer nowadays at the children's books he had arranged, years ago, at one side of the great plate-glass window. Ruth, when she came in from shopping the first time after he had done it, had said nothing. But later when she had brought his tea to him at the desk she had glanced away down the shop.

"I see you are changing our image."

He had denied it but of course it was true. He had seen Stanhope's little girls coming up the street hand-in-hand and quite suddenly he had felt every speck of dust in the shop was made of lead, and that he was made of lead and that life (which he was missing) was bright and innocent like the two children. With a kind of furtive passion he had begun to buy children's books, new ones at that, and arrange them in the left side of the window. Sometimes parents bought a book at Christmas, and rarely, in between, for birthdays, perhaps, but the addition to turnover was imperceptible.

Sim sometimes wondered whether his father's display there had had the same kind of furtive and obscure motivation. His rationalist father had set out a skrying glass, the *I Ching* complete with reeds, and the full set of Tarot cards. Sim understood his own motive only too well. He was using children's books as a bait for the Stanhope twins, who would be some substitute for his own children—Margaret, married but in Canada, and Steven, incurable in that ward where his parents met him week after week for a period of complete non-communication. The brilliant little girls had indeed come in, hardly tall enough to reach the doorknob but with the calm assurance usually connected with privilege. They had examined books with the solemn attention that kittens will give with their noses. They had opened books and turned over page after page, surely faster than not only they but anyone else could read. Yet they seemed to be reading: the fair one—Toni—turning from a child's book to take down an adult one; then the other giggling at a picture while the dark curls shook all over her little head—

Ruth understood though it must have been bitter for her. She had them into the sitting-room for lemonade and cake, but they did not come back. After that, Sim would stand in his doorway when they went to school, first with the au pair and later on their own. He knew exactly when to stand, abstracted, and have his minute gift bestowed on him regally.

"Good morning Mr Goodchild."

"And good morning to the Misses Stanhope!"

So they grew in beauty. It was Wordsworthian.

Ruth emerged from the sitting-room to go shopping.

"I saw Edwin yesterday. I forgot to tell you. He's coming to see you."

Bell lived in part of Sprawson's; they had a flat. Once upon a time, Sim had envied the Bells for living so close to the twins. But that was past. The girls were little girls long ago—ten years ago, not so long after all—and quite beyond children's books.

As if she saw his thought, Ruth nodded at the left-hand side of the shop window.

"You should try something else."

"Any suggestions?"

"Household. BBC Publications. Dressmaking."

"I'll think."

She went away up the High Street among the foreign costumes. Sim nodded and went on nodding, agreeing about the children's books but knowing he wouldn't change them. They would get their dust of lead. They said a stubborn something. Abruptly he turned to the books piled by his desk; the books from Langport Grange to be sorted and priced—work, work, work!

It was work he enjoyed—work that had kept him in his father's business. Bidding was a trial, for he was a coward and not willing to chance his arm. But sorting afterwards—it was almost like panning for gold. You stalked the job lot, your eye having caught the tell-tale glint; and after the dreadful time of bidding—*there* was the first edition of Winstanley's *Introduction to the Study of Painted Glass* in perfect condition!

Well. It happened once.

Sim sat down at his desk but the door flew open, the bell rang and it was Edwin himself, larger than life or would-be larger than life, in his check coat and yellow, dangling scarf—Bell, still dressed as an *undergrad* of the thirties and lacking only the Oxford Bags to be a complete period piece.

"Sim! Sim!"

A gust of wind, a kind of Edward Thomas crossed with George Borrow wind on the heath, great Nature, but all the same, cultivated, cultural and spiritually *sincere*.

"Sim! My good Sim! The man I have met!"

Edwin Bell strode up the shop and sat himself like a lady riding sidesaddle on the corner of the desk. He banged down the text book he was carrying and the copy of the *Bhagavad Gita*. Sim leaned back in his chair, took off his spectacles and blinked at the eager face seen so indistinctly against the light.

"What is it now, Edwin?"

"The man—Ecce homo—if that isn't too disastrously blasphemous and really do you know Sim I don't think it is? The most

196

incredible creature with an effect—I am, do you know, I am—excited!"

"When were you not?"

"At last! I genuinely feel—It's a case of everything comes to him who waits. After all these years—I know what you're going to say—"

"I wasn't going to say anything!"

"You were going to say that my swans were always geese. Well. So they were. I admit it freely."

"Theosophy, Scientism, the Mahatma—"

Edwin subsided a little.

"Edwina implied much the same."

It must have been intended from the beginning of the universe, this marriage between Edwin and Edwina Bell. There was more to the obviousness of the intention than the coincidence of the name. They looked so much like each other that unless a person knew them very well they had a kind of transvestite appearance simply by reference to each other. On top of that, Edwin had a high voice for a man and Edwina a low voice for a woman. Sim still winced at the memory of one of his early telephone conversations with them. A high voice had replied so that he had said "Hullo Edwina!" The voice replied "But Sim, it's Edwin!" Then when next he had been answered by a low voice he had said "Hullo Edwin!" only to hear—"But Sim, it's Edwina." When they walked up the High Street from Sprawson's or from their flat in Sprawson's, they would both have much the same scarf blowing from much the same open overcoat. Edwina's hair was a little shorter than Edwin's and she had rather more bosom. It was a useful distinction.

"Edwina always did have more sense than you, I think."

"Now Sim, you're just saying that because it's what people say about wives when they can't think of anything else. I call it the Little Woman Syndrome."

The phone rang.

"Yes? Yes, we do. Hold on a moment please. It's in good condition. Seven pounds ten, I'm afraid—I mean seven fifty. We have your address? Right. Yes, I will." He put the phone back, made a note in his desk diary, sat back again and looked up at Edwin.

"Well? Out with it!"

Edwin smoothed down the hair at the back of his head with a gesture exactly like Edwina's. Growing together.

"It's this man as I said. The Man in Black."

"I've heard that before. The Man in Black. The Woman in White."

Edwin gave a sudden, triumphant laugh.

"But it's not so, Sim, not so! You couldn't be more wrong if you tried! You see, what you're being is *literary*!"

"Bookseller after all."

"But I haven't told you—"

Edwin was leaning across the desk, sideways, his eyes bright with enthusiasm, mouth open, short nose projecting in search, in passion, in anticipation. Sim shook his head with weary but still good-humoured affection.

"Believe Edwina, Edwin. She has more bosom than you O God why did I say that I mean—"

But once more, as on all the other occasions with all those other people, the thing was irretrievable. There were rumours about the Bells' sex life, everyone knew the rumours and nobody said—surely now Bell was blushing against the light, flushing, rather, the good humour of his excitement changed to anger? Sim jumped up and struck the desk with his fist.

"O curse it curse it curse it! Why do I do it, Edwin? Why in the name of God must I do it?"

Bell was looking away at last.

"You know we once nearly, very nearly, took out a libel writ?"

"Yes. I did. Do. They said so."

"Who's 'They'?"

Sim gestured vaguely.

"People. You know how it is."

"I do indeed, Sim. I do indeed."

Then Sim was silent for a while, not because he had nothing to say but because he had too much. Everything he could think of had a double meaning or was likely to be misunderstood.

At last he looked up.

"Two old men. Got to remember that. Only a few more years. Getting a bit ingrown, silly, perhaps, more than we—more than I am by nature if that's possible. Only it can't, *can't* amount to no more than this, can it? This kind of dull, busy preoccupation with trivialities—I would do this and that but on the other hand there is that and this, have you read the papers, what was on the box, how is Steven, I can let you have it at eighty-five pence with postage and never, never a dive into what must be the deep—I'm sixty-seven. You're—what is it?—Sixty-three. Out there are the Pakis and Blacks, the Chinese, the Whites, the punks and lay-abouts, the—"

He stopped himself, wondering a little why he had gone on so long. Edwin stirred on the corner of the desk, stood up and stared away at Metaphysics.

"I taught the other day for a whole period with my flies open."

Sim kept his lips together but heaved once or twice inside. Edwin appeared not to notice. He was looking clean through the row of books, away and away.

"Edwin. You were telling me about this man."

"Ah yes!"

"A Franciscan friar? A Mahatma? A reincarnation of the first Dalai Lama who wants to build a Potala in Wales?"

"You're jeering."

"Sorry."

"In any case it wasn't the Dalai Lama. Just a Lama."

"Sorry. Sorry."

"The Dalai Lama is still alive so it couldn't have been."

"O God."

"But this—afterwards I found I was—not crying, because the implications of the word are a bit childish, a bit babyish—but weeping. Not for sorrow. For joy."

"One for sorrow."

"Not any more."

"What's his name? I like to have a name to hold on to."

"Then you're out, my dear man, right out. That's the core of it. No names. Rub them off. Ignore them. Think of the mess, the ruckus, the tumultuous, ridiculous, savage complications that language has made for us and we have made for language—oh confound it, now I've started to orate!"

"He wants to get rid of language and has approached two people, you and me via you, who depend on language more than anything else for their existence! Look at these books!"

"I see them."

"Think of your classes."

"Well then!"

199

"Don't you see? You talked once about being more worried by *faux pas* than sin. Precisely at that point you are invited to make a huge sacrifice that would stand our worlds on their—on its—head—the deliberate turning away from the recorded word, printed, radioed, televized, taped, disced—"

"No, no."

"Good God, Sim, you're older than me! How long have you got? How long can you wait about? I tell you—" And Edwin gestured so widely his greatcoat swung open—"this is it!"

"The odd thing is, you know, that I don't care how long or how short I've got. Oh yes. I don't want to die. But then, I'm not going to, am I? Not today, at any rate, with a bit of luck. There'll come a day and I shan't like it. Probably. But not today. Today is infinity and triviality."

"You won't take a chance?"

Sim sighed.

"I foresee the resurrection of the Philosophical Society."

"It was never dead."

"Resumption then. How wordy we are!"

"Transcendentalism—"

The word acted like a pulled trigger on Sim. He simply ceased to listen. The great wheel, of course, and the Hindu universe, alleged to be identical with the one the physicists were uncovering; skandhas and atavars, recession of the galaxies, appearance and illusion—and all the time, Edwin talking more and more like a character in one of Huxley's less successful novels! Sim at this point began silently to rehearse his own particular statement. It is all reasonable. It is all, equally unreasonable. I believe it all as much as I believe anything that is out of sight; as I believe in the expanding universe, which is to say as I believe in the battle of Hastings, as I believe in the life of Jesus, as I believe in—It is a kind of belief which touches nothing in me. It is a kind of second-class believing. My beliefs are me; many and trivial.

Then once more he could hear Edwin and he looked up at him and nodded, a tiny typical dishonesty implying *I see what you mean, yes, I was listening*. The fact that Edwin was still talking sent him spinning away into his customary astonishment at the brute fact of Being and the brute fact that all he believed in as real, as deeply believed in, not as second-class belief, was himself as the man said because he felt himself thinking that he felt himself

200

thinking that he felt awareness without end—

He found himself nodding again. Edwin went on speaking.

"So tell me. How did he know I am a seeker? Where is it written on me? On my forehead like a caste mark? Are there tribal cuts on my cheeks? Put aside all the technicalities, clairvoyance, second sight, extrasensory perception, all the skrying, seeing, the Gift—he simply knew! And as we walked I found myself—now this is the point, I found not that he spoke but—"

Edwin paused and looked as nearly furtive as a man of his open appearance could.

"You're not going to believe this, Sim. He didn't speak. I did."

"But of course!"

"No, no, not for me! For him! Somehow I was finding words for him—I was never at a loss—"

"You never have been. We both have what my mother called tongues hung in the middle that wag both ends—"

"Just so! Just so! He at one end, I at the other. And then—walking along the gravel path towards the elms they haven't cut down yet—as the rain pricked and the wind came and went—"

Edwin stopped. He got up from the desk. He thrust his hands deep into his pockets. The overcoat shut in front of him like drawn curtains.

"—I spoke in more than words."

"You sang, perhaps."

"*Yes*," said Edwin, without a trace of humour. "Exactly so! That is to say I experienced more than words can say; and I experienced it there and then." A small black boy pressed his face to the plate glass, looked into the impenetrable innards of the shop and ran away. Sim looked back at Edwin.

"There's always come a point when I have had to take your say-so. Can't you understand, Edwin, that I'm fettered by a kind of social politeness? I've never been able to say to your face what I actually think about it all."

"I want you to come along. Back to the park."

"Have you arranged a meeting?"

"He'll be there."

Sim passed a hand over his baldness then shook himself in irritation.

"I can't leave the shop whenever I like. You know that. And Ruth is out shopping. I couldn't possibly leave until—"

The shop bell rang and of course it was Ruth. Edwin turned back to Sim triumphantly.

"You see?"

Now Sim was really irritated.

"That's trivial!"

"It all hangs together. Good morning, Ruth."

"Edwin."

"Still going up, dear?"

"Just the penny here and there. Nothing to worry about."

"I was explaining that I can't leave the shop."

"Oh but you can. Cold lunch. I shall be glad to sit."

"And you see again, my dear Sim? Trivial of course!"

Driven, Sim became stubborn.

"I don't want to come!"

"Go with Edwin, dear. Do you good. Fresh air."

"It won't be any good, you know. It never is."

"Up you get."

"I don't see why I—look Ruth, if Graham's comes through tell them we haven't got a full Gibbon after all. One volume of *Miscellaneous* is missing. But we've the full *Decline and Fall* in good condition."

"That's the first edition."

"Price as agreed for the *Decline*. New dicker for the rest."

"I'll remember."

Sim got his overcoat, his scarf, his woollen gloves, his squashy hat. Side by side they walked up the High Street. The bell struck eleven from the tower of the community centre. Edwin nodded at it.

"That's where I met him."

Sim did not answer, and they passed the community centre, from whose graveyard the tombstones had not yet all been moved, in silence. Harold Krishna, Chung and Dethany Clothing, Bartolozzi Dry Cleaning, Mamma Mia Chinese Takeaway. In the door of Sundha Singh's Grocery Store one of the Singh brothers was talking liquidly to a white policeman.

The temple and the new mosque. The Liberal club closed for repairs, graffiti on every available surface. Up the Front. Kill the Bastard Frunt. Fugglestone shoe repairs.

Edwin swerved round a Sikh woman in her brilliant costume only partly hidden by her raincoat. For twelve yards or so Sim

202

followed him among white men and women waiting for a bus. Edwin spoke over his shoulder.

"Different when I came, wasn't it, after the war? London wasn't crawling all over us. The Green was still a village green—"

"If you shut one eye, it was. Ponsonby was vicar. You met this man of yours in there, you said."

"I wanted to see young Steven's wood sculpture. He'll go some distance—not far; but it's already a fallout from using the place as a community centre—there was also an exhibition of what's his name's photographs of insects—you know the man I mean. Fascinating. Oh yes. The Little Theatre Group was rehearsing that thing of Sartre's—you know—*In Camera*—in the, the north annexe—"

"You mean the north transept where they used to reserve the sacrament."

"Now Sim! You old stick-in-the-mud! You weren't even a communicant! Remember we're multi-racial and all religions are one, anyway."

"Try telling them that in the mosque."

"What do I hear? Has the Front been getting to you?"

"Don't be obscene. This man—"

"I met him just where the—no it wasn't. The font was on the other side. But he was standing under the west window, staring down at one of the old inscriptions."

"Epitaphs."

"I teach books, you know. I live by them too. The school does, after all. Yesterday after meeting him, I suddenly thought when I was talking about Shakespeare's own Histories—Good Lord, *that's* why he didn't bother about having his stuff printed! He knew, you see. Well, he would, wouldn't he?"

" 'Venus and Adonis'. 'Rape of Lucrece'. Sonnets, to you."

"A young man. The letter killeth. Who said that?"

*"You found it in print."*

"Some of the time we were both silent. I mean very silent. During one of these silences I found something out. You see, the silence was seared by the passage of these ghastly jets; and I knew that if, *if* we, or he, could find a place with the quality of absolute silence in it—that was why he was in the community centre, I think. Searching for silence—disappointed of course. So we were talking for only part of the time. Or rather I was. Have you ever

203

noticed that I talk a lot, almost logorrhoea, talking for the sake of it? Well I didn't. Not then."

"You're talking about yourself. Not him."

"But that's the point! Part of the time I—well, I spoke *Ursprache*."

"German?"

"Don't be a—God, how lucky they were, those old philosophers and theologians who spoke Latin! But I forgot. No they weren't. It was a kind of print—one remove from. Sim. I spoke the innocent language of the spirit. The language of paradise."

Edwin was looking sideways defiantly and flushing. Sim felt his own face go hot.

"I see," he muttered. "Well—"

"You don't see. And you're embarrassed. I don't see either and I'm embarrassed—"

Edwin covered his privates again with his two fists thrust into the overcoat pockets. He spoke fiercely. "It's not the thing, is it? Awfully bad form, isn't it? A bit methodist, isn't it? Back street stuff isn't it? Just talking with tongues, that's all. Now the moment is gone I can't re-experience it. I can only remember, and what's a memory? Useless clutter! I should have it down and sewn into the lapel of my jacket, here, somewhere. Now we're both blushing like a couple of naughty schoolgirls who've been caught using a bad word. In for a penny in for a pound. You're for it, Sim. Treat it as science, that'll make it feel better. I'm going to describe that memory as exactly as—I said seven words. I said a small sentence and I saw it as a luminous and holy shape before me. Oh, I forgot, we're being scientific aren't we? Luminous would pass. Holy? Right then—the *affect* was one commonly associated in religious phraseology with the word 'Holy'. Well. The light was not of this world. Now laugh."

"I'm not laughing."

They walked on in silence for a while, Edwin with his head turned sideways, in defence and suspicion. He struck a small Eurasian with his shoulder and exploded into the social Edwin which always seemed more real than any other of his private committee.

"I'm so sorry—inexcusable clumsiness—are you sure—oh really it was too bad of me! You're not hurt? Thank you so much, so very very much! Good day. Yes. Good day!"

Then as suddenly switched off, the defensive Edwin looked back at Sim as they walked.

"No. I don't believe you are. Thank you."

"What were the words?"

Astonished, Sim saw a positive tide of red sweep up Edwin's neck, up his face, his low forehead, and vanish under his tough but grizzled hair. Edwin swallowed once and over the knotted scarf it was possible to see how his prominent Adam's apple bobbed up and down. He gave a self-conscious cough.

"I can't remember."

"You—"

"All I have left is a memory of sevenness and a memory of that shape, imprecise as it was, but now crystallized—colourless, now alas—"

"You've done an Annie Besant."

"But that's exactly it! *That*'s exactly the difference! I've done it or rather it's been done—Our geese—have been those whose opinions we thought might be helpful, whose philosophies, whose religions, whose codes might be what we were looking for; and what would eventuate tomorrow or the day after or the year after in some kind of illumination—the difference is that this was it! Was tomorrow, the year after next! I don't have to explain, Sim, I am not looking for anything—I found it, there in the park, sitting beside him. He gave it me."

"I see."

"I was a little downcast you know when you—Dejected. Yes, I was cast down."

"My fault, sorry. Uncivil of me."

"It all falls together as it should. I don't think he would object to a man having and carrying about with him the written word rather than the printed—so, so long as he had copied it out himself—"

"Are you serious?"

"You would write down yourself and keep private to yourself—you know, Sim, I've just remembered. That's coming together. He took my book from me."

"What book?"

"A paperback. Nothing important. He took it and went away into the public lavatory and of course when he came back—well he didn't give it back."

"You've forgotten. Like the seven words."

205

"There was one thing he did, though. He picked up a matchbox and a stone. Then he very carefully balanced the matchbox on the arm of the seat with the stone on top of it."

"What did he say?"

"He's not got a mouth that's intended for speaking. Good Lord, what have I said? That's exactly it! Not intended for speaking!"

"What happened to the matchbox and the stone?"

"I don't know. Perhaps they're still there. Perhaps they fell off. I didn't look."

"We're crazy. Both of us."

"He can speak of course, because he said 'Yes'. I'm nearly sure he said 'Yes'. He must have done. I'm quite sure in my mind that he said some other things. Yes, he said quite a bit concerning 'Secrecy'."

"What secrecy for God's sake?"

"Didn't I tell you? That's the other thing. No reproduced words. No permanent names to anything. And no one must know."

Sim stopped on the pavement so that Edwin had to stop as well and turn to him.

"Look Edwin, this is fantastic nonsense already! It's masonic stuff, inner circle stuff, conspiratorial—don't you understand? Doesn't he understand himself? You could get up in the High Street or the Market Place and speak; you could get up and shout, you could use a loudhailer and no one, but no one, would give a damn! The jets would still come over, the traffic pass, the shoppers the coppers the teeny boppers and all, and no one would even notice. They'd think you were advertising fivepence off at the supermarket. We're damned with our own triviality, that's what it is—secrecy? I've never heard anything so silly in my life!"

"Nevertheless—you see, I have brought you to the gates of the park."

"Let's get it over."

They stood together a few yards inside the gates, while Edwin swung on his heel looking round. Groups of children were playing here and there. The attendant stood only a few yards from the public lavatory, watching the children morosely as they ran in and out or took each other there.

Edwin discovered the man behind them with a great start. Sim, turning as well, found himself looking straight into the man's face. There was something a little stagey about his appearance, as if he were got up to play a part. He wore a broad-brimmed black hat and a long black overcoat, into the pockets of which his hands were thrust as Edwin's were thrust into his. He was, Sim saw, exactly the same size as he was so that they met eye to eye. Yet the man's face was strange. The right side was browner than a European's would be, yet not so distinctly brown as to type him as Hindu or Pakistani and certainly he was no Negro, for his features were quite as Caucasian as Edwin's own. But the left side of his face was a puzzle. It seemed—thought Sim for a moment—as if he held a hand mirror which was casting faint light from the grey, misty day which lowered the colour of that side a tone or two. In that side, the eye was smaller than the right one and then Sim knew that this lighter shade was not a reflection but a different skin. The man, many years before, had had a skin graft that covered most of the left side of his face and was perhaps the reason why Edwin had said he had a mouth not for speaking, because the skin held that side of the mouth closed as it held the eye nearly closed, an eye, perhaps, not for seeing. A fringe of jet-black hair projected down under the black hat all round and on the left side there was a mulberry-coloured thing projecting through rather longer black hair. With a sudden lurch of his stomach Sim saw that this thing was an ear, or what was left of it—an ear imperfectly hidden by the hair and suggesting immediately that its appearance dated from the event that had occasioned the skin graft. Of all sights he had not expected to see such deformation. It made him wince to look at it. His mouth that had opened in the first movement of some social advance, stayed opened and he said nothing. It was not necessary because he could hear Edwin talking eagerly at his side and with that particularly loud, braying note that was a parody teacher's and so often taken off behind his back. But Sim paid no attention to what Edwin was saying. His own gaze was held by the man's one-and-a-half eyes and his half-mouth not meant for speaking and the extraordinary grief that seemed to contract it as much as the pull of the skin. Moreover, the man seemed to be out-lined—but this must be some quirk of psychology—against his background in a way that made him the point of it.

Eyes held, Sim felt the words rising through him, entering his throat, speaking themselves against his own will, evoked, true.

"My inclination is to think that all this is nonsense."

The man's right eye seemed to open wider; and the effect was as if a sudden gleam of light came from it. Anger. Anger and grief. Edwin answered.

"Of course it's not what you expect! The paradox is that if you had thought a bit, Goodchild, you'd have known it couldn't be what you expect!"

A particularly snarling jet soughed louder and louder down over them. At the same moment the High Street seemed to be invaded by a whole string of articulated juggernauts. Sim raised a hand to his ear, more in protest than in hope of keeping the noise out. He glanced sideways. Edwin was still speaking, his short nose lifted, the hectic on his cheeks. It sounded like a comminatory psalm, overthrowing, trampling down.

Sim could only tell what he himself said because he was inside with it.

"What are we getting ourselves into?"

Then the jet had passed, the juggernauts were grinding themselves away, to turn right and go round to the spur of the motorway. He looked back at the man and found with a jolt of surprise that he had gone. A kind of mash of surmises, most of them ridiculous, filled his mind; and then he saw him, ten yards off and striding away, hands in long coat pockets. Edwin was following.

They went like that, the three of them, in single file along the main, gravelled path. Grief and anger. The two so mixed they had become a single, settled quality, a strength. Again, words seemed to find their own way up his body towards his throat like bubbles in a bottle; but with the man's face hidden ahead there he contrived to keep them in.

*I'd expected some kind of Holy Joe.*

As if they shared a mind, Edwin slackened his pace and drew alongside.

"I know it's not what anyone would expect. How are you doing?"

Unwillingly, again, and cautiously—

"I'm—interested."

They were approaching an area where children were playing. There were swings, a see-saw, a small, metal roundabout, a slide. As they moved towards the centre of the park the road noises—and there, now, was the sudden roaring, rattling passage of a train—tended to be muffled as if the trees round the edge of

208

the green did indeed muffle sound as they hindered sight. Only the jets soughed over, one every two or three minutes.

"There! Did you see!"

Edwin had reached sideways and grasped Sim's wrist. They were stopped and looking forward.

"See what?"

"That ball!"

The man had not slackened his pace and was getting ahead of them. Edwin lugged again at Sim's wrist.

"You must have noticed!"

"Noticed what, for—"

As if he were talking to a particularly dim pupil Edwin began to explain.

"The ball that boy kicked. It shot across the gravel and through his feet."

"Nonsense. It went between his feet."

"I tell you. It went *through* them!"

"Optical illusion. I saw as well, you know. It went between them! Be your age, Edwin. You'll be having him levitate next."

"Look, I *saw* it!"

"So did I. And it didn't."

"Did."

Sim burst out laughing and after a moment or two Edwin allowed himself to smile.

"Sorry. But—look. As clearly—"

"It didn't. Because if it did—you see, Edwin the, the miracle would be trivial. More than trivial. What difference would it make if the ball struck and bounced off? Or did in fact, as I am sure it did, happen to find a passage between his feet in an unusually neat but still possible way?"

"You are asking me to doubt the evidence of my own eyes."

"For God's sake! Haven't you seen a conjurer? He's unusual, he's extraordinary, he embarrasses me and so do you, but I'm not going to have a trick of the light or a minimal coincidence stuffed down my throat as a violation of the natural order, as a miracle if you prefer the word."

"I don't know what word to use. It was another dimension, that's all."

"Scientistic top-dressing."

"His life, as far as I have shared it—and that's a matter of

209

minutes—well, it may be hours—is thick with that sort of—phenomenon."

"Why isn't he in a laboratory where the controls are?"

"Because he has something more important to do!"

"More important than the truth?"

"Yes. Yes, if you like!"

"What then?"

"How should I know?"

But the man had stopped by a seat that was set by the gravelled path. Sim and Edwin stopped too, a few yards short of the seat, and Sim had a moment or two of feeling acutely foolish. For now, plainly, they were following the man not as if he were another man but as if he were some rare beast or bird with whom there was no possibility of human intercourse but whose behaviour or plumage or pelt was of interest. It was silly, since the man was no more than some sort of white man dressed all in black, and with a head on him, the one side of which had received severe damage many years ago and been imperfectly repaired; and who—all this Sim told himself with increasing comfort and increasing amusement—who was very reasonably annoyed at what life had done to him.

Edwin had stopped talking and was looking where the man was looking. There was a scatter of children playing, little boys mostly but also a small girl or two on the edge of the group. There was also a man. He was a slender old fellow, seeming, thought Sim, older than I am, the oldest man in the park, this childish morning, a slender, rather bent old fellow with a mop of white hair and an ancient pepper-and-salt suit, a suit far, far older than the children, a good suit, a too good suit, a suit that gentlemen used to have made for them in the days when there were gentlemen and waistcoats were worn; also brown, elastic-sided boots, but no coat on this childish morning, together with an anxious, rather silly face—the old man was playing ball with the children. It was a big ball, of many colours. The old fellow or perhaps old gentleman or just old man was active, springy, and he threw the ball to one boy and had it back and then to another boy and had it back and all the time he was working his way—him and the boys—towards the lavatories, with an anxious and gleaming smile on his thin face.

What am I seeing?

210

Sim swung round on his heel. The park attendant was nowhere to be seen. There were, after all, many groups of children and one man cannot be everywhere. Edwin was looking outraged.

The old man, with an agility that the years had not impaired very much, kicked the ball hard with his shiny boot and laughed and giggled with his thin mouth. The ball beat the boy, beat all the boys. The ball flew and bounced and came as if the old man had intended it, bounce, bounce, and the man in black held up his hands with the ball in them. The old man, giggling and waving, waited for the ball back and the man in black waited and the children. Then the old man with a loping, a springy catlike run came across to the path, but began to slow and stop smiling and even stop panting and he bent a little, just a very little and examined each of them in turn. No one said anything and the children waited.

The old man lowered his chin and looked up at the man from under white, springy eyebrows. He was a clean old man, unnaturally clean in his suit, however worn. His voice was expensively educated.

"My ball, I think, gentlemen."

Still no one said anything. The old man gave his silly, anxious giggle again.

"Virginibus puerisque!"

The man in black held the ball against his chest and looked at the old man over it. Sim could only see the undamaged side of his face, his undamaged eye and ear. The features had been regular, attractive, even.

The old man spoke again.

"If you gentlemen are connected with the Home Office, then I can only assure you that the ball is my ball and that the little men at my back are undamaged. To put the matter clearly, you have nothing on me. So please, give me my ball and go away."

Sim spoke.

"I know you! All those years ago—in my shop! The children's books—"

The old man stared.

"Oh, so it's a meeting of old acquaintances is it? Your shop? Well allow me to tell you, sir, we pay as we go, these days, no credit allowed or given. I paid! Oh yes I paid all right! Not for that but for life you see. You don't understand, do you? Ask Mr

211

Bell, there. He brought you. But I've paid so don't any of you dun me. Give me that ball! I bought it!"

Something was happening to the man in black. It was a kind of slow convulsion, and it shook the ball at his chest. His mouth opened.

"Mr Pedigree."

The old man started. He stared into the melted face, peered, head on one side as if he could look under the white skin of the left side, searched all over, from the drawn mouth to the ear on that side, still so imperfectly hidden. The stare became a glare.

"And I know you, Matty Woodrave! *You*—all those years ago, the one who didn't come and had the face, the cruelty, the gall to, to—Oh I know you! Give me that ball! I have nothing but—it was all your fault!"

Again the convulsion, but this time with the grief and anger made audible—

"I know."

"You heard him! You're my witnesses, gentlemen, I hold you to it! You see? A life wasted, a life that might have been so, so beautiful—"

"No."

The word was low, and grated as if from somewhere that was not accustomed to making speech. The old man gave a kind of snarl.

"I want my ball, I want my ball!"

But the whole attitude of the man before him who held the ball so firmly against his black-clad chest was a refusal. The old man snarled again. He glanced round and cried out as if he had been stung; for the children had run or drifted away and were mixed among the playing groups spread round the park. The old man loped out into the empty space of grass.

"Tommy! Phil! Andy!"

The man in black turned to Sim and faced him over the ball. With great solemnity he held the ball out in both hands and Sim understood that he must take it with an equal solemnity. He even bowed a little as he took the ball between his two hands. The man in black turned away and walked after the old man. As if he knew they had made the first step of following him, he gestured on one side of him in a gesture of admonition, without looking round. Don't follow me.

212

They watched him right across the grass until he disappeared behind the lavatory. Sim turned to Edwin.

"What was all that about?"

"Some of it is clear at any rate. The old man. Pedigree, his name is."

"I said, didn't I? He used to shoplift. Children's books."

"Did you prosecute?"

"Warned him off. I understood him. He wanted the books as bait, the old, old—"

"There, but for the grace of God."

"Don't be sanctimonious. You've never wanted to go round interfering with children, neither have I."

"He's a long time there."

"Spend a penny just like anyone else."

"Unless he's having trouble with the old man."

"It's such a particularly contemptible business. Let's hope we don't see him again."

"Who?"

"The old fellow—what did you call him—Pettifer?"

"Pedigree."

"Pedigree, then. Disgusting."

"Perhaps I'd better have a look—"

"What at?"

"He might be having—"

Edwin trotted across the grass towards the lavatory. Sim waited, feeling not just foolish but disgusted, as if the ball was a contamination. He wondered what to do with it; and the memory of the clean old man with his disgusting appetite made him wince inside. He turned his mind aside to things that were really clean and sweet, thinking of Stanhope's little girls. How exquisite they had been and how well-behaved! What a delight it had been to watch them grow; though no matter how wonderfully *nubile* they became they could never surpass that really fairy delicacy of childhood, a beauty that could make you weep—and of course they hadn't turned out just as they should but that was as much Stanhope's fault as theirs and Sophy was so pretty and so friendly—good morning Mr Goodchild, how is Mrs Goodchild? Yes it is isn't it? There was no doubt about it, the Stanhope twins shone in Greenfield like a light!

Edwin was coming back.

"He's gone. Disappeared."

"You mean he's gone away. Don't exaggerate. There's a gate out to the road among the laurels."

"They've both gone."

"What am I supposed to do with this ball?"

"You'd better keep it, I suppose. We'll see him again."

"Time I was going."

Together they walked back along the gravel path but before they had gone more than fifty yards, Edwin stopped them.

"About here."

"What?"

"Don't you remember? What I saw."

"And I didn't."

But Edwin was not listening. His jaw had dropped.

"Sim! Now I understand. Oh yes, it all hangs together! I'm one step nearer to a complete understanding of—if not what he is—of how he works, what he is doing—That ball that went round or through—He let it go. He knew it was the wrong ball."

# CHAPTER THIRTEEN

Ruth was being fanciful. This was most unusual for her since on the whole she was a down-to-earth woman; but now she had a feverish cold and was staying in bed. The Girl minded the shop now and then, though Sim was always nervous when he did not have both her and the shop in sight, but he had quite often to take hot drinks upstairs and persuade Ruth to drink them. Each time he did this he had to stay a bit because of the fancifulness. She lay on her side of the double-bed where the children had been begotten a generation ago. She kept her eyes closed and her face shone with perspiration. Now and then she muttered.

"What did you say, dear?"

Mutter.

"I've brought you some more hot drink. Wouldn't you like to sit up and drink it?"

Ruth spoke with startling clearness.

"He moved. I saw him."

An almost physical anguish contracted Sim's heart.

"Good. I'm glad. Sit up and drink this."

"She used a knife."

"Ruth! Sit up!"

Her eyes flickered open and he saw them focus on his face. Then she looked round the bedroom and up at the ceiling where the sound of a declining jet was so loud it seemed visible. She put her hands down and heaved herself up.

"Better?"

She shuddered in the bed and he draped a shawl round her shoulders. She drank, sip after sip, then handed the glass back without looking at him.

"Now you're what they used to call all-of-a-glow you'll feel better. Shall I take your temperature again?"

215

She shook her head.

"No point. Know what we know. Too much noise. Which way is north?"

"Why?"

"I want to know. I must know."

"You're a bit hazy still, aren't you?"

"I want to know!"

"Well—"

Sim thought of the road outside, the High Street, the Old Bridge. He pictured the enlacement of canal and rail and motorway and the high jet road searing across them all.

"It's a bit difficult. Where would the sun be?"

"It keeps turning, and the noise!"

"I know."

She lay back again and shut her eyes.

"Try and sleep dear."

"No! Not. Not."

Someone was hooting in the road outside. He glanced down through the window. A juggernaut was trying to get on to the Old Bridge and the cars massing behind it were impatient.

"It'll be quiet later."

"Mind the shop."

"Sandra's there."

"If I want anything I'll thump."

"Better not kiss you."

He laid his forefinger on his lips then transferred it to her forehead. She smiled.

"Go."

He crept away downstairs, through the living-room and into the shop. Sandra was sitting at the desk and staring straight at the big shop window without a trace of expression. The only thing that moved was her lower jaw as it masticated what seemed to be a permanent piece of chewing-gum. She had sandy hair and sandy eyebrows imperfectly concealed by eyebrow pencil. She was rather fat, she wore bulging jeans and Sim disliked her. Ruth had chosen her out of the only three applicants for a job that did not pay much, was dull by modern standards and required no intelligence at all. Sim knew why Ruth had chosen the least attractive, or most unattractive of the applicants and agreed with her, ruefully enough.

216

"Could I have my chair, Sandra, do you think?"

Sarcasm was wasted on her.

"I don't mind."

She got up. He sat down, only to see her wander across to the steps which he used for reaching the high shelves and perch her large bottom on it. Sim watched her savagely.

"Wouldn't it be better, Sandra, if you kept on your feet? It's what people expect you know."

"There isn't any people and there hasn't been. And there won't be not now it's so near lunch. There hasn't been anybody not even the phone."

All that was true. The turnover was becoming ludicrous. If it weren't for the rare books—

Sim experienced a moment of exquisite inferiority. It was no good expecting Sandra to understand the difference between this place and a supermarket or a sweet shop. She had her own idea of that difference and it was all in favour of the supermarket. There was life in the supermarket, fellows, talk, chat, light, noise, even muzak on top of the rest. Here were only the silent books waiting faithfully on their shelves, their words unchanged, century after century from incunabula down to paperbacks. It was a thing so obvious that often Sim found himself astonished at his own capacity for finding it astonishing; and he would move from that point to a generalized state of astonishment that he felt obscurely was, like the man said, the beginning of wisdom. The only trouble was that the astonishment recurred but the wisdom did not follow. Astonished I live; astonished I shall die.

Probably Sandra felt her weight. He looked at her and saw how her broad bottom overflowed the step. Then again, she might be having a period. He stood up.

"OK Sandra. You can have my chair for a bit. Until the phone rings."

She heaved her bottom off the step and wandered down the shop. He saw how her thighs rubbed each other. She sank into the chair, still chewing like a cow.

"Ta."

"Read a book if you like."

She turned her eyes on him, unblinking.

"What for?"

"You can read I suppose?"

217

" 'Course. Your wife asked me. You ought to know that."

Worse and worse. We must get rid of her. Get a Paki, a lad, he'd work. Have to keep an eye on him though.

*Don't* think that! Race relations.

All the same they swarm. With the best will in the world I must say they swarm. They are not what I think, they are what I feel. Nobody knows what I feel, thank God.

But they were to have a visitor, perhaps a customer. He was trying the door now—ting! It was Stanhope, of all people. Sim hurried down the shop, hands washing each other in the appropriate manner, his personalized bit of play-acting.

"Good morning Mr Stanhope! A pleasure to see you. How are you? Well, I hope?"

Stanhope brushed it all aside in his usual manner and went straight to the point, a technical one.

"Sim. Reti. *The Game of Chess*. The nineteen thirty-six reprint. How much please?"

Sim shook his head.

"I'm sorry, Mr Stanhope, but we do not have a copy."

"Sold it? When?"

"We never had one, I'm afraid."

"Oh yes you did."

"You are at perfect liberty—"

"It's a wise bookseller that knows his own stock."

Laughing, Sim shook his head.

"You won't catch me out, Mr Stanhope. Remember I've been here since my father's day."

Stanhope hopped briskly up the steps.

"There you are, poor condition."

"Good Lord."

"Knew I'd seen it. Haven't been in for years, either. How much?"

Sim took the book, blew dust off the top, then looked at the flyleaf. He did a rapid calculation.

"That'll be three pounds ten. I mean three fifty of course."

Stanhope reached into his pocket, grumbling. Sim, unable to resist, heard his own voice going on without, apparently, his volition.

"Yesterday I saw Miss Stanhope. She passed the shop—"

"Who—one of mine? That'll be Sophy, idle little bitch."

"But she's so enchanting—they're both so enchanting—"

"Be your age. That generation's not enchanting, any of it. Here."

"Thank you, sir. They've always been such a pleasure to us, innocence, beauty, manners—"

Stanhope gave a cackle of laughter.

"Innocence? They tried to poison me once, or damn nearly. Left some filthy things in a drawer by the bed. Must have found the spare house-keys and then *plotted*— bitches! I wonder where they found those beastly little monsters?"

"A practical joke. But they've always been so kind to us—"

"Perhaps you'll meet them then, you and Bell at your meetings."

"Meet them?"

"You *are* looking for a quiet place aren't you?"

"Edwin said something."

"Well then."

Stanhope nodded at him, looked briefly towards Sandra then withdrew, ting! A loud thump came from the ceiling. Sim hurried upstairs and held Ruth while she brought up some phlegm. When she was better she asked who he had been talking to.

"Stanhope. Just a chess book. Fortunately we had it in stock."

Her head turned from side to side.

"Dream. Bad dream."

"Just a dream. Next time it'll be a good one."

She drifted off to sleep again and breathed easily. He tiptoed down into the shop. Sandra was still sitting. But then the shop bell tinged again. It was Edwin. Sim made shushing noises and then breathed the reminder melodramatically.

"Ruth's poorly. She's asleep up there—"

Edwin's declension from noise to near silence was as dramatic.

"What is it, dear Sim?"

"Just a cold and she's getting better. But you know at our kind of age—not that she's as old as me, of course; but all the same—"

"I know. We're in the bracket. Look, I have news."

"A meeting?"

"We are all there is, I'm afraid. Yet I'm not afraid, really. Many are called, et cetera."

"Stanhope's place."

"He told you?"

219

"He was here just now. Dropped in."

Sim was faintly proud of Stanhope having dropped in. Stanhope was, after all, a celebrity, with his column, broadcasts and chess displays. Ever since chess had moved out of the grey periphery of the news and with Bobby Fischer edged into the full limelight, Sim had come to an unwilling respect for Stanhope.

"I'm glad you didn't object."

"Who? I? Object to Stanhope?"

"I've always had the feeling that your attitude to him was faintly, shall we say, illiberal."

Sim cogitated.

"That's true, I suppose. After all, I've spent my life here, like him. We're old Greenfield people. You see, there was a bit of scandal and I suppose I'm prudish. When his wife left him. Women, you know. Ruth has no time for him. On the other hand his twin girls—they've been a delight to us all, just to watch them grow up. How he can ignore, could ignore such, such *charmers*— let them grow up any old how—"

"You will be able to sample the charm again, although at second hand."

"They're not!"

"Oh no. You wouldn't expect it, would you? But he says we can use their place."

"A room?"

"It's the stabling at the end of the garden. Have you been in?"

"No, no."

"They used to live there, more or less. Glad enough to get away from Stanhope, if you ask me. And he from them. They took it over. Didn't you know?"

"I don't see what's so special about it."

"I know the place. After all, I live at the top end of the garden. I should, don't you think? When we came here first, the girls even invited us to tea there. It was a kind of dolls' tea party. They were so solemn! The questions Toni asked!"

"I don't see—"

"You old stick-in-the-mud!"

Sim made himself grumble.

"Such an out-of-the-way place. I don't see why you can't use the community centre. After all, that way we might get more members."

220

"It's the quality of the place."

"Feminine?"

Edwin looked at him in surprise. Sim felt himself begin to blush, so he hurried on his explanation.

"I remember when my daughter was at college, once I went into the hostel where she was living—girls from top to bottom—good Lord, you'd never believe perfume could be so penetrating! I just thought, if it's where a couple of—Well. You see."

"Nothing like that at all. Nothing whatsoever."

"Sorry."

"Don't apologize."

"This quality."

Edwin took a turn round one of the middle bookcases. He came back, drawing himself up, beaming. He threw his arms wide.

"Mmm-ah!"

"You seem very pleased with yourself."

"Sim. Have you been in the, the community centre?"

"Not since."

"It's all right of course. Just the thing and it's where I met him—"

"I'm not, you know—not as impressed as you are, no not half as impressed. You'd better understand that, Edwin. I don't doubt that to you in particular—"

"Just listen. Now."

"I am. Go on."

"No, no! Not to me. Just listen."

Sim looked round him, listening. The traffic produced a kind of middle range of noise but nothing unusual. Then the clock struck from the community centre and like an extension of the sound he heard the clang of a fire engine's alarm bell ring as the machine nosed over the Old Bridge. A jet whined down, mile after mile. Edwin opened his mouth to speak, then shut it, holding up one finger.

Sim felt it with his feet, more than heard it—the faint vibration, on and on, as a train rocked across the canal and drew its useful length through the fields towards the midlands.

There came a thump on the ceiling.

"Just a minute. I'll be back."

Ruth wanted him to wait outside the door while she went to the loo. Thought she might come over queer. He sat on the attic stairs, waiting for her. Through the shot-window he could see that men were already opening up the jumbled roofs that had held Frankley's ridiculous stock. Presently the breakers would come with their flailing ball and chain, though it was hardly needed. They had only to lean against the old place and it would collapse. More noise.

He came back to the shop to find Edwin perched on the edge of the desk and talking to Sandra. He felt indignant at the sight.

"You can go along now, Sandra. I know it's early. But I'll lock up."

Sandra, still ruminating, took a kind of loose cardigan from the hook behind the desk.

" 'Bye."

He watched her out of the shop. Edwin laughed.

"Nothing doing there, Sim. I couldn't interest her."

"You—!"

"Why not? All souls are of equal value."

"Oh yes. I believe."

Indeed I do. We are all equal. I believe that. It is more or less a fourth-class belief.

"You were going to explain a crazy idea to me."

"They used to build churches by holy wells. Over them sometimes. They needed it, water, it was stuff you drew up out of the earth in a bucket, the earth gave it you. Not out of a pipe by courtesy of the water board. It was wild, springing, raw stuff."

"Bugs."

"It was holy because men worshipped it. Don't you think that infinite charity would fix that for us?"

"Infinite charity is choosy."

"Water is holiness. Was holiness."

"Today I have not struck a believing streak."

"And now; as water was then, so something as strange and unexpected and necessary in our mess. Silence. Precious, raw silence."

"Double-glazing. Technology has the answer."

"Just as it put the wild holiness in a pen and conducted it demurely through a pipe. No. What I meant was random silence, lucky silence, or destined."

"You've been there now, in the last few days?"

"As soon as Stanhope offered us the place. Certainly. There's a kind of landing passage at the top of the stairs with the rooms opening out. You look through small dormers, that way to the still, untouched canal, the other way into the green of the garden. Silence lives there, Sim. I know it. Silence is there and waiting for us, waiting for him. He's not aware of it yet. I've found it for him. The holiness of silence waiting for us."

"It can't be."

"I wonder how it comes about? Certainly there's a sense of going down, of all the town being built up there and this being, as it were, at the bottom of steps, shut away, a kind of courtyard, a private place farther down into the earth almost holding the sunlight like a cup and the quiet as if someone was there with two hands holding it all—someone who no longer needed to breathe."

"It was innocence. You said—a kind of dolls' tea party. That's sad."

"What's sad about it?"

"They've grown up, you see. Look, Edwin. There's some trick of the building, some way in which sound is reflected away—"

"Even the jets?"

"Why not! Somehow the surfaces will have done it. There'll be a rational explanation."

"You said it was innocence."

"My aged heart was touched."

"Put that way—"

"Have the girls left any traces behind them?"

"The place is still furnished, more or less, if that is what you mean."

"Interesting. Do you think they would be interested? The girls, I mean."

"They aren't home."

Sim was on the point of explaining that he had seen Sophy walking past the shop but thought better of it. There was a touch of curiosity in Edwin's face whenever he heard an inquiry about them—almost as if the non-events, the strange, sensual, delightful and poignant linkage that did not exist except in the world of a man's supposing, were not private, but out there, to be detected, read like a book, no, like a comic strip, part of the generation-long folly of Sim Goodchild.

Because he was old, felt himself to be old and irritable with

223

himself as much as with the world, he did a violence to his accustomed secrecy and revealed a small corner of the comic strip.

"I used to be in love with them."

There—it was out and blinding.

"I mean—not what you might think. They were adorable and to be, be cherished. I don't know—they still are—well she is, the brunette, Sophy, or was still when I last saw her. Of course the fair one—Toni—she's gone."

"You old romantic."

"Paternal instinct. And Stanhope—he really doesn't care about them you know, I'm certain; and then with those women—well that's all a good while ago. One felt they were neglected. I wouldn't have you for the world think—"

"I don't. Oh no—"

"Not that—"

"Quite."

"If you see what I mean."

"Absolutely."

"Of course my child—our children—were so much older."

"Yes. I see that."

"So it was natural with two such decorative little girls living practically on our doorstep."

"Of course."

There was a long pause. Edwin broke it.

"I thought tomorrow night if that's convenient for you. It's his evening off."

"If Ruth is well enough."

"Will she come?"

"I meant if she's well enough to be left. What about Edwina?"

"Oh no. No. Definitely. You know Edwina. She met him, you see. Just for a minute or two. She's so, so—"

"Sensitive. I know. I can't think how she can bear her job as almoner. The things she must see."

"It is a trial. But she makes a distinction. She said plainly afterwards. If he were a patient it would be different. You see."

"Yes I see."

"In her own free time it's different you see."

"Yes."

"Of course if there were an emergency."

"I understand."

224

"So it'll just be the three of us, I'm afraid. Not many is it, when one remembers the old days."

"Perhaps Edwina would care to come and sit with Ruth."

"You know how she is about germs. She's as brave as a lion really, you see, but she has this thing about germs. Not viruses. Just germs."

"Yes, so I believe. Germs are dirtier than viruses. Germs probably have viruses, would you say?"

"She simply has this thing."

"She's not a committee. Women often aren't. Are you a committee Edwin? I am."

"I don't know what you mean."

"Oh Lord. Different standards of belief. Multiply the number of committee members by the number of standards of belief—"

"I'm still not with you, Sim."

"Partitions. One of me believes in partitions. He thinks, for example, that although Frankley's is on the other side of this wall—or is until they knock the place down—the wall remains real and it's no good pretending otherwise. But another of my members—well, what shall I say?"

"Perhaps he'll pierce a partition."

"Your man? Let him do it really, then, and beyond doubt. I know—"

I know how the mind can rise from its bed, go forth, down the stairs, past doors, down the path to the stables that are bright and rosy by the light of two small girls. But they were asleep and remained asleep even if their images performed the silly dance, the witless Arabian thing.

"Know what?"

"It doesn't matter. A committee member."

All is imagination he doth prove.

"Partitions, my majority vote says, remain partitions."

One is one and all alone and ever more shall be so.

Edwin glanced at his watch.

"I must rush. I'll let you know the time when he gets in touch."

"Late evening is best for me."

"For the whole committee. Which one had a thing about the little girls?"

"A sentimental old thing. I doubt he'll bother to come."

225

He ushered Edwin out of the shop door into the street and gestured courteously to his hurrying back.

A sentimental old thing?

Sim sighed to himself. Not a sentimental old thing but the unruly member.

At eight o'clock, Ruth being propped up with a good book and his stomach rather distended with fish fillet and reconstituted potato, together with peas out of a tin, Sim made his way through the shop, relocked the door behind him and walked the few paces to Sprawson's. It was broad daylight but on the right-hand side of the building there was nevertheless a light in Stanhope's window. The town was quiet and only a jukebox in the Keg of Ale disturbed the blue summer evening. Sim thought to himself that the alleged silence of the stables was not really necessary. They might well hold their small meeting—but meeting was hardly the word for three people—might well hold it in the street; but as he thought this, a helicopter, red light sparking away, flew the length of the old canal, and as if to rub in the point a train rumbled over the viaduct. After both machines had passed, his ears, newly sharpened perhaps, detected the faint chatter of a typewriter from the lighted window where Stanhope was still working at his book or a broadcast or his column. Sim ascended the two steps to the glass door and pushed it open. This was familiar ground—solicitors and the Bells to the left, the Stanhope door to the right—at the other end of the short hall the door which gave on to the steps down to the garden. It was all an absurdly romantic area to Sim. He felt, and was aware of, the romance and the absurdity. He had no connection whatsoever with the two little girls, had never had and could expect none. It was all pure fantasy. A few, a very few visits to the shop—

There was a clatter from the stairs on the left. Edwin appeared tumultuously, a man this time of gusto, who threw his long arm round Sim's shoulder and squeezed it tremendously.

"Sim, my dear fellow, here you are!"

It seemed so silly a greeting that Sim detached himself as quickly as he could.

"Where is he?"

"I'm expecting him. He knows where. Or I think so. Shall we go?"

Edwin strode, larger than life, to the end of the hall and opened the door above the garden steps.

"After you, my dear fellow."

Plants and shrubs and smallish trees in flower trespassed on the path that led straight down to the rosy-tiled stables with their ancient dormer windows. Sim had a moment of his usual incredulity at the reality of something that had been so near him and unknown, for so many years. He opened his mouth to speak of this but shut it again.

Each step you took down the steps—there were six of them—had a quite distinct quality. It was a kind of numbing, a muffling. Sim who had swum and snorkeled on the Costa Brava found himself likening the whole process at once to the effect of going under water; but not, as with water, an instant transition from up here to down there, a breaking of a perfect surface, a boundary. Here the boundary was just as indubitable but less distinct. You came down, out of the evening noise of Greenfield, and step by step, you were—numbed was not the right word, nor was muffled. There was not a right word. This oblong of garden, unkempt, abandoned and deserted, was nevertheless like a pool of something, a pool, one could only say, of quiet. Balm. Sim stopped and looked about him as if this effect would reveal itself to the eye as well as the ear but there was nothing—only the over-grown fruit trees, the rioting rose stocks, camomile, nettles, rose-mary, lupins, willowherb and foxgloves. He looked up into the clear air; and there, astonishingly at a great height, a jet was coming down, the noise of its descent wiped away so that it was graceful and innocent as a glider. He looked round him again, buddleia, old man's beard, veronica—and the scents of the garden invaded his nostrils like a new thing.

Edwin's hand was on his shoulder.

"Let's get on."

"I was thinking how preferable all this is to our small patch. I'd forgotten about flowers."

"Greenfield is a country town!"

"It's a question of where one looks. And the silence!"

At the end of the path down the garden they came to the court-yard, shadowed away from the sun. At some time the entrance had been closed by double doors but these had been taken away. Now the only door was the small one, opposite, that led out to the

227

towpath. Stairs went up on their left hand.

"Up here."

Sim followed Edwin up, then stood and looked round him. To call the place a flat would be an exaggeration. There was room for a narrow divan, an ancient sofa, a small table, chairs. There were two cupboards and on either side open entries led to minute bed-rooms. There were dormer windows that looked out over the canal, and back up to the house.

Sim said nothing, but simply stood. It was not the mean size of the room, nor the floor, of one-plank thickness, the interior walls of some sort of cheap boarding. It was not the battered, second-hand furniture, the armchair from which stuffing hung or the stained table. It was the atmosphere, the smell. Someone, Sophy presumably, had been there recently, and the odour of cheap and penetrating scent hung in the air as a kind of cover to an ancient staleness, of food, more scent, of—no, neither a glow nor perspiration—but sweat. There was a mirror surrounded by elaborate gilding on one wall, with a shelf below it on which were bottles, half-used lipsticks, tins, and sprays and powder. Under the dormer, on top of a low cupboard, was a huge doll that leaned and grinned. The central table had a pile of oddments on it—tights, a glove puppet, a pair of pants that needed washing, a woman's magazine and the earplug from a transistor radio. But the velvet cloth on the table was fringed with bobbles, between the patches on the wall where pictures and photographs had once been stuck and left traces of sticking, were ornaments such as china flowers and some bits of coloured material—some of them made into rosettes. There was dust.

Inside Sim, the illusions of twenty years vanished like bubbles. He said to himself yes of course, yes, they weren't looked after and they had to grow up, yes, what was I thinking of? And they had no mother—poor things, poor things! No wonder—

Edwin was delicately removing the objects from the table. He laid them on the cupboard top under the dormer. There was a standard lamp by the cupboard. The shade was pink and had bobbles like the tablecloth.

"Could we get the window open, do you think?"

Sim hardly heard him. He was examining what could only be called his grief. At last he turned to the dormer and examined it. No one had opened it for years but someone had begun to paint

228

the surround, then given up. It was like the cupboard door under the dormer at the other end of the room. Someone had begun to paint that pink and also given up. Sim peered through the dormer that seemed to stare, blearily, back at the house.

Edwin spoke at his side.

"*Feel* the silence!"

Sim looked at him in astonishment.

"Can't you feel the, the—"

"The what, Sim?"

The grief. That's what it must be. Grief. Neglect.

"Nothing."

Then he saw the glass door open at the top of the steps at the other end of the garden. Men came through. He swung round to Edwin.

"Oh no!"

"Did you know about this?"

"Of course I knew the place was here. This is where we had our dolls' tea party."

"You might have told me. I assure you, Edwin, if I'd known I wouldn't have come. Damn it man—we caught him shoplifting! And don't you know where he's been? He's been to jail and you know why. Damn it man!"

"Wildwave."

On the stairs the voice was suddenly near.

"That's what nobody really believes. I don't know where you're taking me and I don't like it. Is this some kind of trap?"

"Look, Edwin—"

The black hat and blasted face rose above the level of the landing. The shock of grey-white hair and the pinched face of the old man in the park followed behind him. The old man stopped on the stairs with a kind of writhing twist.

"Oh no! No you don't Matty! What is this, Pederasts Anonymous? Three cured and one to go?"

The man called Matty had him by the lapel.

"Mr Pedigree—"

"You're as big a fool as ever, Matty! Let me go, d'you hear?"

It was ridiculous. The two strange and unattractive men seemed to be wrestling on the stairs. Edwin was dancing round the top.

"Gentlemen! Gentlemen!"

Sim had a profound wish to be out of it and away from the

ravished building that was so brutally robbed of its silence. But the stairs were blocked. Exhausted for the moment by his efforts to escape, the old man was gasping and trying to speak at the same time.

"You—talk about my condition—it's a beautiful condition—nobody knows. Are you a psychiatrist? I don't *want* to be cured, they know that—so good day to you—" and with an absurd effort at the socially correct thing, he was bowing to Sim and to Edwin above him and at the same time trying to wrench himself away "—a very good day to you—"

"Edwin, let's get out of here for God's sake! It's all a mistake, ridiculous and humiliating!"

"You have nothing on me—any of you—let me go, Matty, I'll, I'll have the law—" And then the man in the black hat had let him go, had dropped his hands. They stood on the stairs, partly visible like bathers on an underwater slope. Pedigree had his face at the level of Windgrove's shoulder. He caught sight of the ear a foot above him. He convulsed with loathing.

"You hideous, hideous creature!"

Slowly and inexorably the blood consumed the right side of Matty's face. He stood, doing nothing, saying nothing. The old man turned away hastily. They heard his feet on the cobbles of the courtyard, saw him appear on the garden path between the over-grown flower beds. He was hurrying away. Half-way up the path he turned, still moving, and glanced under his shoulder at the dormer windows with all the venom of a villain in a melodrama. Sim saw his lips move; but the curious muffling—for after this desecration of the place, that magical quality had declined from a mystery to an impediment—smothered his words. Then he climbed the stairs and went through the hall and out into the street.

Edwin spoke.

"He must have thought we were police."

Windrove's face was white and brown again. His black hat had been pushed a little on one side and the ear was only too visible. As if he knew what Sim was looking at, he took off his hat to settle his hair. Now the reason for the hat was more evident. He smoothed his hair down carefully, then adjusted the black hat to hold it down.

This revelation of a fact seemed to go some way towards making it tolerable for the viewer. Windgraff—Matty, had the old man said?—Matty when he revealed his disability, his deformity, his, one must so call it, handicap, was no longer a forbidding monstrosity but only another man. Sim found himself, before he was aware of making up his mind, sharing round the social small change. He held out his hand.

"I am Sim Goodchild. How do you do."

Windgrove looked down at the hand as if it were an object to be examined and not shaken. Then he took the hand, turned it over and peered into the palm. Sim was slightly disconcerted by this and looked down himself to see if the palm was dirtied in any way, or interesting, or decorated—and by the time the words had fallen through his awareness he understood that his palm was being read, so he stood there, relaxed, and now not a little amused. He looked into his own palm, pale, crinkled, the volume, as it were, most delicately bound in this rarest or at least most expensive of all binding material—and then he fell through into an awareness of his own hand that stopped time in its revolution. The palm was exquisitely beautiful, it was made of light. It was precious and preciously inscribed with a sureness and delicacy beyond art and grounded somewhere else in absolute health.

In a convulsion unlike anything he had ever known, Sim stared into the gigantic world of his own palm and saw that it was holy.

The little room came back, the strange, but no longer forbidding creature still stared down, Edwin was moving chairs to the table.

It was true. The place of silence was magical. And dirty.

Windrave let go his hand and he took it back in all its beauty, its revelation. Edwin spoke. It was possible to detect a little dust on the words, a little touch of jealousy.

"Did you promise him a long life?"

"Don't, Edwin. Nothing like that—"

Windrove went to the other side of the table and that became at once the head of it. Edwin sat down on his right. Sim slid into a chair on his left, three sides of the table and an empty side where Pedigree was not.

Windgrove shut his eyes.

Sim stared round the room, free of it. Here and there, were drawing pins that had held up decorations. A rather poor mirror. The divan by the dormer with its rows of, of *bobbles*—the doll with her frills that sat, propped on the far corner of the cupboard and

231

held there by a cushion—those pony pictures and that photograph of a young man, a pop star probably but now anonymous—

The man laid his hands on the table, palms upward. Sim saw Edwin glance down and take the right-hand one in his own left hand and reach across with the right. He had a moment of embarrassment at the idea, but reached out and took Edwin's hand in his, and laid his right hand on Windrow's left. It was a tough and elastic substance he touched, no universe, but warm, astonishingly warm, hot.

He was shaken by a gust of interior laughter. The Philosophical Society, with its minutes, chairman, committee, its taking of halls and assembly rooms, its distinguished guests, to have come down to this—two old men holding hands with a—what?

It was a time after that—a minute, ten minutes, half an hour, that Sim discovered he wanted to scratch his nose. He wondered whether to be brutal and lift his hands away, thus breaking the small circle, but determined not. It was a small sacrifice after all; and now, if one did detach oneself from the desire to scratch one immediately found how far away those others were, miles, it seemed, so that the circle, instead of being a small one was gigantic, more than a stone circle, county-wide, country-wide—vast.

Sim found he wanted to scratch his nose again. It was provoking to have two such disparate scales, the one of inches, the other, universal more or less—the nose must be *wrestled* with! It was an itch just a fraction to the left of the tip, a tickle fiendishly adjusted to set every nerve of the skin throughout the body tickling in sympathy. He fought resolutely, feeling how hard his right hand was held—and now the left as well, squeezed, who was squeezing who—so that his breath came in great gasps with the effort. His face contorted with the anguish of it and he struggled to get his hands away but they were held firm. All he could do was screw up his face again and again round his nose, trying to reach the tip absurdly with his cheeks, with his lips, his tongue, with anything—and then, inspired, he bent down and rubbed his nose on the wooden surface between his hands. The relief was almost as exquisite as the palm of his hand. He lay, his nose against the wood and let his breathing become even again.

Edwin spoke above his head. Or not Edwin and not speech. Music. Song. It was a single note, golden, radiant, like no singer that ever was. There was, surely, no mere human breath that could sustain the note that spread as Sim's palm had spread before him, widened, became, or was, precious range after range beyond experience, turning itself into pain and beyond pain, taking pain and pleasure and destroying them, being, becoming. It stopped for a while with promise of what was to come. It began, continued, ceased. It had been a word. That beginning, that change of state explosive and vital had been a consonant, and the realm of gold that grew from it a vowel lasting for an aeon; and the semi-vowel of the close was not an end since there was, there could be no end but only a readjustment so that the world of spirit could hide itself again, slowly, slowly fading from sight, reluctant as a lover to go and with the ineffable promise that it would love always and if asked would always come again.

When the man in black let go of Sim's hand, all the hands had become nothing more than just hands again. Sim saw that, because as he lifted his face off the wood, he brought his hands together in front of it; and there was the right palm, a tiny bit sweaty, but not in any sense dirty, and just a palm like any other. He sat up and saw Edwin mopping his face with a paper tissue. With one accord they turned to look at Windrove. He sat, his hands open on the table, his face bowed, his chin on his chest. The brim of the black hat hid his face.

A drop of clear water fell from under the brim and lay on the table. Matty lifted his head; but Sim could read no expression in this blasted side of the face.

Edwin spoke.

"Thank you—thank you a thousand times! God bless you."

Matty looked at Edwin closely, then at Sim who saw that now there was indeed an expression to be read on the brown side of the face. Exhaustion. Windrove stood up, and without speaking moved to the stairs, then began to descend them. Edwin jumped to his feet.

"Windgrove! When? And look—"

He went quickly to the stairs and down them. Sim heard his rapid speech indistinctly from the courtyard.

"When may we meet next?"

"Are you sure? Here?"

"Shall you bring Pedigree?"

"Look here, are you, er, OK for money?"

233

Presently there came the click of the latch from the door leading out to the towpath. Edwin came up the stairs.

Reluctantly Sim stood up, looking round him at the pictures and the places where pictures had been, the doll, the cupboard with the gollywog hanging on it. Side by side they left, courteously insisted on each other going first down the stairs and then side by side again up the garden path, up the stairs, through the hall—the typewriter still clattering in Stanhope's study—and out into the street. Edwin stopped and they faced each other.

Edwin spoke with profound emotion.

"You are such a wonderful team!"

"Who?"

"You and he—in the occult sense."

"I and—he?"

"A wonderful team! I was *so* right you know!"

"What are you talking about?"

"When you went into that trance—I could see the spiritual combat mirrored in your face. Then you passed over, right there, in front of me!"

"It wasn't like that!"

"Sim! Sim! The two of you played on me like an instrument!"

"Look Edwin—"

"You *know* something happened, Sim, don't be modest, it's false humility—"

"Of course something happened but—"

"We broke a barrier, broke down a partition. Didn't we now?"

Sim was about to deny it hotly, when he began to remember. There was no question but that something had happened and likely enough it needed the three of them.

"Perhaps we did."

# CHAPTER FOURTEEN

### 12/6/78

My dear friend Mr Pedigree came as far as the stairs in the stables of Sprawson's but would not stay he is afraid we mean him harm and I do not know what to do. He went off and I was left with Mr Bell who still teaches at Foundlings and Mr Goodchild from the bookshop. They expected something words perhaps. We made a circle with ourselves for protection against evil spirits for there were many in the stables green and purple and black. I held them off as best I could. They stood behind the two gentlemen and clawed at them. How do the two gentlemen live when I am not there I ask myself. Mr Bell offered me money it was funny. But I cried like a child for poor Mr Pedigree who is bound every way by his person it is hideous to see hideous. I can only spare him the time I can spare from being a guardian to the boy. If it were not for worrying about Mr Pedigree I would have a happy life guarding the boy. I will be his servant all the days of my life and look forward to many years of happiness if only I can heal Mr Pedigree and my spiritual face.

### 13/6/78

Great and terrible things are afoot. I thought that only me and Ezekiel had been given the way of showing things to those people who can see (as with matchboxes, thorns, shards, and marrying a wicked woman etc.) because it. I cannot say what I mean.

She had lost her engagement ring she is engaged to Mr Masterman the PT master who is quite famous I am told. We were all looking for it wherever she had been. I told the boys to look under the elms and looked near them myself. Then she came after they had gone and asked had I looked under the elms I said no meaning to go on and say the boys had looked for to say I had looked myself would be a lie but she said before I could speak well I will look and walked off. She is very beautiful and smiling and I gave my foolish person a hard pinch as hard as I could for punishment for what it did and I went on looking for the ring. But looking up (I must remember to give it another hard pinch for that but at the time I did not think) I saw her drop the ring which she said she had lost and then pretend to find it, she threw her arms on both sides and cried bingo. She came to me laughing with the ring held out on the finger of her left hand. I could not say anything but was quite at a stand. She said I must tell everyone where I told her it might be—in fact I ought to tell Mr M I found it. This evening I do not know what to do. Since I vowed to do whatever a person asked me if it is not wicked I do not know whether what she asks is wicked. I am lost like it might be the ring. Now I ask myself what this sign means. Can to lie be a sign I ask myself. She smiled and lied. She lied by doing not by saying. Her saying was true but not true. She did not find it but she found it. I do not know.

14/6/78

All day I was in a daze thinking about the ring and what it meant. She is the terrible woman but why did she give the sign to me? It is a challenge. It means she does not care if her jewel is lost or not. I went to bed after my portion and offering myself to be a sacrifice if it was right. I do not know if what I then had was a vision or a dream. If it was a dream it was not like an ordinary dream they say people have because who could stand such a thing every night I ask myself it may have been like a dream in the Bible. Pharaoh must have been troubled or he would not have sent to find out. It was no ordinary dream. Or perhaps it was a vision and I was really there. It was the woman in the Apocalypse. She came in terrible glory all in colours that hurt she was allowed to torment me because of my bad thoughts about Miss Stanhope. Yet it was not just my fault my thinking about her, she acting so queer with the jewel it took me all day to see she knew about signs and how to show them. But the thing is the woman in the Apocalypse put on Miss Stanhope's face and laughing and caused me to defile myself with much pain which when I woke up I discovered and was

236

frightened and astonished because since Harry Bummer in Northern Territory I thought I could not defile myself and then I could not either be *frightened or ashamed*.

Then on this day (but no dream) 15/6/78 all day as I worked I tried to be ashamed but could not. The finding I can sin like other men. I cannot say what I mean. I listened to the birds to hear if they were laughing and jeering like kookaburras but they were not. Is she then disguised as an angel of light or is she a good spirit. I can see the sky now. I mean I can look into it and it is very slightly coloured all the way up. The boys came but briefly. I tried to tell them these things about everything rejoicing as it might be with Hallelujahs and that. But I could not. It is like going over from black-and-white to colour. There was a bit of sun on a tree over by long meadow and I. The boys went off to music appreciation. I could hear but only a bit. So I *left my work* and went after them and stood by the garage near the music-room window. They played music on the gramophone it came out loud and I heard it like I see the trees and the sky now and the boys like angels it was a big orchestra playing Beethoven a symphony and I for the first time I began to dance there on the gravel outside the music dept window. Mrs Appleby saw me and came so I stood. She looked like an archangel laughing so I stood. She shouted to me marvellous isn't it the Seventh I didn't know you cared for music and I shouted back laughing neither did I. She looked like an archangel laughing so my mouth shouted no matter what I could do. I am a man I could have a son. She said what an extraordinary thing to say are you alright. I remembered then my vow of silence and it seemed very small but I thought I have gone near enough by talking to the boys so I blessed her with my right hand like a priest. She looked surprised and went away quickly. This is all what Mr Pierce used to call a turn up for the book.

Since writing that down, I mean between the word book and the word since I have been shown a great thing. It was not the spirits and it was not a vision or a dream it was an opening. I saw a portion of providence. I hope that one day the boy will read these words. I understand that his reading of them in the years to come is what made me write them down though at the time I had some foolish thought of evidence to show I am not mad (17/5/65). The truth is that between book and Since the eyes of my understanding have been opened. What good is not directly breathed into the

237

world by the holy spirit must come down by and through the nature of men. I saw them, small, wizened, some of them with faces like mine, some crippled, some broken. Behind each was a spirit like the rising of the sun. It was a sight beyond joy and beyond dancing. Then a voice said to me it is the music that frays and breaks the string.

17/6/78

I must take what time I have to tell of the wonderful thing that happened last night after I had repeated my portion. I will write as quick as I can for in a little while I must ride my bike into Greenfield and see Mr Bell and Mr Goodchild and Mr Pedigree for this time I think he will agree to go with me. Last night I thought there was work to do; and I in a way held out the warmth of my person to the spirits and they drew me gently into their presence. The elder in the red robe with a crown and the elder with the blue robe and a coronet was waiting and greeted me kindly. I thanked them for their care of me and hoped for their continued friendship. I thanked them in particular for the years in which they did away in me with the root of a temptation which now of course I am able to see for the small thing it is. When I told them this they brightened wonderfully so that it dazzled my eyes. They showed: We saw how you gazed on the daughters of men and found them fair. I asked them about Miss Stanhope and the sign of her dropping her ring and confessed that I could not see what it meant. Then they showed: All this is hidden from us. Many years ago we called her before us but she did not come.

I had been standing outside the harness room looking up at the sky, but now I went into my bedroom and sat on the edge of the bed. It is difficult my dear, dear boy, to write of what happened after that because of the strangeness and greatness. At once the elders drew me to them. They showed: Now we have answered your questions we will add to your information so that it overflows. The cry that went up to heaven brought you down. Now there is a great spirit that shall stand behind the being of the child you are guarding. That is what you are for. You are to be a burnt offering. Now we shall introduce you to a friend of ours and we shall eat and drink with you.

Although I am now accustomed to them and know my spiritual

238

name and indeed do not go cold when they call me, yet this news was like being in a lower part of heaven as I may say and it made me cold all over again like that time (17/5/65) and all the hair on my person stood up, each on a separate lump. But when every bit of warmth had gone out from me I saw their friend standing between them. He was dressed all in white and with the circle of the sun round his head. The red and blue elders took off their crowns and threw them down and I took off mine and threw it down. I was in great awe of the spirit in white but the red elder showed: This is the spiritual being who shall stand behind the child you are guarding. That child shall bring the spiritual language into the world and nation shall speak it unto nation. When I heard this, my head lowered before them I had such joy for men that the tears fell out of my eyes on the table. Then, still with my eyes lowered I made them welcome at my small table where there seemed to be room. Then the blue elder showed: There is joy in all the heavens today because the like of this meeting has not been seen since the days of Abraham. Then I offered them spiritual food and drink which they accepted. When this was done I had a great desire to sacrifice and asked what I should do and what they now wanted. The red spirit showed: We want nothing but to visit with you and to rejoice with you since you are one of us. And since you are an elder we will share that wisdom with you which though still in the body you ought to have. They did not do this by showing the great book but by a most wonderful opening which even if it was a thing I was able to do it would not be lawful to describe.

All this while the white spirit with the circle of the sun round his head sat across the table from me and after my first being able to see him I had not dared to raise my eyes to his face. Now, because of the glory of the opening and because they had called him their friend and mine I did raise my eyes to his face and the sword proceeded out of his mouth and struck me through the heart with a terrible pain so that as I found out later, I fainted and fell forward across the table. When I woke up again they had put me from them, and

The village clock struck from the church tower. Matty started up from his small table. He shut the exercise book and put it away in the chest of drawers. He hurried down to the harness room and seized his bike from where it leaned against the wall. He drew in his breath with a hiss. The back tyre was flat. He heaved the machine over and stood it on the saddle and handlebars. He hurried to the tap, filled a bucket with water and began to pull out the inner tyre, plunging it under water to find where the puncture was.

# CHAPTER FIFTEEN

Ruth shook her head, smiling. Sim spread his hands in the gesture unconsciously imitated from his grandfather.

"But I want you to come! I *wish* you'd come! You've never objected to making a fool of yourself with me before!"

She said nothing but went on smiling. Sim passed a hand over his baldness.

"You always admired Stanhope—"

"Nonsense!"

"Well—women did—"

"I'm not 'women'."

"But I do wish you'd come. Is it too late in the evening?"

Silence again.

"Is it Pedigree?"

"Go along, dear. Have a good time."

"That's hardly—"

"Well. A successful meeting."

"Edwina's coming."

"Has she said so?"

"Edwin's asking her."

"Give her my love if she's there."

It was a week after the first meeting, and the curious man's free afternoon again. What canvassing Sim had been able to do had produced no result—three refusals and one 'might come' which clearly covered the intention not to. Sim thought ruefully that perhaps it might be worth sending a notice of the demise of the Philosophical Society to be inserted in the *Greenfield Advertiser* among the births and deaths. He was still working out the wording of the notice when he reached the hall of Sprawson's. Edwin was standing on the bottom step of his stairs.

"Where's Ruth?"

"Where's Edwina?"

Then there was another silence. Sim broke it.

"Pedigree."

"I know."

"It's Pedigree. He's why they won't come. Not even Ruth."

"Oh yes. Yes. Edwina would have come in any other circumstances you know."

"So would Ruth."

"She's really a deeply liberal person you know. Only Pedigree—"

"Ruth's the most truly charitable person I know. Charity in its true sense, Greek sense."

"Of course. It was the business over the babies in prams you know. The cruelty to the young mothers. The deliberate psychological torture. She felt so deeply. She said once she'd have castrated him with her own hands if she'd caught him in flagrante delicto."

"She didn't say flagrante delicto!"

"She said assaulting a child. Pushing a pram away with a baby in it can be construed as an assault."

"I thought she meant—"

"Oh no. She wouldn't talk about that would she? I mean she's widely and deeply experienced but there are some things—"

"I remember when she talked about castrating, Ruth agreed with her. Warmly."

Edwin glanced at his watch.

"They're a little late. Shall we go on?"

"After you."

Softly they descended the steps and trod, almost on tiptoe, down the garden path and into the courtyard under the stables. Edwin switched on the light at the bottom of the stairs; and there was a sudden, startled movement in the room at their heads. Sim expected to see Pedigree after all, when he got to the upper level, but it was Sophy, standing by the divan on which she had been sitting and looking, he thought at once, white and strained. But Edwin went straight into action.

"My dear Sophy what a pleasure! How are you? Sitting in the dark? But I'm so sorry—oh dear! Your father you see, he told us we could—"

The girl put her hand up to the curls at the back of her head then took it away again. She was wearing the white sweatshirt with BUY ME stencilled on the front and really, thought Sim, nothing else under it, nothing else whatever, so that—

"We'll go away Sophy dear. Your father must have made a mistake. He told us we could have the room for a meeting of—but how silly! I mean it sounds silly and of course you wouldn't want—"

Then they were all three silent and standing. The single, naked bulb made a black shadow under each nose. Even Sophy looked monstrous, huge, black eye-hollows and the Hitlerian moustache of shadow caught by the light under her nostrils. Sweatshirt, jeans, flip-flops; and surely, some sort of cap? A knitted cap back there, hidden by the curls.

She glanced away from them at shopping bags, plastic ones, leaning against each other on the end of the divan. She touched her hair again, licked her lips and then looked back at Edwin.

"Meeting? You said something about a meeting—"

"Just a silly mistake. Your father, my dear. Sim, d'you think he was pulling our legs? 'Putting us on' I think you'd say, Sophy, according to my latest information. But you've come home to stay, of course. We'll go to the hall and intercept the others."

"Oh no! No! Daddy didn't make a mistake. I'm just going, you see. I'd turned out the light. You can have the place and welcome. Look—just a moment—"

Quickly she moved about the room, switched on a table lamp under the dormer, a table lamp with a pink and bobbled shade. She flicked off the single, naked bulb and the hideous shadows were wiped from her face to be replaced by a rosy and upward glow; and she glowed at them both.

"There! My goodness me! That dreadful top light! Toni used to call it—But I'm glad to see you! It'll be one of your meetings won't it? Make yourselves at home."

"Aren't you taking your, your shopping bags?"

"Those? Oh no! I'm leaving everything! Oh yes indeed! You've no idea. I shan't want any of the stores tonight. Too boring. Just let me put the things out of the way for you—"

Astonished, Sim stared at her face in its rosy glow and could not believe that the smile owed everything to the lamp. She was highly excited—and there, flash from an eye as if it were phosphorescent—and she seemed full of, full of purpose. At once his mind jumped to the usual, dreary conclusion. Sex, of course. An assignation. Interrupted. The really courteous thing, the understanding thing would be to—

But Edwin was talking.

"Au revoir then Sophy dear. Let us see something of you won't you? Or let us hear of you."

"Oh yes. My goodness me."

She had got her shoulder bag and slung it; was sidling round them.

"Remember me to Mrs Bell won't you? And Mrs Goodchild?"

Glow of a smile and then the girl gone away down the stairs, rosy glow left behind, suggestive and empty. They heard the door out to the towpath open, then close. Sim cleared his throat, sank into one of the chairs by the table and looked round him.

"I suppose they call this Brothel Pink."

"I hadn't heard. No."

Edwin sat down too. They were silent for a while. Sim inspected the cardboard box that lay beneath the other dormer. It was full of tinned food, as far as he could see. There was a coil of rope on it.

Edwin had seen it too.

"She must have been going camping. I hope we haven't—"

"Of course not. She has a young man you know. In fact—"

"Edwina's seen her with two young men. At different times, I mean."

"I saw one. Oldish, I thought, for her."

"Edwina said she thought he had a married look about him. The other one she said was younger, much more suitable she said. I mean Edwina's the last person in the world to spread scandal but she said she couldn't help noticing it going on under her nose."

"Dreary. It makes me feel dreary."

"You are such a moral old thing, Sim! Moralistic."

"It makes me feel dreary because I'm not young and with two young men. Well. Two young women."

Then there was silence again. Glancing at Edwin, Sim saw how the feminine lamp was providing him with a delicacy and smiling mouth that he had not got. Perhaps for me too. Here we are, dreary, and with smiles painted on our faces, waiting for— waiting, waiting, waiting. Like the man said.

"They're very late."

Edwin spoke absently.

244

" 'Having if off' they call it nowadays."

He looked quickly back at Sim and perhaps there was a little more intensity under the glow.

"I mean one hears these things. The boys, you see, and then, one reads—"

" 'Getting laid'. Is that American?"

"Incredible isn't it, what you hear? Even on the box!"

Silence again. Then—

"Edwin—we'll need another chair. Four of us."

"There were four chairs last time. Where is it?"

Edwin got up and wandered round the room, peering into corners as if the fourth chair had become not absent but merely less visible and could be seen if you looked closely.

"This used to be their toy-cupboard. I remember when Edwina and I came to tea they showed us every doll—extraordinary the names they had and the stories about them—you know, Sim, there's genius in those girls. Creativity. I don't just mean intelligence. Real, precious creativity. I wonder if their dolls—"

He reached out and opened the cupboard door.

"How very odd!"

"What's odd about keeping dolls in a cupboard?"

"Nothing. But—"

The fourth chair was placed in the centre of the cupboard, facing outward. There were lengths of rope attached to it, to the back and to the legs. Each rope had had the end carefully fused to stop it unravelling.

"Well!"

Edwin shut the door again, came back, laid hold of the table.

"Help me, Sim, please. We'll have to use the divan for the fourth man. Though I must say it won't seem quite, quite seancelike, will it? Takes me right back to the dolls' tea party. I told you about it didn't I?"

"Yes."

"But heaven only knows what she was doing with a chair like that and ropes and things."

"Edwin."

"Yes?"

"Listen carefully. Before the others come. We've stumbled on something, you see. We've no business to have seen that chair."

"What harm—"

245

"Listen. It's sex. Don't you understand? Bondage. Sexual games, private and, and shaming."

"Good God!"

"Before the others come. It's the least I—we—can do. We, you and I must never never never let on, never by the faintest breath—Remember how startled she was when we switched the light on and then when she saw who we were—she was there in the dark, waiting for someone or perhaps getting things ready for someone—and now she's gone away thinking, *Oh God I hope to God they don't ever think to open that cupboard*—"

"Good God!"

"So we must never—"

"Oh but I wouldn't—except to Edwina of course!"

"I mean after all—there but for the grace of God—I mean. After all, we all, I mean."

"What d'you mean?"

"I mean."

Then there was silence in the rosy room for a long, long time. Sim was not thinking about the meeting at all, or the seance, which was what it would be better called. He was thinking about the way in which circumstances could seem to imitate the intuitive understanding that so many people claimed to have and so many others denied was possible. Here, in the rosy light, with the shut cupboard, a few sticks and twists of artificial fibre had betrayed the secret as clearly as if they had spelt it out in print; so that two men, not by a mystic perception but by the warmth of imagination had come simply to a knowledge they were not intended to have and ought not to have. The man who looked too old for Sophy, and the brothel light—His mind dived into the explanation of it all, glamorous and acrid, so fierce an imagination he caught his breath at the scent and stink of it—

"God help us all."

"Yes. All."

More silence. At last Edwin spoke, diffidently, almost.

"They're a long, long time."

"Pedigree won't come without him."

"He won't come without Pedigree."

"What shall we do? Ring the school?"

"We couldn't get hold of him. And I have a feeling he'll be here any minute."

246

"It's too bad. They might have told us, if—"

"We gave our word."

"Wait for an hour, say. Then go."

Edwin reached down and slipped off his shoes. He climbed onto the divan and crossed his legs. He held his arms close to his sides, then extended the forearms, palms upward. He closed his eyes and did a great deal of breathing.

Sim sat and thought to himself. It was all the place, just that and nothing else, the place so often imagined, then found, with its silence but also with its dust and dirt and stink; and now seen to have the brothel image added, the pink lights and bobbled femininity—and at the end, like something out of the furtive book in his desk, the perverted chair.

I know it all, he thought, right to the bitter end.

Yet there was, after all, a certain sad satisfaction, and even a quivering of salt lust by association in this death of an old imagination. They had to grow up, lose the light of their exquisite childhood. They had to go under the harrow like everyone else; and doubtless at the moment it was subsumed under *having a good time* or *being with it* or *being into sex, into bondage.* Heaven lies round us in our infancy.

Edwin honked suddenly. Glancing across at him, Sim saw him jerk his head back up. Edwin had meditated himself asleep then woken himself with his own snore. That reduced everything, too. He felt, in the wake of Edwin's snore, an overwhelming sense of futility. He tried to imagine some deep, significant spiritual drama, some contrivance, some plot that would include them both and be designed solely for the purpose of rescuing Pedigree from his hell; and then had to admit to himself that the whole affair was about Sim the ageing bookseller or no one.

Everything was all right after all, just ordinary. Nothing would happen. It was as usual a matter of living among a whole heap of beliefs, first-class, second-class, third-class, and so on, right through to the blank wall of his daily indifference and ignorance.

Nine o'clock.

"He won't come now, Edwin. Let's go."

Matthew Septimus Windrove had the best of all reasons for not coming. He had mended the tyre slowly and methodically. Then with what for him was an unusual saving of time and energy he had carried the bike over his shoulder to the garages so that he could blow the tyre up in a few seconds with the air pump. But he could not find Mr French to explain to him. He found the garage doors open, which was strange; and he went through to the back of the garages, wondering why Mr French had not turned the lights on. As he moved to the door of the office that opened out of the garage at the back, a man stole round a car and hit him hard on the back of the head with a heavy spanner. He did not even feel himself fall. The man dragged him like a sack into the office and pushed him under the table. Then he returned to his work, which was the placement of a heavy box against the wall of the garage where it backed on to the bookstore. Not long after, the bomb went off. It destroyed the wall, brought down the watertank over the bookstore and broke open the upper face of the nearer petrol tank. The water ran into the burning tank, and instead of putting out the flames, sank down and pushed the petrol up. The burning petrol flooded out in a blazing tide as the fire alarms went off.

There were figures, not known to the school, running towards it. Sophy's idea worked perfectly. Fire drill was not intended for coping with bombs. There was chaos. No one could believe in the extraordinary sounds that were just like shots. In the chaos a strange man dressed as a soldier was able to carry a burden out of the school. It was wrapped in a blanket from the end of which small feet protruded and kicked. This man stumbled on the gravel but ran as fast as he could towards the darkness of the trees. But the flaming tide made him take a curving run and as he did so, a strange thing happened in the fire. It seemed to organize itself into a shape of flame that rushed out of the garage doors and whirled round and round. It made as if on purpose for the man and his burden. It whirled round still and the only noise from it was that of burning. It came so close to the man and it was so monstrous he dropped the bundle and a boy leapt out of it and ran away, ran screaming to where the others were being marshalled. The man dressed as a soldier struck out wildly at the fire-monster, then ran, ran shouting away into the cover of the trees. The fire-monster jigged and whirled. After a time it fell down; and after some more time it lay still.

Sophy, when she left the stables, hurried along the towpath to the Old Bridge and then up into the High Street. She ran to a phone box and dialled a number but the phone rang on and on. She came out. She ran back to the Old Bridge and down to the towpath but there was still a rosy light in the dormers of the stable buildings. She stamped her foot like a child. For a time she seemed lost, taking a few steps towards the green door then coming away, going towards the water then backing off. She ran again towards the Old Bridge then turned round and stood, her fists clenched and up by her shoulders. All the time, in the glare from the street lighting over the bridge, her face was white and ugly. Then she began to run along the towpath, away from the town and the light. She left the stabling, she passed the broken roofline of what had been Frankley's, then the long wall of the almshouses. She passed on, light of step, but panting now, and once, slipping in the mud of the towpath.

A voice talked inside her head.

They must be at the crisis if it's on. I hope it isn't on. Lights out for little boys. Little men. There flashed into her mind the image of a poster the day after tomorrow. BILLION FOR BOY. But no, no. It is impossible that I that we are now at this very moment it may be.

Be your age. Well. Be more than your age.

There was a loud thumping noise in the hedge and it stopped her dead. Something was bouncing and flailing about and then it squeaked and she could make out that it was a rabbit in a snare, down there by the ditch that lay between the towpath and the woods. It was flailing about, not knowing what had caught it and not caring to know but killing itself in an effort just to be free, or it may be, just to be dead. Its passion defiled the night with grotesque and obscene caricature of process, of logical advance through time from one moment to the next where the trap was waiting. She hurried past it, hurried on, a chill on her skin that competed successfully for at least a minute with the warmth from her thrusting speed.

All of a glow.

That was where the children were playing. The rubber boat is still tethered there. That means they will be back, tomorrow, perhaps. I must remember that. What's a girl like etc. And the woman. Family life. Where's Dad? In his column room. Where's Mum? Gone to God or in New Zealand. Well it's much the same thing dearie, innit? That's the lock and that's the bridge and that's the old barge. Those are the downs up there all a-glimmer under.

249

That's the sunken road to the top with trees over. No one would come down that way, not with a car, he wouldn't. Not with a parcel in his arms. Would the water in the canal cover a car? We ought to have found that out. If I walked up the sunken road or along beside it I could see the valley and the slope over the school. That would not be sensible. It is more sensible to stay here where I am placed to warn anyone off. To stay here is sensible.

She turned left and moved into the sunken road. The walking in the groove under the trees was a slower business than walking on the towpath; and some of the things in the air seemed to catch up with her and hang at her shoulder so she hurried as much as she could. The cloudy moon made a dapple everywhere and between the stems and trunks of the trees that had invaded the old road the sides of the downs floated and glimmered, made mostly of two-tone cloud and sliding moonlight.

Then she stopped and stood.

It was a question of direction. You could try to persuade yourself that a straight line to the sky directly over the school was not just *there* and that coincidence could stretch—a real coincidence as the lanky blonde might think it—could stretch to there being two entirely disconnected fires on that line, one, a small, controllable fire, the other—

It was a rose-coloured patch, half-seen over the shoulder of the downs. There was nothing nasty, nothing direct, just a rose petal or two; and now opening and spreading, taking in another cloud corner, the rose lighter and brighter in hue. They said it took the fire engine fifteen minutes to reach the valley by the school when called for. Phone wires cut. But this light in the sky must be beckoning; and in that school of all others there would be some form of communication they could not get at, could not cut—

And he will bring the boy here, down by the canal, to carry him along the towpath to the stables—we could use the old barge, the cupboard up in the front of it, that old loo—

The light brightened over the downs. Suddenly she knew it was her own fire, a thing she had done, a proclamation, a deed in the eye of the world—an outrage, a triumph! The feeling stormed through her, laughter, fierceness, a wild joy at the violation. It was as if the light, shuddering on the other side of the downs, was a loosening thing so that the whole world became weak and melting

250

like the top of a candle. It was then she saw what the last outrage was and knew herself capable of it. She shut her eyes as the image swept round her. She saw how she crawled along the long passage that led from one end of the old barge to the other. She ceased to feel the rough bark of a tree-trunk between her hands and against her body, where she clung with eyes shut. She felt instead the uneven planks of the flooring under her knees, heard the wash of the water under it, felt the wetness well over her hands. Somehow Gerry's commando knife was in her hand. There was a sound like a rabbit thumping that came from that cupboard, that loo right up in front. Then the thumping stopped as if the rabbit was too terrified even to move. Perhaps it was listening to this slow, watery approach.

"All right! All right! I'm coming!"

The thumping would start again, a girl's voice, well, natch.

She addressed the door conversationally.

"Just wait a moment, I'll get you open."

It came easily enough, swung wide. The first thing she could see inside was the ellipse of the little round window, the porthole. But there was also a small white rectangle on the midline of the boat and directly above the seat of the loo, the elsan or whatever. This rectangle was moving violently from side to side and she could smell wee-wee. The boy was there, arms bound behind his back, feet and knees bound. He was seated, bound, on the loo like he might have been in the cupboard and ropes held him on either side to the walls of the boat and there was a huge pad of sticky stuff stuck across his mouth and cheeks. He was jerking as violently as he could and there was a whining noise coming out of his nose. She felt an utter disgust at the creature itself sitting there on the stinking loo, so disgusting, eek and ooh, oh so much part of all weirdness from which you could see that the whole thing was a ruin and

I chose.

Should have brought a gun only I don't know, it is better with the knife—oh much better!

The boy was motionless now, waiting for her on the flat stone. She began to fumble at his jersey with her left hand and he made no move; but when she pulled out the front of his shirt he began to struggle again. But the bonds were beautifully done, Gerry had done a super job, just amazing, the way in which the boy had only

251

a limited kick with his stockinged feet was lovely, should he not have been in his pyjams, the nasty little creature must have been up to something, and she swept her hand over his naked tum and belly button, the navel my dear if you must refer to it at all and she felt paper-thin ribs and a beat, beat, thump, thump at left centre. So she got his trousers undone and held his tiny wet cock in her hand as he struggled and hummed through his nose. She laid the point of the knife on his skin and finding it to be the right place, pushed it a bit so that it pricked. The boy convulsed and flailed in the confinement and she was or someone was, frightened a bit, far off and anxious. So she thrust more still and felt it touch the leaping thing or be touched by it again and again while the body exploded with convulsions and a high humming came out of the nose. She thrust with all the power there was, deliriously; and the leaping thing inside seized the knife so that the haft beat in her hand, and there was a black sun. There was liquid everywhere and strong convulsions and she pulled the knife away to give them free play but they stopped. The boy just sat there in his bonds, the white patch of elastoplast divided down the middle by the dark liquid from his nose.

She came to herself with a terrible start that banged her head against the tree-trunk. There was a roaring and a great clittering of insect stuff and a red, mad light that swirled along the side of the downs. It passed overhead then swung up over the skyline to drop down towards where the fire was. She was trembling with the passion of the mock murder and she began to let herself down the tree-tunnel, back towards the old barge and her knees sagged. She came to the field bridge over the canal—and there was the car coming, no lights, heaving over the uneven track. She could not run, but waited for it. The car stopped, backed, turned and was ready to get away. Then she went to it, giggling and staggering to explain to Gerry about the old men in the stables and how they must use the boat but it was Bill there in the driving seat.

"Bill? Where is he? Where's the boy?"

"There's no bleeding boy. I had him and some burning bugger come out at me and—Sophy it's all gone wrong. We got to get away!"

She stood, staring into his face that was pallid on one side and glowing on the other where a cloud burned in the sky.

"Miss! Sophy—come on for fuck's sake! We got minutes—"

"Gerry!"

"He's all right—they got your boyfriend as a hostage—now come on—"

"They?"

Ever since he saw her without the wig, I knew. Something told me only I refused to believe it. Treachery. They think they've done a swop.

The rage that burst in her overwhelmed triumph and fierceness, bore her up so that she screamed at him, at them, and cursed and spat; and then she was down on hands and knees and screaming and screaming into the grass where there was no boy but a Sophy who had been used and fooled by everyone.

"Sophy!"

"Get lost you dumb beast! Oh shit!"

"For the last time—"

"Sod off!"

And when at last she stopped screaming and began to understand how she had torn her cheeks and how there was hair in her hands and how there was now nothing else, not him nor them nor her but a black night with a dying fire over the crest of the downs the tears rained down her cheeks and washed the blood from them.

Presently she knelt up and spoke, as if he were there.

"It's *no good* you see! All those years, no one—You think she's wonderful, don't you? Men always do at first. But there's nothing there, Gerry, nothing at all. Just the minimum flesh and bones, nothing else, no one to meet, no one to go with, be with, share with. Just ideas. Ghosts. Ideas and emptiness, the perfect terrorist."

She got up, heavily, and glanced across at the old barge where there was no boy, no body. She slung her shoulder bag and wondered how much damage she had done her face. She turned away from the boat and the fire and began to pick her way back along the towpath, where there was now nothing visible but darkness.

"I shall tell. I was used. They'll have nothing on me. Take the ropes off that chair. He said we were going camping, my lord. I've

253

been very foolish my lord I'm sorry I can't help crying. I think my fiancé must have been part of it my lord he was friendly with, with—I'm sure my Daddy had nothing to do with it, my lord. He wanted us out of the stables my lord, said he wanted to use them for something else. No my lord that was after he had been to a chess meeting in Russia. No my lord he never said."

# CHAPTER SIXTEEN

As they let him out of the back of the building Sim adjusted his coloured spectacles with movements so habitual they seemed to have become a part of his automatic life. They were one of three pairs he had acquired during the weeks of the inquiry. His walk was automatic, too, a stately progress. He had learnt that it was fatal—almost literally fatal—to hurry. That way he would attract notice and raise the shout of, *there's one of them*, or, *that's the fellow who gave evidence today*, or even, *that's Goodchild!* It seemed his name was peculiarly attractive to them.

Stately, he walked down the side road to join Fleet Street and thus avoid the queue of those who still were unable to get in. He was inspected by a passing policeman, and even in the twilight of his coloured glasses, he thought the man looked at him with amusement and contempt.

I could do with a cup of tea.

The further you got away from the inquiry, you would have thought, the less there was a chance of being recognized? Not a bit of it! Television made everywhere the same. *There's the fellow who was giving evidence*—No escape. The real ruin, the real public condemnation, was not to be good or bad; either of those had a kind of dignity about them; but to be a fool and to be seen to have been one—

At the end, when we can go away, they will have exonerated us. Until then, we are pilloried. And after?

The woman on the bus—*there's one of them! Aren't you one of the fellows who was in those stables*? And then the spit, incompetent spitting, badly aimed, hanging on the sleeve of his heather-mixture greatcoat—We did nothing! It was a kind of praying!

There was a crowd round a shop. Drawn as he always was, despite himself, to this extension of a place and time, he stopped

255

and stood at the back. By dodging this way and that, he could contrive to see brokenly into the window where at least fifteen television screens were showing their identical pictures; and then he saw a smaller one, high up and at an angle, so he ceased to dodge.

It was the afternoon round-up, he saw. There was a split screen, Mr Justice Mallory and his two coadjutors occupying the bottom third of it, and the smoking school above it, now a very famous film indeed. Athough he had never seen the school itself in the days when it had stood untouched and dignified, he could nevertheless identify the various windows from which various children of this royalty or that princedom or that multinational had jumped or been thrown. The top picture changed. Now it was harking back to London airport—there was Toni, her hair dazzling, there was the young ex-officer (that hurt) who had been her accomplice; there, close to him and at the wrong end of his pistol, the weight-lifter who had been engaged to the other sister—was he part of it? It was unbelievable—what was which and who? There was the plane taking off—the picture changed again and with a dull pain at his heart he saw what was to come. The bug was looking down into a small room where three men were sitting round a table. One of them was writhing and then suddenly laid his head down on the table. Their hands were joined. The man opposite lifted his head and opened his mouth.

The film cut to the inquiry again, everybody laughing, the judge, legal persons, press and those odd bodies whose function he had never quite understood, and who were perhaps special agents as a back-up to the armed soldiers who stood here and there against the walls. There was another cut, back, this time, the film of the three men in slow motion, his own head bowing jerkily, then Edwin's mouth open—and this time the people who stood round the shop window were laughing like the men in the inquiry.

"It wasn't like that!"

Fortunately no one noticed. He hurried away, not able to bear the thought that he might see once more (it was such a popular item) his own evidence that Mr Justice Mallory had described as a moment of low comedy in this terrible affair—

"You say, Mr Goodchild, you were not in a trance?"

"No my lord. My hands were held and I was trying to scratch my nose."

256

And then the roars of laughter, on and on—oh, it must have been for whole seconds.

I wouldn't believe it myself. I wouldn't believe we were—are—innocent.

I heard her in the street, the other woman nodding and talking at the same time the way they do, *there's no smoke without fire that's what I said*. Then they both shut up because they saw me.

The tube was roaring and crowded with rush-hour traffic. He hung on a strap, keeping his head down, looking where he would have seen his feet if a man's stomach hadn't got in the way. It was almost restful to hang there with no one to recognize the fool.

He walked from the station, coming up out of the earth to the street with a sense that once more he was vulnerable. Of course we all had something to do with it! We were there, weren't we?

The man who looked like an accountant but was from the secret service or whatever they call it, the one who did the bugging, said they'd been on to her sister for nearly a year. Who used who?

I had nothing to do with it. Nevertheless I am guilty. My fruitless lust clotted the air and muffled the sounds of the real world.

I am mad.

In the High Street he walked straight and painful, tense. He knew that even the brown women, cloth drawn across the lower part of the face—but in his case as he passed, drawing it higher still, to avoid contamination—even the brown women looked, glinting sideways.

There he goes.

Even Sandra looked. She came fatly, clumsily, but all gleaming and alive with excitement—"My mum wants me not to come but I said as long as Mr Goodchild wants me—"

Sandra wanting to be connected with terror, no matter how far off.

There was a sound of rapid footsteps beside him that slowed to his pace. He glanced sideways and it was Edwin, chin up, fists driven together in the pockets of his greatcoat. He wove a bit and brushed Sim's shoulder. Then they walked on, side by side. People made room for them. Sim turned into the lay-by where he kept his van. Instead of walking the few steps to Sprawson's, Edwin came with him. Sim opened the side door and Edwin followed without saying anything.

In the little sitting-room behind the shop there was dim light. Sim wondered whether to pull the curtains aside but decided against.

Edwin spoke in little more than a whisper.

"Is Ruth all right?"

"What is 'All right'?"

"Edwina's with her sister. Have you heard where Stanhope is?"

"Staying at his club, they say. I don't know."

"Some newspaper's got Sophy."

" 'He stole my heart away, says terrorist's twin.' "

"You're moving I suppose."

"Selling to the shopping-centre people."

"A good price?"

"Oh no. They'll pull the place down and use the ground for access. Big firm."

"Books?"

"Auction. Might make a bit. We're famous for the time being. Roll up!"

"We're innocent. He said so. 'I must state here and now that I think these two gentlemen are the victims of an unfortunate coincidence.' "

"We're not innocent. We're worse than guilty. We're funny. We made the mistake of thinking you could see through a brick wall."

"I'm being encouraged to resign. It's not fair."

Sim laughed.

"I should like to go to my daughter, get the hell out of it."

"Canada?"

"Exile."

"I think, Sim, I shall write a book about the whole affair."

"You'll have the leisure."

"I shall track down and cross-examine everybody who had anything to do with the whole ghastly business and I shall find out the truth."

"He was right, you know. History *is* bunk. History is the nothing people write about a nothing."

"The Akashic records—"

"At least I'm not going to make the mistake of fooling with that kind of idiocy again. No one will *ever* know what happened. There's too much of it, too many people, a sprawling series of events that break apart under their own weight. Those lovely

258

creatures—they have everything—everything in the world, youth, beauty, intelligence—or is there nothing to live for? Crying out about freedom and justice! What freedom? What justice? Oh my God!"

"I don't see what their beauty has to do with it."

"A treasure was poured out for them and they turned their back on it. A treasure not just for them but for all of us."

"Listen!"

"What is it?"

Edwin held up one finger. There was a noise, someone was fiddling with the door of the shop. Sim jumped up and hurried forward. Mr Pedigree was just closing the door behind him.

"We're not open. Good day to you."

Pedigree did not seem so defensive.

"Why was the door open then?"

"It shouldn't have been."

"Well it was."

"Please leave."

"You're in no position, Goodchild, to come the heavy. Oh I know it's only an inquiry, not a trial. But we know, don't we? You're in possession of my small property."

Edwin pushed past Sim.

"You're an informer, aren't you? You did it, didn't you?"

"I don't know what you're talking about."

"That's why you wouldn't stay—"

"I went because I didn't like my company."

"You went to switch the bug on!"

"Edwin, does it matter? That secret service man—"

"I said I'd get the truth!"

"Well. I want my ball. There it is, on your desk. I paid for it. Matty was really honest, you know."

"Just a moment, Sim. We know why you want it don't we? Do you want to go to jail again?"

"We might all go to jail, mightn't we? How do I know I'm not speaking to a very clever pair of terrorists who put those girls up to it? Yes of course she was—as bad as the other! The judge said you were innocent, but we, the great British Public, we—how odd to find myself one of them!—we know, don't we?"

"No, Sim—let me. Pedigree, you're a filthy old thing and you ought to be done away with. Take it and go!"

Mr Pedigree gave a kind of high whinny.

"You think I *like* wandering round lavatories and public parks, desperate for, for—I don't want to, I have to! Have to! Just for, no not even that, just for affection; and more than that, just a touch—It's taken me sixty years to find out what makes me different from other people. I have a rhythm. Perhaps you remember, or are you too young to remember, when it was said that all God's children had rhythm? Mine's a wave motion. You don't know what it's like to live like that, do you? You think I *want* to go to jail? But every so often I can feel the time coming, creeping up on me. You don't know what it's like to want desperately not to and yet know you will, oh yes you will! To feel the denouement, the awful climax, the catastrophe moving and moving and moving—to know that—to say to yourself on Friday it may be, 'I won't, I won't, I won't—' and all the time to *know* with a kind of ghastly astonishment that on Saturday you will, oh yes you will, you'll be fumbling at their flies—"

"For God's sake!"

"And worse; because many years ago a doctor told me what I might become in the end, what with obsession and fear and senility—to keep some child quiet—do I sound verging on senility?"

"Give yourself up. Go to hospital."

"Only they did it while they were young. Willing to kidnap a child—not worrying who got killed—imagine it, those young men, that beautiful girl with all her life before her! No, I'm nowhere near the worst, gentlemen, among the bombings and kidnappings and hijackings all for the highest of motives—what did she say? We know what we are but not what we may be. A favourite character of mine, gentlemen. Well, I won't thank you for your kindness and hospitality. I'm sorry we shan't meet inside—unless of course they turn up more evidence."

They watched him in silence as he wrapped his coat round him, held the big, coloured ball to his chest, and went with his curious springy, tottery step and let himself out of the side door. A moment or two later he shadowed the chinks of boarded-up shop window and was gone.

Sim sat down at the desk, wearily.

"It can't be happening to me."

"It is."

"The real hardship is that there's no end. I sit here. Will they ever stop showing that film of us round the table?"

"Have to, sooner or later."

"Can you stop watching it when it's on?"

"No. Actually not. I have to, like you. Like, like—no, I won't say like Pedigree. But every newstime, every special report, every radio programme—"

Sim stood up and went into the sitting-room. The sound of a man's voice swelled and the screen flickered into brightness. Edwin stood in the doorway. They were going through it all again on the other channel. The shot of the school appeared, was panned slowly, to take in the shattered and smoke-blackened wing. Then, endlessly after that, were Toni and Gerry and Mansfield and Kurtz herding their hostages towards the plane; and again, as a preliminary, before the day's advance, the new News, there was Toni in Africa, broadcasting, beautiful and remote, the long aria in that silvery voice about freedom and justice—

Sim cursed at her.

"She's mad! Why don't people say so? She's mad and bad!"

"She's not human, Sim. We have to face it at last. We're not all human."

"We're all mad, the whole damned race. We're wrapped in illusions, delusions, confusions about the penetrability of partitions, we're all mad and in solitary confinement."

"We think we *know*."

"Know? That's worse than an atom bomb, and always was."

In silence then, they looked and listened; then exclaimed together.

"Journal? Matty's journal? What journal?"

"—has been handed to Mr Justice Mallory. It may throw some light—"

Presently Sim switched the set off. The two men looked at each other and smiled. There would be news of Matty—almost a meeting with him. Somehow and for no reason that he could find, Sim felt heartened by the idea of Matty's journal—happy almost, for the moment. Before he knew what he was about he found himself staring intently into his own palm.

Mr Pedigree, wearing his ancient pepper-and-salt suit, had the overcoat slung over one arm and carried the ball held between his two hands on his way to the park. He was a little breathless and indignant at his breathlessness because he traced it to the talk he had had a few days before with Mr Goodchild and Mr Bell—a talk at which he had voluntarily spoken about his age. Age, then, had leapt out of its ambush somewhere and now went with him, so that he felt in himself even less able than usual to cope with the graph of his obsession. The graph was still there, it was so, no one could deny it, how else do you find yourself at that time of autumn when the day is still warm but these evenings suddenly cold—how else do you still find yourself going towards, despite the desperate words spoken only an hour before, and not just then but here and now as feet took themselves along despite you—no, no, no, not again, Oh God! And still the feet (as you knew they would) took you along and up the long hill to the paradisal, dangerous, damned park where the sons of the morning ran and played—and now, with the still open iron gates ahead, his own breathlessness seemed to matter less; and the *fact*, the undoubted *fact* already standing there, that he would spend tonight in a cell at the police station and overwhelmed with that special contempt they did not feel for murderers—that undoubted *fact* which he tried to rely on to support the 'no, no, no, Oh God!' that versicle without any response, the *fact* was diminishing in importance and was now overlaid quiveringly with an anticipation that really, one could not disguise it, tended to promote the breathlessness of age, not old age, but age, none the less, or its threshold as he said Τηλίκου ὡς περ ἐγών—

Still breathing deeply, astonished and sad, he saw his feet move him forward now again up the steep lip of his obsession, up to the gate on to the gravel, the feet themselves looking, peering at that far side where the boys shouted and played—only half an hour and they will be home with mum. Only another half hour and I would have held out for another whole day!

A wind took a scurry of autumn leaves across his feet but they ignored them and went on fast, too fast—

"Wait! I said wait!"

But it was all reasonable. Only the body has its reasons and feet are selfish, so that as they tried to pass the seat he was able for a while to arrest them and he pulled the coat round him, then slumped on the iron slats.

"Overdone it, you two."

The two did nothing inside their shining boots and he came to himself a little, feeling sheepish and wrapped in a cloud of illusion. Heart was more important than feet and protested. He hung over it, hoping that something nasty was not going to happen with its thump, thump, thump; and as he detected the first slowing of the beat he said inside, not daring even to risk giving the words air, since air was what heart wanted and must have to the exclusion of any other activity—

*That was a narrow escape!*

Presently he opened his eyes and made the brilliant colours of the ball take firm shape. The boys would not stay at the farther end of the park. Some of them would come this way, they must, to get to the main gate, they would come down the road and they would see the brilliant ball, bring it back to him when he threw it—the ploy was infallible, at worst would lead to a moment's banter, at best—

A cloud moved away from the sun and the sun itself seized him with many golden hands and warmed him. He was surprised to find how grateful he was to the sun for his mercy and that there was a little while to wait until the children came. If thought and decision was an exciting affair it was also a tiring one, hysterical sometimes and dangerous. He thought his heart would be the better for a little rest until he had to go into action, so he nestled into the huge coat and leaned his head down on his chest. The golden hands of the sun stroked him warmly and he was conscious of sunlight like waves as if someone were stirring it with a paddle. This was impossible of course but he was happy to find that light was a positive thing, an element on its own and what was more, one lying very close to the skin. This led him to open his eyes and look about. Then he discovered it was a function of this sunlight not merely to soak things in gold but also to hide them for he seemed to be sitting up to his very eyes in a sea of light. He looked to the left and saw nothing; and then to the right and saw without any surprise at all that Matty was coming. He knew this ought to surprise him because Matty was dead. But here Matty was, entering the park through the main gate and as usual dressed in black. He came slowly to Mr Pedigree who found his approach not only natural but even agreeable for the boy was not really as awful to look at as one might think, there where he

263

waded along waist deep in gold. He came and stood before
Pedigree and looked down at him. Pedigree understood that they
were in a park of mutuality and closeness where the sunlight lay
right on the skin.

"You know it was all your fault Matty."

Matty seemed to agree; and really the boy was quite pleasant to
look at!

"So I'm not going to be preached at Matty. We'll say no more
about it. Eh?"

Windrove continued to weave and hold on to his hat. Mr
Pedigree saw that it was the extraordinarily lively nature of this
gold, this wind, this wonderful light and warmth that kept
Windrove moving rhythmically in order to stay in one place. There
was a long period then, when he felt that the situation was so
enjoyable as to make it unnecessary to think of anything else. But
after a time, random thoughts began to perform themselves in the
volume that Mr Pedigree was accustomed to regard as himself.

He spoke out of this thinking.

"I don't want to wake up and find I'm inside, you know. That's
happened so often. What they used to call chokey in my young
day."

Windrove appeared to agree; and then, without words, Mr
Pedigree knew that Windrove *did* agree—and this was such a joy
of certainty that Mr Pedigree felt the tears streaming down his
face. Presently, when he was more himself, he spoke out of the
certainty.

"You're an odd chap, Matty, you always were. You have this
habit of popping up. There've been times when I wondered if you
actually existed when no one else was looking and listening if you
see what I mean. Times when I thought—is he all connected with
everything else or does he kind of drift through; I wonder!"

Then there was another long silence. Mr Pedigree was the one
to break it at last.

"They call it so many things, don't they, sex, money, power,
knowledge—and all the time it lies right on their skin! The thing
they all want without knowing it—yet that it should be you, ugly
little Matty, who really loved me! I tried to throw it away you
know, but it wouldn't go. Who are you, Matty? There've been
such people in this neighbourhood, such monsters, that girl and
her men, Stanhope, Goodchild, Bell even, and his ghastly

264

wife—I'm not like them, bad but not as bad, I never hurt anybody—*they* thought I hurt children but I didn't, I hurt myself. And you know about the last thing the thing I shall be scared into doing if I live long enough—just to keep a child quiet, keep it from telling—that's hell Matty, that'll be hell—help me!''

It was at this point that Sebastian Pedigree found he was not dreaming. For the golden immediacy of the wind altered at its heart and began first to drift upwards, then swirl upwards then rush upwards round Matty. The gold grew fierce and burned. Sebastian watched in terror as the man before him was consumed, melted, vanished like a guy in a bonfire; and the face was no longer two-tone but gold as the fire and stern and everywhere there was a sense of the peacock eyes of great feathers and the smile round the lips was loving and terrible. This being drew Sebastian towards him so that the terror of the golden lips jerked a cry out of him—

"Why? Why?"

The face looming over him seemed to speak or sing but not in human speech.

*Freedom.*

Then Sebastian, feeling the many-coloured ball that he held against his chest, and knowing what was to happen, cried out in agony.

"No! No! No!"

He clutched the ball closer, drew it in to avoid the great hands that were reaching towards him. He drew the ball closer than the gold on the skin, he could feel how it beat between his hands with terror and he clutched it and screamed again and again. But the hands came in through his. They took the ball as it beat and drew it away so that the strings that bound it to him tore as he screamed. Then it was gone.

The park keeper coming from the other gate saw him where he sat with his head on his chest. The park keeper was tired and irritated for he could see the brilliant ball lying a few yards from the old man's feet where it had rolled when he dropped it. He knew the filthy old thing would never be cured and he was more than twenty yards away when he began talking at him bitterly.

265

WILLIAM FAULKNER

*The Sound and*
*the Fury*

with an Introduction by
Nicholas Shakespeare

EVERYMAN'S LIBRARY

*69*

This book is one of 250 volumes in Everyman's Library
which have been distributed to 4500 state schools
throughout the United Kingdom.
The project has been supported by a grant of £4 million
from the Millennium Commission.

First published in the USA, 1929
First published in Great Britain, 1931
First included in Everyman's Library, 1992
Copyright, 1929, and renewed 1956, by William Faulkner
Introduction and Bibliography © Everyman Publishers plc, 2000
Chronology by Richard Godden © David Campbell Publishers Ltd.,
1992
Typography by Peter B. Willberg

ISBN 1-85715-069-4

A CIP catalogue record for this book is available from the
British Library

Published by Everyman Publishers plc,
Gloucester Mansions, 140A Shaftesbury Avenue,
London WC2H 8HD

Distributed by Random House (UK) Ltd.,
20 Vauxhall Bridge Road, London SW1V 2SA

# THE  SOUND  AND
THE  FURY

———

# INTRODUCTION

*'The South,' said Shreve. 'The South. Jesus.'*

I remember Oxford, Mississippi, as a small, prim town of white-painted metal bedsteads and on the lawns the brass of fallen leaves. There was a fine bookshop in the square and a university. Otherwise, the place was as remote as could be from Oxford, Oxfordshire, where I had been at boarding school. The town had the air of a stage set hauled out into the flat and viewless swampland by a people with a feverish appetite for theatrics.

Already dead thirty-five years, William Faulkner was still the main act. You could not help but cross his tracks: in the four-faced courthouse clock which was said to tell the time in his fiction, in the round tower where he wrote his novels on yellow legal pads, in the university where, in charge of the campus post office, he used to play cards after dumping copies of the *Baptist Record* in the garbage. It was impossible to ignore Oxford's most famous son, and I was ashamed that I wanted to. The truth was, I had not read a line of Faulkner.

There are paths to the sea that once avoided you do not take. There's nothing wrong with the path-not-taken: it's just that you chose another, and a decision, perhaps made lightly, firms into the natural order. It is the way in which patterns and people are formed, and seas are carved out. As wide and obvious as he was, Faulkner failed to beckon. It would be several years before I became intimate with his image: the aquiline nose, the moustache brushing down the corners of a tightly closed mouth, the implacable, unfrivolous and daunting expression. Later, I heard a recording of his voice and it seemed to support my disinterest. He speaks without inflexion in a high-pitched timbre that renders all it utters into a lulling and monotonous chant, rather as if saying a rosary. At a time when I was looking for plot, for clarity, for romantic passion, Faulkner required too much patience. I preferred to encounter him through his effect on South American writers like Borges and García Márquez. I was not ready to listen.

# THE SOUND AND THE FURY

You can read *Romeo and Juliet* before you fall in love, but certain books require you to fall out of love before you are able to enjoy them. When eventually I came to Faulkner I was an adult and it was an electrifying experience to meet, later than most, a writer who turns your head so fast you get a burn down your neck. The book was *The Sound and the Fury*. I didn't understand fully what was going on, yet I knew something was going on that mattered. I was baffled by the first page, but as I sank into it the prose began to send its charge through me, and I recognized one of those spasms that involves all the nerves.

*

It is still extraordinary to think that Faulkner began writing *The Sound and the Fury* in the belief he might not be published again. He had just turned thirty and his third novel, on which he pinned elaborate hopes, had been rejected by his publisher with a recommendation that he did not offer it elsewhere. 'I had,' he said, 'stopped thinking of myself in publishing terms.'

Not unlike his admired Balzac (whose *Cromwell* was turned down with the advice 'the author should do anything he likes, but not literature'), Faulkner needed to be scared into his skin. His most powerful novel – the one he regarded with most tenderness – sprang out of intense anguish, personal as well as professional. His response to failure is a consolation to all writers. *To hell with everyone, I'll do what I want.*

The rejection of the book with which he expected to make his critical and commercial reputation had the effect of a purification. Putting aside his 600-page manuscript of *Flags in the Dust*, he embarked on a new story, a 'dark story of madness and hatred'. He told no one what he was doing (as far as anyone in Oxford knew, he spent these days earning money by painting signs). He likened his new novel to a vase he had made so he could escape into it. 'One day I seemed to shut a door between me and all publishers' addresses and book lists. I said to myself, Now I can write. Now I can make myself a vase like that which the old Roman kept at his bedside and wore the rim slowly away with kissing it.' He would look back on this period, early 1928, as the most rapturous of his writing career. He wrote for his own pleasure, 'without any accompanying feeling of drive or effort, or any following feeling of exhaustion or relief or distaste.' He had no plan. 'I was thinking of books, publication, only ... in reverse, in saying to myself, I won't have to worry about publishers liking or not liking this at all.' He wrote quickly, fluently and the novel reads as it was written, as if he was composing chamber music for one.

Published on 7 October 1929, *The Sound and the Fury* sold less than 3,000 copies over the next seventeen years. By 1945 almost all of its author's work was out of print. Commercially, his publishers had been right.

So why has the novel taken its grip on the dark complexities of our psyche?

*

In *The Sound and the Fury*, Faulkner continued the process begun in the abandoned manuscript, a narrative of the decay and disintegration of his Mississippi family. The novel is humid and difficult, heavy with the kind of sad dampness found in Joyce. You can smell the breath: adolescent, losing the sweetness of childhood, on the sour edge of turning. But where Joyce placed himself in exile to find his voice, essentially urban, Faulkner needed to return to his source, to the 'country folks' in and about the town of Oxford, his home since he was five.

'You're a country boy,' said an early mentor, Sherwood Anderson. 'All you know is that little patch up there in Mississippi where you started from.'

As a younger writer Faulkner had condemned Anderson for exploiting those around him: 'I think that when a writer reaches the point when he's to write about people he knows, his friends, then he has reached the tragic point.' Reaching the tragic point would, however, be Faulkner's salvation. 'I discovered that my own little postage stamp of native soil was worth writing about and that I would never live long enough to exhaust it and that by sublimating the actual into the apocryphal I would have complete liberty to use whatever talent I might have to its absolute top.' Nor would he find it sufficient simply to reflect the lives of those close to hand. In order to create an authentic cosmos of his own, Faulkner had

THE SOUND AND THE FURY

to mine the most intimate, troubling veins of a childhood he
might have preferred to forget. 'I realized that to make it truly
evocative it must be personal.' From a child, he had been shy
and aloof and rattling with 'back-looking' southern ghosts. The
novel he never expected to see published was an exploration of
what haunted him.

*

When, twenty years later, the world discovered William
Cuthbert Faulkner, it found a soft-spoken and stonily remote
figure in his late forties. He once described his lifetime's
ambition to be the last private individual on earth. 'Mr
Faulkner tole me to tell you he ain't here,' his houseboy
informed those who telephoned Rowan Oak. To a publisher
who requested contributor information, Faulkner wrote: 'Tell
them I was born of an alligator and a nigger slave at the
Geneva peace conference two years ago.' And to Malcolm
Cowley, who did more than anyone to resuscitate his work:
'It is my ambition to be, as a private individual, abolished and
voided from history, leaving it markless, no refuse save the
printed books.' He wished his epitaph to be: 'He made the
books and he died.'

Regarding his books, his 'native soil' remained hugely
ambivalent. Faulkner's father denied reading anything he
wrote. Buyers of his novels at the local drugstore in Oxford
habitually wanted their copies wrapped before they stepped
back into the square. Within the community, his name was
spoken through cupped hands. 'We don't talk about him
around here,' said a dean on the university's nine-hole golf
course where Faulkner had sold soft drinks. One man who
did succeed in talking to him, Henry Nash Smith, was forced
to resign from the Southern Methodist University for associating with 'so obscene a writer'.

Where his friends and family were ambivalent, the American literary scene alternated between indifference and hostil-
ity. The London *Times* might choose to dub Oxford 'the
literary capital of the English speaking world', but in the
opinion of the *Jackson Daily News* Faulkner had sullied his
community by populating it with perverts, murderers and

idiots. 'He is a propagandist of degradation and properly belongs in the privy school of literature.' Even after the announcement of his Nobel prize in 1950, the *New York Times* judged his world 'too often vicious, depraved, decadent, corrupt.' Incest and rape might be common in Faulkner's fictional Jefferson, but nowhere else in the United States.

In September 1945, a year before his work was reprinted, Faulkner won $250 for second prize in *Ellery Queen Mystery Magazine*. 'In France, I am the father of a literary movement. In Europe I am considered the best modern American and among the first of all writers in America. In America I eke out a hack's motion pictures wages by winning second prize in a manufactured mystery story contest.' He complained: 'All my native land did for me was to invade my privacy over my protest and my plea.'

Yet his best work, of which *The Sound and the Fury* is the outstanding example, invited the invasion. 'I am telling the same story over and over, which is myself and the world.'

*

Faulkner had known his vocation since he was nine. 'I want to be a writer like my great-granddaddy.' He was speaking of Colonel William Clerk Falkner, the family founder who had met a violent death eight years before he was born. Named after him, Faulkner grew up feeling at every turn the giant's tread of this first William: slave-owner, planter, brigadier in the militia, lawyer, railroad king ('he built the first railroad in our county'), author.

The 'Old Colonel', as the family referred to him, had arrived in Mississippi in 1842, an outcast. After injuring his brother with a hoe in St Genevieve, Missouri, he set out on foot, aged seventeen, to find his aunt in Ripley. He wrote his first book three years later, the life of a convicted axe-murderer in Ripley gaol – with whose family he split the profits. In 1851 he published at his own expense *The Siege of Monterey*, an amateur poem about his experience as a Lieutenant in the Mexican War, where he had lost the tips of three fingers. He also paid for a novel, *The Spanish Heroine*, and a play, *The Lost Diamond*. But his indisputable success was *The White Rose of*

*Memphis*, a gaudy, humourless romance set on a Mississippi riverboat and shot through with quotations from the Bible, Shakespeare and Walter Scott. The novel went into thirty-five editions and sold, apparently, 160,000 copies.

He was a Márquez colonel, dynamic and haughty. He knew what it was to kill and on one occasion knifed a man who pulled a pistol on him, complaining Falkner had blackballed him from the Knights Temperance. As a Confederate soldier, he was strict and fearless. He repulsed General Irwin at the battle of First Manassas, losing two horses under him. General Beauregard, observing Falkner gallop by on a third, was compelled to shout: 'Go ahead, you hero with the black plume; *history shall never forget you!*' But history did forget him as it tended to cold-shoulder heroes from the south. 'He rode through that country like a living force,' wrote Faulkner, who lamented that nothing remained of his great-grandfather's work save an imported statue. The expression in the marble beard failed to suggest its subject's complexity or his tragedy. The Old Colonel died on 5 November 1889, in Ripley, after a former partner from the railroad shot him with a .44, point blank in his mouth. As a child, Faulkner used to play with the pipe he had been smoking.

*

In later life Faulkner would visit the statue in Ripley and repair it. The monument was of Carrara marble, eight foot high on a fourteen foot pediment, the face, long-nosed and vacant, chiselled in Italy from a photograph. As if he would quite like to join him on the pediment, Faulkner identified with the Old Colonel to the extent of altering his surname. Born William Cuthbert Falkner, he rescued the 'u' dropped by his ancestor and set himself apart from the rest of his family (rather as Nathaniel Hathorne had done by changing his name). The smallest of men – he never grew to more than five foot five – Faulkner had always the energy of a pug dog straining to be eight feet tall.

He was filial to Colonel Falkner's spirit right to the end: he even died on that man's birthday, 6 July. His allegiance had skipped two generations. He described his father as a dull man.

xii

# INTRODUCTION

Murry Falkner was bitter, awkward and inadequate: an uneasy man to love who loved railways, cowboy books and hunting in the woods. Thwarted in his ambitions to be a Texas rancher or the president of his father's railroad company – 'his first and lasting love' – he tottered from one business to another. He sold coal-oil for lamps and ran an unsuccessful hardware store on the square in Oxford ('Father was not a natural salesman – of hardware or anything else,' said Faulkner's younger brother, Jack). To William, his eldest child, he bequeathed a taste for bonded bourbon and for binge drinking. Unable to support his family, Murry would grow violent and profane on hunter's whisky. His nickname for his son was 'snake-lips'. Faulkner drew on him in *The Sound and the Fury*, both for the morose, unshockable father and for Jason, his hopeless storekeeper son. 'He talks just like my husband did,' said Maud Falkner.

Faulkner's mother had had a difficult marriage with Murry. 'I never did like him,' Maud admitted shortly before her death. A Baptist who practised Methodism, she hoped not to meet her husband in the afterlife.

Church was important to Maud, and literature. While Murry pored over westerns and comic strips, his wife read Shakespeare, Balzac, Conrad. She passed on her tastes to her favourite son. Physically, she resembled the matriarch of his novel, 'her eyes so dark as to appear all pupil or all iris', and her feelings towards Faulkner are of a parcel with Mrs Compson's towards Jason: she believed in him unswervingly. He, in his turn, looked up to proud and determined women like her, small, bird-headed, with a tart reserve ('DON'T COMPLAIN DON'T EXPLAIN' was the sign she hung in her kitchen). From Maud Butler, Faulkner inherited his size, his inflexible self-conviction and his silences. She had first-hand experience of growing up exposed to shame and scandal, and of harbouring corrosive secrets. Her mother had been married to a sheriff of Lafayette County, but he ran off soon after their marriage, leaving his young family pennilesss – rather in the circumstances Sydney Herbert deserts Caddy in *The Sound and the Fury*. Faulkner's abandoned grandmother would come and stay in 1902, teaching him to paint. Faulkner

THE SOUND AND THE FURY

called her Damuddy, and it is her funeral which provides the focal point of his novel.

Lastly, there was Caroline Barr who worked in the kitchen. Known as Mammy Callie, she was Faulkner's second mother and his model for Dilsey. Born into slavery in 1840, she 'gave to my family a fidelity without stint or calculation of recompense and to my childhood an immeasurable devotion and love.' She could neither read nor write, but she could tell stories. From Mammy Callie, who called him 'Memmy', Faulkner first heard the incantatory cadences of the negro spiritual; and in the stories she embroidered in the kitchen, of plantation life before the Civil War, she taught Faulkner the power of dialect, the short steps but large rhythms which sway his prose. Just as Dilsey does, he never has to describe a character in the book. He goes inside their voice so quickly they are there.

*

*To be a writer like my great-granddaddy.* From his first writing, almost until he started *The Sound and the Fury*, Faulkner could be a congested and erratic imitator. In 1924, he published, at his own expense, *The Marble Faun*, a volume of poetry inspired by his dandyish enthusiasm for A.E. Housman: 'Here was reason for being born into a fantastic world: discovering the splendour of fortitude, the beauty of being of the soil like a tree about which fools might howl and which winds of disillusion and death and despair might strip, leaving it bleak, without bitterness, beautiful in sadness.' But Faulkner never convinced as a poet ('warm in dark between the breasts of Death'). Nor did he cut a plausible figure of a young man rooted indomitably in his landscape – a land, he wrote, of great swamps lurking with alligators and water moccasins. He spent his one year at university imitating French Symbolists, sporting a trim moustache and carrying a cane and a handkerchief up his sleeve. He might champ to take after his marble colonel. He more accurately resembled his marble faun: able to observe life being lived under his nose, yet powerless to break out of the stone and enjoy it.

Like Benjy, the passive idiot child whose voice begins the

novel, Faulkner found it a tremendous effort to participate in the universe. He played truant at school, where he was known as 'quair'. As book-keeper in his grandfather's bank, he earned the distancing nickname of 'Count' – after the spickness of his clothes. In another image Joseph Blotner records in his biography, Faulkner dresses like a punctual tramp. A student tracks his progress across the campus, unshaven, his shirt unbuttoned, in sandals without socks: 'That is Bill Faulkner and he will never amount to a damn.'

Faulkner in those days viewed Oxford simply as a 'temporary address'. He seized the Great War as an opportunity to leave town and to follow in the footprints of his reckless ancestor 'and be glorious and beribboned too'. But his machinations to become a war hero were ludicrous. Judged too small and weak, he stuffed himself with bananas. He was accepted as a pilot cadet only after pretending to be a 'God-fearing' young Englishman from Finchley. As a pilot he was grounded for the rest of the war on an airfield near Toronto, learning callisthenics. He achieved his desired status in imagination only. In biographical notes for *The Marble Faun* he wrote of his career as a man at arms: 'During the war he was with the British Air Force and made a brilliant record. He was severely wounded.' In fact, he was taking for himself his younger brother's injury and bravery: aged nineteen, Jack had been gassed in Champagne and wounded by shrapnel on the edge of Argonne Forest. Not only did Faulkner not see combat, no record exists for him having flown at all. There is not even a record for the mysterious accident in which he claims to have ploughed into a hangar after drinking a crock of bourbon, ending up hanging upside-down from the rafters. But the story reveals how he viewed the world, the peculiar angle of his vision: awry, suspended, trapped. And it shows the writer's muscle already at work, that 'completely amoral' tic which allowed Faulkner to take what he needed to make his characters: 'They are partly composed from what they were in actual life and partly from what they should have been and were not: thus I improved on God, who, dramatic though He be, has no sense, no feeling for, theatre.'

He applied this *maquillage* in his relationships with women.

The wounded air-ace who returned from Toronto with a limp and a swagger stick insinuated Jason Compson's seasoned acquaintance with the Memphis underworld. Faulkner told the madam of one bordello that he was 'vacationing from sex', even putting it about that he had fathered two illegitimate children. More likely, his eyes did the doing. They were the eyes of a vigorous observer, not a vigorous lover, and they reflected the pain of what they missed. His hawk-like gaze, according to one admirer, 'burned through the flesh and bone of everyone in front of him'. Tennessee Williams could not rid himself of the memory of Faulkner's expression: 'Those terrible, distraught eyes,' he wrote to Hemingway. 'They moved me to tears.'

In point of fact, Faulkner's private life had much in common with his war record: it failed to take off. He was a man who responded to women who did not respond to him; sullen-jawed, flat-chested flappers like Helen Baird who sat on other men's balconies and ignored him, 'not thinking even a hell of a little bit of me'. About Helen, he confided to a friend: 'It's hell being in love, ain't it?' He converted his erotic longing into more verse:

> '. . . can breasts be ever small as these
> Twin timorous rabbits' quisitive soft repose?'

Whatever the truth of his antics in Memphis, Faulkner reverted back home to tongue-tied immobility. His first love, whom he was to marry after completing *The Sound and the Fury*, was the pretty and over-emotional Estelle Oldham. He had courted her since adolescence, when his attitude echoed his love-stunned faun At parties in Oxford, he sat penitently watching while Estelle danced in other men's arms. She suggested they elope, run off, but he could not muster the courage. Only on paper could he play the lover. He and Estelle were united between the covers of his poetry and in Beardsley-like drawings (some printed in the university magazine) of a scantily-dressed nymph, a satyr playing his pipe for her, a couple dancing the Charleston.

In April 1918, Estelle married a handsome lawyer and gambler, Cornell Sidney Franklin, and went to live in Shanghai. Her elopement plunged Faulkner into an agony of sexual jealousy. Ten years later, he would pour his ache and his seethe into the character of Benjy's febrile brother, Quentin. 'His world went to pieces,' said his brother John. According to Jack, 'I don't think Bill ever stopped thinking of her.' His thoughts showed even to strangers. 'I felt that Faulkner had been deeply hurt – probably in some love affair,' said the architect Buckminster Fuller. 'I felt that he had something that kept hurting him – that drove him to write very very beautifully to overcome the pain ...' As Faulkner put it in *Mosquitoes*: 'You don't commit suicide when you are disappointed in love. You write a book.'

Estelle's marriage with Franklin did not work out (she had burst into tears on her wedding day). In January 1927, she returned with her two children to Oxford. Soon Faulkner was a regular visitor. He received his rejection of *Flags in the Dust* ('THE book' he had told his publisher) at a period when Estelle was entangled in her divorce. Now she reached out to him. Together they might pull back the hands of the clock. Already a hard drinker, she began to pressure her first love into doing what he should have done all along and marry her.

The return of his virgin nymph as a whisky-swilling mother and imminent divorcee, together with the marriage, in March 1927, of his second muse Helen Baird, might explain Faulkner's comment to his French translator that he was suffering at this time from 'des difficultés d'ordre intime'. There may have been, in addition, a third woman. Early in 1928, when he had begun *The Sound and the Fury*, he wrote a cryptic message to his Aunt Bama: 'I have something – someone I mean – to show you, if only you would. Of course, it's a woman. I would like to see you taken with her utter charm, and intrigued by her utter shallowness. Like a lovely vase ...' The woman is unnamed and, of course, it is possible she existed. But this is the period when he was kissing his bedside vase, as he called his fourth novel, in which he would discover the woman who would become the first of all his women, whom he was to christen his 'heart's darling'.

*

Faulkner shapes his Caddy, the Lolita of the 1920s, from the women he had loved: the chaste and chastened Estelle, Helen Baird, his cousin Sallie Murry. She is an uncontrollable charac-ter absolutely under his domination, but where Nabokov puts Lolita on the run, out in the world, Faulkner sets Caddy sizzling at the dining-room table. Until she disappears entirely, her wick is only as long as the Compson household and garden.

'I was worst to him I loved the most,' goes the line of an Icelandic saga. To be the darling of Faulkner's heart is not an enviable fate. Caddy is his favourite character but, as David Minter observes, he lays upon her 'frail and unbowed shoul-ders the whole burden of man's history of his impossible heart's desire.' He infuses her with his frustrated longing and out of the process moulds someone with the backbone to carry his terrible load and somehow retain her dignity. Dilsey might be bowed down by the weight. Caddy stands straight and speaks straight, authority and virtue still clinging to her.

She evolves out of three stories he had been writing about the Compson children. In each story they are let out to play at the Faulknerian hour, three brothers and a sister moving through a 'strange, slightly sinister suspension of twilight'. At their head, like an adolescent piper, scampers Caddy.

Faulkner called the third story, *Twilight*. 'I thought it could be done in ten pages.' He based it on his grandmother's funeral in June 1907: a story without a plot, he wrote, of some children being sent away from the house because they were too young to know what was going on. In the central scene, the brothers look up their sister's legs as she climbs a tree to observe what it is they have been forbidden to see. That image becomes critical for Faulkner, 'the only thing in literature which would ever move me very much: Caddy climbing the pear tree to look in the window at her grandmother's funeral while Quentin and Jason and Benjy and the negroes looked up at the muddy seat of her drawers.' When Caddy stoops in her wet garments to comfort her smallest brother, who is crying, 'the entire story ... seemed to explode on paper before me.' The soiled drawers – familiar, private, tender – would become a metaphor for 'the shame she was to engender'.

Of Caddy, Faulkner wrote: 'I loved her so much ... I

couldn't decide to give her life just for the duration of a short story. She deserved more than that. So my novel was created almost in spite of myself.' For the rest of his life, he called her 'the daughter' of his mind.

*

The forbidden sight Caddy glimpses from the pear tree is the adult world of her parents. It is a bold disappointment. 'They're not doing anything in there,' she complains. 'Just sitting in chairs and looking.'

Caddy sees behind the window into a gathering of typical Faulkner grown-ups, desiccated and lethargic creatures defined by what they are not, by negatives: 'volitionless', 'substanceless', 'unwived', 'unmeditant', 'talonless', 'fangless', 'destinationless'. The air they breathe is vitiated and enervating, their inactivity a kind of death.

In *The Sound and the Fury*, adulthood manifests itself as illness. 'Bad health is the primary reason for all life,' Mr Compson teaches his children. One by one the adults in the book fall ill: 'Damuddy was sick ... Father was sick ... Uncle Maury was sick ... Mother's sick again.'

Poised on her branch outside, Caddy looks into a rotting house where there exists no credible authority. Incapacitated, her parents have deserted their posts. Her father stares at his decanter while her neurotic mother lies in an upstairs room, hand perpetually over forehead. The only moral centre is someone not of their blood: the black servant Dilsey, who is old, weak and ultimately indulgent rather than corrective.

Unparented, the children are left to run wild and in doing so the sap spills over.

*

For Faulkner, adolescence is a prodromal world where the softest touch to the flesh leaves an imprint, the faintest smell is saturated with 'the heavy rifeness of honeysuckle' and every sight installs itself. Passions are at their darkest because at their most inexplicable. But this is the age when passions direct behaviour, when to gaze up a young girl's legs is to have longing made palpable and tantalizingly within reach.

Benjy entering the house to eat feels 'a hunger in itself inarticulate, not knowing it is hunger'. All the Compson children ache with this hunger. Their appetites go unsated at the dinner table. Unnourished, they need to pick their fruit where they can. Caddy most of all.

A young girl coming into flower is a dangerous thing. 'Parasitic and potent and serene' is how Faulkner describes 'that transition stage between childhood and womanhood'. When that girl is as delectable and sexually charismatic as Caddy, it disrupts the natural order. To satisfy her hunger, she becomes mother to Benjy, lover to Quentin. As Faulkner writes in his second novel about Quentin, *Absalom, Absalom!*: 'Let flesh touch with flesh and watch the fall of all the eggshell shibboleth of caste and colour too.'

The Compson adults do not know what to do with this sap and fail to contain it. They substitute surveillance for love, making others responsible. The children are handed over to non-kin like Dilsey or her son Luster, or when matters get really out of hand, to the least loving, least loveable member of the Compson family, Jason – who is set upon to watch his sister and brother, exactly as he will watch his niece, Caddy's daughter.

The only child who can be contained behind the gate is the retarded one, who cannot pass into adulthood. Benjy, the primal force of the book, responds to this drive at the most primal level. When he tries to articulate its power, he is castrated.

Through their neglect and inactivity, the Compson parents emotionally mutilate each of their children. In Jason, the sap simply hardens: in his attempt to contain it, he carries it around in his meanness. Out of this drive Caddy gets pregnant, seeking the love she cannot find at home, because her mother is too ill to supply it, her father too drunk and misogynist. Out of this drive, which liquefies into sexual jealousy for his sister, Quentin kills himself.

'Dese funny folks,' says Dilsey's son, Luster. 'Glad I aint none of em.'

We know from the first page this garden is doomed. The softness in the fruit is over-readiness, the first sign it is going bad. We do not expect any of the characters to cope with the cards Faulkner has dealt them, or escape. The mother will not be woken up by Quentin's death. If anything, his death fixes her forever at the top of the stairs, calling Dilsey's name. In the same way, Jason does not stop lying, Benjy does not stop bellowing, Caddy does not stop running.

Caddy is as absent from Faulkner's novel as she is from his life. Hers is the voice we never hear except indirectly, but we are complicit in her fate. Her silence is the black hole into which we all lean. We watch her clamber up the fence hemming in the rest of us, and reappear on the other side, free. She is still at large, eighteen years after Faulkner created her. In an Appendix he wrote for the novel, she stands beside a sports car in the company of a German general. And hers is the photograph over which Dilsey weeps 'because she knows Caddy doesn't want to be saved hasn't anything anymore worth being saved for nothing worth being lost that she can lose'.

*

Those who know Faulkner's South will be familiar with its people's capacity for bare-fisted rage. On the last pages of the novel, Jason lashes out at Benjy in an act of ruthlessness, and hitting kin he hits himself. Faulkner makes all his children transgress: they spy, they lie, they steal, they commit incest. Their transgression enacts their author's transgression of the novel form. Driven by failure and disappointment, Faulkner falls back into his own arms. By sealing himself off, he repudiates the heritage of Balzac, Dostoevsky, Conrad and breaks out of the restraints of conventional narrative. He wrote, he said, his guts into *The Sound and the Fury*. In so doing, he wrote a book that creates out 'of the materials of the human spirit something which didn't exist before'.

The novel is not plotless, but it soon compels you to discard all expectations of plot and to listen, instead, to Faulkner's voice, the voice of someone moving at the rapt, absorbed pace of a discoverer. The undergrowth is dense and claustrophobic, springing back after it is parted, and the path through this new realm is sometimes obscure. Faulkner's attention is so concentrated on the prospect before him that he makes limited concessions to lucidity. He has the audacity to throw at you two different Jasons, two different Quentins without telling you how to figure them out. Nor does he help with a continuous narrative. Rather, he relies on four separate narrators who span eight periods of time. (For one edition, he proposed using three coloured inks to differentiate between Benjy's childhood, adolescence and present). Skip a line, a word even, and you risk losing his trail altogether. Arnold Bennett found the novel 'exasperatingly, unimaginably difficult to read'. He was not alone. Taxed about a certain passage, Faulkner told his French translator: 'I have absolutely no idea what I meant.' After finishing the first chapter, he realized that what he had just written was, as he put it, 'incomprehensible, even I could not have told what was going on then, so I had to write another chapter. Then I decided to let Quentin tell his version of the same day, or that same occasion, so he told it.'

Faulkner's confusion propels him onward. And gradually it becomes clear that the difficulty of reading the first chapter mimics the turmoil of adolescence for its four principal characters: an unfiltered and searing experience which the rest of the novel labours to clarify.

\*

Faulkner once made the distinction between books you can read fast and those you must read slowly. You read *The Sound and the Fury* aware that you will have to re-read every line. Its first reader, his friend Phil Stone, read the manuscript sitting in Faulkner's room in the tower of his parents' house in Oxford. He could not make head nor tail of it.

'Wait, just wait,' said Faulkner. He demanded the same patience of himself. 'The damndest book I ever read,' he wrote to Aunt Bama.

Most writers go in, turn on the light, leave. Faulkner keeps you in the dark, in the mess. He lowers your face to the soil, to his peculiar line of vision, from where everything comes into startling contour, like Caddy's nose seen rising above the apple. Even his sky presses down with a distorting weight: 'It was so low that all smells and sounds of night seemed to have been crowded down like under a slack tent especially the honeysuckle.'

He observes no boundaries. Surfaces are permeable, light turns into oil. In this odd exchange between matter and air, people dissolve into their surrounds. There is no skin on anybody. Everything is hyper-focused and distorted. This is true most especially of time, which operates as a hot vacuum keeping old wounds and grievances alive, poised to sting even in death.

Faulkner's South is its own world. His idiosyncratic punctuation slips you into its time-frame. His narrative moves at the pace of a disturbed dream, beating to the tock of Quentin's fractured watch, or the cabinet clock in the Compson kitchen, seen only by lamplight, at night, and 'evincing an enigmatic profundity because it had but one hand'. The phrase 'enigmatic profundity' captures the gravitas of the prose – at once incomprehensible and urgent. There is little difference between dreaming and reading Faulkner. He removes the membrane dividing moment from moment so that there are only significant moments and these run together and blur. 'There is no such thing as memory,' he wrote in *Absalom, Absalom!*, 'the brain recalls just what the muscles grope for: no more, no less: and its resultant sum is usually incorrect and false and worthy only of the name of dream.'

As every undergraduate has learnt, perhaps the only foothold a first-time reader can secure in this world is to register the patterns from which meaning might emerge. Faulkner tempts you into making lists. Of smells: wisteria, gasoline, honeysuckle, camphor, cigar smoke, perfume. Of words: suppurating, suspenseful, gaunt, unflagging, aghast, outrageous, attenuated, impervious, invincible. Of those images and sensations that spark the narrative: Benjy, clinging to the fence to keep pace with the golfers who call for their caddy, which is also the forbidden name of his sister. The quarter lost by Luster through a hole in his pocket. The quarter found by Quentin who gives it to a little Italian girl. The girl, with her 'black secret friendly gaze' who reminds Quentin of himself at that age with Caddy in the barn. The girl's enraged brother who accuses him of stealing his sister and reacts exactly as did Quentin when he tried to punch Dalton Ames for seducing Caddy. And so on, until the moment dawns that everything is linked and that repetition is the order of things, both in the novel's plot (being the same story told four times) and in the language Faulkner uses to tell it. He is saying: *If you want to know my meaning, here it is. We are doomed to repetition.*

It is hard, once heard, to forget Faulkner's voice. His rhythms and cadences attract and draw us in. He reiterates the important lesson of invoking character through action and dialogue, and he repeats his dialogue to hallucinatory effect. Not until the final section does the author, in a kind of delayed objectivity, present us with a description of his characters. There is a sense of release suddenly to see them corporeal, but we already know what they smell like, their madnesses and obsessions.

Near the end of the novel, Dilsey goes with Benjy to church and they listen to a sermon given by an undersized visiting clergyman. In his best writing, Faulkner can achieve the trance-inducing rhetoric of the small, monkey-faced preacher. 'It [the voice] sounded too big to have come from him ... They even forgot his insignificant appearance in the virtuosity with which he ran and poised and swooped upon the cold inflexionless wire of his voice ... The voice consumed him, until he was nothing and they were nothing and there was not even a voice but instead their hearts were speaking to one another in chanting measures beyond the need for words.'

Reading Faulkner can also brace and intoxicate, like drinking good whisky for the first time. He might not be to everyone's taste, but his flavour – mossy, unsettling, all his own – has permeated the literature of the twentieth century, from Thomas Bernhard's Vienna to Haldor Laxness's Iceland to the Macondo of Gabriel García Márquez. His fellow southerner, Flannery O'Connor, likened him to a railroad such as his great-grandfather might have built. 'When you hear the Dixie Special coming down the line, you'd better get off the track.'

This is the tremor you feel when you begin reading *The Sound and the Fury*. It is not a question of argument or applause. You can hate Faulkner. You can love Faulkner. It doesn't matter. He's coming through.

Nicholas Shakespeare

# SELECT BIBLIOGRAPHY

BLOTNER, JOSEPH, *Faulkner, A Biography*, Random House, 1974.

BLOTNER, JOSEPH, ed., *Selected Letters of William Faulkner*, Random House, 1977.

BROWN, CALVIN S., 'Colonel Falkner as General Reader: *The White Rose of Memphis*', *Mississippi Quarterly*, 30, 1977.

COWLEY, MALCOLM, ed., *The Faulkner-Cowley File: Letters and Memories, 1944–1962*, Viking, 1966.

COINDREAU, MAURICE-EDGAR, 'Preface to *The Sound and the Fury*', *Mississippi Quarterly*, 19, 1966.

FALKNER, MURRY C., *The Falkners of Mississippi: A Memoir*, Louisiana State University Press, 1967.

FAULKNER, JOHN, *My Brother Bill: An Affectionate Reminiscence*, Trident, 1963.

FAULKNER, WILLIAM, *Absalom, Absalom!*, Random House, 1936.

FAULKNER, WILLIAM, 'Appendix: Compson. 1699–1945', in Malcolm Cowley, ed., *The Portable Faulkner*, Viking, 1946.

FAULKNER, WILLIAM, *Collected Stories*, Random House, 1950.

FAULKNER, WILLIAM, *Essays, Speeches & Public Letters*, ed. James B. Meriwether, Random House, 1965.

FAULKNER, WILLIAM, *Flags in the Dust*, Random House, 1973.

FAULKNER, WILLIAM, 'An Introduction to *The Sound and the Fury*', *Mississippi Quarterly*, 26, 1973.

FAULKNER, WILLIAM, *Lion in the Garden: Interviews with William Faulkner*, ed. James Meriwether and Michael Millgate, Random House, 1968.

FAULKNER, WILLIAM, *The Marble Faun*, The Four Seasons Company, 1924.

FAULKNER, WILLIAM, *Mosquitoes*, Boni & Liveright, 1927.

MINTER, DAVID, *William Faulkner, His Life and Work*, John Hopkins, University Press, 1997.

STEIN, JEAN, 'William Faulkner: An Interview', *Paris Review*, 1956.

STONE, PHIL, 'William Faulkner: The Man and His Work', *Oxford Magazine*, 1, 1934.

WILDE, META CARPENTER, and BORSTEN, ORIN, *A Loving Gentleman: The Love Story of William Faulkner and Meta Carpenter*, Simon & Schuster, 1976.

# CHRONOLOGY

———

| DATE | AUTHOR'S LIFE | LITERARY CONTEXT |
|---|---|---|
| | Recalling my own needs as a first- and second-time reader, I concentrated less on Faulkner's life than on that of the Compsons.* In dating the novel's key events I draw on the work of Brooks, Volpe and Matthews (Compson dates are marked 'C'). | |
| 1861–5 | | |
| 1866 | | Swinburne: *Poems and Ballads*. |
| 1880 | | Cable: *The Grandissimes*. |
| 1889–1945 | | |
| 1890(C) | Quentin Compson born. | |
| 1892–3 | | |
| 1893 | | Wilde (illustrated by Beardsley): *Salomé*. |
| 1894(C) | Jason Compson born. | Twain: *Pudd'nhead Wilson*. |
| 1895(C) | Benjy (first named Maury) Compson born. | |
| 1896 | | Housman: *A Shropshire Lad*. |
| 1897 | William Cuthbert Faulkner (the first of four sons) is born in New Albany, Mississippi. He was to live a large part of his life in Oxford, Mississippi. | Conrad: *The Nigger of the 'Narcissus'*. |
| 1898(C) | Damuddy's death and Caddy's subsequent tree-climbing. | |
| 1899 | | Chopin: *The Awakening*. |
| 1900(C) | Benjy's name changed. | Dreiser: *Sister Carrie*. |
| 1900–10 | | |
| 1900–30 | | |
| 1901 | | Washington: *Up From Slavery*. |
| 1903 | | Du Bois: *The Souls of Black Folk*. |

*This chronology was compiled by Richard Godden.

The Civil War.

The 'lynching era', during which Mississippi had 13 per cent of the nation's recorded lynchings (peaks 1889–1908 and 1918–22).
Census: enumerators instructed to distinguish between 'blacks', 'mulattoes', 'quadroons' and 'octoroons'. New constitution of the state of Mississippi prohibits interracial union (the prohibition stands for seventy-five years).
Depression: drastic fall in agricultural prices.

Census: Northern population 50 per cent urban, Southern population 82 per cent rural.
8 million immigrants arrive in US.
Annual wage levels in the ten Southern states hover at between 60 per cent and 70 per cent of those in the rest of the country.

| DATE | AUTHOR'S LIFE | LITERARY CONTEXT |
|---|---|---|
| 1905–6(C) | Caddy uses perfume. | |
| 1907 | | |
| 1908(C) | Benjy is first required to sleep alone. | |
| 1909(C) | Caddy's loss of virginity. | Stein: *Three Lives.* |
| 1910(C) | Sydney Herbert Head marries Candace Compson (briefly). | |
| 1911(C) | Ms Quentin Compson born. | Dreiser: *Jennie Gerhardt.* |
| 1912(C) | Mr Compson dies. | |
| 1914 | | |
| 1915 (approx.) | | |
| 1916 | | Joyce: *A Portrait of the Artist as a Young Man.* Twain: *The Mysterious Stranger.* |
| 1917 | | Eliot: 'The Love Song of J. Alfred Prufrock'. |
| 1919 | | Anderson: *Winesburg, Ohio.* |
| 1920 | | Anderson: *Poor White.* Fitzgerald: *This Side of Paradise.* Lewis: *Main Street.* |
| 1921 | | |
| 1922 | | Eliot: *The Waste Land.* Lewis: *Babbitt.* |
| 1923 | | Toomer: *Cane.* |
| 1924 | *The Marble Faun*, a book of poems. | Hemingway: *In Our Time.* |
| 1925 | *Soldiers' Pay.* | Anderson: *Dark Laughter.* Dos Passos: *Manhattan Transfer.* Dreiser: *An American Tragedy.* Fitzgerald: *The Great Gatsby.* Glasgow: *Barren Ground.* |
| 1927 | *Mosquitoes.* | Cather: *Death Comes for the Archbishop.* |
| 1928 | Liveright rejects the manuscript of the third novel, *Flags in the Dust* (published in revised form as *Sartoris* in 1929). Begins to write *The Sound and the Fury* in the spring and finishes by early fall. | |

# CHRONOLOGY

Immigration at its highest (1,285,000).

Freud and Jung visit America, lecturing at Harvard. First Model T Ford marketed.
Date of Old South's termination, according to C. Vann Woodward.

Margaret Sangar indicted and forced to leave America for sending birth control information through the mail.
Start of black exodus to the North (half a million by 1920).

The United Daughters of the Confederacy and the Daughters of the American Revolution work openly for women's suffrage in Mississippi.

Eighteenth Amendment (Prohibition).
Nineteenth Amendment (Female Suffrage) passed by the House, but blocked in the Senate for a year by Southerners.
First advertisements showing a woman holding a cigarette.
Mississippi state legislature outlaws advocacy of 'social equality' in printed form.
Spring seeding of largest Southern cotton crop since 1914. December, most drastic price collapse in Southern history.
Emergency immigration restriction law.
Three-year government survey into cotton concludes, 'New York is the most important source of cotton loans' (i.e. South still an internal colony).

The 'Monkey Trial' in Dayton, Tennessee, finds for *Genesis* and signals the withdrawal of Southern culture into other-worldliness.

Lindbergh flies Atlantic. Sacco and Vanzetti executed.

First television broadcast. First full-length sound film.

| DATE | AUTHOR'S LIFE | LITERARY CONTEXT |
|------|---------------|------------------|
| 1929 | After rejection by Harcourt, Brace, the new firm of Cape and Smith publishes *The Sound and the Fury* in an edition of 1,789 copies. Faulkner marries Estelle Oldham Franklin after her divorce is finalized in April. Takes copy of *Ulysses* on honeymoon, suggesting that Estelle should read it. The Faulkner's first child, Alabama, is born prematurely and dies after only a few days. | Hemingway: *A Farewell to Arms*. Wolfe: *Look Homeward, Angel*. |
| 1930 | *As I Lay Dying*. | Twelve Southerners: *I'll Take My Stand: The South and the Agrarian Tradition*. |
| 1931 | *Sanctuary*. | |
| 1932 | *Light in August*. Accepts first contract as a scriptwriter in Hollywood with Metro-Goldwyn-Mayer (May–October). | Caldwell: *Tobacco Road*. |
| 1933 | The Faulkners' daughter Jill is born. There is a discussion of a reissue of *The Sound and the Fury* that would follow the author's suggestion that different coloured inks be used to indicate various time periods in section one. Faulkner writes an introduction, but the project collapses. | West: *Miss Lonelyhearts*. Hemingway: *Winner Take Nothing*. |
| 1934 | | Fitzgerald: *Tender is the Night*. |
| 1935 | *Pylon*. | |
| 1936 | *Absalom, Absalom!* | |
| 1937 | | Steinbeck: *Of Mice and Men*. |
| 1938 | | Tate: *The Fathers*. Dos Passos: *U.S.A.* |
| 1939 | *The Wild Palms*. | Steinbeck: *The Grapes of Wrath*. |
| 1940 | *The Hamlet* (first of three-volume Snopes Trilogy). | Hemingway: *For Whom the Bell Tolls*. Wright: *Native Son*. Stead: *The Man Who Loved Children*. |
| 1941 | | Fitzgerald: *The Last Tycoon*. |

# CHRONOLOGY

HISTORICAL EVENTS

Wall Street Crash.

Lindbergh kidnapping.
Roosevelt elected President.

Roosevelt announces 'New Deal'.

Trans-continental air-service begins in US.

US enters World War.

| DATE | AUTHOR'S LIFE | LITERARY CONTEXT |
|------|---------------|------------------|
| 1942 | *Go Down, Moses.* In desperate financial circumstances from the mid '30s to the mid '40s, Faulkner writes short stories for quick returns. *Go Down Moses* is a novel reworked from earlier stories. Accepts a long but low-paying contract for scriptwriting from Warner Brothers. | |
| 1943 | | |
| 1948 | *Intruder in the Dust.* | |
| 1950 | *Collected Stories.* Wins the 1949 Nobel Prize for Literature. Financial security follows wide recognition for the first time in his career. Increasingly a public figure. | |
| 1951 | *Requiem for a Nun.* | |
| 1952 | | O'Connor: *Wise Blood.* |
| 1954 | *A Fable.* | |
| 1957 | *The Town* (second volume of Snopes Trilogy). | |
| 1959 | *The Mansion* (final Snopes volume). | |
| 1960 | | O'Connor: *The Violent Bear It Away.* |
| 1962 | *The Reivers.* Faulkner dies. | |
| 1963 | | |

# CHRONOLOGY

HISTORICAL EVENTS

Mechanical cotton-harvester (patented late nineteenth century) first used in Mississippi.

Korean War.

Kennedy becomes President.

Kennedy assassinated.

# *April Seventh*
## 1928

THROUGH the fence, between the curling flower spaces, I could see them hitting. They were coming toward where the flag was and I went along the fence. Luster was hunting in the grass by the flower tree. They took the flag out, and they were hitting. Then they put the flag back and they went to the table, and he hit and the other hit. Then they went on, and I went along the fence. Luster came away from the flower tree and we went along the fence and they stopped and we stopped and I looked through the fence while Luster was hunting in the grass.

'Here, caddie.' He hit. They went away across the pasture. I held to the fence and watched them going away.

'Listen at you, now.' Luster said. 'Ain't you something, thirty-three years old, going on that way. After I done went all the way to town to buy you that cake. Hush up that moaning. Ain't you going to help me find that quarter so I can go to the show tonight.'

They were hitting little, across the pasture. I went back along the fence to where the flag was. It flapped on the bright grass and the trees.

'Come on.' Luster said. 'We done looked there. They ain't no more coming right now. Let's go down to the branch and find that quarter before them niggers finds it.'

It was red, flapping on the pasture. Then there was a bird slanting and tilting on it. Luster threw. The flag flapped on the bright grass and the trees. I held to the fence.

'Shut up that moaning.' Luster said. 'I can't make

them come if they ain't coming, can I. If you don't hush up, mammy ain't going to have no birthday for you. If you don't hush, you know what I going to do. I going to eat that cake all up. Eat them candles, too. Eat all them thirty-three candles. Come on, let's go down to the branch. I got to find my quarter. Maybe we can find one of they balls. Here. Here they is. Way over yonder. See.' He came to the fence and pointed his arm. 'See them. They ain't coming back here no more. Come on.'

We went along the fence and came to the garden fence, where our shadows were. My shadow was higher than Luster's on the fence. We came to the broken place and went through it.

'Wait a minute.' Luster said. 'You snagged on that nail again. Can't you never crawl through here without snagging on that nail.'

*Caddy uncaught me and we crawled through. Uncle Maury said to not let anybody see us, so we better stoop over, Caddy said. Stoop over, Benjy. Like this, see. We stooped over and crossed the garden, where the flowers rasped and rattled against us. The ground was hard. We climbed the fence, where the pigs were grunting and snuffing. I expect they're sorry because one of them got killed today, Caddy said. The ground was hard, churned and knotted.*

*Keep your hands in your pockets, Caddy said. Or they'll get froze. You don't want your hands froze on Christmas, do you.*

'It's too cold out there.' Versh said. 'You don't want to go out doors.'

'What is it now.' Mother said.

'He want to go out doors.' Versh said.

'Let him go.' Uncle Maury said.

'It's too cold.' Mother said. 'He'd better stay in. Benjamin. Stop that, now.'

'It won't hurt him.' Uncle Maury said.

'You, Benjamin.' Mother said. 'If you don't be good, you'll have to go to the kitchen.'

'Mammy say keep him out the kitchen today.' Versh said. 'She say she got all that cooking to get done.'

'Let him go, Caroline.' Uncle Maury said. 'You'll worry yourself sick over him.'

'I know it.' Mother said. 'It's a judgment on me. I sometimes wonder'

'I know, I know.' Uncle Maury said. 'You must keep your strength up. I'll make you a toddy.'

'It just upsets me that much more.' Mother said. 'Don't you know it does.'

'You'll feel better.' Uncle Maury said. 'Wrap him up good, boy, and take him out for a while.'

Uncle Maury went away. Versh went away.

'Please hush.' Mother said. 'We're trying to get you out as fast as we can. I don't want you to get sick.'

Versh put my overshoes and overcoat on and we took my cap and went out. Uncle Maury was putting the bottle away in the sideboard in the dining-room.

'Keep him out about half an hour, boy.' Uncle Maury said. 'Keep him in the yard, now.'

'Yes, sir.' Versh said. 'We don't never let him get off the place.'

We went out doors. The sun was cold and bright.

'Where you heading for.' Versh said. 'You don't think you going to town, does you.' We went through the rattling leaves. The gate was cold. 'You better keep them hands in your pockets.' Versh said, 'You get them froze onto that gate, then what you do. Whyn't you wait for them in the house.' He put my hands into my pockets. I could hear him rattling in the leaves. I could smell the cold. The gate was cold.

'Here some hickeynuts. Whooey. Git up that tree. Look here at this squirl, Benjy.'

I couldn't feel the gate at all, but I could smell the bright cold.

'You better put them hands back in your pockets.'

Caddy was walking. Then she was running, her booksatchel swinging and jouncing behind her.

'Hello, Benjy.' Caddy said. She opened the gate and came in and stooped down. Caddy smelled like leaves.

'Did you come to meet me.' she said. 'Did you come to meet Caddy. What did you let him get his hands so cold for, Versh.'

'I told him to keep them in his pockets.' Versh said. 'Holding onto that ahun gate.'

'Did you come to meet Caddy.' she said, rubbing my hands. 'What is it. What are you trying to tell Caddy.' Caddy smelled like trees and like when she says we were asleep.

*What are you moaning about, Luster said. You can watch them again when we get to the branch. Here. Here's you a jim-son weed. He gave me the flower. We went through the fence, into the lot.*

'What is it.' Caddy said. 'What are you trying to tell Caddy. Did they send him out, Versh.'

'Couldn't keep him in.' Versh said. 'He kept on until they let him go and he come right straight down here, looking through the gate.'

'What is it.' Caddy said. 'Did you think it would be Christmas when I came home from school. Is that what you thought. Christmas is the day after tomorrow. Santy Claus, Benjy. Santy Claus. Come on, let's run to the house and get warm.' She took my hand and we ran through the bright rustling leaves. We ran up the steps and out of the bright cold, into the dark cold. Uncle Maury was putting the bottle back in the sideboard. He called Caddy. Caddy said,

'Take him in to the fire, Versh. Go with Versh.' she said. 'I'll come in a minute.'

We went to the fire. Mother said,

'Is he cold, Versh.'

'Nome.' Versh said.

'Take his overcoat and overshoes off.' Mother said. 'How many times do I have to tell you not to bring him into the house with his overshoes on.

'Yessum.' Versh said. 'Hold still, now.' He took my overshoes off and unbuttoned my coat. Caddy said,

'Wait, Versh. Can't he go out again, Mother. I want him to go with me.'

'You'd better leave him here.' Uncle Maury said. 'He's been out enough today.'

'I think you'd both better stay in.' Mother said. 'It's getting colder, Dilsey says.'

'Oh, Mother.' Caddy said.

'Nonsense.' Uncle Maury said. 'She's been in school all day. She needs the fresh air. Run along, Candace.'

'Let him go, Mother.' Caddy said. 'Please. You know he'll cry.'

'Then why did you mention it before him.' Mother said. 'Why did you come in here. To give him some excuse to worry me again. You've been out enough today. I think you'd better sit down here and play with him.'

'Let them go, Caroline.' Uncle Maury said. 'A little cold won't hurt them. Remember, you've got to keep your strength up.'

'I know.' Mother said. 'Nobody knows how I dread Christmas. Nobody knows. I am not one of those women who can stand things. I wish for Jason's and the children's sakes I was stronger.'

'You must do the best you can and not let them worry you.' Uncle Maury said. 'Run along, you two. But don't stay out long, now. Your mother will worry.'

'Yes, sir.' Caddy said. 'Come on, Benjy. We're going out doors again.' She buttoned my coat and we went toward the door.

'Are you going to take that baby out without his overshoes.' Mother said. 'Do you want to make him sick, with the house full of company.'

'I forgot.' Caddy said. 'I thought he had them on.'

We went back. 'You must think.' Mother said. *Hold still now* Versh said. He put my overshoes on. 'Someday I'll be gone, and you'll have to think for him.' *Now stomp* Versh said. 'Come here and kiss Mother, Benjamin.'

Caddy took me to Mother's chair and Mother took

my face in her hands and then she held me against her.

'My poor baby.' she said. She let me go. 'You and Versh take good care of him, honey.'

'Yessum.' Caddy said. We went out. Caddy said,

'You needn't go, Versh. I'll keep him for a while.'

'All right.' Versh said. 'I ain't going out in that cold for no fun.' He went on and we stopped in the hall and Caddy knelt and put her arms around me and her cold bright face against mine. She smelled like trees.

'You're not a poor baby. Are you. You've got your Caddy. Haven't you got your Caddy.'

*Can't you shut up that moaning and slobbering, Luster said. Ain't you shamed of yourself, making all this racket. We passed the carriage house, where the carriage was. It had a new wheel.*

'Git in, now, and set still until your maw come.' Dilsey said. She shoved me into the carriage. T. P. held the reins. ''Clare I don't see how come Jason won't get a new surrey.' Dilsey said. 'This thing going to fall to pieces under you all some day. Look at them wheels.'

Mother came out, pulling her veil down. She had some flowers.

'Where's Roskus.' she said.

'Roskus can't lift his arms, today.' Dilsey said. 'T. P. can drive all right.'

'I'm afraid to.' Mother said. 'It seems to me you all could furnish me with a driver for the carriage once a week. It's little enough I ask, Lord knows.'

'You know just as well as me that Roskus got the rheumatism too bad to do more than he have to, Miss Cahline.' Dilsey said. 'You come on and get in, now. T. P. can drive you just as good as Roskus.'

'I'm afraid to.' Mother said. 'With the baby.'

Dilsey went up the steps. 'You calling that thing a baby,' she said. She took Mother's arm. 'A man big as T. P. Come on, now, if you going.'

'I'm afraid to.' Mother said. They came down the steps and Dilsey helped Mother in. 'Perhaps it'll be the best thing, for all of us.' Mother said.

'Ain't you shamed, talking that way.' Dilsey said.
'Don't you know it'll take more than a eighteen year old
nigger to make Queenie run away. She older than him
and Benjy put together. And don't you start no projecking with Queenie, you hear me, T. P. If you don't drive to
suit Miss Cahline, I going to put Roskus on you. He ain't
too tied up to do that.'

'Yessum.' T. P. said.

'I just know something will happen.' Mother said.
'Stop, Benjamin.'

'Give him a flower to hold.' Dilsey said, 'That what he
wanting.' She reached her hand in.

'No, no.' Mother said. 'You'll have them all scattered.'

'You hold them.' Dilsey said. 'I'll get him one out.'
She gave me a flower and her hand went away.

'Go on now, 'fore Quentin see you and have to go too.'
Dilsey said.

'Where is she.' Mother said.

'She down to the house playing with Luster.' Dilsey
said. 'Go on, T. P. Drive that surrey like Roskus told you,
now.'

'Yessum.' T. P. said. 'Hum up, Queenie.'

'Quentin.' Mother said. 'Don't let'

'Course I is.' Dilsey said.

The carriage jolted and crunched on the drive. 'I'm
afraid to go and leave Quentin.' Mother said. 'I'd better
not go. T. P.' We went through the gate, where it didn't
jolt any more. T. P. hit Queenie with the whip.

'You, T. P.' Mother said.

'Got to get her going.' T. P. said. 'Keep her wake up
till we get back to the barn.'

'Turn around.' Mother said. 'I'm afraid to go and leave
Quentin.'

'Can't turn here.' T. P. said. Then it was broader.

'Can't you turn here.' Mother said.

'All right.' T. P. said. We began to turn.

'You, T. P.' Mother said, clutching me.

7

'I got to turn around somehow.' T. P. said. 'Whoa, Queenie.' We stopped.

'You'll turn us over.' Mother said.

'What you want to do, then.' T. P. said.

'I'm afraid for you to try to turn around.' Mother said.

'Get up, Queenie.' T. P. said. We went on.

'I just know Dilsey will let something happen to Quentin while I'm gone.' Mother said. 'We must hurry back.'

'Hum up, there.' T. P. said. He hit Queenie with the whip.

'You, T. P.' Mother said, clutching me. I could hear Queenie's feet and the bright shapes went smooth and steady on both sides, the shadows of them flowing across Queenie's back. They went on like the bright tops of wheels. Then those on one side stopped at the tall white post where the soldier was. But on the other side they went on smooth and steady, but a little slower.

'What do you want.' Jason said. He had his hands in his pockets and a pencil behind his ear.

'We're going to the cemetery.' Mother said.

'All right.' Jason said. 'I don't aim to stop you, do I. Was that all you wanted with me, just to tell me that.'

'I know you won't come.' Mother said. 'I'd feel safer if you would.'

'Safe from what.' Jason said. 'Father and Quentin can't hurt you.'

Mother put her handkerchief under her veil. 'Stop it, Mother.' Jason said. 'Do you want to get that damn loony to bawling in the middle of the square. Drive on, T. P.'

'Hum up, Queenie.' T. P. said.

'It's a judgment on me.' Mother said. 'But I'll be gone too, soon.'

'Here.' Jason said.

'Whoa.' T. P. said. Jason said,

'Uncle Maury's drawing on you for fifty. What do you want to do about it.'

'Why ask me.' Mother said. 'I don't have any say so. I

try not to worry you and Dilsey. I'll be gone soon, and then you'

'Go on, T. P.' Jason said.

'Hum up, Queenie.' T. P. said. The shapes flowed on. The ones on the other side began again, bright and fast and smooth, like when Caddy says we are going to sleep.

*Cry baby, Luster said. Ain't you shamed. We went through the barn. The stalls were all open. You ain't got no spotted pony to ride now, Luster said. The floor was dry and dusty. The roof was falling. The slanting holes were full of spinning yellow. What do you want to go that way for. You want to get your head knocked off with one of them balls.*

'Keep your hands in your pockets.' Caddy said, 'Or they'll be froze. You don't want your hands froze on Christmas, do you.'

We went around the barn. The big cow and the little one were standing in the door, and we could hear Prince and Queenie and Fancy stomping inside the barn. 'If it wasn't so cold, we'd ride Fancy.' Caddy said, 'But it's too cold to hold on today.' Then we could see the branch, where the smoke was blowing. 'That's where they are killing the pig.' Caddy said. 'We can come back by there and see them.' We went down the hill.

'You want to carry the letter.' Caddy said. 'You can carry it.' She took the letter out of her pocket and put it in mine. 'It's a Christmas present.' Caddy said. 'Uncle Maury is going to surprise Mrs. Patterson with it. We got to give it to her without letting anybody see it. Keep your hands in your pockets good, now.' We came to the branch.

'It's froze.' Caddy said, 'Look.' She broke the top of the water and held a piece of it against my face. 'Ice. That means how cold it is.' She helped me across and we went up the hill. 'We can't even tell Mother and Father. You know what I think it is. I think it's a surprise for Mother and Father and Mr. Patterson both, because Mr. Patterson sent you some candy. Do you remember when Mr. Patterson sent you some candy last summer.'

There was a fence. The vine was dry, and the wind rattled in it.

'Only I don't see why Uncle Maury didn't send Versh.' Caddy said. 'Versh won't tell.' Mrs. Patterson was looking out the window. 'You wait here.' Caddy said. 'Wait right here, now. I'll be back in a minute. Give me the letter.' She took the letter out of my pocket. 'Keep your hands in your pockets.' She climbed the fence with the letter in her hand and went through the brown, rattling flowers. Mrs. Patterson came to the door and opened it and stood there.

*Mr. Patterson was chopping in the green flowers. He stopped chopping and looked at me. Mrs. Patterson came across the garden, running. When I saw her eyes I began to cry. You idiot, Mrs. Patterson said, I told him never to send you alone again. Give it to me. Quick. Mr. Patterson came fast, with the hoe. Mrs. Patterson leaned across the fence, reaching her hand. She was trying to climb the fence. Give it to me, she said, Give it to me. Mr. Patterson climbed the fence. He took the letter. Mrs. Patterson's dress was caught on the fence. I saw her eyes again and I ran down the hill.*

'They ain't nothing over yonder but houses.' Luster said. 'We going down to the branch.'

They were washing down at the branch. One of them was singing. I could smell the clothes flapping, and the smoke blowing across the branch.

'You stay down here.' Luster said. 'You ain't got no business up yonder. Them folks hit you, sho.'

'What he want to do.'

'He don't know what he want to do.' Luster said. 'He think he want to go up yonder where they knocking that ball. You sit down here and play with your jimson weed. Look at them chillen playing in the branch, if you got to look at something. How come you can't behave yourself like folks.' I sat down on the bank, where they were washing, and the smoke blowing blue.

'Is you all seen anything of a quarter down here.' Luster said.

'What quarter.'

'The one I had here this morning.' Luster said. 'I lost it somewhere. It fell through this here hole in my pocket. If I don't find it I can't go to the show tonight.'

'Where'd you get a quarter, boy. Find it in white folks' pocket while they ain't looking.'

'Got it at the getting place.' Luster said. 'Plenty more where that one come from. Only I got to find that one. Is you all found it yet.'

'I ain't studying no quarter. I got my own business to tend to.'

'Come on here.' Luster said. 'Help me look for it.'

'He wouldn't know a quarter if he was to see it, would he.'

'He can help look just the same.' Luster said. 'You all going to the show tonight.'

'Don't talk to me about no show. Time I get done over this here tub I be too tired to lift my hand to do nothing.'

'I bet you be there.' Luster said. 'I bet you was there last night. I bet you all be right there when that tent open.'

'Be enough niggers there without me. Was last night.'

'Nigger's money good as white folks, I reckon.'

'White folks gives nigger money because know first white man comes along with a band going to get it all back, so nigger can go to work for some more.'

'Ain't nobody going make you go to that show.'

'Ain't yet. Ain't thought of it, I reckon.'

'What you got against white folks.'

'Ain't got nothing against them. I goes my way and lets white folks go theirs. I ain't studying that show.'

'Got a man in it can play a tune on a saw. Play it like a banjo.'

'You go last night.' Luster said. 'I going tonight. If I can find where I lost that quarter.'

'You going take him with you, I reckon.'

'Me.' Luster said. 'You reckon I be found anywhere with him, time he start bellering.'

*11*

'What does you do when he start bellering.'

'I whips him.' Luster said. He sat down and rolled up his overalls. They played in the branch.

'You all found any balls yet.' Luster said.

'Ain't you talking biggity. I bet you better not let your grandmammy hear you talking like that.'

Luster got into the branch, where they were playing. He hunted in the water, along the bank.

'I had it when we was down here this morning.' Luster said.

'Where 'bouts you lose it.'

'Right out this here hole in my pocket.' Luster said. They hunted in the branch. Then they all stood up quick and stopped, then they splashed and fought in the branch. Luster got it and they squatted in the water, looking up the hill through the bushes.

'Where is they.' Luster said.

'Ain't in sight yet.'

Luster put it in his pocket. They came down the hill.

'Did a ball come down here.'

'It ought to be in the water. Didn't any of you boys see it or hear it.'

'Ain't heard nothing come down here.' Luster said. 'Heard something hit that tree up yonder. Don't know which way it went.'

They looked in the branch.

'Hell. Look along the branch. It came down here. I saw it.'

They looked along the branch. Then they went back up the hill.

'Have you got that ball.' the boy said.

'What I want with it.' Luster said. 'I ain't seen no ball.'

The boy got in the water. He went on. He turned and looked at Luster again. He went on down the branch.

The man said 'Caddie' up the hill. The boy got out of the water and went up the hill.

'Now, just listen at you.' Luster said. 'Hush up.'

'What he moaning about now.'

'Lawd knows.' Luster said. 'He just starts like that. He been at it all morning. Cause it his birthday, I reckon.'

'How old he.'

'He thirty-three.' Luster said. 'Thirty-three this morning.'

'You mean, he been three years old thirty years.'

'I going by what mammy say.' Luster said. 'I don't know. We going to have thirty-three candles on a cake, anyway. Little cake. Won't hardly hold them. Hush up. Come on back here.' He came and caught my arm. 'You old loony.' he said. 'You want me to whip you.'

'I bet you will.'

'I is done it. Hush, now.' Luster said. 'Ain't I told you you can't go up there. They'll knock your head clean off with one of them balls. Come on, here.' He pulled me back. 'Sit down.' I sat down and he took off my shoes and rolled up my trousers. 'Now, git in that water and play and see can you stop that slobbering and moaning.'

I hushed and got in the water *and Roskus came and said to come to supper and Caddy said,*

*It's not supper time yet. I'm not going.*

She was wet. We were playing in the branch and Caddy squatted down and got her dress wet and Versh said,

'Your mommer going to whip you for getting your dress wet.'

'She's not going to do any such thing.' Caddy said.

'How do you know.' Quentin said.

'That's all right how I know.' Caddy said. 'How do you know.'

'She said she was.' Quentin said. 'Besides, I'm older than you.'

'I'm seven years old.' Caddy said, 'I guess I know.'

'I'm older than that.' Quentin said. 'I go to school. Don't I, Versh.'

'I'm going to school next year.' Caddy said, 'When it comes. Ain't I, Versh.'

'You know she whip you when you get your dress wet.' Versh said.

'It's not wet.' Caddy said. She stood up in the water and looked at her dress. 'I'll take it off,' she said. 'Then it'll dry.'

'I bet you won't.' Quentin said.

'I bet I will.' Caddy said.

'I bet you better not.' Quentin said.

Caddy came to Versh and me and turned her back.

'Unbutton it, Versh.' she said.

'Don't you do it, Versh.' Quentin said.

'Tain't none of my dress.' Versh said.

'You unbutton it, Versh.' Caddy said, 'Or I'll tell Dilsey what you did yesterday.' So Versh unbuttoned it.

'You just take your dress off.' Quentin said. Caddy took her dress off and threw it on the bank. Then she didn't have on anything but her bodice and drawers, and Quentin slapped her and she slipped and fell down in the water. When she got up she began to splash water on Quentin, and Quentin splashed water on Caddy. Some of it splashed on Versh and me and Versh picked me up and put me on the bank. He said he was going to tell on Caddy and Quentin, and then Quentin and Caddy began to splash water at Versh. He got behind a bush.

'I'm going to tell mammy on you all.' Versh said.

Quentin climbed up the bank and tried to catch Versh, but Versh ran away and Quentin couldn't. When Quentin came back Versh stopped and hollered that he was going to tell. Caddy told him that if he wouldn't tell, they'd let him come back. So Versh said he wouldn't, and they let him.

'Now I guess you're satisfied.' Quentin said, 'We'll both get whipped now.'

'I don't care.' Caddy said. 'I'll run away.'

'Yes you will.' Quentin said.

'I'll run away and never come back.' Caddy said. I began to cry. Caddy turned around and said 'Hush.' So I

hushed. Then they played in the branch. Jason was playing too. He was by himself further down the branch.
Versh came around the bush and lifted me down into the
water again. Caddy was all wet and muddy behind, and I
started to cry and she came and squatted in the water.

'Hush now.' she said. 'I'm not going to run away.' So I
hushed. Caddy smelled like trees in the rain.

*What is the matter with you, Luster said. Can't you get done
with that moaning and play in the branch like folks.*

*Whyn't you take him on home. Didn't they told you not to
take him off the place.*

*He still think they own this pasture, Luster said. Can't
nobody see down here from the house, noways.*

*We can. And folks don't like to look at a loony. Tain't no
luck in it.*

Roskus came and said to come to supper and Caddy
said it wasn't supper time yet.

'Yes 'tis.' Roskus said. 'Dilsey say for you all to come
on to the house. Bring them on, Versh.' He went up the
hill, where the cow was lowing.

'Maybe we'll be dry by the time we get to the house.'
Quentin said.

'It was all your fault.' Caddy said. 'I hope we do get
whipped.' She put her dress on and Versh buttoned it.

'They won't know you got wet.' Versh said. 'It don't
show on you. Less me and Jason tells.'

'Are you going to tell, Jason.' Caddy said.

'Tell on who.' Jason said.

'He won't tell.' Quentin said. 'Will you, Jason.'

'I bet he does tell.' Caddy said. 'He'll tell Damuddy.'

'He can't tell her.' Quentin said. 'She's sick. If we
walk slow it'll be too dark for them to see.'

'I don't care whether they see or not.' Caddy said. 'I'm
going to tell, myself. You carry him up the hill, Versh.'

'Jason won't tell.' Quentin said. 'You remember that
bow and arrow I made you, Jason.'

'It's broke now.' Jason said.

'Let him tell.' Caddy said. 'I don't give a cuss. Carry

*15*

Maury up the hill, Versh.' Versh squatted and I got on his back.

*See you all at the show tonight, Luster said. Come on, here. We got to find that quarter.*

'If we go slow, it'll be dark when we get there.' Quentin said.

'I'm not going slow.' Caddy said. We went up the hill, but Quentin didn't come. He was down at the branch when we got to where we could smell the pigs. They were grunting and snuffing in the trough in the corner. Jason came behind us, with his hands in his pockets. Roskus was milking the cow in the barn door.

*The cows came jumping out of the barn.*

'Go on.' T. P. said. 'Holler again. I going to holler myself. Whooey.' Quentin kicked T. P. again. He kicked T. P. into the trough where the pigs ate and T. P. lay there. 'Hot dog.' T. P. said, 'Didn't he get me then. You see that white man kick me that time. Whooey.'

I wasn't crying, but I couldn't stop. I wasn't crying, but the ground wasn't still, and then I was crying. The ground kept sloping up and the cows ran up the hill. T. P. tried to get up. He fell down again and the cows ran down the hill. Quentin held my arm and we went toward the barn. Then the barn wasn't there and we had to wait until it came back. I didn't see it come back. It came behind us and Quentin set me down in the trough where the cows ate. I held on to it. It was going away too, and I held to it. The cows ran down the hill again, across the door. I couldn't stop. Quentin and T. P. came up the hill, fighting. T. P. was falling down the hill and Quentin dragged him up the hill. Quentin hit T. P. I couldn't stop.

'Stand up.' Quentin said, 'You stay right here. Don't you go away until I get back.'

'Me and Benjy going back to the wedding.' T. P. said. 'Whooey.'

Quentin hit T. P. again. Then he began to thump T. P. against the wall. T. P. was laughing. Every time Quentin thumped him against the wall he tried to say Whooey, but he couldn't say it for laughing. I quit crying, but I couldn't stop. T. P. fell on me and the barn door went away. It went down the hill and T. P. was fighting by himself and he fell down again. He was still laughing, and I couldn't stop, and I tried to get up and fell down, and I couldn't stop. Versh said,

'You sho done it now. I'll declare if you ain't. Shut up that yelling.'

T. P. was still laughing. He flopped on the door and laughed. 'Whooey.' he said, 'Me and Benjy going back to the wedding. Sassprilluh.' T. P. said.

'Hush.' Versh said. 'Where you get it.'

'Out the cellar.' T. P. said. 'Whooey.'

'Hush up.' Versh said, 'Where'bouts in the cellar.'

'Anywhere.' T. P. said. He laughed some more. 'More'n a hundred bottles left. More'n a million. Look out, nigger, I going to holler.'

Quentin said, 'Lift him up.'

Versh lifted me up.

'Drink this, Benjy.' Quentin said. The glass was hot. 'Hush, now.' Quentin said. 'Drink it.'

'Sassprilluh.' T. P. said. 'Lemme drink it, Mr. Quentin.'

'You shut your mouth.' Versh said, 'Mr. Quentin wear you out.

'Hold him, Versh.' Quentin said.

They held me. It was hot on my chin and on my shirt. 'Drink.' Quentin said. They held my head. It was hot inside me, and I began again. I was crying now, and something was happening inside me and I cried more, and they held me until it stopped happening. Then I hushed. It was still going around, and then the shapes began. 'Open the crib, Versh.' They were going slow. 'Spread those empty sacks on the floor.' They were going faster, almost fast enough. 'Now. Pick up his feet.' They went on, smooth and bright. I could hear T. P. laughing. I went on with them, up the bright hill.

*At the top of the hill Versh put me down.* 'Come on here,

17

Quentin.' he called, looking back down the hill. Quentin was still standing there by the branch. He was chunking into the shadows where the branch was.

'Let the old skizzard stay there.' Caddy said. She took my hand and we went on past the barn and through the gate. There was a frog on the brick walk, squatting in the middle of it. Caddy stepped over it and pulled me on.

'Come on, Maury.' she said. It still squatted there until Jason poked at it with his toe.

'He'll make a wart on you.' Versh said. The frog hopped away.

'Come on, Maury.' Caddy said.

'They got company tonight.' Versh said.

'How do you know.' Caddy said.

'With all them lights on.' Versh said, 'Light in every window.'

'I reckon we can turn all the lights on without company, if we want to.' Caddy said.

'I bet it's company.' Versh said. 'You all better go in the back and slip upstairs.'

'I don't care.' Caddy said. 'I'll walk right in the parlour where they are.'

'I bet your pappy whip you if you do.' Versh said.

'I don't care.' Caddy said. 'I'll walk right in the parlour; I'll walk right in the dining-room and eat supper.'

'Where you sit.' Versh said.

'I'd sit in Damuddy's chair.' Caddy said. 'She eats in bed.'

'I'm hungry.' Jason said. He passed us and ran on up the walk. He had his hands in his pockets and he fell down. Versh went and picked him up.

'If you keep them hands out your pockets, you could stay on your feet.' Versh said. 'You can't never get them out in time to catch yourself, fat as you is.'

Father was standing by the kitchen steps.

'Where's Quentin.' he said.

'He coming up the walk.' Versh said. Quentin was coming slow. His shirt was a white blur.

'Oh.' Father said. Light fell down the steps, on him.

'Caddy and Quentin threw water on each other.' Jason said.

We waited.

'They did.' Father said. Quentin came, and Father said, 'You can eat supper in the kitchen tonight.' He stopped and took me up, and the light came tumbling down the steps on me too, and I could look down at Caddy and Jason and Quentin and Versh. Father turned toward the steps. 'You must be quiet, though.' he said.

'Why must we be quiet, Father.' Caddy said. 'Have we got company.'

'Yes.' Father said.

'I told you they was company.' Versh said.

'You did not.' Caddy said, 'I was the one that said there was. I said I would'

'Hush.' Father said. They hushed and Father opened the door and we crossed the back porch and went in to the kitchen. Dilsey was there, and Father put me in the chair and closed the apron down and pushed it to the table, where supper was. It was steaming up.

'You mind Dilsey, now.' Father said. 'Don't let them make any more noise than they can help, Dilsey.'

'Yes, sir.' Dilsey said. Father went away.

'Remember to mind Dilsey, now.' he said behind us. I leaned my face over where the supper was. It steamed up on my face.

'Let them mind me tonight, Father.' Caddy said.

'I won't.' Jason said. 'I'm going to mind Dilsey.'

'You'll have to, if Father says so.' Caddy said. 'Let them mind me, Father.'

'I won't.' Jason said, 'I won't mind you.'

'Hush.' Father said. 'You all mind Caddy, then. When they are done, bring them up the back stairs, Dilsey.'

'Yes, sir.' Dilsey said.

'There.' Caddy said, 'Now I guess you'll mind me.'

'You all hush, now.' Dilsey said. 'You got to be quiet tonight.'

'Why do we have to be quiet tonight.' Caddy whispered.

'Never you mind.' Dilsey said, 'You'll know in the Lawd's own time.' She brought my bowl. The steam from it came and tickled my face. 'Come here, Versh.' Dilsey said.

'When is the Lawd's own time, Dilsey.' Caddy said.

'It's Sunday.' Quentin said. 'Don't you know anything.'

'Shhhhhh.' Dilsey said. 'Didn't Mr. Jason say for you all to be quiet. Eat your supper, now. Here, Versh. Git his spoon.' Versh's hand came with the spoon, into the bowl. The spoon came up to my mouth. The steam tickled into my mouth. Then we quit eating and we looked at each other and we were quiet, and then we heard it again and I began to cry.

'What was that.' Caddy said. She put her hand on my hand.

'That was Mother.' Quentin said. The spoon came up and I ate, then I cried again.

'Hush.' Caddy said. But I didn't hush and she came and put her arms around me. Dilsey went and closed both the doors and then we couldn't hear it.

'Hush, now.' Caddy said. I hushed and ate. Quentin wasn't eating, but Jason was.

'That was Mother.' Quentin said. He got up.

'You set right down.' Dilsey said. 'They got company in there, and you in them muddy clothes. You set down too, Caddy, and get done eating.'

'She was crying.' Quentin said.

'It was somebody singing.' Caddy said. 'Wasn't it, Dilsey.'

'You all eat your supper, now, like Mr. Jason said.' Dilsey said. 'You'll know in the Lawd's own time.' Caddy went back to her chair.

'I told you it was a party.' she said.

Versh said, 'He done et all that.'

'Bring his bowl here.' Dilsey said. The bowl went away.

'Dilsey.' Caddy said, 'Quentin's not eating his supper. Hasn't he got to mind me.'

'Eat your supper, Quentin.' Dilsey said, 'You all got to get done and get out of my kitchen.'

'I don't want any more supper.' Quentin said.

'You've got to eat if I say you have.' Caddy said. 'Hasn't he, Dilsey.'

The bowl steamed up to my face, and Versh's hand dipped the spoon in it and the steam tickled into my mouth.

'I don't want any more.' Quentin said. 'How can they have a party when Damuddy's sick.'

'They'll have it downstairs.' Caddy said. 'She can come to the landing and see it. That's what I'm going to do when I get my nightie on.'

'Mother was crying.' Quentin said. 'Wasn't she crying, Dilsey.'

'Don't you come pestering at me, boy.' Dilsey said. 'I got to get supper for all them folks soon as you all get done eating.'

After a while even Jason was through eating, and he began to cry.

'Now you got to tune up.' Dilsey said.

'He does it every night since Damuddy was sick and he can't sleep with her.' Caddy said. 'Cry baby.'

'I'm going to tell on you.' Jason said.

He was crying. 'You've already told.' Caddy said. 'There's not anything else you can tell, now.'

'You all needs to go to bed.' Dilsey said. She came and lifted me down and wiped my face and hands with a warm cloth. 'Versh, can you get them up the back stairs quiet. You, Jason, shut up that crying.'

'It's too early to go to bed now.' Caddy said. 'We don't ever have to go to bed this early.'

'You is tonight.' Dilsey said. 'Your pa say for you to come right on upstairs when you et supper. You heard him.'

'He said to mind me.' Caddy said.

'I'm not going to mind you.' Jason said.

'You have to.' Caddy said. 'Come on, now. You have to do like I say.'

'Make them be quiet, Versh.' Dilsey said. 'You all going to be quiet, ain't you.'

'What do we have to be so quiet for, tonight.' Caddy said.

'Your mommer ain't feeling well.' Dilsey said. 'You all go on with Versh, now.'

'I told you Mother was crying.' Quentin said. Versh took me up and opened the door onto the back porch. We went out and Versh closed the door black. I could smell Versh and feel him. 'You all be quiet, now. We're not going upstairs yet. Mr. Jason said for you to come right upstairs. He said to mind me. I'm not going to mind you. But he said for all of us to. Didn't he, Quentin.' I could feel Versh's head. I could hear us. 'Didn't he, Versh. Yes, that's right. Then I say for us to go out doors a while. Come on.' Versh opened the door and we went out.

We went down the steps.

'I expect we'd better go down to Versh's house, so we'll be quiet.' Caddy said. Versh put me down and Caddy took my hand and we went down the brick walk.

'Come on.' Caddy said, 'That frog's gone. He's hopped way over to the garden, by now. Maybe we'll see another one.' Roskus came with the milk buckets. He went on. Quentin wasn't coming with us. He was sitting on the kitchen steps. We went down to Versh's house. I liked to smell Versh's house. *There was a fire in it and T. P. squatting in his shirt tail in front of it, chunking it into a blaze.*

Then I got up and T. P. dressed me and we went to the kitchen and ate. Dilsey was singing and I began to cry and she stopped.

'Keep him away from the house, now.' Dilsey said.

'We can't go that way.' T. P. said.

We played in the branch.

'We can't go around yonder.' T. P. said. 'Don't you know mammy say we can't.'

Dilsey was singing in the kitchen and I began to cry.

'Hush.' T. P. said. 'Come on. Let's go down to the barn.'

Roskus was milking at the barn. He was milking with one hand, and groaning. Some birds sat on the barn door and watched him. One of them came down and ate with the cows. I watched Roskus milk while T. P. was feeding Queenie and Prince. The calf was in the pig pen. It nuzzled at the wire, bawling.

'T. P.' Roskus said. T. P. said Sir, in the barn. Fancy held her head over the door, because T. P. hadn't fed her yet. 'Gid done there.' Roskus said. 'You got to do this milking. I can't use my right hand no more.'

T. P. came and milked.

'Whyn't you get the doctor.' T. P. said.

'Doctor can't do no good.' Roskus said. 'Not on this place.'

'What wrong with this place.' T. P. said.

'Tain't no luck on this place.' Roskus said. 'Turn that calf in if you done.'

*Tain't no luck on this place, Roskus said. The fire rose and fell behind him and Versh, sliding on his and Versh's face. Dilsey finished putting me to bed. The bed smelled like T. P. I liked it.*

'What you know about it.' Dilsey said. 'What trance you been in.'

'Don't need no trance.' Roskus said. 'Ain't the sign of it laying right there on that bed. Ain't the sign of it been here for folks to see fifteen years now.'

'S'pose it is.' Dilsey said. 'It ain't hurt none of you and yourn, is it. Versh working and Frony married off your hands and T. P. getting big enough to take your place when rheumatism finish getting you.'

'They been two, now.' Roskus said. 'Going to be one more. I seen the sign, and you is too.'

'I heard a squinch owl that night.' T. P. said. 'Dan wouldn't come and get his supper, neither. Wouldn't come no closer than the barn. Begun howling right after dark. Versh heard him.'

'Going to be more than one more.' Dilsey said. 'Show me the man what ain't going to die, bless Jesus.'

'Dying ain't all.' Roskus said.

'I knows what you thinking.' Dilsey said. 'And they ain't going to be no luck in saying that name, lessen you going to set up with him while he cries.'

'They ain't no luck on this place.' Roskus said. 'I seen it at first but when they changed his name I knowed it.'

'Hush your mouth.' Dilsey said. She pulled the covers up. It smelled like T. P. 'You all shut up now, till he get to sleep.'

'I seen the sign.' Roskus said.

'Sign T. P. got to do all your work for you.' Dilsey said. *Take him and Quentin down to the house and let them play with Luster, where Frony can watch them, T. P., and go and help your pa.*

We finished eating. T. P. took Quentin up and we went down to T. P.'s house. Luster was playing in the dirt. T. P. put Quentin down and she played in the dirt too. Luster had some spools and he and Quentin fought and Quentin had the spools. Luster cried and Frony came and gave Luster a tin can to play with, and then I had the spools and Quentin fought me and I cried.

'Hush.' Frony said, 'Ain't you shamed of yourself. Taking a baby's play pretty.' She took the spools from me and gave them back to Quentin.

'Hush, now.' Frony said, 'Hush, I tell you.'

'Hush up.' Frony said. 'You needs whipping, that's what you needs.' She took Luster and Quentin up. 'Come on here.' she said. We went to the barn. T. P. was milking the cow. Roskus was sitting on the box.

'What's the matter with him now.' Roskus said.

'You have to keep him down here.' Frony said. 'He fighting these babies again. Taking they play things. Stay here with T. P. now, and see can you hush a while.'

'Clean that udder good now.' Roskus said. 'You

milked that young cow dry last winter. If you milk this one dry, they ain't going to be no more milk.'

Dilsey was singing.

'Not around yonder.' T. P. said. 'Don't you know mammy say you can't go around there.'

They were singing.

'Come on.' T. P. said. 'Let's go play with Quentin and Luster. Come on.'

Quentin and Luster were playing in the dirt in front of T. P.'s house. There was a fire in the house, rising and falling, with Roskus sitting black against it.

'That's three, thank the Lawd.' Roskus said. 'I told you two years ago. They ain't no luck on this place.'

'Whyn't you get out, then.' Dilsey said. She was undressing me. 'Your bad luck talk got them Memphis notions into Versh. That ought to satisfy you.'

'If that all the bad luck Versh have.' Roskus said.

Frony came in.

'You all done.' Dilsey said.

'T. P. finishing up.' Frony said. 'Miss Cahline want you to put Quentin to bed.'

'I'm coming just as fast as I can.' Dilsey said. 'She ought to know by this time I ain't got no wings.'

'That's what I tell you.' Roskus said. 'They ain't no luck going be on no place where one of they own chillens' name ain't never spoke.'

'Hush.' Dilsey said. 'Do you want to get him started.'

'Raising a child not to know its own mammy's name.' Roskus said.

'Don't you bother your head about her.' Dilsey said. 'I raised all of them and I reckon I can raise one more. Hush now. Let him get to sleep if he will.'

'Saying a name.' Frony said. 'He don't know nobody's name.'

'You just say it and see if he don't.' Dilsey said. 'You say it to him while he sleeping and I bet he hear you.'

'He know lot more than folks thinks.' Roskus said. 'He knowed they time was coming, like that pointer done. He could tell you when hisn coming, if he could talk. Or yours. Or mine.'

'You take Luster outen that bed, mammy.' Frony said. 'That boy conjure him.'

'Hush your mouth.' Dilsey said, 'Ain't you got no better sense than that. What you want to listen to Roskus for, anyway. Get in, Benjy.'

Dilsey pushed me and I got in the bed, where Luster already was. He was asleep. Dilsey took a long piece of wood and laid it between Luster and me. 'Stay on your side now.' Dilsey said. 'Luster little, and you don't want to hurt him.'

*You can't go yet, T. P. said. Wait.*

We looked around the corner of the house and watched the carriages go away.

'Now.' T. P. said. He took Quentin up and we ran down to the corner of the fence and watched them pass. 'There he go,' T. P. said. 'See that one with the glass in it. Look at him. He laying in there. See him.'

*Come on, Luster said, I going to take this here ball down home, where I won't lose it. Naw, sir, you can't have it. If them men sees you with it, they'll say you stole it. Hush up, now. You can't have it. What business you got with it. You can't play no ball.*

Frony and T. P. were playing in the dirt by the door. T. P. had lightning bugs in a bottle.

'How did you all get back out.' Frony said.

'We've got company.' Caddy said. 'Father said for us to mind me tonight. I expect you and T. P. will have to mind me too.'

'I'm not going to mind you.' Jason said. 'Frony and T. P. don't have to either.'

'They will if I say so.' Caddy said. 'Maybe I won't say for them to.'

'T. P. don't mind nobody.' Frony said. 'Is they started the funeral yet.'

'What's a funeral.' Jason said.

'Didn't mammy tell you not to tell them.' Versh said.

'Where they moans.' Frony said. 'They moaned two days on Sis Beulah Clay.'

*They moaned at Dilsey's house. Dilsey was moaning. When Dilsey moaned Luster said, Hush, and we hushed, and then I began to cry and Blue howled under the kitchen steps. Then Dilsey stopped and we stopped.*

'Oh.' Caddy said, 'That's niggers. White folks don't have funerals.'

'Mammy said us not to tell them, Frony.' Versh said.

'Tell them what.' Caddy said.

*Dilsey moaned, and when it got to the place I began to cry and Blue howled under the steps. Luster, Frony said in the window, Take them down to the barn. I can't get no cooking done with all that racket. That hound too. Get them outen here.*

*I ain't going down there, Luster said. I might meet pappy down there. I seen him last night, waving his arms in the barn.*

'I like to know why not.' Frony said. 'White folks dies too. Your grandmammy dead as any nigger can get, I reckon.'

'Dogs are dead.' Caddy said, 'And when Nancy fell in the ditch and Roskus shot her and the buzzards came and undressed her.'

The bones rounded out of the ditch, where the dark vines were in the black ditch, into the moonlight, like some of the shapes had stopped. Then they all stopped and it was dark, and when I stopped to start again I could hear Mother, and feet walking fast away, and I could smell it. Then the room came, but my eyes went shut. I didn't stop. I could smell it. T. P. unpinned the bedclothes.

'Hush.' he said, 'Shhhhhhhh.'

But I could smell it. T. P. pulled me up and he put on my clothes fast.

'Hush, Benjy.' he said. 'We going down to our house. You want to go down to our house, where Frony is. Hush. Shhhhh.'

He laced my shoes and put my cap on and we went

*27*

out. There was a light in the hall. Across the hall we could hear Mother.

'Shhhhhh, Benjy.' T. P. said, 'We'll be out in a minute.'

A door opened and I could smell it more than ever, and a head came out. It wasn't Father. Father was sick there.

'Can you take him out of the house.'

'That's where we going.' T. P. said. Dilsey came up the stairs.

'Hush.' she said, 'Hush. Take him down home, T. P. Frony fixing him a bed. You all look after him, now. Hush, Benjy. Go on with T. P.'

She went where we could hear Mother.

'Better keep him there.' It wasn't Father. He shut the door, but I could still smell it.

We went downstairs. The stairs went down into the dark and T. P. took my hand, and we went out the door, out of the dark. Dan was sitting in the backyard, howling.

'He smell it.' T. P. said. 'Is that the way you found it out.'

We went down the steps, where our shadows were.

'I forgot your coat.' T. P. said. 'You ought to had it. But I ain't going back.'

Dan howled.

'Hush now.' T. P. said. Our shadows moved, but Dan's shadow didn't move except to howl when he did.

'I can't take you down home, bellering like you is.' T. P. said. 'You was bad enough before you got that bull-frog voice. Come on.'

We went along the brick walk, with our shadows. The pig pen smelled like pigs. The cow stood in the lot, chewing at us. Dan howled.

'You going to wake the whole town up.' T. P. said. 'Can't you hush.'

We saw Fancy, eating by the branch. The moon shone on the water when we got there.

'Naw, sir.' T. P. said, 'This too close. We can't stop

here. Come on. Now, just look at you. Got your whole leg wet. Come on, here.' Dan howled.

The ditch came up out of the buzzing grass. The bones rounded out of the black vines.

'Now.' T. P. said. 'Beller your head off if you want to. You got the whole night and a twenty-acre pasture to beller in.'

T. P. lay down in the ditch and I sat down, watching the bones where the buzzards ate Nancy, flapping black and slow and heavy out of the ditch.

*I had it when we was down here before, Luster said. I showed it to you. Didn't you see it. I took it out of my pocket right here and showed it to you.*

'Do you think buzzards are going to undress Damuddy.' Caddy said. 'You're crazy.'

'You're a skizzard.' Jason said. He began to cry.

'You're a knobnot.' Caddy said. Jason cried. His hands were in his pockets.

'Jason going to be rich man.' Versh said. 'He holding his money all the time.'

Jason cried.

'Now you've got him started.' Caddy said. 'Hush up, Jason. How can buzzards get in where Damuddy is. Father wouldn't let them. Would you let a buzzard undress you. Hush up, now.'

Jason hushed. 'Frony said it was a funeral.' he said.

'Well it's not.' Caddy said. 'It's a party. Frony don't know anything about it. He wants your lightning bugs, T. P. Let him hold it a while.'

T. P. gave me the bottle of lightning bugs.

'I bet if we go around to the parlour window we can see something.' Caddy said. 'Then you'll believe me.'

'I already knows.' Frony said. 'I don't need to see.'

'You better hush your mouth, Frony.' Versh said. 'Mammy going whip you.'

'What is it.' Caddy said.

'I knows what I knows.' Frony said.

'Come on.' Caddy said, 'Let's go around to the front.

*29*

We started to go.

'T. P. wants his lightning bugs.' Frony said.

'Let him hold it a while longer, T. P.' Caddy said. 'We'll bring it back.'

'You all never caught them.' Frony said.

'If I say you and T. P. can come too, will you let him hold it.' Caddy said.

'Ain't nobody said me and T. P. got to mind you.' Frony said.

'If I say you don't have to, will you let him hold it.' Caddy said.

'All right.' Frony said. 'Let him hold it, T. P. We going to watch them moaning.'

'They ain't moaning.' Caddy said. 'I tell you it's a party. Are they moaning, Versh.'

'We ain't going to know what they doing, standing here.' Versh said.

'Come on.' Caddy said. 'Frony and T. P. don't have to mind me. But the rest of us do. You better carry him, Versh. It's getting dark.'

Versh took me up and we went on around the kitchen.

*When we looked around the corner we could see the lights coming up the drive. T. P. went back to the cellar door and opened it.*

*You know what's down there, T. P. said. Soda water. I seen Mr. Jason come up with both hands full of them. Wait here a minute.*

*T. P. went and looked in the kitchen door. Dilsey said, What are you peeping in here for. Where's Benjy.*

*He out here, T. P. said.*

*Go on and watch him, Dilsey said. Keep him out the house now.*

*Yessum, T. P. said. Is they started yet.*

*You go on and keep that boy out of sight, Dilsey said. I got all I can tend to.*

A snake crawled out from under the house. Jason said he wasn't afraid of snakes and Caddy said he was but she wasn't and Versh said they both were and Caddy said to be quiet, like father said.

*You ain't got to start bellering now, T. P. said. You want some this sassprilluh.*

*It tickled my nose and eyes.*

*If you ain't going to drink it, let me get to it, T. P. said. All right, here 'tis. We better get another bottle while ain't nobody bothering us. You be quiet, now.*

We stopped under the tree by the parlour window. Versh set me down in the wet grass. It was cold. There were lights in all the windows.

'That's where Damuddy is.' Caddy said. 'She's sick every day now. When she gets well we're going to have a picnic.'

'I knows what I knows.' Frony said.

The trees were buzzing, and the grass.

'The one next to it is where we have the measles.' Caddy said. 'Where do you and T. P. have the measles, Frony.'

'Has them just wherever we is, I reckon.' Frony said.

'They haven't started yet.' Caddy said.

*They getting ready to start, T. P. said. You stand right here now while I get that box so we can see in the window. Here, les finish drinking this here sassprilluh. It make me feel just like a squinch owl inside.*

We drank the sassprilluh and T. P. pushed the bottle through the lattice, under the house, and went away. I could hear them in the parlour and I clawed my hands against the wall. T. P. dragged the box. He fell down, and he began to laugh. He lay there, laughing into the grass. He got up and dragged the box under the window, trying not to laugh.

'I skeered I going to holler.' T. P. said. 'Git on the box and see is they started.'

'They haven't started because the band hasn't come yet.' Caddy said.

'They ain't going to have no band.' Frony said.

'How do you know.' Caddy said.

'I knows what I knows.' Frony said.

'You don't know anything.' Caddy said. She went to the tree. 'Push me up, Versh.'

'Your paw told you to stay out that tree.' Versh said.

'That was a long time ago.' Caddy said. 'I expect he's forgotten about it. Besides, he said to mind me tonight. Didn't he say to mind me tonight.'

'I'm not going to mind you.' Jason said. 'Frony and T. P. are not going to either.'

'Push me up, Versh.' Caddy said.

'All right.' Versh said. 'You the one going to get whipped. I ain't.' He went and pushed Caddy up into the tree to the first limb. We watched the muddy bottom of her drawers. Then we couldn't see her. We could hear the tree thrashing.

'Mr. Jason said if you break that tree he whip you.' Versh said.

'I'm going to tell on her too.' Jason said.

The tree quit thrashing. We looked up into the still branches.

'What you seeing.' Frony whispered.

*I saw them. Then I saw Caddy, with flowers in her hair, and a long veil like shining wind. Caddy. Caddy.*

'Hush.' T. P. said, 'They going to hear you. Get down quick.' He pulled me. Caddy. I clawed my hands against the wall Caddy. T. P. pulled me.

'Hush.' he said, 'Hush. Come on here quick.' He pulled me on. Caddy 'Hush up, Benjy. You want them to hear you. Come on, les drink some more sassprilluh, then we can come back if you hush. We better get one more bottle or we both be hollering. We can say Dan drunk it. Mr. Quentin always saying he so smart, we can say he sassprilluh dog, too.'

The moonlight came down the cellar stairs. We drank some more sassprilluh.

'You know what I wish.' T. P. said. 'I wish a bear would walk in that cellar door. You know what I do. I walk right up to him and spit in he eye. Gimme that bottle to stop my mouth before I holler.'

T. P. fell down. He began to laugh, and the cellar door and the moonlight jumped away and something hit me.

'Hush up.' T. P. said, trying not to laugh, 'Lawd, they'll all hear us. Get up.' T. P. said, 'Get up, Benjy, quick.' He was thrashing about and laughing and I tried to get up. The cellar steps ran up the hill in the moonlight and T. P. fell up the hill, into the moonlight, and I ran against the fence and T. P. ran behind me saying 'Hush up hush up.' Then he fell into the flowers, laughing, and I ran into the box. But when I tried to climb onto it it jumped away and hit me on the back of the head and my throat made a sound. It made the sound again and I stopped trying to get up, and it made the sound again and I began to cry. But my throat kept on making the sound while T. P. was pulling me. It kept on making it and I couldn't tell if I was crying or not, and T. P. fell down on top of me, laughing, and it kept on making the sound and Quentin kicked T. P. and Caddy put her arms around me, and her shining veil, and I couldn't smell trees any more and I began to cry.

*Benjy, Caddy said, Benjy. She put her arms around me again, but I went away.* 'What is it, Benjy.' she said, 'Is it this hat.' She took her hat off and came again, and I went away.

'Benjy.' she said, 'What is it, Benjy. What has Caddy done.'

'He don't like that prissy dress.' Jason said. 'You think you're grown up, don't you. You think you're better than anybody else, don't you. Prissy.'

'You shut your mouth.' Caddy said, 'You dirty little beast. Benjy.'

'Just because you are fourteen, you think you're grown up, don't you.' Jason said. 'You think you're something. Don't you.'

'Hush, Benjy.' Caddy said. 'You'll disturb Mother. Hush.'

But I didn't hush, and when she went away I

followed, and she stopped on the stairs and waited and I stopped too.

'What is it, Benjy.' Caddy said, 'Tell Caddy. She'll do it. Try.'

'Candace.' Mother said.

'Yessum.' Caddy said.

'Why are you teasing him.' Mother said. 'Bring him here.'

We went to Mother's room, where she was lying with the sickness on a cloth on her head.

'What is the matter now.' Mother said. 'Benjamin.'

'Benjy.' Caddy said. She came again, but I went away.

'You must have done something to him.' Mother said. 'Why won't you let him alone, so I can have some peace. Give him the box and please go on and let him alone.'

Caddy got the box and set it on the floor and opened it. It was full of stars. When I was still, they were still. When I moved, they glinted and sparkled. I hushed.

Then I heard Caddy walking and I began again.

'Benjamin.' Mother said, 'Come here.' I went to the door. 'You Benjamin.' Mother said.

'What is it now.' Father said, 'Where are you going.'

'Take him downstairs and get someone to watch him, Jason.' Mother said. 'You know I'm ill, yet you'

Father shut the door behind us.

'T. P.' he said.

'Sir.' T. P. said downstairs.

'Benjy's coming down.' Father said. 'Go with T. P.'

I went to the bathroom door. I could hear the water.

'Benjy.' T. P. said downstairs.

I could hear the water. I listened to it.

'Benjy.' T. P. said downstairs.

I listened to the water.

I couldn't hear the water, and Caddy opened the door.

'Why, Benjy.' she said. She looked at me and I went and she put her arms around me. 'Did you find Caddy again.' she said. 'Did you think Caddy had run away.' Caddy smelled like trees.

We went to Caddy's room. She sat down at the mirror. She stopped her hands and looked at me.

'Why, Benjy. What is it.' she said. 'You mustn't cry. Caddy's not going away. See here.' she said. She took up the bottle and took the stopper out and held it to my nose. 'Sweet. Smell. Good.'

I went away and I didn't hush, and she held the bottle in her hand, looking at me.

'Oh.' she said. She put the bottle down and came and put her arms around me. 'So that was it. And you were trying to tell Caddy and you couldn't tell her. You wanted to, but you couldn't, could you. Of course Caddy won't. Of course Caddy won't. Just wait till I dress.'

Caddy dressed and took up the bottle again and we went down to the kitchen.

'Dilsey.' Caddy said, 'Benjy's got a present for you.' She stooped down and put the bottle in my hand. 'Hold it out to Dilsey, now.' Caddy held my hand out and Dilsey took the bottle.

'Well I'll declare.' Dilsey said, 'If my baby ain't give Dilsey a bottle of perfume. Just look here, Roskus.'

Caddy smelled like trees. 'We don't like perfume ourselves.' Caddy said.

*She smelled like trees.*

'Come on, now.' Dilsey said, 'You too big to sleep with folks. You a big boy now. Thirteen years old. Big enough to sleep by yourself in Uncle Maury's room.' Dilsey said.

Uncle Maury was sick. His eye was sick, and his mouth. Versh took his supper up to him on the tray.

'Maury says he's going to shoot the scoundrel.' Father said. 'I told him he'd better not mention it to Patterson beforehand.' He drank.

'Jason.' Mother said.

'Shoot who, Father.' Quentin said. 'What's Uncle Maury going to shoot him for.'

'Because he couldn't take a little joke.' Father said.

'Jason.' Mother said, 'How can you. You'd sit right there and see Maury shot down in ambush, and laugh.'

'Then Maury'd better stay out of ambush.' Father said.

'Shoot who, Father.' Quentin said, 'Who's Uncle Maury going to shoot.'

'Nobody.' Father said. 'I don't own a pistol.'

Mother began to cry. 'If you begrudge Maury your food, why aren't you man enough to say so to his face. To ridicule him before the children, behind his back.'

'Of course I don't.' Father said, 'I admire Maury. He is invaluable to my own sense of racial superiority. I wouldn't swap Maury for a matched team. And do you know why, Quentin.'

'No, sir.' Quentin said.

'*Et ego in arcadia* I have forgotten the latin for hay.' Father said. 'There, there.' he said, 'I was just joking.' He drank and set the glass down and went and put his hand on Mother's shoulder.

'It's no joke.' Mother said. 'My people are every bit as well born as yours. Just because Maury's health is bad.'

'Of course.' Father said. 'Bad health is the primary reason for all life. Created by disease, within putrefaction, into decay. Versh.'

'Sir.' Versh said behind my chair.

'Take the decanter and fill it.'

'And tell Dilsey to come and take Benjamin up to bed.' Mother said.

'You a big boy.' Dilsey said, 'Caddy tired sleeping with you. Hush now, so you can go to sleep.' The room went away, but I didn't hush, and the room came back and Dilsey came and sat on the bed, looking at me.

'Ain't you going to be a good boy and hush.' Dilsey said. 'You ain't, is you. See you can wait a minute, then.'

She went away. There wasn't anything in the door. Then Caddy was in it.

'Hush.' Caddy said. 'I'm coming.'

I hushed and Dilsey turned back the spread and Caddy got in between the spread and the blanket. She didn't take off her bathrobe.

'Now.' she said, 'Here I am.' Dilsey came with a blanket and spread it over her and tucked it around her.

'He be gone in a minute.' Dilsey said. 'I leave the light on in your room.'

'All right.' Caddy said. She snuggled her head beside mine on the pillow. 'Good night, Dilsey.'

'Good night, honey.' Dilsey said. The room went black. *Caddy smelled like trees.*

We looked up into the tree where she was.

'What she seeing, Versh.' Frony whispered.

'Shhhhhhh.' Caddy said in the tree. Dilsey said, 'You come on here.' She came around the corner of the house. 'Why'n't you all go on upstairs, like your paw said, stead of slipping out behind my back. Where's Caddy and Quentin.'

'I told her not to climb up that tree.' Jason said. 'I'm going to tell on her.'

'Who in what tree.' Dilsey said. She came and looked up into the tree. 'Caddy.' Dilsey said. The branches began to shake again.

'You, Satan.' Dilsey said. 'Come down from there.'

'Hush.' Caddy said, 'Don't you know Father said to be quiet.' Her legs came in sight and Dilsey reached up and lifted her out of the tree.

'Ain't you got any better sense than to let them come around here.' Dilsey said.

'I couldn't do nothing with her.' Versh said.

'What you all doing here.' Dilsey said. 'Who told you to come up to the house.'

'She did.' Frony said. 'She told us to come.'

'Who told you you got to do what she say.' Dilsey said. 'Get on home, now.' Frony and T. P. went on. We couldn't see them when they were still going away.

'Out here in the middle of the night.' Dilsey said. She took me up and we went to the kitchen.

'Slipping out behind my back.' Dilsey said. 'When you knowed it's past your bedtime.'

*37*

'Shhhh, Dilsey.' Caddy said. 'Don't talk so loud. We've got to be quiet.'

'You hush your mouth and get quiet then.' Dilsey said. 'Where's Quentin.'

'Quentin's mad because he had to mind me tonight.' Caddy said. 'He's still got T. P.'s bottle of lightning bugs.'

'I reckon T. P. can get along without it.' Dilsey said. 'You go and find Quentin, Versh. Roskus say he seen him going towards the barn.' Versh went on. We couldn't see him.

'They're not doing anything in there.' Caddy said. 'Just sitting in chairs and looking.'

'They don't need no help from you all to do that.' Dilsey said. We went around the kitchen.

*Where you want to go now, Luster said. You going back to watch them knocking ball again. We done looked for it over there. Here. Wait a minute. You wait right here while I go back and get that ball. I done thought of something.*

The kitchen was dark. The trees were black on the sky. Dan came waddling out from under the steps and chewed my ankle. I went around the kitchen, where the moon was. Dan came scuffling along, into the moon.

'Benjy.' T. P. said in the house.

The flower tree by the parlour window wasn't dark, but the thick trees were. The grass was buzzing in the moonlight where my shadow walked on the grass.

'You, Benjy.' T. P. said in the house. 'Where you hiding. You slipping off. I knows it.'

*Luster came back. Wait, he said. Here. Don't go over there. Miss Quentin and her beau in the swing yonder. You come on this way. Come back here, Benjy.*

It was dark under the trees. Dan wouldn't come. He stayed in the moonlight. Then I could see the swing and I began to cry.

*Come away from there, Benjy, Luster said. You know Miss Quentin going to get mad.*

It was two now, and then one in the swing. Caddy came fast, white in the darkness.

'Benjy.' she said, 'How did you slip out. Where's Versh.'

She put her arms around me and I hushed and held to her dress and tried to pull her away.

'Why, Benjy.' she said. 'What is it. T. P.' she called.

The one in the swing got up and came, and I cried and pulled Caddy's dress.

'Benjy.' Caddy said. 'It's just Charlie. Don't you know Charlie.'

'Where's his nigger.' Charlie said. 'What do they let him run around loose for.'

'Hush, Benjy.' Caddy said. 'Go away, Charlie. He doesn't like you.' Charlie went away and I hushed. I pulled at Caddy's dress

'Why, Benjy.' Caddy said. 'Aren't you going to let me stay here and talk to Charlie a while.'

'Call that nigger.' Charlie said. He came back. I cried louder and pulled at Caddy's dress.

'Go away, Charlie.' Caddy said. Charlie came and put his hands on Caddy and I cried more. I cried loud.

'No, no.' Caddy said. 'No. No.'

'He can't talk.' Charlie said. 'Caddy.'

'Are you crazy.' Caddy said. She began to breathe fast. 'He can see. Don't. Don't.' Caddy fought. They both breathed fast. 'Please. Please.' Caddy whispered.

'Send him away.' Charlie said.

'I will.' Caddy said. 'Let me go.'

'Will you send him away.' Charlie said.

'Yes.' Caddy said. 'Let me go.' Charlie went away. 'Hush.' Caddy said. 'He's gone.' I hushed. I could hear her and feel her chest going.

'I'll have to take him to the house.' she said. She took my hand. 'I'm coming.' she whispered.

'Wait.' Charlie said. 'Call the nigger.'

'No.' Caddy said. 'I'll come back. Come on, Benjy.'

'Caddy.' Charlie whispered, loud. We went on. 'You better come back. Are you coming back.' Caddy and I were running. 'Caddy.' Charlie said. We ran out into the moonlight, toward the kitchen.

'Caddy.' Charlie said.

Caddy and I ran. We ran up the kitchen steps, onto the porch, and Caddy knelt down in the dark and held me. I could hear her and feel her chest. 'I won't.' she said. 'I won't any more, ever. Benjy. Benjy.' Then she was crying, and I cried, and we held each other. 'Hush.' she said. 'Hush. I won't any more.' So I hushed and Caddy got up and we went into the kitchen and turned the light on and Caddy took the kitchen soap and washed her mouth at the sink, hard. Caddy smelled like trees.

*I kept a-telling you to stay away from there, Luster said. They sat up in the swing, quick. Quentin had her hands on her hair. He had a red tie.*

*You old crazy loon, Quentin said. I'm going to tell Dilsey about the way you let him follow everywhere I go. I'm going to make her whip you good.*

'I couldn't stop him.' Luster said. 'Come on here, Benjy.'

'Yes you could.' Quentin said. 'You didn't try. You were both snooping around after me. Did Grandmother send you all out here to spy on me.' She jumped out of the swing. 'If you don't take him right away this minute and keep him away, I'm going to make Jason whip you.'

'I can't do nothing with him.' Luster said. 'You try it if you think you can.'

'Shut your mouth.' Quentin said. 'Are you going to get him away.'

'Ah, let him stay.' he said. He had a red tie. The sun was red on it. 'Look here, Jack.' He struck a match and put it in his mouth. Then he took the match out of his mouth. It was still burning. 'Want to try it.' he said. I went over there. 'Open your mouth.' he said. I opened my mouth. Quentin hit the match with her hand and it went away.

'Goddamn you.' Quentin said. 'Do you want to get him started. Don't you know he'll beller all day. I'm going to tell Dilsey on you.' She went away running.

'Here, kid.' he said. 'Hey. Come on back. I ain't going to fool with him.'

Quentin ran on to the house. She went around the kitchen.

'You played hell then, Jack.' he said. 'Ain't you.'

'He can't tell what you saying.' Luster said. 'He deef and dumb.'

'Is.' he said. 'How long's he been that way.'

'Been that way thirty-three years today.' Luster said. 'Born looney. Is you one of them show folks.'

'Why.' he said.

'I don't ricklick seeing you around here before.' Luster said.

'Well, what about it.' he said.

'Nothing.' Luster said. 'I going tonight.'

He looked at me.

'You ain't the one can play a tune on that saw, is you.' Luster said.

'It'll cost you a quarter to find that out.' he said. He looked at me. 'Why don't they lock him up.' he said. 'What'd you bring him out here for.'

'You ain't talking to me.' Luster said. 'I can't do nothing with him. I just come over here looking for a quarter I lost so I can go to the show tonight. Look like now I ain't going to get to go.' Luster looked on the ground. 'You ain't got no extra quarter, is you.' Luster said.

'No.' he said. 'I ain't.'

'I reckon I have just to find that other one, then.' Luster said. He put his hand in his pocket. 'You don't want to buy no golf ball neither, does you.' Luster said.

'What kind of ball.' he said.

'Golf ball.' Luster said. 'I don't want but a quarter.'

'What for.' he said. 'What do I want with it.'

'I didn't think you did.' Luster said. 'Come on here, mulehead.' he said. 'Come on here and watch them knocking that ball. Here. Here something you can play with along with that jimson weed.' Luster picked it up and gave it to me. It was bright.

*41*

'Where'd you get that.' he said. His tie was red in the sun, walking.

'Found it under this here bush.' Luster said. 'I thought for a minute it was that quarter I lost.'

He came and took it.

'Hush.' Luster said. 'He going to give it back when he done looking at it.'

'Agnes Mabel Becky.' he said. He looked toward the house.

'Hush.' Luster said. 'He fixing to give it back.'

He gave it to me and I hushed.

'Who come to see her last night.' he said.

'I don't know.' Luster said. 'They comes every night she can climb down that tree. I don't keep no track of them.'

'Damn if one of them didn't leave a track.' he said. He looked at the house. Then he went and lay down in the swing. 'Go away.' he said. 'Don't bother me.'

'Come on here.' Luster said. 'You done played hell now. Time Miss Quentin get done telling on you.'

We went to the fence and looked through the curling flower spaces. Luster hunted in the grass.

'I had it right here.' he said. I saw the flag flapping, and the sun slanting on the broad grass.

'They'll be some along soon.' Luster said. 'There some now, but they going away. Come on and help me look for it.'

We went along the fence.

'Hush.' Luster said. 'How can I make them come over here, if they ain't coming. Wait. They'll be some in a minute. Look yonder. Here they come.'

I went along the fence, to the gate, where the girls passed with their booksatchels. 'You, Benjy.' Luster said. 'Come back here.'

*You can't do no good looking through the gate, T. P. said. Miss Caddy done gone long ways away. Done got married and left you. You can't do no good, holding to the gate and crying. She can't hear you.*

*What is it he wants, T. P. Mother said. Can't you play with him and keep him quiet.*

*He want to go down yonder and look through the gate, T. P. said.*

*Well, he cannot do it, Mother said. It's raining. You will just have to play with him and keep him quiet. You, Benjamin.*

*Ain't nothing going to quiet him, T. P. said. He think if he down to the gate, Miss Caddy come back.*

*Nonsense, Mother said.*

I could hear them talking. I went out the door and I couldn't hear them, and I went down to the gate, where the girls passed with their booksatchels. They looked at me, walking fast, with their heads turned. I tried to say, but they went on, and I went along the fence, trying to say, and they went faster. Then they were running and I came to the corner of the fence and I couldn't go any further, and I held to the fence, looking after them and trying to say.

'You, Benjy.' T. P. said. 'What you doing, slipping out. Don't you know Dilsey whip you.'

'You can't do no good, moaning and slobbering through the fence.' T. P. said. 'You done skeered them chillen. Look at them, walking on the other side of the street.'

*How did he get out, Father said. Did you leave the gate unlatched when you came in, Jason.*

*Of course not, Jason said. Don't you know I've got better sense than to do that. Do you think I wanted anything like this to happen. This family is bad enough, God knows. I could have told you, all the time. I reckon you'll send him to Jackson, now. If Mrs. Burgess don't shoot him first.*

*Hush, Father said.*

*I could have told you, all the time, Jason said.*

It was open when I touched it, and I held to it in the twilight. I wasn't crying, and I tried to stop, watching the girls coming along in the twilight. I wasn't crying.

'There he is.'

They stopped.

'He can't get out. He won't hurt anybody, anyway. Come on.'

'I'm scared to. I'm scared. I'm going to cross the street.'

'He can't get out.'

I wasn't crying.

'Don't be a 'fraid cat. Come on.'

They came on in the twilight. I wasn't crying, and I held to the gate. They came slow.

'I'm scared.'

'He won't hurt you. I pass here every day. He just runs along the fence.'

They came on. I opened the gate and they stopped, turning. I was trying to say, and I caught her, trying to say, and she screamed and I was trying to say and trying and the bright shapes began to stop and I tried to get out. I tried to get it off of my face, but the bright shapes were going again. They were going up the hill to where it fell away and I tried to cry. But when I breathed in, I couldn't breathe out again to cry, and I tried to keep from falling off the hill and I fell off the hill into the bright, whirling shapes.

*Here, loony, Luster said. Here come some. Hush your slobbering and moaning, now.*

They came to the flag. He took it out and they hit, then he put the flag back.

'Mister.' Luster said.

He looked around. 'What.' he said.

'Want to buy a golf ball.' Luster said.

'Let's see it.' he said. He came to the fence and Luster reached the ball through.

'Where'd you get it.' he said.

'Found it.' Luster said.

'I know that.' he said. 'Where. In somebody's golf bag.'

'I found it laying over here in the yard.' Luster said. 'I'll take a quarter for it.'

'What makes you think it's yours.' he said.

'I found it.' Luster said.

'Then find yourself another one.' he said. He put it in his pocket and went away.

'I got to go to that show tonight.' Luster said.

'That so.' he said. He went to the table. 'Fore, caddie.' he said. He hit.

'I'll declare.' Luster said. 'You fusses when you don't see them and you fusses when you does. Why can't you hush. Don't you reckon folks gets tired of listening to you all the time. Here. You dropped your jimson weed.' He picked it up and gave it back to me. 'You needs a new one. You 'bout wore that one out.' We stood at the fence and watched them.

'That white man hard to get along with.' Luster said. 'You see him take my ball.' They went on. We went on along the fence. We came to the garden and we couldn't go any further. I held to the fence and looked through the flower spaces. They went away.

'Now you ain't got nothing to moan about.' Luster said. 'Hush up. I the one got something to moan over, you ain't. Here. Whyn't you hold on to that weed. You be bellering about it next.' He gave me the flower. 'Where you heading now.'

Our shadows were on the grass. They got to the trees before we did. Mine got there first. Then we got there, and then the shadows were gone. There was a flower in the bottle. I put the other flower in it.

'Ain't you a grown man, now.' Luster said. 'Playing with two weeds in a bottle. You know what they going to do with you when Miss Cahline die. They going to send you to Jackson, where you belong. Mr. Jason say so. Where you can hold the bars all day long with the rest of the looneys and slobber. How you like that.'

Luster knocked the flowers over with his hand. 'That's what they'll do to you at Jackson when you starts bellering.'

I tried to pick up the flowers. Luster picked them up, and they went away. I began to cry.

'Beller.' Luster said. 'Beller. You want something to beller about. All right, then. Caddy.' he whispered. 'Caddy. Beller now. Caddy.'

'Luster.' Dilsey said from the kitchen.

The flowers came back.

'Hush.' Luster said. 'Here they is. Look. It's fixed back just like it was at first. Hush, now.'

'You, Luster.' Dilsey said.

'Yessum.' Luster said. 'We coming. You done played hell. Get up.' He jerked my arm and I got up. We went out of the trees. Our shadows were gone.

'Hush.' Luster said. 'Look at all them folks watching you. Hush.'

'You bring him on here.' Dilsey said. She came down the steps.

'What you done to him now.' she said.

'Ain't done nothing to him.' Luster said. 'He just started bellering.'

'Yes you is.' Dilsey said. 'You done something to him. Where you been.'

'Over yonder under them cedars.' Luster said.

'Getting Quentin all riled up.' Dilsey said. 'Why can't you keep him away from her. Don't you know she don't like him where she at.'

'Got as much time for him as I is.' Luster said. 'He ain't none of my uncle.'

'Don't you sass me, nigger boy.' Dilsey said.

'I ain't done nothing to him.' Luster said. 'He was playing there, and all of a sudden he started bellering.'

'Is you been projecking with his graveyard.' Dilsey said.

'I ain't touched his graveyard.' Luster said.

'Don't lie to me, boy.' Dilsey said. We went up the steps and into the kitchen. Dilsey opened the fire-door and drew a chair up in front of it and I sat down. I hushed.

*What you want to get her started for, Dilsey said. Whyn't you keep him out of there.*

*He was just looking at the fire, Caddy said. Mother was telling him his new name. We didn't mean to get her started.*

*I knows you didn't, Dilsey said. Him at one end of the house and her at the other. You let my things alone, now. Don't you touch nothing till I get back.*

'Ain't you shamed of yourself.' Dilsey said. 'Teasing him.' She set the cake on the table.

'I ain't been teasing him.' Luster said. 'He was playing with that bottle full of dogfennel and all of a sudden he started up bellering. You heard him.'

'You ain't done nothing to his flowers.' Dilsey said.

'I ain't touched his graveyard.' Luster said. 'What I want with his truck. I was just hunting for that quarter.

'You lost it, did you.' Dilsey said. She lit the candles on the cake. Some of them were little ones. Some were big ones cut into little pieces. 'I told you to go put it away. Now I reckon you want me to get you another one from Frony.'

'I got to go to that show, Benjy or no Benjy.' Luster said. 'I ain't going to follow him around day and night both.'

'You going to do just what he want you to, nigger boy.' Dilsey said. 'You hear me.'

'Ain't I always done it.' Luster said. 'Don't I always does what he wants. Don't I, Benjy.'

'Then you keep it up.' Dilsey said. 'Bringing him in here, bawling and getting her started too. You all go ahead and eat this cake, now, before Jason come. I don't want him jumping on me about a cake I bought with my own money. Me baking a cake here, with him counting every egg that comes into this kitchen. See can you let him alone now, less you don't want to go to that show tonight.'

Dilsey went away.

'You can't blow out no candles.' Luster said. 'Watch me blow them out.' He leaned down and puffed his face. The candles went away. I began to cry. 'Hush.' Luster said. 'Here. Look at the fire while I cuts this cake.'

*I could hear the clock, and I could hear Caddy standing behind me, and I could hear the roof. It's still raining, Caddy said. I hate rain. I hate everything. And then her head came into my lap and she was crying, holding me, and I began to cry. Then I looked at the fire again and the bright, smooth shapes went again. I could hear the clock and the roof and Caddy.*

I ate some cake. Luster's hand came and took another piece. I could hear him eating. I looked at the fire.

A long piece of wire came across my shoulder. It went to the door, and then the fire went away. I began to cry.

'What you howling for now.' Luster said. 'Look there.' The fire was there. I hushed. 'Can't you set and look at the fire and be quiet like mammy told you.' Luster said. 'You ought to be ashamed of yourself. Here. Here's you some more cake.'

'What you done to him now.' Dilsey said. 'Can't you never let him alone.'

'I was just trying to get him to hush up and not sturb Miss Cahline.' Luster said. 'Something got him started again.'

'And I know what that something name.' Dilsey said. 'I'm going to get Versh to take a stick to you when he comes home. You just trying yourself. You been doing it all day. Did you take him down to the branch.'

'Nome.' Luster said. 'We been right here in this yard all day, like you said.'

His hand came for another piece of cake. Dilsey hit his hand. 'Reach it again, and I chop it right off with this here butcher knife.' Dilsey said. 'I bet he ain't had one piece of it.'

'Yes he is.' Luster said. 'He already had twice as much as me. Ask him if he ain't.'

'Reach hit one more time.' Dilsey said. 'Just reach it.'

*That's right, Dilsey said. I reckon it'll be my time to cry next. Reckon Maury going to let me cry on him a while, too.*

*His name's Benjy now, Caddy said.*

*How come it is, Dilsey said. He ain't wore out the name he was born with yet, is he.*

*Benjamin came out of the bible, Caddy said. It's a better
name for him than Maury was.*

*How come it is, Dilsey said.*

*Mother says it is, Caddy said.*

*Huh, Dilsey said. Name ain't going to help him. Hurt him
neither. Folks don't have no luck, changing names. My name
been Dilsey since fore I could remember and it be Dilsey when
they's long forgot me.*

*How will they know it's Dilsey, when it's long forgot, Dilsey,
Caddy said.*

*It'll be in the Book, honey, Dilsey said. Writ out.*

*Can you read it, Caddy said.*

*Won't have to, Dilsey said. They'll read it for me. All I got to
do is say Ise here.*

The long wire came across my shoulder, and the fire
went away. I began to cry.

Dilsey and Luster fought.

'I seen you.' Dilsey said. 'Oho, I seen you.' She
dragged Luster out of the corner, shaking him. 'Wasn't
nothing bothering him, was they. You just wait till your
pappy come home. I wish I was young like I use to be,
I'd tear them years right off your head. I good mind to
lock you up in that cellar and not let you go to that show
tonight, I sho is.'

'Ow, mammy.' Luster said. 'Ow, mammy.'

I put my hand out to where the fire had been.

'Catch him.' Dilsey said. 'Catch him back.'

My hand jerked back and I put it in my mouth and
Dilsey caught me. I could still hear the clock between
my voice. Dilsey reached back and hit Luster on the
head. My voice was going loud every time.

'Get that soda.' Dilsey said. She took my hand out of
my mouth. My voice went louder then and my hand
tried to go back to my mouth, but Dilsey held it. My
voice went loud. She sprinkled soda on my hand.

'Look in the pantry and tear a piece off of that rag
hanging on the nail.' she said. 'Hush, now. You don't
want to make your ma sick again, does you. Here, look at

*49*

the fire. Dilsey make your hand stop hurting in just a minute. Look at the fire.' She opened the fire-door. I looked at the fire, but my hand didn't stop and I didn't stop. My hand was trying to go to my mouth, but Dilsey held it.

She wrapped the cloth around it. Mother said,

'What is it now. Can't I even be sick in peace. Do I have to get up out of bed to come down to him, with two grown negroes to take care of him.'

'He all right now.' Dilsey said. 'He going to quit. He just burnt his hand a little.'

'With two grown negroes, you must bring him into the house, bawling.' Mother said. 'You got him started on purpose, because you know I'm sick.' She came and stood by me. 'Hush.' she said. 'Right this minute. Did you give him this cake.'

'I bought it.' Dilsey said. 'It never come out of Jason's pantry. I fixed him some birthday.'

'Do you want to poison him with that cheap store cake.' Mother said. 'Is that what you are trying to do. Am I never to have one minute's peace.'

'You go on back upstairs and lay down.' Dilsey said. 'It'll quit smarting him in a minute now, and he'll hush. Come on, now.'

'And leave him down here for you all to do something else to.' Mother said. 'How can I lie there, with him bawling down here. Benjamin. Hush this minute.'

'They ain't nowhere else to take him.' Dilsey said. 'We ain't got the room we use to have. He can't stay out in the yard, crying where all the neighbours can see him.'

'I know, I know.' Mother said. 'It's all my fault. I'll be gone soon, and you and Jason will both get along better.' She began to cry.

'You hush that, now.' Dilsey said. 'You'll get yourself down again. You come on back upstairs. Luster going to take him to the liberry and play with him till I get his supper done.'

Dilsey and Mother went out.

'Hush up.' Luster said. 'You hush up. You want me to burn your other hand for you. You ain't hurt. Hush up.'

'Here.' Dilsey said. 'Stop crying, now.' She gave me the slipper, and I hushed. 'Take him to the liberry,' she said. 'And if I hear him again, I going to whip you myself.'

We went to the library, Luster turned on the light. The windows went black, and the dark tall place on the wall came and I went and touched it. It was like a door, only it wasn't a door.

The fire came behind me and I went to the fire and sat on the floor, holding the slipper. The fire went higher. It went onto the cushion in Mother's chair.

'Hush up.' Luster said. 'Can't you never get done for a while. Here I done built you a fire, and you won't even look at it.'

*Your name is Benjy. Caddy said. Do you hear. Benjy. Benjy.*

*Don't tell him that, Mother said. Bring him here.*

*Caddy lifted me under the arms.*

*Get up, Mau—I mean Benjy, she said.*

*Don't try to carry him, Mother said. Can't you lead him over here. Is that too much for you to think of.*

*I can carry him*, Caddy said. 'Let me carry him up, Dilsey.'

'Go on, Minute.' Dilsey said. 'You ain't big enough to tote a flea. You go on and be quiet, like Mr. Jason said.'

There was a light at the top of the stairs. Father was there, in his shirt sleeves. The way he looked said Hush. Caddy whispered,

'Is Mother sick.'

*Versh set me down and we went into Mother's room. There was a fire. It was rising and falling on the walls. There was another fire in the mirror. I could smell the sickness. It was a cloth folded on Mother's head. Her hair was on the pillow. The fire didn't reach it, but it shone on her hand, where her rings were jumping.*

'Come and tell Mother good night.' Caddy said. We went to the bed. The fire went out of the mirror. Father got up from the bed and lifted me up and Mother put her hand on my head.

'What time is it.' Mother said. Her eyes were closed.

'Ten minutes to seven.' Father said.

'It's too early for him to go to bed.' Mother said.

'He'll wake up at daybreak, and I simply cannot bear another day like to-day.'

'There, there.' Father said. He touched Mother's face.

'I know I'm nothing but a burden to you.' Mother said. 'But I'll be gone soon. Then you will be rid of my bothering.'

'Hush.' Father said. 'I'll take him downstairs awhile.' He took me up. 'Come on, old fellow. Let's go downstairs awhile. We'll have to be quiet while Quentin is studying, now.'

Caddy went and leaned her face over the bed and Mother's hand came into the firelight. Her rings jumped on Caddy's back.

*Mother's sick, Father said. Dilsey will put you to bed. Where's Quentin.*

*Versh getting him, Dilsey said.*

Father stood and watched us go past. We could hear Mother in her room. Caddy said 'Hush.' Jason was still climbing the stairs. He had his hands in his pockets.

'You all must be good tonight.' Father said. 'And be quiet, so you won't disturb Mother.'

'We'll be quiet.' Caddy said. 'You must be quiet now, Jason.' she said. We tiptoed.

*We could hear the roof. I could see the fire in the mirror too. Caddy lifted me again.*

'Come on, now.' she said. 'Then you can come back to the fire. Hush, now.'

'Candace.' Mother said.

'Hush, Benjy.' Caddy said. 'Mother wants you a minute. Like a good boy. Then you can come back, Benjy.'

Caddy let me down, and I hushed.

'Let him stay here, Mother. When he's through looking at the fire, then you can tell him.'

'Candace.' Mother said. Caddy stooped and lifted me.
We staggered. 'Candace.' Mother said.

'Hush.' Caddy said. 'You can still see it. Hush.'

'Bring him here.' Mother said. 'He's too big for you to
carry. You must stop trying. You'll injure your back. All of
our women have prided themselves on their carriage. Do
you want to look like a washer-woman.'

'He's not too heavy.' Caddy said. 'I can carry him.'

'Well, I don't want him carried, then.' Mother said. 'A
five year old child. No, no. Not in my lap. Let him stand
up.'

'If you'll hold him, he'll stop.' Caddy said. 'Hush.' she
said. 'You can go right back. Here. Here's your cushion.
See.'

'Don't, Candace,' Mother said.

'Let him look at it and he'll be quiet.' Caddy said.
'Hold up just a minute while I slip it out. There, Benjy.
Look.'

I looked at it and hushed.

'You humour him too much.' Mother said. 'You and
your father both. You don't realize that I am the one who
has to pay for it. Damuddy spoiled Jason that way and it
took him two years to outgrow it, and I am not strong
enough to go through the same thing with Benjamin.'

'You don't need to bother with him.' Caddy said. 'I
like to take care of him. Don't I, Benjy.'

'Candace.' Mother said. 'I told you not to call him
that. It was bad enough when your father insisted on calling you by that silly nickname, and I will not have him
called by one. Nicknames are vulgar. Only common
people use them. Benjamin.' she said.

'Look at me.' Mother said.

'Benjamin.' she said. She took my face in her hands
and turned it to hers.

'Benjamin.' she said. 'Take that cushion away,
Candace.'

'He'll cry.' Caddy said.

'Take that cushion away, like I told you.' Mother said. 'He must learn to mind.'

The cushion went away.

'Hush, Benjy.' Caddy said.

'You go over there and sit down.' Mother said. 'Benjamin.' She held my face to hers.

'Stop that.' she said. 'Stop it.'

But I didn't stop and Mother caught me in her arms and began to cry, and I cried. Then the cushion came back and Caddy held it above Mother's head. She drew Mother back in the chair and Mother lay crying against the red-and-yellow cushion.

'Hush, Mother.' Caddy said. 'You go upstairs and lay down, so you can be sick. I'll go get Dilsey.' She led me to the fire and I looked at the bright, smooth shapes. I could hear the fire and the roof.

Father took me up. He smelled like rain.

'Well, Benjy.' he said. 'Have you been a good boy today.'

Caddy and Jason were fighting in the mirror.

'You, Caddy.' Father said.

They fought. Jason began to cry.

'Caddy.' Father said. Jason was crying. He wasn't fighting any more, but we could see Caddy fighting in the mirror and Father put me down and went into the mirror and fought too. He lifted Caddy up. She fought. Jason lay on the floor, crying. He had the scissors in his hand. Father held Caddy.

'He cut up all Benjy's dolls.' Caddy said. 'I'll slit his gizzle.'

'Candace.' Father said.

'I will.' Caddy said. 'I will.' She fought. Father held her. She kicked at Jason. He rolled into the corner, out of the mirror. Father brought Caddy to the fire. They were all out of the mirror. Only the fire was in it. Like the fire was in a door.

'Stop that.' Father said. 'Do you want to make Mother sick in her room.'

Caddy stopped. 'He cut up all the dolls Mau –
Benjy and I made.' Caddy said. 'He did it just for
meanness.'

'I didn't.' Jason said. He was sitting up, crying. 'I
didn't know they were his. I just thought they were some
old papers.'

'You couldn't help but know.' Caddy said. 'You did it
just.'

'Hush.' Father said. 'Jason.' he said.

'I'll make you some more tomorrow.' Caddy said.
'We'll make a lot of them. Here, you can look at the
cushion, too.'

*Jason came in.*

*I kept telling you to hush, Luster said.*

*What's the matter now, Jason said.*

'He just trying hisself.' Luster said. 'That the way he
been going on all day.'

'Why don't you let him alone, then.' Jason said. 'If you
can't keep him quiet, you'll have to take him out to the
kitchen. The rest of us can't shut ourselves up in a room
like Mother does.'

'Mammy say keep him out the kitchen till she get
supper.' Luster said.

'Then play with him and keep him quiet.' Jason said.
'Do I have to work all day and then come home to a mad
house.' He opened the paper and read it.

*You can look at the fire and the mirror and the cushion too,
Caddy said. You won't have to wait until supper to look at the
cushion, now. We could hear the roof. We could hear Jason too,
crying loud beyond the wall.*

Dilsey said, 'You come, Jason. You letting him alone, is
you.'

'Yessum.' Luster said.

'Where Quentin.' Dilsey said. 'Supper near bout
ready.'

'I don't know'm.' Luster said. 'I ain't seen her.'

Dilsey went away. 'Quentin.' she said in the hall.
'Quentin. Supper ready.'

*We could hear the roof. Quentin smelled like rain, too.*

*What did Jason do, he said.*

*He cut up all Benjy's dolls, Caddy said.*

*Mother said to not call him Benjy, Quentin said. He sat on the rug by us. I wish it wouldn't rain, he said. You can't do anything.*

*You've been in a fight, Caddy said. Haven't you.*

*It wasn't much, Quentin said.*

*You can tell it, Caddy said. Father'll see it.*

*I don't care, Quentin said. I wish it wouldn't rain.*

Quentin said, 'Didn't Dilsey say supper was ready.'

'Yessum.' Luster said. Jason looked at Quentin. Then he read the paper again. Quentin came in. 'She say it bout ready.' Luster said. Quentin jumped down in Mother's chair. Luster said,

'Mr. Jason.'

'What.' Jason said.

'Let me have two bits.' Luster said.

'What for.' Jason said.

'To go to the show tonight.' Luster said.

'I thought Dilsey was going to get a quarter from Frony for you.' Jason said.

'She did.' Luster said. 'I lost it. Me and Benjy hunted all day for that quarter. You can ask him.'

'Then borrow one from him.' Jason said. 'I have to work for mine.' He read the paper. Quentin looked at the fire. The fire was in her eyes and on her mouth. Her mouth was red.

'I tried to keep him away from there.' Luster said.

'Shut your mouth.' Quentin said. Jason looked at her.

'What did I tell you I was going to do if I saw you with that show fellow again.' he said. Quentin looked at the fire. 'Did you hear me.' Jason said.

'I heard you.' Quentin said. 'Why don't you do it, then.'

'Don't you worry.' Jason said.

'I'm not.' Quentin said. Jason read the paper again.

*I could hear the roof. Father leaned forward and looked at Quentin.*

*Hello, he said. Who won.*

'Nobody.' Quentin said. 'They stopped us. Teachers.'

'Who was it.' Father said. 'Will you tell.'

'It was all right.' Quentin said. 'He was as big as me.'

'That's good.' Father said. 'Can you tell what it was about.'

'It wasn't anything.' Quentin said. 'He said he would put a frog in her desk and she wouldn't dare to whip him.'

'Oh.' Father said. 'She. And then what.'

'Yes, sir.' Quentin said. 'And then I kind of hit him.'

We could hear the roof and the fire and a snuffling outside the door.

'Where was he going to get a frog in November.' Father said.

'I don't know, sir.' Quentin said.

We could hear them.

'Jason.' Father said. We could hear Jason.

'Jason.' Father said. 'Come in here and stop that.'

We could hear the roof and the fire and Jason.

'Stop that, now.' Father said. 'Do you want me to whip you again.' Father lifted Jason up into the chair by him. Jason snuffled. We could hear the fire and the roof. Jason snuffled a little louder.

'One more time.' Father said. We could hear the fire and the roof.

*Dilsey said, All right. You all can come on to supper.*

*Versh smelled like rain. He smelled like a dog, too. We could hear the fire and the roof.*

We could hear Caddy walking fast. Father and Mother looked at the door. Caddy passed it, walking fast. She didn't look. She walked fast.

'Candace.' Mother said. Caddy stopped walking.

'Yes, Mother.' she said.

'Hush, Caroline.' Father said.

'Come here.' Mother said.

'Hush, Caroline.' Father said. 'Let her alone.'

Caddy came to the door and stood there, looking at Father and Mother. Her eyes flew at me, and away. I began to cry. It went loud and I got up. Caddy came in and stood with her back to the wall, looking at me. I went toward her, crying, and she shrank against the wall and I saw her eyes and I cried louder and pulled at her dress. She put her hands out but I pulled at her dress. Her eyes ran.

*Versh said, Your name Benjamin now. You know how come your name Benjamin now. They making a bluegum out of you. Mammy say in old time your granpa changed nigger's name, and he turn preacher, and when they look at him, he bluegum too. Didn't use to be bluegum, neither. And when family woman look him in the eye in the full of the moon, chile born bluegum. And one evening, when they was about a dozen them bluegum chillen running round the place, he never come home. Possum hunters found him in the woods, et clean. And you know who et him. Them bluegum chillen did.*

We were in the hall. Caddy was still looking at me. Her hand was against her mouth and I saw her eyes and I cried. We went up the stairs. She stopped again, against the wall, looking at me and I cried and she went on and I came on, crying, and she shrank against the wall, looking at me. She opened the door to her room, but I pulled at her dress and we went to the bathroom and she stood against the door, looking at me. Then she put her arm across her face and I pushed at her, crying.

*What are you doing to him, Jason said. Why can't you let him alone.*

*I ain't touching him, Luster said. He been doing this way all day long. He needs whipping.*

*He needs to be sent to Jackson, Quentin said. How can anybody live in a house like this.*

*If you don't like it, young lady, you'd better get out, Jason said.*

*I'm going to, Quentin said. Don't you worry.*

Versh said, 'You move back some, so I can dry my legs off.' He shoved me back a little. 'Don't you start

*58*

bellering, now. You can still see it. That's all you have to do. You ain't had to be out in the rain like I is. You's born lucky and don't know it.' He lay on his back before the fire.

'You know how come your name Benjamin now.' Versh said. 'Your mamma too proud for you. What mammy say.'

'You be still there and let me dry my legs off.' Versh said. 'Or you know what I'll do. I'll skin your rinktum.'

We could hear the fire and the roof and Versh.

Versh got up quick and jerked his legs back. Father said, 'All right, Versh.'

'I'll feed him tonight.' Caddy said. 'Sometimes he cries when Versh feeds him.'

'Take this tray up.' Dilsey said. 'And hurry back and feed Benjy.'

'Don't you want Caddy to feed you.' Caddy said.

*Has he got to keep that old dirty slipper on the table, Quentin said. Why don't you feed him in the kitchen. It's like eating with a pig.*

*If you don't like the way we eat, you'd better not come to the table, Jason said.*

Steam came off of Roskus. He was sitting in front of the stove. The oven door was open and Roskus had his feet in it. Steam came off the bowl. Caddy put the spoon into my mouth easy. There was a black spot on the inside of the bowl.

*Now, now, Dilsey said. He ain't going to bother you no more.*

It got down below the mark. Then the bowl was empty. It went away. 'He's hungry tonight.' Caddy said. The bowl came back. I couldn't see the spot. Then I could. 'He's starved, tonight.' Caddy said. 'Look how much he's eaten.'

*Yes he will, Quentin said. You all send him out to spy on me. I hate this house. I'm going to run away.*

Roskus said, 'It going to rain all night.'

*You've been running a long time, not to 've got any further off than mealtime, Jason said.*

*See if I don't, Quentin said.*

'Then I don't know what I going to do.' Dilsey said. 'It caught me in the hip so bad now I can't scarcely move. Climbing them stairs all evening.'

*Oh, I wouldn't be surprised, Jason said. I wouldn't be surprised at anything you'd do.*

*Quentin threw her napkin on the table.*

*Hush your mouth, Jason, Dilsey said. She went and put her arm around Quentin. Sit down, honey, Dilsey said. He ought to be ashamed of hisself, throwing what ain't your fault up to you.*

'She sulling again, is she.' Roskus said.

'Hush your mouth.' Dilsey said.

*Quentin pushed Dilsey away. She looked at Jason. Her mouth was red. She picked up her glass of water and swung her arm back, looking at Jason. Dilsey caught her arm. They fought. The glass broke on the table, and the water ran into the table. Quentin was running.*

'Mother's sick again.' Caddy said.

'Sho she is.' Dilsey said. 'Weather like this make anybody sick. When you going to get done eating, boy.'

*Goddamn you, Quentin said. Goddamn you. We could hear her running on the stairs. We went to the library.*

Caddy gave me the cushion, and I could look at the cushion and the mirror and the fire.

'We must be quiet while Quentin's studying.' Father said. 'What are you doing, Jason.'

'Nothing.' Jason said.

'Suppose you come over here to do it, then.' Father said.

Jason came out of the corner.

'What are you chewing.' Father said.

'Nothing.' Jason said.

'He's chewing paper again.' Caddy said.

'Come here, Jason.' Father said.

Jason threw into the fire. It hissed, uncurled, turning black. Then it was grey. Then it was gone. Caddy and

Father and Jason were in Mother's chair. Jason's eyes were puffed shut and his mouth moved, like tasting. Caddy's head was on Father's shoulder. Her hair was like fire, and little points of fire were in her eyes, and I went and Father lifted me into the chair too, and Caddy held me. She smelled like trees.

*She smelled like trees. In the corner it was dark, but I could see the window. I squatted there, holding the slipper. I couldn't see it, but my hands saw it, and I could hear it getting night, and my hands saw the slipper but I couldn't see myself, but my hands could see the slipper, and I squatted there, hearing it getting dark.*

*Here you is, Luster said. Look what I got. He showed it to me. You know where I got it. Miss Quentin gave it to me. I knowed they couldn't keep me out. What you doing, off in here. I thought you done slipped back out doors. Ain't you done enough moaning and slobbering today, without hiding off in this here empty room, mumbling and taking on. Come on here to bed, so I can get up there before it starts. I can't fool with you all night tonight. Just let them horns toot the first toot and I done gone.*

We didn't go to our room.

'This is where we have the measles.' Caddy said. 'Why do we have to sleep in here tonight.'

'What you care where you sleep.' Dilsey said. She shut the door and sat down and began to undress me. Jason began to cry. 'Hush.' Dilsey said.

'I want to sleep with Damuddy.' Jason said.

'She's sick.' Caddy said. 'You can sleep with her when she gets well. Can't he, Dilsey.'

'Hush, now.' Dilsey said. Jason hushed.

'Our nighties are here, and everything.' Caddy said. 'It's like moving.'

'And you better get into them.' Dilsey said. 'You be unbuttoning Jason.'

Caddy unbuttoned Jason. He began to cry.

'You want to get whipped.' Dilsey said. Jason hushed.

*Quentin, Mother said in the hall.*

*What, Quentin said beyond the wall. We heard Mother lock*

*the door. She looked in our door and came in and stooped over the bed and kissed me on the forehead.*

When you get him to bed, go and ask Dilsey if she objects to my having a hot water bottle, Mother said. Tell her that if she does, I'll try to get along without it. Tell her I just want to know.

Yessum, Luster said. Come on. Get your pants off.

Quentin and Versh came in. Quentin had his face turned away. 'What are you crying for.' Caddy said.

'Hush.' Dilsey said. 'You all get undressed, now. You can go on home, Versh.'

*I got undressed and I looked at myself, and I began to cry. Hush, Luster said. Looking for them ain't going to do no good. They're gone. You keep on like this, and we ain't going have you no more birthday. He put my gown on. I hushed, and then Luster stopped, his head toward the window. Then he went to the window and looked out. He came back and took my arm. Here she come, he said. Be quiet, now. We went to the window and looked out. It came out of Quentin's window and climbed across into the tree. We watched the tree shaking. The shaking went down the tree, then it came out and we watched it go away across the grass. Then we couldn't see it. Come on, Luster said. There now. Hear them horns. You get in that bed while my foots behaves.*

There were two beds. Quentin got in the other one. He turned his face to the wall. Dilsey put Jason in with him. Caddy took her dress off.

'Just look at your drawers.' Dilsey said. 'You better be glad your ma ain't seen you .

'I already told on her.' Jason said.

'I bound you would.' Dilsey said.

'And see what you got by it.' Caddy said. 'Tattletale.'

'What did I get by it.' Jason said.

'Whyn't you get your nightie on.' Dilsey said. She went and helped Caddy take off her bodice and drawers. 'Just look at you.' Dilsey said. She wadded the drawers and scrubbed Caddy behind with them. 'It done soaked clean through onto you.' she said. 'But you won't get no bath this night. Here.' She put Caddy's nightie on her and Caddy climbed into the bed and Dilsey went to the door and stood with her hand on the light. 'You all be quiet now, you hear.' she said.

'All right.' Caddy said. 'Mother's not coming in tonight.' she said. 'So we still have to mind me.'

'Yes.' Dilsey said. 'Go to sleep, now.'

'Mother's sick.' Caddy said. 'She and Damuddy are both sick.'

'Hush.' Dilsey said. 'You go to sleep.'

The room went black, except the door. Then the door went black. Caddy said, 'Hush, Maury,' putting her hand on me. So I stayed hushed. We could hear us. We could hear the dark.

It went away, and Father looked at us. He looked at Quentin and Jason, then he came and kissed Caddy and put his hand on my head.

'Is Mother very sick.' Caddy said.

'No.' Father said. 'Are you going to take good care of Maury.'

'Yes.' Caddy said.

Father went to the door and looked at us again. Then the dark came back, and he stood black in the door, and then the door turned black again. Caddy held me and I could hear us all, and the darkness, and something I could smell. And then I could see the windows, where the trees were buzzing. Then the dark began to go in smooth, bright shapes, like it always does, even when Caddy says that I have been asleep.

# *June Second*
## 1910

WHEN the shadow of the sash appeared on the curtains it was between seven and eight o'clock and then I was in time again, hearing the watch. It was Grandfather's and when Father gave it to me he said, Quentin, I give you the mausoleum of all hope and desire; it's rather excruciatingly apt that you will use it to gain the reducto absurdum of all human experience which can fit your individual needs no better than it fitted his or his father's. I give it to you not that you may remember time, but that you might forget it now and then for a moment and not spend all your breath trying to conquer it. Because no battle is ever won he said. They are not even fought. The field only reveals to man his own folly and despair, and victory is an illusion of philosophers and fools.

It was propped against the collar box and I lay listening to it. Hearing it, that is, I don't suppose anybody ever deliberately listens to a watch or a clock. You don't have to. You can be oblivious to the sound for a long while, then in a second of ticking it can create in the mind unbroken the long diminishing parade of time you didn't hear. Like Father said down the long and lonely light-rays you might see Jesus walking, like. And the good Saint Francis that said Little Sister Death, that never had a sister.

Through the wall I heard Shreve's bed-springs and then his slippers on the floor hishing. I got up and went to the dresser and slid my hand along it and touched the watch and turned it face-down and went back to bed. But the shadow of the sash was still there and I had learned to tell almost to the minute, so I'd have to turn my back to it, feeling the eyes animals used to have in the back of their heads when it was on top, itching. It's always the idle habits you acquire which you will regret. Father said that. That Christ was not crucified: he was worn away by a minute clicking of little wheels. That had no sister.

And so as soon as I knew I couldn't see it, I began to wonder what time it was. Father said that constant speculation regarding the position of mechanical hands on an arbitrary dial which is a symptom of mind-function. Excrement Father said like sweating. And I saying All right. Wonder. Go on and wonder.

If it had been cloudy I could have looked at the window, thinking what he said about idle habits. Thinking it would be nice for them down at New London if the weather held up like this. Why shouldn't it? The month of brides, the voice that breathed *She ran right out of the mirror, out of the banked scent. Roses. Roses. Mr. and Mrs. Jason Richmond Compson announce the marriage of.* Roses. Not virgins like dogwood, milkweed. I said I have committed incest, Father I said. Roses. Cunning and serene. If you attend Harvard one year, but don't see the boat-race, there should be a refund. Let Jason have it. Give Jason a year at Harvard.

Shreve stood in the door, putting his collar on, his glasses glinting rosily, as though he had washed them with his face. 'You taking a cut this morning?'

'Is it that late?

He looked at his watch. 'Bell in two minutes.'

'I didn't know it was that late.' He was still looking at the watch, his mouth shaping. 'I'll have to hustle. I can't stand another cut. The dean told me last week –' He put the watch back into his pocket. Then I quit talking.

'You'd better slip on your pants and run,' he said. He went out.

I got up and moved about, listening to him through the wall. He entered the sitting-room, toward the door.

'Aren't you ready yet?'

'Not yet. Run along. I'll make it.'

He went out. The door closed. His feet went down the corridor. Then I could hear the watch again. I quit moving around and went to the window and drew the curtains aside and watched them running for chapel, the same ones fighting the same heaving coat-sleeves, the same books and flapping collars flushing past like debris on a flood, and Spoade. Calling Shreve my husband. Ah let him alone, Shreve said, if he's got better sense than to chase after the little dirty sluts, whose business. In the South you are ashamed of being a virgin. Boys. Men. They lie about it. Because it means less to women, Father said. He said it was men invented virginity not women. Father said it's like death: only a state in which the others are left and I said, But to believe it doesn't matter and he said, That's what's so sad about anything: not only virginity, and I said, Why couldn't it have been me and not her who is unvirgin and he said, That's why that's sad too; nothing is even worth the changing of it, and Shreve said if he's got better sense than to chase after the little dirty sluts and I said Did you ever have a sister? Did you? Did you?

Spoade was in the middle of them like a terrapin in a street full of scuttering dead leaves, his collar about his ears, moving at his customary unhurried walk. He was from South Carolina, a senior. It was his club's boast that he never ran for chapel and had never got there on time and had never been absent in four years and had never made either chapel or first lecture with a shirt on his back and socks on his feet. About ten o'clock he'd come in Thompson's, get two cups of coffee, sit down and take his socks out of his pocket and remove his shoes and put them on while the coffee cooled. About noon you'd see him with a shirt and collar on, like anybody else. The others passed him running, but he never increased his pace at all. After a while the quad was empty.

A sparrow slanted across the sunlight, onto the window ledge, and cocked his head at me. His eye was round and bright. First he'd watch me with one eye, then flick! and it would be the other one, his throat pumping faster than any pulse. The hour began to strike. The sparrow quit swapping eyes and watched me steadily with the same one until the chimes ceased, as if he were listening too. Then he flicked off the ledge and was gone.

It was a while before the last stroke ceased vibrating. It stayed in the air, more felt than heard, for a long time. Like all the bells that ever rang still ringing in the long dying light-rays and Jesus and Saint Francis talking about his sister. Because if it were just to hell; if that were all of it. Finished. If things just finished themselves. Nobody else there but her and me. If we could just have done something so dreadful that they would have fled hell except us. *I have committed incest I said Father it was I it was not Dalton Ames* And when he put Dalton Ames. Dalton Ames. Dalton Ames. When he put the pistol in my hand I didn't. That's why I didn't. He would be there and she would and I would. Dalton Ames. Dalton Ames. Dalton Ames. If we could have just done something so dreadful and Father said That's sad too, people cannot do anything that dreadful they cannot do anything very dreadful at all they cannot even remember tomorrow what seemed dreadful today and I said, You can shirk all things and he said, Ah can you. And I will look down and see my murmuring bones and the deep water like wind, like a roof of wind, and after a long time they cannot distinguish even bones upon the lonely and inviolate sand. Until on the Day when He says Rise only the flat-iron would come floating up. It's not when you realize that nothing can help you – religion, pride, anything – it's when you realize that you don't need any aid. Dalton Ames. Dalton Ames. Dalton Ames. If I could have been his mother lying with open body lifted laughing, holding his father with my hand refraining, seeing, watching him die before he lived. *One minute she was standing in the door.*

I went to the dresser and took up the watch, with the face still down. I tapped the crystal on the corner of the dresser and caught the fragments of glass in my hand and put them into the ashtray and twisted the hands off and put them in the tray. The watch ticked on. I turned the face up, the blank dial with little wheels clicking and clicking behind it, not knowing any better. Jesus walking on Galilee and Washington not telling lies. Father brought back a watch-charm from the Saint Louis Fair to Jason: a tiny opera glass into which you squinted with one eye and saw a skyscraper, a ferris wheel all spidery, Niagara Falls on a pinhead. There was a red smear on the dial. When I saw it my thumb began to smart. I put the watch down and went into Shreve's room and got the iodine and painted the cut. I cleaned the rest of the glass out of the rim with the towel.

I laid out two suits of underwear, with socks, shirts, collars and ties, and packed my trunk. I put in everything except my new suit and an old one and two pairs of shoes and two hats, and my books. I carried the books into the sitting-room and stacked them on the table, the ones I had brought from home and the ones *Father said it used to be a gentleman was known by his books; nowadays he is known by the ones he has not returned* and locked the trunk and addressed it. The quarter-hour sounded. I stopped and listened to it until the chimes ceased.

I bathed and shaved. The water made my finger smart a little, so I painted it again. I put on my new suit and put my watch on and packed the other suit and the accessories and my razor and brushes in my hand bag, and wrapped the trunk key into a sheet of paper and put it in an envelope and addressed it to Father, and wrote the two notes and sealed them.

The shadow hadn't quite cleared the stoop. I stopped inside the door, watching the shadow move. It moved almost perceptibly, creeping back inside the door, driving the shadow back into the door. *Only she was running already when I heard it. In the mirror she was running before I knew what it was. That quick, her train caught up over her arm she ran out of the mirror like a cloud, her veil swirling in long glints her heels brittle and fast clutching her dress onto her shoulder with the other hand, running out of the mirror the smells roses roses the voice that breathed o'er Eden. Then she was across the porch I couldn't hear her heels then in the moonlight like a cloud, the floating shadow of the veil running across the grass, into the bellowing. She ran out of her dress, clutching her bridal, running into the bellowing where T. P. in the dew Whooey Sassprilluh Benjy under the box bellowing. Father had a V-shaped silver cuirass on his running chest*

Shreve said, 'Well, you didn't ... Is it a wedding or a wake?'

'I couldn't make it,' I said.

'Not with all that primping. What's the matter? You think this was Sunday?'

'I reckon the police won't get me for wearing my new suit one time,' I said.

'I was thinking about the Square students. Have you got too proud to attend classes too?'

'I'm going to eat first.' The shadow on the stoop was gone. I stepped into sunlight, finding my shadow again. I walked down the steps just ahead of it. The half-hour went. Then the chimes ceased and died away.

Deacon wasn't at the post office either. I stamped the two envelopes and mailed the one to Father and put Shreve's in my inside pocket, and then I remembered where I had last seen the Deacon. It was on Decoration Day, in a G. A. R. uniform, in the middle of the parade. If you waited long enough on any corner you would see him in whatever parade came along. The one before was on Columbus' or Garibaldi's or somebody's birthday. He was in the Street Sweeper's section, in a stovepipe hat, carrying a two-inch Italian flag, smoking a cigar among the brooms and scoops. But the last time was the G. A. R. one, because Shreve said:

'There now. Just look at what your grandpa did to that poor old nigger.'

'Yes,' I said, 'Now he can spend day after day marching in parades. If it hadn't been for my grandfather, he'd have to work like white folks.'

I didn't see him anywhere. But I never knew even a working nigger that you could find when you wanted him, let alone one that lived off the fat of the land. A car came along. I went over to town and went to Parker's and had a good breakfast. While I was eating I heard a clock strike the hour. But then I suppose it takes at least one hour to lose time in, who has been longer than history getting into the mechanical progression of it.

When I finished breakfast I bought a cigar. The girl said a fifty cent one was the best, so I took one and lit it and went out to the street. I stood there and took a couple of puffs, then I held it in my hand and went on toward the corner. I passed a jeweller's window, but I looked away in time. At the corner two bootblacks caught me, one on either side, shrill and raucous, like blackbirds. I gave the cigar to one of them, and the other one a nickel. Then they let me alone. The one with the cigar was trying to sell it to the other for the nickel.

There was a clock, high up in the sun, and I thought about how, when you don't want to do a thing, your body will try to trick you into doing it, sort of unawares. I could feel the muscles in the back of my neck, and then I could hear my watch ticking away in my pocket and after a while I had all the other sounds shut away, leaving only the watch in my pocket. I turned back up the street, to the window. He was working at the table behind the window. He was going bald. There was a glass in his eye – a metal tube screwed into his face. I went in.

The place was full of ticking, like crickets in September grass, and I could hear a big clock on the wall above his head. He looked up, his eye big and blurred and rushing beyond the glass. I took mine out and handed it to him.

'I broke my watch.'

He flipped it over in his hand. 'I should say you have. You must have stepped on it.'

'Yes, sir. I knocked it off the dresser and stepped

on it in the dark. It's still running though.'

He pried the back open and squinted into it. 'Seems to be all right. I can't tell until I go over it, though. I'll go into it this afternoon.'

'I'll bring it back later.' I said. 'Would you mind telling me if any of those watches in the window are right?'

He held my watch on his palm and looked up at me with his blurred rushing eye.

'I made a bet with a fellow,' I said, 'And I forgot my glasses this morning.'

'Why, all right,' he said. He laid the watch down and half rose on his stool and looked over the barrier. Then he glanced up at the wall. 'It's twen – '

'Don't tell me,' I said, 'please sir. Just tell me if any of them are right.'

He looked at me again. He sat back on the stool and pushed the glass up on to his forehead. It left a red circle around his eye and when it was gone his whole face looked naked. 'What're you celebrating today?' he said. 'That boat race ain't until next week, is it?'

'No, sir. This is just a private celebration. Birthday. Are any of them right?'

'No. But they haven't been regulated and set yet. If you're thinking of buying one of them – '

'No, sir. I don't need a watch. We have a clock in our sitting-room. I'll have this one fixed when I do.' I reached my hand.

'Better leave it now.'

'I'll bring it back later.' He gave me the watch. I put it in my pocket. I couldn't hear it now, above all the others. 'I'm much obliged to you. I hope I haven't taken up your time.'

'That's all right. Bring it in when you are ready. And you better put off this celebration until after we win that boat race.'

'Yes, sir. I reckon I had.'

I went out, shutting the door upon the ticking. I looked back into the window. He was watching me across

71

the barrier. There were about a dozen watches in the window, a dozen different hours and each with the same assertive and contradictory assurance that mine had, without any hands at all. Contradicting one another. I could hear mine, ticking away inside my pocket, even though nobody could see it, even though it could tell nothing if anyone could.

And so I told myself to take that one. Because Father said clocks slay time. He said time is dead as long as it is being clicked off by little wheels; only when the clock stops does time come to life. The hands were extended, slightly off the horizontal at a faint angle, like a gull tilting into the wind. Holding all I used to be sorry about like the new moon holding water, niggers say. The jeweller was working again, bent over his bench, the tube tunnelled into his face. His hair was parted in the centre. The part ran up into the bald spot, like a drained marsh in December.

I saw the hardware store from across the street. I didn't know you bought flat-irons by the pound.

The clerk said, 'These weigh ten pounds.' Only they were bigger than I thought. So I got two six-pound little ones, because they would look like a pair of shoes wrapped up. They felt heavy enough together, but I thought again how Father had said about the reducto absurdum of human experience, thinking how the only opportunity I seemed to have for the application of Harvard. Maybe by next year; thinking maybe it takes two years in school to learn to do that properly.

But they felt heavy enough in the air. A street car came. I got on. I didn't see the placard on the front. It was full, mostly prosperous looking people reading newspapers. The only vacant seat was beside a nigger. He wore a derby and shined shoes and he was holding a dead cigar stub. I used to think that a Southerner had to be always conscious of niggers. I thought that Northerners would expect him to. When I first came East I kept thinking You've got to remember to think of them as coloured people not niggers, and if it hadn't happened that I wasn't thrown with many of them, I'd have wasted a lot of time and trouble before I learned that the best way to take all people, black or white, is to take them for what they think they are, then leave them alone. That was when I realized that a nigger is not a person so much as a form of behaviour; a sort of obverse reflection of the white people he lives among. But I thought at first that I ought to miss having a lot of them around me because I thought that Northerners thought I did, but I didn't know that I really had missed Roskus and Dilsey and them until that morning in Virginia. The train was stopped when I waked and I raised the shade and looked out. The car was blocking a road crossing, where two white fences came down a hill and then sprayed outward and downward like part of a skeleton of a horn, and there was a nigger on a mule in the middle of the stiff ruts, waiting for the train to move. How long he had been there I didn't know, but he sat straddle of the mule, his head wrapped in a piece of blanket, as if they had been built there with the fence and the road, or with the hill, carved out of the hill itself, like a sign put there saying You are home again. He didn't have a saddle and his feet dangled almost to the ground. The mule looked like a rabbit. I raised the window.

'Hey, Uncle,' I said, 'Is this the way?'

'Suh?' He looked at me, then he loosened the blanket and lifted it away from his ear.

'Christmas gift!' I said.

'Sho comin, boss. You done caught me, ain't you?'

'I'll let you off this time.' I dragged my pants out of the little hammock and got a quarter out. 'But look out next time. I'll be coming back through here two days after New Year, and look out then.' I threw the quarter out the window. 'Buy yourself some Santy Claus.'

'Yes, suh,' he said. He got down and picked up the quarter and rubbed it on his leg. 'Thanky, young marster. Thanky.' Then the train began to move. I leaned out the

73

window, into the cold air, looking back. He stood there beside the gaunt rabbit of a mule, the two of them shabby and motionless and unimpatient. The train swung around the curve, the engine puffing with short, heavy blasts, and they passed smoothly from sight that way, with that quality about them of shabby and timeless patience, of static serenity: that blending of childlike and ready incompetence and paradoxical reliability that tends and protects them it loves out of all reason and robs them steadily and evades responsibility and obligations by means too barefaced to be called subterfuge even and is taken in theft or evasion with only that frank and spon-taneous admiration for the victor which a gentleman feels for anyone who beats him in a fair contest, and withal a fond and unflagging tolerance for white folks' vagaries like that of a grandparent for unpredictable and troublesome children, which I had forgotten. And all that day, while the train wound through rushing gaps and along ledges where movement was only a labouring sound of the exhaust and groaning wheels and the eter-nal mountains stood fading into the thick sky, I thought of home, of the bleak station and the mud and the nig-gers and country folks thronging slowly about the square, with toy monkeys and wagons and candy in sacks and roman candles sticking out, and my insides would move like they used to do in school when the bell rang.

I wouldn't begin counting until the clock struck three. Then I would begin, counting to sixty and folding down one finger and thinking of the other fourteen fingers waiting to be folded down, or thirteen or twelve or eight or seven, until all of a sudden I'd realize silence and the unwinking minds, and I'd say 'Ma'am?' 'Your name is Quentin, isn't it?' Miss Laura said. Then more silence and the cruel unwinking minds and hands jerking into the silence. 'Tell Quentin who discovered Mississippi River, Henry.' 'DeSoto.' Then the minds would go away, and after a while I'd be afraid I had gotten behind and I'd count fast and fold down another finger, then I'd be afraid I was going too fast and I'd slow up, then I'd get afraid and count fast again. So I never could come out even with the bell, and the released surging of feet moving already, feeling earth in the scuffed floor, and the day like a pane of glass struck a light, sharp blow, and my insides would move, sitting still. *Moving sitting still. One minute she was standing in the door. Benjy. Bellowing. Benjamin the child of mine old age bellowing. Caddy! Caddy!*

*I'm going to run away. He began to cry she went and touched him. Hush. I'm not going to. Hush. He hushed. Dilsey.*

*He smell what you tell him when he want to. Don't have to listen nor talk.*

*Can he smell that new name they give him? Can he smell bad luck?*

*What he want to worry about luck for? Luck can't do him no hurt.*

*What they change his name for then if ain't trying to help his luck?*

The street car stopped, started, stopped again. Below the window I watched the crowns of people's heads passing beneath new straw hats not yet unbleached. There were women in the car now, with market baskets, and men in work-clothes were beginning to outnumber the shined shoes and collars.

The nigger touched my knee. 'Pardon me,' he said. I swung my legs out and let him pass. We were going beside a blank wall, the sound clattering back into the car, at the women with market baskets on their knees and a man in a stained hat with a pipe stuck in the band. I could smell water, and in a break in the wall I saw a glint of water and two masts, and a gull motionless in mid-air, like on an invisible wire between the masts, and I raised my hand and through my coat touched the letters I had written. When the car stopped I got off.

The bridge was open to let a schooner through. She was in tow, the tug nudging along under her quarter, trailing smoke, but the ship herself was like she was moving without visible means. A man naked to the waist

75

was coiling down a line on the fo'c'sle head. His body was burned the colour of leaf tobacco. Another man in a straw hat without any crown was at the wheel. The ship went through the bridge, moving under bare poles like a ghost in broad day, with three gulls hovering above the stern like toys on invisible wires.

When it closed I crossed to the other side and leaned on the rail above the boathouses. The float was empty and the doors were closed. The crew just pulled in the late afternoon now, resting up before. The shadow of the bridge, the tiers of railing, my shadow leaning flat upon the water, so easily had I tricked it that would not quit me. At least fifty feet it was, and if I only had something to blot it into the water, holding it until it was drowned, the shadow of the package like two shoes wrapped up lying on the water. Niggers say a drowned man's shadow was watching for him in the water all the time. It twinkled and glinted, like breathing, the float slow like breathing too, and debris half submerged, healing out to the sea, and the caverns and the grottoes of the sea. The displacement of water is equal to the something of something. Reducto absurdum of all human experience, and two six-pound flat-irons weigh more than one tailor's goose. What a sinful waste Dilsey would say. Benjy knew it when Damuddy died. He cried. *He smell hit. He smell hit.*

The tug came back downstream, the water shearing in long rolling cylinders, rocking the float at last with the echo of passage, the float lurching on to the rolling cylinder with a plopping sound and a long jarring noise as the door rolled back and two men emerged, carrying a shell. They set it in the water and a moment later Bland come out, with the sculls. He wore flannels, a grey jacket and a stiff straw hat. Either he or his mother had read somewhere that Oxford students pulled in flannels and stiff hats, so early one March they bought Gerald a one pair shell and in his flannels and stiff hat he went on the river. The folks at the boathouses threatened to call a policeman, but he went anyway. His mother came down in a hired motor, in a fur suit like an arctic explorer's, and saw him off in a twenty-five mile wind and a steady drove of ice floes like dirty sheep. Ever since then I have believed that God is not only a gentleman and a sport; He is a Kentuckian too. When he sailed away she made a detour and came down to the river again and drove along parallel with him, the car in low gear. They said you couldn't have told they'd ever seen one another before, like a King and Queen, not even looking at one another, just moving side by side across Massachusetts on parallel courses like a couple of planets.

He got in and pulled away. He pulled pretty well now. He ought to. They said his mother tried to make him give rowing up and do something else the rest of his class couldn't or wouldn't do, but for once he was stubborn. If you could call it stubbornness, sitting in his attitudes of princely boredom, with his curly yellow hair and his violet eyes and his eyelashes and his New York clothes, while his mamma was telling us about Gerald's horses and Gerald's niggers and Gerald's women. Husbands and fathers in Kentucky must have been awful glad when she carried Gerald off to Cambridge. She had an apartment over in town, and Gerald had one there too, besides his rooms in college. She approved of Gerald associating with me because I at least revealed a blundering sense of noblesse oblige by getting myself born below Mason and Dixon, and a few others whose geography met the requirements (minimum). Forgave, at least. Or condoned. But since she met Spoade coming out of chapel one He said she couldn't be a lady no lady would be out at that hour of the night she never had been able to forgive him for having five names, including that of a present English ducal house. I'm sure she solaced herself by being convinced that some misfit Maingault or Mortemar had got mixed up with the lodge-keeper's daughter. Which was quite probable, whether she invented it or not. Spoade was the world's champion sitter-a-round, no holds barred and gouging discretionary.

The shell was a speck now, the oars catching the sun in spaced glints, as if the hull were winking itself along. *Did you ever have a sister? No but they're all bitches. Did you ever have a sister? One minute she was. Bitches. Not bitch one minute she stood in the door* Dalton Ames. Dalton Ames. Dalton Shirts. I thought all the time they were khaki, army issue khaki, until I saw they were of heavy Chinese silk or finest flannel because they made his face so brown his eyes so blue. Dalton Ames. It just missed gentility. Theatrical fixture. Just papier mâché, then touch. Oh. Asbestos. Not quite bronze. *But won't see him at the house.*

*Caddy's a woman too, remember. She must do things for women's reasons, too.*

*Why won't you bring him to the house, Caddy? Why must you do like nigger women do in the pasture the ditches the dark woods hot hidden furious in the dark woods.*

And after a while I had been hearing my watch for some time and I could feel the letters crackle through my coat, against the railing, and I leaned on the railing, watching my shadow, how I had tricked it. I moved along the rail, but my suit was dark too and I could wipe my hands, watching my shadow, how I had tricked it. I walked it into the shadow of the quay. Then I went east.

*Harvard my Harvard boy Harvard harvard* That pimple-faced infant she met at the field-meet with coloured ribbons. Skulking along the fence trying to whistle her out like a puppy. Because they couldn't cajole him into the dining-room Mother believed he had some sort of spell he was going to cast on her when he got her alone. Yet any blackguard *He was lying beside the box under the window bellowing* that could drive up in a limousine with a flower in his buttonhole. *Harvard. Quentin this is Herbert. My Harvard boy. Herbert will be a big brother has already promised Jason a position in the bank.*

Hearty, celluloid like a drummer. Face full of teeth white but not smiling. *I've heard of him up there.* All teeth but not smiling. *You going to drive?*

*Get in Quentin.*

*You going to drive.*

*It's her car aren't you proud of your little sister owns first auto in town Herbert his present. Louis has been giving her lessons every morning didn't you get my letter* Mr. and Mrs. Jason Richmond Compson announce the marriage of their daughter Candace to Mr. Sydney Herbert Head on the twenty-fifth of April one thousand nine hundred and ten at Jefferson Mississippi. At home after the first of August number Something Something Avenue South Bend Indiana. Shreve said Aren't you even going to open it? *Three days. Times. Mr. and Mrs. Jason Richmond Compson* Young Lochinvar rode out of the west a little too soon, didn't he?

I'm from the south. You're funny, aren't you.

O yes I knew it was somewhere in the country.

You're funny, aren't you. You ought to join the circus.

I did. That's how I ruined my eyes watering the elephant's fleas. *Three times* These country girls. You can't even tell about them, can you. Well, anyway Byron never had his wish, thank God. *But not hit a man in glasses.* Aren't you even going to open it? *It lay on the table a candle burning at each corner upon the envelope tied in a soiled pink garter two artificial flowers. Not hit a man in glasses.*

Country people poor things they never saw an auto before lots of them honk the horn Candace so *She wouldn't look at me* they'll get out of the way *wouldn't look at me* your father wouldn't like it if you were to injure one of them I declare your father will simply have to get an auto now I'm almost sorry you brought it down Herbert I've enjoyed it so much of course there's the carriage but so often when I'd like to go out Mr. Compson has the darkies doing something it would be worth my head to interrupt he insists that Roskus is at my call all the time but I know what that means I know how often people make promises just to satisfy their consciences are you going to treat my little baby girl that way Herbert but I know you won't Herbert has spoiled us all to death

Quentin did I write you that he is going to take Jason into his bank when Jason finishes high school Jason will make a splendid banker he is the only one of my children with any practical sense you can thank me for that he takes after my people the others are all Compson. *Jason furnished the flour. They made kites on the back porch and sold them for a nickle a piece, he and the Patterson boy. Jason was treasurer.*

There was no nigger in this street car, and the hats unbleached as yet flowing past under the window. Going to Harvard. We have sold Benjy's *He lay on the ground under the window, bellowing. We have sold Benjy's pasture so that Quentin may go to Harvard* a brother to you. Your little brother.

You should have a car it's done you no end of good don't you think so Quentin I call him Quentin at once you see I have heard so much about him from Candace.

Why shouldn't you I want my boys to be more than friends yes Candace and Quentin more than friends *Father I have committed* what a pity you had no brother or sister *No sister no sister had no sister* Don't ask Quentin he and Mr. Compson both feel a little insulted when I am strong enough to come down to the table I am going on nerve now I'll pay for it after it's all over and you have taken my little daughter away from me *My little sister had no. If I could say Mother. Mother*

Unless I do what I am tempted to and take you instead I don't think Mr. Compson could overtake the car.

Ah Herbert Candace do you hear that *She wouldn't look at me soft stubborn jaw-angle not back-looking* You needn't be jealous though it's just an old woman he's flattering a grown married daughter I can't believe it.

Nonsense you look like a girl you are lots younger than Candace colour in your cheeks like a girl *A face reproachful tearful an odour of camphor and of tears a voice weeping steadily and softly beyond the twilit door the twilight-coloured smell of honeysuckle. Bringing empty trunks down the attic stairs they sounded like coffins*

*French Lick. Found not death at the salt lick*

Hats not unbleached and not hats. In three years I cannot wear a hat. I could not. Will there be hats then since I was not and not Harvard then. Where the best of thought Father said clings like dead ivy vines upon old dead brick. Not Harvard then. Not to me, anyway. Again. Sadder than was. Again. Saddest of all. Again.

Spoade had a shirt on; then it must be. When I can see my shadow again if not careful that I tricked into the water shall tread again upon my impervious shadow. But no sister. I wouldn't have done it. *I won't have my daughter spied on* I wouldn't have.

*How can I control any of them when you have always taught them to have no respect for me and my wishes I know you look down on my people but is that any reason for teaching my children my own children I suffered for to have no respect* Trampling my shadow's bones into the concrete with hard heels and then I was hearing the watch, and I touched the letters through my coat.

*I will not have my daughter spied on by you or Quentin or anybody no matter what you think she has done*

*At least you agree there is reason for having her watched*

I wouldn't have I wouldn't have. *I know you wouldn't I didn't mean to speak so sharply but women have no respect for each other for themselves*

*But why did she* The chimes began as I stepped on my shadow, but it was the quarter-hour. The Deacon wasn't in sight anywhere. *think I would have could have*

*She didn't mean that that's the way women do things it's because she loves Caddy*

*The street lamps would go down the hill then rise toward town* I walked upon the belly of my shadow. I could extend my hand beyond it. *feeling Father behind me beyond the rasping darkness of summer and August the street lamps* Father and I protect women from one another from themselves our women *Women are like that they don't acquire knowledge of people we are for that they are just born with a practical fertility of suspicion that makes a crop every so often and usually right they have an affinity for evil for supplying whatever the evil lacks in itself for drawing it about them instinctively as you do bed-clothing in slumber fertilizing the mind for it until the evil has served its purpose whether it ever existed or no* He was coming along between a couple of freshmen. He hadn't quite recovered from the parade, for he gave me a salute, a very superior-officerish kind.

'I want to see you a minute,' I said, stopping.

'See me? All right. See you again, fellows,' he said, stopping and turning back; 'glad to have chatted with you.' That was the Deacon, all over. Talk about your natural psychologists. They said he hadn't missed a train at the beginning of school in forty years, and that he could pick out a Southerner with one glance. He never missed, and once he had heard you speak, he could name your state. He had a regular uniform he met trains in, a sort of Uncle Tom's cabin outfit, patches and all.

'Yes, suh. Right dis way, young marster, hyer we is,' taking your bags. 'Hyer, boy, come hyer and git dese grips.' Whereupon a moving mountain of luggage would edge up, revealing a white boy of about fifteen, and the Deacon would hang another bag on him somehow and drive him off. 'Now, den, don't you drap hit. Yes, suh, young marster, jes give de old nigger yo room number, and hit'll be done got cold dar when you arrives.'

From then on until he had you completely subjugated he was always in or out of your room, ubiquitous and garrulous, though his manner gradually moved northward as his raiment improved, until at last when he had bled you until you began to learn better he was calling you Quentin or whatever, and when you saw him next he'd be wearing a cast-off Brooks suit and a hat with a Princeton club I forget which band that someone had given him and which he was pleasantly and unshakably convinced was a part of Abe Lincoln's military sash. Someone spread the story years ago, when he first appeared around college from wherever he came from, that he was a graduate of the divinity school. And when

he came to understand what it meant he was so taken
with it that he began to retail the story himself, until at
last he must come to believe he really had. Anyway he
related long pointless anecdotes of his undergraduate
days, speaking familiarly of dead and departed professors
by their first names, usually incorrect ones. But he had
been guide mentor and friend to unnumbered crops of
innocent and lonely freshmen, and I suppose that with
all his petty chicanery and hypocrisy he stank no higher
in heaven's nostrils than any other.

'Haven't seen you in three-four days,' he said, staring
at me from his still military aura. 'You been sick?'

'No. I've been all right. Working, I reckon. I've seen
you, though.'

'Yes?'

'In the parade the other day.'

'Oh, that. Yes, I was there. I don't care nothing about
that sort of thing, you understand, but the boys likes to
have me with them, the vet'runs does. Ladies wants all
the old vet'runs to turn out, you know. So I has to oblige
them.'

'And on that Wop holiday, too,' I said. 'You were oblig-
ing the W.C.T.U. then, I reckon.'

'That? I was doing that for my son-in-law. He aims to
get a job on the city forces. Street cleaner. I tells him all
he wants is a broom to sleep on. You saw me, did you?'

'Both times. Yes.'

'I mean, in uniform. How'd I look?'

'You looked fine. You looked better than any of them.
They ought to make you a general, Deacon.'

He touched my arm, lightly, his hand that worn, gentle quality of niggers' hands. 'Listen. This ain't for outside talking. I don't mind telling you because you and
me's the same folk, come long and short.' He leaned a little to me, speaking rapidly, his eyes not looking at me.
'I've got strings out, right now. Wait till next year. Just
wait. Then see where I'm marching. I won't need to tell
you how I'm fixing it; I say, just wait and see, my boy.'

He looked at me now and clapped me lightly on the shoulder and rocked back on his heels, nodding at me. 'Yes, sir. I didn't turn Democrat three years ago for nothing. My son-in-law on the city; me – Yes, sir. If just turning Democrat'll make that son of a bitch go to work … And me: just you stand on that corner yonder a year from two days ago, and see.'

'I hope so. You deserve it, Deacon. And while I think about it – ' I took the letter from my pocket. 'Take this around to my room to-morrow and give it to Shreve. He'll have something for you. But not till to-morrow, mind.'

He took the letter and examined it. 'It's sealed up.'

'Yes. And it's written inside, Not good until tomorrow.'

'H'm,' he said. He looked at the envelope, his mouth pursed. 'Something for me, you say?'

'Yes. A present I'm making you.'

He was looking at me now, the envelope white in his black hand, in the sun. His eyes were soft and irisless and brown, and suddenly I saw Roskus watching me from behind all his white folks' claptrap of uniforms and politics and Harvard manner, diffident, secret, inarticulate and sad. 'You ain't playing a joke on the old nigger, is you?'

'You know I'm not. Did any Southerner ever play a joke on you?'

'You're right. They're fine folks. But you can't live with them.'

'Did you ever try?' I said. But Roskus was gone. Once more he was that self he had long since taught himself to wear in the world's eye, pompous, spurious, not quite gross.

'I'll confer to your wishes, my boy.'

'Not until to-morrow, remember.'

'Sure,' he said; 'understand, my boy. Well – '

'I hope – ' I said. He looked down at me, benignant, profound. Suddenly I held out my hand and we shook, he gravely, from the pompous height of his municipal and military dream. 'You're a good fellow, Deacon. I hope ... You've helped a lot of young fellows, here and there.'

'I've tried to treat all folks right,' he said. 'I draw no petty social lines. A man to me is a man, wherever I find him.'

'I hope you'll always find as many friends as you've made.'

'Young fellows. I get along with them. They don't forget me, neither,' he said, waving the envelope. He put it into his pocket and buttoned his coat. 'Yes, sir,' he said, 'I've had good friends.'

The chimes began again, the half-hour. I stood in the belly of my shadow and listened to the strokes spaced and tranquil along the sunlight, among the thin, still little leaves. Spaced and peaceful and serene, with that quality of autumn always in bells even in the month of brides. *Lying on the ground under the window bellowing* He took one look at her and knew. Out of the mouths of babes. *The street lamps* The chimes ceased. I went back to the post office, treading my shadow into pavement. *go down the hill then they rise toward town like lanterns hung one above another on a wall.* Father said because she loves Caddy she loves people through their shortcomings. Uncle Maury straddling his legs before the fire must remove one hand long enough to drink Christmas. Jason ran on, his hands in his pockets fell down and lay there like a trussed fowl until Versh set him up. *Whyn't you keep them hands outen your pockets when you running you could stand up then* Rolling his head in the cradle rolling it flat across the back. Caddy told Jason Versh said that the reason Uncle Maury didn't work was that he used to roll his head in the cradle when he was little.

Shreve was coming up the walk, shambling, fatly earnest, his glasses glinting beneath the running leaves like little pools.

'I gave Deacon a note for some things. I may not be in this afternoon, so don't you let him have anything until to-morrow, will you?'

'All right.' He looked at me. 'Say, what're you doing to-day, anyhow? All dressed up and mooning around like the prologue to a suttee. Did you go to Psychology this morning?'

'I'm not doing anything. Not until to-morrow, now.'

'What's that you got there?'

'Nothing. Pair of shoes I had half-soled. Not until to-morrow, you hear?'

'Sure. All right. Oh, by the way, did you get a letter off the table this morning?'

'No.'

'It's there. From Semiramis. Chauffeur brought it before ten o'clock.'

'All right. I'll get it. Wonder what she wants now.'

'Another band recital, I guess. Tumpty ta ta Gerald blah. "A little louder on the drum, Quentin." God, I'm glad I'm not a gentleman.' He went on, nursing a book, a little shapeless, fatly intent. *The street lamps* do you think so because one of our forefathers was a governor and three were generals and Mother's weren't

any live man is better than any dead man but no live or dead man is very much better than any other live or dead man *Done in Mother's mind though. Finished. Finished. Then we were all poisoned* you are confusing sin and morality women don't do that your Mother is thinking of morality whether it be sin or not has not occurred to her

Jason I must go away you keep the others I'll take Jason and go where nobody knows us so he'll have a chance to grow up and forget all this the others don't love me they have never loved anything with that streak of Compson selfishness and false pride Jason was the only one my heart went out to without dread

nonsense Jason is all right I was thinking that as soon as you feel better you and Caddy might go up to French Lick

and leave Jason here with nobody but you and the darkies

she will forget him then all the talk will die away *found not death at the salt licks*

maybe I could find a husband for her *not death at the salt licks*

The car came up and stopped. The bells were still ringing the half-hour. I got on and it went on again, blotting the half-hour. No: the three-quarters. Then it would be ten minutes anyway. To leave Harvard *your Mother's dream for sold Benjy's pasture for*

what have I done to have been given children like these Benjamin was punishment enough and now for her to have no more regard for me her own mother I've suffered for her dreamed and planned and sacrificed I went down into the valley yet never since she opened her eyes has she given me one unselfish thought at times I look at her I wonder if she can be my child except Jason he has never given me one moment's sorrow since I first held him in my arms I knew then that he was to be my joy and my salvation I thought that Benjamin was punishment enough for any sins I have committed I thought he was my punishment for putting aside my pride and marrying a man who held himself above me I don't complain I loved him above all of them because of it because my duty though Jason pulling at my heart all the while but I see now that I have not suffered enough I see now that I must pay for your sins as well as mine what have you done what sins have your high and mighty people visited upon me but you'll take up for them you always have found excuses for your own blood only Jason can do wrong because he is more Bascomb than Compson while your own daughter my little daughter my baby girl she is she is no better than that when I was a girl I was unfortunate I was only a Bascomb I was taught that there is no half-way ground that a woman is either a lady or not but I never dreamed when I held her in my arms that any daughter of mine could let herself don't you know I can look at her eyes and tell you may think she'd tell you but she doesn't tell things she is secretive you don't know her I know things she's done that I'd die before I'd have

you know that's it go on criticize Jason accuse me of setting him to watch her as if it were a crime while your own
daughter can I know you don't love him that you wish to
believe faults against him you never have yes ridicule
him as you always have Maury you cannot hurt me any
more than your children already have and then I'll be
gone and Jason with no one to love him shield him from
this I look at him every day dreading to see this
Compson blood beginning to show in him at last with his
sister slipping out to see what do you call it then have
you ever laid eyes on him will you even let me try to find
out who he is it's not for myself I couldn't bear to see him
it's for your sake to protect you but who can fight against
bad blood you won't let me try we are to sit back with our
hands folded while she not only drags your name in the
dirt but corrupts the very air your children breathe Jason
you must let me go away I cannot stand it let me have
Jason and you keep the others they're not my flesh and
blood like he is strangers nothing of mine and I am afraid
of them I can take Jason and go where we are not known
I'll go down on my knees and pray for the absolution of
my sins that he may escape this curse try to forget that
the others ever were

   If that was the three-quarters, not over ten minutes
now. One car had just left, and people were already waiting for the next one. I asked, but he didn't know whether
another one would leave before noon or not because
you'd think that interurbans. So the first one was another
trolley. I got on. You can feel noon. I wonder if even min-
ers in the bowels of the earth. That's why whistles:
because people that sweat, and if just far enough from
sweat you won't hear whistles and in eight minutes
you should be that far from sweat in Boston. Father
said a man is the sum of his misfortunes. One day
you'd think misfortune would get tired, but then time
is your misfortune Father said. A gull on an invisible
wire attached through space dragged. You carry the
symbol of your frustration into eternity. Then the

wings are bigger Father said only who can play a harp.

I could hear my watch whenever the car stopped, but not often they were already eating *Who would play a* Eating the business of eating inside of you space too space and time confused Stomach saying noon brain saying eat o'clock All right I wonder what time it is what of it. People were getting out. The trolley didn't stop so often now, emptied by eating.

Then it was past. I got off and stood in my shadow and after a while a car came along and I got on and went back to the interurban station. There was a car ready to leave, and I found a seat next the window and it started and I watched it sort of frazzle out into slack tide flats, and then trees. Now and then I saw the river and I thought how nice it would be for them down at New London if the weather and Gerald's shell going solemnly up the glinting forenoon and I wondered what the old woman would be wanting now, sending me a note before ten o'clock in the morning. What picture of Gerald I to be one of the *Dalton Ames oh asbestos Quentin has shot* background. Something with girls in it. Women do have *always his voice above the gabble voice that breathed* an affinity for evil, for believing that no woman is to be trusted, but that some men are too innocent to protect themselves. Plain girls. Remote cousins and family friends whom mere acquaintanceship invested with a sort of blood obligation noblesse oblige. And she sitting there telling us before their faces what a shame it was that Gerald should have all the family looks because a man didn't need it, was better off without it but without it a girl was simply lost. Telling us about Gerald's women in a *Quentin has shot Herbert he shot his voice through the floor of Caddy's room* tone of smug approbation. 'When he was seventeen I said to him one day "What a shame that you should have a mouth like that it should be on a girl's face" and can you imagine *the curtains leaning in on the twilight upon the odour of the apple tree her head against the twilight her arms behind her head kimono-winged the voice that breathed o'er eden clothes upon the bed by the nose seen above the apple* what he said? just seventeen, mind. "Mother" he said "it often is." ' And him sitting there in attitudes regal watching two or three of them through his eyelashes. They gushed like swallows swooping his eyelashes. Shreve said he always had *Are you going to look after Benjy and Father*

*The less you say about Benjy and Father the better when have you ever considered them Caddy*

*Promise*

*You needn't worry about them you're getting out in good shape*

*Promise I'm sick you'll have to promise* wondered who invented that joke but then he always had considered Mrs. Bland a remarkably preserved woman he said she was grooming Gerald to seduce a duchess sometime. She called Shreve that fat Canadian youth twice she arranged a new room-mate for me without consulting me at all, once for me to move out, once for

He opened the door in the twilight. His face looked like a pumpkin pie.

'Well, I'll say a fond farewell. Cruel fate may part us, but I will never love another. Never.'

'What are you talking about?'

'I'm talking about cruel fate in eight yards of apricot silk and more metal pound for pound than a galley slave and the sole owner and proprietor of the unchallenged peripatetic john of the late Confederacy.' Then he told me how she had gone to the proctor to have him moved out and how the proctor had revealed enough low stubbornness to insist on consulting Shreve first. Then she suggested that he send for Shreve right off and do it, and he wouldn't do that, so after that she was hardly civil to Shreve. 'I make it a point never to speak harshly of females,' Shreve said, 'but that woman has got more ways like a bitch than any lady in these sovereign states and dominions.' and now Letter on the table by hand, command orchid scented coloured If she knew I had

passed almost beneath the window knowing it there
without My dear Madam I have not yet had an opportunity of receiving your communication but I beg in
advance to be excused today or yesterday and tomorrow
or when As I remember that the next one is to be how
Gerald throws his nigger downstairs and how the nigger
plead to be allowed to matriculate in the divinity school
to be near marster marse gerald and How he ran all the
way to the station beside the carriage with tears in his
eyes when marse gerald rid away I will wait until the day
for the one about the sawmill husband came to the
kitchen door with a shotgun Gerald went down and bit
the gun in two and handed it back and wiped his hands
on a silk handkerchief threw the handkerchief in the
stove I've only heard that one twice

*shot him through the* I saw you come in here so I
watched my chance and came along thought we might
get acquainted have a cigar

Thanks I don't smoke

No things must have changed up there since my day
mind if I light up

Help yourself

Thanks I've heard a lot I guess your mother won't
mind if I put the match behind the screen will she a lot
about you Candace talked about you all the time up
there at the Licks. I got pretty jealous I says to myself
who is this Quentin anyway I must see what this animal
looks like because I was hit pretty hard see soon as I saw
the little girl I don't mind telling you it never occurred to
me it was her brother she kept talking about she couldn't
have talked about you any more if you'd been the only
man in the world husband wouldn't have been in it you
won't change your mind and have a smoke

I don't smoke

In that case I won't insist even though it is a pretty fair
weed cost me twenty-five bucks a hundred wholesale
friend in Havana yes I guess there are lots of changes up
there I keep promising myself a visit but I never get

around to it been hitting the ball now for ten years I can't get away from the bank during school fellow's habits change things that seem important to an undergraduate you know tell me about things up there

I'm not going to tell Father and Mother if that's what you are getting at

Not going to tell not going to oh that that's what you are talking about is it you understand that I don't give a damn whether you tell or not understand that a thing like that unfortunate but no police crime I wasn't the first or the last I was just unlucky you might have been luckier

You lie

Keep your shirt on I'm not trying to make you tell anything you don't want to meant no offence of course a young fellow like you would consider a thing of that sort a lot more serious than you will in five years

I don't know but one way to consider cheating I don't think I'm likely to learn different at Harvard

We're better than a play you must have made the Dramat well you're right no need to tell them we'll let bygones be bygones eh no reason why you and I should let a little thing like that come between us I like you Quentin I like your appearance you don't look like these other hicks I'm glad we're going to hit it off like this I've promised your mother to do something for Jason but I would like to give you a hand too Jason would be just as well off here but there's no future in a hole like this for a young fellow like you

Thanks you'd better stick to Jason he'd suit you better than I would

I'm sorry about that business but a kid like I was then I never had a mother like yours to teach me the finer points it would just hurt her necessarily to know it yes you're right to need to that includes Candace of course

I said Mother and Father

Look here take a look at me how long do you think you'd last with me

I won't have to last long if you learned to fight up at school too try and see how long I would

You damned little        what do you think you're
getting at

Try and see

My God the cigar what would your mother say if she
found a blister on her mantel just in time too look here
Quentin we're about to do something we'll both regret I
like you liked you as soon as I saw you I says he must be
a damned good fellow whoever he is or Candace
wouldn't be so keen on him listen I've been out in the
world now for ten years things don't matter so much then
you'll find that out let's you and I get together on this
thing sons of old Harvard and all I guess I wouldn't know
the place now best place for a young fellow in the world
I'm going to send my sons there give them a better
chance than I had wait don't go yet let's discuss this thing
a young man gets these ideas and I'm all for them does
him good while he's in school forms his character good
for tradition the school but when he gets out into the
world he'll have to get his the best way he can because
he'll find that everybody else is doing the same thing and
be damned to here let's shake hands and let bygones be
bygones for your mother's sake remember her health
come on give me your hand here look at it it's just out of
convent look not a blemish not even been creased yet
see here

To hell with your money

No no come on I belong to the family now see I know
how it is with a young fellow he has lots of private affairs
it's always pretty hard to get the old man to stump up for
I know haven't I been there and not so long ago either
but now I'm getting married and all specially up there
come on don't be a fool listen when we get a chance for a
real talk I want to tell you about a little widow over in
town

I've heard that too keep your damned money

Call it a loan then just shut your eyes a minute and
you'll be fifty

Keep your hands off of me you'd better get
that cigar off the mantel

Tell and be damned than see what it gets you if you were not a damned fool you'd have seen that I've got them too tight for any half-baked Galahad of a brother your mother's told me about your sort with your head swelled up come in oh come in dear Quentin and I were just getting acquainted talking about Harvard did you want me can't stay away from the old man can she

Go out a minute Herbert I want to talk to Quentin

Come in come in let's all have a gabfest and get acquainted I was just telling Quentin

Go on Herbert go out a while

Well all right than I suppose you and bubber do want to see one another once more eh

You'd better take that cigar off the mantel

Right as usual my boy then I'll toddle along let them order you around while they can Quentin after day after tomorrow it'll be pretty please to the old man won't it dear give us a kiss honey

Oh stop that save that for day after tomorrow

I'll want interest then don't let Quentin do anything he can't finish oh by the way did I tell Quentin the story about the man's parrot and what happened to it a sad story remind me of that think of it yourself ta-ta see you in the funny paper

Well

Well

What are you up to now

Nothing

You're meddling in my business again didn't you get enough of that last summer

Caddy you've got fever *You're sick how are you sick*

*I'm just sick. I can't ask.*

*Shot his voice through the*

Not that blackguard Caddy

Now and then the river glinted beyond things in sort of swooping glints, across noon and after. Well after now, though we had passed where he was still pulling upstream majestical in the face of god gods. Better.

Gods. God would be canaille too in Boston in Massachusetts. Or maybe just not a husband. The wet oars winking him along in bright winks and female palms. Adulant. Adulant if not a husband he'd ignore God. *That blackguard, Caddy* The river glinted away beyond a swooping curve.

*I'm sick you'll have to promise*

*Sick how are you sick*

*I'm just sick I can't ask anybody yet promise you will*

*If they need any looking after it's because of you how are you sick* Under the window we could hear the car leaving for the station, the 8:10 train. To bring back cousins. Heads. Increasing himself head by head but not barbers. Manicure girls. We had a blood horse once. In the stable yes, but under leather a cur. *Quentin has shot all of their voices through the floor of Caddy's room*

The car stopped. I got off, into the middle of my shadow. A road crossed the track. There was a wooden marquee with an old man eating something out of a paper bag, and then the car was out of hearing too. The road went into the trees, where it would be shady, but June foliage in New England not much thicker than April at home in Mississippi. I could see a smoke stack. I turned my back to it, tramping my shadow into the dust. *There was something terrible in me sometimes at night I could see it grinning at me I could see it through them grinning at me through their faces it's gone now and I'm sick*

*Caddy*

*Don't touch me just promise*

*If you're sick you can't*

*Yes I can after that it'll be all right it won't matter don't let them send him to Jackson promise*

*I promise Caddy Caddy*

*Don't touch me don't touch me*

*What does it look like Caddy*

*What*

*That that grins at you that thing through them*

I could still see the smoke stack. That's where the

95

water would be, heading out to the sea and the peaceful grottoes. Tumbling peacefully they would, and when He said Rise only the flat-irons. When Versh and I hunted all day we wouldn't take any lunch, and at twelve o'clock I'd get hungry. I'd stay hungry until about one, then all of a sudden I'd even forget that I wasn't hungry any more. *The street lamps go down the hill then heard the car go down the hill. The chair-arm flat cool smooth under my fore-head shaping the chair the apple tree leaning on my hair above the eden clothes by the nose seen* You've got fever I felt it yesterday it's like being near a stove.

Don't touch me.

Caddy you can't do it if you are sick. That blackguard.

I've got to marry somebody. *Then they told me the bone would have to be broken again*

At last I couldn't see the smoke stack. The road went beside a wall. Trees leaned over the wall, sprayed with sunlight. The stone was cool. Walking near it you could feel the coolness. Only our country was not like this country. There was something about just walking through it. A kind of still and violent fecundity that satisfied ever bread-hunger like. Flowing around you, not brooding and nursing every niggard stone. Like it were put to makeshift for enough green to go around among the trees and even the blue of distance not that rich chimaera. *told me the bone would have to be broken again and inside me it began to say Ah Ah Ah and I began to sweat. What do I care I know what a broken leg is all it is it won't be anything I'll just have to stay in the house a little longer that's all and my jaw-muscles getting numb and my mouth saying Wait Wait just a minute through the sweat ah ah ah behind my teeth and Father damn that horse damn that horse. Wait it's my fault. He came along the fence every morning with a basket toward the kitchen dragging a stick along the fence every morning I dragged myself to the window cast and all and laid for him with a piece of coal Dilsey said you goin to ruin yoself ain't you got no mo sense than that not fo days since you bruck hit. Wait I'll get used to it in a minute wait just a minute I'll get*

Even sound seemed to fail in this air, like the air was worn out with carrying sounds so long. A dog's voice carries further than a train, in the darkness anyway. And some people's. Niggers. Louis Hatcher never even used his horn carrying it and that old lantern. I said, 'Louis, when was the last time you cleaned that lantern?'

'I cleant hit a little while back. You member when all dat flood-watter wash dem folks away up yonder? I cleant hit dat ve'y day. Old woman and me setting fore de fire dat night and she say "Louis, whut you gwine do ef dat flood git out dis fur?" and I say "Dat's a fack. I reckon I had better clean dat lantun up." So I cleant hit dat night.'

'That flood was way up in Pennsylvania,' I said. 'It couldn't even have got down this far.'

'Dat's whut you says,' Louis said. 'Watter kin git des ez high en wet in Jefferson ez hit kin in Pennsylvaney, I reckon. Hit's de folks dat says de high watter can't git dis fur dat comes floatin out on de ridge-pole, too.'

'Did you and Martha get out that night?'

'We done jest that. I cleant dat lantun and me and her sot de balance of de night on top o dat knoll back de graveyard. En ef I'd knowed of aihy one higher, we'd a been on hit instead.'

'And you haven't cleaned that lantern since then.'

'Whut I want to clean hit when dey ain't no need?'

'You mean, until another flood comes along?'

'Hit kep us outen dat un.'

'Oh, come on, Uncle Louis,' I said.

'Yes, suh. You do you way en I do mine. Ef all I got to do to keep outen de high watter is to clean dis yere lantun, I wont quoil wid no man.'

'Unc' Louis wouldn't ketch nothin wid a light he could see by,' Versh said.

'I wuz huntin possums in dis country when dey was still drowndin nits in yo pappy's head wid coal oil, boy,' Louis said. 'Ketchin um, too.'

'Dat's de troof,' Versh said. 'I reckon Unc' Louis done caught mo possums than aihy man in dis country.'

'Yes, suh,' Louis said, 'I got plenty light fer possums to see, all right. I ain't heard none o dem complainin. Hush, now. Dar he. Whooey. Hum awn, dawg.' And we'd sit in the dry leaves that whispered a little with the slow respiration of our waiting and with the slow breathing of the earth and the windless October, the rank smell of the lantern fouling the brittle air, listening to the dogs and to the echo of Louis' voice dying away. He never raised it, yet on a still night we have heard it from our front porch. When he called the dogs in he sounded just like the horn he carried slung on his shoulder and never used, but clearer, mellower, as though his voice were a part of darkness and silence, coiling out of it, coiling into it again. WhoOoooo. WhoOoooo. WhoOooooooooooooooo. *Got to marry somebody*

*Have there been very many Caddy*

*I don't know too many will you look after Benjy and Father*

*You don't know whose it is then does he know*

*Don't touch me will you look after Benjy and Father*

I began to feel the water before I came to the bridge. The bridge was of grey stone, lichened, dappled with slow moisture where the fungus crept. Beneath it the water was clear and still in the shadow, whispering and clucking about the stone in fading swirls of spinning sky. *Caddy that*

*I've got to marry somebody* Versh told me about a man mutilated himself. He went into the woods and did it with a razor, sitting in a ditch. A broken razor flinging them backward over his shoulder the same motion complete the jerked skein of blood backward not looping. But that's not it. It's not not having them. It's never to have had them then I could say O That That's Chinese I don't know Chinese. And Father said it's because you are a virgin: don't you see? Women are never virgins. Purity is a negative state and therefore contrary to nature. It's nature is hurting you not Caddy and I said That's just words and he said So is virginity and I said you don't know. You can't know and he said Yes. On the instant when we come to realize that tragedy is second-hand.

Where the shadow of the bridge fell I could see down for a long way, but not as far as the bottom. When you leave a leaf in water a long time after awhile the tissue will be gone and the delicate fibres waving slow as the motion of sleep. They don't touch one another, no matter how knotted up they once were, no matter how close they lay once to the bones. And maybe when He says Rise the eyes will come floating up too, out of the deep quiet and the sleep, to look on glory. And after a while the flat-irons would come floating up. I hid them under the end of the bridge and went back and leaned on the rail.

I could not see the bottom, but I could see a long way into the motion of the water before the eye gave out, and then I saw a shadow hanging like a fat arrow stemming into the current. Mayflies skimmed in and out of the shadow of the bridge just above the surface. *If it could just be a hell beyond that: the clean flame the two of us more than dead. Then you will have only me then only me then the two of us amid the pointing and the horror beyond the clean flame* The arrow increased without motion, then in a quick swirl the trout lipped a fly beneath the surface with that sort of gigantic delicacy of an elephant picking up a peanut. The fading vortex drifted away down stream and then I saw the arrow again, nose into the current, wavering delicately to the motion of the water above which the Mayflies slanted and poised. *Only you and me then amid the pointing and the horror walled by the clean flame*

The trout hung, delicate and motionless among the wavering shadows. Three boys with fishing poles came on to the bridge and we leaned on the rail and looked down at the trout. They knew the fish. He was a neighbourhood character.

'They've been trying to catch that trout for twenty-five years. There's a store in Boston offers a twenty-five dollar fishing rod to anybody that can catch him.'

'Why don't you all catch him, then? Wouldn't you

like to have a twenty-five dollar fishing rod?'

'Yes,' they said. They leaned on the rail, looking down at the trout. 'I sure would,' one said.

'I wouldn't take the rod,' the second said. 'I'd take the money instead.'

'Maybe they wouldn't do that,' the first said. 'I bet he'd make you take the rod.'

'Then I'd sell it.'

'You couldn't get twenty-five dollars for it.'

'I'd take what I could get then. I can catch just as many fish with this pole as I could with a twenty-five dollar one.' Then they talked about what they would do with twenty-five dollars. They all talked at once, their voices insistent and contradictory and impatient, making of unreality a possibility, then a probability, then an incontrovertible fact, as people will when their desires become words.

'I'd buy a horse and wagon,' the second said.

'Yes, you would,' the others said.

'I would. I know where I can buy one for twenty-five dollars. I know the man.'

'Who is it?'

'That's all right who it is. I can buy it for twenty-five dollars.'

'Yah,' the others said, 'He don't know any such thing. He's just talking.'

'Do you think so?' the boy said. They continued to jeer at him, but he said nothing more. He leaned on the rail, looking down at the trout which he had already spent, and suddenly the acrimony, the conflict, was gone from their voices, as if to them too it was as though he had captured the fish and bought his horse and wagon, they too partaking of that adult trait of being convinced of anything by an assumption of silent superiority. I suppose that people using themselves and each other so much by words, are at least consistent in attributing wisdom to a still tongue, and for a while I could feel the other two seeking swiftly for some means by which to cope with him, to rob him of his horse and wagon.

'You couldn't get twenty-five dollars for that pole,' the first said. 'I bet anything you couldn't.'

'He hasn't caught that trout yet,' the third said suddenly, then they both cried:

'Yah, wha'd I tell you? What's the man's name? I dare you to tell. There ain't any such man.'

'Ah, shut up,' the second said. 'Look, Here he comes again.' They leaned on the rail, motionless, identical, their poles slanting slenderly in the sunlight, also identical. The trout rose without haste, a shadow in faint wavering increase; again the little vortex faded slowly downstream. 'Gee,' the first one murmured.

'We don't try to catch him any more,' he said. 'We just watch Boston folks that come out and try.'

'Is he the only fish in this pool?'

'Yes. He ran all the others out. The best place to fish around here is down at the Eddy.'

'No it ain't,' the second said. 'It's better at Bigelow's Mill two to one.' Then they argued for a while about which was the best fishing and then left off all of a sudden to watch the trout rise again and the broken swirl of water suck down a little of the sky. I asked how far it was to the nearest town. They told me.

'But the closest car line is that way,' the second said, pointing back down the road. 'Where are you going?'

'Nowhere. Just walking.'

'You from the college?'

'Yes. Are there any factories in that town?'

'Factories?' They looked at me.

'No,' the second said. 'Not there.' They looked at my clothes. 'You looking for work?'

'How about Bigelow's Mill?' the third said. 'That's a factory.'

'Factory my eye. He means a sure enough factory.'

'One with a whistle,' I said. 'I haven't heard any one o'clock whistles yet.'

'Oh,' the second said. 'There's a clock in the Unitarian

steeple. You can find out the time from that. Haven't you got a watch on that chain?'

'I broke it this morning.' I showed them my watch. They examined it gravely.

'It's still running,' the second said. 'What does a watch like that cost?'

'It was a present,' I said. 'My father gave it to me when I graduated from high school.'

'Are you a Canadian?' the third said. He had red hair.

'Canadian?'

'He don't talk like them,' the second said. 'I've heard them talk. He talks like they do in minstrel shows.'

'Say,' the third said. 'Ain't you afraid he'll hit you?'

'Hit me?'

'You said he talks like a coloured man.'

'Ah, dry up,' the second said. 'You can see the steeple when you get over that hill there.'

I thanked them. 'I hope you have good luck. Only don't catch that old fellow down there. He deserves to be let alone.'

'Can't anybody catch that fish,' the first said. They leaned on the rail, looking down into the water, the three poles like three slanting threads of yellow fire in the sun. I walked upon my shadow, tramping it into the dappled shade of trees again. The road curved, mounting away from the water. It crossed the hill, then descended winding, carrying the eye, the mind on ahead beneath a still green tunnel, and the square cupola above the trees and the round eye of the clock but far enough. I sat down at the roadside. The grass was ankle deep, myriad. The shadows on the road were as still as if they had been put there with a stencil, with slanting pencils of sunlight. But it was only a train, and after a while it died away beyond the trees, the long sound, and then I could hear my watch and the train dying away, as though it were running through another month or another summer somewhere, rushing away under the poised gull and all things rushing. Except Gerald. He would be sort of grand too, pulling in lonely state across the noon, rowing himself right out of noon, up the long bright air like an apotheosis, mounting into a drowsing infinity where only he and the gull, the one terrifically motionless, the other in a steady and measured pull and recover that partook of inertia itself, the world punily beneath their shadows on the sun. Caddy that blackguard that blackguard Caddy

Their voices came over the hill, and the three slender poles like balanced threads of running fire. They looked at me passing, not slowing.

'Well,' I said, 'I don't see him.'

'We didn't try to catch him,' the first said. 'You can't catch that fish.'

'There's the clock,' the second said, pointing. 'You can tell the time when you get a little closer.'

'Yes,' I said, 'All right.' I got up. 'You all going to town?'

'We're going to the Eddy for chub,' the first said.

'You can't catch anything at the Eddy,' the second said.

'I guess you want to go to the mill, with a lot of fellows splashing and scaring all the fish away.'

'You can't catch any fish at the Eddy.'

'We won't catch none nowhere if we don't go on,' the third said.

'I don't see why you keep on talking about the Eddy,' the second said. 'You can't catch anything there.'

'You don't have to go,' the first said. 'You're not tied to me.'

'Let's go to the mill and go swimming,' the third said.

'I'm going to the Eddy and fish,' the first said. 'You can do as you please.'

'Say, how long has it been since you heard of anybody catching a fish at the Eddy?' the second said to the third.

'Let's go to the mill and go swimming,' the third said. The cupola sank slowly beyond the trees, with the round face of the clock far enough yet. We went on in the dappled shade. We came to an orchard, pink and white.

It was full of bees; already we could hear them.

'Let's go to the mill and go swimming,' the third said. A lane turned off beside the orchard. The third boy slowed and halted. The first went on, flecks of sunlight slipping along the pole across his shoulder and down the back of his shirt. 'Come on,' the third said. The second boy stopped too. *Why must you marry somebody Caddy*

*Do you want me to say it do you think that if I say it it won't be*

'Let's go up to the mill,' he said. 'Come on.'

The first boy went on. His bare feet made no sound, falling softer than leaves in the thin dust. In the orchard the bees sounded like a wind getting up, a sound caught by a spell just under crescendo and sustained. The lane went along the wall, arched over, shattered with bloom, dissolving into trees. Sunlight slanted into it, sparse and eager. Yellow butterflies flickered along the shade like flecks of sun.

'What do you want to go to the Eddy for?' the second boy said. 'You can fish at the mill if you want to.'

'Ah, let him go,' the third said. They looked after the first boy. Sunlight slid patchily across his walking shoulders, glinting along the pole like yellow ants.

'Kenny,' the second said. *Say it to Father will you I will am my fathers Progenitive I invented him created I him Say it to him it will not be for he will say I was not and then you and I since philoprogenitive*

'Ah, come on,' the boy said. 'They're already in.' They looked after the first boy. 'Yah,' they said suddenly, 'go on then, mamma's boy. If he goes swimming he'll get his head wet and then he'll get a licking.' They turned into the lane and went on, the yellow butterflies slanting about them along the shade.

*it is because there is nothing else I believe there is something else but there may not be and then I You will find that even injustice is scarcely worthy of what you believe yourself to be.* He paid me no attention, his jaw set in profile, his face turned a little away beneath his broken hat.

'Why don't you go swimming with them?' I said. *that blackguard Caddy*

*Were you trying to pick a fight with him were you*

*A liar and a scoundrel Caddy was dropped from his club for cheating at cards got sent to Coventry caught cheating at midterm exams and expelled*

*Well what about it I'm not going to play cards with*

'Do you like fishing better than swimming?' I said. The sound of the bees diminished, sustained yet, as though instead of sinking into silence, silence merely increased between us, as water rises. The road curved again and became a street between shady lawns with white houses. *Caddy that blackguard can you think of Benjy and Father and do it not of me*

*What else can I think about what else have I thought about* The boy turned from the street. He climbed a picket fence without looking back and crossed the lawn to a tree and laid the pole down and climbed into the fork of the tree and sat there, his back to the road and the dappled sun motionless at last upon his white shirt. *Else have I thought about I can't even cry I died last year I told you I had but I didn't know then what I meant I didn't know what I was saying* Some days in late August at home are like this, the air thin and eager like this, with something in it sad and nostalgic and familiar. Man the sum of his climatic experiences Father said. Man the sum of what have you. A problem in impure properties carried tediously to an unvarying nil: stalemate of dust and desire. *But now I know I'm dead I tell you*

*Then why must you listen we can go away you and Benjy and me where nobody knows us where* The buggy was drawn by a white horse, his feet clopping in the thin dust; spidery wheels chattering thin and dry, moving uphill beneath a rippling shawl of leaves. Elm. No: ellum. Ellum.

*On what on your school money the money they sold the pasture for so you could go to Harvard don't you see you've got to finish now if you don't finish he'll have nothing*

*Sold the pasture* His white shirt was motionless in the fork, in the flickering shade. The wheels were spidery. Beneath the sag of the buggy the hooves neatly rapid like the motions of a lady doing embroidery, diminishing without progress like a figure on a treadmill being drawn rapidly off stage. The street turned again. I could see the white cupola, the round stupid assertion of the clock. *Sold the pasture*

*Father will be dead in a year they say if he doesn't stop drinking and he won't stop he can't stop since I since last summer and then they'll send Benjy to Jackson I can't cry I can't even cry one minute she was standing in the door the next minute he was pulling at her dress and bellowing his voice hammered back and forth between the walls in waves and she shrinking against the wall getting smaller and smaller with her white face her eyes like thumbs dug into it until he pushed her out of the room his voice hammering back and forth as though its own momentum would not let it stop as though there were no place for it in silence bellowing*

When you opened the door a bell tinkled, but just once, high and clear and small in the neat obscurity above the door, as though it were gauged and tempered to make that single clear small sound so as not to wear the bell out nor to require the expenditure of too much silence in restoring it when the door opened upon the recent warm scent of baking; a little dirty child with eyes like a toy bear's and two patent-leather pig-tails.

'Hello, sister.' Her face was like a cup of milk dashed with coffee in the sweet warm emptiness. 'Anybody here?'

But she merely watched me until a door opened and the lady came. Above the counter where the ranks of crisp shapes behind the glass her neat grey face her hair tight and sparse from her neat grey skull, spectacles in neat grey rims riding approaching like something on a wire, like a cash box in a store. She looked like a librarian. Something among dusty shelves of ordered certitudes long divorced from reality, desiccating peacefully, as if a breath of that air which sees injustice done

'Two of these, please, ma'am.'

From under the counter she produced a square cut from a newspaper and laid it on the counter and lifted the two buns out. The little girl watched them with still and unwinking eyes like two currants floating motionless in a cup of weak coffee Land of the kike home of the wop. Watching the bread, the neat grey hands, a broad gold band on the left forefinger, knuckled there by a blue knuckle.

'Do you do your own baking, ma'am?'

'Sir?' she said. Like that. Sir? Like on the stage. Sir? 'Five cents. Was there anything else?'

'No, ma'am. Not for me. This lady wants something.' She was not tall enough to see over the case, so she went to the end of the counter and looked at the little girl.

'Did you bring her in here?'

'No, ma'am. She was here when I came.'

'You little wretch,' she said. She came out around the counter, but she didn't touch the little girl. 'Have you got anything in your pockets?'

'She hasn't got many pockets,' I said. 'She wasn't doing anything. She was just standing here, waiting for you.'

'Why didn't the bell ring, then?' She glared at me. She just needed a bunch of switches, a blackboard behind her 2 x 2 e 5. 'She'll hide it under her dress and a body'd never know it. You, child. How'd you get in here?'

The little girl said nothing. She looked at the woman, then she gave me a flying black glance and looked at the woman again. 'Them foreigners,' the woman said. 'How'd she get in without the bell ringing?'

'She came in when I opened the door,' I said. 'It rang once for both of us. She couldn't reach anything from here, anyway. Besides, I don't think she would. Would you, sister?' The little girl looked at me, secretive, contemplative. 'What do you want? Bread?'

She extended her fist. It uncurled upon a nickel, moist

and dirty, moist dirt ridged into her flesh. The coin was damp and warm. I could smell it, faintly metallic.

'Have you got a five cent loaf, please, ma'am?'

From beneath the counter she produced a square cut from a newspaper sheet and laid it on the counter and wrapped a loaf into it. I laid the coin and another one on the counter. 'And another one of those buns, please, ma'am.'

She took another bun from the case. 'Give me that parcel,' she said. I gave it to her and she unwrapped it and put the third bun in and wrapped it and took up the coins and found two coppers in her apron and gave them to me. I handed them to the little girl. Her fingers closed about them, damp and hot, like worms.

'You going to give her that bun?' the woman said.

'Yessum,' I said. 'I expect your cooking smells as good to her as it does to me.'

I took up the two packages and gave the bread to the little girl, the woman all iron-grey behind the counter, watching us with cold certitude. 'You wait a minute,' she said. She went to the rear. The door opened again and closed. The little girl watched me, holding the bread against her dirty dress.

'What's your name?' I said. She quit looking at me, but she was still motionless. She didn't even seem to breathe. The woman returned. She had a funny looking thing in her hand. She carried it sort of like it might have been a dead pet rat.

'Here,' she said. The child looked at her. 'Take it,' the woman said, jabbing it at the little girl. 'It just looks peculiar. I calculate you won't know the difference when you eat it. Here. I can't stand here all day.' The child took it, still watching her. The woman rubbed her hands on her apron. 'I got to have that bell fixed,' she said. She went to the door and jerked it open. The little bell tinkled once, faint and clear and invisible. We moved toward the door and the woman's peering back.

'Thank you for the cake,' I said.

'Them foreigners,' she said, staring up into the obscurity where the bell tinkled. 'Take my advice and stay clear of them, young man.'

'Yessum,' I said. 'Come on, sister.' We went out. 'Thank you, ma'am.'

She swung the door to, then jerked it open again, making the bell give forth its single small note. 'Foreigners,' she said, peering up at the bell.

We went on. 'Well,' I said, 'How about some ice cream?' She was eating the gnarled cake. 'Do you like ice cream?' She gave me a black still look, chewing. 'Come on.'

We came to the drug-store and had some ice cream. She wouldn't put the loaf down. 'Why not put it down so you can eat better?' I said, offering to take it. But she held to it, chewing the ice cream like it was taffy. The bitten cake lay on the table. She ate the ice cream steadily, then she fell to on the cake again, looking about at the showcases. I finished mine and we went out.

'Which way do you live?' I said.

A buggy, the one with the white horse it was. Only Dog Peabody is fat. Three hundred pounds. You ride with him on the uphill side, holding on. Children. Walking easier than holding uphill. *Seen the doctor yet have you seen Caddy*

*I don't have to I can't ask now afterward it will be all right, it won't matter*

Because women so delicate so mysterious Father said. Delicate equilibrium of periodical filth between two moons balanced. Moons he said full and yellow as harvest moons her hips thighs. Outside outside of them always but. Yellow. Feet soles with walking like. Then know that some man that all those mysterious and imperious concealed. With all that inside of them shapes an outward suavity waiting for a touch to. Liquid putrefaction like drowned things floating like pale rubber flabbily filled getting the odour of honeysuckle all mixed up.

'You'd better take your bread on home, hadn't you?'

She looked at me. She chewed quietly and steadily; at regular intervals a small distension passed smoothly down her throat. I opened my package and gave her one of the buns. 'Good-bye,' I said.

I went on. Then I looked back. She was behind me. 'Do you live down this way?' She said nothing. She walked beside me, under my elbow sort of, eating. We went on. It was quiet, hardly anyone about *getting the odour of honeysuckle all mixed She would have told me not to let me sit there on the steps hearing her door twilight slamming hearing Benjy still crying Supper she would have to come down then getting honeysuckle all mixed up in it* We reached the corner.

'Well, I've got to go down this way,' I said. 'Good-bye.' She stopped too. She swallowed the last of the cake, then she began on the bun, watching me across it. 'Good-bye,' I said. I turned into the street and went on, but I went to the next corner before I stopped.

'Which way do you live?' I said. 'This way?' I pointed down the street. She just looked at me. 'Do you live over that way? I bet you live close to the station, where the trains are. Don't you?' She just looked at me, serene and secret and chewing. The street was empty both ways, with quiet lawns and houses neat among the trees, but no one at all except back there. We turned and went back. Two men sat in chairs in front of a store.

'Do you all know this little girl? She sort of took up with me and I can't find where she lives.'

They quit looking at me and looked at her.

'Must be one of them new Italian families,' one said. He wore a rusty frock coat. 'I've seen her before. What's your name, little girl?' She looked at them blackly for awhile, her jaws moving steadily. She swallowed without ceasing to chew.

'Maybe she can't speak English,' the other said.

'They sent her after bread,' I said. 'She must be able to speak something.'

'What's your pa's name?' the first said. 'Pete? Joe?

name John huh?' She took another bite from the bun.

'What must I do with her?' I said. 'She just follows me. I've got to get back to Boston.'

'You from the college?'

'Yes, sir. And I've got to get on back.'

'You might go up the street and turn her over to Anse. He'll be up at the livery stable. The marshal.'

'I reckon that's what I'll have to do,' I said. 'I've got to do something with her. Much obliged. Come on sister.'

We went up the street, on the shady side, where the shadow of the broken façade blotted slowly across the road. We came to the livery stable. The marshal wasn't there. A man sitting in a chair tilted in the broad low door, where a dark cool breeze smelling of ammonia blew among the ranked stalls, said to look at the post office. He didn't know her either.

'Them furriners. I can't tell one from another. You might take her across the tracks where they live, and maybe somebody'll claim her.'

We went to the post office. It was back down the street. The man in the frock coat was opening a newspaper.

'Anse just drove out of town,' he said. 'I guess you'd better go down past the station and walk past them houses by the river. Somebody there'll know her.'

'I guess I'll have to,' I said. 'Come on, sister.' She pushed the last piece of the bun into her mouth and swallowed it. 'Want another?' I said. She looked at me, chewing, her eyes black and unwinking and friendly. I took the other two buns out and gave her one and bit into the other. I asked a man where the station was and he showed me. 'Come on, sister.'

We reached the station and crossed the tracks, where the river was. A bridge crossed it, and a street of jumbled frame houses followed the river, backed on to it. A shabby street, but with an air heterogeneous and vivid too. In the centre off an untrimmed plot enclosed by a fence of gaping and broken pickets stood an ancient lopsided surrey and a weathered house from an upper window of which hung a garment of vivid pink.

'Does that look like your house?' I said. She looked at me over the bun. 'This one?' I said, pointing. She just chewed, but it seemed to me that I discerned something affirmative, acquiescent even if it wasn't eager, in her air. 'This one?' I said. 'Come on, then.' I entered the broken gate. I looked back at her. 'Here?' I said. 'This look like your house?'

She nodded her head rapidly, looking at me, gnawing into the damp half moon of the bread. We went on. A walk of broken random flags, speared by fresh coarse blades of grass, led to the broken stoop. There was no movement about the house at all, and the pink garment hanging in no wind from the upper window. There was a bell pull with a porcelain knob, attached to about six feet of wire when I stopped pulling and knocked. The little girl had the crust edgeways in her chewing mouth.

A woman opened the door. She looked at me, then she spoke rapidly to the little girl in Italian, with a rising inflexion, then a pause, interrogatory. She spoke to her again, the little girl looking at her across the end of the crust, pushing it into her mouth with a dirty hand.

'She says she lives here,' I said. 'I met her downtown. Is this your bread?'

'No spika,' the woman said. She spoke to the little girl again. The little girl just looked at her.

'No live here?' I said. I pointed to the girl, then at her, then at the door. The woman shook her head. She spoke rapidly. She came to the edge of the porch and pointed down the road, speaking.

I nodded violently too. 'You come show?' I said. I took her arm, waving my other hand toward the road. She spoke swiftly, pointing. 'You come show,' I said, trying to lead her down the steps.

'Si, si,' she said, holding back, showing me whatever it was. I nodded again.

'Thanks. Thanks. Thanks.' I went down the steps

and walked toward the gate, not running, but pretty fast. I reached the gate and stopped and looked at her for a while. The crust was gone now, and she looked at me with her black friendly stare. The woman stood on the stoop, watching us.

'Come on, then,' I said. 'We'll have to find the right one sooner or later.'

She moved along just under my elbow. We went on. The houses all seemed empty. Not a soul in sight. A sort of breathlessness that empty houses have. Yet they couldn't all be empty. All the different rooms, if you could just slice the walls away all of a sudden Madam, your daughter, if you please. No. Madam, for God's sake, your daughter. She moved along just under my elbow, her shiny pigtails, and then the last house played out and the road curved out of sight beyond a wall, following the river. The woman was emerging from the broken gate, with a shawl over her head and clutched under her chin. The road curved on, empty. I found a coin and gave it to the little girl. A quarter. 'Good-bye, sister,' I said. Then I ran.

I ran fast, not looking back. Just before the road curved away I looked back. She stood in the road, a small figure clasping the loaf of bread to her filthy little dress, her eyes still and black and unwinking. I ran on.

A lane turned from the road. I entered it and after a while I slowed to a fast walk. The lane went between back premises – unpainted houses with more of those gay and startling coloured garments on lines, a barn broken-backed, decaying quietly among rank orchard trees, unpruned and weed-choked, pink and white and murmurous with sunlight and with bees. I looked back. The entrance to the lane was empty. I slowed still more my shadow pacing me, dragging its head through the weeds that hid the fence.

The lane went back to a barred gate, became defunctive in grass, a mere path scarred quietly into new grass. I climbed the gate into a wood-lot and crossed it and came to another wall and followed that one, my shadow behind me now. There were vines and creepers where at home would be honeysuckle. Coming and coming especially in the dusk when it rained, getting honeysuckle all mixed up in it as though it were not enough without that, not unbearable enough. *What did you let him for kiss kiss*

*I didn't let him I made him watching me getting mad What do you think of that? Red print of my hand coming up through her face like turning a light on under your hand her eyes going bright*

*It's not for kissing I slapped you. Girl's elbows at fifteen Father said you swallow like you had a fishbone in your throat what's the matter with you and Caddy across the table not to look at me. It's for letting it be some darn town squirt I slapped you you will will you now I guess you say calf rope. My red hand coming up out of her face. What do you think of that scouring her head into the. Grass sticks criss-crossed into the flesh tingling scouring her head. Say calf rope say it*

*I didn't kiss a dirty girl like Natalie anyway* The wall went into shadow, and then my shadow, I had tricked it again. I had forgot about the river curving along the road. I climbed the wall. And then she watched me jump down, holding the loaf against her dress.

I stood in the weeds and we looked at one another for a while.

'Why didn't you tell me you lived out this way, sister?' The loaf was wearing slowly out of the paper; already it needed a new one. 'Well, come on then and show me the house.' *not a dirty girl like Natalie. It was raining we could hear it on the roof, sighing through the high sweet emptiness of the barn.*

*There? touching her*

*Not there*

*There? not raining hard but we couldn't hear anything but the roof and as if it was my blood or her blood*

*She pushed me down the ladder and ran off and left me Caddy did*

*Was it there it hurt you when Caddy did ran off was it there*

*Oh* She walked just under my elbow, the top of her patent leather head, the loaf fraying out of the news-paper.

'If you don't get home pretty soon you're going to wear that loaf out. And then what'll your mamma say?' *I bet I can lift you up*

*You can't I'm too heavy*

*Did Caddy go away did she go to the house you can't see the barn from our house did you ever try to see the barn from*

*It was her fault she pushed me she ran away*

*I can lift you up see how I can*

*Oh her blood or my blood Oh* We went on in the thin dust, our feet silent as rubber in the thin dust where pen-cils of sun slanted in the trees. And I could feel water again running swift and peaceful in the secret shade.

'You live a long way, don't you. You're mighty smart to go this far to town by yourself.' *It's like dancing sitting down did you ever dance sitting down? We could hear the rain, a rat in the crib, the empty barn vacant with horses. How do you hold to dance do you hold like this*

*Oh*

*I used to hold like this you thought I wasn't strong enough didn't you*

*Oh Oh Oh Oh*

*I hold to use like this I mean did you hear what I said I said oh oh oh oh*

The road went on, still and empty, the sun slanting more and more. Her stiff little pigtails were bound at the tips with bits of crimson cloth. A corner of the wrapping flapped a little as she walked, the nose of the loaf naked. I stopped.

'Look here. Do you live down this road? We haven't passed a house in a mile, almost.'

She looked at me, black and secret and friendly.

'Where do you live, sister? Don't you live back there in town?'

There was a bird somewhere in the woods, beyond the broken and infrequent slanting of sunlight.

'Your papa's going to be worried about you. Don't you reckon you'll get a whipping for not coming straight home with that bread?'

The bird whistled again, invisible, a sound meaning-less and profound, inflexionless, ceasing as though cut off with the blow of a knife, and again, and that sense of water swift and peaceful above secret places, felt, not seen not heard.

'Oh, hell, sister.' About half the paper hung limp. 'That's not doing any good now.' I tore it off and dropped it beside the road. 'Come on. We'll have to go to town. We'll go back along the river.'

We left the road. Among the moss little pale flowers grew, and the sense of water mute and unseen. *I hold to use like this I mean I use to hold She stood in the door looking at us her hands on her hips*

*You pushed me it was your fault it hurt me too*

*We were dancing sitting down I bet Caddy can't dance sitting down*

*Stop that stop that*

*I was just brushing the trash off the back of your dress*

*You keep your nasty old hands off of me it was your fault you pushed me down I'm mad at you*

*I don't care she looked at us stay mad she went away* We began to hear the shouts, the splashings; I saw a brown body gleam for an instant.

*Stay mad. My shirt was getting wet and my hair. Across the roof hearing the roof loud now I could see Natalie going through the garden among the rain. Get wet I hope you catch pneumonia go on home Cowface. I jumped hard as I could into the hog-wallow the mud yellowed up to my waist stinking I kept on plunging until I fell down and rolled over in it* 'Hear them in swimming, sister? I wouldn't mind doing that myself.' If I had time. When I have time. I could hear my watch. *mud was warmer than the rain it smelled awful. She had her back turned I went around in front of her. You know what I was doing? She turned her back I went around in front of her the rain creeping into the mud flatting her bodice through her dress it smelled horrible. I was hugging her that's what I was doing. She turned her back I went around in front of her. I was hugging her I tell you.*

*I don't give a damn what you were doing.*

*You don't you don't I'll make you I'll make you give a damn. She hit my hands away I smeared mud on her with the other hand I couldn't feel the wet smacking of her hand I wiped mud from my legs smeared it on her wet hard turning body hearing her fingers going into my face but I couldn't feel it even when the rain began to taste sweet on my lips*

They saw us from the water first, heads and shoulders. They yelled and one rose squatting and sprang among them. They looked like beavers, the water lipping about their chins, yelling.

'Take that girl away! What did you want to bring a girl here for? Go on away!'

'She won't hurt you. We just want to watch you for a while.'

They squatted in the water. Their heads drew into a clump, watching us, then they broke and rushed toward us, hurling water with their hands. We moved quick.

'Look out, boys; she won't hurt you.'

'Go on away, Harvard!' It was the second boy, the one that thought the horse and wagon back there at the bridge. 'Splash them, fellows!'

'Let's get out and throw them in,' another said. 'I ain't afraid of any girl.'

'Splash them! Splash them!' They rushed toward us, hurling water. We moved back. 'Go on away!' they yelled. 'Go on away!'

We went away. They huddled just under the bank, their slick heads in a row against the bright water. We went on. 'That's not for us, is it.' The sun slanted through to the moss here and there, leveller. 'Poor kid, you're just a girl.' Little flowers grew among the moss, littler than I had ever seen. 'You're just a girl. Poor kid.' There was a path, curving along beside the water. Then the water was still again, dark and still and swift.

'Nothing but a girl. Poor sister.' *We lay in the wet grass panting the rain like cold shot on my back. Do you care now do you do you*

*My Lord we sure are in a mess get up. Where the rain touched my forehead it began to smart my hand came red away streaking off pink in the rain. Does it hurt*

*Of course it does what do you reckon*

*I tried to scratch your eyes out my Lord we sure do stink we better try to wash it off in the branch* 'There's town again, sister. You'll have to go home now. I've got to get back to school. Look how late it's getting. You'll go home now, won't you?' But she just looked at me with her black, secret, friendly gaze, the half-naked loaf clutched to her breast. 'It's wet. I thought we jumped back in time.' I took my handkerchief and tried to wipe the loaf, but the crust began to come off, so I stopped. 'We'll just have to let it dry itself. Hold it like this.' She held it like that. It looked kind of like rats had been eating it now. *and the water building and building up the squatting back the sloughed mud stinking surfaceward pocking the pattering surface like grease on a hot stove. I told you I'd make you*

*I don't give a goddam what you do*

Then we heard the running and we stopped and looked back and saw him coming up the path running, the level shadows flicking upon his legs.

'He's in a hurry. We'd –' then I saw another man, an oldish man running heavily, clutching a stick, and a boy naked from the waist up, clutching his pants as he ran.

'There's Julio,' the little girl said, and then I saw his Italian face and his eyes as he sprang upon me. We went down. His hands were jabbing at my face and he was saying something and trying to bite me, I reckon, and then they hauled him off and held him heaving and thrashing and yelling and they held his arms and he tried to kick me until they dragged him back. The little girl was howling, holding the loaf in both arms. The half-naked boy was darting and jumping up and down, clutching his trousers and someone pulled me up in time to see another stark naked figure come around the tranquil bend in the path running and change direction in mid-stride and leap into the woods, a couple of garments rigid as boards behind it. Julio still struggled. The man who had pulled me up said, 'Whoa, now. We got you.' He wore a vest but no coat. Upon it was a metal shield. In his other hand he clutched a knotted, polished stick.

'You're Anse, aren't you?' I said. 'I was looking for you. What's the matter?'

'I warn you that anything you say will be used against you,' he said. 'You're under arrest.'

'I killa heem,' Julio said. He struggled. Two men held him. The little girl howled steadily, holding the bread. 'You steala my seester,' Julio said. 'Let go, meesters.'

'Steal his sister?' I said. 'Why, I've been –'

'Shet up,' Anse said. 'You can tell that to Squire.'

'Steal his sister?' I said. Julio broke from the men and sprang at me again, but the marshal met him and they struggled until the other two pinioned his arms again. Anse released him, panting.

'You durn furriner,' he said, 'I've a good mind to take you up too, for assault and battery.' He turned to me again. 'Will you come peaceable, or do I handcuff you?'

'I'll come peaceable,' I said. 'Anything, just so I can find someone – do something with – Stole his sister,' I said. 'Stole his – '

'I've warned you,' Anse said. 'He aims to charge you with meditated criminal assault. Here, you, make that gal shut up that noise.'

'Oh,' I said. Then I began to laugh. Two more boys with plastered heads and round eyes came out of the bushes buttoning shirts that had already dampened on to their shoulders and arms, and I tried to stop the laughter, but I couldn't.

'Watch him, Anse, he's crazy, I believe.'

'I'll have to qu-quit,' I said, 'it'll stop in a mu-minute. The other time it said ah ah ah,' I said, laughing. 'Let me sit down a while.' I sat down, they watching me, and the little girl with her streaked face and the gnawed-looking loaf, and the water swift and peaceful below the path. After a while the laughter ran out. But my throat wouldn't quit trying to laugh, like retching after your stomach is empty.

'Whoa, now,' Anse said. 'Get a grip on yourself.'

'Yes,' I said, tightening my throat. There was another yellow butterfly, like one of the sunflecks had come loose. After a while I didn't have to hold my throat so tight. I got up. 'I'm ready. Which way?'

We followed the path, the two others watching Julio and the little girl and the boys somewhere in the rear. The path went along the river to the bridge. We crossed it and the tracks, people coming to the doors to look at us and more boys materializing from somewhere until when we turned into the main street we had quite a procession. Before the drug-store stood a motor, a big one, but I didn't recognize them until Mrs. Bland said:

'Why, Quentin! Quentin Compson!' Then I saw Gerald, and Spoade in the back seat, sitting on the back of his neck. And Shreve. I didn't know the two girls.

'Quentin Compson!' Mrs. Bland said.

'Good afternoon,' I said, raising my hat. 'I'm under arrest. I'm sorry I didn't get your note. Did Shreve tell you?'

'Under arrest?' Shreve said. 'Excuse me,' he said.

He heaved himself up and climbed over their feet and got out. He had on a pair of my flannel pants, like a glove. I didn't remember forgetting them. I didn't remember how many chins Mrs. Bland had, either. The prettiest girl was with Gerald in front, too. They watched me through veils, with a kind of delicate horror. 'Who's under arrest?' Shreve said. 'What's this, mister?'

'Gerald,' Mrs. Bland said, 'Send these people away. You get in this car, Quentin.'

Gerald got out. Spoade hadn't moved.

'What's he done, Cap?' he said. 'Robbed a hen house?'

'I warn you,' Anse said. 'Do you know the prisoner?'

'Know him,' Shreve said. 'Look here – '

'Then you can come along to the squire's. You're obstructing justice. Come along.' He shook my arm.

'Well, good afternoon,' I said. 'I'm glad to have seen you all. Sorry I couldn't be with you.'

'You, Gerald,' Mrs. Bland said.

'Look here, constable,' Gerald said.

'I warn you you're interfering with an officer of the law,' Anse said. 'If you've anything to say, you can come to the squire's and make cognizance of the prisoner.' We went on. Quite a procession now, Anse and I leading. I could hear them telling them what it was, and Spoade asking questions, and then Julio said something violently in Italian and I looked back and saw the little girl standing at the curb, looking at me with her friendly, inscrutable regard.

'Git on home,' Julio shouted at her, 'I beat hell outa you.'

We went down the street and turned into a bit of lawn in which, set back from the street, stood a one-storey building of brick trimmed with white. We went up the rock path to the door, where Anse halted everyone except us and made them remain outside. We entered a bare room smelling of stale tobacco. There was a sheet iron stove in the centre of a wooden frame filled with sand, and a faded map on the wall and the dingy plat of a township. Behind a scarred littered table a man with a fierce roach of iron grey hair peered at us over steel spectacles.

'Got him, did ye, Anse?' he said.

'Got him, Squire.'

He opened a huge dusty book and drew it to him and dipped a foul pen into an inkwell filled with what looked like coal dust.

'Look here, mister,' Shreve said.

'The prisoner's name,' the squire said. I told him. He wrote it slowly into the book, the pen scratching with excruciating deliberation.

THE SOUND AND THE FURY

'Look here, mister,' Shreve said, 'We know this fellow. We – '

'Order in the court,' Anse said.

'Shut up, bud,' Spoade said. 'Let him do it his way. He's going to anyhow.'

'Age,' the squire said. I told him. He wrote that, his mouth moving as he wrote. 'Occupation.' I told him. 'Harvard student, hey?' he said. He looked up at me, bowing his neck a little to see over the spectacles. His eyes were clear and cold, like a goat's. 'What are you up to, coming out here kidnapping children?'

'They're crazy, Squire,' Shreve said. 'Whoever says this boy's kidnapping – '

Julio moved violently. 'Crazy?' he said. 'Don't I catcha heem, eh? Don't I see weetha my own eyes – '

'You're a liar,' Shreve said. 'You never – '

'Order, order,' Anse said, raising his voice.

'You fellers shet up,' the squire said. 'If they don't stay quiet, turn 'em out, Anse.' They got quiet. The squire looked at Shreve, then at Spoade, then at Gerald. 'You know this young man?' he said to Spoade.

'Yes, your honour,' Spoade said. 'He's just a country boy in school up there. He don't mean any harm. I think the marshal'll find it's a mistake. His father's a congregational minister.'

'H'm,' the squire said. 'What was you doing, exactly?' I told him, he watching me with his cold, pale eyes. 'How about it, Anse?'

'Might have been,' Anse said. 'Them durn furriners.'

'I American,' Julio said. 'I gotta da pape'.'

'Where's the gal?'

'He sent her home,' Anse said.

'Was she scared or anything?'

'Not till Julio there jumped on the prisoner. They were just walking along the river path, towards town. Some boys swimming told us which way they went.'

'It's a mistake, Squire,' Spoade said. 'Children and

dogs are always taking up with him like that. He can't help it.'

'H'm,' the squire said. He looked out of the window for a while. We watched him. I could hear Julio scratching himself. The squire looked back.

'Air you satisfied the gal ain't took any hurt, you, there?'

'No hurt now,' Julio said sullenly.

'You quit work to hunt for her?'

'Sure I quit. I run. I run like hell. Looka here, looka there, then man tella me he seen him giva her she eat. She go weetha.'

'H'm,' the squire said. 'Well, son, I calculate you owe Julio something for taking him away from his work.'

'Yes, sir,' I said. 'How much?'

'Dollar, I calculate.'

I gave Julio a dollar.

'Well,' Spoade said, 'If that's all – I reckon he's discharged, your honour?'

The squire didn't look at him. 'How far'd you run him, Anse?'

'Two miles, at least. It was about two hours before we caught him.'

'H'm,' the squire said. He mused a while. We watched him, his stiff crest, the spectacles riding low on his nose. The yellow shape of the window grew slowly across the floor, reached the wall, climbing. Dust motes whirled and slanted. 'Six dollars.'

'Six dollars?' Shreve said. 'What's that for?'

'Six dollars,' the squire said. He looked at Shreve a moment, then at me again.

'Look here,' Shreve said.

'Shut up,' Spoade said. 'Give it to him, bud, and let's get out of here. The ladies are waiting for us. You got six dollars?'

'Yes,' I said. I gave him six dollars.

'Case dismissed,' he said.

'You get a receipt,' Shreve said. 'You get a signed receipt for that money.'

The squire looked at Shreve mildly. 'Case dismissed,' he said without raising his voice.

'I'll be damned – ' Shreve said.

'Come on here,' Spoade said, taking his arm. 'Good afternoon, Judge. Much obliged.' As we passed out the door Julio's voice rose again, violent, then ceased. Spoade was looking at me, his brown eyes quizzical, a little cold. 'Well, bud, I reckon you'll do your girl chasing in Boston after this.'

'You damned fool,' Shreve said. 'What the hell do you mean anyway, straggling off here, fooling with these damn wops?'

'Come on,' Spoade said, 'They must be getting impatient.'

Mrs. Bland was talking to them. They were Miss Holmes and Miss Daingerfield and they quit listening to her and looked at me again with that delicate and curious horror, their veils turned back upon their little white noses and their eyes fleeing and mysterious beneath the veils.

'Quentin Compson,' Mrs. Bland said. 'What would your mother say? A young man naturally gets into scrapes, but to be arrested on foot by a country policeman. What did they think he'd done, Gerald?'

'Nothing,' Gerald said.

'Nonsense. What was it, you, Spoade?'

'He was trying to kidnap that little dirty girl, but they caught him in time,' Spoade said.

'Nonsense,' Mrs. Bland said, but her voice sort of died away and she stared at me for a moment, and the girls drew their breaths in with a soft concerted sound. 'Fiddlesticks,' Mrs. Bland said briskly. 'If that isn't just like these ignorant low class Yankees. Get in, Quentin.'

Shreve and I sat on two small collapsible seats. Gerald cranked the car and got in and we started.

'Now, Quentin, you tell me what all this foolishness is

about,' Mrs. Bland said. I told them, Shreve hunched and furious on his little seat and Spoade sitting again on the back of his neck beside Miss Daingerfield.

'And the joke is, all the time Quentin had us all fooled,' Spoade said. 'All the time we thought he was the model youth that anybody could trust a daughter with, until the police showed him up at his nefarious work.'

'Hush up, Spoade,' Mrs. Bland said. We drove down the street and crossed the bridge and passed the house where the pink garment hung in the window. 'That's what you get for not reading my note. Why didn't you come and get it? Mr. MacKenzie says he told you it was there.'

'Yessum. I intended to, but I never went back to the room.'

'You'd have let us sit there waiting I don't know how long, if it hadn't been for Mr. MacKenzie. When he said you hadn't come back, that left an extra place, so we asked him to come. We're very glad to have you anyway, Mr. MacKenzie.' Shreve said nothing. His arms were folded and he glared straight ahead past Gerald's cap. It was a cap for motoring in England. Mrs. Bland said so. We passed that house, and three others, and another yard where the little girl stood by the gate. She didn't have the bread now, and her face looked like it had been streaked with coal-dust. I waved my hand, but she made no reply, only her head turned slowly as the car passed, following us with her unwinking gaze. Then we ran beside the wall, our shadows running along the wall, and after a while we passed a piece of torn newspaper lying beside the road and I began to laugh again. I could feel it in my throat and I looked off into the trees where the afternoon slanted, thinking of afternoon and of the bird and the boys in swimming. But still I couldn't stop it and then I knew that if I tried too hard to stop it I'd be crying and I thought about how I'd thought about I could not be a virgin, with so many of them walking along in the shadows and whispering with their soft girl voices lingering in

the shadowy places and the words coming out and perfume and eyes you could feel not see, but if it was that
simple to do it wouldn't be anything and if it wasn't anything, what was I and then Mrs. Bland said, 'Quentin? Is
he sick, Mr. MacKenzie?' and then Shreve's fat hand
touched my knee and Spoade began talking and I quit
trying to stop it.

'If that hamper is in his way, Mr. MacKenzie, move it
over on your side. I brought a hamper of wine because I
think young gentlemen should drink wine, although my
father, Gerald's grandfather' *ever do that Have you ever
done that In the grey darkness a little light her hands locked
about*

'They do, when they can get it,' Spoade said. 'Hey,
Shreve?' *her knees her face looking at the sky the smell of honeysuckle upon her face and throat*

'Beer, too,' Shreve said. His hand touched my knee
again. I moved my knee again. *like a thin wash of lilac
coloured paint talking about him bringing*

'You're not a gentleman,' Spoade said. *him between us
until the shape of her blurred not with dark*

'No. I'm Canadian,' Shreve said. *talking about him the
oar blades winking him along winking the Cap made for
motoring in England and all time rushing beneath and they two
blurred within the other for ever more he had been in the army
had killed men*

'I adore Canada,' Miss Daingerfield said. 'I think it's
marvellous.'

'Did you ever drink perfume?' Spoade said. *with one
hand he could lift her to his shoulder and run with her running
Running*

'No,' Shreve said. *running the beast with two backs and
she blurred in the winking oars running the swine of Euboeleus
running coupled within how many Caddy*

'Neither did I,' Spoade said. *I don't know too many there
was something terrible in me terrible in me Father I have committed Have you ever done that We didn't we didn't do that did
we do that*

'and Gerald's grandfather always picked his own mint before breakfast, while the dew was still on it. He wouldn't even let old Wilkie touch it do you remember Gerald but always gathered it himself and made his own julep. He was as crotchety about his julep as an old maid, measuring everything by a recipe in his head. There was only one man he ever gave that recipe to; that was' *we did how can you not know it if you'll just wait I'll tell you how it was it was a crime we did a terrible crime it cannot be hid you think it can but wait Poor Quentin you've never done that have you and I'll tell you how it was I'll tell Father then it'll have to be because you love Father then we'll have to go away amid the pointing and the horror the clean flame I'll make you say we did I'm stronger than you I'll make you know we did you thought it was them but it was me listen I fooled you all the time it was me you thought I was in the house where that damn honeysuckle try-ing not to think the swing the cedars the secret surges the breath-ing locked drinking the wild breath the yes Yes Yes yes* 'never be got to drink wine himself, but he always said that a ham-per what book did you read that in the one where Gerald's rowing suit of wine was a necessary part of any gentlemen's picnic basket' *did you love them Caddy did you love them When they touched me I died*
one minute she was standing there the next he was yelling and pulling at her dress they went into the hall and up the stairs yelling and shoving at her up the stairs to the bathroom door and stopped her back against the door and her arm across her face yelling and trying to shove her into the bathroom when she came in to supper T. P. was feeding him he started again just whimpering at first until she touched him then he yelled she stood there her eyes like cornered rats then I was running in the grey darkness it smelled of rain and all flower scents the damp warm air released and crickets sawing away in the grass pacing me with a small travelling island of silence Fancy watched me across the fence blotchy like a quilt on a line I thought damn that nigger he forgot to feed her again I ran down the hill in that vacuum of crickets like a breath

travelling across a mirror she was lying in the water her head on the sand spit the water flowing about her hips there was a little more light in the water her skirt half saturated flopped along her flanks to the water's motion in heavy ripples going nowhere renewed themselves of their own movement I stood on the bank I could smell the honeysuckle on the water gap the air seemed to drizzle with honeysuckle and with the rasping of crickets a substance you could feel on the flesh

is Benjy still crying

I dont know yes I dont know

poor Benjy

I sat down on the bank the grass was damp a little then I found my shoes wet

get out of that water are you crazy

but she didnt move her face was a white blur framed out of the blur of the sand by her hair

get out now

she sat up then she rose her skirt flopped against her draining she climbed the bank her clothes flopping sat down

why dont you wring it out do you want to catch cold

yes

the water sucked and gurgled across the sand spit and on in the dark among the willows across the shallow the water rippled like a piece of cloth holding still a little light as water does

hes crossed all the oceans all around the world

then she talked about him clasping her wet knees her face tilted back in the grey light the smell of honeysuckle there was a light in mothers room and in Benjys where T. P. was putting him to bed

do you love him

her hand came out I didnt move it fumbled down my arm and she held my hand flat against her chest her heart thudding

no no

did he make you then he made you do it let him he

*128*

was stronger than you and he tomorrow Ill kill him I swear I will father neednt know until afterward and then you and I nobody need ever know we can take my school money we can cancel my matriculation Caddy you hate him dont you dont you

she held my hand against her chest her heart thudding I turned and caught her arm

Caddy you hate him dont you

she moved my hand up against her throat her heart was hammering there

poor Quentin

her face looked at the sky it was low so low that all smells and sounds of night seemed to have been crowded down like under a slack tent especially the honeysuckle it had got into my breathing it was on her face and throat like paint her blood pounded against my hand I was leaning on my other arm it began to jerk and jump and I had to pant to get any air at all out of that thick grey honeysuckle

yes I hate him I would die for him Ive already died for him I die for him over and over again every time this goes

when I lifted my hand I could still feel criss-crossed twigs and grass burning into the palm

poor Quentin

she leaned back on her arms her hands locked about her knees

youve never done that have you

what done what

that what I have what I did

yes yes lots of times with lots of girls

then I was crying her hand touched me again and I was crying against her damp blouse then she lying on her back looking past my head into the sky I could see a rim of white under her irises I opened my knife

do you remember the day damuddy died when you sat down in the water in your drawers

yes

I held the point of the knife at her throat
it wont take but a second just a second then I can do
mine I can do mine then
all right can you do yours by yourself
yes the blades long enough Benjys in bed by now
yes
it wont take but a second Ill try not to hurt
all right
will you close your eyes
no like this you'll have to push it harder
touch your hand to it
but she didnt move her eyes were wide open looking
past my head at the sky
Caddy do you remember how Dilsey fussed at you
because your drawers were muddy
dont cry
Im not crying Caddy
push it are you going to
do you want me to
yes push it
touch your hand to it
dont cry poor Quentin
but I couldnt stop she held my head against her damp
hard breast I could hear her heart going firm and slow
now not hammering and the water gurgling among the
willows in the dark and waves of honeysuckle coming up
the air my arm and shoulder were twisted under me
what is it what are you doing
her muscles gathered I sat up
its my knife I dropped it
she sat up
what time is it
I dont know
she rose to her feet I fumbled along the ground
Im going let it go
I could feel her standing there I could smell her damp
clothes feeling her there
its right here somewhere

let it go you can find it tomorrow come on
wait a minute Ill find it
are you afraid to
here it is it was right here all the time
was it come on
I got up and followed we went up the hill the crickets
hushing before us
its funny how you can sit down and drop something
and have to hunt all around for it
the grey it was grey with dew slanting up into the grey
sky then the trees beyond
damn that honeysuckle I wish it would stop
you used to like it
we crossed the crest and went on toward the trees she
walked into me she gave over a little the ditch was a
black scar on the grey grass she walked into me again she
looked at me and gave over we reached the ditch
lets go this way
what for
lets see if you can still see Nancys bones I havent
thought to look in a long time have you
it was matted with vines and briers dark
they were right here you cant tell whether you see
them or not can you
stop Quentin
come on
the ditch narrowed closed she turned toward the trees
stop Quentin
Caddy
I got in front of her again
Caddy
stop it
I held her
Im stronger than you
she was motionless hard unyielding but still
I wont fight stop youd better stop
Caddy dont Caddy
it wont do any good dont you know it wont let me go

the honeysuckle drizzled and drizzled I could hear the crickets watching us in a circle she moved back went around me on toward the trees

you go on back to the house you neednt come

I went on

why dont you go on back to the house

damn that honeysuckle

we reached the fence she crawled through I crawled through when I rose from stooping he was coming out of the trees into the grey toward us coming toward us tall and flat and still even moving like he was still she went to him

this is Quentin Im wet Im wet all over you dont have to if you dont want to

their shadows one shadow her head rose it was above his on the sky higher their two heads

you dont have to if you dont want to

then not two heads the darkness smelled of rain of damp grass and leaves the grey light drizzling like rain the honeysuckle coming up in damp waves I could see her face a blur against his shoulder he held her in one arm like she was no bigger than a child he extended his hand

glad to know you

we shook hands then we stood there her shadow high against his shadow one shadow

whatre you going to do Quentin

walk a while I think Ill go through the woods to the road and come back through town

I turned away going

good night

Quentin

I stopped

what do you want

in the woods the tree frogs were going smelling rain in the air they sounded like toy music boxes that were hard to turn and the honeysuckle

come here

what do you want
come here Quentin
I went back she touched my shoulder leaning down
her shadow the blur of her face leaning down from his
high shadow I drew back
look out
you go on home
Im not sleepy Im going to take a walk
wait for me at the branch
Im going for a walk
Ill be there soon wait for me you wait
no Im going through the woods
I didnt look back the tree frogs didnt pay me any
mind the grey light like moss in the trees drizzling but
still it wouldnt rain after a while I turned went back to
the edge of the woods as soon as I got there I began to
smell honeysuckle again I could see the lights on the
courthouse clock and the glare of town the square on the
sky and the dark willows along the branch and the light
in mother's windows the light still on in Benjys room and
I stooped through the fence and went across the pasture
running I ran in the grey grass among the crickets the
honeysuckle getting stronger and stronger and the smell
of water then I could see the water the colour of grey
honeysuckle I lay down on the bank with my face close
to the ground so I couldnt smell the honeysuckle I
couldnt smell it then and I lay there feeling the earth
going through my clothes listening to the water and after
a while I wasnt breathing so hard and lay there thinking
that if I didnt move my face I wouldnt have to breathe
hard and smell it and then I wasnt thinking about anything at all she came along the bank and stopped I didnt
move
its late you go on home
what
you go on home its late
all right
her clothes rustled I didnt move they stopped rustling

*133*

are you going in like I told you
I didnt hear anything
Caddy
yes I will if you want me to I will
I sat up she was sitting on the ground her hands
clasped about her knee
go on to the house like I told you
yes Ill do anything you want me to anything yes
she didnt even look at me I caught her shoulder and
shook her hard
you shut up
I shook her
you shut up you shut up
yes
she lifted her face then I saw she wasnt even looking
at me at all I could see that white rim
get up
I pulled her she was limp I lifted her to her feet
go on now
was Benjy still crying when you left
go on
we crossed the branch the roof came in sight then the
windows upstairs
hes asleep now
I had to stop and fasten the gate she went on in the
grey light the smell of rain and still it wouldnt rain and
honeysuckle beginning to come from the garden fence
beginning she went into the shadow I could hear her feet
then
Caddy
I stopped at the steps I couldnt hear her feet
Caddy
I heard her feet then my hand touched her not warm
not cool just still her clothes a little damp still
do you love him now
not breathing except slow like far away breathing
Caddy do you love him now
I dont know

outside the grey light the shadows of things like dead things in stagnant water

I wish you were dead

do you you coming in now

are you thinking about him now

I dont know

tell me what youre thinking about tell me

stop stop Quentin

you shut up you shut up you hear me you shut up are you going to shut up

all right I will stop well make too much noise

Ill kill you do you hear

lets go out to the swing theyll hear you here

Im not crying do you say Im crying

no hush now well wake Benjy up

you go on into the house go on now

I am dont cry Im bad anyway you cant help it

theres a curse on us its not our fault is it our fault

hush come on and go to bed now

you cant make me theres a curse on us

finally I saw him he was just going into the barber-shop he looked out I went on and waited

Ive been looking for you two or three days

you wanted to see me

Im going to see you

he rolled the cigarette quickly with about two motions he struck the match with his thumb

we cant talk here suppose I meet you somewhere Ill come to your room are you at the hotel no thats not so good you know that bridge over the creek in there back of

yes all right

at one oclock right

yes

I turned away

Im obliged to you

look

I stopped looked back

she all right

he looked like he was made out of bronze his khaki shirt

she need me for anything now

Ill be there at one

she heard me tell T.P. to saddle Prince at one oclock she kept watching me not eating much she came too

what are you going to do

nothing cant I go for a ride if I want to

youre going to do something what is it

none of your business whore whore

T. P. had Prince at the side door

I wont want him Im going to walk

I  went down the drive and out the gate I turned into the lane then I ran before I reached the bridge I saw him leaning on the rail the horse was hitched in the woods he looked over his shoulder then he turned his back he didnt look up until I came on to the bridge and stopped he had a piece of bark in his hands breaking pieces from it and dropping them over the rail into the water

I came to tell you to leave town

he broke a piece of bark deliberately dropped it carefully into the water watched it float away

I said you must leave town

he looked at me

did she send you to me

I say you must go not my father not anybody I say it

listen save this for a while I want to know if shes all right have they been bothering her up there

thats something you dont need to trouble yourself about

then I heard myself saying Ill give you until sundown to leave town

he broke a piece of bark and dropped it into the water then he laid the bark on the rail and rolled a cigarette with those two swift motions spun the match over the rail

what will you do if I dont leave

Ill kill you dont think that just because I look like a
kid to you
      the smoke flowed in two jets from his nostrils across
his face
      how old are you
      I began to shake my hands were on the rail I thought
if I hid them hed know why
      Ill give you until tonight
      listen buddy whats your name Benjys the natural isnt
he you are
      Quentin
      my mouth said it I didnt say it at all
      Ill give you till sundown
      Quentin
      he raked the cigarette ash carefully off against the rail
he did it slowly and carefully like sharpening a pencil my
hands had quit shaking
      listen no good taking it so hard its not your fault kid it
would have been some other fellow
      did you ever have a sister did you
      no but theyre all bitches
      I hit him my open hand beat the impulse to shut it to
his face his hand moved as fast as mine the cigarette
went over the rail I swung with the other hand he caught
it too before the cigarette reached the water he held both
my wrists in the same hand his other hand flicked to his
arm pit under his coat behind him the sun slanted and a
bird singing somewhere beyond the sun we looked at
one another while the bird singing he turned my hands
loose
      look here
      he took the bark from the rail and dropped it into the
water it bobbed up the current took it floated away his
hand lay on the rail holding the pistol loosely we
waited
      you cant hit it now
      no
      it floated on it was quite still in the woods I heard the

bird again and the water afterward the pistol came up he didnt aim at all the bark disappeared then pieces of it floated up spreading he hit two more of them pieces of bark no bigger than silver dollars

thats enough I guess

he swung the cylinder out and blew into the barrel a thin wisp of smoke dissolved he reloaded the three chambers shut the cylinder he handed it to me butt first

what for I wont try to beat that

youll need it from what you said Im giving you this one because youve seen what itll do

to hell with your gun

I  hit him I was still trying to hit him long after he was holding my wrists but I still tried then it was like I was looking at him through a piece of coloured glass I could hear my blood and then I could see the sky again and branches against it and the sun slanting through them and he holding me on my feet

did you hit me

I couldnt hear

what

yes how do you feel

all right let go

he let me go I leaned against the rail

do you feel all right

let me alone Im all right

can you make it home all right

go on let me alone

youd better not try to walk take my horse

no you go on

you can hang the reins on the pommel and turn him loose hell go back to the stable

let me alone you go on and let me alone

I leaned on the rail looking at the water I heard him untie the horse and ride off and after a while I couldnt hear anything but the water and then the bird again I left the bridge and sat down with my back against a tree and leaned my head against the tree and shut my eyes a patch of sun came through and fell across my eyes and I moved a little further around the tree I heard the bird again and the water and then everything sort of rolled away and I didnt feel anything at all I felt almost good after all those days and the nights with honeysuckle coming up out of the darkness into my room where I was trying to sleep even when after a while I knew that he hadnt hit me that he had lied about that for her sake too and that I had just passed out like a girl but even that didnt matter any more and I sat there against the tree with little flecks of sunlight brushing across my face like yellow leaves on a twig listening to the water and not thinking about anything at all even when I heard the horse coming fast I sat there with my eyes closed and heard its feet bunch scuttering the hissing sand and feet running and her hard running hands

fool fool are you hurt

I opened my eyes her hands running on my face

I didnt know which way until I heard the pistol I didnt know where I didnt think he and you running off slipping I didnt think he would have

she held my face between her hands bumping my head against the tree

stop stop that

I caught her wrists

quit that quit it

I knew he wouldnt I knew he wouldnt

she tried to bump my head against the tree

I told him never to speak to me again I told him

she tried to break her wrists free

let me go

stop it Im stronger than you stop it now

let me go I've got to catch him and ask his let me go Quentin please let me go let me go

all at once she quit her wrists went lax

yes I can tell him I can make him believe any time I can make him

Caddy

*139*

she hadnt hitched Prince he was liable to strike out for home if the notion took him

any time he will believe me

do you love him Caddy

do I what

she looked at me then everything emptied out of her eyes and they looked like the eyes in the statues blank and unseeing and serene

put your hand against my throat

she took my hand and held it flat against her throat

now say his name

Dalton Ames

I felt the first surge of blood there it surged in strong accelerating beats

say it again

her face looked off into the trees where the sun slanted and where the bird

say it again

Dalton Ames

her blood surged steadily beating and beating against my hand

It kept on running for a long time, but my face felt cold and sort of dead, and my eye, and the cut place on my finger was smarting again. I could hear Shreve working the pump, then he came back with the basin and a round blob of twilight wobbling in it, with a yellow edge like a fading balloon, then my reflection. I tried to see my face in it.

'Has it stopped?' Shreve said. 'Give me the rag.' He tried to take it from my hand.

'Look out,' I said, 'I can do it. Yes, it's about stopped now.' I dipped the rag again, breaking the balloon. The rag stained the water. 'I wish I had a clean one.'

'You need a piece of beefsteak for that eye,' Shreve said. 'Damn if you won't have a shiner to-morrow. The son of a bitch,' he said.

'Did I hurt him any?' I wrung out the handkerchief and tried to clean the blood off of my vest.

'You can't get that off,' Shreve said. 'You'll have to send it to the cleaner's. Come on, hold it on your eye, why don't you.'

'I can get some of it off,' I said. But I wasn't doing much good. 'What sort of shape is my collar in?'

'I don't know,' Shreve said. 'Hold it against your eye. Here.'

'Look out,' I said. 'I can do it. Did I hurt him any?'

'You may have hit him. I may have looked away just then or blinked or something. He boxed the hell out of you. He boxed you all over the place. What did you want to fight him with your fists for? You goddamn fool. How do you feel?'

'I feel fine,' I said. 'I wonder if I can get something to clean my vest.'

'Oh, forget your damn clothes. Does your eye hurt?'

'I feel fine,' I said. Everything was sort of violet and still, the sky green paling into gold beyond the gable of the house and a plume of smoke rising from the chimney without any wind. I heard the pump again. A man was filling a pail, watching us across his pumping shoulder. A woman crossed the door, but she didn't look out. I could hear a cow lowing somewhere.

'Come on,' Shreve said. 'Let your clothes alone and put that rag on your eye. I'll send your suit out first thing to-morrow.'

'All right. I'm sorry I didn't bleed on him a little, at least.'

'Son of a bitch,' Shreve said. Spoade came out of the house, talking to the woman I reckon, and crossed the yard. He looked at me with his cold, quizzical eyes.

'Well, bud,' he said, looking at me, 'I'll be damned if you don't go to a lot of trouble to have your fun. Kidnapping, then fighting. What do you do on your holidays? Burn houses?'

'I'm all right,' I said. 'What did Mrs. Bland say?'

'She's giving Gerald hell for bloodying you up. She'll give you hell for letting him, when she sees you. She don't object to the fighting, it's the blood that annoys her. I think you lost caste with her a little by not holding your blood better. How do you feel?'

'Sure,' Shreve said, 'If you can't be a Bland, the next best thing is to commit adultery with one or get drunk and fight him, as the case may be.'

'Quite right,' Spoade said. 'But I didn't know Quentin was drunk.'

'He wasn't,' Shreve said. 'Do you have to be drunk to want to hit that son of a bitch?'

'Well, I think I'd have to be pretty drunk to try it, after seeing how Quentin came out. Where'd he learn to box?'

'He's been going to Mike's every day, over in town,' I said.

'He has?' Spoade said. 'Did you know that when you hit him?'

'I don't know,' I said. 'I guess so. Yes.'

'Wet it again,' Shreve said. 'Want some fresh water?'

'This is all right,' I said. I dipped the cloth again and held it to my eye. 'Wish I had something to clean my vest.' Spoade was still watching me.

'Say,' he said, 'What did you hit him for? What was it he said?'

'I don't know. I don't know why I did.'

'The first I knew was when you jumped up all of a sudden and said, "Did you ever have a sister? did you?" and when he said No, you hit him. I noticed you kept on looking at him, but you didn't seem to be paying any attention to what anybody was saying until you jumped up and asked him if he had any sisters.'

'Ah, he was blowing off as usual,' Shreve said, 'about his women. You know: like he does, before girls, so they don't know exactly what he's saying. All his damn innuendo and lying and a lot of stuff that don't make sense even. Telling us about some wench that he made date with to meet at a dance hall in Atlantic City and stood her up and went to the hotel and went to bed and how he lay there being sorry for her waiting on the pier for him, without him there to give her what she wanted. Talking about the body's beauty and the sorry ends thereof and how tough women have it, without anything else they can do except lie on their backs. Leda lurking in the bushes, whimpering and moaning for the swan, see. The son of a bitch. I'd hit him myself. Only I'd grabbed up her damn hamper of wine and done it if it had been me.'

'Oh,' Spoade said, 'the champion of dames. Bud, you excite not only admiration, but horror.'

He looked at me, cold and quizzical. 'Good God,' he said.

'I'm sorry I hit him,' I said. 'Do I look too bad to go back and get it over with?'

'Apologies, hell,' Shreve said, 'Let them go to hell. We're going to town.'

'He ought to go back so they'll know he fights like a gentleman,' Spoade said. 'Gets licked like one, I mean.'

'Like this?' Shreve said, 'With his clothes all over blood?'

'Why, all right,' Spoade said, 'You know best.'

'He can't go around in his undershirt,' Shreve said, 'He's not a senior yet. Come on, let's go to town.'

'You needn't come,' I said. 'You go on back to the picnic.'

'Hell with them,' Shreve said. 'Come on here.'

'What'll I tell them?' Spoade said. 'Tell them you and Quentin had a fight too?'

'Tell them nothing,' Shreve said. 'Tell her her option expired at sunset. Come on, Quentin. I'll ask that woman where the nearest interurban –'

'No,' I said, 'I'm not going back to town.'

Shreve stopped, looking at me. Turning, his glasses looked like small yellow moons.

'What are you going to do?'

'I'm not going back to town yet. You go on back to the picnic. Tell them I wouldn't come back because my clothes were spoiled.'

143

'Look here,' he said, 'What are you up to?'

'Nothing. I'm all right. You and Spoade go on back. 'I'll see you to-morrow.' I went on across the yard toward the road.

'Do you know where the station is?' Shreve said.

'I'll find it. I'll see you all to-morrow. Tell Mrs. Bland I'm sorry I spoiled her party.' They stood watching me. I went around the house. A rock path went down to the road. Roses grew on both sides of the path. I went through the gate, onto the road. It dropped downhill, toward the woods, and I could make out the motor beside the road. I went up the hill. The light increased as I mounted, and before I reached the top I heard a car. It sounded far away across the twilight and I stopped and listened to it. I couldn't make out the motor any longer, but Shreve was standing in the road before the house, looking up the hill. Behind him the yellow light lay like a wash of paint on the roof of the house. I lifted my hand and went on over the hill, listening to the car. Then the house was gone and I stopped in the green and yellow light and heard the car growing louder and louder, until just as it began to die away it ceased all together. I waited until I heard it start again. Then I went on.

As I descended the light dwindled slowly, yet at the same time without altering its quality, as if I and not light were changing, decreasing, though even when the road ran into trees you could have read a newspaper. Pretty soon I came to a lane. I turned into it. It was closer and darker than the road, but when it came out at the trolley stop – another wooden marquee – the light was still unchanged. After the lane it seemed brighter, as though I had walked through night in the lane and come out into morning again. Pretty soon the car came. I got on it, they turning to look at my eye, and found a seat on the left side.

The lights were on in the car, so while we ran between trees I couldn't see anything except my own face and a woman across the aisle with a hat sitting right on top of her head, with a broken feather in it, but when we ran out of the trees I could see the twilight again, that quality of light as if time really had stopped for a while, with the sun hanging just under the horizon, and then we passed the marquee where the old man had been eating out of the sack, and the road going on under the twilight, into twilight and the sense of water peaceful and swift beyond. Then the car went on, the draught building steadily up in the open door until it was drawing steadily through the car with the odour of summer and darkness except honeysuckle. Honeysuckle was the saddest odour of all, I think. I remember lots of them. Wistaria was one. On the rainy days when Mother wasn't feeling quite bad enough to stay away from the windows we used to play under it. When Mother stayed in bed Dilsey would put old clothes on us and let us go out in the rain because she said rain never hurt young folks. But if Mother was up we always began by playing on the porch until she said we were making too much noise, then we went out and played under the wistaria frame.

This was where I saw the river for the last time this morning, about here. I could feel water beyond the twilight, smell. When it bloomed in the spring and it rained the smell was everywhere you didn't notice it so much at other times but when it rained the smell began to come into the house at twilight either it would rain more at twilight or there was something in the light itself but it always smelled strongest then until I would lie in bed thinking when will it stop when will it stop. The draught in the door smelled of water, a damp steady breath. Sometimes I could put myself to sleep saying that over and over until after the honeysuckle got all mixed up in it the whole thing came to symbolize night and unrest seemed to be lying neither asleep nor awake looking down a long corridor of grey half-light where all stable things had become shadowy paradoxical all I had done shadows all I had felt suffered taking visible form antic and perverse mocking without relevance inherent themselves with the denial of the significance they should have affirmed thinking I was I was not who was not was not who.

I could smell the curves of the river beyond the dusk and I saw the last light supine and tranquil upon tide-flats like pieces of broken mirror, then beyond them lights began in the pale clear air, trembling a little like butterflies hovering a long way off. Benjamin the child of. How he used to sit before that mirror. Refuge unfailing in which conflict tempered silenced reconciled. Benjamin the child of mine old age held hostage into Egypt. O Benjamin. Dilsey said it was because Mother was too proud for him. They come into white people's lives like that in sudden sharp black trickles that isolate white facts for an instant in unarguable truth like under a microscope; the rest of the time just voices that laugh when you see nothing to laugh at, tears when no reason for tears. They will bet on the odd or even number of mourners at a funeral. A brothel full of them in Memphis went into a religious trance ran naked into the street. It took three policemen to subdue one of them. Yes Jesus O good man Jesus O that good man.

The car stopped. I got out, with them looking at my eye. When the trolley came it was full. I stopped on the back platform.

'Seats up front,' the conductor said. I looked into the car. There were no seats on the left side.

'I'm not going far,' I said. 'I'll just stand here.'

We crossed the river. The bridge, that is, arching slow and high into space, between silence and nothingness where lights – yellow and red and green – trembled in the clear air, repeating themselves.

'Better go up front and get a seat,' the conductor said,

'I get off pretty soon,' I said. 'A couple of blocks.'

I got off before we reached the post office. They'd all be sitting around somewhere by now though, and then I was hearing my watch and I began to listen for the chimes and I touched Shreve's letter through my coat, the bitten shadows of the elms flowing upon my hand. And then as I turned into the quad the chimes did begin and I went on while the notes came up like ripples on a pool and passed me and went on, saying Quarter to what? All right. Quarter to what.

Our windows were dark. The entrance was empty. I walked close to the left wall when I entered, but it was empty: just the stairs curving up into shadows echoes of feet in the sad generations like light dust upon the shadows, my feet waking them like dust, lightly to settle again.

I could see the letter before I turned the light on, propped against a book on the table so I would see it. Calling him my husband. And then Spoade said they were going somewhere, would not be back until late, and Mrs. Bland would need another cavalier. But I would have seen him and he cannot get another car for an hour because after six o'clock. I took out my watch and listened to it clicking away, not knowing it couldn't even lie. Then I laid it face up on the table and took Mrs. Bland's letter and tore it across and dropped the pieces into the waste basket and took off my coat, vest, collar, tie and shirt. The tie was spoiled too, but then niggers. Maybe a pattern of blood he could call that the one Christ was wearing. I found the gasoline in Shreve's room and spread the vest on the table, where it would be flat, and opened the gasoline.

*the first car in town a girl Girl that's what Jason couldn't bear smell of gasoline making him sick then got madder than ever because a girl had no sister but Benjamin Benjamin the child of my sorrowful if I'd just had a mother so I could say Mother Mother* It took a lot of gasoline, and then I couldn't tell if it was still the stain or just the gasoline. It had started the cut to smarting again so when I went to wash I hung the vest on a chair and lowered the light cord so that the bulb would be drying the splotch. I washed my face and hands, but even then I could smell it within the soap stinging, constricting the nostrils a little. Then I

*147*

opened the bag and took the shirt and collar and tie out and put the bloody ones in and closed the bag, and dressed. While I was brushing my hair the half-hour went. But there was until the three-quarters anyway except suppose *seeing on the rushing darkness only his own face no broken feather unless two of them but not two like that going to Boston the same night then my face his face for an instant across the crashing when out of darkness two lighted windows in rigid fleeing crash gone his face and mine just I see saw did I see not good-bye the marquee empty of eating the road empty in darkness in silence the bridge arching into silence darkness sleep the water peaceful and swift not goodbye*

I turned out the light and went into my bedroom, out of the gasoline but I could still smell it. I stood at the window the curtains moved slow out of the darkness touching my face like someone breathing asleep, breathing slow into the darkness again, leaving the touch. *After they had gone upstairs Mother lay back in her chair, the camphor handkerchief to her mouth. Father hadn't moved he still sat beside her holding her hand the bellowing hammering away like no place for it in silence* When I was little there was a picture in one of our books, a dark place into which a single weak ray of light came slanting upon two faces lifted out of the shadow. *You know what I'd do if I were King?* she never was a queen or a fairy she was always a king or a giant or a general *I'd break that place open and drag them out and I'd whip them good* It was torn out, jagged out. I was glad. I'd have to turn back to it until the dungeon was Mother herself she and Father upward into weak light holding hands and us lost somewhere below even them without even a ray of light. Then the honeysuckle got into it. As soon as I turned off the light and tried to go to sleep it would begin to come into the room in waves building and building up until I would have to pant to get any air at all out of it until I would have to get up and feel my way like when I was a little boy *hands can see touching in the mind shaping unseen door Door now nothing hands can see* My nose could see gasoline, the vest on the table, the door. The corridor was still empty of all the feet in sad generations seeking water. *yet the eyes unseeing clenched like teeth not disbelieving doubting even the absence of pain shin ankle knee the long invisible flowing of the stair-railing where a misstep in the darkness filled with sleeping Mother Father Caddy Jason Maury door I am not afraid only Mother Father Caddy Jason Maury getting so far ahead sleeping I will sleep fast when I door Door door* It was empty too, the pipes, the porcelain, the stained quiet walls, the throne of contemplation. I had forgotten the glass, but I could *hands can see cooling fingers invisible swan-throat where less than Moses rod the glass touch tentative not to drumming lean cool throat drumming cooling the metal the glass full overfull cooling the glass the fingers flushing sleep leaving the taste of dampened sleep in the long silence of the throat* I returned up the corridor, waking the lost feet in whispering battalions in the silence, into the gasoline, the watch telling its furious lie on the dark table. Then the curtains breathing out of the dark upon my face, leaving the breathing upon my face. A quarter-hour yet. And then I'll not be. The peacefullest words. Peacefullest words. *Non fui. Sum. Fui. Nom sum.* Somewhere I heard bells once. Mississippi or Massachusetts. I was. I am not. Massachusetts or Mississippi. Shreve has a bottle in his trunk. *Aren't you even going to open it* Mr. and Mrs. Jason Richmond Compson announce the *Three Times. Days. Aren't you even going to open it* marriage of their daughter Candace *that liquor teaches you to confuse the means with the end.* I am. Drink. I was not. Let us sell Benjy's pasture so that Quentin may go to Harvard and I may knock my bones together and together. I will be dead in. Was it one year Caddy said. Shreve has a bottle in his trunk. Sir I will not need Shreve's I have sold Benjy's pasture and I can be dead in Harvard Caddy said in the caverns and the grottoes of the sea tumbling peacefully to the wavering tides because Harvard is such a fine sound forty acres is no high price for a fine sound. A fine dead sound we will swap Benjy's pasture for a fine dead sound. It will last him a long time because he cannot hear it unless he can smell it *as soon as she came in the door he began to cry* I thought all the time it was just one of those town squirts that Father was always teasing her about until. I didn't notice him any more than any other stranger drummer or what thought they were army shirts until all of a sudden I knew he wasn't thinking of me at all as a potential source of harm, but was thinking of her when he looked at me was looking at me through her like through a piece of coloured glass *why must you meddle with me don't you know it won't do any good I thought you'd have left that for Mother and Jason*

*did Mother set Jason to spy on you* I wouldn't have.

*Women only use other people's codes of honour it's because she loves Caddy* staying downstairs even when she was sick so Father couldn't kid Uncle Maury before Jason Father said Uncle Maury was too poor a classicist to risk the blind immortal boy in person he should have chosen Jason because Jason would have made only the same kind of blunder Uncle Maury himself would have made not one to get him a black eye the Patterson boy was smaller than Jason too they sold the kites for a nickel apiece until the trouble over finances Jason got a new partner still smaller one small enough anyway because T. P. said Jason still treasurer but Father said why should Uncle Maury work if he father could support five or six niggers that did nothing at all but sit with their feet in the oven he certainly could board and lodge Uncle Maury now and then and lend him a little money who kept his Father's belief in the celestial derivation of his own species at such a fine heat then Mother would cry and say that Father believed his people were better than hers that he was ridiculing Uncle Maury to teach us the same thing she couldn't see that Father was teaching us that all men are just accumulations dolls stuffed with sawdust swept up from the trash heaps where all previous dolls had been thrown away the sawdust flowing from what wound in what side that not for me died not.

It used to be I thought of death as a man something like Grandfather a friend of his a kind of private and particular friend like we used to think of Grandfather's desk not to touch it not even to talk loud in the room where it was I always thought of them as being together somewhere all the time waiting for old Colonel Sartoris to come down and sit with them waiting on a high place beyond cedar trees Colonel Sartoris was on a still higher place looking out across at something and they were waiting for him to get done looking at it and come down Grandfather wore his uniform and we could hear the murmur of their voices from beyond the cedars they were always talking and Grandfather was always right

The three-quarters began. The first note sounded, measured and tranquil, serenely peremptory, emptying the unhurried silence for the next one and that's it if people could only change one another for ever that way merge like a flame swirling up for an instant then blown cleanly out along the cool eternal dark instead of lying there trying not to think of the swing until all cedars came to have that vivid dead smell of perfume that Benjy hated so. Just by imagining the clump it seemed to me that I could hear whispers secret surges smell the beating of hot blood under wild unsecret flesh watching against red eyelids the swine untethered in pairs rushing coupled into the sea and he we must just stay awake and see evil done for a little while its not always and it doesnt have to be even that long for a man of courage and he do you consider that courage and i yes sir dont you and he every man is the arbiter of his own virtues whether or not you consider it courageous is of more importance than the act itself than any act otherwise you could not be in earnest and i you dont believe i am serious and he i think you are too serious to give me any cause for alarm you wouldnt have felt driven to the expedient of telling me you have committed incest otherwise and i i wasnt lying i wasnt lying and he you wanted to sublimate a piece of natural human folly into a horror and then exorcize it

with truth and i it was to isolate her out of the loud world
so that it would have to flee us of necessity and then the
sound of it would be as though it had never been and he
did you try to make her do it and i i was afraid to i was
afraid she might and then it wouldnt have done any good
but if i could tell you we did it would have been so and
then the others wouldnt be so and then the world would
roar away and he and now this other you are not lying
now either but you are still blind to what is in yourself to
that part of general truth the sequence of natural events
and their causes which shadows every mans brow even
benjys you are not thinking of finitude you are contemplating an apotheosis in which a temporary state of mind
will become symmetrical above the flesh and aware both
of itself and of the flesh it will not quite discard you will
not even be dead and i temporary and he you cannot bear
to think that some day it will no longer hurt you like this
now were getting at it you seem to regard it merely as an
experience that will whiten your hair overnight so to
speak without altering your appearance at all you wont
do it under these conditions it will be a gamble and the
strange thing is that man who is conceived by accident
and whose every breath is a fresh cast with dice already
loaded against him will not face that final main which he
knows beforehand he has assuredly to face without
essaying expedients ranging all the way from violence to
petty chicanery that would not deceive a child until some
day in very disgust he risks everything on a single blind
turn of a card no man ever does that under the first fury
of despair or remorse or bereavement he does it only
when he has realized that even the despair or remorse or
bereavement is not particularly important to the dark
diceman and i temporary and he it is hard believing to
think that a love or a sorrow is a bond purchased without
design and which matures willynilly and is recalled without warning to be replaced by whatever issue the gods
happen to be floating at the time no you will not do that
until you come to believe that even she was not quite

worth despair perhaps and i i will never do that nobody knows what i know and he i think you'd better go on up to cambridge right away you might go up into maine for a month you can afford it if you are careful it might be a good thing watching pennies has healed more scars than jesus and i suppose i realize what you believe i will realize up there next week or next month and he then you will remember that for you to go to harvard has been your mothers dream since you were born and no compson has ever disappointed a lady and i temporary it will be better for me for all of us and he every man is the arbiter of his own virtues but let no man prescribe for another mans well-being and i temporary and he was the saddest word of all there is nothing else in the world its not despair until time its not even time until it was

The last note sounded. At last it stopped vibrating and the darkness was still again. I entered the sitting-room and turned on the light. I put my vest on. The gasoline was faint now, barely noticeable, and in the mirror the stain didn't show. Not like my eye did, anyway. I put on my coat. Shreve's letter crackled through the cloth and I took it out and examined the address, and put it in my side pocket. Then I carried the watch into Shreve's room and put it in his drawer and went to my room and got a fresh handkerchief and went to the door and put my hand on the light switch. Then I remembered I hadn't brushed my teeth, so I had to open the bag again. I found my toothbrush and got some of Shreve's paste and went out and brushed my teeth. I squeezed the brush as dry as I could and put it back in the bag and shut it, and went to the door again. Before I snapped the light out I looked around to see if there was anything else, then I saw that I had forgotten my hat. I'd have to go by the post office and I'd be sure to meet some of them, and they'd think I was a Harvard Square student making like he was a senior. I had forgotten to brush it too, but Shreve had a brush, so I didn't have to open the bag any more.

# *April Sixth*

## 1928

ONCE a bitch always a bitch, what I say. I says you're lucky if her playing out of school is all that worries you. I says she ought to be down there in that kitchen right now, instead of up there in her room, gobbing paint on her face and waiting for six niggers that can't even stand up out of a chair unless they've got a panful of bread and meat to balance them, to fix breakfast for her. And Mother says,

'But to have the school authorities think that I have no control over her, that I can't – '

'Well,' I says, 'You can't, can you? You never have tried to do anything with her,' I says, 'How do you expect to begin this late, when she's seventeen years old?'

She thought about that for a while.

'But to have them think that … I didn't even know she had a report card. She told me last fall that they had quit using them this year. And now for Professor Junkin to call me on the telephone and tell me if she's absent one more time, she will have to leave school. How does she do it? Where does she go? You're downtown all day; you ought to see her if she stays on the streets.'

'Yes,' I says, 'If she stayed on the streets. I don't reckon she'd be playing out of school just to do something she could do in public,' I says.

'What do you mean?' she says.

'I don't mean anything,' I says. 'I just answered your question.' Then she begun to cry again, talking about how her own flesh and blood rose up to curse her.

'You asked me,' I says.

'I don't mean you,' she says. 'You are the only one of them that isn't a reproach to me.'

'Sure,' I says, 'I never had time to be. I never had time to go to Harvard like Quentin or drink myself into the ground like Father. I had to work. But of course if you want me to follow her around and see what she does, I can quit the store and get a job where I can work at night. Then I can watch her during the day and you can use Ben for the night shift.'

'I know I'm just a trouble and a burden to you,' she says, crying on the pillow.

'I ought to know it,' I says. 'You've been telling me that for thirty years. Even Ben ought to know it now. Do you want me to say anything to her about it?'

'Do you think it will do any good?' she says.

'Not if you come down there interfering just when I get started,' I says. 'If you want me to control her, just say so and keep your hands off. Every time I try to, you come butting in and then she gives both of us the laugh.'

'Remember she's your own flesh and blood,' she says.

'Sure,' I says, 'that's just what I'm thinking of – flesh. And a little blood too, if I had my way. When people act like niggers, no matter who they are the only thing to do is treat them like a nigger.'

'I'm afraid you'll lose your temper with her,' she says.

'Well,' I says, 'You haven't had much luck with your system. You want me to do anything about it, or not? Say one way or the other; I've got to get on to work.'

'I know you have to slave your life away for us,' she says. 'You know if I had my way, you'd have an office of your own to go to, and hours that became a Bascomb. Because you are a Bascomb, despite your name. I know that if your father could have foreseen – '

'Well,' I says, 'I reckon he's entitled to guess wrong now and then, like anybody else, even a Smith or a Jones.' She begun to cry again.

'To hear you speak bitterly of your dead father,' she says.

'All right,' I says, 'All right. Have it your way. But as I haven't got an office, I'll have to get on to what I have

155

got. Do you want me to say anything to her?'

'I'm afraid you'll lose your temper with her,' she says.

'All right,' I says. 'I won't say anything, then.'

'But something must be done,' she says. 'To have people think I permit her to stay out of school and run about the streets, or that I can't prevent her doing it . ... Jason, Jason,' she says, 'How could you. How could you leave me with these burdens.'

'Now, now,' I says, 'You'll make yourself sick. Why don't you either lock her up all day too, or turn her over to me and quit worrying over her?'

'My own flesh and blood,' she says, crying. So I says,

'All right. I'll tend to her. Quit crying, now.'

'Don't lose your temper,' she says. 'She's just a child, remember.'

'No,' I says, 'I won't.' I went out, closing the door.

'Jason,' she says. I didn't answer. I went down the hall. 'Jason,' she says beyond the door. I went on downstairs. There wasn't anybody in the dining-room, then I heard her in the kitchen. She was trying to make Dilsey let her have another cup of coffee. I went in.

'I reckon that's your school costume, is it?' I says. 'Or maybe today's a holiday?'

'Just a half a cup, Dilsey,' she says. 'Please.'

'No, suh,' Dilsey says, 'I ain't gwine do it. You ain't got no business wid mo'n one cup, a seventeen year old gal, let lone whut Miss Cahline say. You go on and git dressed for school, so you kin ride to town wid Jason. You fixin to be late again.'

'No she's not,' I says. 'We're going to fix that right now.' She looked at me, the cup in her hand. She brushed her hair back from her face, her kimono slipping off her shoulder. 'You put that cup down and come in here a minute,' I says.

'What for?' she says.

'Come on,' I says. 'Put that cup in the sink and come in here.'

'What you up to now, Jason?' Dilsey says.

'You may think you can run over me like you do your grandmother and everybody else,' I says, 'But you'll find out different. I'll give you ten seconds to put that cup down like I told you.'

She quit looking at me. She looked at Dilsey. 'What time is it, Dilsey?' she says. 'When it's ten seconds, you whistle. Just a half a cup. Dilsey, pl – '

I grabbed her by the arm. She dropped the cup. It broke on the floor and she jerked back, looking at me, but I held her arm. Dilsey got up from her chair.

'You, Jason,' she says.

'You turn me lose,' Quentin says, 'I'll slap you.'

'You will, will you?' I says, 'You will, will you?' She slapped at me. I caught that hand too and held her like a wildcat. 'You will, will you?' I says. 'You think you will?'

'You, Jason!' Dilsey says. I dragged her into the dining-room. Her kimono came unfastened, flapping about her, damn near naked. Dilsey came hobbling along. I turned and kicked the door shut in her face.

'You keep out of here,' I says.

Quentin was leaning against the table, fastening her kimono. I looked at her.

'Now,' I says, 'I want to know what you mean, playing out of school and telling your grandmother lies and forging her name on your report and worrying her sick. What do you mean by it?'

She didn't say anything. She was fastening her kimono up under her chin, pulling it tight around her, looking at me. She hadn't got around to painting herself yet and her face looked like she had polished it with a gun rag. I went and grabbed her wrist. 'What do you mean?' I says.

'None of your damn business,' she says. 'You turn me loose.'

Dilsey came in the door. 'You, Jason,' she says.

'You get out of here, like I told you,' I says, not even looking back. 'I want to know where you go when you play out of school,' I says. 'You keep off the streets, or I'd

*157*

see you. Who do you play out with? Are you hiding out in the woods with one of those damn slick-headed jelly-beans? Is that where you go?'

'You – you old goddamn!' she says. She fought, but I held her. 'You damn old goddamn!' she says.

'I'll show you,' I says. 'You may can scare an old woman off, but I'll show you who's got hold of you now.' I held her with one hand, then she quit fighting and watched me, her eyes getting wide and black.

'What are you going to do?' she says.

'You wait until I get this belt out and I'll show you,' I says, pulling my belt out. Then Dilsey grabbed my arm.

'Jason,' she says, 'You, Jason! Ain't you ashamed of yourself.'

'Dilsey,' Quentin says, 'Dilsey.'

'I ain't gwine let him,' Dilsey says, 'Don't you worry, honey.' She held to my arm. Then the belt came out and I jerked loose and flung her away. She stumbled into the table. She was so old she couldn't do any more than move hardly. But that's all right: we need somebody in the kitchen to eat up the grub the young ones can't tote off. She came hobbling between us, trying to hold me again. 'Hit me, den,' she says, 'ef nothin else but hittin somebody won't do you. Hit me,' she says.

'You think I won't?' I says.

'I don't put no devilment beyond you,' she says. Then I heard Mother on the stairs. I might have known she wasn't going to keep out of it. I let go. She stumbled back against the wall, holding her kimono shut.

'All right,' I says, 'We'll just put this off a while. But don't think you can run it over me. I'm not an old woman, nor an old half dead nigger, either. You damn little slut,' I says.

'Dilsey,' she says, 'Dilsey, I want my mother.'

Dilsey went to her. 'Now, now,' she says, 'He ain't gwine so much as lay his hand on you while Ise here.' Mother came on down the stairs.

'Jason,' she says, 'Dilsey.'

'Now, now,' Dilsey says, 'I ain't gwine let him tech you.' She put her hand on Quentin. She knocked it down.

'You damn old nigger,' she says. She ran toward the door.

'Dilsey,' Mother says on the stairs. Quentin ran up the stairs, passing her. 'Quentin,' Mother says, 'You, Quentin.' Quentin ran on. I could hear her when she reached the top, then in the hall. Then the door slammed.

Mother had stopped. Then she came on. 'Dilsey,' she says.

'All right,' Dilsey says, 'Ise coming. You go on and git dat car and wait now,' she says, 'so you kin cahy her to school.'

'Don't you worry,' I says. 'I'll take her to school and I'm going to see that she stays there. I've started this thing, and I'm going through with it.'

'Jason,' Mother says on the stairs.

'Go on, now,' Dilsey says, going toward the door. 'You want to git her started too? Ise comin, Miss Cahline.'

I went on out. I could hear them on the steps. 'You go on back to bed now,' Dilsey was saying, 'Don't you know you ain't feeling well enough to git up yet? Go on back, now. I'm gwine to see she gits to school in time.'

I went on out the back to back the car out, then I had to go all the way round to the front before I found them.

'I thought I told you to put that tyre on the back of the car,' I says.

'I ain't had time,' Luster says. 'Ain't nobody to watch him till mammy git done in de kitchen.'

'Yes,' I says, 'I feed a whole damn kitchenful of niggers to follow around after him, but if I want an automobile tyre changed, I have to do it myself.'

'I ain't had nobody to leave him wid,' he says. Then he begun moaning and slobbering.

'Take him on round to the back,' I says. 'What the hell makes you want to keep him around here where people

can see him?' I made them go on, before he got started
bellowing good. It's bad enough on Sundays, with that
damn field full of people that haven't got a sideshow and
six niggers to feed, knocking a damn oversize mothball
around. He's going to keep on running up and down that
fence and bellowing every time they come in sight until
first thing I know they're going to begin charging me golf
dues, then Mother and Dilsey'll have to get a couple of
china door knobs and a walking-stick and work it out,
unless I play at night with a lantern. Then they'd send us
all to Jackson, maybe. God knows, they'd hold Old
Home week when that happened.

I went on back to the garage. There was the tyre, leaning against the wall, but be damned if I was going to put
it on. I backed out and turned around. She was standing
by the drive. I says,

'I know you haven't got any books: I just want to ask
you what you did with them, if it's any of my business.
Of course I haven't got any right to ask,' I says, 'I'm just
the one that paid $11.65 for them last September.'

'Mother buys my books,' she says. 'There's not a cent
of your money on me. I'd starve first.'

'Yes?' I says. 'You tell your grandmother that and see
what she says. You don't look all the way naked,' I says,
'even if that stuff on your face does hide more of you
than anything else you've got on.'

'Do you think your money or hers either paid for a
cent of this?' she says.

'Ask your grandmother,' I says. 'Ask her what became
of those cheques. You saw her burn one of them, as I
remember.' She wasn't even listening, with her face all
gummed up with paint and her eyes hard as a fice dog's.

'Do you know what I'd do if I thought your money or
hers either bought one cent of this?' she says, putting her
hand on her dress.

'What would you do?' I says, 'Wear a barrel?'

'I'd tear it right off and throw into the street,' she
says. 'Don't you believe me?'

'Sure you would,' I says. 'You do it every time.'

'See if I wouldn't,' she says. She grabbed the neck of her dress in both hands and made like she would tear it.

'You tear that dress,' I says, 'And I'll give you a whipping right here that you'll remember all your life.'

'See if I don't,' she says. Then I saw that she really was trying to tear it, to tear it right off of her. By the time I got the car stopped and grabbed her hands there was about a dozen people looking. It made me so mad for a minute it kind of blinded me.

'You do a thing like that again and I'll make you sorry you ever drew breath,' I says.

'I'm sorry now,' she says. She quit, then her eyes turned kind of funny and I says to myself if you cry here in this car, on the street, I'll whip you. I'll wear you out. Lucky for her she didn't, so I turned her wrists loose and drove on. Luckily we were near an alley, where I could turn into the back street and dodge the square. They were already putting the tent up in Beard's lot. Earl had already given me the two passes for our show windows. She sat there with her face turned away, chewing her lip. 'I'm sorry now,' she says. 'I don't see why I was ever born.'

'And I know of at least one other person that don't understand all he knows about that,' I says. I stopped in front of the school house. The bell had rung, and the last of them were just going in. 'You're on time for once, anyway,' I says. 'Are you going in there and stay there, or am I coming with you and make you?' She got out and banged the door. 'Remember what I say,' I says. 'I mean it. Let me hear one more time that you are slipping up and down back alleys with one of those damn squirts.'

She turned back at that. 'I don't slip around,' she says. 'I dare anybody to know everything I do.'

'And they all know it, too,' I says. 'Everybody in this town knows what you are. But I won't have it any more, you hear? I don't care what you do, myself,' I says, 'But I've got a position in this town, and I'm not going to have any member of my family going on like a nigger wench. You hear me?'

'I don't care,' she says, 'I'm bad and I'm going to hell, and I don't care. I'd rather be in hell than anywhere where you are.'

'If I hear one more time that you haven't been to school, you'll wish you were in hell,' I says. She turned and ran on across the yard. 'One more time, remember,' I says. She didn't look back.

I went to the post office and got the mail and drove on to the store and parked. Earl looked at me when I came in. I gave him a chance to say something about my being late, but he just said,

'Those cultivators have come. You'd better help Uncle Job put them up.'

I went on to the back, where old Job was uncrating them, at the rate of about three bolts to the hour.

'You ought to be working for me,' I says. 'Every other no-count nigger in town eats in my kitchen.'

'I works to suit de man whut pays me Sat'dy night,' he says. 'When I does dat, it don't leave me a whole lot of time to please other folks.' He screwed up a nut. 'Ain't nobody works much in dis country cep de boll-weevil, noways,' he says.

'You'd better be glad you're not a boll-weevil waiting on those cultivators,' I says. 'You'd work yourself to death before they'd be ready to prevent you.'

'Dat's de troof,' he says, 'Boll-weevil got tough time. Work ev'y day in de week out in de hot sun, rain er shine. Ain't got no front porch to set on en watch de watter-milyuns growin and Sat'dy don't mean nothin a-tall to him.'

'Saturday wouldn't mean nothing to you, either,' I says, 'if it depended on me to pay you wages. Get those things out of the crates now and drag them inside.'

I opened her letter first and took the cheque out. Just like a woman. Six days late. Yet they try to make men believe that they're capable of conducting a business.

How long would a man that thought the first of the
month came on the sixth last in business. And like as not,
when they sent the bank statement out, she would want
to know why I never deposited my salary until the sixth.
Things like that never occur to a woman.

'I had no answer to my letter about Quentin's easter
dress. Did it arrive all right? I've had no answer to the
last two letters I wrote her, though the cheque in the
second one was cashed with the other cheque. Is she
sick? Let me know at once or I'll come there and see
for myself. You promised you would let me know when
she needed things. I will expect to hear from you
before the 10th. No you'd better wire me at once. You
are opening my letters to her. I know that as well as if I
were looking at you. You'd better wire me at once
about her to this address.'

About that time Earl started yelling at Job, so I put
them away and went over to try to put some life into him.
What this country needs is white labour. Let these damn
trifling niggers starve for a couple of years, then they'd
see what a soft thing they have.

Along toward ten o'clock I went up front. There was a
drummer there. It was a couple of minutes to ten, and I
invited him up the street to get a cocacola. We got to
talking about crops.

'There's nothing to it,' I says, 'Cotton is a speculator's
crop. They fill the farmer full of hot air and get him to
raise a big crop for them to whipsaw on the market, to
trim the suckers with. Do you think the farmer gets anything out of it except a red neck and a hump in his back?
You think the man that sweats to put it into the ground
gets a red cent more than a bare living,' I says. 'Let him
make a big crop and it won't be worth picking; let him
make a small crop and he won't have enough to gin. And
what for? So a bunch of damn eastern jews, I'm not talking about men of the jewish religion,' I says, 'I've known

*163*

some jews that were fine citizens. You might be one yourself,' I says.

'No,' he says, 'I'm an American.'

'No offence,' I says. 'I give every man his due, regardless of religion or anything else. I have nothing against jews as an individual,' I says. 'It's just the race. You'll admit that they produce nothing. They follow the pioneers into a new country and sell them clothes.'

'You're thinking of Armenians,' he says, 'aren't you. A pioneer wouldn't have any use for new clothes.'

'No offence,' I says. 'I don't hold a man's religion against him.'

'Sure,' he says, 'I'm an American. My folks have some French blood, why I have a nose like this. I'm an American, all right.'

'So am I,' I says. 'Not many of us left. What I'm talking about is the fellows that sit up there in New York and trim the sucker gamblers.'

'That's right,' he says. 'Nothing to gambling, for a poor man. There ought to be a law against it.'

'Don't you think I'm right?' I says.

'Yes,' he says, 'I guess you're right. The farmer catches it coming and going.'

'I know I'm right,' I says. 'It's a sucker game, unless a man gets inside information from somebody that knows what's going on. I happen to be associated with some people who're right there in the ground. They have one of the biggest manipulators in New York for an adviser. Way I do it,' I says, 'I never risk much at a time. It's the fellow that thinks he knows it all and is trying to make a killing with three dollars that they're laying for. That's why they are in the business.'

Then it struck ten. I went up to the telegraph office. It opened up a little, just like they said. I went into the corner and took out the telegram again, just to be sure. While I was looking at it a report came in. It was up two points. They were all buying. I could tell that from what they were saying. Getting aboard. Like they didn't know

it could go but one way. Like there was a law or something against doing anything but buying. Well, I reckon
those eastern jews have got to live too. But I'll be
damned if it hasn't come to a pretty pass when any damn
foreigner that can't make a living in the country where
God put him, can come to this one and take money right
out of an American's pockets. It was up two points more.
Four points. But hell, they were right there and knew
what was going on. And if I wasn't going to take the
advice, what was I paying them ten dollars a month for. I
went out, then I remembered and came back and sent
the wire. 'All well. Q writing today.'

'Q?' the operator says.

'Yes,' I says, 'Q. Can't you spell Q?'

'I just asked to be sure,' he says.

'You send it like I wrote it and I'll guarantee you to be
sure,' I says. 'Send it collect.'

'What you sending, Jason?' Doc Wright says,
looking over my shoulder. 'Is that a code message to
buy?'

'That's all right about that,' I says. 'You boys use your
own judgment. You know more about it than those New
York folks do.'

'Well, I ought to,' Doc says, 'I'd a saved money this
year raising it at two cents a pound.'

Another report came in. It was down a point.

'Jason's selling,' Hopkins says. 'Look at his face.'

'That's all right about what I'm doing,' I says. 'You
boys follow your own judgment. Those rich New York
jews have got to live like everybody else,' I says.

I went on back to the store. Earl was busy up front. I
went on back to the desk and read Lorraine's letter.
'Dear daddy wish you were here. No good parties when
daddys out of town I miss my sweet daddy.' I reckon she
does. Last time I gave her forty dollars. Gave it to her. I
never promise a woman anything nor let her know what
I'm going to give her. That's the only way to manage
them. Always keep them guessing. If you can't think of

any other way to surprise them, give them a bust in the jaw.

I tore it up and burned it over the spittoon. I make it a rule never to keep a scrap of paper bearing a woman's hand, and I never write them at all. Lorraine is always after me to write to her but I says anything I forgot to tell you will save till I get to Memphis again but I says I don't mind you writing me now and then in a plain envelope, but if you ever try to call me up on the telephone, Memphis won't hold you I says. I says when I'm up there I'm one of the boys, but I'm not going to have any woman calling me on the telephone. Here I says, giving her the forty dollars. If you ever get drunk and take a notion to call me on the phone, just remember this and count ten before you do it.

'When'll that be?' she says.

'What?' I says.

'When you're coming back,' she says.

'I'll let you know,' I says. Then she tried to buy a beer, but I wouldn't let her. 'Keep your money,' I says. 'Buy yourself a dress with it.' I gave the maid a five, too. After all, like I say money has no value; it's just the way you spend it. It don't belong to anybody, so why try to hoard it. It just belongs to the man that can get it and keep it. There's a man right here in Jefferson made a lot of money selling rotten goods to niggers, lived in a room over the store about the size of a pig-pen, and did his own cooking. About four or five years ago he was taken sick. Scared the hell out of him so that when he was up again he joined the church and bought himself a Chinese missionary, five thousand dollars a year. I often think how mad he'll be if he was to die and find out there's not any heaven, when he thinks about that five thousand a year. Like I say, he'd better go on and die now and save money.

When it was burned good I was just about to shove the others into my coat when all of a sudden something told me to open Quentin's before I went home, but about that time Earl started yelling for me up front, so I put them away and went and waited on the damn redneck while he spent fifteen minutes deciding whether he wanted a twenty cent hame string or a thirty-five cent one.

'You'd better take that good one,' I says. 'How do you fellows ever expect to get ahead, trying to work with cheap equipment?'

'If this one ain't any good,' he says, 'why have you got it on sale?'

'I didn't say it wasn't any good,' I says, 'I said it's not as good as that other one.'

'How do you know it's not,' he says. 'You ever use airy one of them?'

'Because they don't ask thirty-five cents for it,' I says. 'That's how I know it's not as good.'

He held the twenty cent one in his hands, drawing it through his fingers. 'I reckon I'll take this hyer one,' he says. I offered to take it and wrap it, but he rolled it up and put it in his overalls. Then he took out a tobacco sack and finally got it untied and shook some coins out. He handed me a quarter. 'That fifteen cents will buy me a snack of dinner,' he says.

'All right,' I says. 'You're the doctor. But don't come complaining to me next year when you have to buy a new outfit.'

'I ain't makin' next year's crop yit,' he says. Finally I got rid of him, but every time I took that letter out something would come up. They were all in town for the show, coming in in droves to give their money to something that brought nothing to the town and wouldn't leave anything except what those grafters in the Mayor's office will split among themselves, and Earl chasing back and forth like a hen in a coop, saying 'Yes, ma'am, Mr. Compson will wait on you. Jason, show this lady a churn or a nickel's worth of screen hooks.'

Well, Jason likes work. I says no I never had university advantages because at Harvard they teach you how to go for a swim at night without knowing how to swim and at

Sewanee they don't even teach you what water is. I says you might send me to the state University; maybe I'll learn how to stop my clock with a nose spray and then you can send Ben to the Navy I says or to the cavalry anyway, they use geldings in the cavalry. Then when she sent Quentin home for me to feed too I says I guess that's right too, instead of me having to go way up north for a job they sent the job down here to me and then Mother begun to cry and I says it's not that I have any objection to having it here; if it's any satisfaction to you I'll quit work and nurse it myself and let you and Dilsey keep the flour barrel full, or Ben. Rent him out to a sideshow; there must be folks somewhere that would pay a dime to see him, then she cried more and kept saying my poor afflicted baby and I says yes he'll be quite a help to you when he gets his growth not being more than one and a half times as high as me now and she says she'd be dead soon and then we'd all be better off and so I says all right, all right, have it your way. It's your grandchild, which is more than any other grandparents it's got can say for certain. Only I says it's only a question of time. If you believe she'll do what she says and not try to see it, you fool yourself because the first time that was that Mother kept on saying thank God you are not a Compson except in name, because you are all I have left now, you and Maury, and I says well I could spare Uncle Maury myself and then they came and said they were ready to start. Mother stopped crying then. She pulled her veil down and we went downstairs. Uncle Maury was coming out of the dining-room, his handkerchief to his mouth. They kind of made a lane and we went out the door just in time to see Dilsey driving Ben and T. P. back around the corner. We went down the steps and got in. Uncle Maury kept saying Poor little sister, poor little sister, talking around his mouth and patting Mother's hand. Talking around whatever it was.

'Have you got your band on?' she says. 'Why don't they go on, before Benjamin comes out and makes a spectacle. Poor little boy. He doesn't know. He can't even realize.'

'There, there,' Uncle Maury says, patting her hand, talking around his mouth. 'It's better so. Let him be unaware of bereavement until he has to.'

'Other women have their children to support them in times like this,' Mother says.

'You have Jason and me,' he says.

'It's so terrible to me,' she says, 'Having the two of them like this, in less than two years.'

'There, there,' he says. After a while he kind of sneaked his hand to his mouth and dropped them out the window. Then I knew what I had been smelling. Clove stems. I reckon he thought that the least he could do at Father's funeral or maybe the sideboard thought it was still Father and tripped him up when he passed. Like I say, if he had to sell something to send Quentin to Harvard we'd all been a damn sight better off if he'd sold that sideboard and bought himself a one-armed strait-jacket with part of the money. I reckon the reason all the Compson gave out before it got to me like Mother says, is that he drank it up. At least I never heard of him offering to sell anything to send me to Harvard.

So he kept on patting her hand and saying 'Poor little sister,' patting her hand with one of the black gloves that we got the bill for four days later because it was the twenty-sixth because it was the same day one month that Father went up there and got it and brought it home and wouldn't tell anything about where she was or anything and Mother crying and saying 'And you didn't even see him? You didn't even try to get him to make any provision for it?' and Father says 'No she shall not touch his money not one cent of it' and Mother says 'He can be forced to by law. He can prove nothing, unless – Jason Compson,' she says, 'Were you fool enough to tell – '

'Hush, Caroline,' Father says, then he sent me to help Dilsey get that old cradle out of the attic and I says,

'Well, they brought my job home tonight' because all

THE SOUND AND THE FURY

the time we kept hoping they'd get things straightened out and he'd keep her because Mother kept saying she would at least have enough regard for the family not to jeopardize my chance after she and Quentin had had theirs.

'And whar else do she belong?' Dilsey says, 'Who else gwine raise her cep me? Ain't I raised ev'y one of y'all?'

'And a damn fine job you made of it,' I says. 'Anyway it'll give her something to sure enough worry over now.' So we carried the cradle down and Dilsey started to set it up in her old room. Then Mother started sure enough.

'Hush, Miss Cahline,' Dilsey says, 'You gwine wake her up.'

'In there?' Mother says, 'To be contaminated by that atmosphere? It'll be hard enough as it is, with the heritage she already has.'

'Hush,' Father says, 'Don't be silly.'

'Why ain't she gwine sleep in here,' Dilsey says, 'In the same room whar I put her ma to bed ev'y night of her life since she was big enough to sleep by herself.'

'You don't know,' Mother says, 'To have my own daughter cast off by her husband. Poor little innocent baby,' she says, looking at Quentin. 'You will never know the suffering you've caused.'

'Hush, Caroline,' Father says.

'What you want to go on like that fo Jason fer?' Dilsey says.

'I've tried to protect him.' Mother says. 'I've always tried to protect him from it. At least I can do my best to shield her.'

'How sleepin in dis room gwine hurt her, I like to know,' Dilsey says.

'I can't help it,' Mother says. 'I know I'm just a troublesome old woman. But I know that people cannot flout God's laws with impunity.'

'Nonsense,' Father said. 'Fix it in Miss Caroline's room then, Dilsey.'

'You can say nonsense,' Mother says. 'But she must

never know. She must never even learn that name. Dilsey, I forbid you ever to speak that name in her hearing. If she could grow up never to know that she had a mother, I would thank God.'

'Don't be a fool,' Father says.

'I have never interfered with the way you brought them up,' Mother says, 'But now I cannot stand any more. We must decide this now, tonight. Either that name is never to be spoken in her hearing, or she must go, or I will go. Take your choice.'

'Hush,' Father says, 'You're just upset. Fix it in here, Dilsey.'

'En you's about sick too,' Dilsey says. 'You looks like a hant. You git in bed and I'll fix you a toddy and see kin you sleep. I bet you ain't had a full night's sleep since you lef.'

'No,' Mother says, 'Don't you know what the doctor says? Why must you encourage him to drink? That's what's the matter with him now. Look at me, I suffer too, but I'm not so weak that I must kill myself with whisky.'

'Fiddlesticks,' Father says, 'What do doctors know? They make their livings advising people to do whatever they are not doing at the time, which is the extent of anyone's knowledge of the degenerate ape. You'll have a minister in to hold my hand next.' Then Mother cried, and he went out. Went downstairs, and then I heard the sideboard. I woke up and heard him going down again. Mother had gone to sleep or something, because the house was quiet at last. He was trying to be quiet too, because I couldn't hear him, only the bottom of his nightshirt and his bare legs in front of the sideboard.

Dilsey fixed the cradle and undressed her and put her in it. She never had waked up since he brought her in the house.

'She pretty near too big fer it,' Dilsey says. 'Dar now. I gwine spread me a pallet right acrost de hall, so you won't need to git up in de night.'

'I won't sleep,' Mother says. 'You go on home. I won't mind. I'll be happy to give the rest of my life to her, if I can just prevent – '

'Hush, now,' Dilsey says. 'We gwine take keer of her. En you go on to bed too,' she says to me, 'You got to go to school tomorrow.'

So I went out, then Mother called me back and cried on me a while.

'You are my only hope,' she says. 'Every night I thank God for you.' While we were waiting there for them to start she says Thank God if he had to be taken too, it is you left me and not Quentin. Thank God you are not a Compson, because all I have left now is you and Maury and I says, Well I could spare Uncle Maury myself. Well, he kept on patting her hand with his black glove, talking away from her. He took them off when his turn with the shovel came. He got up near the first, where they were holding the umbrellas over them, stamping every now and then and trying to kick the mud off their feet and sticking to the shovels so they'd have to knock it off, making a hollow sound when it fell on it, and when I stepped back around the hack I could see him behind a tombstone, taking another one out of a bottle. I thought he never was going to stop because I had on my new suit too, but it happened that there wasn't much mud on the wheels yet, only Mother saw it and says I don't know when you'll ever have another one and Uncle Maury says, 'Now, now. Don't you worry at all. You have me to depend on, always.'

And we have. Always. The fourth letter was from him. But there wasn't any need to open it. I could have written it myself, or recited it to her from memory, adding ten dollars just to be safe. But I had a hunch about that other letter. I just felt that it was about time she was up to some of her tricks again. She got pretty wise after that first time. She found out pretty quick that I was a different breed of cat from Father. When they begun to get it filled up toward the top Mother started crying sure enough, so Uncle Maury got in with her and drove off. He says You can come in with somebody; they'll be glad to give you a lift. I'll have to take your mother on and I thought about saying, Yes you ought to brought two bottles instead of just one only I thought about where we were so I let them go on. Little they cared how wet I got, because then Mother could have a whale of a time being afraid I was taking pneumonia.

Well, I got to thinking about that and watching them throwing dirt into it, slapping it on anyway like they were making mortar or something or building a fence, and I began to feel sort of funny and so I decided to walk around a while. I thought that if I went toward town they'd catch up and be trying to make me get in one of them, so I went on back toward the nigger graveyard. I got under some cedars, where the rain didn't come much, only dripping now and then, where I could see when they got through and went away. After a while they were all gone and I waited a minute and came out.

I had to follow the path to keep out of the wet grass so I didn't see her until I was pretty near there, standing there in a black cloak, looking at the flowers, I knew who it was right off, before she turned and looked at me and lifted up her veil.

'Hello, Jason,' she says, holding out her hand. We shook hands.

'What are you doing here?' I says. 'I thought you promised her you wouldn't come back here. I thought you had more sense than that.'

'Yes?' she says. She looked at the flowers again. There must have been fifty dollars' worth. Somebody had put one bunch on Quentin's. 'You did?' she says.

'I'm not surprised though,' I says. 'I wouldn't put anything past you. You don't mind anybody. You don't give a damn about anybody.'

'Oh,' she says, 'that job.' She looked at the grave. 'I'm sorry about that, Jason.'

'I bet you are,' I says. 'You'll talk mighty meek now.

But you needn't have come back. There's not anything left. Ask Uncle Maury, if you don't believe me.'

'I don't want anything,' she says. She looked at the grave. 'Why didn't they let me know?' she says. 'I just happened to see it in the paper. On the back page. Just happened to.'

I didn't say anything. We stood there, looking at the grave, and then I got to thinking about when we were little and one thing and another and I got to feeling funny again, kind of mad or something, thinking about now we'd have Uncle Maury around the house all the time, running things like the way he left me to come home in the rain by myself. I says,

'A fine lot you care, sneaking in here soon as he's dead. But it won't do you any good. Don't think that you can take advantage of this to come sneaking back. If you can't stay on the horse you've got, you'll have to walk,' I says. 'We don't even know your name at that house,' I says. 'Do you know that? We don't even know you with him and Quentin,' I says. 'Do you know that?'

'I know it,' she says. 'Jason,' she says, looking at the grave, 'if you'll fix it so I can see her a minute I'll give you fifty dollars.'

'You haven't got fifty dollars,' I says.

'Will you?' she says, not looking at me.

'Let's see it,' I says. 'I don't believe you've got fifty dollars.'

I could see where her hands were moving under her cloak, then she held her hand out. Damn if it wasn't full of money. I could see two or three yellow ones.

'Does he still give you money?' I says. 'How much does he send you?'

'I'll give you a hundred,' she says. 'Will you?'

'Just a minute,' I says, 'And just like I say I wouldn't have her know it for a thousand dollars.'

'Yes,' she says. 'Just like you say do it. Just so I see her a minute. I won't beg or do anything. I'll go right on away.'

'Give me the money,' I says.

'I'll give it to you afterwards,' she says.

'Don't you trust me?' I says.

'No,' she says. 'I know you. I grew up with you.'

'You're a fine one to talk about trusting people,' I says. 'Well,' I says, 'I got to get on out of the rain. Good-bye.' I made to go away.

'Jason,' she says. I stopped.

'Yes?' I says. 'Hurry up. I'm getting wet.'

'All right,' she says. 'Here.' There wasn't anybody in sight. I went back and took the money. She still held to it. 'You'll do it?' she says, looking at me from under the veil, 'You promise?'

'Let go,' I says, 'You want somebody to come along and see us?'

She let go. I put the money in my pocket. 'You'll do it, Jason?' she says. 'I wouldn't ask you, if there was any other way.'

'You're damn right there's no other way,' I says. 'Sure I'll do it. I said I would, didn't I? Only you'll have to do just like I say, now.'

'Yes,' she says, 'I will.' So I told her where to be, and went to the livery stable. I hurried and got there just as they were unhitching the hack. I asked if they had paid for it yet and he said No and I said Mrs. Compson forgot something and wanted it again, so they let me take it. Mink was driving. I bought him a cigar, so we drove around until it begun to get dark on the back streets where they wouldn't see him. Then Mink said he'd have to take the team on back and so I said I'd buy him another cigar and so we drove into the lane and I went across the yard to the house. I stopped in the hall until I could hear Mother and Uncle Maury upstairs, then I went on back to the kitchen. She and Ben were there with Dilsey. I said Mother wanted her and I took her into the house. I found Uncle Maury's raincoat and put it around her and picked her up and went back to the lane and got in the hack. I told Mink to drive to the depot. He

was afraid to pass the stable, so we had to go the back
way and I saw her standing on the corner under the light
and I told Mink to drive close to the walk and when I
said Go on, to give the team a bat. Then I took the raincoat off of her and held her to the window and Caddy
saw her and sort of jumped forward.

'Hit em Mink!' I says, and Mink gave them a cut and
we went past her like a fire-engine. 'Now get on that
train like you promised,' I says. I could see her running
after us through the back window. 'Hit em again,' I says,
'Let's get on home.' When we turned the corner she was
still running.

And so I counted the money again that night and put
it away, and I didn't feel so bad. I says I reckon that'll
show you. I reckon you'll know now that you can't beat
me out of a job and get away with it. It never occurred to
me she wouldn't keep her promise and take that train.
But I didn't know much about them then; I didn't have
any more sense than to believe what they said, because
the next morning damn if she didn't walk right into the
store, only she had sense enough to wear the veil and not
speak to anybody. It was Saturday morning, because I
was at the store, and she came right on back to the desk
where I was, walking fast.

'Liar,' she says, 'Liar.'

'Are you crazy?' I says. 'What do you mean? Coming
in here like this?' She started in, but I shut her off. I says,
'You already cost me one job; do you want me to lose this
one too? If you've got anything to say to me, I'll meet
you somewhere after dark. What have you got to say to
me?' I says, 'Didn't I do everything I said? I said see her
a minute, didn't I? Well, didn't you?' She just stood there
looking at me, shaking like an ague-fit, her hands
clenched and kind of jerking. 'I did just what I said I
would,' I says, 'You're the one that lied. You promised to
take that train. Didn't you? Didn't you promise? If you
think you can get that money back, just try it,' I says. 'If
it'd been a thousand dollars, you'd still owe me after the

risk I took. And if I see or hear you're still in town after number 17 runs,' I says, 'I'll tell Mother and Uncle Maury. Then hold your breath until you see her again.' She just stood there, looking at me, twisting her hands together.

'Damn you,' she says, 'Damn you.'

'Sure,' I says, 'That's all right too. Mind what I say, now. After number 17, and I tell them.'

After she was gone I felt better. I says I reckon you'll think twice before you deprive me of a job that was promised me. I was a kid then. I believed folks when they said they'd do things. I've learned better since. Besides, like I say I guess I don't need any man's help to get along I can stand on my own feet like I always have. Then all of a sudden I thought of Dilsey and Uncle Maury. I thought how she'd get around Dilsey and that Uncle Maury would do anything for ten dollars. And there I was, couldn't even get away from the store to protect my own Mother. Like she says, if one of you had to be taken, thank God it was you left me I can depend on you and I says well I don't reckon I'll ever get far enough from the store to get out of your reach. Somebody's got to hold on to what little we have left, I reckon.

So as soon as I got home I fixed Dilsey. I told Dilsey she had leprosy and I got the bible and read where a man's flesh rotted off and I told her that if she ever looked at her or Ben or Quentin they'd catch it too. So I thought I had everything all fixed until that day when I came home and found Ben bellowing. Raising hell and nobody could quiet him. Mother said, Well, get him the slipper then. Dilsey made out she didn't hear. Mother said it again and I says I'd go I couldn't stand that damn noise. Like I say I can stand lots of things I don't expect much from them but if I have to work all day long in a damn store damn if I don't think I deserve a little peace and quiet to eat dinner in. So I says I'd go and Dilsey says quick, 'Jason!'

Well, like a flash I knew what was up, but just to make

sure I went and got the slipper and brought it back, and just like I thought, when he saw it you'd thought we were killing him. So I made Dilsey own up, then I told Mother. We had to take her up to bed then, and after things got quieted down a little I put the fear of God into Dilsey. As much as you can into a nigger, that is. That's the trouble with nigger servants, when they've been with you for a long time they get so full of self-importance that they're not worth a damn. Think they run the whole family.

'I like to know whut's de hurt in lettin dat po chile see her own baby,' Dilsey says. 'If Mr. Jason was still here hit ud be different.'

'Only Mr. Jason's not here,' I says. 'I know you won't pay me any mind, but I reckon you'll do what Mother says. You keep on worrying her like this until you get her into the graveyard too, then you can fill the whole house full of ragtag and bobtail. But what did you want to let that damn idiot see her for?'

'You's a cold man, Jason, if man you 'is,' she says. 'I thank de Lawd I got mo heart dan dat, even ef hit is black.'

'At least I'm man enough to keep that flour barrel full,' I says. 'And if you do that again, you won't be eating out of it either.'

So the next time I told her that if she tried Dilsey again, Mother was going to fire Dilsey and send Ben to Jackson and take Quentin and go away. She looked at me for a while. There wasn't any street light close and I couldn't see her face much. But I could feel her looking at me. When we were little when she'd get mad and couldn't do anything about it her upper lip would begin to jump. Every time it jumped it would leave a little more of her teeth showing, and all the time she'd be as still as a post, not a muscle moving except her lip jerking higher and higher up her teeth. But she didn't say anything. She just said,

'All right. How much?'

'Well, if one look through a hack window was worth a hundred,' I says. So after that she behaved pretty well, only one time she asked to see a statement of the bank account.

'I know they have Mother's endorsement on them,' she says, 'But I want to see the bank statement. I want to see myself where those cheques go.'

'That's in mother's private business,' I says. 'If you think you have any right to pry into her private affairs I'll tell her you believe those cheques are being misappropriated and you want an audit because you don't trust her.'

She didn't say anything or move. I could hear her whispering Damn you oh damn you oh damn you.

'Say it out,' I says, 'I don't reckon it's any secret what you and I think of one another. Maybe you want the money back,' I says.

'Listen, Jason,' she says, 'Don't lie to me now. About her. I won't ask to see anything. If that isn't enough, I'll send more each month. Just promise that she'll – that she – You can do that. Things for her. Be kind to her. Little things that I can't, they won't let. ... But you won't. You never had a drop of warm blood in you. Listen,' she says, 'If you'll get Mother to let me have her back, I'll give you a thousand dollars.'

'You haven't got a thousand dollars,' I says, 'I know you're lying now.'

'Yes I have. I will have. I can get it.'

'And I know how you'll get it,' I says, 'You'll get it the same way you got her. And when she gets big enough – ' Then I thought she really was going to hit at me, and then I didn't know what she was going to do. She acted for a minute like some kind of a toy that's wound up too tight and about to burst all to pieces.

'Oh, I'm crazy,' she says, 'I'm insane. I can't take her. Keep her. What am I thinking of. Jason,' she says, grabbing my arm. Her hands were hot as fever. 'You'll have to promise to take care of her, to – She's kin to you; your

179

own flesh and blood. Promise, Jason. You have Father's name: do you think I'd have to ask him twice? Once, even?'

'That's so,' I says, 'He did leave me something. What do you want me to do,' I says, 'Buy an apron and a go-cart? I never got you into this,' I says. 'I run more risk than you do, because you haven't got anything at stake. So if you expect – '

'No,' she says, then she begun to laugh and to try to hold it back all at the same time. 'No. I have nothing at stake,' she says, making that noise, putting her hands to her mouth. 'Nuh-nuh-nothing,' she says.

'Here,' I says, 'Stop that!'

'I'm tr-trying to,' she says, holding her hands over her mouth. 'Oh God, oh God.'

'I'm going away from here,' I says, 'I can't be seen here. You get on out of town now, you hear?'

'Wait,' she says, catching my arm. 'I've stopped. I won't again. You promise, Jason?' she says, and me feel-ing her eyes almost like they were touching my face, 'You promise? Mother – that money – if sometimes she needs things – If I send cheques for her to you, other ones besides those, you'll give them to her? You won't tell? You'll see that she has things like other girls?'

'Sure,' I says, 'As long as you behave and do like I tell you.'

And so when Earl came up front with his hat on he says, 'I'm going to step up to Rogers' and get a snack. We won't have time to go home to dinner, I reckon.'

'What's the matter we won't have time?' I says.

'With this show in town and all,' he says. 'They're going to give an afternoon performance too, and they'll all want to get done trading in time to go to it. So we'd better just run up to Rogers'.'

'All right,' I says, 'It's your stomach. If you want to make a slave of yourself to your business, it's all right with me.'

'I reckon you'll never be a slave to any business,' he says.

'Not unless it's Jason Compson's business,' I says.

So when I went back and opened it the only thing that surprised me was it was a money order not a cheque. Yes, sir. You can't trust a one of them. After all the risk I'd taken, risking Mother finding out about her coming down here once or twice a year sometimes, and me having to tell Mother lies about it. That's gratitude for you. And I wouldn't put it past her to try to notify the post office not to let anyone except her cash it. Giving a kid like that fifty dollars. Why I never saw fifty dollars until I was twenty-one years old, with all the other boys with the afternoon off and all day Saturday and me working in a store. Like I say, how can they expect anybody to control her, with her giving her money behind our backs. She has the same home you had I says, and the same raising. I reckon Mother is a better judge of what she needs than you are, that haven't even got a home. 'If you want to give her money,' I says, 'You send it to Mother, don't be giving it to her. If I've got to run this risk every few months, you'll have to do like I say, or it's out.'

And just about the time I got ready to begin on it because if Earl thought I was going to dash up the street and gobble two bits' worth of indigestion on his account he was bad fooled. I may not be sitting with my feet on a mahogany desk but I am being paid for what I do inside this building and if I can't manage to live a civilized life outside of it I'll go where I can. I can stand on my own feet; I don't need any man's mahogany desk to prop me up. So just about the time I got ready to start. I'd have to drop everything and run to sell some redneck a dime's worth of nails or something, and Earl up there gobbling a sandwich and half-way back already, like as not, and then I found that all the blanks were gone. I remembered then that I had aimed to get some more, but it was too late now, and then I looked up and there Quentin came. In the back door. I heard her asking old Job if I was there. I just had time to stick them in the drawer and close it.

She came around to the desk. I looked at my watch.

'You been to dinner already?' I says. 'It's just twelve; I just heard it strike. You must have flown home and back.'

'I'm not going home to dinner,' she says. 'Did I get a letter today?'

'Were you expecting one?' I says. 'Have you got a sweetie that can write?'

'From Mother,' she says. 'Did I get a letter from Mother?' she says, looking at me.

'Mother got one from her,' I says. 'I haven't opened it. You'll have to wait until she opens it. She'll let you see it, I imagine.'

'Please, Jason,' she says, not paying any attention, 'Did I get one?'

'What's the matter?' I says. 'I never knew you to be this anxious about anybody. You must expect some money from her.'

'She said she – ' she says. 'Please, Jason,' she says, 'Did I?'

'You must have been to school today, after all,' I says, 'Somewhere where they taught you to say please. Wait a minute, while I wait on that customer.'

I went and waited on him. When I turned to come back she was out of sight behind the desk. I ran. I ran around the desk and caught her as she jerked her hand out of the drawer. I took the letter away from her, beating her knuckles on the desk until she let go.

'You would, would you?' I says.

'Give it to me,' she says, 'You've already opened it. Give it to me. Please, Jason. It's mine. I saw the name.'

'I'll take a hame string to you,' I says. 'That's what I'll give you. Going into my papers.'

'Is there some money in it?' she says, reaching for it. 'She said she would send me some money. She promised she would. Give it to me.'

'What do you want with money?' I says.

'She said she would,' she says, 'Give it to me. Please,

*182*

Jason. I won't ever ask you anything again if you'll give it to me this time.'

'I'm going to, if you'll give me time,' I says. I took the letter and the money order out and gave her the letter. She reached for the money order, not hardly glancing at the letter. 'You'll have to sign it first,' I says.

'How much is it?' she says.

'Read the letter,' I says. 'I reckon it'll say.'

She read it fast, in about two looks.

'It don't say,' she says, looking up. She dropped the letter to the floor. 'How much is it?'

'It's ten dollars,' I says.

'Ten dollars?' she says, staring at me.

'And you ought to be damn glad to get that,' I says, 'A kid like you. What are you in such a rush for money all of a sudden for?'

'Ten dollars?' she says, like she was talking in her sleep, 'Just ten dollars?' She made a grab at the money order. 'You're lying,' she says. 'Thief!' she says, 'Thief!'

'You would, would you?' I says, holding her off.

'Give it to me!' she says, 'It's mine. She sent it to me. I will see it. I will.'

'You will?' I says, holding her, 'How're you going to do it?'

'Just let me see it, Jason,' she says, 'Please. I won't ask you for anything again.'

'Think I'm lying, do you?' I says. 'Just for that you won't see it.'

'But just ten dollars,' she says, 'She told me she – she told me – Jason, please please please. I've got to have some money. I've just got to. Give it to me, Jason. I'll do anything if you will.'

'Tell me what you've got to have money for,' I says.

'I've got to have it,' she says. She was looking at me. Then all of a sudden she quit looking at me without moving her eyes at all. I knew she was going to lie. 'It's some money I owe,' she says. 'I've got to pay it. I've got to pay it today.'

'Who to?' I says. Her hands were sort of twisting. I could watch her trying to think of a lie to tell. 'Have you been charging things at stores again?' I says. 'You needn't bother to tell me that. If you can find anybody in this town that'll charge anything to you after what I told them, I'll eat it.'

'It's a girl,' she says, 'It's a girl. I borrowed some money from a girl. I've got to pay it back. Jason, give it to me. Please. I'll do anything. I've got to have it. Mother will pay you. I'll write to her to pay you and that I won't ever ask her for anything again. You can see the letter. Please, Jason. I've got to have it.'

'Tell me what you want with it, and I'll see about it,' I says. 'Tell me.' She just stood there, with her hands working against her dress. 'All right,' I says, 'If ten dollars is too little for you, I'll just take it home to Mother, and you know what'll happen to it then. Of course, if you're so rich you don't need ten dollars – '

She stood there, looking at the floor, kind of mumbling to herself. 'She said she would send me some money. She said she sends money here and you say she don't send any. She said she's sent a lot of money here. She says it's for me. That it's for me to have some of it. And you say we haven't got any money.'

'You know as much about that as I do,' I says. 'You've seen what happens to those cheques.'

'Yes,' she says, looking at the floor. 'Ten dollars,' she says, 'Ten dollars.'

'And you'd better thank your stars it's ten dollars,' I says. 'Here,' I says. I put the money order face down on the desk, holding my hand on it, 'Sign it.'

'Will you let me see it?' she says. 'I just want to look at it. Whatever it says, I won't ask for but ten dollars. You can have the rest. I just want to see it.'

'Not after the way you've acted,' I says. 'You've got to learn one thing, and that is that when I tell you to do something, you've got it to do. You sign your name on that line.'

She took the pen, but instead of signing it she just stood there with her head bent and the pen shaking in her hand. Just like her mother. 'Oh, God,' she says, 'oh, God.'

'Yes,' I says, 'That's one thing you'll have to learn if you never learn anything else. Sign it now, and get on out of here.'

She signed it. 'Where's the money?' she says. I took the order and blotted it and put it in my pocket. Then I gave her the ten dollars.

'Now you go on back to school this afternoon, you hear?' I says. She didn't answer. She crumpled the bill up in her hand like it was a rag or something and went on out the front door just as Earl came in. A customer came in with him and they stopped up front. I gathered up the things and put on my hat and went up front.

'Been much busy?' Earl says.

'Not much,' I says. He looked out the door.

'That your car over yonder?' he says. 'Better not try to go out home to dinner. We'll likely have another rush just before the show opens. Get you a lunch at Rogers' and put a ticket in the drawer.'

'Much obliged,' I says. 'I can still manage to feed myself, I reckon.'

And right there he'd stay, watching that door like a hawk until I came through it again. Well, he'd just have to watch it for a while; I was doing the best I could. The time before I says that's the last one now; you'll have to remember to get some more right away. But who can remember anything in all this hurrah. And now this damn show had to come here the one day I'd have to hunt all over town for a blank cheque, besides all the other things I had to do to keep the house running, and Earl watching the door like a hawk.

I went to the printing shop and told him I wanted to play a joke on a fellow, but he didn't have anything. Then he told me to have a look in the old opera house, where somebody had stored a lot of papers and junk out of the old Merchants' and Farmers' Bank when it failed, so I dodged up a few more alleys so Earl couldn't see me and finally found old man Simmons and got the key from him and went up there and dug around. At last I found a pad on a Saint Louis bank. And of course she'd pick this one time to look at it close. Well, it would have to do. I couldn't waste any more time now.

I went back to the store. 'Forgot some papers Mother wants to go to the bank,' I says. I went back to the desk and fixed the cheque. Trying to hurry and all, I says to myself it's a good thing her eyes are giving out, with that little whore in the house, a Christian forbearing woman like Mother. I says you know just as well as I do what she's going to grow up into but I says that's your business, if you want to keep her and raise her in your house just because of Father. Then she would begin to cry and say it was her own flesh and blood so I just says All right. Have it your own way. I can stand it if you can.

I fixed the letter up again and glued it back and went out.

'Try not to be gone any longer than you can help,' Earl says.

'All right,' I says. I went to the telegraph office. The smart boys were all there.

'Any of you boys made your million yet?' I says.

'Who can do anything, with a market like that?' Doc says.

'What's it doing?' I says. I went in and looked. It was three points under the opening. 'You boys are not going to let a little thing like the cotton market beat you, are you?' I says. 'I thought you were too smart for that.'

'Smart, hell,' Doc says. 'It was down twelve points at twelve o'clock. Cleaned me out.'

'Twelve points?' I says. 'Why the hell didn't somebody let me know? Why didn't you let me know?' I says to the operator.

'I take it as it comes in,' he says. 'I'm not running a bucket shop.'

'You're smart, aren't you?' I says. 'Seems to me, with the money I spend with you, you could take time to call me up. Or maybe your damn company's in a conspiracy with those damn eastern sharks.'

He didn't say anything. He made like he was busy.

'You're getting a little too big for your pants,' I says. 'First thing you know you'll be working for a living.'

'What's the matter with you?' Doc says. 'You're still three points to the good.'

'Yes,' I says, 'If I happened to be selling. I haven't mentioned that yet, I think. You boys all cleaned out?'

'I got caught twice,' Doc says. 'I switched just in time.'

'Well,' I. O. Snopes says, 'I've picked hit; I reckon tain't no more than fair fer hit to pick me once in a while.'

So I left them buying and selling among themselves at a nickel a point. I found a nigger and sent him for my car and stood on the corner and waited. I couldn't see Earl looking up and down the street, with one eye on the clock, because I couldn't see the door from here. After about a week he got back with it.

'Where the hell have you been?' I says, 'Riding around where the wenches could see you?'

'I come straight as I could,' he says, 'I had to drive clean around the square, wid all dem wagons.'

I never found a nigger yet that didn't have an airtight alibi for whatever he did. But just turn one loose in a car and he's bound to show off. I got in and went on around the square. I caught a glimpse of Earl in the door across the square.

I went straight to the kitchen and told Dilsey to hurry up with dinner.

'Quentin ain't come yit,' she says.

'What of that?' I says. 'You'll be telling me next that Luster's not quite ready to eat yet. Quentin knows when meals are served in this house. Hurry up with it, now.'

Mother was in her room. I gave her the letter. She

opened it and took the cheque out and sat holding it in her hand. I went and got the shovel from the corner and gave her a match. 'Come on,' I says, 'Get it over with. You'll be crying in a minute.'

She took the match, but she didn't strike it. She sat there, looking at the cheque. Just like I said it would be.

'I hate to do it,' she says, 'To increase your burden by adding Quentin ...'

'I guess we'll get along,' I says. 'Come on. Get it over with.'

But she just sat there, holding the cheque.

'This one is on a different bank,' she says. 'They have been on an Indianapolis bank.'

'Yes,' I says. 'Women are allowed to do that too.'

'Do what?' she says.

'Keep money in two different banks,' I says.

'Oh,' she says. She looked at the cheque a while. 'I'm glad to know she's so ... she has so much ... God sees that I am doing right,' she says.

'Come on,' I says, 'finish it. Get the fun over.'

'Fun?' she says, 'When I think – '

'I thought you were burning this two hundred dollars a month for fun,' I says. 'Come on, now. Want me to strike the match?'

'I could bring myself to accept them,' she says, 'For my children's sake. I have no pride.'

'You'd never be satisfied,' I says, 'You know you wouldn't. You've settled that once, let it stay settled. We can get along.'

'I leave everything to you,' she says. 'But sometimes I become afraid that in doing this I am depriving you all of what is rightfully yours. Perhaps I shall be punished for it. If you want me to, I will smother my pride and accept them.'

'What would be the good in beginning now, when you've been destroying them for fifteen years?' I says. 'If you keep on doing it, you have lost nothing, but if you'd begin to take them now, you'll have lost fifty thousand dollars. We've got along so far, haven't we?' I says. 'I haven't seen you in the poor-house yet.'

'Yes,' she says, 'We Bascombs need nobody's charity. Certainly not that of a fallen woman.'

She struck the match and lit the cheque and put it in the shovel, and then the envelope, and watched them burn.

'You don't know what it is,' she says, 'Thank God you will never know what a mother feels.'

'There are lots of women in this world no better than her,' I says.

'But they are not my daughters,' she says. 'It's not myself,' she says, 'I'd gladly take her back, sins and all, because she is my flesh and blood. It's for Quentin's sake.'

Well, I could have said it wasn't much chance of anybody hurting Quentin much, but like I say I don't expect much but I do want to eat and sleep without a couple of women squabbling and crying in the house.

'And yours,' she says. 'I know how you feel toward her.'

'Let her come back,' I says, 'far as I'm concerned.'

'No,' she says. 'I owe that to your father's memory.'

'When he was trying all the time to persuade you to let her come home when Herbert threw her out?' I says.

'You don't understand,' she says. 'I know you don't intend to make it more difficult for me. But it's my place to suffer for my children,' she says. 'I can bear it.'

'Seems to me you go to a lot of unnecessary trouble doing it,' I says. The paper burned out. I carried it to the grate and put it in. 'It just seems a shame to me to burn up good money,' I says.

'Let me never see the day when my children will have to accept that, the wages of sin,' she says. 'I'd rather see even you dead in your coffin first.'

'Have it your way,' I says. 'Are we going to have dinner soon?' I says, 'Because if we're not, I'll have to go on back. We're pretty busy today.' She got up. 'I've told her once,' I says. 'It seems she's waiting on Quentin or Luster or somebody. Here, I'll call her. Wait.' But she went to the head of the stairs and called.

'Quentin ain't come yit,' Dilsey says.

'Well, I'll have to get on back,' I says. 'I can get a sandwich downtown. I don't want to interfere with Dilsey's arrangements,' I says. Well, that got her started again, with Dilsey hobbling and mumbling back and forth, saying,

'All right, all right, Ise puttin hit on fast as I kin.'

'I try to please you all,' Mother says, 'I try to make things as easy for you as I can.'

'I'm not complaining, am I?' I says. 'Have I said a word except I had to go back to work?'

'I know,' she says, 'I know you haven't had the chance the others had, that you've had to bury yourself in a little country store. I wanted you to get ahead. I knew your father would never realize that you were the only one who had any business sense, and then when everything else failed I believed that when she married, and Herbert … after his promise …'

'Well, he was probably lying too,' I says. 'He may not have even had a bank. And if he had, I don't reckon he'd have to come all the way to Mississippi to get a man for it.'

We ate a while. I could hear Ben in the kitchen, where Luster was feeding him. Like I say, if we've got to feed another mouth and she won't take that money, why not send him down to Jackson. He'll be happier there, with people like him. I says God knows there's little enough room for pride in this family, but it don't take much pride to not like to see a thirty year old man playing around the yard with a nigger boy, running up and down the fence and lowing like a cow whenever they play golf over there. I says if they'd sent him to Jackson at first we'd all be better off today. I says, you've done your duty by him; you've done all anybody can expect of you and more than most folks would do, so why not send him there and get that much benefit out of the taxes we pay. Then she says, 'I'll be gone soon. I know I'm just a burden to you' and I says 'You've been saying that so long that I'm beginning to believe you' only I says you'd better be sure and not let me know you're gone because I'll sure have him on number seventeen that night and I says I think I know a place where they'll take her too and the name of it's not Milk street and Honey avenue either. Then she begun to cry and I says All right all right I have as much pride about my kinfolks as anybody even if I don't always know where they come from.

We ate for a while. Mother sent Dilsey to the front to look for Quentin again.

'I keep telling you she's not coming to dinner,' I says.

'She knows better than that,' Mother says, 'She knows I don't permit her to run about the streets and not come home at meal time. Did you look good, Dilsey?'

'Don't let her, then,' I says.

'What can I do,' she says. 'You have all of you flouted me. Always.'

'If you wouldn't come interfering, I'd make her mind,' I says. 'It wouldn't take me but about one day to straighten her out.'

'You'd be too brutal with her,' she says. 'You have your Uncle Maury's temper.'

That reminded me of the letter. I took it out and handed it to her. 'You won't have to open it,' I says. 'The bank will let you know how much it is this time.'

'It's addressed to you,' she says.

'Go on and open it,' I says. She opened it and read it and handed it to me.

'"My dear young nephew," it says,

'"You will be glad to learn that I am now in a position to avail myself of an opportunity regarding which, for reasons which I shall make obvious to you, I shall not go into details until I have an opportunity to divulge it to you in a more secure manner. My business experience

*191*

has taught me to be chary of committing anything of a confidential nature to any more concrete medium than speech, and my extreme precaution in this instance should give you some inkling of its value. Needless to say, I have just completed a most exhaustive examination of all its phases, and I feel no hesitancy in telling you that it is that sort of golden chance that comes but once in a lifetime, and I now see clearly before me that goal toward which I have long and unflaggingly striven, i.e., the ultimate solidification of my affairs by which I may restore to its rightful position that family of which I have the honour to be the sole remaining male descendant; that family in which I have ever included your lady mother and her children.

' "As it so happens, I am not quite in a position to avail myself of this opportunity to the uttermost which it warrants, but rather than go out of the family to do so, I am today drawing upon your Mother's bank for the small sum necessary to complement my own initial investment, for which I herewith enclose, as a matter of formality, my note of hand at eight per cent per annum. Needless to say, this is merely a formality, to secure your Mother in the event of that circumstance of which man is ever the plaything and sport. For naturally I shall employ this sum as though it were my own and so permit your Mother to avail herself of this opportunity which my exhaustive investigation has shown to be a bonanza – if you will permit the vulgarism – of the first water and purest ray serene.

' "This is in confidence, you will understand, from one business man to another; we will harvest our own vineyards, eh? And knowing your Mother's delicate health and that timorousness which such delicately nurtured Southern ladies would naturally feel regarding matters of business, and their charming proneness to divulge unwittingly such matters in conversation, I would suggest that you do not mention it to her at all. On second thought, I advise you not to do so. It might be better to simply restore this sum to the bank at some future date, say, in a lump sum with the other small sums for which I am indebted to her, and say nothing about it at all. It is our duty to shield her from the crass material world as much as possible.

'"Your affectionate Uncle,

'"Maury L. Bascomb."'

'What do you want to do about it?' I says, flipping it across the table.

'I know you grudge what I give him,' she says.

'It's your money,' I says. 'If you want to throw it to the birds even, it's your business.'

'He's my own brother,' Mother says. 'He's the last Bascomb. When we are gone there won't be any more of them.'

'That'll be hard on somebody, I guess,' I says. 'All right, all right,' I says. 'It's your money. Do as you please with it. You want me to tell the bank to pay it?'

'I know you begrudge him,' she says. 'I realize the burden on your shoulders. When I'm gone it will be easier on you.'

'I could make it easier right now,' I says. 'All right, all right, I won't mention it again. Move all bedlam in here if you want to.'

'He's your own brother,' she says, 'Even if he is afflicted.'

'I'll take your bank book,' I says, 'I'll draw my cheque today.'

'He kept you waiting six days,' she says. 'Are you sure the business is sound? It seems strange to me that a solvent business cannot pay its employees promptly.'

'He's all right,' I says, 'Safe as a bank. I tell him not to bother about mine until we get done collecting every month. That's why it's late sometimes.'

'I just couldn't bear to have you lose the little I had to invest for you,' she says. 'I've often thought that Earl is not a good business man. I know he doesn't take you into his confidence to the extent that your investment in the business should warrant. I'm going to speak to him.'

'No, you let him alone,' I says. 'It's his business.'

'You have a thousand dollars in it.'

'You let him alone,' I says, 'I'm watching things. I have your power of attorney. It'll be all right.'

'You don't know what a comfort you are to me,' she says. 'You have always been my pride and joy, but when you came to me of your own accord and insisted on banking your salary each month in my name, I thanked God it was you left me if they had to be taken.'

'They were all right,' I says. 'They did the best they could, I reckon.'

'When you talk that way I know you are thinking bitterly of your father's memory,' she says. 'You have a right to, I suppose. But it breaks my heart to hear you.'

I got up. 'If you've got any crying to do,' I says, 'you'll have to do it alone, because I've got to get on back. I'll get the bank book.'

'I'll get it,' she says.

'Keep still,' I says, 'I'll get it.' I went upstairs and got the bank book out of her desk and went back to town. I went to the bank and deposited the cheque and the money order and the other ten, and stopped at the telegraph office. It was one point above the opening. I had already lost thirteen points, all because she had to come helling in there at twelve, worrying me about that letter.

'What time did that report come in?' I says.

'About an hour ago,' he says.

'An hour ago?' I says. 'What are we paying you for?' I says, 'Weekly reports? How do you expect a man to do anything? The whole damn top could blow off and we'd not know it.'

'I don't expect you to do anything,' he says. 'They changed that law making folks play the cotton market.'

'They have?' I says. 'I hadn't heard. They must have sent the news out over the Western Union.'

I went back to the store. Thirteen points. Damn if I

believe anybody knows anything about the damn thing
except the ones that sit back in those New York offices
and watch the country suckers come up and beg them to
take their money. Well, a man that just calls shows he has
no faith in himself, and like I say if you aren't going to
take the advice, what's the use in paying money for it.
Besides, these people are right up there on the ground;
they know everything that's going on. I could feel the
telegram in my pocket. I'd just have to prove that they
were using the telegraph company to defraud. That
would constitute a bucket shop. And I wouldn't hesitate
that long, either. Only be damned if it doesn't look like a
company as big and rich as the Western Union could get
a market report out on time. Half as quick as they'll get a
wire to you saying Your account closed out. But what the
hell do they care about the people. They're hand in
glove with that New York crowd. Anybody could see
that.

When I came in Earl looked at his watch. But he
didn't say anything until the customer was gone. Then
he says,

'You go home to dinner?'

'I had to go to the dentist,' I says because it's not any
of his business where I eat but I've got to be in the store
with him all the afternoon. And with his jaw running off
after all I've stood. You take a little two by four country
storekeeper like I say it takes a man with just five hundred dollars to worry about it fifty thousand dollars'
worth.

'You might have told me,' he says, 'I expected you
back right away.'

'I'll trade you this tooth and give you ten dollars to
boot, any time,' I says. 'Our arrangement was an hour for
dinner,' I says, 'and if you don't like the way I do, you
know what you can do about it.'

'I've known that some time,' he says. 'If it hadn't
been for your mother I'd have done it before now, too.
She's a lady I've got a lot of sympathy for, Jason. Too

bad some other folks I know can't say as much.'

'Then you can keep it,' I says. 'When we need any sympathy I'll let you know in plenty of time.'

'I've protected you about that business a long time, Jason,' he says.

'Yes?' I says, letting him go on. Listening to what he would say before I shut him up.

'I believe I know more about where that automobile came from than she does.'

'You think so, do you?' I says. 'When are you going to spread the news that I stole it from my mother?'

'I don't say anything,' he says, 'I know you have her power of attorney. And I know she still believes that thousand dollars is in this business.'

'All right,' I says, 'Since you know so much, I'll tell you a little more: go to the bank and ask them whose account I've been depositing a hundred and sixty dollars on the first of every month for twelve years.'

'I don't say anything,' he says, 'I just ask you to be a little more careful after this.'

I never said anything more. It doesn't do any good. I've found that when a man gets into a rut the best thing you can do is let him stay there. And when a man gets it in his head that he's got to tell something on you for your own good, good night. I'm glad I haven't got the sort of conscience I've got to nurse like a sick puppy all the time. If I'd ever be as careful over anything as he is to keep his little shirt tail full of business from making him more than eight per cent. I reckon he thinks they'd get him on the usury law if he netted more than eight per cent. What the hell chance has a man got, tied down in a town like this and to a business like this. Why I could take his business in one year and fix him so he'd never have to work again, only he'd give it all away to the church or something. If there's one thing gets under my skin, it's a damn hypocrite. A man that thinks anything he don't understand all about must be crooked and that first chance he gets he's morally bound to tell the third party what's none of his business to tell. Like I say if I thought every time a man did something I didn't know all about he was bound to be a crook, I reckon I wouldn't have any trouble finding something back there on those books that you wouldn't see any use for running and telling somebody I thought ought to know about it, when for all I knew they might know a damn sight more about it now than I did, and if they didn't it was damn little of my business anyway and he says, 'My books are open to anybody. Anybody that has any claim or believes she has any claim on this business can go back there and welcome.'

'Sure, you won't tell,' I says, 'You couldn't square your conscience with that. You'll just take her back there and let her find it. You won't tell, yourself.'

'I'm not trying to meddle in your business,' he says. 'I know you missed out on some things like Quentin had. But your mother has had a misfortunate life too, and if she was to come in here and ask me why you quit, I'd have to tell her. It ain't that thousand dollars. You know that. It's because a man never gets anywhere if fact and his ledgers don't square. And I'm not going to lie to anybody, for myself or anybody else.'

'Well, then,' I says, 'I reckon that conscience of yours is a more valuable clerk than I am; it don't have to go home at noon to eat. Only don't let it interfere with my appetite,' I says, because how the hell can I do anything right, with that damn family and her not making any effort to control her nor any of them, like that time when she happened to see one of them kissing Caddy and all next day she went around the house in a black dress and a veil and even Father couldn't get her to say a word except crying and saying her little daughter was dead and Caddy about fifteen then only in three years she'd been wearing haircloth or probably sandpaper at that rate. Do you think I can afford to have her running about the streets with every drummer that comes to town, I says, and them telling the new ones up and down the road where to pick up a hot one when they made Jefferson. I haven't got much pride, I can't afford it with a kitchenful of niggers to feed and robbing the state asylum of its star freshman. Blood, I says, governors and generals. It's a damn good thing we never had any kings and presidents; we'd all be down there at Jackson chasing butterflies. I say it'd be bad enough if it was mine; I'd at least be sure it was a bastard to begin with, and now even the Lord doesn't know that for certain probably.

So after a while I heard the band start up, and then they began to clear out. Headed for the show, every one of them. Haggling over a twenty cent hame string to save fifteen cents, so they can give it to a bunch of Yankees that come in and pay maybe ten dollars for the privilege. I went on out to the back.

'Well,' I says, 'If you don't look out, that bolt will grow into your hand. And then I'm going to take an axe and chop it out. What do you reckon the boll-weevils'll eat if you don't get those cultivators in shape to raise them a crop?' I says, 'sage grass?'

'Dem folks sho do play dem horns,' he says. 'Tell me man in dat show kin play a tune on a handsaw. Pick hit like a banjo.'

'Listen,' I says. 'Do you know how much that show'll spend in this town? About ten dollars,' I says. 'The ten dollars Buck Turpin has in his pocket right now.'

'Whut dey give Mr. Buck ten dollars fer?' he says.

'For the privilege of showing here,' I says. 'You can put the balance of what they'll spend in your eye.'

'You mean dey pays ten dollars jest to give dey show here?' he says.

'That's all,' I says. 'And how much do you reckon …'

'Gret day,' he says, 'You mean to tell me dey chargin um to let um show here? I'd pay ten dollars to see dat man pick dat saw, ef I had to. I figures dat to-morrow mawnin I be still owin um nine dollars and six bits at dat rate.'

And then a Yankee will talk your head off about

niggers getting ahead. Get them ahead, what I say. Get them so far ahead you can't find one south of Louisville with a bloodhound. Because when I told him about how they'd pick up Saturday night and carry off at least a thousand dollars out of the county, he says,

'I don't begrudge um. I kin sho afford my two bits.'

'Two bits hell,' I says. 'That don't begin it. How about the dime or fifteen cents you'll spend for a damn two cent box of candy or something. How about the time you're wasting right now, listening to that band.'

'Dat's de troof,' he says. 'Well, ef I lives twell night hit's gwine to be two bits mo dey takin out of town, dat's sho.'

'Then you're a fool,' I says.

'Well,' he says, 'I don't spute dat neither. Ef dat uz a crime, all chain-gangs wouldn't be black.'

Well, just about that time I happened to look up the alley and saw her. When I stepped back and looked at my watch I didn't notice at the time who he was because I was looking at the watch. It was just two thirty, forty-five minutes before anybody but me expected her to be out. So when I looked around the door the first thing I saw was the red tie he had on and I was thinking what the hell kind of a man would wear a red tie. But she was sneaking along the alley, watching the door, so I wasn't thinking anything about him until they had gone past. I was wondering if she'd have so little respect for me that she'd not only play out of school when I told her not to, but would walk right past the store, daring me not to see her. Only she couldn't see into the door because the sun fell straight into it and it was like trying to see through an automobile searchlight, so I stood there and watched her go on past, with her face painted up like a damn clown's and her hair all gummed and twisted and a dress that if a woman had come out doors even on Gayoso or Beale Street when I was a young fellow with no more than that to cover her legs and behind, she'd been thrown in jail. I'll be damned if they don't dress like they were trying to make every man they passed on the street want to reach out and clap his hand on it. And so I was thinking what kind of a damn man would wear a red tie when all of a sudden I knew he was one of those show folks well as if she'd told me. Well, I can stand a lot; if I couldn't, damn if I wouldn't be in a hell of a fix, so when they turned the corner I jumped down and followed. Me, without any hat, in the middle of the afternoon, having to chase up and down back alleys because of my mother's good name. Like I say you can't do anything with a woman like that, if she's got it in her. If it's in her blood, you can't do anything with her. The only thing you can do is to get rid of her, let her go on and live with her own sort.

I went on to the street, but they were out of sight. And there I was, without any hat, looking like I was crazy too. Like a man would naturally think, one of them is crazy and another one drowned himself and the other one was turned out into the street by her husband, what's the reason the rest of them are not crazy too. All the time I could see them watching me like a hawk, waiting for a chance to say Well I'm not surprised I expected it all the time the whole family's crazy. Selling land to send him to Harvard and paying taxes to support a state University all the time that I never saw except twice at a baseball game and not letting her daughter's name be spoken on the place until after a while Father wouldn't even come downtown any more but just sat there all day with the decanter I could see the bottom of his nightshirt and his bare legs and hear the decanter clinking until finally T. P. had to pour it for him and she says You have no respect for your Father's memory and I says I don't know why not it sure is preserved well enough to last only if I'm crazy too God knows what I'll do about it just to look at water makes me sick and I'd just as soon swallow gasoline as a glass of whisky and Lorraine telling them he may not drink but if you don't believe he's a man I can tell you how to find out she says If I catch you fooling with any of these whores you know what I'll do she says

I'll whip her grabbing at her I'll whip her as long as I can find her she says and I says if I don't drink that's my business but have you ever found me short I says I'll buy you enough beer to take a bath in if you want it because I've got every respect for a good honest whore because with Mother's health and the position I try to uphold to have her with no more respect for what I try to do for her than to make her name and my name and my Mother's name a byword in the town.

She had dodged out of sight somewhere. Saw me coming and dodged into another alley, running up and down the alleys with a damn show man in a red tie that everybody would look at and think what kind of a damn man would wear a red tie. Well, the boy kept speaking to me and so I took the telegram without knowing I had taken it. I didn't realize what it was until I was signing for it, and I tore it open without even caring much what it was. I knew all the time what it would be, I reckon. That was the only thing else that could happen, especially holding it up until I had already had the cheque entered on the pass book.

I don't see how a city no bigger than New York can hold enough people to take the money away from us country suckers. Work like hell all day every day, send them your money and get a little piece of paper back, Your account closed at 20.62. Teasing you along, letting you pile up a little paper profit, then bang! Your account closed at 20.62. And if that wasn't enough, paying ten dollars a month to somebody to tell you how to lose it fast, that either don't know anything about it or is in cahoots with the telegraph company. Well, I'm done with them. They've sucked me in for the last time. Any fool except a fellow that hasn't got any more sense than to take a jew's word for anything could tell the market was going up all the time, with the whole damn delta about to be flooded again and the cotton washed right out of the ground like it was last year. Let it wash a man's crop out of the ground year after year, and them up there in

Washington spending fifty thousand dollars a day keeping an army in Nicaragua or some place. Of course it'll overflow again, and then cotton'll be worth thirty cents a pound. Well, I just want to hit them one time and get my money back. I don't want a killing; only these small town gamblers are out for that, I just want my money back that these damn jews have got with all their guaranteed inside dope. Then – I'm through; they can kiss my foot for every other red cent of mine they get.

I went back to the store. It was half-past three almost. Damn little time to do anything in, but then I am used to that. I never had to go to Harvard to learn that. The band had quit playing. Got them all inside now, and they wouldn't have to waste any more wind. Earl says,

'He found you, did he? He was in here with it a while ago. I thought you were out back somewhere.'

'Yes,' I says, 'I got it. They couldn't keep it away from me all afternoon. The town's too small. I've got to go out home a minute,' I says. 'You can dock me if it'll make you feel any better.'

'Go ahead,' he says, 'I can handle it now. No bad news, I hope.'

'You'll have to go to the telegraph office and find that out,' I says. 'They'll have time to tell you. I haven't.'

'I just asked,' he says. 'Your mother knows she can depend on me.'

'She'll appreciate it,' I says. 'I won't be gone any longer than I have to.'

'Take your time,' he says. 'I can handle it now. You go ahead.'

I got the car and went home. Once this morning, twice at noon, and now again, with her and having to chase all over town and having to beg them to let me eat a little of the food I am paying for. Sometimes I think what's the use of anything. With the precedent I've been set I must be crazy to keep on. And now I reckon I'll get home just in time to take a nice long drive after a basket of tomatoes or something and then have to go back to town smelling like a camphor factory so my head won't explode right on my shoulders. I keep telling her there's not a damn thing in that aspirin except flour and water for imaginary invalids. I says you don't know what a headache is. I says you think I'd fool with that damn car at all if it depended on me. I says I can get along without one I've learned to get along without lots of things but if you want to risk yourself in that old worn out surrey with a half grown nigger boy all right because I says God looks after Ben's kind, God knows He ought to do something for him but if you think I'm going to trust a thousand dollars' worth of delicate machinery to a half grown nigger or a grown one either, you'd better buy him one yourself because I says you like to ride in the car and you know you do.

Dilsey said Mother was in the house. I went on into the hall and listened, but I didn't hear anything. I went upstairs, but just as I passed her door she called me.

'I just wanted to know who it was,' she says. 'I'm here alone so much that I hear every sound.'

'You don't have to stay here,' I says. 'You could spend the whole day visiting like other women, if you wanted to.' She came to the door.

'I thought maybe you were sick,' she says. 'Having to hurry through your dinner like you did.'

'Better luck next time,' I says. 'What do you want?'

'Is anything wrong?' she says.

'What could be?' I says. 'Can't I come home in the middle of the afternoon without upsetting the whole house?'

'Have you seen Quentin?' she says.

'She's in school,' I says.

'It's after three,' she says. 'I heard the clock strike at least a half an hour ago. She ought to be home by now.'

'Ought she?' I says. 'When have you ever seen her before dark?'

'She ought to be home,' she says. 'When I was a girl ...'

'You had somebody to make you behave yourself,' I says. 'She hasn't.'

'I can't do anything with her,' she says. 'I've tried and I've tried.'

'And you won't let me, for some reason,' I says, 'So you ought to be satisfied.' I went on to my room. I turned the key easy and stood there until the knob turned. Then she says,

'Jason.'

'What,' I says.

'I just thought something was wrong.'

'Not in here,' I says. 'You've come to the wrong place.'

'I don't mean to worry you,' she says.

'I'm glad to hear that,' I says. 'I wasn't sure. I thought I might have been mistaken. Do you want anything?'

After a while she says, 'No. Not any thing.' Then she went away. I took the box down and counted out the money and hid the box again and unlocked the door and went out. I thought about the camphor, but it would be too late now, anyway. And I'd just have one more round trip. She was at her door, waiting.

'You want anything from town?' I says.

'No,' she says. 'I don't mean to meddle in your affairs. But I don't know what I'd do if anything happened to you, Jason.'

'I'm all right,' I says. 'Just a headache.'

'I wish you'd take some aspirin,' she says. 'I know you're not going to stop using the car.'

'What's the car got to do with it?' I says. 'How can a car give a man a headache?'

'You know gasoline always made you sick,' she says. 'Ever since you were a child. I wish you'd take some aspirin.'

'Keep on wishing it,' I says. 'It won't hurt you.'

I got in the car and started back to town. I had just turned on to the street when I saw a ford coming helling toward me. All of a sudden it stopped. I could hear the wheels sliding and it slewed around and backed and whirled and just as I was thinking what the hell they were up to, I saw that red tie. Then I recognized her face looking back through the window. It whirled into the alley. I saw it turn again, but when I got to the back street it was just disappearing, running like hell.

I saw red. When I recognized that red tie, after all I had told her, I forgot about everything. I never thought about my head even until I came to the first forks and had to stop. Yet we spend money and spend money on roads and damn if it isn't like trying to drive over a sheet of corrugated iron roofing. I'd like to know how a man could be expected to keep up with even a wheelbarrow. I think too much of my car; I'm not going to hammer it to pieces like it was a ford. Chances were they had stolen it, anyway, so why should they give a damn. Like I say blood always tells. If you've got blood like that in you, you'll do anything. I says whatever claim you believe she has on you has already been discharged; I says from now on you have only yourself to blame because you know what any sensible person would do. I says if I've got to spend half my time being a damn detective, at least I'll go where I can get paid for it.

So I had to stop there at the forks. Then I remembered it. It felt like somebody was inside with a hammer, beating on it. I says I've tried to keep you from being worried by her; I says far as I'm concerned, let her go to hell as fast as she pleases and the sooner the better. I says what else do you expect except every drummer and cheap show that comes to town because even these town jelly-beans give her the go-by now. You don't know what goes on I says, you don't hear the talk that I hear and you can just bet I shut them up too. I says my people owned slaves here when you all were running little shirt tail country stores and farming land no nigger would look at on shares.

If they ever farmed it. It's a good thing the Lord did something for this country; the folks that live on it never have. Friday afternoon, and from right here I could see three miles of land that hadn't even been broken, and every able-bodied man in the county in town at that show. I might have been a stranger starving to death, and there wasn't a soul in sight to ask which way to town even. And she trying to get me to take aspirin. I says when I eat bread I'll do it at the table. I says you always talking about how much you give up for us when you could buy ten new dresses a year on the money you spend for those damn patent medicines. It's not something to cure it I need it's just an even break not to have to have them but as long as I have to work ten hours a day to support a kitchenful of niggers in the style they're accustomed to and send them to the show with every other nigger in the county, only he was late already. By the time he got there it would be over.

After a while he got up to the car and when I finally got it through his head if two people in a ford had passed him, he said yes. So I went on, and when I came to where the wagon road turned off I could see the tyre tracks. Ab Russell was in his lot, but I didn't bother to ask him and I hadn't got out of sight of his barn hardly when I saw the ford. They had tried to hide it. Done about as well at it as she did at everything else she did. Like I say it's not that I object to so much; maybe she can't help that, it's because she hasn't even got enough consideration for her own family to have any discretion. I'm afraid all the time I'll run into them right in the middle of the street or under a wagon on the square, like a couple of dogs.

I parked and got out. And now I'd have to go way around and cross a ploughed field, the only one I had seen since I left town, with every step like somebody was walking along behind me, hitting me on the head with a club. I kept thinking that when I got across the field at least I'd have something level to walk on, that wouldn't jolt me every step, but when I got into the woods it was full of underbrush and I had to twist around through it, and then I came to a ditch full of briars. I went along it for a while, but it got thicker and thicker, and all the time Earl probably telephoning home about where I was and getting Mother all upset again.

When I finally got through I had had to wind around so much that I had to stop and figure out just where the car would be. I knew they wouldn't be far from it, just under the closest bush, so I turned and worked back toward the road. Then I couldn't tell just how far I was, so I'd have to stop and listen, and then with my legs not using so much blood, it all would go into my head like it would explode any minute, and the sun getting down just to where it could shine straight into my eyes and my ears ringing so I couldn't hear anything. I went on, trying to move quiet, then I heard a dog or something and I knew that when he scented me he'd have to come helling up, then it would be all off.

I had got beggar lice and twigs and stuff all over me, inside my clothes and shoes and all, and then I happened to look around and I had my hand right on a bunch of poison oak. The only thing I couldn't understand was why it was just poison oak and not a snake or something. So I didn't even bother to move it. I just stood there until the dog went away. Then I went on.

I didn't have any idea where the car was now. I couldn't think about anything except my head, and I'd just stand in one place and sort of wonder if I had really seen a ford even, and I didn't even care much whether I had or not. Like I say, let her lay out all day and all night with everything in town that wears pants, what do I care. I don't owe anything to anybody that has no more consideration for me, that wouldn't be a damn bit above planting that ford there and making me spend a whole afternoon and Earl taking her back there and showing her the books just because he's too damn virtuous for this world. I says you'll have one hell of a time in heaven, without anybody's business to meddle in only don't you ever let me catch you at it I says, I close my eyes to it because of your grandmother, but just you let me catch you doing it one time on this place, where my mother lives. These

*207*

damn little slick-haired squirts, thinking they are raising so much hell, I'll show them something about hell I says, and you too. I'll make him think that damn red tie is the latch string to hell, if he thinks he can run the woods with my niece.

With the sun and all in my eyes and my blood going so I kept thinking every time my head would go on and burst and get it over with, with briars and things grabbing at me, then I came on to the sand ditch where they had been and I recognized the tree where the car was, and just as I got out of the ditch and started running I heard the car start. It went off fast, blowing the horn. They kept on blowing it, like it was saying Yah. Yah. Yaaahhhhhhhh, going out of sight. I got to the road just in time to see it go out of sight.

By the time I got up to where my car was, they were clean out of sight, the horn still blowing. Well, I never thought anything about it except I was saying Run. Run back to town. Run home and try to convince Mother that I never saw you in that car. Try to make her believe that I don't know who he was. Try to make her believe that I didn't miss ten feet of catching you in that ditch. Try to make her believe you were standing up, too.

It kept on saying Yahhhhh, Yahhhhh, Yaaahhhhhhhhhh, getting fainter and fainter. Then it quit, and I could hear a cow lowing up at Russell's barn. And still I never thought. I went up to the door and opened it and raised my foot. I kind of thought then that the car was leaning a little more than the slant of the road would be, but I never found it out until I got in and started off.

Well, I just sat there. It was getting on toward sundown, and town was about five miles. They never even had guts enough to puncture it, to jab a hole in it. They just let the air out. I just stood there for a while, thinking about that kitchenful of niggers and not one of them had time to lift a tyre on to the rack and screw up a couple of bolts. It was kind of funny because even she couldn't have seen far enough ahead to take the pump out or purpose, unless she thought about it while he was letting out the air maybe. But what it probably was, was somebody took it out and gave it to Ben to play with for a squirt gun because they'd take the whole car to pieces if he wanted it and Dilsey says, Ain't nobody teched yo car. What we want to fool with hit fer? and I says You're a nigger. You're lucky, do you know it? I says I'll swap with you any day because it takes a white man not to have any more sense than to worry about what a little slut of a girl does.

I walked up to Russell's. He had a pump. That was just an oversight on their part, I reckon. Only I still couldn't believe she'd have had the nerve to. I kept thinking that. I don't know why it is I can't seem to learn that a woman'll do anything. I kept thinking, Let's forget for a while how I feel toward you and how you feel toward me: I just wouldn't do you this way. I wouldn't do you this way no matter what you had done to me. Because like I say blood is blood and you can't get around it. It's not playing a joke that any eight year old boy could have thought of, it's letting your own uncle be laughed at by a man that would wear a red tie. They come into town and call us all a bunch of hicks and think it's too small to hold them. Well he doesn't know just how right he is. And her too. If that's the way she feels about it, she'd better keep right on going and a damn good riddance.

I stopped and returned Russell's pump and drove on to town. I went to the drug-store and got a cocacola and then I went to the telegraph office. It had closed at 12.21, forty points down. Forty times five dollars; buy something with that if you can, and she'll say, I've got to have it I've just got to and I'll say that's too bad you'll have to try somebody else, I haven't got any money; I've been too busy to make any.

I just looked at him.

'I'll tell you some news,' I says, 'You'll be astonished to learn that I am interested in the cotton market,' I says. 'That never occurred to you, did it?'

'I did my best to deliver it,' he says. 'I tried the store twice and called up your house, but they didn't know where you were,' he says, digging in the drawer.

'Deliver what?' I says. He handed me a telegram. 'What time did this come?' I says.

'About half-past three,' he says.

'And now it's ten minutes past five,' I says.

'I tried to deliver it,' he says. 'I couldn't find you.'

'That's not my fault, is it?' I says. I opened it, just to see what kind of a lie they'd tell me this time. They must be in one hell of a shape if they've got to come all the way to Mississippi to steal ten dollars a month. Sell, it says. The market will be unstable, with a general downward tendency. Do not be alarmed following government report.

'How much would a message like this cost?' I says. He told me.

'They paid it,' he says.

'Then I owe them that much,' I says. 'I already knew this. Send this collect,' I says, taking a blank. Buy, I wrote, Market just on point of blowing its head off. Occasional flurries for purpose of hooking a few more country suckers who haven't got in to the telegraph office yet. Do not be alarmed. 'Send that collect,' I says.

He looked at the message, then he looked at the clock. 'Market closed an hour ago,' he says.

'Well,' I says, 'That's not my fault either. I didn't invent it; I just bought a little of it while under the impression that the telegraph company would keep me informed as to what it was doing.'

'A report is posted whenever it comes in,' he says.

'Yes,' I says, 'And in Memphis they have it on a blackboard every ten seconds,' I says. 'I was within sixty-seven miles of there once this afternoon.'

He looked at the message. 'You want to send this?' he says.

'I still haven't changed my mind,' I says. I wrote the

other one out and counted the money. 'And this one too, if you're sure you can spell b-u-y.'

I went back to the store. I could hear the band from down the street. Prohibition's a fine thing. Used to be they'd come in Saturday with just one pair of shoes in the family and him wearing them, and they'd go down to the express office and get his package; now they all go to the show barefooted, with the merchants in the door like a row of tigers or something in a cage, watching them pass. Earl says,

'I hope it wasn't anything serious.'

'What?' I says. He looked at his watch. Then he went to the door and looked at the courthouse clock. 'You ought to have a dollar watch,' I says. 'It won't cost you so much to believe it's lying each time.'

'What?' he says.

'Nothing,' I says. 'Hope I haven't inconvenienced you.'

'We were not busy much,' he says. 'They all went to the show. It's all right.'

'If it's not all right,' I says, 'You know what you can do about it.'

'I said it was all right,' he says.

'I heard you,' I says. 'And if it's not all right, you know what you can do about it.'

'Do you want to quit?' he says.

'It's not my business,' I says. 'My wishes don't matter. But don't get the idea that you are protecting me by keeping me.'

'You'd be a good business man if you'd let yourself, Jason,' he says.

'At least I can tend to my own business and let other people's alone,' I says.

'I don't know why you are trying to make me fire you,' he says. 'You know you could quit any time and there wouldn't be any hard feelings between us.'

'Maybe that's why I don't quit,' I says. 'As long as I tend to my job, that's what you are paying me for.' I went on to the back and got a drink of water and went on out to the back door. Job had the cultivators all set up at last. It was quiet there, and pretty soon my head got a little easier. I could hear them singing now, and then the band played again. Well, let them get every quarter and dime in the county; it was no skin off my back. I've done what I could; a man that can live as long as I have and not know when to quit is a fool. Especially as it's no business of mine. If it was my own daughter now it would be different, because she wouldn't have time to; she'd have to work some to feed a few invalids and idiots and niggers, because how could I have the face to bring anybody there. I've too much respect for anybody to do that. I'm a man, I can stand it, it's my own flesh and blood and I'd like to see the colour of the man's eyes that would speak disrespectful of any woman that was my friend it's these damn good women that do it I'd like to see the good, church-going woman that's half as square as Lorraine, whore or no whore. Like I say if I was to get married you'd go up like a balloon and you know it and she says I want you to be happy to have a family of your own not to slave your life away for us. But I'll be gone soon and then you can take a wife but you'll never find a woman who is worthy of you and I says yes I could. You'd get right up out of your grave you know you would. I says no thank you I have all the women I can take care of now if I married a wife she'd probably turn out to be a hophead or something. That's all we lack in this family, I says.

The sun was down beyond the Methodist church now, and the pigeons were flying back and forth around the steeple, and when the band stopped I could hear them cooing. It hadn't been four months since Christmas, and yet they were almost as thick as ever. I reckon Parson Walthall was getting a bellyful of them now. You'd have thought we were shooting people, with him making speeches and even holding on to a man's gun when they came over. Talking about peace on earth good will toward all and not a sparrow can fall to earth. But what does he care how thick they get, he hasn't got anything to do what does he care what time it is. He pays no taxes, he doesn't have to see his money going every year to have the courthouse clock cleaned to where it'll run. They had to pay a man forty-five dollars to clean it. I counted over a hundred half-hatched pigeons on the ground. You'd think they'd have sense enough to leave town. It's a good thing I don't have any more ties than a pigeon, I'll say that.

The band was playing again, a loud fast tune, like they were breaking up. I reckon they'd be satisfied now. Maybe they'd have enough music to entertain them while they drove fourteen or fifteen miles home and unharnessed in the dark and fed the stock and milked. All they'd have to do would be to whistle the music and tell the jokes to the live stock in the barn, and then they could count up how much they'd made by not taking the stock to the show too. They could figure that if a man had five children and seven mules, he cleared a quarter by taking his family to the show. Just like that. Earl came back with a couple of packages.

'Here's some more stuff going out,' he says. 'Where's Uncle Job?'

'Gone to the show, I imagine,' I says. 'Unless you watched him.'

'He doesn't slip off,' he says. 'I can depend on him.'

'Meaning me by that,' I says.

He went to the door and looked out, listening.

'That's a good band,' he says. 'It's about time they were breaking up, I'd say.'

'Unless they're going to spend the night there,' I says. The swallows had begun, and I could hear the sparrows beginning to swarm in the trees in the courthouse yard. Every once in a while a bunch of them would come swirling around in sight above the roof, then go away. They are as big a nuisance as the pigeons, to my notion. You can't even sit in the courthouse yard for them. First thing you know, bing. Right on your hat. But it would take a millionaire to afford to shoot them at five cents a shot. If they'd just put a little poison out there in the square, they'd get rid of them in a day, because if a merchant can't keep his stock from running around the square, he'd better try to deal in something besides chickens, something that don't eat, like ploughs or onions. And if a man don't keep his dogs up, he either don't want it or he hasn't any business with one. Like I say if all the businesses in a town are run like country businesses, you're going to have a country town.

'It won't do you any good if they have broke up,' I says. 'They'll have to hitch up and take out to get home by midnight as it is.'

'Well,' he says, 'They enjoy it. Let them spend a little money on a show now and then. A hill farmer works pretty hard and gets mighty little for it.'

'There's no law making them farm in the hills,' I says, 'Or anywhere else.'

'Where would you and me be, if it wasn't for the farmers?' he says.

'I'd be home right now,' I says, 'Lying down, with an ice pack on my head.'

'You have these headaches too often,' he says. 'Why don't you have your teeth examined good? Did he go over them all this morning?'

'Did who?' I says.

'You said you went to the dentist this morning.'

'Do you object to my having the headache on your time?' I says. 'Is that it?' They were crossing the alley now, coming up from the show.

'There they come,' he says. 'I reckon I better get up front.' He went on. It's a curious thing how no matter what's wrong with you, a man'll tell you to have your teeth examined and a woman'll tell you to get married. It always takes a man that never made much at anything to tell you how to run your business, though. Like these college professors without a whole pair of socks to their name, telling you how to make a million in ten years, and a woman that couldn't even get a husband can always tell you how to raise a family.

Old man Job came up with the wagon. After a while he got through wrapping the lines around the whip socket.

'Well,' I says, 'Was it a good show?'

'I ain't been yit,' he says. 'But I kin be arrested in dat tent tonight, dough.'

'Like hell you haven't,' I says. 'You've been away from here since three o'clock. Mr. Earl was just back here looking for you.'

'I been tendin to my business,' he says. 'Mr. Earl knows whar I been.'

'You may can fool him,' I says. 'I won't tell on you.'

'Den he's de onliest man here I'd try to fool,' he says. 'Whut I want to waste my time foolin a man whut I don't keer whether I sees him Sat'dy night er not? I won't try to fool you,' he says. 'You too smart fer me. Yes, suh,' he says, looking busy as hell, putting five or six little packages into the wagon, 'You's too smart fer me. Ain't a man in dis town kin keep up wid you fer smartness. You fools a man whut so smart he can't even keep up wid hisself,' he says, getting in the wagon and unwrapping the reins.

'Who's that?' I says.

'Dat's Mr. Jason Compson,' he says. 'Git up dar, Dan!'

One of the wheels was just about to come off. I watched to see if he'd get out of the alley before it did. Just turn any vehicle over to a nigger, though. I says that old rattle-trap's just an eyesore, yet you'll keep it standing there in the carriage house a hundred years just so that boy can ride to the cemetery once a week. I says he's not the first fellow that'll have to do things he doesn't want to. I'd make him ride in that car like a civilized man or stay at home. What does he know about where he goes or what he goes in, and us keeping a carriage and a horse so he can take a ride on Sunday afternoon.

A lot Job cared whether the wheel came off or not, long as he wouldn't have too far to walk back. Like I say the only place for them is in the field, where they'd have to work from sunup to sundown. They can't stand prosperity or an easy job. Let one stay around white people for a while and he's not worth killing. They get so they can outguess you about work before your very eyes, like Roskus the only mistake he ever made was he got careless one day and died. Shirking and stealing and giving you a little more lip and a little more lip until some day you have to lay them out with a scantling or something. Well, it's Earl's business. But I'd hate to have my business advertised over this town by an old doddering nigger and a wagon that you thought every time it turned a corner it would come all to pieces.

The sun was all high up in the air now, and inside it was beginning to get dark. I went up front. The square was empty. Earl was back closing the safe, and then the clock begun to strike.

'You lock the back door,' he says. I went back and locked it and came back. 'I suppose you're going to the show tonight,' he says. 'I gave you those passes yesterday, didn't I?'

'Yes,' I said. 'You want them back?'

'No, no,' he says. 'I just forgot whether I gave them to you or not. No sense in wasting them.'

He locked the door and said Good night and went on. The sparrows were still rattling away in the trees, but the square was empty except for a few cars. There was a ford in front of the drug-store, but I didn't even look at it. I know when I've had enough of anything. I don't mind trying to help her, but I know when I've had enough. I guess I could teach Luster to drive it, then they could chase her all day long if they wanted to, and I could stay home and play with Ben.

I went in and got a couple of cigars. Then I thought I'd have another headache shot for luck, and I stood and talked with them a while.

'Well,' Mac says, 'I reckon you've got your money on the Yankees this year.'

'What for?' I says.

'The Pennant,' he says. 'Not anything in the League can beat them.'

'Like hell there's not,' I says. 'They're shot,' I says. 'You think a team can be that lucky for ever?'

'I don't call it luck,' Mac says.

'I wouldn't bet on any team that fellow Ruth played on,' I says. 'Even if I knew it was going to win.'

'Yes?' Mac says.

'I can name you a dozen men in either League who're more valuable than he is,' I says.

'What have you got against Ruth?' Mac says.

'Nothing,' I says. 'I haven't got anything against him. I don't even like to look at his picture.' I went on out. The lights were coming on, and people going along the streets toward home. Sometimes the sparrows never got still until full dark. The night they turned on the new lights around the courthouse it waked them up and they were flying around and blundering into the lights all night long. They kept it up two or three nights, then one morning they were all gone. Then after about two months they all came back again.

I drove on home. There were no lights in the house yet, but they'd all be looking out the windows, and Dilsey jawing away in the kitchen like it was her own food she was having to keep hot until I got there. You'd think to hear her that there wasn't but one supper in the world, and that was the one she had to keep back a few minutes on my account. Well at least I could come home one time without finding Ben and that nigger hanging on the gate like a bear and a monkey in the same cage. Just let it come toward sundown and he'd head for the gate like a cow for the barn, hanging on to it and bobbing his head and sort of moaning to himself. That's a hog for punishment for you. If what had happened to him for fooling with open gates had happened to me, I never would want to see another one. I often wondered what he'd be thinking about, down there at the gate, watching the girls going home from school, trying to want something he couldn't even remember he didn't and couldn't want any longer. And what he'd think when they'd be undressing him and he'd happen to take a look at himself and begin to cry like he'd do. But like I say they never did enough of that. I says I know what you need, you need what they did to Ben then you'd behave. And if you don't know what that was I says, ask Dilsey to tell you.

There was a light in Mother's room. I put the car up and went on into the kitchen. Luster and Ben were there.

'Where's Dilsey?' I says. 'Putting supper on?'

'She upstairs wid Miss Cahline,' Luster says. 'Dey been goin hit. Ever since Miss Quentin come home. Mammy up there keepin um fum fightin. Is dat show come, Mr. Jason?'

'Yes,' I says.

'I thought I heard de band,' he says. 'Wish I could go,' he says. 'I could ef I jes had a quarter.'

Dilsey came in. 'You come, is you?' she says. 'Whut you been up to dis evenin? You knows how much work I got to do; whyn't you git here on time?'

'Maybe I went to the show,' I says. 'Is supper ready?'

'Wish I could go,' Luster said. 'I could ef I jes had a quarter.'

'You ain't got no business at no show,' Dilsey says. 'You go on in de house and set down,' she says. 'Don't you go upstairs and git um started again, now.'

'What's the matter?' I says.

'Quentin come in a while ago and says you been follerin her around all evenin and den Miss Cahline jumped on her. Whyn't you let her alone? Can't you live in de same house wid you own blood niece widout quoilin?'

'I can't quarrel with her,' I says, 'because I haven't seen her since this morning. What does she say I've done now? Made her go to school? That's pretty bad,' I says.

'Well, you tend to yo business and let her alone,'

Dilsey says, 'I'll take keer of her ef you'n Miss Cahline'll let me. Go on in dar now and behave yoself twell I git supper on.'

'Ef I jes had a quarter,' Luster says, 'I could go to dat show.'

'En ef you had wings you could fly to heaven,' Dilsey says. 'I don't want to hear another word about dat show.'

'That reminds me,' I says, 'I've got a couple of tickets they gave me.' I took them out of my coat.

'You fixin to use um?' Luster says.

'Not me,' I says. 'I wouldn't go to it for ten dollars.'

'Gimme one of um, Mr. Jason,' he says.

'I'll sell you one,' I says. 'How about it?'

'I ain't got no money,' he says.

'That's too bad,' I says. I made to go out.

'Gimme one of um, Mr. Jason,' he says. 'You ain't gwine need um bofe.'

'Hush yo mouf,' Dilsey says, 'Don't you know he ain't gwine give nothing away?'

'How much you want fer hit?' he says.

'Five cents,' I says.

'I ain't got dat much,' he says.

'How much you got?' I says.

'I ain't got nothing,' he says.

'All right,' I says. I went on.

'Mr. Jason,' he says.

'Whyn't you hush up?' Dilsey says. 'He jes teasin you. He fixin to use dem tickets hisself. Go on, Jason, and let him lone.'

'I don't want them,' I says. I came back to the stove. 'I came in here to burn them up. But if you want to buy one for a nickel?' I says, looking at him and opening the stove lid.

'I ain't got dat much,' he says.

'All right,' I says. I dropped one of them in the stove.

'You, Jason,' Dilsey says, 'Ain't you shamed?'

'Mr. Jason,' he says, 'Please, suh, I'll fix dem tyres ev'y day fer a mont'.'

'I need the cash,' I says. 'You can have it for a nickel.'

'Hush, Luster,' Dilsey says. She jerked him back. 'Go on,' she says, 'Drop hit in. Go on. Git hit over with.'

'You can have it for a nickel,' I says.

'Go on,' Dilsey says. 'He ain't got no nickel. Go on. Drop hit in.'

'All right,' I says. I dropped it in and Dilsey shut the stove.

'A big growed man like you,' she says. 'Git on outen my kitchen. Hush,' she says to Luster. 'Don't you git Benjy started. I'll git you a quarter fum Frony to-night and you kin go to-morrow night. Hush up, now.'

I went on into the living-room. I couldn't hear anything from upstairs. I opened the paper. After a while Ben and Luster came in. Ben went to the dark place on the wall where the mirror used to be, rubbing his hands on it and slobbering and moaning. Luster begun punching at the fire.

'What're you doing?' I says. 'We don't need any fire to-night.'

'I trying to keep him quiet,' he says. 'Hit always cold Easter,' he says.

'Only this is not Easter,' I says. 'Let it alone.'

He put the poker back and got the cushion out of Mother's chair and gave it to Ben, and he hunkered down in front of the fireplace and got quiet.

I read the paper. There hadn't been a sound from upstairs when Dilsey came in and sent Ben and Luster on to the kitchen and said supper was ready.

'All right,' I says. She went out. I sat there, reading the paper. After a while I heard Dilsey looking in at the door.

'Whyn't you come on and eat?' she says.

'I'm waiting for supper,' I says.

'Hit's on the table,' she says. 'I done told you.'

'Is it?' I says. 'Excuse me. I didn't hear anybody come down.'

'They ain't comin,' she says. 'You come on and eat, so I can take something up to them.'

'Are they sick?' I says. 'What did the doctor say it was? Not smallpox, I hope.'

'Come on here, Jason,' she says, 'So I kin git done.'

'All right,' I says, raising the paper again. 'I'm waiting for supper now.'

I could feel her watching me at the door. I read the paper.

'Whut you want to act like this fer?' she says. 'When you knows how much bother I has anyway.'

'If Mother is any sicker than she was when she came down to dinner, all right,' I says. 'But as long as I am buying food for people younger than I am, they'll have to come down to the table to eat it. Let me know when supper's ready,' I says, reading the paper again. I heard her climbing the stairs, dragging her feet and grunting and groaning like they were straight up and three feet apart. I heard her at Mother's door, then I heard her calling Quentin, like the door was locked, then she went back to Mother's room and then Mother went and talked to Quentin. Then they came downstairs. I read the paper.

Dilsey came back to the door. 'Come on,' she says, 'fo you kin think up some mo devilment. You just tryin yoself tonight.'

I went to the dining-room. Quentin was sitting with her head bent. She had painted her face again. Her nose looked like a porcelain insulator.

'I'm glad you feel well enough to come down,' I says to Mother.

'It's little enough I can do for you, to come to the table,' she says. 'No matter how I feel. I realize that when a man works all day he likes to be surrounded by his family at the supper table. I want to please you. I only wish you and Quentin got along better. It would be easier for me.'

'We get along all right,' I says. 'I don't mind her staying locked up in her room all day if she wants to. But I can't have all this whoop-de-do and sulking at meal times. I know that's a lot to ask her, but I'm that way in my own house. Your house, I meant to say.'

'It's yours,' Mother says, 'You are the head of it now.'

Quentin hadn't looked up. I helped the plates and she begun to eat.

'Did you get a good piece of meat?' I says. 'If you didn't, I'll try to find you a better one.'

She didn't say anything.

'I say, did you get a good piece of meat?' I says.

'What?' she says. 'Yes. It's all right.'

'Will you have some more rice?' I says.

'No,' she says.

'Better let me give you some more,' I says.

'I don't want any more,' she says.

'Not at all,' I says, 'You're welcome.'

'Is your headache gone?' Mother says.

'Headache?' I says.

'I was afraid you were developing one,' she says. 'When you came in this afternoon.'

'Oh,' I says. 'No, it didn't show up. We stayed so busy this afternoon I forgot about it.'

'Was that why you were late?' Mother says. I could see Quentin listening. I looked at her. Her knife and fork were still going, but I caught her looking at me, then she looked at her plate again. I says,

'No. I loaned my car to a fellow about three o'clock and I had to wait until he got back with it.' I ate for a while.

'Who was it?' Mother says.

'It was one of those show men,' I says. 'It seems his sister's husband was out riding with some town woman, and he was chasing them.'

Quentin sat perfectly still, chewing.

'You ought not to lend your car to people like that,' Mother says. 'You are too generous with it. That's why I never call on you for it if I can help it.'

'I was beginning to think that myself, for a while,' I says. 'But he got back, all right. He says he found what he was looking for.'

'Who was the woman?' Mother says.

'I'll tell you later.' I says. 'I don't like to talk about such things before Quentin.'

Quentin had quit eating. Every once in a while she'd take a drink of water, then she'd sit there crumbling a biscuit up, her face bent over her plate.

'Yes,' Mother says, 'I suppose women who stay shut up like I do have no idea what goes on in this town.'

'Yes,' I says, 'They don't.'

'My life has been so different from that,' Mother says. 'Thank God I don't know about such wickedness. I don't even want to know about it. I'm not like most people.'

I didn't say any more. Quentin sat there, crumbling the biscuit until I quit eating, then she says,

'Can I go now?' without looking at anybody.

'What?' I says. 'Sure, you can go. Were you waiting on us?'

She looked at me. She had crumbled all the biscuit, but her hands still went on like they were crumbling it yet and her eyes looked like they were cornered or something and then she started biting her mouth like it ought to have poisoned her, with all that red lead.

'Grandmother,' she says, 'Grandmother – '

'Did you want something else to eat?' I says.

'Why does he treat me like this, Grandmother?' she says. 'I never hurt him.'

'I want you all to get along with one another,' Mother says, 'You are all that's left now, and I do want you all to get along better.'

'It's his fault,' she says, 'He won't let me alone, and I have to. If he doesn't want me here, why won't he let me go back to – '

'That's enough,' I says, 'Not another word.'

'Then why won't he let me alone?' she says. 'He – he just – '

'He is the nearest thing to a father you've ever had,' Mother says. 'It's his bread you and I eat. It's only right that he should expect obedience from you.'

'It's his fault,' she says. She jumped up. 'He makes me do it. If he would just – ' she looked at us, her eyes cornered, kind of jerking her arms against her sides.

'If I would just what?' I says.

'Whatever I do, it's your fault,' she says. 'If I'm bad, it's because I had to be. You made me. I wish I was dead. I wish we were all dead.' Then she ran. We heard her run up the stairs. Then a door slammed.

'That's the first sensible thing she ever said,' I says.

'She didn't go to school today,' Mother says.

'How do you know?' I says. 'Were you downtown?'

'I just know,' she says. 'I wish you could be kinder to her.'

'If I did that I'd have to arrange to see her more than once a day,' I says. 'You'll have to make her come to the table every meal. Then I could give her an extra piece of meat every time.'

'There are little things you could do,' she says.

'Like not paying any attention when you ask me to see that she goes to school?' I says.

'She didn't go to school today,' she says. 'I just know she didn't. She says she went for a car ride with one of the boys this afternoon and you followed her.'

'How could I,' I says, 'When somebody had my car all afternoon? Whether or not she was in school today is already past,' I says. 'If you've got to worry about it, worry next Monday.'

'I wanted you and she to get along with one another,' she says. 'But she has inherited all of the headstrong traits. Quentin's too. I thought at the time, with the heritage she would already have, to give her that name, too. Sometimes I think she is the judgment of Caddy and Quentin upon me.'

'Good Lord,' I says, 'You've got a fine mind. No wonder you kept yourself sick all the time.'

'What?' she says. 'I don't understand.'

'I hope not,' I says. 'A good woman misses a lot she's better off without knowing.'

'They were both that way,' she says, 'They would make interest with your father against me when I tried to correct them. He was always saying they didn't need controlling, that they already knew what cleanliness and honesty were, which was all that anyone could hope to be taught. And now I hope he's satisfied.'

'You've got Ben to depend on,' I says, 'Cheer up.'

'They deliberately shut me out of their lives,' she says, 'It was always her and Quentin. They were always conspiring against me. Against you, too, though you were too young to realize it. They always looked on you and me as outsiders, like they did your Uncle Maury. I always told your father that they were allowed too much freedom, to be together too much. When Quentin started to school we had to let her go the next year, so she could be with him. She couldn't bear for any of you to do anything she couldn't. It was vanity in her, vanity and false pride. And then when her troubles began I knew that Quentin would feel that he had to do something just as bad. But I didn't believe that he could have been so selfish as to – I didn't dream that he – '

'Maybe he knew it was going to be a girl,' I says, 'And that one more of them would be more than he could stand.'

'He could have controlled her,' she says. 'He seemed to be the only person she had any consideration for. But that is a part of the judgment too, I suppose.'

'Yes,' I says, 'Too bad it wasn't me instead of him. You'd be a lot better off.'

'You say things like that to hurt me,' she says. 'I deserve it though. When they began to sell the land to send Quentin to Harvard I told your father that he must make an equal provision for you. Then when Herbert offered to take you into the bank I said, Jason is provided for now, and when all the expense began to pile up and I was forced to sell our furniture and the rest of the pasture, I wrote her at once because I said she will realize that she and Quentin have had their share and part of

Jason's too and that it depends on her now to compensate him. I said she will do that out of respect for her father. I believed that, then. But I'm just a poor old woman; I was raised to believe that people would deny themselves for their own flesh and blood. It's my fault. You were right to reproach me.'

'Do you think I need any man's help to stand on my feet?' I says, 'Let alone a woman that can't name the father of her own child.'

'Jason,' she says.

'All right,' I says. 'I didn't mean that. Of course not.'

'If I believed that were possible, after all my suffering.'

'Of course it's not,' I says. 'I didn't mean it.'

'I hope that at least is spared me,' she says.

'Sure it is,' I says, 'She's too much like both of them to doubt that.'

'I couldn't bear that,' she says.

'Then quit thinking about it,' I says. 'Has she been worrying you any more about getting out at night?'

'No. I made her realize that it was for her own good and that she'd thank me for it some day. She takes her books with her and studies after I lock the door. I see the light on as late as eleven o'clock some nights.'

'How do you know she's studying?' I says.

'I don't know what else she'd do in there alone,' she says. 'She never did read any.'

'No,' I says, 'You wouldn't know. And you can thank your stars for that,' I says. Only what would be the use in saying it aloud. It would just have her crying on me again.

I heard her go upstairs. Then she called Quentin and Quentin says What? through the door. 'Good night,' Mother says. Then I heard the key in the lock, and Mother went back to her room.

When I finished my cigar and went up, the light was still on. I could see the empty keyhole, but I couldn't hear a sound. She studied quiet. Maybe she learned that

in school. I told Mother good night and went on to my
room and got the box out and counted it again. I could
hear the Great American Gelding snoring away like a
planing mill. I read somewhere they'd fix men that way
to give them women's voices. But maybe he didn't know
what they'd done to him. I don't reckon he even knew
what he had been trying to do, or why Mr. Burgess
knocked him out with the fence picket. And if they'd
just sent him on to Jackson while he was under the ether,
he'd never have known the difference. But that would
have been too simple for a Compson to think of. Not half
complex enough. Having to wait to do it at all until he
broke out and tried to run a little girl down on the street
with her own father looking at him. Well, like I say they
never started soon enough with their cutting, and they
quit too quick. I know at least two more that needed
something like that, and one of them not over a mile
away, either. But then I don't reckon even that would do
any good. Like I say once a bitch always a bitch. And just
let me have twenty-four hours without any damn New
York jew to advise me what it's going to do. I don't want
to make a killing; save that to suck in the smart gamblers
with. I just want an even chance to get my money back.
And once I've done that they can bring all Beale Street
and all bedlam in here and two of them can sleep in my
bed and another one can have my place at the table too.

# *April Eighth*
## 1928

THE day dawned bleak and chill, a moving wall of grey light out of the north-east which, instead of dissolving into moisture, seemed to disintegrate into minute and venomous particles, like dust that, when Dilsey opened the door of the cabin and emerged, needled laterally into her flesh, precipitating not so much a moisture as a substance partaking of the quality of thin, not quite congealed oil. She wore a stiff black straw hat perched upon her turban, and a maroon velvet cape with a border of mangy and anonymous fur above a dress of purple silk, and she stood in the door for a while with her myriad and sunken face lifted to the weather, and one gaunt hand flat-soled as the belly of a fish, then she moved the cape aside and examined the bosom of her gown.

The gown fell gauntly from her shoulders, across her fallen breasts, then tightened upon her paunch and fell again, ballooning a little above the nether garments which she would remove layer by layer as the spring accomplished and the warm days, in colour regal and moribund. She had been a big woman once but now her skeleton rose, draped loosely in unpadded skin that tightened again upon a paunch almost dropsical, as though muscle and tissue had been courage or fortitude which the days or the years had consumed until only the indomitable skeleton was left rising like a ruin or a landmark above the somnolent and impervious guts, and above that the collapsed face that gave the impression of the bones themselves being outside the flesh, lifted into the driving day with an expression at once fatalistic and of a child's astonished disappointment, until she turned and entered the house again and closed the door.

The earth immediately about the door was bare. It had a patina, as though from the soles of bare feet in generations, like old silver or the walls of Mexican houses which have been plastered by hand. Beside the house, shading it in summer, stood three mulberry trees, the fledged leaves that would later be broad and placid as the palms of hands streaming flatly undulant upon the driving air. A pair of jaybirds came up from nowhere, whirled up on the blast like gaudy scraps of cloth or paper and lodged in the mulberries, where they swung in raucous tilt and recover, screaming into the wind that ripped their harsh cries onward and away like scraps of paper or of cloth in turn. Then three more joined them and they swung and tilted in the wrung branches for a time, screaming. The door of the cabin opened and Dilsey emerged once more, this time in a man's felt hat and an army overcoat, beneath the frayed skirts of which her blue gingham dress fell in uneven balloonings, streaming too about her as she crossed the yard and mounted the steps to the kitchen door.

A moment later she emerged, carrying an open umbrella now, which she slanted ahead into the wind, and crossed to the woodpile and laid the umbrella down, still open. Immediately she caught at it and arrested it and held to it for a while, looking about her. Then she closed it and laid it down and stacked stovewood into her crooked arm, against her breast, and picked up the umbrella and got it open at last and returned to the steps and held the wood precariously balanced while she contrived to close the umbrella, which she propped in the corner just within the door. She dumped the wood into the box behind the stove. Then she removed the overcoat and hat and took a soiled apron down from the wall and put it on and built a fire in the stove. While she was doing so, rattling the grate bars and clattering the lids, Mrs. Compson began to call her from the head of the stairs.

She wore a dressing gown of quilted black satin,

holding it close under her chin. In the other hand she held a red rubber hot water bottle and she stood at the head of the back stairway, calling 'Dilsey' at steady and inflexionless intervals into the quiet stairwell that descended into complete darkness, then opened again where a grey window fell across it. 'Dilsey,' she called, without inflexion or emphasis or haste, as though she were not listening for a reply at all. 'Dilsey.'

Dilsey answered and ceased clattering the stove, but before she could cross the kitchen Mrs. Compson called her again, and before she crossed the dining-room and brought her head into relief against the grey splash of the window, still again.

'All right,' Dilsey said, 'All right, here I is. I'll fill hit soon ez I git some hot water.' She gathered up her skirts and mounted the stairs, wholly blotting the grey light. 'Put hit down dar en g'awn back to bed.'

'I couldn't understand what was the matter,' Mrs. Compson said. 'I've been lying awake for an hour at least, without hearing a sound from the kitchen.'

'You put hit down and g'awn back to bed,' Dilsey said. She toiled painfully up the steps, shapeless, breathing heavily. 'I'll have de fire gwine in a minute, en de water hot in two mo'.'

'I've been lying there for an hour, at least,' Mrs. Compson said. 'I thought maybe you were waiting for me to come down and start the fire.'

Dilsey reached the top of the stairs and took the water bottle. 'I'll fix hit in a minute,' she said. 'Luster oversleep dis mawnin, up half de night at dat show. I gwine build de fire myself. Go on now, so you won't wake de others twell I ready.'

'If you permit Luster to do things that interfere with his work, you'll have to suffer for it yourself,' Mrs. Compson said. 'Jason won't like this if he hears about it. You know he won't.'

'Twusn't none of Jason's money he went on,' Dilsey said. 'Dat's one thing sho.' She went on down the stairs.

Mrs. Compson returned to her room. As she got into bed again she could hear Dilsey yet descending the stairs with a sort of painful and terrific slowness that would have become maddening had it not presently ceased beyond the flapping diminishment of the pantry door.

She entered the kitchen and built up the fire and began to prepare breakfast. In the midst of this she ceased and went to the window and looked out toward her cabin, then she went to the door and opened it and shouted into the driving weather.

'Luster!' she shouted, standing to listen, tilting her face from the wind, 'You, Luster?' She listened, then as she prepared to shout again Luster appeared around the corner of the kitchen.

'Ma'am?' he said innocently, so innocently that Dilsey looked down at him, for a moment motionless, with something more than mere surprise.

'Whar you at?' she said.

'Nowhere,' he said. 'Jes in de cellar.'

'Whut you doing in de cellar?' she said. 'Don't stand dar in de rain, fool,' she said.

'Ain't doin nothing,' he said. He came up the steps.

'Don't you dare come in dis do' widout a armful of wood,' she said. 'Here I done had to tote yo wood en build yo fire bofe. Didn't I tole you not to leave dis place last night befo dat woodbox wus full to de top?'

'I did,' Luster said, 'I filled hit.'

'Whar hit gone to, den?'

'I don't know'm. I ain't teched hit.'

'Well, you git hit full up now,' she said. 'And git on up den en see bout Benjy.'

She shut the door. Luster went to the woodpile. The five jaybirds whirled over the house, screaming, and into the mulberries again. He watched them. He picked up a rock and threw it. 'Whoo,' he said, 'Git on back to hell, whar you belong to. Tain't Monday yit.'

He loaded himself mountainously with stovewood. He could not see over it, and he staggered to the steps

*231*

and up them and blundered crashing against the door, shedding billets. Then Dilsey came and opened the door for him and he blundered across the kitchen. 'You, Luster!' she shouted, but he had already hurled the wood into the box with a thunderous crash. 'Hah!' he said.

'Is you tryin to wake up de whole house?' Dilsey said. She hit him on the back of his head with the flat of her hand. 'Go on up dar and git Benjy dressed, now.'

'Yessum,' he said. He went towards the outer door.

'Whar you gwine?' Dilsey said.

'I thought I better go round de house en in by de front, so I won't wake up Miss Cahline en dem.'

'You go on up dem back stairs like I tole you en git Benjy's clothes on him,' Dilsey said. 'Go on, now.'

'Yessum,' Luster said. He returned and left by the dining-room door. After a while it ceased to flap. Dilsey prepared to make biscuit. As she ground the sifter steadily above the bread board, she sang, to herself at first, something without particular tune or words, repetitive, mournful and plaintive, austere, as she ground a faint, steady snowing of flour onto the bread board. The stove had begun to heat the room and to fill it with murmurous minors of the fire, and presently she was singing louder, as if her voice too had been thawed out by the growing warmth, and then Mrs. Compson called her name again from within the house. Dilsey raised her face as if her eyes could and did penetrate the walls and ceiling and saw the old woman in her quilted dressing gown at the head of the stairs, calling her name with machine-like regularity.

'Oh, Lawd,' Dilsey said. She set the sifter down and swept up the hem of her apron and wiped her hands and caught up the bottle from the chair on which she had laid it and gathered her apron about the handle of the kettle which was now jetting faintly. 'Jes a minute,' she called, 'De water jes dis minute got hot.'

It was not the bottle which Mrs. Compson wanted,

however, and clutching it by the neck like a dead hen Dilsey went to the foot of the stairs and looked upward.

'Ain't Luster up dar wid him?' she said.

'Luster hasn't been in the house. I've been lying here listening for him. I knew he would be late, but I did hope he'd come in time to keep Benjamin from disturbing Jason on Jason's one day in the week to sleep in the morning.'

'I don't see how you expect anybody to sleep, wid you standin in de hall, holl'in at folks fum de crack of dawn,' Dilsey said. She began to mount the stairs, toiling heavily. 'I sont dat boy up dar half-hour ago.'

Mrs. Compson watched her, holding the dressing gown under her chin. 'What are you going to do?' she said.

'Gwine git Benjy dressed en bring him down to de kitchen, whar he won't wake Jason en Quentin,' Dilsey said.

'Haven't you started breakfast yet?'

'I'll tend to dat too,' Dilsey said. 'You better git back in bed twell Luster make yo fire. Hit cold dis mawnin.'

'I know it,' Mrs. Compson said. 'My feet are like ice. They were so cold they waked me up.' She watched Dilsey mount the stairs. It took her a long while. 'You know how it frets Jason when breakfast is late,' Mrs. Compson said.

'I can't do but one thing at a time,' Dilsey said. 'You git on back to bed, fo I has you on my hands dis mawnin too.'

'If you're going to drop everything to dress Benjamin, I'd better come down and get breakfast. You know as well as I do how Jason acts when it's late.'

'En who gwine eat yo messin?' Dilsey said. 'Tell me dat. Go on now,' she said, toiling upward. Mrs. Compson stood watching her as she mounted, steadying herself against the wall with one hand, holding her skirts up with the other.

'Are you going to wake him up just to dress him?' she said.

Dilsey stopped. With her foot lifted to the next step she stood there, her hand against the wall and the grey splash of the window behind her, motionless and shapeless she loomed.

'He ain't awake den?' she said.

'He wasn't when I looked in,' Mrs. Compson said. 'But it's past his time. He never does sleep after half-past seven. You know he doesn't.'

Dilsey said nothing. She made no further move, but though she could not see her save as a blobby shape without depth, Mrs. Compson knew that she had lowered her face a little and that she stood now like a cow in the rain, as she held the empty water bottle by its neck.

'You're not the one who has to bear it,' Mrs. Compson said. 'It's not your responsibility. You can go away. You don't have to bear the brunt of it day in and day out. You owe nothing to them, to Mr. Compson's memory. I know you have never had any tenderness for Jason. You've never tried to conceal it.'

Dilsey said nothing. She turned slowly and descended, lowering her body from step to step, as a small child does, her hand against the wall. 'You go on and let him alone,' she said. 'Don't go in dar no mo, now. I'll send Luster up soon as I find him. Let him alone, now.'

She returned to the kitchen. She looked into the stove, then she drew her apron over her head and donned the overcoat and opened the outer door and looked up and down the yard. The weather drove upon her flesh, harsh and minute, but the scene was empty of all else that moved. She descended the steps, gingerly, as if for silence, and went around the corner of the kitchen. As she did so Luster emerged quickly and innocently from the cellar door.

Dilsey stopped. 'Whut you up to?' she said.

'Nothing,' Luster said, 'Mr. Jason say fer me to find out whar dat water leak in de cellar fum.'

'En when wus hit he say fer you to do dat?' Dilsey

234

said. 'Last New Year's day, wasn't hit?'

'I thought I jes be lookin whiles dey sleep,' Luster said. Dilsey went to the cellar door. He stood aside and she peered down into the obscurity odorous of dank earth and mould and rubber.

'Huh,' Dilsey said. She looked at Luster again. He met her gaze blandly, innocent and open. 'I don't know whut you up to, but you ain't got no business doin hit. You jes tryin me too dis mawnin cause de others is, ain't you? You git on up dar en see to Benjy, you hear?'

'Yessum,' Luster said. He went on toward the kitchen steps, swiftly.

'Here,' Dilsey said, 'You git me another armful of wood while I got you.'

'Yessum,' he said. He passed her on the steps and went to the woodpile. When he blundered again at the door a moment later, again invisible and blind within and beyond his wooden avatar, Dilsey opened the door and guided him across the kitchen with a firm hand.

'Jes thow hit at dat box again,' she said, 'Jes thow hit.'

'I got to,' Luster said, panting, 'I can't put hit down no other way.'

'Den you stand dar en hold hit a while,' Dilsey said. She unloaded him a stick at a time. 'Whut got into you dis mawnin? Here I sont you fer wood en you ain't never brought mo'n six sticks at a time to save yo life twell today. Whut you fixin to ax me kin you do now? Ain't dat show lef town yit?'

'Yessum. Hit done gone.'

She put the last stick into the box. 'Now you go on up dar wid Benjy, like I tole you befo,' she said. 'And I don't want nobody else yellin down dem stairs at me twell I rings de bell. You hear me.'

'Yessum,' Luster said. He vanished through the swing door. Dilsey put some more wood in the stove and returned to the bread board. Presently she began to sing again.

The room grew warmer. Soon Dilsey's skin had taken

on a rich, lustrous quality as compared with that as of a faint dusting of wood ashes which both it and Luster's had worn, as she moved about the kitchen, gathering about her the raw materials of food, co-ordinating the meal. On the wall above the cupboard, invisible save at night, by lamplight and even then evincing an enigmatic profundity because it had but one hand, a cabinet clock ticked, then with a preliminary sound as if it had cleared its throat, struck five times.

'Eight o'clock,' Dilsey said. She ceased and tilted her head upward, listening. But there was no sound save the clock and the fire. She opened the oven and looked at the pan of bread, then stooping she paused while someone descended the stairs. She heard the feet cross the dining-room, then the swing door opened and Luster entered, followed by a big man who appeared to have been shaped of some substance whose particles would not or did not cohere to one another or to the frame which supported it. His skin was dead-looking and hairless; dropsical too, he moved with a shambling gait like a trained bear. His hair was pale and fine. It had been brushed smoothly down upon his brow like that of children in daguerrotypes. His eyes were clear, of the pale sweet blue of cornflowers, his thick mouth hung open, drooling a little.

'Is he cold?' Dilsey said. She wiped her hands on her apron and touched his hand.

'Ef he ain't, I is,' Luster said. 'Always cold Easter. Ain't never seen hit fail. Miss Cahline say ef you ain't got time to fix her hot water bottle to never mind about hit.'

'Oh, Lawd,' Dilsey said. She drew a chair into the corner between the woodbox and the stove. The man went obediently and sat in it. 'Look in de dining-room and see whar I laid dat bottle down,' Dilsey said. Luster fetched the bottle from the dining-room and Dilsey filled it and gave it to him. 'Hurry up, now,' she said. 'See ef Jason wake now. Tell em hit's all ready.'

Luster went out. Ben sat beside the stove. He sat

loosely, utterly motionless save for his head, which made a continual bobbing sort of movement as he watched Dilsey with his sweet vague gaze as she moved about. Luster returned.

'He up,' he said, 'Miss Cahline say put hit on de table.' He came to the stove and spread his hands palm down above the firebox. 'He up, too,' he said, 'Gwine hit wid bofe feet dis mawnin.'

'Whut's de matter now?' Dilsey said. 'Git away fum dar. How kin I do anything wid you standin over de stove?'

'I cold,' Luster said.

'You ought to thought about dat whiles you wus down dar in dat cellar,' Dilsey said. 'Whut de matter wid Jason?'

'Sayin me en Benjy broke dat winder in his room.'

'Is dey one broke?' Dilsey said.

'Dat's whut he sayin,' Luster said. 'Say I broke hit.'

'How could you, when he keep hit locked all day en night?'

'Say I broke hit chunkin rocks at hit,' Luster said.

'En did you?'

'Nome,' Luster said.

'Don't lie to me, boy,' Dilsey said.

'I never done hit,' Luster said. 'Ask Benjy ef I did. I ain't stud'in dat winder.'

'Who could a broke hit, den?' Dilsey said. 'He jes tryin hisself, to wake Quentin up,' she said, taking the pan of biscuits out of the stove.

'Reckin so,' Luster said. 'Dese is funny folks. Glad I ain't none of em.'

'Ain't none of who?' Dilsey said. 'Lemme tell you somethin, nigger boy, you got jes es much Compson devilment in you es any of em. Is you right sho you never broke dat window?'

'Whut I want to break hit fur?'

'Whut you do any of yo devilment fur?' Dilsey said.

'Watch him now, so he can't burn his hand again twell I git de table set.'

She went to the dining-room, where they heard her moving about, then she returned and set a plate at the kitchen table and set food there. Ben watched her, slobbering, making a faint, eager sound.

'All right, honey,' she said, 'Here yo breakfast. Bring his chair, Luster.' Luster moved the chair up and Ben sat down, whimpering and slobbering. Dilsey tied a cloth about his neck and wiped his mouth with the end of it. 'And see kin you kep fum messin up his clothes one time,' she said, handing Luster a spoon.

Ben ceased whimpering. He watched the spoon as it rose to his mouth. It was as if even eagerness were muscle-bound in him too, and hunger itself inarticulate, not knowing it is hunger. Luster fed him with skill and detachment. Now and then his attention would return long enough to enable him to feint the spoon and cause Ben to close his mouth upon the empty air, but it was apparent that Luster's mind was elsewhere. His other hand lay on the back of the chair and upon that dead surface it moved tentatively, delicately, as if he were picking an inaudible tune out of the dead void, and once he even forgot to tease Ben with the spoon while his fingers teased out of the slain wood a soundless and involved arpeggio until Ben recalled him by whimpering again.

In the dining-room Dilsey moved back and forth. Presently she rang a small clear bell, then in the kitchen Luster heard Mrs. Compson and Jason descending, and Jason's voice, and he rolled his eyes whitely with listening.

'Sure, I know they didn't break it,' Jason said. 'Sure, I know that. Maybe the change of weather broke it.'

'I don't see how it could have,' Mrs. Compson said. 'Your room stays locked all day long, just as you leave it when you go to town. None of us ever go in there except Sunday, to clean it. I don't want you to think that I would

go where I'm not wanted, or that I would permit anyone
else to.'

'I never said you broke it, did I?' Jason said.

'I don't want to go in your room,' Mrs. Compson said.
'I respect anybody's private affairs. I wouldn't put my
foot over the threshold, even if I had a key.'

'Yes,' Jason said, 'I know your keys won't fit. That's
why I had the lock changed. What I want to know is, how
that window got broken.'

'Luster say he didn't do hit,' Dilsey said.

'I knew that without asking him,' Jason said. 'Where's
Quentin?' he said.

'Where she is ev'y Sunday mawnin,' Dilsey said.
'Whut got into you de last few days, anyhow?'

'Well, we're going to change all that,' Jason said. 'Go
up and tell her breakfast is ready.'

'You leave her alone now, Jason,' Dilsey said. 'She gits
up fear breakfast ev'y week mawnin, en Cahline lets her
stay in bed ev'y Sunday. You knows dat.'

'I can't keep a kitchenful of niggers to wait on her
pleasure, much as I'd like to,' Jason said. 'Go and tell her
to come down to breakfast.'

'Ain't nobody have to wait on her,' Dilsey said. 'I puts
her breakfast in de warmer en she – '

'Did you hear me?' Jason said.

'I hears you,' Dilsey said. 'All I been hearin, when you
in de house. Ef hit ain't Quentin er yo maw, hit's Luster
en Benjy. Whut you let him go on dat way fer, Miss
Cahline?'

'You'd better do as he says,' Mrs. Compson said, 'He's
head of the house now. It's his right to require us to
respect his wishes. I try to do it, and if I can, you can too.'

'Tain't no sense in him being so bad tempered he got
to make Quentin git up jes to suit him,' Dilsey said.
'Maybe you think she broke dat window.'

'She would, if she happened to think of it,' Jason said.
'You go and do what I told you.'

'En I wouldn't blame her none ef she did,' Dilsey

239

said, going toward the stairs. 'Wid you naggin at her all de blessed time you in de house.'

'Hush, Dilsey,' Mrs. Compson said, 'It's neither your place nor mine to tell Jason what to do. Sometimes I think he is wrong, but I try to obey his wishes for you alls' sakes. If I'm strong enough to come to the table, Quentin can too.'

Dilsey went out. They heard her mounting the stairs. They heard her a long while on the stairs.

'You've got a prize set of servants,' Jason said. He helped his mother and himself to food. 'Did you ever have one that was worth killing? You must have had some before I was big enough to remember.'

'I have to humour them,' Mrs. Compson said. 'I have to depend on them so completely. It's not as if I were strong. I wish I were. I wish I could do all the housework myself. I could at least take that much off your shoulders.'

'And a fine pigsty we'd live in, too,' Jason said. 'Hurry up, Dilsey,' he shouted.

'I know you blame me,' Mrs. Compson said, 'for letting them off to go to church today.'

'Go where?' Jason said. 'Hasn't that damn show left yet?'

'To church,' Mrs. Compson said. 'The darkies are having a special Easter service. I promised Dilsey two weeks ago that they could get off.'

'Which means we'll eat cold dinner,' Jason said, 'or none at all.'

'I know it's my fault,' Mrs. Compson said. 'I know you blame me.'

'For what?' Jason said. 'You never resurrected Christ, did you?'

They heard Dilsey mount the final stair, then her slow feet overhead.

'Quentin,' she said. When she called the first time Jason laid his knife and fork down and he and his mother appeared to wait across the table from one another, in identical attitudes; the one cold and shrewd, with close-thatched brown hair curled into two stubborn hooks, one on either side of his forehead like a bartender in carica-ture, and hazel eyes with black-ringed irises like marbles, the other cold and querulous, with perfectly white hair and eyes pouched and baffled and so dark as to appear to be all pupil or all iris.

'Quentin,' Dilsey said, 'Get up, honey. Dey waitin breakfast on you.'

'I can't understand how that window got broken,' Mrs. Compson said. 'Are you sure it was done yesterday? It could have been like that a long time, with the warm weather. The upper sash, behind the shade like that.'

'I've told you for the last time that it happened yester-day,' Jason said. 'Don't you reckon I know the room I live in? Do you reckon I could have lived in it a week with a hole in the window you could stick your hand – ' his voice ceased, ebbed, left him staring at his mother with eyes that for an instant were quite empty of anything. It was as though his eyes were holding their breath, while his mother looked at him, her face flaccid and querulous, interminable, clairvoyant yet obtuse. As they sat so Dilsey said,

'Quentin. Don't play wid me, honey. Come on to breakfast, honey. Dey waitin fer you.'

'I can't understand it,' Mrs. Compson said, 'It's just as if somebody had tried to break into the house – ' Jason sprang up. His chair crashed over backward. 'What – ' Mrs. Compson said, staring at him as he ran past her and went jumping up the stairs, where he met Dilsey. His face was now in shadow, and Dilsey said,

'She sullin. Yo ma ain't unlocked – ' But Jason ran on past her and along the corridor to a door. He didn't call. He grasped the knob and tried it, then he stood with the knob in his hand and his head bent a little, as if he were listening to something much further away than the dimensioned room beyond the door, and which he already heard. His attitude was that of one who goes through the motions of listening in order to deceive him-self as to what he already hears. Behind him Mrs. Compson mounted the stairs, calling his name. Then she saw Dilsey and she quit calling him and began to call Dilsey instead.

'I told you she ain't unlocked dat do' yit,' Dilsey said.

When she spoke he turned and ran toward her, but his voice was quiet, matter of fact. 'She carry the key with her?' he said. 'Has she got it now, I mean, or will she have – '

'Dilsey,' Mrs. Compson said on the stairs.

'Is which?' Dilsey said. 'Whyn't you let – '

'The key,' Jason said, 'To that room. Does she carry it with her all the time. Mother.' Then he saw Mrs. Compson and he went down the stairs and met her. 'Give me the key,' he said. He fell to pawing at the pock-ets of the rusty black dressing sacque she wore. She resisted.

'Jason,' she said, 'Jason! Are you and Dilsey trying to put me to bed again?' she said, trying to fend him off, 'Can't you even let me have Sunday in peace?'

'The key,' Jason said, pawing at her, 'Give it here.' He looked back at the door, as if he expected it to fly open before he could get back to it with the key he did not yet have.

'You, Dilsey!' Mrs. Compson said, clutching her sacque about her.

'Give me the key, you old fool!' Jason cried suddenly. From her pocket he tugged a huge bunch of rusted keys on an iron ring like a medieval jailer's and ran back up the hall with the two women behind him.

'You, Jason!' Mrs. Compson said. 'He will never find the right one,' she said, 'You know I never let anyone take my keys, Dilsey,' she said. She began to wail.

'Hush,' Dilsey said, 'He ain't gwine do nothin to her. I ain't gwine let him.'

'But on Sunday morning, in my own house,' Mrs. Compson said, 'When I've tried so hard to raise them

Christians. Let me find the right key, Jason,' she said. She put her hand on his arm. Then she began to struggle with him, but he flung her aside with a motion of his elbow and looked around at her for a moment, his eyes cold and harried, then he turned to the door again and the unwieldy keys.

'Hush,' Dilsey said, 'You, Jason!'

'Something terrible has happened,' Mrs. Compson said, wailing again, 'I know it has. You, Jason,' she said, grasping at him again. 'He won't even let me find the key to a room in my own house!'

'Now, now,' Dilsey said, 'Whut kin happen? I right here. I ain't gwine let him hurt her. Quentin,' she said, raising her voice, 'don't you be skeered, honey, Ise right here.'

The door opened, swung inward. He stood in it for a moment, hiding the room, then he stepped aside. 'Go in,' he said in a thick, light voice. They went in. It was not a girl's room. It was not anybody's room, and the faint scent of cheap cosmetics and the few feminine objects and the other evidences of crude and hopeless efforts to feminize it but added to its anonymity, giving it that dead and stereotyped transience of rooms in assignation houses. The bed had not been disturbed. On the floor lay a soiled undergarment of cheap silk a little too pink; from a half open bureau drawer dangled a single stocking. The window was open. A pear tree grew there, close against the house. It was in bloom and the branches scraped and rasped against the house and the myriad air, driving in the window, brought into the room the forlorn scent of the blossoms.

'Dar now,' Dilsey said, 'Didn't I told you she all right?'

'All right?' Mrs. Compson said. Dilsey followed her into the room and touched her.

'You come on and lay down, now,' she said. 'I find her in ten minutes.'

Mrs. Compson shook her off. 'Find the note,' she said. 'Quentin left a note when he did it.'

'All right,' Dilsey said, 'I'll find hit. You come on to yo room, now.'

'I knew the minute they named her Quentin this would happen,' Mrs. Compson said. She went to the bureau and began to turn over the scattered objects there – scent bottles, a box of powder, a chewed pencil, a pair of scissors with one broken blade lying upon a darned scarf dusted with powder and stained with rouge. 'Find the note,' she said.

'I is,' Dilsey said. 'You come on, now. Me and Jason'll find hit. You come on to yo room.'

'Jason,' Mrs. Compson said, 'Where is he?' She went to the door. Dilsey followed her on down the hall, to another door. It was closed. 'Jason,' she called through the door. There was no answer. She tried the knob, then she called him again. But there was still no answer, for he was hurling things backward out of the closet: garments, shoes, a suitcase. Then he emerged carrying a sawn section of tongue-and-groove planking and laid it down and entered the closet again and emerged with a metal box. He set it on the bed and stood looking at the broken lock while he dug a key ring from his pocket and selected a key, and for a time longer he stood with the selected key in his hand, looking at the broken lock, then he put the keys back in his pocket and carefully tilted the contents of the box out upon the bed. Still carefully he sorted the papers, taking them up one at a time and shaking them. Then he upended the box and shook it too and slowly replaced the papers and stood again, looking at the broken lock, with the box in his hands and his head bent. Outside the window he heard some jaybirds swirl shrieking past, and away, their cries whipping away along the wind, and an automobile passed somewhere and died away also. His mother spoke his name again beyond the door, but he didn't move. He heard Dilsey lead her away up the hall, and then a door closed. Then he replaced the box in the closet and flung the garments back into it and went downstairs to the telephone. While he stood there with the receiver to his ear, waiting, Dilsey came down the stairs. She looked at him, without stopping, and went on.

The wire opened. 'This is Jason Compson,' he said, his voice so harsh and thick that he had to repeat himself. 'Jason Compson,' he said, controlling his voice. 'Have a car ready, with a deputy, if you can't go, in ten minutes. I'll be there – What? – Robbery. My house. I know who it – Robbery, I say. Have a car read – What? Aren't you a paid law enforcement – Yes, I'll be there in five minutes. Have that car ready to leave at once. If you don't, I'll report it to the governor.'

He clapped the receiver back and crossed the dining-room, where the scarce-broken meal now lay cold on the table, and entered the kitchen. Dilsey was filling the hot water bottle. Ben sat, tranquil and empty. Beside him Luster looked like a fice dog, brightly watchful. He was eating something. Jason went on across the kitchen.

'Ain't you going to eat no breakfast?' Dilsey said. He paid her no attention. 'Go on and eat yo breakfast, Jason.' He went on. The outer door banged behind him. Luster rose and went to the window and looked out.

'Whoo,' he said, 'Whut happenin up dar? He been beatin' Miss Quentin?'

'You hush yo mouf,' Dilsey said. 'You git Benjy started now en I beat yo head off. You keep him quiet es you kin twell I get back, now.' She screwed the cap on the bottle and went out. They heard her go up the stairs, then they heard Jason pass the house in his car. Then there was no sound in the kitchen save the simmering murmur of the kettle and the clock.

'You know whut I bet?' Luster said. 'I bet he beat her. I bet he knock her in de head en now he gone fer de doctor. Dat's whut I bet.' The clock tick-tocked, solemn and profound. It might have been the dry pulse of the decaying house itself; after a while it whirred and cleared its throat and struck six times. Ben looked up at it, then he looked at the bullet-like silhouette of Luster's head in the window and he begun to bob his head again, drooling. He whimpered.

'Hush up, loony,' Luster said without turning. 'Look like we ain't gwine git to go to no church today.' But Ben sat in the chair, his big soft hands dangling between his knees, moaning faintly. Suddenly he wept, a slow bellowing sound, meaningless and sustained. 'Hush,' Luster said. He turned and lifted his hand. 'You want me to whup you?' But Ben looked at him, bellowing slowly with each expiration. Luster came and shook him. 'You hush dis minute!' he shouted. 'Here,' he said. He hauled Ben out of the chair and dragged the chair around facing the stove and opened the door to the firebox and shoved Ben into the chair. They looked like a tug nudging at a clumsy tanker in a narrow dock. Ben sat down again facing the rosy door. He hushed. Then they heard the clock again, and Dilsey slow on the stairs. When she entered he began to whimper again. Then he lifted his voice.

'Whut you done to him?' Dilsey said. 'Why can't you let him lone dis mawnin, of all times?'

'I ain't doin nothin to him,' Luster said. 'Mr. Jason skeered him, dat's whut hit is. He ain't kilt Miss Quentin, is he?'

'Hush, Benjy,' Dilsey said. He hushed. She went to the window and looked out. 'Is it quit raining?' she said.

'Yessum,' Luster said. 'Quit long time ago.'

'Den y'all go out do's a while,' she said. 'I jes got Miss Cahline quiet now.'

'Is we gwine to church?' Luster said.

'I let you know bout dat when de time come. You keep him away fum de house twell I calls you.'

'Kin we go to de pastuh?' Luster said.

'All right. Only you keep him away fum de house. I done stood all I kin.'

'Yessum,' Luster said. 'Whar Mr. Jason gone, mammy?'

'Dat's some mo of yo business, ain't it?' Dilsey said. She began to clear the table. 'Hush, Benjy. Luster gwine take you out to play.'

'Whut he done to Miss Quentin, mammy?' Luster said.

'Ain't done nothin to her. You all git on outen here?'

'I bet she ain't here,' Luster said.

Dilsey looked at him. 'How you know she ain't here?'

'Me and Benjy seed her clamb out de window last night. Didn't us, Benjy?'

'You did?' Dilsey said, looking at him.

'We sees her doin hit ev'y night,' Luster said, 'Clamb right down dat pear tree.'

'Don't you lie to me, nigger boy,' Dilsey said.

'I ain't lying. Ask Benjy ef I is.'

'Whyn't you say somethin about it, den?'

'Twarn't none o my business,' Luster said. 'I ain't gwine git mixed up in white folks' business. Come on here, Benjy, les go out do's.'

They went out. Dilsey stood for a while at the table, then she went and cleared the breakfast things from the dining-room and ate her breakfast and cleaned up the kitchen. Then she removed her apron and hung it up and went to the foot of the stairs and listened for a moment. There was no sound. She donned the overcoat and the hat and went across to her cabin.

The rain had stopped. The air now drove out of the south-east, broken overhead into blue patches. Upon the crest of a hill beyond the trees and roofs and spires of town sunlight lay like a pale scrap of cloth, was blotted away. Upon the air a bell came, then as if at a signal, other bells took up the sound and repeated it.

The cabin door opened and Dilsey emerged, again in the maroon cape and the purple gown, and wearing soiled white elbow-length gloves and minus her head-cloth now. She came into the yard and called Luster. She waited a while, then she went to the house and around it to the cellar door, moving close to the wall, and looked into the door. Ben sat on the steps. Before him Luster squatted on the damp floor. He held a saw in his left hand, the blade sprung a little by pressure of his hand,

and he was in the act of striking the blade with the worn wooden mallet with which she had been making beaten biscuit for more than thirty years. The saw gave forth a single sluggish twang that ceased with lifeless alacrity, leaving the blade in a thin clean curve between Luster's hand and the floor. Still, inscrutable, it bellied.

'Dat's de way he done hit,' Luster said. 'I jes ain't foun de right thing to hit it wid.'

'Dat's whut you doin, is it?' Dilsey said. 'Bring me dat mallet,' she said.

'I ain't hurt hit,' Luster said.

'Bring hit here,' Dilsey said. 'Put dat saw whar you got hit first.'

He put the saw away and brought the mallet to her. Then Ben wailed again, hopeless and prolonged. It was nothing. Just sound. It might have been all time and injustice and sorrow become vocal for an instant by a conjunction of planets.

'Listen at him,' Luster said, 'He been gwine on dat way ev'y since you sont us outen de house. I don't know whut got into him dis mawnin.'

'Bring him here,' Dilsey said.

'Come on, Benjy,' Luster said. He went back down the steps and took Ben's arm. He came obediently, wailing, that slow hoarse sound that ships make, that seems to begin before the sound itself has started, seems to cease before the sound itself has stopped.

'Run and git his cap,' Dilsey said. 'Don't make no noise Miss Cahline kin hear. Hurry, now. We already late.'

'She gwine hear him anyhow, ef you don't stop him.' Luster said.

'He stop when we git off de place,' Dilsey said. 'He smellin hit. Dat's whut hit is.'

'Smell whut, mammy?' Luster said.

'You go git dat cap,' Dilsey said. Luster went on. They stood in the cellar door, Ben one step below her. The sky was broken now into scudding patches that dragged their swift shadows up out of the shabby garden, over the broken fence and across the yard. Dilsey stroked Ben's head, slowly and steadily, smoothing the bang upon his brow. He wailed quietly, unhurriedly. 'Hush,' Dilsey said, 'Hush, now. We be gone in a minute. Hush, now.' He wailed quietly and steadily.

Luster returned, wearing a stiff new straw hat with a coloured band and carrying a cloth cap. The hat seemed to isolate Luster's skull, in the beholder's eyes as a spotlight would, in all its individual planes and angles. So peculiarly individual was its shape that at first glance the hat appeared to be on the head of someone standing immediately behind Luster. Dilsey looked at the hat.

'Whyn't you wear yo old hat?' she said.

'Couldn't find hit,' Luster said.

'I bet you couldn't. I bet you fixed hit last night so you couldn't find hit. You fixin to ruin dat un.'

'Aw, mammy,' Luster said. 'Hit ain't gwine rain.'

'How you know? You go git dat old hat en put dat new un away.'

'Aw, mammy.'

'Den you go git de umbreller.'

'Aw, mammy.'

'Take yo choice,' Dilsey said. 'Git yo old hat, er de umbreller. I don't keer which.'

Luster went to the cabin. Ben wailed quietly.

'Come on,' Dilsey said, 'Dey kin ketch up wid us. We gwine to hear de singin.' They went around the house, toward the gate. 'Hush,' Dilsey said from time to time as they went down the drive. They reached the gate. Dilsey opened it. Luster was coming down the drive behind them, carrying the umbrella. A woman was with him. 'Here dey come,' Dilsey said. They passed out the gate. 'Now den,' she said. Ben ceased. Luster and his mother overtook them. Frony wore a dress of bright blue silk and a flowered hat. She was a thin woman, with a flat, pleasant face.

'You got six weeks' work right dar on yo back,' Dilsey said. 'Whut you gwine do ef hit rain?'

'Git wet, I reckon,' Frony said. 'I ain't never stopped no rain yit.'

'Mammy always talkin bout hit gwine rain,' Luster said.

'Ef I don't worry bout y'all, I don't know who is,' Dilsey said. 'Come on, we already late.'

'Rev'un Shegog gwine preach today,' Frony said.

'Is?' Dilsey said. 'Who him?'

'He fum Saint Looey,' Frony said. 'Dat big preacher.'

'Huh,' Dilsey said, 'Whut dey needs is a man kin put de fear of God into dese here triflin young niggers.'

'Rev'un Shegog gwine preach today,' Frony said. 'So dey tells.'

They went on along the street. Along its quiet length white people in bright clumps moved churchward, under the windy bells, walking now and then in the random and tentative sun. The wind was gusty, out of the southeast, chill and raw after the warm days.

'I wish you wouldn't keep on bringin him to church, mammy,' Frony said. 'Folks talkin.'

'Whut folks?' Dilsey said.

'I hears em,' Frony said.

'And I know whut kind of folks,' Dilsey said, 'Trash white folks. Dat's who it is. Thinks he ain't good enough fer white church, but nigger church ain't good enough fer him.'

'Dey talks, jes de same,' Frony said.

'Den you send um to me,' Dilsey said. 'Tell em de good Lawd don't keer whether he smart er not. Don't nobody but white trash keer dat.'

A street turned off at right angles, descending, and became a dirt road. On either hand the land dropped more sharply; a broad flat dotted with small cabins whose weathered roofs were on a level with the crown of the road. They were set in small grassless plots littered with broken things, bricks, planks, crockery, things of a once utilitarian value. What growth there was consisted of rank weeds and the trees were mulberries and locusts and sycamores – trees that partook also of the foul desic-cation which surrounded the houses; trees whose very burgeoning seemed to be the sad and stubborn remnant of September, as if even spring had passed them by, leav-ing them to feed upon the rich and unmistakable smell of negroes in which they grew.

From the doors negroes spoke to them as they passed, to Dilsey usually:

'Sis' Gibson! How you dis mawnin?'

'I'm well. Is you well?'

'I'm right well, I thank you.'

They emerged from the cabins and struggled up the shading levee to the road – men in staid, hard brown or black, with gold watch chains and now and then a stick; young men in cheap violent blues or stripes and swagger-ing hats; women a little stiffly sibilant, and children in garments bought second hand off white people, who looked at Ben with the covertness of nocturnal animals:

'I bet you won't go up en tech him.'

'How come I won't?'

'I bet you won't. I bet you skeered to.'

'He won't hurt folks. He des a loony.'

'How come a loony won't hurt folks?'

'Dat un won't. I teched him.'

'I bet you won't now.'

'Case Miss Dilsey lookin.'

'You won't noways.'

'He don't hurt folks. He des a loony.'

And steadily the older people speaking to Dilsey, though, unless they were quite old, Dilsey permitted Frony to respond.

'Mammy ain't feeling well dis mawnin.'

'Dat's too bad. But Rev'un Shegog'll cure dat. He'll give her de comfort en de unburdenin.'

The road rose again, to a scene like a painted back-drop. Notched into a cut of red clay crowned with oaks the road appeared to stop short off, like a cut ribbon. Beside it a weathered church lifted its crazy steeple like a painted church, and the whole scene was as flat and without perspective as a painted cardboard set upon the ultimate edge of the flat earth, against the windy sunlight of space and April and a midmorning filled with bells. Toward the church they thronged with slow sabbath deliberation. The women and children went on in, the men stopped outside and talked in quiet groups until the bell ceased ringing. Then they too entered.

The church had been decorated, with sparse flowers from kitchen gardens and hedgerows, and with streamers of coloured crepe paper. Above the pulpit hung a battered Christmas bell, the accordion sort that collapses. The pulpit was empty, though the choir was already in place, fanning themselves although it was not warm.

Most of the women were gathered on one side of the room. They were talking. Then the bell struck one time and they dispersed to their seats and the congregation sat for an instant, expectant. The bell struck again one time. The choir rose and began to sing and the congregation turned its head as one, as six small children – four girls with tight pigtails bound with small scraps of cloth like butterflies, and two boys with close napped heads – entered and marched up the aisle, strung together in a harness of white ribbons and flowers, and followed by two men in single file. The second man was huge, of a light coffee colour, imposing in a frock coat and white tie. His head was magisterial and profound, his neck rolled above his collar in rich folds. But he was familiar to them, and so the heads were still reverted when he had passed, and it was not until the choir ceased singing that they realized that the visiting clergyman had already entered, and when they saw the man who had preceded their minister enter the pulpit still ahead of him an indescribable sound went up, a sigh, a sound of astonishment and disappointment.

The visitor was undersized, in a shabby alpaca coat. He had a wizened black face like a small, aged monkey. And all the while that the choir sang again and while the six children rose and sang in thin, frightened, tuneless whispers, they watched the insignificant looking man sitting dwarfed and countrified by the minister's imposing bulk, with something like consternation. They were still looking at him with consternation and unbelief when the minister rose and introduced him in rich, rolling tones whose very unction served to increase the visitor's insignificance.

'En dey brung dat all de way fum Saint Looey,' Frony whispered.

'I've knowed de Lawd to use cuiser tools dan dat,' Dilsey said. 'Hush, now,' she said to Ben, 'Dey fixin to sing again in a minute.'

When the visitor rose to speak he sounded like a white man. His voice was level and cold. It sounded too big to have come from him and they listened at first through curiosity, as they would have to a monkey talking. They began to watch him as they would a man on a tight rope. They even forgot his insignificant appearance in the virtuosity with which he ran and poised and swooped upon the cold inflexionless wire of his voice, so that at last, when with a sort of swooping glide he came to rest again beside the reading desk with one arm resting upon it at shoulder height and his monkey body as reft of all motion as a mummy or an emptied vessel, the congregation sighed as if it waked from a collective dream and moved a little in its seats. Behind the pulpit the choir fanned steadily. Dilsey whispered, 'Hush, now. Dey fixin to sing in a minute.'

Then a voice said, 'Brethren.'

The preacher had not moved. His arm lay yet across the desk, and he still held that pose while the voice died in sonorous echoes between the walls. It was as different as day and dark from his former tone, with a sad, timbrous quality like an alto horn, sinking into their hearts and speaking there again when it had ceased in fading and cumulate echoes.

'Brethren and sisteren,' it said again. The preacher removed his arm and he began to walk back and forth before the desk, his hands clasped behind him, a meagre figure, hunched over upon itself like that of one long immured in striving with the implacable earth, 'I got the recollection and the blood of the Lamb!' He tramped steadily back and forth beneath the twisted paper and the Christmas bell, hunched, his hands clasped behind him. He was like a worn small rock whelmed by the successive waves of his voice. With his body he seemed to feed the voice that, succubus like, has fleshed its teeth in him. And the congregation seemed to watch with its own eyes while the voice consumed him, until he was nothing and they were nothing and there was not even a voice but instead their hearts were speaking to one another in chanting measures beyond the need for words, so that when he came to rest against the reading desk, his monkey face lifted and his whole attitude that of a serene, tortured crucifix that transcended its shabbiness and insignificance and made it of no moment, a long moaning expulsion of breath rose from them, and a woman's single soprano: 'Yes, Jesus!'

As the scudding day passed overhead the dingy windows glowed and faded in ghostly retrograde. A car passed along the road outside, labouring in the sand, died away. Dilsey sat bolt upright, her hand on Ben's knee. Two tears slid down her fallen cheeks, in and out of the myriad coruscations of immolation and abnegation and time.

'Brethren,' the minister said in a harsh whisper, without moving.

'Yes, Jesus!' the woman's voice said, hushed yet.

'Breddren en sistuhn!' His voice rang again, with the horns. He removed his arm and stood erect and raised his hands. 'I got de ricklickshun en de blood of de Lamb!' They did not mark just when his intonation, his pronunciation, became negroid, they just sat swaying a little in their seats as the voice took them into itself.

'When de long, cold – Oh, I tells you, breddren, when de long, cold – I sees de light en I sees de word, po sinner! Dey passed away in Egypt, de swingin chariots; de generations passed away. Wus a rich man: whar he now, O breddren? Wus a po man: whar he now, O sistuhn? Oh I tells you, ef you ain't got de milk en de dew of de old salvation when de long, cold years rolls away!'

'Yes, Jesus!'

'I tells you, breddren, en I tells you, sistuhn, dey'll come a time. Po sinner sayin Let me lay down wid de Lawd, lemme lay down my load. Den whut Jesus gwine say, O breddren? O sistuhn? Is you got de ricklickshun en de blood of de Lamb? Case I ain't gwine load down heaven!'

He fumbled in his coat and took out a handkerchief and mopped his face. A low concerted sound rose from the congregation: 'Mmmmmmmmmmmmmm!' The woman's voice said, 'Yes, Jesus! Jesus!'

'Breddren! Look at dem little chillen settin dar. Jesus wus like dat once. He mammy suffered de glory en de pangs. Sometime maybe she helt him at de nightfall, whilst de angels singin him to sleep; maybe she look out de do' en see de Roman po-lice passin.' He tramped back and forth, mopping his face. 'Listen, breddren! I sees de day. Ma'y settin in de do' wid Jesus on her lap, de little Jesus. Like dem chillen dar, de little Jesus. I hears de angels singing de peaceful songs en de glory; I sees de closin eyes; sees Mary jump up, sees de sojer face: We gwine to kill! We gwine to kill! We gwine to kill yo little Jesus! I hears de weepin en de lamentation of de po mammy widout de salvation en de word of God!'

'Mmmmmmmmmmmmmmmmmm! Jesus! Little Jesus!' and another voice, rising:

'I sees, O Jesus! Oh I sees!' and still another, without words, like bubbles rising in water.

'I sees hit, breddren! I sees hit! Sees de blastin,

blindin sight! I sees Calvary, wid de sacred trees, sees de thief en de murderer en de least of dese; I hears de boastin en de braggin: Ef you be Jesus, lif up yo tree en walk! I hears de wailin of women en de evenin lamentations; I hears de weepin en de crying en de turnt-away face of God: dey done kilt Jesus; dey done kilt my Son!'

'Mmmmmmmmmmmmmm! Jesus! I sees, O Jesus!'

'O blind sinner! Breddren, I tells you; sistuhn, I says to you, when de Lawd did turn His mighty face, say, Ain't gwine overload heaven! I can see de widowed God shet His do'; I sees de whelmin flood roll between; I sees de darkness en de death everlastin upon de generations. Den, lo! Breddren! Yes, breddren! Whut I see? Whut I see, O sinner? I sees de resurrection en de light; sees de meek Jesus sayin Dey kilt Me dat ye shall live again; I died dat dem whut sees en believes shall never die. Breddren, O breddren! I sees de doom crack en hears de golden horns shoutin down de glory, en de arisen dead whut got de blood en de ricklickshun of de Lamb!'

In the midst of the voices and the hands Ben sat, rapt in his sweet blue gaze. Dilsey sat bolt upright beside, crying rigidly and quietly in the annealment and the blood of the remembered Lamb.

As they walked through the bright noon, up the sandy road with the dispersing congregation talking easily again group to group, she continued to weep, unmindful of the talk.

'He sho a preacher, mon! He didn't look like much at first, but hush!'

'He seed de power en de glory.'

'Yes, suh. He seed hit. Face to face he seed hit.'

Dilsey made no sound, her face did not quiver as the tears took their sunken and devious courses, walking with her head up, making no effort to dry them away even.

'Whyn't you quit dat, mammy?' Frony said. 'Wid all dese people lookin. We be passin white folks soon.'

'I've seed de first en de last,' Dilsey said. 'Never you mind me.'

'First en last whut?' Frony said.

'Never you mind,' Dilsey said. 'I seed de beginnin, en now I sees de endin.'

Before they reached the street, though, she stopped and lifted her skirt and dried her eyes on the hem of her topmost underskirt. Then they went on. Ben shambled along beside Dilsey, watching Luster who anticked along ahead, the umbrella in his hand and his new straw hat slanted viciously in the sunlight, like a big foolish dog watching a small clever one. They reached the gate and entered. Immediately Ben began to whimper again, and for a while all of them looked up the drive at the square, paintless house with its rotting portico.

'Whut's gwine on up dar today?' Frony said. 'Something is.'

'Nothin,' Dilsey said. 'You tend to yo business en let de white folks tend to deir'n.'

'Somethin is,' Frony said. 'I heard him first thing dis mawnin. Tain't none of my business, dough.'

'En I knows whut, too,' Luster said.

'You knows mo dan you got any use fer,' Dilsey said. 'Ain't you jes heard Frony say hit ain't none of yo business? You take Benjy on to de back and keep him quiet twell I put dinner on.'

'I knows whar Miss Quentin is,' Luster said.

'Den jes keep hit,' Dilsey said. 'Soon es Quentin need any of you egvice, I'll let you know. Y'all g'awn en play in de back, now.'

'You know whut gwine happen soon es dey start playing dat ball over yonder,' Luster said.

'Dey won't start fer a while yit. By dat time T. P. be here to take him ridin. Here, you gimme dat new hat.'

Luster gave her the hat and he and Ben went on across the back yard. Ben was still whimpering, though not loud. Dilsey and Frony went to the cabin. After a while Dilsey emerged, again in the faded calico dress, and went to the kitchen. The fire had died down. There was no sound in the house. She put on the apron and went upstairs. There was no sound anywhere. Quentin's room was as they had left it. She entered and picked up the under-garment and put the stocking back in the drawer and closed it. Mrs. Compson's door was closed. Dilsey stood beside it for a moment, listening. Then she opened it and entered, entered a pervading reek of camphor. The shades were drawn, the room in half-light, and the bed, so that at first she thought Mrs. Compson was asleep and was about to close the door when the other spoke.

'Well?' she said, 'What is it?'

'Hit's me,' Dilsey said. 'You want anything?'

Mrs. Compson didn't answer. After a while, without moving her head at all, she said: 'Where's Jason?'

'He ain't come back yit,' Dilsey said. 'Whut you want?'

Mrs. Compson said nothing. Like so many cold, weak people, when faced at last by the incontrovertible disaster she exhumed from somewhere a sort of fortitude, strength. In her case it was an unshakable conviction regarding the yet unplumbed event. 'Well,' she said presently, 'Did you find it?'

'Find whut? Whut you talkin about?'

'The note. At least she would have enough consideration to leave a note. Even Quentin did that.'

'Whut you talkin about?' Dilsey said, 'Don't you know she all right? I bet she be walkin right in dis do' befo dark.'

'Fiddlesticks,' Mrs. Compson said, 'It's in the blood. Like uncle, like niece. Or mother. I don't know which would be worse. I don't seem to care.'

'Whut you keep on talking that way fur?' Dilsey said. 'Whut she want to do anything like that fur?'

'I don't know. What reason did Quentin have? Under God's heaven what reason did he have? It can't be simply to flout and hurt me. Whoever God is, He would not permit that. I'm a lady. You might not believe that from my offspring, but I am.'

'You des wait en see,' Dilsey said. 'She be here by night, right dar in her bed.' Mrs. Compson said nothing. The camphor-soaked cloth lay upon her brow. The black robe lay across the foot of the bed. Dilsey stood with her hand on the door knob.

'Well,' Mrs. Compson said. 'What do you want? Are you going to fix some dinner for Jason and Benjamin, or not?'

'Jason ain't come yit,' Dilsey said. 'I gwine fix somethin. You sho you don't want nothing? Yo bottle still hot enough?'

'You might hand me my Bible.'

'I give hit to you dis mawnin, befo I left.'

'You laid it on the edge of the bed. How long did you expect it to stay there?'

Dilsey crossed to the bed and groped among the shadows beneath the edge of it and found the Bible, face down. She smoothed the bent pages and laid the book on the bed again. Mrs. Compson didn't open her eyes. Her hair and the pillow were the same colour, beneath the wimple of the medicated cloth she looked like an old nun praying. 'Don't put it there again,' she said, without opening her eyes. 'That's where you put it before. Do you want me to have to get out of bed to pick it up?'

Dilsey reached the book across her and laid it on the broad side of the bed. 'You can't see to read, noways,' she said. 'You want me to raise de shade a little?'

'No. Let them alone. Go on and fix Jason something to eat.'

Dilsey went out. She closed the door and returned to the kitchen. The stove was almost cold. While she stood there the clock above the cupboard struck ten times. 'One o'clock,' she said aloud, 'Jason ain't comin home. Ise seed de first en de last,' she said, looking at the cold stove, 'I seed de first en de last.' She set out some cold food on a table. As she moved back and forth she sang a hymn. She sang the first two lines over and over to the complete tune. She arranged the meal and went to the door and called Luster, and after a time Luster and Ben entered. Ben was still moaning a little, as to himself.

'He ain't never quit,' Luster said.

'Y'all come on en eat,' Dilsey said. 'Jason ain't coming to dinner.' They sat down at the table. Ben could manage solid food pretty well for himself, though even now, with cold food before him, Dilsey tied a cloth about his neck. He and Luster ate. Dilsey moved about the kitchen, singing the two lines of the hymn which she remembered. 'Y'all kin g'awn en eat,' she said, 'Jason ain't comin home.'

He was twenty miles away at that time. When he left the house he drove rapidly to town, overreaching the slow sabbath groups and the peremptory bells along the broken air. He crossed the empty square and turned into a narrow street that was abruptly quieter even yet, and stopped before a frame house and went up the flower-bordered walk to the porch.

Beyond the screen door people were talking. As he lifted his hand to knock he heard steps, so he withheld his hand until a big man in black broadcloth trousers and a stiff-bosomed white shirt without collar opened the door. He had vigorous untidy iron-grey hair and his grey eyes were round and shiny like a little boy's. He took Jason's hand and drew him into the house, still shaking it.

'Come right in,' he said, 'Come right in.'

'You ready to go now?' Jason said.

'Walk right in,' the other said, propelling him by the elbow into a room where a man and a woman sat. 'You know Myrtle's husband, don't you? Jason Compson, Vernon.'

'Yes,' Jason said. He did not even look at the man, and as the sheriff drew a chair across the room the man said,

'We'll go out so you can talk. Come on, Myrtle.'

'No, no,' the sheriff said, 'You folks keep your seat. I

reckon it ain't that serious, Jason? Have a seat.'

'I'll tell you as we go along,' Jason said. 'Get your hat and coat.'

'We'll go out,' the man said, rising.

'Keep your seat,' the sheriff said. 'Me and Jason will go out on the porch.'

'You get your hat and coat,' Jason said. 'They've already got a twelve hour start.' The sheriff led the way back to the porch. A man and a woman passing spoke to him. He responded with a hearty florid gesture. Bells were still ringing, from the direction of the section known as Nigger Hollow. 'Get your hat, Sheriff,' Jason said. The sheriff drew up two chairs.

'Have a seat and tell me what the trouble is.'

'I told you over the phone,' Jason said, standing. 'I did that to save time. Am I going to have to go to law to compel you to do your sworn duty?'

'You sit down and tell me about it,' the sheriff said. 'I'll take care of you all right.'

'Care, hell,' Jason said. 'Is this what you call taking care of me?'

'You're the one that's holding us up,' the sheriff said. 'You sit down and tell me about it.'

Jason told him, his sense of injury and impotence feeding upon its own sound, so that after a time he forgot his haste in the violent cumulation of his self justification and his outrage. The sheriff watched him steadily with his cold shiny eyes.

'But you don't know they done it,' he said. 'You just think so.'

'Don't know?' Jason said. 'When I spent two damn days chasing her through alleys, trying to keep her away from him, after I told her what I'd do to her if I ever caught her with him, and you say I don't know that that little b – '

'Now, then,' the sheriff said, 'That'll do. That's enough of that.' He looked out across the street, his hands in his pockets.

'And when I come to you, a commissioned officer of the law,' Jason said.

'That show's in Mottson this week,' the sheriff said.

'Yes,' Jason said, 'And if I could find a law officer that gave a solitary damn about protecting the people that elected him to office, I'd be there too by now.' He repeated his story, harshly recapitulant, seeming to get an actual pleasure out of his outrage and impotence. The sheriff did not appear to be listening at all.

'Jason,' he said, 'What were you doing with three thousand dollars hid in the house?'

'What?' Jason said. 'That's my business where I keep my money. Your business is to help me get it back.'

'Did your mother know you had that much on the place?'

'Look here,' Jason said, 'My house has been robbed. I know who did it and I know where they are. I come to you as the commissioned officer of the law, and I ask you once more, are you going to make any effort to recover my property, or not?'

'What do you aim to do with that girl, if you catch them?'

'Nothing,' Jason said, 'Not anything. I wouldn't lay my hand on her. The bitch that cost me a job, the one chance I ever had to get ahead, that killed my father and is shortening my mother's life every day and made my name a laughing stock in the town. I won't do anything to her,' he said. 'Not anything.'

'You drove that girl into running off, Jason,' the sheriff said.

'How I conduct my family is no business of yours,' Jason said. 'Are you going to help me or not?

'You drove her away from home,' the sheriff said. 'And I have some suspicions about who that money belongs to that I don't reckon I'll ever know for certain.'

Jason stood, slowly wringing the brim of his hat in his hands. He said quietly: 'You're not going to make any effort to catch them for me?'

'That's not any of my business, Jason. If you had any actual proof, I'd have to act. But without that I don't figger it's any of my business.'

'That's your answer, is it?' Jason said. 'Think well, now.'

'That's it, Jason.'

'All right,' Jason said. He put his hat on. 'You'll regret this. I won't be helpless. This is not Russia, where just because he wears a little metal badge, a man is immune to law.' He went down the steps and got in his car and started the engine. The sheriff watched him drive away, turn, and rush past the house toward town.

The bells were ringing again, high in the scudding sunlight in bright disorderly tatters of sound. He stopped at a filling station and had his tyres examined and the tank filled.

'Gwine on a trip, is you?' the negro asked him. He didn't answer. 'Look like hit gwine fair off, after all,' the negro said.

'Fair off, hell,' Jason said, 'It'll be raining like hell by twelve o'clock.' He looked at the sky, thinking about rain, about the slick clay roads, himself stalled somewhere miles from town. He thought about it with a sort of triumph, of the fact that he was going to miss dinner, that by starting now and so serving his compulsion of haste, he would be at the greatest possible distance from both towns when noon came. It seemed to him that, in this, circumstance was giving him a break, so he said to the negro:

'What the hell are you doing? Has somebody paid you to keep this car standing here as long as you can?'

'Dis here ty' ain't got no air a-tall in hit,' the negro said.

'Then get the hell away from there and let me have that tube,' Jason said.

'Hit up now,' the negro said, rising. 'You kin ride now.'

Jason got in and started the engine and drove off. He went into second gear, the engine spluttering and gasping, and he raced the engine, jamming the throttle down and snapping the choker in and out savagely. 'It's goin to rain,' he said, 'Get me half-way there, and rain like hell.' And he drove on out of the bells and out of town, thinking of himself slogging through the mud, hunting a team. 'And every damn one of them will be at church.' He thought of how he'd find a church at last and take a team and of the owner coming out, shouting at him and of himself striking the man down. 'I'm Jason Compson. See if you can stop me. See if you can elect a man to office that can stop me,' he said, thinking of himself entering the courthouse with a file of soldiers and dragging the sheriff out. 'Thinks he can sit with his hands folded and see me lose my job. I'll show him about jobs.' Of his niece he did not think at all, nor of the arbitrary valuation of the money. Neither of them had had entity or individuality for him for ten years; together they merely symbolized the job in the bank of which he had been deprived before he ever got it.

The air brightened, the running shadow patches were not the obverse, and it seemed to him that the fact that the day was clearing was another cunning stroke on the part of the foe, the fresh battle toward which he was carrying ancient wounds. From time to time he passed churches, unpainted frame buildings with sheet iron steeples, surrounded by tethered teams and shabby motor-cars, and it seemed to him that each of them was a picket-post where the rear guards of Circumstance peeped fleetingly back at him. 'And damn You, too,' he said, 'See if You can stop me,' thinking of himself, his file of soldiers with the manacled sheriff in the rear, dragging Omnipotence down from His throne, if necessary; of the embattled legions of both hell and heaven through which he tore his way and put his hands at last on his fleeing niece.

The wind was out of the south-east. It blew steadily upon his cheek. It seemed that he could feel the prolonged blow of it sinking through his skull, and suddenly with an old premonition he clapped the brakes on and stopped and sat perfectly still. Then he lifted his hand to his neck and began to curse, and sat there, cursing in a harsh whisper. When it was necessary for him to drive for any length of time he fortified himself with a handker-chief soaked in camphor, which he would tie about his throat when clear of town, thus inhaling the fumes, and he got out and lifted the seat cushion on the chance that there might be a forgotten one there. He looked beneath both seats and stood again for a while, cursing, seeing himself mocked by his own triumphing. He closed his eyes, leaning on the door. He could return and get the forgotten camphor, or he could go on. In either case, his head would be splitting, but at home he could be sure of finding camphor on Sunday, while if he went on he could not be sure. But if he went back, he would be an hour and a half later in reaching Mottson. 'Maybe I can drive slow,' he said. 'Maybe I can drive slow, thinking of some-thing else – '

He got in and started. 'I'll think of something else,' he said, so he thought about Lorraine. He imagined himself in bed with her, only he was just lying beside her, plead-ing with her to help him, then he thought of the money again, and that he had been outwitted by a woman, a girl. If he could just believe it was the man who had robbed him. But to have been robbed of that which was to have compensated him for the lost job, which he had acquired through so much effort and risk, by the very symbol of the lost job itself, and worst of all, by a bitch of a girl. He drove on, shielding his face from the steady wind with the corner of his coat.

He could see the opposed forces of his destiny and his will drawing swiftly together now, toward a junction that would be irrevocable; he became cunning. I can't make a blunder, he told himself. There would be just one right thing, without alternatives: he must do that. He believed that both of them would know him on sight, while he'd have to trust to seeing her first, unless the man still wore the red tie. And the fact that he must depend on that red tie seemed to be the sum of the impending disaster; he could almost smell it, feel it above the throbbing of his head.

He crested the final hill. Smoke lay in the valley, and roofs, a spire or two above trees. He drove down the hill and into the town, slowing, telling himself again of the need for caution, to find where the tent was located first. He could not see very well now, and he knew that it was the disaster which kept telling him to go directly and get something for his head. At a filling station they told him that the tent was not up yet, but that the show cars were on a siding at the station. He drove there.

Two gaudily painted pullman cars stood on the track. He reconnoitred them before he got out. He was trying to breathe shallowly, so that the blood would not beat so in his skull. He got out and went along the station wall, watching the cars. A few garments hung out of the windows, limp and crinkled, as though they had been recently laundered. On the earth beside the steps of one sat three canvas chairs. But he saw no sign of life at all until a man in a dirty apron came to the door and emptied a pan of dishwater with a broad gesture, the sunlight glinting on the metal belly of the pan, then entered the car again.

Now I'll have to take him by surprise, before he can warn them, he thought. It never occurred to him that they might not be there, in the car. That they should not be there, that the whole result should not hinge on whether he saw them first or they saw him first, would be opposed to all nature and contrary to the whole rhythm of events. And more than that: he must see them first, get the money back, then what they did would be of no importance to him, while otherwise the whole world would know that he, Jason Compson, had been robbed by Quentin, his niece, a bitch.

He reconnoitred again. Then he went to the car and mounted the steps, swiftly and quietly, and paused at the door. The galley was dark, rank with stale food. The man was a white blur, singing in a cracked, shaky tenor. An old man, he thought, and not as big as I am. He entered the car as the man looked up.

'Hey?' the man said, stopping his song.

'Where are they?' Jason said. 'Quick, now. In the sleeping car?'

'Where's who?' the man said.

'Don't lie to me,' Jason said. He blundered on in the cluttered obscurity.

'What's that?' the other said, 'Who you calling a liar?' And when Jason grasped his shoulder he exclaimed, 'Look out, fellow!'

'Don't lie,' Jason said, 'Where are they?'

'Why, you bastard,' the man said. His arm was frail and thin in Jason's grasp. He tried to wrench free, then he turned and fell to scrabbling on the littered table behind him.

'Come on,' Jason said, 'Where are they?'

'I'll tell you where they are,' the man shrieked, 'Lemme find my butcher knife.'

'Here,' Jason said, trying to hold the other, 'I'm just asking you a question.'

'You bastard,' the other shrieked, scrabbling at the table. Jason tried to grasp him in both arms, trying to prison the puny fury of him. The man's body felt so old, so frail, yet so fatally single-purposed that for the first time Jason saw clear and unshadowed the disaster toward which he rushed.

'Quit it!' he said, 'Here! Here! I'll get out. Give me time, and I'll get out.'

'Call me a liar,' the other wailed, 'Lemme go. Lemme go just one minute. I'll show you.'

Jason glared wildly about, holding the other. Outside it was now bright and sunny, swift and bright and empty, and he thought of the people soon to be going quietly home to Sunday dinner, decorously festive, and of himself trying to hold the fatal, furious little old man whom he dared not release long enough to turn his back and run.

'Will you quit long enough for me to get out?' he said, 'Will you?' But the other still struggled, and Jason freed one hand and struck him on the head. A clumsy, hurried blow, and not hard, but the other slumped immediately and slid clattering among pans and buckets to the floor. Jason stood above him, panting, listening. Then he turned and ran from the car. At the door he restrained himself and descended more slowly and stood there again. His breath made a hah hah hah sound and he stood there trying to repress it, darting his gaze this way and that, when at a scuffling sound behind him he turned in time to see the little old man leaping awkwardly and furiously from the vestibule, a rusty hatchet high in his hand.

He grasped at the hatchet, feeling no shock but knowing that he was falling, thinking So this is how it'll end, and he believed that he was about to die and when something crashed against the back of his head he thought How did he hit me there? Only maybe he hit me a long time ago, he thought, And I just now felt it, and he thought Hurry. Hurry. Get it over with, and then a furious desire not to die seized him and he struggled, hearing the old man wailing and cursing in his cracked voice.

He still struggled when they hauled him to his feet, but they held him and he ceased.

'Am I bleeding much?' he said, 'The back of my head. Am I bleeding?' He was still saying that while he felt himself being propelled rapidly away, heard the old man's thin furious voice dying away behind him. 'Look at my head,' he said, 'Wait, I – '

'Wait, hell,' the man who held him said, 'That damn little wasp'll kill you. Keep going. You ain't hurt.'

'He hit me,' Jason said. 'Am I bleeding?'

'Keep going,' the other said. He led Jason on around the corner of the station, to the empty platform where an express truck stood, where grass grew rigidly in a plot bordered with rigid flowers and a sign in electric lights:

Keep your  on Mottson, the gap filled by a human eye with an electric pupil. The man released him.

'Now,' he said, 'You get on out of here and stay out. What were you trying to do? Commit suicide?'

'I was looking for two people,' Jason said. 'I just asked him where they were.'

'Who you looking for?'

'It's a girl,' Jason said. 'And a man. He had on a red tie in Jefferson yesterday. With this show. They robbed me.'

'Oh,' the man said. 'You're the one, are you. Well, they ain't here.'

'I reckon so,' Jason said. He leaned against the wall and put his hand to the back of his head and looked at his palm. 'I thought I was bleeding,' he said. 'I thought he hit me with that hatchet.'

'You hit your head on the rail,' the man said. 'You better go on. They ain't here.'

'Yes. He said they were not here. I thought he was lying.'

'Do you think I'm lying?' the man said.

'No,' Jason said. 'I know they're not here.'

'I told him to get the hell out of there, both of them,' the man said. 'I won't have nothing like that in my show. I run a respectable show, with a respectable troupe.'

'Yes,' Jason said. 'You don't know where they went?'

'No. And I don't want to know. No member of my show can pull a stunt like that. You her – brother?'

'No,' Jason said. 'It don't matter. I just wanted to see them. You sure he didn't hit me? No blood, I mean.'

'There would have been blood if I hadn't got there when I did. You stay away from here, now. That little bastard'll kill you. That your car yonder?'

'Yes.'

'Well, you get in it and go back to Jefferson. If you find

them, it won't be in my show, I run a respectable show. You say they robbed you?'

'No,' Jason said, 'It don't make any difference.' He went to the car and got in. What is it I must do? he thought. Then he remembered. He started the engine and drove slowly up the street until he found a drug-store. The door was locked. He stood for a while with his hand on the knob and his head bent a little. Then he turned away and when a man came along after a while he asked if there was a drug-store open anywhere, but there was not. Then he asked when the northbound train ran, and the man told him at two-thirty. He crossed the pavement and got in the car again and sat there. After a while two negro lads passed. He called to them.

'Can either of you boys drive a car?'

'Yes, suh.'

'What'll you charge to drive me to Jefferson right away?'

They looked at one another, murmuring.

'I'll pay a dollar,' Jason said.

They murmured again. 'Couldn't go fer dat,' one said.

'What will you go for?'

'Kin you go?' one said.

'I can't git off,' the other said. 'Whyn't you drive him up dar? You ain't got nothin to do.'

'Yes, I is.'

'Whut you got to do?'

They murmured again, laughing.

'I'll give you two dollars,' Jason said. 'Either of you.'

'I can't git away neither,' the first said.

'All right,' Jason said. 'Go on.'

He sat there for some time. He heard a clock strike the half-hour, then people began to pass, in Sunday and Easter clothes. Some looked at him as they passed, at the man sitting quietly behind the wheel of a small car, with his invisible life ravelled out about him like a wornout sock. After a while a negro in overalls came up.

'Is you de one wants to go to Jefferson?' he said.

'Yes,' Jason said. 'What'll you charge me?'

'Fo dollars.'

'Give you two.'

'Can't go fer no less'n fo.' The man in the car sat quietly. He wasn't even looking at him. The negro said, 'You want me er not?'

'All right,' Jason said, 'Get in.'

He moved over and the negro took the wheel. Jason closed his eyes. I can get something for it at Jefferson, he told himself, easing himself to the jolting, I can get something there. They drove on, along the streets where people were turning peacefully into houses and Sunday dinners, and on out of town. He thought that. He wasn't thinking of home, where Ben and Luster were eating cold dinner at the kitchen table. Something – the absence of disaster, threat, in any constant evil – permitted him to forget Jefferson as any place which he had ever seen before, where his life must resume itself.

When Ben and Luster were done Dilsey sent them out doors. 'And see kin you keep let him alone twell fo o'clock. T. P. be here den.'

'Yessum,' Luster said. They went out. Dilsey ate her dinner and cleared up the kitchen. Then she went to the foot of the stairs and listened, but there was no sound. She returned through the kitchen and out the outer door and stopped on the steps. Ben and Luster were not in sight, but while she stood there she heard another sluggish twang from the direction of the cellar door and she went to the door and looked down upon a repetition of the morning's scene.

'He done it jes dat way,' Luster said. He contemplated the motionless saw with a kind of hopeful dejection. 'I ain't got de right thing to hit it wid yit,' he said.

'En you ain't gwine find hit down here, neither,' Dilsey said. 'You take him on out in de sun. You bofe get pneumonia down here on dis wet flo.'

She waited and watched them cross the yard toward a

271

clump of cedar trees near the fence. Then she went on to her cabin.

'Now, don't you git started,' Luster said, 'I had enough trouble wid you to-day.' There was a hammock made of barrel staves slatted into woven wires. Luster lay down in the swing, but Ben went on vaguely and purposelessly. He began to whimper again. 'Hush, now, Luster said, 'I fixin to whup you.' He lay back in the swing. Ben had stopped moving, but Luster could hear him whimpering. 'Is you gwine hush, er ain't you?' Luster said. He got up and followed and came upon Ben squatting before a small mound of earth. At either end of it an empty bottle of blue glass that once contained poison was fixed in the ground. In one was a withered stalk of jimson weed. Ben squatted before it, moaning, a slow, inarticulate sound. Still moaning he sought vaguely about and found a twig and put it in the other bottle. 'Whyn't you hush?' Luster said, 'You want me to give you somethin' to sho nough moan about? Sposin I does dis.' He knelt and swept the bottle suddenly up and behind him. Ben ceased moaning. He squatted, looking at the small depression where the bottle had sat, then as he drew his lungs full Luster brought the bottle back into view. 'Hush!' he hissed, 'Don't you dast to beller! Don't you. Dar hit is. See? Here. You fixin to start ef you stays here. Come on, les go see ef dey started knockin ball yit.' He took Ben's arm and drew him up and they went to the fence and stood side by side there, peering between the matted honeysuckle not yet in bloom.

'Dar,' Luster said, 'Dar come some. See um?'

They watched the foursome play on to the green and out, and move to the tee and drive. Ben watched, whimpering, slobbering. When the foursome went on he followed along the fence, bobbing and moaning. One said,

'Here, caddie. Bring the bag.'

'Hush, Benjy,' Luster said, but Ben went on at his shambling trot, clinging to the fence, wailing in his hoarse, hopeless voice. The man played and went on,

Ben keeping pace with him until the fence turned at right angles, and he clung to the fence, watching the people move on and away.

'Will you hush now?' Luster said, 'Will you hush now?' He shook Ben's arm. Ben clung to the fence, wailing steadily and hoarsely. 'Ain't you gwine stop?' Luster said, 'Or is you?' Ben gazed through the fence. 'All right, den,' Luster said, 'You want somethin to beller about?' He looked over his shoulder, toward the house. Then he whispered: 'Caddy! Beller now. Caddy! Caddy! Caddy!'

A moment later, in the slow intervals of Ben's voice, Luster heard Dilsey calling. He took Ben by the arm and they crossed the yard toward her.

'I tole you he warn't gwine stay quiet,' Luster said.

'You vilyun!' Dilsey said, 'Whut you done to him?'

'I ain't done nothin. I tole you when dem folks start playin, he git started up.'

'You come on here,' Dilsey said. 'Hush, Benjy. Hush, now.' But he wouldn't hush. They crossed the yard quickly and went to the cabin and entered. 'Run git dat shoe,' Dilsey said. 'Don't you sturb Miss Cahline, now. Ef she say anything, tell her I got him. Go on, now; you kin sho do dat right, I reckon.' Luster went out. Dilsey led Ben to the bed and drew him down beside her and she held him, rocking back and forth, wiping his drooling mouth upon the hem of her skirt. 'Hush, now,' she said, stroking his head, 'Hush. Dilsey got you.' But he bellowed slowly, abjectly, without tears; the grave hopeless sound of all voiceless misery under the sun. Luster returned, carrying a white satin slipper. It was yellow now, and cracked and soiled, and when they placed it into Ben's hand he hushed for a while. But he still whimpered, and soon he lifted his voice again.

'You reckon you kin find T. P.?' Dilsey said.

'He say yistiddy he gwine out to St. John's today. Say he be back at fo.'

Dilsey rocked back and forth, stroking Ben's head.

'Dis long time, O Jesus,' she said, 'Dis long time.'

'I kin drive dat surrey, mammy,' Luster said.

'You kill bofe y'all,' Dilsey said, 'You do hit fer devil-ment. I knows you got plenty sense to. But I can't trust you. Hush, now,' she said. 'Hush. Hush.'

'Nome I won't,' Luster said. 'I drives wid T. P.' Dilsey rocked back and forth, holding Ben. 'Miss Cahline say ef you can't quiet him, she gwine git up en come down en do hit.'

'Hush, honey,' Dilsey said, stroking Ben's head. 'Luster, honey,' she said, 'Will you think about yo ole mammy en drive dat surrey right?'

'Yessum,' Luster said. 'I drive hit jes like T. P.'

Dilsey stroked Ben's head, rocking back and forth. 'I does de bes I kin,' she said, 'Lawd knows dat. Go git it, den,' she said, rising. Luster scuttled out. Ben held the slipper, crying. 'Hush, now. Luster gone to git de surrey en take you to de graveyard. We ain't gwine risk gittin yo cap,' she said. She went to a closet contrived of a calico curtain hung across a corner of the room and got the felt hat she had worn. 'We's down to worse'n dis, ef folks jes knowed,' she said. 'You's de Lawd's chile, anyway. En I be His'n too, fo long, praise Jesus. Here.' She put the hat on his head and buttoned his coat. He wailed steadily. She took the slipper from him and put it away and they went out. Luster came up, with an ancient white horse in a battered and lopsided surrey.

'You gwine be careful, Luster?' she said.

'Yessum,' Luster said. She helped Ben into the back seat. He had ceased crying, but now he began to whim-per again.

'Hit's his flower,' Luster said. 'Wait, I'll git him one.'

'You set right dar,' Dilsey said. She went and took the cheekstrap. 'Now, hurry en git him one.' Luster ran around the house, toward the garden. He came back with a single narcissus.

'Dat un broke,' Dilsey said, 'Whyn't you git him a goodun?'

'Hit de onliest one I could find,' Luster said. 'Y'all

took all of um Friday to dec'rate de church. Wait, I'll fix hit.' So while Dilsey held the horse Luster put a splint on the flower stalk with a twig and two bits of string and gave it to Ben. Then he mounted and took the reins. Dilsey still held the bridle.

'You knows de way now?' she said, 'Up de street, round de square, to de graveyard, den straight back home.'

'Yessum,' Luster said, 'Hum up, Queenie.'

'You gwine be careful, now?'

'Yessum.' Dilsey released the bridle.

'Hum up, Queenie,' Luster said.

'Here,' Dilsey said, 'You han me dat whup.'

'Aw, mammy,' Luster said.

'Give hit here,' Dilsey said, approaching the wheel. Luster gave it to her reluctantly.

'I won't never git Queenie started now.'

'Never you mind about dat,' Dilsey said. 'Queenie know mo bout whar she gwine dan you does. All you got to do is set dar en hold dem reins. You knows de way, now?'

'Yessum. Same way T. P. goes ev'y Sunday.'

'Den you do de same thing dis Sunday.'

'Cose I is. Ain't I drove fer T. P. mo'n a hund'ed times?'

'Den do hit again,' Dilsey said. 'G'awn, now. En ef you hurts Benjy, nigger boy, I don't know whut I do. You bound fer de chain-gang, but I'll send you dar fo even chain-gang ready fer you.'

'Yessum,' Luster said. 'Hum up, Queenie.'

He flapped the lines on Queenie's broad back and the surrey lurched into motion.

'You, Luster!' Dilsey said.

'Hum up, dar!' Luster said. He flapped the lines again. With subterranean rumblings Queenie jogged slowly down the drive and turned into the street, where Luster exhorted her into a gait resembling a prolonged and suspended fall in a forward direction.

Ben quit whimpering. He sat in the middle of the seat, holding the repaired flower upright in his fist, his eyes serene and ineffable. Directly before him Luster's bullet head turned backward continually until the house passed from view, then he pulled to the side of the street and while Ben watched him he descended and broke a switch from a hedge. Queenie lowered her head and fell to cropping the grass until Luster mounted and hauled her head up and harried her into motion again, then he squared his elbows and with the switch and the reins held high he assumed a swaggering attitude out of all proportion to the sedate clopping of Queenie's hoofs and the organlike basso of her internal accompaniment. Motors passed them, and pedestrians; once a group of half grown negroes:

'Dar Luster. Whar you gwine, Luster? To de bone-yard?'

'Hi,' Luster said, 'Ain't de same boneyard y'all headed fer. Hum up, elefump.'

They approached the square, where the Confederate soldier gazed with empty eyes beneath his marble hand into wind and weather. Luster took still another notch in himself and gave the impervious Queenie a cut with the switch, casting his glance about the square. 'Dar Mr. Jason's car,' he said then he spied another group of negroes. 'Les show dem niggers how quality does, Benjy,' he said, 'Whut you say?' He looked back. Ben sat, holding the flower in his fist, his gaze empty and un-troubled. Luster hit Queenie again and swung her to the left at the monument.

For an instant Ben sat in an utter hiatus. Then he bel-lowed. Bellow on bellow, his voice mounted, with scarce interval for breath. There was more than astonishment in it, it was horror; shock; agony eyeless, tongueless; just sound, and Luster's eyes backrolling for a white instant. 'Gret God,' he said, 'Hush! Hush! Gret God!' He whirled again and struck Queenie with the switch. It broke and he cast it away and with Ben's voice mounting

276

toward its unbelievable crescendo Luster caught up the end of the reins and leaned forward as Jason came jumping across the square and on to the step.

With a backhanded blow he hurled Luster aside and caught the reins and sawed Queenie about and doubled the reins back and slashed her across the hips. He cut her again and again, into a plunging gallop, while Ben's hoarse agony roared about them, and swung her about to the right of the monument. Then he struck Luster over the head with his fist.

'Don't you know any better than to take him to the left?' he said. He reached back and struck Ben, breaking the flower stalks again. 'Shut up!' he said, 'Shut up!' He jerked Queenie back and jumped down. 'Get to hell on home with him. If you ever cross that gate with him again, I'll kill you!'

'Yes, suh!' Luster said. He took the reins and hit Queenie with the end of them. 'Git up! Git up, dar! Benjy, fer God's sake!'

Ben's voice roared and roared. Queenie moved again, her feet began to clop-clop steadily again, and at once Ben hushed. Luster looked quickly back over his shoulder, then he drove on. The broken flower drooped over Ben's fist and his eyes were empty and blue and serene again as cornice and façade flowed smoothly once more from left to right; post and tree, window and doorway, and signboard, each in its ordered place.

## ABOUT THE INTRODUCER

NICHOLAS SHAKESPEARE grew up in Latin America and is the author of *The Vision of Elena Silves*, *The High Flyer* and *The Dancer Upstairs*. He has recently published a biography of Bruce Chatwin.

FYODOR DOSTOEVSKY
The Brothers Karamazov
Crime and Punishment
Demons

GEORGE ELIOT
Adam Bede
Daniel Deronda
Middlemarch
The Mill on the Floss
Silas Marner

WILLIAM FAULKNER
The Sound and the Fury

HENRY FIELDING
Joseph Andrews and Shamela
Tom Jones

F. SCOTT FITZGERALD
The Great Gatsby
This Side of Paradise

GUSTAVE FLAUBERT
Madame Bovary

FORD MADOX FORD
The Good Soldier
Parade's End

E. M. FORSTER
Howards End
A Passage to India

ELIZABETH GASKELL
Mary Barton

EDWARD GIBBON
The Decline and Fall of the
Roman Empire
Vols 1 to 3: The Western Empire
Vols 4 to 6: The Eastern Empire

J. W. VON GOETHE
Selected Works

IVAN GONCHAROV
Oblomov

GÜNTER GRASS
The Tin Drum

GRAHAM GREENE
Brighton Rock
The Human Factor

DASHIELL HAMMETT
The Maltese Falcon
The Thin Man
Red Harvest
(in 1 vol.)

THOMAS HARDY
Far From the Madding Crowd
Jude the Obscure
The Mayor of Casterbridge
The Return of the Native
Tess of the d'Urbervilles
The Woodlanders

JAROSLAV HAŠEK
The Good Soldier Švejk

NATHANIEL HAWTHORNE
The Scarlet Letter

JOSEPH HELLER
Catch-22

ERNEST HEMINGWAY
A Farewell to Arms
The Collected Stories

GEORGE HERBERT
The Complete English Works

HERODOTUS
The Histories

PATRICIA HIGHSMITH
The Talented Mr. Ripley
Ripley Under Ground
Ripley's Game
(in 1 vol.)

HINDU SCRIPTURES
(tr. R. C. Zaehner)

JAMES HOGG
Confessions of a Justified Sinner

HOMER
The Iliad
The Odyssey

VICTOR HUGO
Les Misérables

HENRY JAMES
The Awkward Age
The Bostonians
The Golden Bowl
The Portrait of a Lady
The Princess Casamassima
The Wings of the Dove
Collected Stories (2 vols)

JAMES JOYCE
Dubliners
A Portrait of the Artist as
a Young Man
Ulysses